"Tell It to Us Easy"
and Other Stories

ALSO BY JUDITH MUSSER
AND FROM MCFARLAND

*"Girl, Colored" and Other Stories: A Complete
Short Fiction Anthology of African American Women
Writers in* The Crisis *Magazine, 1910–2010* (2011)

"Tell It to Us Easy" and Other Stories

A Complete Short Fiction Anthology of African American Women Writers in Opportunity *Magazine (1923–1948)*

Edited by JUDITH MUSSER

McFarland & Company, Inc., Publishers
Jefferson, North Carolina, and London

The present work is a reprint of the illustrated case bound edition of "Tell It to Us Easy" and Other Stories: A Complete Short Fiction Anthology of African American Women Writers in Opportunity *Magazine (1923–1948), first published in 2008 by McFarland.*

LIBRARY OF CONGRESS CATALOGUING-IN-PUBLICATION DATA

"Tell it to us easy" and other stories : a complete short fiction anthology of African American women writers in Opportunity magazine (1923–1948) / edited by Judith Musser.
p. cm.
Includes bibliographical references and index.

ISBN 978-0-7864-6619-1
softcover : acid free paper ∞

1. Short stories, American.
2. American fiction—African American authors.
3. American fiction—Women authors.
4. African American women—Fiction.
5. American fiction—20th century.
I. Musser, Judith, 1959–
II. Opportunity magazine.

PS647.A35T43   2012   813'.0108928708996073—dc20   2007050805

BRITISH LIBRARY CATALOGUING DATA ARE AVAILABLE

© 2008 Judith Musser. All rights reserved

No part of this book may be reproduced or transmitted in any form or by any means, electronic or mechanical, including photocopying or recording, or by any information storage and retrieval system, without permission in writing from the publisher.

Front cover: *Red, Yellow, and White Roses*, 1941. Oil on fabric, 16⅜ × 20⅛ in. Collection Mrs. Robert Montgomery

Manufactured in the United States of America

*McFarland & Company, Inc., Publishers
Box 611, Jefferson, North Carolina 28640
www.mcfarlandpub.com*

To David, Katie, Emily,
Sydney, Owen, and Ian

Acknowledgments

There are many people who have made this book possible. I thank the National Endowment for the Humanities for granting me a summer stipend. In addition, I am grateful for La Salle University's assistance in providing both a summer stipend and part-time research leave. I particularly appreciate the guidance and creative scheduling of Dr. Kevin Harty, chair of English at La Salle University, as well as the faithful support of my colleagues. Able assistance was also provided by the librarians at the Library of Congress. I also thank the National Urban League for granting permission to publish these stories.

I am grateful for the refreshing and invigorating sustenance provided by the Bethany Beach group of friends and the empowerment engendered by those amazing women in Massachusetts who gather together at Thanksgiving. Barb, thank you for your editing skills. Thank you Dan, Bob, Kathleen, Susan, Barbara, Beth, Fabrizio, Linda, and Thomas, for your enduring support. Last, but certainly not least, I am particularly grateful to Kathy, my sister and friend, who continues to inspire and create confidence.

TABLE OF CONTENTS

Introduction 1

DIGRESSION Eunice Roberta Hunton	7		THE TYPEWRITER Dorothy West	62
REPLICA Eunice Roberta Hunton	9		MUTTSY Zora Neale Hurston	67
SLACKENED CAPRICE Ottie B. Graham	10		THE PINK HAT Caroline Bond Day	76
DRENCHED IN LIGHT Zora Neale Hurston	15		MASKS: A STORY Eloise Bibb Thompson	79
WHO GIVES HIMSELF Eunice Roberta Hunton	21		BLACK Nellie R. Bright	84
THE TEARS OF THE ALMOND TREE Isabelle Eberhardt	22		HIGH FALUTIN' Pearl Fisher	89
ELISE Julia Rumford	25		A SLAVE FOR LIFE: A STORY OF THE LONG AGO Coralie Franklin Cook	95
ONE NIGHT IN AFRICA Isabelle Eberhardt	26		DARK LAUGHTER Ethel Riley	102
THE CORNER Eunice Hunton Carter	29		BEYOND THE YEARS Mary Etta Spencer	108
SPUNK Zora Neale Hurston	30		RECOMPENSE Lilith Shell	114
THE HANDS: A STORY Marita Bonner	34		CROSS CROSSINGS CAUTIOUSLY Anita Scott Coleman	121
MADEMOISELLE 'TASIE—A STORY Eloise Bibb Thompson	37		PRODIGAL Laura D. Nichols	123
JOHN REDDING GOES TO SEA Zora Neale Hurston	44		FAITH: A STORY Thelma T. Clement	125
THE LEGEND OF NGURANGURANE (THE SON OF THE CROCODILE) Violette De Mazia	54		THE ETERNAL QUEST Anita Scott Coleman	128

x Table of Contents

EBONY—A STORY Isabel M. Thompson	130
THE NOOSE Octavia B. Wynbush	134
THERE WERE THREE Marita O. Bonner	138
OF JIMMIE HARRIS Marita O. Bonner	142
CORNER STORE Marita O. Bonner	146
THE BLACK DRESS: A SHORT SHORT STORY Dorothy West	150
TIN CAN Marita Bonner Occomy	152
PART OF THE PACK: ANOTHER VIEW OF NIGHT LIFE IN HARLEM Hazel V. Campbell	165
WHITE ONLY: A STORY OF THE COLOR LINE Helen Faw Mull	172
STREET OF THE MORTAR AND PESTLE: A STORY OF COLOR IN THE CAPITAL Florence Jackson Stoddard	175
A SEALED POD Marita Bonner	180
THE PARASITES Hazel Vivian Campbell	185
TOO MUCH PIGMENT Effie Carrow	192
THE MAKIN'S Marita B. Bonner	199
ACROSS THE LINE Grace W. Tompkins	204
A STREET CAR RIDE Frances Eisenberg	205
HALL OF LIBERTY Manet Fowler	210
INCIDENT A'lelia Ransom	216
NOTHING CHANGES Mary Louise Bohanon	217
BLACK FRONTS Marita Bonner	223
SOUTHERN CIRCUMSTANCE Manet Fowler	229
THE FUGITIVE Grace W. Tompkins	233
BLACK BROTHER Cordelia T. Smith	237
CONDEMNED HOUSE: A SHORT STORY Lucille Boehm	241
TWO-BIT PIECE Lucille Boehm	244
THE FINE LINE: A STORY OF THE COLOR LINE Marian Minus	246
UNCLE BEN Helen Faw Mull	254
THE WOMAN IN THE WINDOW Ramona Lowe	257
A DAY'S PAY: A SHORT STORY Elise D. Challeno	261
THE RED DRESS: A SHORT STORY Grace W. Tompkins	264
HALF-BRIGHT: A SHORT STORY Marian Minus	269
MAMMY (A SHORT STORY) Dorothy West	275
THE BISHOP AND THE LANDLADY Patsy Graves	281
EXCESS BAGGAGE Helen Faw Mull	287
SALLY Duanna Dungye	290
THE LITTLE THAT IS EVERYTHING Elsie A. Parry	292
PORTRAIT OF A CITIZEN Zora L. Barnes	295
THE SIMPLE ONE Alice I. Murray	299
CITIZEN IN THE SOUTH Ruby Rohrlich	303

"Faith"		Mrs. Millennium	
Doris Peters	308	Frances Evans Layer	329
Two Worlds		Dark Quarry	
Helen Bayne Anthony	312	Babette Stiefel	333
Requiem		Concerto	
Zora L. Barnes	314	Shirley Nelson Shuman	339
Big Joe: A Short Short Story		The Bones of Louella Brown	
Stella Kamp	318	Ann Petry	340
Tell It to Us Easy		Gold Is Where You Find It	
Eleanor Simms	319	Alberta Thomas	349
One Blue Star		A Change of Scenery	
May Miller	322	Rosalie Lieberman	351
The Souls of White Children		Not in the Record	
Mary Capotosto	325	Elizabeth Walker Reeves	353

Index 357

INTRODUCTION

The Harlem Renaissance was a time period and movement which brought an unprecedented degree of recognition to African American writers. There were more books published by African Americans in the 1920s than ever before and it would not be until the 1960s that African American literary activity would again exhibit equal or greater vitality. In the late 1920s and 1930s, literary magazines became an important resource for these new black writers. The black literary journals included "little magazines" such as *The Messenger, Metropolitan, Fire!!, Harlem, Abbott's Monthly, Black Opals, Challenge, New Challenge* and *The Saturday Evening Quill*.[1] Not only did the little magazines reflect the culture and ideology of this new literary movement, but the two major journals with the longest publication history and the largest readership fundamentally influenced the work of young writers. *Opportunity*, supported by The National Urban League, continued publishing a monthly journal until 1948; *The Crisis*, funded by the NAACP, is still in publication today. It was through these magazines that women short story writers in particular responded to the call to create literature that would reflect the life of the African American. To one who reads the 81 stories published by women in *Opportunity*,[2] it becomes evident that African American women's writing made significant contributions to the academic study of the Harlem Renaissance, to understanding the popular culture of America for the first half of the twentieth century, and to the progressive thematic and stylistic connections embedded in the history of African American women's writing.

Opportunity began its monthly editions in 1923 and ended in 1948 and, in various ways, the journal was in stark contrast to *The Crisis*. To begin, the epigraph for the journal comes from Galatians 6:10 and reads: "As we have therefore opportunity let us do good unto all men." As both the epigraph and title indicate, the magazine's message reflected a positive and uplifting agenda. In addition, *Opportunity* followed the National Urban League's doctrines of self-help and support for the arts. *Opportunity* published literary works of various genres, including poetry, sketches, short stories, plays, and essays. Poetry submissions were the most frequent and regular of the literary examples with one to three poems appearing in each monthly edition. Short stories were the second most popular genre represented.

The title, the motto, and the National Urban League's agenda may suggest that the literature selected for publication in the magazine would reflect sentimentality, romanticism and accommodationist perspectives. Surprisingly, this is not the case and this is most likely due to the editorial skills of Charles S. Johnson. Johnson was a well-known sociologist whose publications included scientific research on race relations and sociological work which emphasized a study of the process of shifting from the folk culture of the rural South to the industrial culture of urban America. He believed that African Americans had to suspend their identities in a marginal situation because their rural heritage did not survive transplantation to the city. Johnson identified the development of intense frustrations and hostilities, including a deep-seated feeling of inferiority in the transplanted African American. Johnson's solution to this problem was direct—African Americans must concern themselves with reality and real possibilities, not impossible dreams. As editor of *Opportunity*, Johnson applied his sociological philosophy to literary criticism. His emphasis on scientific objectivity and realism is first seen in his opening editorial comments. He announced that *Opportunity* was dedicated to depicting "Negro life as it is with no exaggerations." It was crucial that Black writers be given a vehicle to express both their frustrations and unromanticized situations. Johnson's important editorial contributions to the Harlem Renaissance were noted by both Langston Hughes and Zora Neale Hurston. Hughes wrote in *The Big Sea* that Johnson "did more to encourage and develop Negro writers during the 1920's than anyone else in America" (218). Hurston's notoriety began with her publications in *Opportunity* and through the *Opportunity* Awards Dinners. In her autobiography, *Dust Tracks on a Road*, she particularly notes Johnson's influence not only on her literary career, but on the development of the New Negro movement:

> Charles Johnson ... was just then founding *Opportunity Magazine*.... He explained that he was writing to all of the Negro colleges with the idea of introducing new writers and new material to the public.... He wrote me a kind letter and said something about New York. So, beginning to feel the urge to write, I wanted to be in New York.
> This move on the part of Dr. Johnson was the root of the so-called Negro Renaissance. It was his work, and only his hush-mouth nature has caused it to be attributed to many others. The success of *Opportunity* Award dinners was news. Later on, the best of this material was collected in a book called *The New Negro* and edited by Dr. Alain Locke, but it was the same material, for the most part, gathered and published by Dr. Charles Spurgeon Johnson ... [Hurston 121–122].

The Literary Contests sponsored by *Opportunity* and the *Opportunity* Award dinners were probably the most influential and effective events which stimulated and empowered Black writers, and in particular, women short story writers such as Zora Neale Hurston and Marita Bonner. *Opportunity*'s Literary Contests were first announced in August of 1924. In the next issue, the objectives of the contest were stated clearly:

> It hopes to stimulate creative literary effort among Negroes; to locate and orient Negro writers of ability; to stimulate and encourage interest in the serious development of a body of literature about Negro life, drawing deeply upon these tremendously rich sources; to encourage the reading of literature both by Negro authors and about Negro life, not merely because they are Negro authors but because what they write is literature and because the literature is interesting; to foster a market for Negro writers and for literature by and about Negroes; to bring these writers into contact with the general world of letters to which they have been for the most part timid and inarticulate strangers; to stimulate and foster a type of writing by Negroes which shakes itself free of deliberate propaganda and protest [258].

Entries were at first slow in coming despite the reassurance that "if you can write, this is your *Opportunity*." In December, the editors quoted Robert H. Davis who expressed a hope "that the Contest will reveal 'some rare first note' worthy of development and of free incorporation into the stream of American letters." These words must have been encouraging for two months later, the editors announced that the contributions outstripped expectation. Before December, the number of submissions was only 231; by the deadline in February, the final count for the first contest was 732. Contributions for the second contest rose to 1,276, and although the number of submissions was not revealed for the third contest, the editors were particularly encouraged by the geographical distribution suggesting that the boundaries of the Renaissance were expanding beyond Harlem.

Among all of the categories, it was the short story which was highlighted in all three contests. The short story category received the highest monetary prize each of the three years. Submissions were also greatest in this category. From the manuscripts submitted in 1925, "the short stories alone ... are enough to fill twelve solid volumes" (*Opportunity* 1925: 36). In addition, when the winning contestants were announced in the May 1925 issue, the editors noted the following about the short story submissions: "In the field of short story there was a most intense interest, probably, because the creative ability of Negroes has not often been expressed through this medium" (130). In addition to the editors, the judges were profuse with their compliments of this genre's creativity. The stories displayed "extraordinary imaginative gifts"; they were "remarkably good" and "revealed great treasure." Some comments were distinctly race-conscious: "I liked that writers [are] sticking to their people, to the subjects about which they should be familiar" (130). Another judge wrote

> I fancy these stories mark an epoch in the history of American letters—the entrance into the domain of art of a new race, differently dowered, but with something we can not well do without. In the future we must learn to look—more and more—to the black races for art, because joy—its mainspring—is dying so rapidly now in the Great Caucasian Race [130].

In spite of this endorsement of the Black artist as entertainer, it is clear that the short stories made a distinct impression as a significant genre in the development of American literature.

African American women were successful in receiving prizes and honorable mentions in the short story category. Those receiving awards included the following: Zora Neale Hurston for "Spunk," "Black Death," "Muttsy"; Dorothy West for "The Typewriter"; Marita Bonner for "The Hands"; and Pearl Fisher for "High Falutin.'" Later contests were held and Marita Bonner was again honored for her story "Tin Can." *Opportunity* editors were also quick to point out that many of the short story contributions were highlighted in Edward J. O'Brien's analysis of the best short stories of 1925. Four of the six titles were written by women: Zora Neale Hurston's "Spunk" and "Drenched in Light"; Eloise Bibb Thompson's "Mademoiselle Tasie"' Marita Bonner's "The Hands"; and Isabelle Eberhardt's two African stories titled "One Night in Africa" and "Tears of the Almond Tree."

Thus, the objectives that Charles Johnson set out in 1924 were fulfilled through the award ceremonies. And although the most notorious contests lasted for only three years, *Opportunity* continued to announce other smaller contests and publish short stories. In fact, the number of short stories written by women writers gradually increased after the third contest in 1927. Most of these women were new writers and made their first, and in some cases, only appearance in the pages of *Opportunity*.[3] These stories, what the editors of *Opportunity* referred to as "the fugitive work of our scattered writers," are the pieces that students, literary critics, historians, and social anthropologists will want to read. Roses and Randolph in their own introduction to a collection of Harlem Renaissance women's texts claim that "the right of African-American women to exist in the realm of their own experience is acknowledged and honored. They can be studied in their own context and identified as a group apart from the traditional hierarchies of power, as 'haves' instead of 'have nots'" (4–5).[4]

Literary historians, especially those interested in the definition and description of the Harlem Renaissance, will want to note how these women's stories expand the time frame of the Harlem Renaissance. For example, most of the stories were published after the stock market crash in 1929, a year that is often used to mark the end of white patronage and thus the end of the Harlem Renaissance era. These women continued to write and submit their creative work in spite of the lack of financial support by white readers. Descriptions of the Harlem Renaissance have also indicated that most of the writers were living in or around Harlem, the Mecca of African American publishing. As indicated in Johnson's sociological attention to the transplanted African American and from the settings of the stories, geographical origins of the writers were diverse. Anita Scott Coleman was raised in New Mexico and later moved to Los Angeles, Marita Bonner wrote almost exclusively of Chicago, Dorothy West sets her stories in Boston, Eloise Bibb Thompson represented the Creole culture of the South, and various women grounded their fiction in the Caribbean and Africa. In addition, critical scholarship has suggested that most of the stories written during the Harlem Renaissance were modeled on literature written by white men. Robert Bone (xv–xx) supports this argument in *Down Home* by suggesting that Harlem Renaissance literature gravitated towards the pastoral tradition including characteristics of satire and picaresque, highlighting regional settings in the rural South, and emphasizing the Protestant religion. After reading women's stories from *Opportunity*, Bone's generalizations will have limited applications. The stories written by African American women contain themes, settings, ideals and events largely outside this list of characteristics.

Women writers in these stories reflect diversity in setting, style, characterization, speech representation, realism, and audience. The content of the stories can be examined in light of the historical shifts taking place in American culture. For example, the earlier stories include testimonials of characters who can remember the conditions of slavery; there are references to the lynchings that were prevalent in the early twentieth century; one story documents the race riots in Harlem during the 1940s; later stories reflect America's entrance into World War II and how recruitment and military service affected African American families. Variable class representation is demonstrated—from wealthy African American characters who travel first class to Europe to child laborers and itinerant farmers. There is an emphasis on the possibilities and restrictions of education from early elementary school children who cling to their dialect to African American college graduates who struggle to see their educational success confront limited employment opportunities. The arts are reflected in stories about classical musicians, opera singers, church choirs, and street musicians. The stories reflect the societal challenges facing African Americans such as health care, housing disenfranchisement, and discrimination in the justice system. Many of the stories remind readers that Black Americans represent a vast cultural diversity. The characters range from the Creoles of New Orleans, Haitian voodoo witchdoctors, a German mulatto, West Indian immigrants, and African nationals. In particular, some of the stories recount the African oral mythologies and place their stories in Algiers and the Sahara Desert. In summary, these stories provide endless insight into the everyday living of African Americans in the first half of the 20th century.

Readers who are interested in studying the thematic and stylistic features of African American women will find in the stories a connection between the slave and ante-bellum stories of the 19th century and the fiction of the writers of the Black Arts Movement. There is a strong self-reflexive element to the stories written by women. Many of the characters are artists, musicians, actors and writers and their stories provide insight into the hardships and failures of the struggling African American artists who do not experience the enthusiastic success some critics believe characterize this era. Black women writers frequently utilize dialect in representing a character's voice. In addition, the character of the tragic mulatto is common in the literature of this time period; however, women writers do not idolize or romanticize the mulatto's condition, a trait that is often seen in African American male writers. Many of these stories reflect a rejection of stereotypes of African American women, much as Locke had advocated in *The New Negro* (5): "The day of 'Aunties,' 'uncles,' and 'mammies,' is ... gone ... it is time to scrap the fictions, garret the bogeys and settle down to a realistic facing of facts." Finally, the characters in women's short fiction, the majority of which are female, are far more attentive to issues which affect their lives personally than on the large question of African American and American destiny. Women's stories in *Opportunity* concentrate on the realities of shifting to an industrial culture and under the editorial skills of Johnson, this may not be surprising. Many of the stories imitate the characteristics of proletarian fiction which emphasize women's working conditions as well as the challenges of living in a multi-ethnic neighborhood populated with foreign immigrants. These characters face conflicts on a daily basis, such as how to find and keep a job, save enough money, feed, clothe, and educate children, deal with a spouse (or life without a spouse), and maintain personal dignity in the face of routine oppression and prejudice. This is where Johnson's sociological ideology continued even after he left the magazine in 1928. Editorial comments attached to the stories, though rare, emphasize the importance of realistic portrayals of African American life. For example, the editor comments on Hazel V. Campbell's story "Part of the Pack" as follows: "The Harlem riots in fiction that approaches the truth. A vivid portrayal of the basic cause of the outbreak that recently swept over Harlem, destroying life and property." Another of Campbell's stories, "The Parasites," is described as a "realistic story by a young writer showing the administration of Relief among Negroes, from a viewpoint almost wholly new in stories of this kind." Finally, Alberta Thomas's story "Gold Is Where You Find It" needs the Editor's confirmation that the plot of the story is not fictitious: "The facts in this story, we have been assured, are true, with only the names being fictitious."

There are many excellent anthologies of literature from the Harlem Renaissance. Some are collections of various genres of the time-period (essays, poetry, short stories, and plays).[5] There are a few that include only short stories: Craig Gable's *Ebony Rising* is the most recent and Marcy Knopf's book *The Sleeper Wakes* is a collection of 27 short stories by women from various magazines. This anthology contains all of the short stories by African American women from *Opportunity*'s complete publication history. The importance of a complete collection is that no editorial preference, no critical bias, and no preconceived image is utilized in presenting stories from a magazine that was dedicated to depicting the lives of African American people "with no exaggerations." Likewise, I have presented these stories with little editing. Occasional typographical errors were corrected, but spellings have been unchanged.

These short stories by women are an integral part of literary tradition and any study of the first half of the twentieth century must incorporate these stories in order to broaden temporal, geographical, cultural, and critical boundaries. Johnson's list of goals for *Opportunity* written 84 years ago have application today. This anthology likewise hopes "to stimulate and encourage interest in the serious development of a body of literature about Negro life, drawing deeply upon these tremendously rich sources ... because what they write is literature and because the literature is interesting ... [and] ... to bring these writers into contact with the general world of letters to which they have been for the most part timid and inarticulate strangers."

Notes

1. Abby Ann Johnson and Ronald M. Johnson explore the publication histories of these early magazines in their article entitled "Forgotten Pages: Black Literary Magazines in the 1920's."
2. This collection does not include stories distinguished as written "for Young Readers." In addition, six stories were not included because the authors were identified by the editors of *Opportunity* as white (Minnie Hite Moody, Virginia Harris, Mabel Thompson Rauch, and Sarah Walmsley Eldridge).
3. Very little is known about most of these writers. The best resource for biographical information is *Harlem's Glory*, edited by Lorraine Roses and Ruth Randolph. This text includes information on Eunice Hunton, Ottie Graham, Zora Neale Hurston, Marita Bonner, Eloise Bibb Thompson, Dorothy West, Caroline Bond Day, Nellie Bright, Anita Scott Coleman, Octavia Wynbrush, Hazel Campbell, May Miller, and Ann Petry.
4. The title of this collection, "Tell It to Us Easy" comes from one of the stories; this title validates the importance of storytelling, it acknowledges an audience, and it affirms a straightforward style to literature as exemplified by this collection.
5. See Sondra Kathryn Wilson's *The Opportunity Reader*, Patton and Honey's *Double-Take*, David Levering Lewis' *The Portable Harlem Renaissance Reader*, Roses and Randolph's *Harlem's Glory*.

Works Cited

Bone, Robert. *Down Home: A History of Afro-American Short Fiction from Its Beginnings to the End of the Harlem Renaissance*. New York: Putnam, 1975.
Gable, Craig, ed. *Ebony Rising: Short Fiction of the Greater Harlem Renaissance*. Bloomington: Indiana UP, 2004.
Hughes, Langston. *The Big Sea*. New York: Hill and Wang, 1963.
Hurston, Zora Neale. *Dust Tracks on a Road*. New York: Harper Perennial, 1991.
Johnson, Abby Ann, and Ronald M. Johnson. "Forgotten Pages: Black Literary Magazines in the 1920's." *Journal of American Studies* 8 (1974): 363–382.
Johnson, Charles S. "An Opportunity for Negro Writers." *Opportunity* 2 (1924): 258.
Knopf, Marcy. *The Sleeper Wakes: Harlem Renaissance Stories by Women*. New Brunswick: Rutgers UP, 1993.
Lewis, David Levering, ed. *The Portable Harlem Renaissance Reader*. New York: Penguin, 1994.
Locke, Alain, ed. *The New Negro: An Interpretation*. 1925. New York: Johnson Reprint, 1968.
Patton, Venetria K., and Maureen Honey, ed. *Double-Take: A Revisionist Harlem Renaissance Anthology*. New Brunswick: Rutgers UP, 2001.
Roses, Lorraine Elena, and Ruth Elizabeth Randolph. *Harlem's Glory: Black Women Writing, 1900–1950*. Cambridge: Harvard, UP, 1996.

DIGRESSION

by Eunice Roberta Hunton*

It was April and the sickle of a new moon hung low in a star-studded sky as our car sped through the soft-scented stillness of a southern night. Past miles of ghostly peach orchards in full bloom, through a sweet, cool wood of cedar, down a hill and through a gully cut in a bank of damp, red clay and then a cluster of gaunt, wooden structure sparsely dotted with lights—Martinsville. As the motor turned more cautiously into a narrow lane and stopped suddenly before a long, brilliantly lighted shanty high on a bank, the air was torn with the throbbing sound of that music peculiar to these United States—Negro string music. We alighted; ascended rickety, wooden stairs to the railless veranda of the cabin and pushed open the door. We were at a country dance in Georgia.

The room which we entered was a large, unplastered one scrupulously clean but crowded with furniture and women, old women in large part, dressed in stiff gingham dresses and stiffer yet gingham aprons with starched white turbans crowning their costumes. A few of these women were young enough to retain traces of a golden yellow or smooth brown beauty. One of these stepped forward; looked at us intently yet with a face devoid of expression; collected a tax of two cents a piece; placed our wraps on one of the three spotless beds crowded into the room and invited us to "go on in."

The door to which she pointed opened into a fair sized room bare of furnishings save for a large kerosene lamp hanging from the ceiling and in a far corner of the room a chair and two boxes upon which were seated the blind 'cellist, the wooden-legged violinist, and the banjo-man who was with them. The room was crowded with men and boys and fewer girls. The larger number were at the moment lounging against the walls, for the musicians were mechanically grinding out a waltz or rather a hash of all waltzes popular during the last five years, and the few couples left on the floor were in the process of what is known as "dancing down." They were engaged in a test of pure physical endurance. The music was accompanied by the sound of irregular panting breaths from the dancers, the rhythmical scraping of their feet, and an

---

*To three companions in adventure on a Spring night.

occasional sigh of defeat as a worn down couple dropped out. Otherwise there was a tense silence as the dance, which had plainly been going on over a long period of time, drew to a close. Couple after couple left the floor, finally leaving a solitary pair dancing on and on. For about fifteen long minutes these two continued the dance until, amid much hand clapping, the man, half reeling, led the girl, still fresh, to a place beside the wall. And such a girl—barely out of her teens, scarcely more than an inch or two over five feet, slim and lithe, with short black curls framing an oval face of rare olive richness. Dressed in a short blue skirt and white sailor blouse, she looked like some child playing with grown-ups—that is, she looked that way until one saw her vivid red mouth so alluringly full, and those dark eyes whose depths revealed a glimpse of things...

When the excitement over the waltz was ended, the revelers realized for the first time that there were outsiders in their midst. There was a hush that was broken only when the blind 'cellist, with a word to his companions, started a tune that seemed to be popular. Immediately there were grins and each sought his favorite partner. There was a scramble for the girls. There were not enough to go around, and boys seized each other eagerly and joined the crowd of dancers. There never was, nor will there ever be again, music like that. It stirred the blood; it blinded reason; it stripped away the veneer of civilization; and leaving the senses bare and unprotected, it played upon them tauntingly, temptingly, cruelly. The air was stiflingly heavy and there was quiet. None of that levity and mirthful chatter, which is usually a part of dances, prevailed. No, everyone was completely submerged by the music. And then the banjo-man began to chant some words; the group one by one took them up until, dancing with a mad and passionate frenzy, all were singing:

> "I'd sigh, I'd cry,
> I'd lay me down an' die
> If I should ever lose my lovin' man,
> If I should ever lose my lovin' man."

Over and over the tune was played. On and on they danced, the air growing more fetid, the dancing growing more and more abandoned, men and women clinging passionately to each other in savage caresses until, when it seemed as if the emotional tension might easily madden, the music stopped with an abruptness that had the effect of a sudden dash of cold water.

There were other dances after that, but they were all anti-climax. And so after firmly refusing numerous invitations to partake the "white lightnin'" which was served by dipper from a wooden bucket, we started away. As we left the crowded rooms with the eyes of little scarlet lips desirously intent upon a member of our party, it seemed as though we were entering another world; and yet as we sped once more through the sweet, clean night, there suddenly came to me on the air the fragment of a song:

> "I'd sigh, I'd cry,
> I'd lay me down an' die
> If I------" [*Opportunity* 1.12 (December 1923): 359, 381]

REPLICA

by Eunice Roberta Hunton

Noonday sun scorched a treeless ribbon of brick red road; a breeze hot and languid stirred fitfully; angry red dust rose in great puffs only to settle back heavily on all who dared the road, and then—*impasse*. For the way ended quite suddenly in a cordon of vehicles. There was a wheelbarrow of anti-bellum origin wedged in between a fifth hand Packard and a delivery wagon of doubtful age. A Ford, shining and new, rubbed shoulders with a road mender's pitch cart. They were all there, these and dozens of others barricading the entrance to a grove of Georgia oaks.

In the cool shadow of the mammoth trees the heat of the road was forgotten. Life was a pleasant bustle—shouts of merriment from youths in holiday attire, shrill cries from romping children, mellow peals of laughter from slim brown girls, whose comely bodies stood silhouetted as streaks of light pierced thin and clinging garments; the pungent fumes of charcoal fires mingling with savory odors of barbecue; tables groaning beneath their weight of food, the food of the great Negro South—ham, pink and juicy, platters of rich brown chicken, pans of golden rolls, steaming pigs' feet, deep, flaky pies, yellow corn bread with fish fried crisp and brown, cake in profusion, and everywhere pails of lemonade beside ice cream freezers oozing streams of brackish water. But suddenly from the heart of the grove, there came a throbbing, a pulsing that dominated the whole, that stilled laughter, that quenched appetites, that pulled and drew until presently the whole assembly stood ringed in a circle at the feet of the three on the little raised platform. And they who stood above were in truth exalted. With eyes closed and an expression of mysticism about their faces they beat their drums, a large bass drum and two smaller ones throbbing in the irregular beats of a monotonous syncopation,—the same measure over and over again. They wove a spell and took possession of one, yet all the while one was conscious of a certain familiarity. Those drumbeats seemed but the echo of some well known theme.

But the train of reflection and self searching was broken, for into the center of the circle had leaped a weird figure, an old woman, burnt black with the suns of many summers and worn thin with the burdens of years; but her turbaned figure was as straight as an arrow and the eyes which she now closed in ecstasy were clear and bright. Her apron flapped grotesquely in the breeze as she began a dance of astounding agility and abandon. In a moment or two she was joined by a girl barely out of her teens. The girl was barefooted and her short gingham dress was cut low at the throat. Her bare skin gleamed like burnished copper in the sunlight. As she began to dance the dusky mane of her hair tumbled down, her full red lips drooped slightly apart, the swell of her ripe young breasts rose and fell with drumbeat after drumbeat, and the youths in the circle watched spellbound. Soon woman after woman, throwing away restraint, joined the dancers and the dance itself increased in abandon and barbarity as the minutes slipped away.

And then memory came flooding back. It was the memory of jungle nights, of stagnant heat, of prowling beasts, of glowing fires, of the tom tom's pulsing beat, of naked bodies gleaming in the firelight, dancing, dancing, dancing, and the strong black arms of a belted chief. [*Opportunity* 2.21 (September 1924): 276]

SLACKENED CAPRICE

by Ottie B. Graham

Coming home from a long journey, I stopped with Carlotta at a southern city to visit an old friend of her mother's. The trip had been wearisome and we were glad of the few hours to stretch our limbs and rest. The place we wanted was easily reached, and when we arrived there it was so beautiful and still that a feeling of rest came over us in spite of our fatigue.

On the porch was a man standing before a bird cage. He was quiet, with his hands behind him, and he saw only the bird. We walked up the steps and spoke to him before he turned to notice us. He was too old to be young and too young to be even middle-aged. His eyes were soft, very kind and soft, and his smile was slow. He started to speak, but a woman came hurriedly out of the house, interrupting with a laugh and a greeting. She was his mother and the friend Carlotta had come to see. She welcomed us and led us to a sitting-room; then she asked us to excuse her for a few minutes. Her girl was burning something.

As she left the room by one door, her son entered by another. He had us make ourselves comfortable and brought us a cool drink of fruit juice. He sat and talked with us, saying himself very little but making us say much. I believe we were talking about a relative of his or about somebody's new position when he asked very abruptly, "How do you find people as you travel? Are they at all care-free?" His question was directed to Carlotta, but she had chance only for a philosophical, "Well," before he had apparently forgotten that the question was ever in his mind.

"Do you like music?" he asked quite as suddenly as he had made the first query. We said yes, of course.

"Then I shall play for you," he announced very quietly, and without more ado went to the piano. Once seated, he thought no more about us, and his long, bony fingers lifted and sped across the keyboard. For a moment they reminded me of slender, swiftly driven horses. I remember smiling inwardly as I thought that, because the idea seemed far-fetched; but there was something about him that made me draw far-fetched figures. He trilled and lilted through passages as light and airy as flying fairy down. There was something of Grieg wonder in them, but they were not Grieg. Glad, laughing measures repeated themselves, splashing in patches of sharp brilliancy throughout the ascending movement. Then, with what seemed something of reluctance in the long, bony fingers, the allegro stopped its prancing and quieted to a soberer swing. It did not cease descending; it came down, down, losing its gay fire, until only a sweet, crying melody remained. This melody was not at all akin to the start of the composition. Sweet and soft, even yearning, as though it would dance but could not, it merely sang. Here was something of Taylor plaintiveness, but it was not Taylor. And the slender fingers, stopped in their fleet gallop, caressed now tenderly the keys over which they had just sped.

This change of tone and tempo, though beautiful, was to me unusual and I wondered about it as I listened. So engrossed in his rendition was the man, he seemed actually to suffer from his tenseness. His brows raised in despairing frowns which wavered and settled again. He began to sway so that I looked at Carlotta and she at me, both afraid that he would fall from his seat. Just then his mother called to him, cheerily and as though she would check his sad song. Somehow I had imagined he would not leave the instrument even if he stopped playing to answer, but he did. He whirled from the piano, stood a moment, and passed through the door with what seemed a single stride. He said nothing to us—nothing whatever; but before we got over the shock of his leaving he had returned by the other door. He appeared to be annoyed—exceedingly annoyed, and he made a slight glance in our direction as he took his seat again.

The bony, long fingers rested once more upon the keys, impatient to be driven; and the light, dashing measures arose once more—arose and danced away. Then again came the gradual down-toning, and the slackening of pace, down, down, until a mere song remained. A mere song, but a sad one, which sang since it could not dance. The man, as he played on, suffered again, losing himself in the strains that went floating away. This time his mother came into the room, cheerily interrupting him at the place where she had called before. He turned, slowly this time, excusing himself, and quietly left our presence.

The woman made some passing mention of her son's absorbing fondness for the piano, and with an apology for her delay, set upon other conversation. We had well launched upon some interesting thing when the son returned again. He sat close by, listening but saying little, and smiling here and there his slow smile. A woman was mentioned, a master of some instrument, and we turned to talking of music. This made for our hostess' son a livening interest. In a short while he had taken the discussion into details of execution, and arrested the whole with his offer to play again. As though he had not touched the piano for us before, he said very simply, "I will play for you."

His mother seemed a bit nervous as he arose and approached the piano; but he was seated, we were forgotten, and the slender steeds were ready again to obey the will of their master. So splendid a musician was the man, we found ourselves too firmly held by his skill to become amused. A third time he set out upon the same thing—the thing which started swift beauty and descended, down, down, to a simple, plaintive song.

His mother wanted to stop him again. It was easy to see that she wanted to, but a third time would be too significant of the strange uneasiness which lay behind her son's playing this thing beyond a certain point. Here again I wondered, as I listened, about the gradual, depressing change in the composition, and I wondered whether it pleased me. It was beautiful, to be sure, but I decided that I did not like it. There came then the end of the number. Quite suddenly it ended, and with a crash! A crash in high treble, like a quick, shrill scream. It did something to me that I could never explain; I will never forget that crash.

The son staggered from the piano and out to the porch. He murmured as he went, clutching at his breast and at his head. When his mother reached him, he had stopped at the bird's cage. He was standing still, very still, as though he had never been unsteady. To the bird he talked confidingly, saying low things we could not understand. But when he saw Carlotta and me, he lifted the cage down, quietly excusing himself and walked away, down the veranda steps and out to the back of the lawn. All the way he talked to the bird.

"He's been this way now for sometime," his mother said resignedly, looking after him. "He went with the army—volunteered. He came back to me a wreck from gas. His nerves were almost gone, and sometimes his head was wrong; but he began to get back to normal after a while. His music helped a lot—dear boy. He started on his composing again and became wrapped up in a Caprice. That was what he just played. Oh, he was doing so well and I was so proud of him, and one little incident ruined everything. It's strange how it affected him." She stopped a minute as it all came back to her, and when she started again her southern drawl seemed sweeter and sad.

"He went walking one day with me down through the grove. We were just a'laughing and talking, and he kept singing snatches of his Caprice. We stopped to watch a group of children playing in a pretty little park. My boy said that he would work better on his Caprice now that he had seen them. Oh, they were happy little mites. They ran and skipped about, and fell over one another, and laughed and sang as though nothing was anything but their little game. I picked out one who reminded me of the way my boy used to look—brown face and brown curls—brown eyes full of sparkle. Oh, my!" she said, and she sighed.

"Then just as we started to move away, we noticed a sudden hush come over them. There stood a big, burly white man, a watchman or keeper or something, snarling at them and telling them they couldn't stay there. 'No niggers in there.' Well, the poor little things just sauntered away. Nothing else to do. It was mean. Children are such lovely things—who could hurt them? As they moved away down the grove, one tried to start the others skipping again. They tried it, but it didn't do. They went along their way, several trying to stop the youngest little fellow from crying. He wanted to play in the park.

"Well, my boy didn't talk any more all the way home. He was like something hit in the face. I found him looking at this khaki next day, and later saying something to the bird about his song. He said the cage took something from the bird's song. Then he worked on his Caprice, but it wouldn't go. The first part kept up, but it would just change, it seemed, of itself. My poor boy, he couldn't do a thing with it. It stopped on him every time. Then he got so his head was wrong again. The doctors didn't do much good. They still come, but what's the use? I'm afraid it's all over with him. He can't play anything else. Nothing else but that half Caprice. Funny how one little thing can do so much harm."

Soon we left, as best we could, trying to smile again. Carlotta said later that always within her she could hear that woman saying, "Children are such lovely things—who could hurt them?" And I could hear, and can hear now, the scream in that final crash!

Last year I returned to that city for a longer visit, this time alone. Soon after my arrival there I inquired about the Jaimesons. The mother had died of grief sometime back, upon the son's failure to return home. He had wandered away five years ago without saying anything at all. His mother had stood talking to visitors, bidding them good-bye. The son, bearing a bird in a cage, had gone off through the back garden gate and had not been seen since. This, of course, was like the firing of a cannon to me. I was completely stunned to know that I had figured unknowingly in so grave a tragedy. Had Carlotta and I not been there to take the good woman's time, she might have kept better watch over her demented son.

I asked about their home. It had been sold at auction and torn down, and a theatre now stood in its place. I expressed a desire to see the structure—to attend the theatre, and I was surprised to learn that it was actually possible for me to be admitted. This was the South, and no place in America was any too kind. Always they said the Negro had little or no culture; yet they closed to him, as a rule, all roads to culture. Soon there was to be a concert at this theatre, held through the efforts to a certain music club. Anybody could go. A brown face could not appear on the main floor, to be sure, but a brown face could *appear*. I would go.

I sat, on the night of the concert, awaiting the beginning of the program. To a friend I talked of the Jaimeson's. The theatre was pretty—just pretty. It seemed a great shame that so beautiful a home as that of the Jaimeson's should have been destroyed. Oh, well. My friend seemed not to mind. Soon she opened her program and I remembered that I had not looked at mine. The artist of the evening was a well known pianist. He would give a group of his own arrangements of rare and unfinished compositions. In a footnote the name Jaimeson caught my eye. Then I could not believe what I read. An unfinished Caprice by a little known Negro composer had furnished the theme of a number which was very dear to the artist. This thing was next to the last number, and I could scarcely enjoy what went before it. I tried to feel ashamed of not becoming sufficiently absorbed in what at some other time would have taken me from the earth. But I wanted now only to hear this Caprice—to see it executed—and I was not at all ashamed. It was only natural that the rest of the numbers were minor to Jaimeson's.

Finally the Caprice was played and encored. I almost choked to keep from screaming. The old picture came before me, and all that this thing had meant and had failed to mean to its composer whirled round and round in my brain, and I could hear the crash before it came. I waited for the crash. This man did not make it. Then it had not been written in the manuscript. Why should I have thought it had?

The last rendition was a tremendous thing. I tried to concentrate upon it, but instead I sat and wondered about what had gone before it. I supposed that the manuscript of the Caprice had fallen into the hands of the music club during the moving and auctioning of the household goods of the Jaimeson home. Through them it had come into the hands of this artist, no doubt. Thus I pondered and listened at intervals until the music ceased. The artist refused an encore, so the audience started filing out. Now I was wondering why monsieur would not play again. We had reached the lower floor, when there broke upon the air that Caprice.

It was not the artist of the evening. One knew that immediately. I heard three men half whisper, "My God!" I may have said it too. Everyone turned back into the auditorium—also we, even we. Downstairs. Jaimeson sat at the piano. Jaimeson himself. I knew him as soon as I looked. He was like a ghost, long kept from some material thing which he had needed. He was taller, it seemed, and gaunt. His hair had grown long and his profile keener. Like a rail he looked as he leaned forward, driving once more the thing, fiery steeds, his fingers. Nobody stopped him—nobody dared. He played with the frenzy of madness—played as though he were trying to atone for an ill-given rendition of this thing which was his.

The pianist of the concert stood midway to the stage, staring and bewildered. Almost the entire audience had returned. They stood staring and astounded. Nobody stopped the player. Midway its dashing course, as five years before it had done, the Caprice checked its wild capering. It changed to something slower, softer, yearning—then came the crash! Like a great mark of exclamation in the midst of a sad, smoothly flowing voice it came. It smote the dazed listeners and I could feel them start—a shortened breath, quickly drawn, *en masse*.

Jaimeson had obeyed his urge; it had taken all his strength; now he collapsed. No one had noticed the bird cage on the floor beside him until he reached for it at the end of his playing. He must have intended to leave as suddenly as he had come, but he missed the cage (it was empty now), and crumpled to the floor.

There was great and immediate excitement, of course. It was not until special appeals were made to the curious crowd by both the manager and the artist that peace and quiet were secured. Then the curtains were drawn and the onlookers cut off from the little scene. But I held a feeling of intimacy for this poor, crazed soul, hurt forever beyond cure, and I ran, almost unconsciously, to him. Somehow I found my way backstage where they had taken him. The friend who was with me had thought me daring, but I had dismissed her, not caring what she thought. This man was alone and I would help him.

Someone I took to be a doctor asked who I was. "His sister," I answered.

"This fellow was an only child. I knew the family." Here was a tangle. The person speaking was sure of what he said. I knew that certainly.

"Wife, huh?" from someone else, and the words meant more than they asked.

They ignored the glance of defiance I had flashed and accepted my silence for affirmative response. I made no answer, but went to the couch where Jaimeson lay. No one forbade me to touch him so I sat beside him and rested his head on my breast. He stirred and looked at me, and tears stole down my face. He reached up and fingered a loose ringlet of my hair. I found myself gazing at a man who stood beside me. I was hardly aware of his presence, yet I was speaking to him. "Children are such lovely things—who could hurt them?"

"Was he injured when he was a child?" the man inquired.

"No," I said, "but such a little thing caused it. *Not* a little thing either."

"What was it?" the man asked quickly, and I knew that I had better cease talking while I could.

"Please don't ask me now," I whispered. "It will upset him again." Then, laying Jaimeson's head back upon the couch, I stood up.

"How did he get here tonight? Why wasn't he more closely watched?" the man continued. I had known this question was coming, though I had not prepared an answer.

"I don't know how he came," I said. "I thought he was safe in bed." I felt my face burn, and dropped down upon the couch again beside my strange charge. "I think I can move him now," I ventured, "if you will get me a cab." Heaven knows where I would have taken him. I had not the faintest idea.

"Better wait until the doctor gets here. We've sent for him." Just slightly I trembled.

"Where has he been all these years? In a sanitarium?" the man asked. He seemed wound up to ask questions forever.

"Yes," I whispered again. Anything which sounded plausible would do.

Just then Jaimeson sat up and stared across the room. A piano stood in the corner. Again he was like a ghost. I moved that he might arise. He wanted to. And I motioned to the others not to interfere. I must show some authority, and it would satisfy him to play, even if the result were adverse. So he moved to the instrument, two of the men and I keeping close behind him. He did not notice us. Once seated, he leaned forward to play. He started the Caprice and stopped. Started again and stopped. Something was wrong. Something was wrong. The steeds would not obey their master. First time. First time? I wondered. They started on their dash; then stopped. Started; then stopped. The man looked at me. There was something he knew, yet something he could not understand. He smiled his slow smile and shook his head. Then he played. But it was not the first part he played. That part he could not do. Instead he brought forth the sad, low-singing melody which seemed not at all a part of the Caprice.

Over and over this thing he played, his head sometimes dropped low and forward—sometimes pitched back and high. I stood behind him, and a little to the side. His mouth was partly open. His mouth watered. With a soft, silk kerchief I wiped his watering mouth. Over and over he played the softly wailing measures, his head sometimes dropped low and forward—sometimes pitched back and high.

The others stood watching—simply watching. No one spoke. Finally an arrival was announced. "Here's the doctor," someone called.

Jaimeson stopped short. I imagined he wanted the bird cage, for he looked around for something. However, he turned and clung to me. He knew that I was someone who cared.

The doctor came toward us. Jaimeson's hold on me relaxed. The doctor spoke lightly. "What seems to be the trouble?"

Jaimeson slipped down and crumpled again to the floor. I answered the doctor. "Nothing now."

I knew without the doctor's word, that the man was dead. I just knew somehow. Just knew. And I was glad for him. It was better that he escape. The others straightway looked to me. I had seen it this far, I would finish. I sold my rings and paid for the burial.

[*Opportunity* 2.23 (November 1924): 332–335.]

DRENCHED IN LIGHT

by Zora Neale Hurston

"You Isie Watts! git 'own offen dat gate post an' rake up dis yahd!"

The little brown figure perched upon the gate post looked yearningly up the gleaming shell road that led to Orlando, and down the road that led to Sanford and shrugged her thin shoulders. This heaped kindling on Grandma Potts' already burning ire.

"Lawd a-mussy!" she screamed, enraged—"Heah Joel, gimme dat wash stick. Ah'll show dat limb of Satan she kain't shake huhseff at *me*. If she ain't down by de time Ah gets dere, Ah'll break huh down in de lines." (loins)

"Aw Gran'ma, ah see Mist' George and Jim Robinson comin' and Ah wanted to wave at 'em," the child said petulantly.

"You jes wave dat rake at dis heah yayd, madame, else Ah'll take you down a button hole lower. You'se too 'oomanish jumpin' up in everybody's face dat pass."

This struck the child in a very sore spot for nothing pleased her so much as to sit atop of the gate post and hail the passing vehicles on their way South to Orlando, or North to Sanford. That white shell road was her great attraction. She raced up and down the stretch of it that lay before her gate like a round eyed puppy hailing gleefully all travelers. Everybody in the country, white and colored, knew little Isis Watts, the joyful. The Robinson brothers, white cattlemen, were particularly fond of her and always extended a stirrup for her to climb up behind one of them for a short ride, or let her try to crack the long bull whips and yee whoo at the cows.

Grandma Potts went inside and Isis literally waved the rake at the "chaws" of ribbon cane that lay so bountifully about the yard in company with the knots and peelings, with a thick sprinkling of peanut hulls.

The herd of cattle in their envelope of gray dust came alongside and Isis dashed out to the nearest stirrup and was lifted up.

"Hello theah Snidlits, I was wonderin' wheah you was," said Jim Robinson as she snuggled down behind him in the saddle. They were almost out of the danger zone when Grandma emerged.

"You Isie-s!" she bawled.

The child slid down on the opposite side from the house and executed a flank movement through the corn patch that brought her into the yard from behind the privy.

"You lil' hasion you! Wheah you been?"

"Out in de back yahd," Isis lied and did a cart wheel and a few fancy steps on her way to the front again.

"If you doan git tuh dat yahd, Ah make a mommuk of you!" Isis observed that Grandma was cutting a fancy assortment of switches from peach, guana and cherry trees.

She finished the yard by raking everything under the edge of the porch and began a romp with the dogs, those lean, floppy eared 'coon hounds that all country folks keep. But Grandma vetoed this also.

"Isie, you set 'own on dat porch! Uh great big 'leven yeah old gal racin' an' rompin' lak day—set 'own!"

Isis impatiently flung herself upon the steps.

"Git up offa dem steps, you aggravatin' limb, 'fore Ah git dem hick'ries tuh you, an' set yo' seff on a cheah."

Isis petulantly arose and sat down as violently as possible in a chair, but slid down until she all but sat upon her shoulder blades.

"Now look atcher," Grandma screamed. "Put yo' knees together, an' git up offen yo' backbone! Lawd, you know dis hellion is gwine make me stomp huh insides out."

Isis sat bolt upright as if she wore a ramrod down her back and began to whistle. Now there are certain things that Grandma Potts felt no one of this female persuasion should do—one was to sit with the knees separated, "settin' brazen" she called it; another was whistling, another playing with boys, neither must a lady cross her legs.

Up she jumped from her seat to get the switches.

"So youse whistlin' in mah face, huh!" She glared till her eyes were beady and Isis bolted for safety. But the noon hour brought John Watts, the widowed father, and this excused the child from sitting for criticism.

Being the only girl in the family, of course she must wash the dishes, which she did in intervals between frolics with the dogs. She even gave Jake, the puppy, a swim in the dishpan by holding him suspended above the water that reeked of "pot likker"— just high enough so that his feet would be immersed. The deluded puppy swam and swam without ever crossing the pan, much to his annoyance. Hearing Grandma she hurriedly dropped him on the floor, which he tracked up with feet wet with dishwater.

Grandma took her patching and settled down in the front room to sew. She did this every afternoon, and invariably slept in the big red rocker with her head lolled back over the back, the sewing falling from her hand.

Isis had crawled under the center table with its red plush cover with little round balls for fringe. She was lying on her back imagining herself various personages. She wore trailing robes, golden slippers with blue bottoms. She rode white horses with flaring pink nostrils to the horizon, for she still believed that to be land's end. She was picturing herself gazing over the edge of the world into the abyss when the spool of cotton fell from Grandma's lap and rolled away under the whatnot. Isis drew back from her contemplation of the nothingness at the horizon and glanced up at the sleeping woman. Her head had fallen far back. She breathed with a regular "snark" intake and soft "poosah" exhaust. But Isis was a visual minded child. She heard the snores only subconsciously but she saw straggling beard on Grandma's chin, trembling a little with every "snark" and "poosah." They were long gray hairs curled here and there against the dark brown skin. Isis was moved with pity for her mother's mother.

"Poah Gran-ma needs a shave," she murmured, and set about it. Just then Joel, next older than Isis, entered with a can of bait.

"Come on Isie, le's we all go fishin'. The perch is bitin' fine in Blue Sink."

"Sh-sh—" cautioned his sister, "Ah got to shave Gran'ma."

"Who say so?" Joel asked, surprised.

"Nobody doan hafta tell me. Look at her chin. No ladies don't weah no whiskers if they kin help it. But Gran'ma gittin' ole an' she doan know how to shave like me."

The conference adjourned to the back porch lest Grandma wake.

"Aw, Isie, you doan know nothin' 'bout shavin' a-tall—but a *man* lak *me*—"

"Ah do so know."

"You don't not. Ah'm goin' shave her mahseff."

"Naw, you won't neither, Smarty. Ah saw her first an' thought it all up first," Isis declared, and ran to the calico covered box on the wall above the wash basin and seized her father's razor. Joel was quick and seized the mug and brush.

"Now!" Isis cried defiantly, "Ah got the razor."

"Goody, goody, goody, pussy cat, Ah got the brush an' you can't shave 'thought lather—see! Ah know mo' than you," Joel retorted.

"Aw, who don't know dat?" Isis pretended to scorn. But seeing her progress blocked for lack of lather she compromised.

"Ah know! Les' we all shave her. You lather an' Ah shave."

This was agreeable to Joel. He made mountains of lather and anointed his own chin, and the chin of Isis and the dogs, splashed the walls and at last was persuaded to lather Grandma's chin. Not that he was loath but he wanted his new plaything to last as long as possible.

Isis stood on one side of the chair with the razor clutched cleaver fashion. The niceties of razor-handling had passed over her head. The thing with her was to *hold* the razor—sufficient in itself.

Joel splashed on the lather in great gobs and Grandma awoke.

For one bewildered moment she stared at the grinning boy with the brush and mug but sensing another presence, she turned to behold the business face of Isis and the razor-clutching hand. Her jaw dropped and Grandma, forgetting years of rheumatism, bolted from the chair and fled the house, screaming.

"She's gone to tell papa, Isie. You didn't have no business wid his razor and he's gonna lick yo hide," Joel cried, running to replace mug and brush.

"You too, chucklehead, you, too," retorted Isis. "You was playin' wid his brush and put it all over the dogs—Ah seen you put it on Ned an' Beullah." Isis shaved some slivers from the door jamb with the razor and replaced it in the box. Joel took his bait and pole and hurried to Blue Sink. Isis crawled under the house to brood over the whipping she knew would come. She had meant well.

But sounding brass and tinkling cymbal drew her forth. The local lodge of the Grand United Order of Odd Fellows led by a braying, thudding band, was marching in full regalia down the road. She had forgotten the barbecue and log-rolling to be held today for the benefit of the new hall.

Music to Isis meant motion. In a minute razor and whipping forgotten, she was doing a fair imitation of the Spanish dancer she had seen in a medicine show some time before. Isis' feet were gifted—she could dance most anything she saw.

Up, up went her spirits, her brown little feet doing all sorts of intricate things and her body in rhythm, hand curving above her head. But the music was growing faint. Grandma was nowhere in sight. She stole out of the gate, running and dancing after the band.

Then she stopped. She couldn't dance at the carnival. Her dress was torn and dirty. She picked a long stemmed daisy and thrust it behind her ear. But the dress, no better. Oh, an idea! In the battered round topped trunk in the bedroom!

She raced back to the house, then, happier, raced down the white dusty road to the picnic grove, gorgeously clad. People laughed good naturedly at her, the band played and Isis danced because she couldn't help it. A crowd of children gathered admiringly about her as she wheeled lightly about, hand on hip, flower between her teeth with the red and white fringe of the table-cloth—Grandma's new red tablecloth that she wore in lieu of a Spanish shawl—trailing in the dust. It was too ample for her meager form, but she wore it like a gypsy. Her brown feet twinkled in and out of the fringe. Some grown people joined the children about her. The Grand Exalted Ruler rose to speak; the band was hushed, but Isis danced on, the crowd clapping their hands for her. No one listened to the Exalted One, for little by little the multitude had surrounded the brown dancer.

An automobile drove up to the Crown and halted. The white men and a lady got out and pushed into the crowd, suppressing mirth discreetly behind gloved hands. Isis looked up and waved them a magnificent hail and went on dancing until—

Grandma had returned to the house and missed Isis and straightway sought her at the festivities expecting to find her in her soiled dress, shoeless, gaping at the crowd, but what she saw drove her frantic. Here was her granddaughter dancing before a gaping crowd in her brand new red tablecloth, and reeking of lemon extract, for Isis had added the final touch to her costume. She *must* have perfume.

Isis saw Grandma and bolted. She heard her cry: "Mah Gawd, mah brand new table cloth Ah jus' bought f'um O'landah!" as she fled through the crowd and on into the woods.

II

She followed the little creek until she came to the ford in a rutty wagon road that led to Apopka and laid down on the cool grass at the roadside. The April sun was quite hot.

Misery, misery and woe settled down upon her and the child wept. She knew another whipping was in store for her.

"Oh, Ah wish Ah could die, then Gran'ma an' papa would be sorry they beat me so much. Ah b'leeve Ah'll run away an' never go home no mo'. Ah'm goin' drown mahseff in the creek!" Her woe grew attractive.

Isis got up and waded into the water. She routed out a tiny 'gator and a huge bull frog. She splashed and sang, enjoying herself immensely. The purr of a motor struck her ear and she saw a large, powerful car jolting along the rutty road toward her. It stopped at the water's edge.

"Well, I declare, it's our little gypsy," exclaimed the man at the wheel. "What are you doing here, now?"

"Ah'm killin' mahseff," Isis declared dramatically, "Cause Gran'ma beats me too much."

There was a hearty burst of laughter from the machine.

"You'll last sometime the way you are going about it. Is this the way to Maitland? We want to go to the Park Hotel."

Isis saw no longer any reason to die. She came up out of the water, holding up the dripping fringe of the tablecloth.

"Naw, indeedy. You go to Maitlan' by the shell road—it goes my mah house—and turn off at Lake Sebelia to the clay road that takes you right to the do'."

"Well," went on the driver, smiling furtively, "Could you quit dying long enough to go with us?"

"Yessuh," she said thoughtfully, "Ah wanta go wid you."

The door of the car swung open. She was invited to a seat beside the driver. She had often dreamed of riding in one of these heavenly chariots but never thought she would, actually.

"Jump in then, Madame Tragedy, and show us. We lost ourselves after we left your barbecue."

During the drive Isis explained to the kind lady who smelt faintly of violets and to the indifferent men that she was really a princess. She told them about her trips to the horizon, about the trailing gowns, the gold shoes with blue bottoms—she insisted on the blue bottoms—the white charger, the time when she was Hercules and had slain numerous dragons and sundry giants. At last the car approached her gate over which stood the umbrella China-berry tree. The car was abreast of the gate and had all but passed when Grandma spied her glorious tablecloth lying back against the upholstery of the Packard.

"You Isie-e!" she bawled. "You lil' wretch you! come heah *dis instant.*"

"That's me," the child confessed, mortified, to the lady on the rear seat.

"Oh, Sewell, stop the car. This is where the child lives. I hate to give her up though."

"Do you wanta keep me?" Isis brightened.

"Oh, I wish I could, you shinning little morsel. Wait, I'll try to save you a whipping this time.

She dismounted with the gaudy lemon flavored culprit and advanced to the gate where Grandma stood glowering, switches in hand.

"You're gointuh ketchit f'um you haid to yo' heels m' lady. Jes' come in heah."

"Why, good afternoon," she accosted the furious grandparent. "You're not going to whip this poor little thing, are you?" the lady asked in conciliatory tones.

"Yes, Ma'am. She's de wustest lil' limb dat ever drawed bref. Jes' look at mah new table cloth, dat ain't never been washed. She done traipsed all over de woods, uh dancin' an' uh prancin' in it. She done took a razor to me t'day an' Lawd knows whut mo'."

Isis clung to the white hand fearfully.

"Ah wuzn't gointer hurt Gran'ma, miss—Ah wuz jus' gointer shave her whiskers fuh huh 'cause she's old an' can't."

The white hand closed tightly over the little brown one that was quite soiled. She could understand a voluntary act of love even though it miscarried.

"Now, Mrs. er—er—I didn't get the name—how much did your tablecloth cost?"

"One whole big silvah dollar down at O'landah—ain't had it a week yit."

"Now here's five dollars to get another one. The little thing loves laughter. I want her to go on to the hotel and dance in that tablecloth for me. I can stand a little light today—"

"Oh, yessum, yessum," Grandma cut in, "Everything's alright, sho' she kin go, yessum."

The lady went on: "I want brightness and this Isis is joy itself, why she's drenched in light!"

Isis for the first time in her life, felt herself appreciated and danced up and down in an ecstasy of joy for a minute.

"Now, behave you'seff, Isie, ovah at de hotel wid de white folks," Grandma cautioned, pride in her voice, though she strove to hide it. "Lawd, ma'am, dat gal keeps me so fractious, Ah doan know mah haid f'um mah feet. Ah orter comb huh haid, too, befo' she go wid you all."

"No, no, don't bother. I like her as she is. I don't think she'd like it either, being combed and scrubbed. Come on, Isis."

Feeling that Grandma had been somewhat squelched did not detract from Isis' spirit at all. She pranced over to the waiting motor and this time seated herself on the rear seat between the sweet, smiling lady and the rather aloof man in gray.

"Ah'm gointer stay wid you all," she said with a great deal of warmth, and snuggled up to her benefactress. "Want me tuh sing a song fuh you?"

"There, Helen, you've been adopted," said the man with a short, harsh laugh.

"Oh, I hope so, Harry." She put her arm about the red draped figure at her side and drew it close until she felt the warm puffs of the child's breath against her side. She looked hungrily ahead of her and spoke into space rather than to anyone in the car. "I want a little of her sunshine to soak into my soul. I need it."

[*Opportunity* 2.24 (December 1924): 371–374]

WHO GIVES HIMSELF

by Eunice Roberta Hunton

"Who gives himself with his gift, feeds three;
Himself, his hungry neighbor, and me."

It was Christmas Eve by the calendar and the customs of men. But Christmas isn't Christmas when you're marooned in a boarding school in the far South in Louisiana. It's just one more day. Moreover, it simply could not be Christmas Eve. It was too hot; home was too far away; and as I crept into bed I half expected to hear a rising bell break in upon sweet dreams at the unholy hour of 6:30 the next morning. And then I began to remember that I couldn't even wait until six-thirty. I must rise with the dawn. Now, I have seen dawn in all its mysteries and promise breaking over shadowing mountains and limitless plains, over peaceful deep and turbulent streams; I have seen it creep upon the crowded skylines of the great cities of the world and gild the steeple of a village church. But to these dawns, dawn in the swamp lands of Louisiana is as Hades to Heaven—antitheses. For dawn in Louisiana is not a lovely thing, dew-pearled or even dew-drenched. It is sullen and soggy; gnarled and groggy. It comes grudgingly, relapsing now and again into dank shadows and leaving in its wake a long interval of gray chill before the arrival of the sun.

On Christmas morning, then, I was to fare forth in such a dawn, for the task of directing some students in the distribution of Christmas baskets to the poor of the neighboring countryside was mine. The anticipation of this evoked no particular pleasure and I fell asleep with visions of sugar cane stalks, muddy roads, draughty cabins and Christmas baskets chasing each other through my head....

Was I dreaming? No, I could hear it coming nearer, the sound of horns blending beautifully the strains of the century old paean, louder and louder the music grew and then just outside my window, passing into yet another Christmas carol, it began to grow more soft as the school brass quartet went on into the village a scant half mile away. With yet three quarters of an hour before I was needed to be ready on my way I settled down for a short nap and was on that drowsy borderland between sleep and consciousness when once more music broke the stillness of the early morning. This time, it was mixed voices, so soft that one just barely heard them, but soon they came nearer. "Hark, the herald angels sing!" I was wide awake and slowly I caught the spirit. It *was* Christmas morning.

There were two trucks loaded with baskets to be distributed far and wide that morning and I was a bit dismayed on leaving the school as I surveyed the itinerary in my hands. But my heart was light; I had forgotten the dawn; for was it not Christmas morning? A part of the chorus that had caroled earlier in the morning was with us as leaving the trucks in the road we turned up the pathway to leave our first basket and the fifty-cent piece which the Sunday School had sent. They began to chant "Christmas time is here, Noel we gladly sing." At the sound the door of the cabin flew open and a gaunt black woman in a drab and faded gingham dress, clasping a new born babe to her breast, stared wonderingly. Then seeing that we came to her she cried, "Christmas gift" in a voice that trembled with excitement and emotion. She received our gifts regally but her thanks were broken and breathless. As she blessed the gift bearers, silent tears coursed down her cheeks.

One of our group, a girl just turned fifteen, begged to hold the infant for just one minute. The mother surrendered her child, and with trembling hands, broke a white rose from the one bush that grew near her door and, stripping it of thorns, placed it midst the holly that was on my coat. It was Christmas morning and the mother of a new born babe had given me a rose. [*Opportunity* 2.24 (December 1924): 374]

The Tears of the Almond Tree

by Isabelle Eberhardt*

Bou-Saada, the tawny queen clothed with dim gardens and guarded by violet hills, sleeps voluptuously by the rough edge of the ravine in the depths of which the little water tinkles away over pebble stones that are rose hued or white. Leaning nonchalantly as if in a dream over low mud-baked walls, the almond trees weep, and their tears are white—white petals—kissed away by the wind—. Their sweet perfume floats in the warm and gentle air evoking a sort of tender melancholy—

It is spring. Under this external appearance of languor of the melting affecting

---

*Dedicated to Maxime Noire painter of fiery skies and the almond trees when they flower.

end of everything, life is breeding; a life that is violent, filled with the ardor of love; a powerful sap mounting mightily from mysterious reservoirs of creation in order to burst all of a sudden into the intoxication of renewal—flowers born in the light.

The silence of the cities of the South rests upon Bou-Saada. In the little Arab village the passers are few. Down in the ravine however there are groups of women, groups of girls in dazzling costume.

Mlahfa violet hued, emerald green, flashing rose, the green of the citron, sky blue orange, red or white embroidered with multi colored stars and flowers. Their heads are coifed with the towering heavy headdresses of the Sahara. They are composed of tresses of hair, gold and silver ornaments, little chains, mirrors and amulets, or crowned with diadems trimmed with black ostrich feathers. All of this passes and shimmers in the sunlight; groups of women unite and separate in a ceaseless changing rainbow. They resemble bands of charming butterflies.

There are groups of men, too, hooded and draped in white, of grave bronzed faces who turn suddenly the corner of an ochre colored street.

For years and years in front of a dilapidated dwelling of baked mud, two women have seated themselves morning and evening. They wear the *mlafha* too; but it is of somber red, and its heavy folds of wool weigh down their bodies, which are thin and dry as the bodies of mummies. Their heads are dressed with long tresses of red wool intermingled with tresses of gray hair tinted with henna; there are heavy rings swinging from their weary ears, which also hold up little chains of silver, which serve to hold in place the silk kerchiefs that cover their headdresses. Necklaces made of pieces of gold and of hardened aromatic paste heavy plaques chiseled silver cover their wrinkled breasts. Whenever they move, which is rarely and slowly, the headdress and necklace, the bracelets and the ear rings, begin to tinkle.

As motionless as antique and forgotten idols, they watch through the thick blue smoke of their cigarettes—men pass, who now have no eyes for them. They watch the gay cavaliers, the wedding processions, the long caravans of camels or mules, and the decrepit old men who used to be their lovers, in fact all this great dazzling movement of life which can touch them no more.

Their dull eyes monstrously painted and enlarged with *kehol*, their painted cheeks, their painted lips all this forced decoration of youth flings a sort of sinister shadow across their toothless emaciated faces.

But long ago they were young, Saadia, whose fine thin face looked like chiseled bronze, and Habiba, white skinned, and frail, delighted the idle hours of pleasure of Bou-Saadi, and the hearts of the nomads.

Now rich, decked out with the results of the greed of their youth, they look out peacefully upon the decorative, richly hued, changing picture of the great city where the Tell meets the Sahara, and where all the races of Africa meet and blend. They sit there and smile—smile at life which is changeless, and goes on without them—smile at their memories—

When at the hour when the slow and plaintive voice of the muezzin calls the faithful to prayer, the two old friends get up, and then prostrate themselves upon a spotless rug, their heads to the ground with a great clanking of jewels. After that they take up their old places again and their interrupted dreams, just as if they were waiting for someone who can never come.

Rarely they exchange a few words. "Look O Saadia, down there! That is Si

Chalal, the *cadi*—Do you remember when he used to be my lover? What a dashing man he was in those days! How generous he was, although in those days he was only a simple *adel*. He's old now—it takes two men to lift him to his mule. The women don't care to look at his face any more—Just think—the face of him—whose eyes I used to cover with kisses.

"Yes—And how Ali, the lieutenant in those days, merely a *spahi* always came with Si Chalal—and how I used to love him? You remember do you not? He too—he was a pretty boy, and good—how I wept the day he went away to Medeah! But he—he laughed, he was happy and did not care, because they had just made him a brigadier. He forgot me then—that's the way men are. He died only last year—God be merciful unto his soul!"

Sometimes they try to sing together the couplets of some old love song. It sounded strangely in their trembling voices. It became something tarnished and dull.

And thus they lived together, without cares or regrets, amid the faded phantoms of past happiness, awaiting—the end.

The red sun is beginning to rise slowly behind the mountain draped magnificently in mist. A purple glow sweeps the face of the earth like a veil of shade. The increasing rays of light scatter aigrettes of flame on top of the date-palm, and the cupolas of silver of the *marabouts* have become massive gold. For the space of an instant all this ancient tawny city flames as if a great conflagration dwelled within it, while down low on the ground of the gardens, in the bed of the little river, the narrow pathways, vague shadows float like thin blue smoke, softening the angles, opening up mysterious distances between little walls in narrow street, and the chiseled trunks of tall date palms. On the edge of the little river the increasing daylight turns to crimson and rose the scattered tears—heaped upon the ground like snow—of the pensive almond tree.

In front of the dwelling of the two old ladies the fresh winds of morning finished scattering the ashes of a little fire, it sweeps them away in a little blue whirlwind. Saddia and Habiba are not in their accustomed place.

Inside the dwelling there is a strident song of grief. Upon the mat upon the floor Habiba is now merely a shapeless bundle of dark red wool. Upon her immobile stiffened body the great gems scintillate strangely. Saadia and other women of her class of long ago are lamenting her death. The tinkle, tinkle, of their heavy jewels accompanies the lament of the mourners.

At dawn Habiba—old and exhausted—had died gently because the springs of life are dried up. Toward mid-day some men come. They bear her away to one of the little cemeteries, which are never enclosed, and where the great waves of the desert sand roll eternally toward the little sunbaked, bud dwellings of man.

That is all—now Saadia, alone, sits in front of her door, in the dawn, in the twilight. With the dim blue smoke of her eternal cigarette she is breathing out the little life that is left, while down there on the edge of the ravine—in the sunlight, and in the shadows of the gardens the almond trees finish weeping their eternal tears—the tears of pale petals in the sweet smile of spring.

[*Opportunity* 3.25 (January 1925): 11–12]

ELISE

by Julia Rumford

Now you're me and I'm Anna O'Malley that always calls me "nigger." Elise, bless the little five-year-old, was talking to her reflection in the mirror.

"Make a circle, children." It was amusing to see her try to imitate the elder-sisterly tones of her kindergarten teacher without moving the lips of the "nigger" in the mirror.

She extended her graceful little brown arms to close an imaginary circle. The "nigger" did likewise. Elise, her big, black eyes alight with indignation, drew back her hand in scorn:—

"*I'm* not going to take *your* hand. "I'm—," but the little "nigger" also drew back in evident disdain!

"No, no—," her baby voice was quite distressed. "You mustn't do what I do, *I'm* Anna O'Malley!"

Again and again she tried to show contempt without having the "nigger" do likewise.

Poor darling! There she lay before the mirror, a crumpled golden brown heap, sobbing away her disappointment. And the "nigger" in the mirror sobbed in sympathy.

* * *

Elise was on her way home from school alone for the first time. She felt very proud and grownup. A small crowd of children had gathered not far from the school-yard. *She* would go and see what the trouble was.

As she approached, she recognized Anna O'Malley and Rita Kornowitz in a furious face-slapping, hair-pulling combat. The small spectators evidently thought it great fun. There were frequent calls of "Give it to 'er, Anna," or "Dontcher be afraid, Rita."

Elise watched the progress of the battle a moment, painfully conscious of taking care of herself. Then switching off with a disdainful glance over her shoulder, she addressed the air, and whom it might concern in general:

"I wouldn't be white if I could!"

Elise was coaxing her dolly to take a nap.

"Come, now, if you promise to go to sleep right away afterward, Mother will tell you a story."

She pressed her beloved hazel-cheeked Lucinda close to her.

"Long, long ago, there was a king who had seven princesses. Kings' little girls are called princesses, Lucinda. One of the princesses was black. Not like the stove, Lucinda, but like me. Did you know they call this black, too?" Elise held up her dimpled hand for Lucinda's inspection.

"The other four, no five, no *six* little girls, princesses, I mean, were white. The name of the black princess was Ambra. The white princesses were very wicked, and so they wouldn't let Ambra play in their ring, or bite their candy, or come to their birthday parties.

"One day a prince—a most awfully beautiful prince—came. He was very tall and dignified, like the man at Tracy's that tells them when they can take the elevator up; and his face was soft and kind, like the animal in the picture over the mantel. They call that animal a dough, Mother says. And he was the color of the dough, too.

"The prince said, 'I have come from a far country, where all the little girls are black. They have dolls and dishes and candy and everything. I have come to find a princess for my country, but she must be black.'

"And then all the white princesses were sorry they weren't black. And Ambra said to the prince, 'I would like to be your princess, but I do not want to leave my dear father, who is white.' And the prince said, 'Oh, that is all right. Only the children must be black. The fathers can be any color.'

"So Ambra and her father went away with the prince, and left the six wicked, white sisters by themselves, because they didn't have any mother, Lucinda. She died—just like my mama did." [*Opportunity* 3.26 (February 1925): 56]

ONE NIGHT IN AFRICA

by Isabelle Eberhardt*

One morning the sad rains ceased and the sun rose in a sky that was clear, washed free of the tarnishing mists of winter, and showing its blue profound.

In the sheltered garden a giant tree stretched out arms laden with flowers the hue of rose-porcelain.

Toward the right, the voluptuous curves of the hills of Mustapha stretched out until they vanished in the infinite transparencies of distance.

There were little sparkling dots of gold upon the small white facades of the valleys.

In the distance the dim wings of Neopolitan fishing boats spread out upon the tranquil satin of the gulf. The warm wind passed like a breath that caressed. Inanimate objects trembled with joy. Then the illusion of waiting for something, of being happy, awoke again in the heart of the Vagabond.

He had run away with the one whom he loved, to the humble white-washed dwelling where time passed insensibly, with something of delicious languor in it, behind the carved wood, behind the curtains with their faded colors.

In front of them spread out that splendid decoration which is Algiers.

Why think of going away again, why seek happiness elsewhere, since the

*Translated by Edna Worthley Underwood

Vagabond had it in front of him in the unsoundable depths of the changing eyes of this woman whom he loved. He plunged his eyes into hers for long, long periods until an anguish that became joy mingled their two beings.

Why set out again on the chase of space when this retreat of theirs confronted horizons that were so immense, when here they were able to feel the universe mirrored and centered within themselves?

All that was not related to his love now fell away from the Vagabond and receded gradually into vague distance.

He renounced his dream of vague, ascetic solitude. He renounced the pleasure he had had in the chance habitations of the night, and the long road—the tyrannical mistress—which had taken him prisoner and which when he was drunk with the sunlight he had adored so.

The Vagabond with his ardent heart was letting himself be cradled here for hours and days, cradled with a happiness which symbolized reality.

Life and the objects which surrounded life seemed lovely. It seemed to him that he had become better because the too brutal strength of his weary body and the too fierce energy of his will were touched with languor. He was gentler.

Long ago—in years of exile—in the crushing boredom of sedentary city life, the heart of the Vagabond had contracted with grief whenever he happened to think of the fairylands of sun, of the great free plains.

Now curled up on his bed, touched by the light that came in through one of the little windows, he was evoking in the ear of this woman whom he loved, visions of the land of his dreams, touched with the sweet melancholy of the past, which is really the perfume of things which are dead.

The Vagabond did not regret anything any more. He wanted only the infinite duration of that which was.

* * *

Night fell warm upon the gardens; silence reigned. In this silence there was something felt like an immense sigh, the sigh perhaps of the sea which slept, slept down there under the stars—a sigh of the earth, perhaps, oppressed with the heat of love.

Like jewels, fires glittered on the languorous slope of the hills. Other fires grouped themselves together like beads—rosaries of gold-flung against the land; other fires jumped up and sparkled like trembling eyes in the velvet blackness of gigantic trees.

The Vagabond and the woman he loved got up from the bed and went out upon the long highway. It was empty. They grasped each other's hands. They smiled there—alone in the night.

They did not speak because they understood so much better what each other said by silence.

Slowly, slowly, side by side, they climbed the slopes of the Sahil, while a belated moon began to disentangle itself from the eucalyptus trees and light a little the gentle undulations of the Mitidja.

They sat down upon a rock.

A bluish light slipped over the vast fields of night and aigrettes of silver began to tremble among the branches.

Long, long the Vagabond looked upon the road; the road broad, white and which led into the unknown.

It was the road of the South.

In the suddenly awakened soul of the Vagabond a world of memories began to live again. He closed his eyes to try to chase the visions away. He clenched his hand around the woman he loved. But in spite of himself he opened his eyes again and his eyes looked upon the road. His native inclination for the old tyrannical mistress who had made him drunk with sunlight took possession of him again. Again he belonged to her. Every fiber of his being was hers again. Once again—this time when they got up—he threw a longing glance upon the road, and his heart left him and went out to it just as of old.

They came back to their dwelling; they entered through the vital silence of their garden. They went to bed again in the silence—under the spreading camphor tree.

Above their heads, the great tree spread out its branches laden with rose hued flowers which had turned to violet in the blue pallor of night.

The Vagabond looked at the woman he loved, so close beside him. She was scarcely more than a vaporous vision, unreal, something ready to disappear, to blend with the diaphanous light of the moon.

The form of the woman he loved was vague now and distant. Then the Vagabond who still loved her, knew that with the dawn he would go away, and grief entered his heart.

He picked up one of the huge flowers of the camphor tree which are so much like human flesh and kissed it in order to stifle a sob.

* * *

The great red sun had plunged down into its sunset-ocean of blood, there beyond the black line which was the horizon.

Quickly day—like a light—went out. Quickly the desert of stone was drowned in soft cold transparency.

In one far corner of the level of the plain a few little fires were kindled.

Some nomads armed with long guns were moving about restlessly, their long, white draperies floating about in the bright points of the flame.

A hobbled horse whinnied. A man crouched upon the ground, head thrown back, eyes closed, as if in a dream, was chanting over and over again an ancient song of the desert, in which the word love and the word death alternated, and rang against each other.... After that there was no sound in the great dull immensity.

* * *

Beside a fire that was all but extinguished now, the Vagabond was sleeping rolled in his burnous. His head rested upon his folded arm, his relaxed and weary limbs were given over to the speedy forgetfulness of sleep. The unique pleasure of falling asleep all alone and unknown, among a crowd of men who are simple of heart and crude—like the earth itself, the old, good, patiently cradling Mother-Earth. He had given himself up to the pleasure of falling asleep for one night in the corner of a desert which had no name and to which he knew he would never come back again.

(Written down at Ain Taga in the Month of April)

THE CORNER

by Eunice Hunton Carter

My friend lives in the house on the corner. She lives high above the street in a doll's house of white enamel and soft blues with lovely old furniture and oriental rugs of faded brilliance on dark polished floors; in a miniature home with a real fireplace and polished grasses and flowers all about in crystal bowls. She lives high up there but below are the street and the avenue. And one Fall night as I waited for her in the loveliest room of all, I turned from watching the fire flicker and dart across the room and great chrysanthemums casting sleeping shadows on the wall. I turned from this and watched the street. It was alive with light and sound, the light and sound of the city, the black city. Motor cars whizzed by carrying throngs of pleasure seekers, aliens many of them, in search of novelty and thrill, come to the black city for something new. And in the small morning hours they went back to their homes in Westchester and the Bronx, on Park Avenue and Riverside Drive, back to their haunts on Broadway and thereabouts, serene in the belief that in Harlem cabarets they had found something new, that in black and tan replicas of downtown cabarets, roofs and supper clubs, promoted by quacks of every race, they had seen life in the black city.

In reality as their cars swept past the corner, they were passing life by. They had missed a chance of seeing life when they didn't stop and watch the boy on the corner who for clapping companions in front of the drug store was doing a dance that was a bit of Buck and Wing, a bit of "Charleston" and many other things. They didn't hear the errand boy who came out of the drugstore singing a song that had drifted out of the cabaret to come from him purified by the sheer joy and spontaneity of his singing.

Around the corner on the Avenue, a man mounted on a soap box was making a political speech in which he was putting race first and country after and the crowd around him was eager and interested—until a pair of detectives passed leading a troupe of gypsies toward the police station.

A group of school girls, bright felt hats perched jauntily on sleek bobbed heads, with short fur coats from which bright scarves fluttered in the night, passed by linked arm in arm, chattering as they went home from a late moving picture. To me, from my high perch, they looked like school girls the town over, but a passerby would have seen skins of olive, tan and copper beneath the bright felt hats.

A man without legs wheeled himself along on a wooden platform and with an instrument or two gave the effect of a whole brass band as he attracted attention to the box for largess fastened onto his platform. A girl of the town dropped a coin or two as she went on her way but slim brown girl and boy passed him by unheedingly as with eyes locked, they walked on into the night.

Across the street the crowd around an automobile from which a swarthy man in morning clothes and a fez was displaying gruesome pictures and dispensing patent medicines parted to let a girl, glitteringly shod and swathed in furs, enter a waiting taxicab.

Beneath the window a crowd of youths were in heated argument gesticulating fiercely. I leaned from the window and listened. For want of a better meeting place a group of college youths were discussing philosophy.

Inside the lovely room, the fire had burned low. The silver chimed clock on the mantle struck many times. I decided not to wait longer for my friend. I took my hat and coat and went down into the street and turned into the Avenue. I started to cross. A taxicab filled with alien pleasure-seekers crossed my path. As they passed the tower, they heard nothing but their own maudlin laughter, they saw nothing but their own vacuous faces. They passed on to the cabarets, illegitimate offspring of their own resorts, looking for life, Harlem life, and blindly, feverishly, rushing by it.

[*Opportunity* 3.28 (April 1925): 114–115]

SPUNK

by Zora Neale Hurston

A giant of a brown-skinned man sauntered up the one street of the Village and out into the palmetto thickets with a small pretty woman clinging lovingly to his arm.

"Looka theah, folkses!" cried Elijah Mosley, slapping his leg gleefully. "Theh they go, big as life an' brassy as tacks."

All the loungers in the store tried to walk to the door with an air of nonchalance but with small success.

"Now pee-eople!" Walter Thomas gasped. "Will you look at 'em!"

"But that's one thing Ah likes about Spunk Banks—he ain't skeered of nothing' on God's green footstool—*nothin'*! He rides that log down at saw-mill jus' like he struts 'round wid another man's wife—jus' don't give a kitty. When Tes' Miller got cut to giblets on that circle-saw, Spunk steps right up and starts ridin'. The rest of us was skeered to go near it."

A round-shouldered figure in overalls much too large, came nervously in the door and the talking ceased. The men looked at each other and winked.

"Gimme some soda-water. Sass'prilla Ah reckon," the newcomer ordered, and stood far down the counter near the open pickled pig-feet tub to drink it.

Elijah nudged Walter and turned with mock gravity to the new-comer.

"Say, Joe, how's everything up yo' way? How's yo' wife?"

Joe started and all but dropped the bottle he held in his hands. He swallowed several times painfully and his lips trembled.

"Aw 'Lige, you oughtn't to do nothin' like that," Walter grumbled. Elijah ignored him.

"She jus' passed heah a few minutes ago goin' thata way," with a wave of his hand in the direction of the woods.

Now Joe knew his wife had passed that way. He knew that the men lounging in the general store had seen her, moreover, he knew that the men knew *he* knew. He stood there silent for a long moment staring blankly, with his Adam's apple twitching nervously up and down his throat. One could actually *see* the pain he was suffering, his eyes, his face, his hands and even the dejected slump of his shoulders. He set the bottle down upon the counter. He didn't bang it, just eased it out of his hand silently and fiddled with his suspender buckle.

"Well, Ah'm goin' after her to-day. Ah'm going' an' fetch her back. Spunk's done gone too fur."

He reached deep down into his trouser pocket and drew out a hollow ground razor, large and shiny, and passed his moistened thumb back and forth over the edge.

"Talkin' like a man, Joe. Course that's *yo'* fambly affairs, but Ah like to see grit in anybody."

Joe Kanty laid down a nickel and stumbled out into the street.

Dusk crept in from the woods. Ike Clarke lit the swinging oil lamp that was almost immediately surrounded by candleflies. The men laughed boisterously behind Joe's back as they watched him shamble woodward.

"You oughtn't to said whut you did to him, Lige—look how it worked him up," Walter chided.

"And Ah hope it did work him up. 'Tain't even decent for a man to take and take like he do."

"Spunk will sho' kill him."

"Aw, Ah doan't know. You never kin tell. He might turn him up an' spank him fur gettin' in the way, but Spunk wouldn't shoot no unarmed man. Dat razor he carried outa heah ain't gonna run Spunk down an' cut him, an' Joe ain't got the nerve to go up to Spunk with it knowing he totes that Army .45. He makes that break outa heah to bluff us. He's gonna hide that razor behind the first likely palmetto root an' sneak back home to bed. Don't tell me nothin' 'bout that rabbit-foot colored man. Didn't he meet Spunk an' Lena face to face one day las' week an' mumble sumthin' to Spunk 'bout lettin' his wife alone?"

"What did Spunk say?" Walter broke in—"Ah like him fine but 'tain't right the way he carries on wid Lena Kanty, jus' cause Joe's timid 'bout fightin'."

"You wrong theah, Walter. 'Tain't cause Joe's timid at all, it's cause Spunk wants Lena. If Joe was a passle of wile cats Spunk would tackle the job just the same. He'd go after *anything* he wanted the same way. As Ah wuz sayin' a minute ago, he tole Joe right to his face that Lena was his. 'Call her,' he says to Joe. 'Call her and see if she'll come. A woman knows her boss an' she answers when he calls.' 'Lena, ain't I yo' husband?' Joe sorter whines out. Lena looked at him real disgusted but she don't answer and she don't move outa her tracks. Then Spunk reaches out an' takes hold of her arm an' says: 'Lena, youse mine. From now on Ah works for you an' fights for you an' Ah never wants you to look to nobody for a crumb of bread, a stitch of close or a shingle to go over yo' head, but *me* long as Ah live. Ah'll git the lumber foh owah house to-morrow. Go home an' git you' things together!'

"'Thass mah house,' Lena speaks up. 'Papa gimme that.'

"'Well,' says Spunk, 'doan give up whut's yours, but when youse inside don't for-git youse mine, an' let no other man git outa his place wid you!"

"Lena looked up at him with her eyes so full of love that they wuz runnin' over, an' Spunk seen it an' Joe seen it too, and his lip started to tremblin' and his Adam's apple was galloping up and down his neck like a race horse. Ah bet he's wore out half a dozen Adam's apples since Spunk's been on the job with Lena. That's all he'll do. He'll be back heah after while swallowing' an' workin' his lips like he wants to say somethin' an' can't."

"But didn't he do *nothin*' to stop 'em?"

"Nope, not a frazzlin' thing—jus' stood there. Spunk took Lena's arm and walked off jus' like nothin' ain't happened and he stood there gazin' after them till they was outa sight. Now you know woman don't want no man like that. I'm jus' waitin' to see whut he's goin' to say when he gits back."

II

But Joe Kanty never came back, never. The men in the store heard the sharp report of a pistol somewhere distant in the palmetto thicket and soon Spunk came walking leisurely, with his big black Stetson set at the same rakish angle and Lena clinging to his arm, came walking right into the general store. Lena wept in a frightened manner.

"Well," Spunk announced calmly, "Joe came out there wid a meatax an' made me kill him."

He sent Lena home and led the men back to Joe—Joe crumpled and limp with his right hand still clutching his razor.

"See mah back? Mah cloes cut clear through. He sneaked up an' tried to kill me from the back, but Ah got him, an' got him good, first shot," Spunk said.

The men glared at Elijah, accusingly.

"Take him up an' plant him in 'Stoney lonesome,'" Spunk said in a careless voice. "Ah didn't wanna shoot him but he made me do it. He's a dirty coward, jumpin' on a man from behind."

Spunk turned on his heel and sauntered away to where he knew his love wept in fear for him and no man stopped him. At the general store later on, they all talked of locking him up until the sheriff should come from Orlando, but no one did anything but talk.

A clear case of self-defense, the trial was a short one, and Spunk walked out of the court house to freedom again. He could work again, ride the dangerous log-carriage that fed the singing, snarling, biting, circle-saw; he could stroll the soft dark lanes with his guitar. He was free to roam the woods again; he was free to return to Lena. He did all of these things.

III

"Whut you reckon, Walt?" Elijah asked one night later. "Spunk's gittin' ready to marry Lena!"

"Naw! Why, Joe ain't had time to git cold yit. Nohow Ah didn't figger Spunk was the marrin' kind."

"Well, he is," rejoined Elijah. "He done moved most of Lena's things—and her along wid 'em—over to the Bradley house. He's buying it. Jus' like Ah told yo' all right in heah the night Joe wuz kilt. Spunk's crazy 'bout Lena. He don't want folks to keep on talkin' 'bout her—thass reason he's rushin' so. Funny thing 'bout that bob-cat, wan't it?"

"Whut bob-cat, 'Lige? Ah ain't heered 'bout none."

"Ain't cher? Well, night befo' las' was the fust night Spunk an' Lena moved together an' jus' as they was goin' to bed, a big black bob-cat, black all over, you hear me, *black*, walked round and round that house and holwed like forty, an' when Spunk got his gun an' went to the winder to shoot it, he ways it stood right still an' looked him in the eye, an' howled right at him. The thing got Spunk so nervoused up he couldn't shoot. But Spunk says twan't no bob-cat nohow. He ways it was Joe done sneaked back from Hell!"

"Humph!" sniffed Walter, "he oughter be nervous after what he done. Ah reckon Joe come back to dare him to marry Lena, or to come out an' fight. Ah bet he'll be back time and agin, too. Know what Ah think? Joe wuz a braver man than Spunk."

There was a general shout of derision from the group.

"Thass a fact," went on Walter. "Lookit whut he done; took a razor an' went out to fight a man he knowed toted a gun an' wuz a crack shot, too; 'nother thing Joe wuz skeered of Spunk, skeered plumb stiff! But he went jes' the same. It took him a long time to get his nerve up. 'Tain't nothin' for Spunk to fight when he ain't skeered of nothin'. Now, Joe's done come back to have it out wid the man that's got all he ever had. Y'll know Joe ain't never had nothin' nor wanted nothin' besides Lena. It must been a h'ant cause ain' nobody never seen no black bob-cat."

"'Nother thing," cut in one of the men, "Spunk wuz cussin' a blue streak to-day 'cause he 'lowed dat saw wuz wobblin'—almos' got 'im once. The machinist come, looked it over an' said it wuz alright. Spunk musta been leanin' t'wards it some. Den he claimed somebody pushed 'im but 'twant nobody close to 'im. Ah wuz glad when knockin' off time come. I'm skeered of dat man when he gits hot. He'd beat you full of button holes as quick as he's look atcher."

IV

The men gathered the next evening in a different mood, no laughter. No badinage this time.

"Look, 'Lige, you goin' to set up wid Spunk?"

"Naw, Ah reckon not, Walter. Tell yuh the truth, Ah'm a lil bit skittish. Spunk died too wicket—died cussin', he did. You know he thought he wuz done out life."

"Good Lawd, who'd he think done it?"

"Joe."

"Joe Kanty? How come?"

"Walter, Ah b'leeve Ah will walk up thata way an' set. Lena would like it Ah reckon."

"But whut did he say, 'Lige?"

Elijah did not answer until they had left the lighted store and were strolling down the dark street.

"Ah wuz loadin' a wagon wid scantlin' right near the saw when Spunk fell on the carriage but 'fore Ah could git to him the saw got him in the body—awful sight. Me an' Skint Miller got him off but it was too late. Anybody could see that. The fust thing he said wuz: 'He pushed me, 'Lige—the dirty hound pushed me in the back!'"—

He was spittin' blood at ev'ry breath. We laid him on the sawdust pile with his face to the East so's he could die easy. He helt mah han' till the last, Walter, and said: 'It was Joe, 'Lige—the dirty sneak shoved me ... he didn't dare come to mah face ... but A'll git the son-of-a-wood louse soon's Ah get there an' make hell too hot for him.... Ah felt him shove me...!" Thass how he died."

"If spirits kin fight, there's a powerful tussle goin' on somewhere ovah Jordan 'cause Ah b'leeve Joe's ready for Spunk an' ain't skeered any more—yas, Ah b'leeve Joe pushed 'im mahself."

They had arrived at the house. Lena's lamentations were deep and loud. She had filled the room with magnolia blossoms that gave off a heavy sweet odor. The keepers of the wake tipped about whispering in frightened tones. Everyone in the village was there, even old Jeff Kanty, Joe's father, who a few hours before would have been afraid to come within ten feet of him, stood leering triumphantly down upon the fallen giant as if his fingers had been the teeth of steel that laid him low.

The cooling board consisted of three sixteen-inch boards on saw horses, a dingy sheet was his shroud.

The women ate heartily of the funeral baked meats and wondered who would be Lena's next. The men whispered coarse conjectures between guzzles of whiskey.

[*Opportunity* 3.30 (June 1925): 171–173]

THE HANDS: A STORY

by Marita Bonner

I saw his hands as soon as I skipped on the car at Vesey Avenue. Dark Brown, gnarled, knotted, bumping arm, in quirky knots like old brown bark on a cherry tree.

I skipped on the car real quickly. I wanted to cry, so I skipped. Someone had hurt my feelings and I wanted to cry—but I would not. I stared at everyone opposite me.

I am not rude. I can stare at people without their noticing me. Women only glance at me in pity or in grim scorn. Men never see me; so I stare safely.

You see, I am tallish and my bones poke out in subduable angles. I have no complexion—no hair. Of course there are some features and something atop my head, but the one is not complexion and the other not hair. My clothes look well when they are not on me. I have good taste in selecting things but I cannot wear them well. Nothing seems to belong to me, nor I to anything. I guess I am merely unfortunately ugly.

There are games I have to play by myself when I feel particularly ugly, particularly unfortunate.

I tried them all as soon as I had sat in my seat, for tears were coming up from behind, from each side and from below my eyes and I was breathing in quick rushes—with long pauses in between—around lumps in my throat, that kept rising and sinking like mercury in a thermometer. I plunged headlong into my first game: Being-where-I-was-not....

There was all around me a crushing dark forest with a crooked ribbon of water in its midst. There was a cheese-colored moon and a wind playing a flighty dance rhythm through the trees. Vines draped low to the water's edge and the cold black slender loops of snakes were strung like bracelets on the boughs of trees. Spicy flowers and fruit and the tanging odor of crushed green leaves and water, too, still in its basin. Snakes—and no people snakes. Where were the people? I in the forest and the forest peopled by snakes....

One of the mercurial lumps caught my breath and choked me out of my game. I started unmolested and struggled over another lump into my second game: Christ-in-all-men.

The lumps were closer together now—almost consolidating. Christ-in-all-men.

In the woman in the corner with the purple-scarlet painted cheeks and the purple blotched lips and the hungry restless light quick-snapping like fox-fire, in her eyes!

Maybe the tears were run together. I could not see Christ-in-all-men there.

Then I saw the hands: dark brown skin laid in thin grey-rimmed patches, like an alligator's back. Joints jutting like nodes on a bough; hands laid carefully, one on the other on blue denim trousers.

Working hands. Hands that had toiled.

Christ-in-all-men. Christ, the carpenter.

Now the game could be played in earnest....

He started to work when he was seven. Ran errands, lugged coal, lugged oil, lugged washing, sold papers. In the summer when the sun baked the flesh on your hands; in the winter when the blood stands still in your hands; when the wind blows.

Went to school sometimes and labored hard to keep the pen from wavering between the round end fingers.

Worked after school: Labored as hard with shovel as with pencil. Ran elevators; shoveled coal; washed windows; scrubbed; dug.

Graduated from "grades" and "got a job."

Worked.

Up at five; swallowed coffee.

Slumbered down town, through a city half asleep, half preparing to go to bed. Scraped square-toed across a wharf, across a plank, down into a ship.

A strange ship that never moved, never went anywhere. Just stood at the wharf like a Christmas toy, with its insides fractured. All around, other ships whisked, frittered, floated—according to their bulk—in and out.

This one stood unashamed and motionless while you shoveled and shoveled and shoveled until the step from bin to boiler seemed a pit in which your feet were fastened. Until the blood in your arms and the blood in your head met together and your heart seemed crowded out of it all.

Shoveled until sooty sweat stood in pools on the floor and shrank the few garments on your back into a back that shoved them off at once with the hard quiver of muscles. Shoveled and shoveled—until it was dinner time.

Sometimes he washed his hands; sometimes he did not. Days there were when he went above; then there were days when he dragged to a pile of coal close by the bin and sat to eat.

Slices of bread, half a loaf thick. Slabs of meat too wide to swallow well. Cold coffee in a flanked bottle—something sweet at the end.

Perhaps a snatch of sleep; perhaps a friendly smoke—then the shovel.

The feel in the handle for the "good grip" and then from bin to boiler—from boiler to bin until six.

World in dim twilight when he went down; world in dim twilight when he came up.

Home. At first one narrow room with a trough bed, a jig-saw mirror and a gas-light with an asthmatic flaw in it. A light that sputtered and flickered to hide from the hateful brassy brown paper on the wall and the piece of shade at the window that was pretending to be what it wasn't.

He washed his hands now and spread vaseline on spots where the skin wore thin. Then he set forth into a world deliciously dark now. To dance halls, where violins and pianos wooed melody, syncopation and one another with a breath-taking seduction. Where made a deal wood floor glassy and an over-robust figure a pleasing armful and made your teeth show whether you would or not.

Shovels were shovels; with music, lights, perfume and gay colors, a mere poke in the ribs worthy of a deep-seated laugh. A brown face, ashy with white powder and dyed with too-bright rouge make your breath draw in twice to once coming out.

Sometimes he played at pool and cards.

Sometimes it was lodge night and he added new dignity as carefully as he adjusted his white apron.

At church he took collection, balancing the basket carefully between thumb and forefinger. One night in June there was a revival and all the lost found Christ and themselves. As usher he helped most of them to and from the forward bench—politely ministering, protecting, urging on at once.

One slight brown girl, crying as if she had truly melted in tears wavered up from a back seat. His sturdy hands steadied her and their strength only made her cry the more.

He guided her into a bench and looked down into her round, plump, seal-smooth face with its tilted eyes too far apart and a nose, flat and yet up-turned. A face full of the strangely unrelated features found only in a race as marred by tampering, crossing and back-crossing as the Negro.

"Don't worry, Christ ain't hard to find if you're looking for Him," the hand said.

"I'm afraid of everything! Life. Religion. Help me! Where is God? Where is Christ? Tell me! What shall I do to be saved?" pleaded the eyes.

Of course, it was but a second, but he felt very, very strong and knowing and weak and awkward all at the same time. He withdrew rapidly and came back to be sick just as rapidly after the service—and stayed.

Patted her arm one dazing night as she mouthed almost in a whisper: "I do."

Patted her when she trembled into the unspeakable uncertainty of birth.

Patted little brown cheeks, wreathed in smiles. Wiped snubbed brown noses and patted young heads flung care-free and unknowing; high.

Shoveled. Sometimes with soul out of the ship and at home. Shoveled desperately, almost frantic with fear lest they lay him off at the wrong time.

Shoveled the children out of two rooms into four. Out of grades into high school. Out of gingham and into crepe-de-chine.

Shoveled and dreamed about some day with its hours of ease, its house with a yard and garden; its plenty to eat; its plenty to drink and something in the bank to put 'him and her away decent.'

Shoveled, patted, soothed, smoothed, steadied souls welcoming back from the fearsome darkness of the unknown and Judgment.

Shoveled, patted, smoothed, smoothed—steadied.

Laid carefully one upon the other on a lap of blue denim.

Snakes, peopling the forest. Christ-in-all-men.

Which game, Oh God, must I play most? ...   *Opportunity* 3.32 (August 1925): 235–237.

MADEMOISELLE 'TASIE—A STORY

by Eloise Bibb Thompson

It was all on account of that last Mardi Gras Ball. Mlle. 'Tasie felt it. Indeed she was absolutely sure of it. The night had been cold and damp and she had not had a wrap suited for such weather. So she had gone in a thin blue organdy dress, the best she owned, with simply a white scarf thrown over her shoulders. A "white" scarf, and a "blue" organdy. It was scandalous! And her "tante" but one year dead. No wonder bad luck in the shape of ill health had followed her ever since—putting off her mourning so soon to go to a Mardi Gras ball. Well, what was the use of thinking of it now? "De milk has been speel, so to speak," she mused, "eet ees a grat wonder, yes, as de doctah say, I deed not go into decline."

But try as she would Mlle. 'Tasie could not stop thinking of it. The heavy cold caught at that Mardi Gras ball was the direct cause of her being about to take the momentous step that she was planning to take to-day. And momentous it was, for a fact; there was not the slightest doubt about that. How it would all end, she was at a loss to comprehend.

Not that it counted so much with her now; for ill health and depravation had forced her to accept with resignation many things that before had seemed unendurable. But her neighbors ah! and her relatives who knew how thoroughly she had formerly hated the very thing that she was about to do. Mon Dieu! What were they not saying of her now?

Yes, there was a time in her life when Mlle. 'Tasie would rather have fainted, actually, than to even so much as have been seen on the street with a certain kind of individual, which she and her class designated as an "Negre Americain" aux grosses oreilles"—an American Negro with large ears. In a word, with a black American. How many times had she not said of such a contingency, "h-eet h-ees a thing not to be thought h-of h-at h-all." And now—O, now see what she was fixing to do!

For Mlle. 'Tasie was a Creole lady of much less color than a black American. Be pleased to know first of all, that there are colored Creoles as well as white Creoles, just as there are Creole eggs and Creole cabbages. Any person or article brought up in the French Quarter of old New Orleans, the downtown section across Canal street, is strictly Creole. And to carry the thought to its final conclusion is, in the highest sense of the word, Superior. Mlle. 'Tasie was what was designated by her lightly colored contemporaries, in a whisper, as "un briquet," that is, she had a reddish yellow complexion, and very crinkled red hair. "In a whisper," because the hair of a "briquet" is usually so short and so crinkled that no one feels flattered at being called one. Yet in spite of all that, Mlle. 'Tasie was a Creole, came of a good family, and spoke "patois French" for the most part, sometimes English, and hence, thinking herself superior, had not mingled with English–speaking Negroes known as Americans. And being yellow, she had never been accustomed, until now, to even be on speaking terms with blacks.

It was positive fact, Mlle. 'Tasie had come of an exceptional Creole family. Everyone with whom she came in contact knew that well. How could they help knowing it when they had heard it so often? As for the corner grocer from whom Mlle. 'Tasie bought charcoal for her diminutive furnace—she couldn't afford a stove—and various other sundries for her almost empty larder, why, had you awakened him from the soundest sort of sleep, he could have told you about her family, word for word, as she had told it, embellished it with glowing incidents, as she had done. In a word, he could have torn that family tree to pieces for you, from root to apex at the shortest possible notice. That was because, of course, so many circumstances had given rise there in his store, for the frequent telling of her history; having incurred, as she had, the hostility of her English–speaking black neighbors, at whom she rarely ever glanced. By some strange trick of fortune, these black neighbors were much better off than she, and loved to put their little ones up to poking fun at her whenever she came to the store for the small purchases that she made—beans and rice, almost invariably, with a whispered request for meat-scrapings, thrown in by way of courtesy. Poking their heads in roguishly, thru the half-opened door, these taunting, little urchins were wont to scream at her, "Dere she goes, fellahs, look at 'er. A picayune o' red beans, a picayune o' rice, lagricappe salt meat to make it taste nice." Then Mlle. 'Tasie would laugh loudly to hide her embarrassment. Pityingly she would say with up-lifted shoulders and outwardly turned palms, "'Ow you ken h-expec' any bettah fum dem? My own fadda h-own plenty lak dat.—But h-I know, me. H-eet ees dey madda, yes, teach 'em lak dat. She ees mad 'cause h-I doan associate wid 'her. But 'her mahster wheep 'er back plenty, yes. Me—h-I nevva know a mahster, me. H-ask h-any one eef h-eet ees de trufe, and dey will tell you."

None knew better of Mlle. 'Tasie's family than Paul Donseigneur, the clothier of Orleans Street. Paul had been owned by Mlle. 'Tasie's father, Jose Gomez, who belonged to that class of mulattoes known before the Civil War as free men of color. Escaping from the island of Guadeloupe, during a West Indian insurrection, Gomez had settled in New Orleans, purchased a number of slaves and a goodly portion of land, ultimately becoming a "rentier" of some importance. Paul, a tailor by trade, had been assigned to the making of his master's clothes. Because of his efficiency and estimable character, he had rapidly risen in favor. But Paul was aspiring also. He longed for his freedom and begged permission of Gomez to purchase it from him. After much deliberation, the latter surprised him one day with a gift of himself,—that is, with free papers showing a complete bestowal of Paul and all that he possessed, upon himself.

Paul was deeply grateful. It was not in his nature, as it was with so many of his race, to hate the hand that lifted him, when that hand was black. He never forgot the generosity of his master, nor his subsequent assistance in the way of influence, immediately after the Civil War, toward the foundation of the very business into which he was still engaged.

But times had been precarious in New Orleans for any business venture during the early years of reconstruction. Especially so for Paul, efficient and alert though he was, yet an ex-slave, with no capital and no business experience. During the general upheaval, he saw nothing of his master who, like many men of his class, had kept well out of the way of all danger. When the smoke and powder of wrought-up feelings had at last cleared away, Paul again looked about for his old master, with the hope that things had not gone so badly with him. But alas! There was not the slightest trace of him to be found. Had he left the city, or had he only gone uptown? Either step would have been fatal for Paul's finding him. For people in the Faubourg Ste. Marie—the American quarter—were as completely lost at any time, to the people of the French quarter, as if they had gone to New York.

Paul knew that out of that great family of many sons and daughters, only two remained. At least there had been two when last he saw them—his master and Mlle. 'Tasie, the youngest daughter. How had they fared during all those troublous times? Wherever they were, he knew that they were poorer; for the Civil War had stripped them of most of their possessions, and unprepared as they were for service, they would never be able to retrieve them, he was certain. It was all very sad. But there was nothing to be done, since he knew not where to find them.

Chance, however, some ten years later, just before the opening of our story, discovered to him one member of that family at least, Mlle. 'Tasie. He was crossing over to the French Market, one morning, from the old Place D' Armes, en route to his clothing store, when he heard the guttural tones of a Gascon restauranteur raised in heated discussion. Hastening to the spot he saw seated upon one of the high stools, before the oil cloth-covered counter of the "coffee stand," a shabby, little colored woman in a black calico dress, much-worn but speckless gaiters, and a long, cotton crepe veil thrown back from a faded straw hat—a perfect picture of bitter poverty trying to be genteel.

Thru the cracked and much be-scratched mirror that ran around the wall of the "coffee stand" in front of her, he saw reflected her small pinched face, courageously rouged and powdered, and recognized Mlle. 'Tasie.

Wonderingly, Paul took in the situation. The merchant's prices, it seems, were higher than some of the others in the market, or more, anyhow, than Mlle. 'Tasie had been aware of. When the time came to pay for what she had eaten, small tho' it was, she was unprepared to do so completely. Hence the Gasconian war of words.

Mlle. 'Tasie's embarrassment at the turn of affairs was beyond description. With trembling fingers peeping out from cotton lace mittens that time had worn from black to green, she hurriedly lowered her veil, then fumbled about in her lace-covered reticule as if seeking the desired change with absolute fright. Going forward, Paul touched the enraged Gascon on the elbow. The sight of his proffered coin was like oil poured upon troubled waters. Mlle. 'Tasie was saved.

When she lifted her tearful eyes to Paul's pitying face, he saw even through the faded veil what privation had done for her. Gently he took her by the arm and led her to the Place D'Armes thru which he had but just passed. And there upon one of the benches, he coaxed out of her, her whole tragic story. She told him how their poverty becoming greater and greater, she and her father had hidden themselves as he had feared, in the American quarter across Canal Street, away from the people who had known them in brighter days; of her father's subsequent death, and her struggles to support herself with her needle; of her many failures at doing so, because of her complete unpreparedness. To his reproachful query as to why she had not appealed to him, she had answered, shoulders up-lifted and mitten-covered palms turned outward, "'Ow h-I could do dat, my deah? Come wid my 'and h-open to you? Me? H-eet was h-impossible."

But he assured her that the success of his tailoring business slow, to be sure, but very promising always, was such that he might have aided them at the time and was in a still better position of doing so now. She shook her head sadly at the suggestion, and her tears began to flow anew. "Me, h-I would die first!" she exclaimed passionately, "befo' h-I come to dat."

When she grew calmer, he told her of an innovation that he was planning to bring into his business—the making of blue jeans into trousers for the roustabouts on the Levee, and for other workmen. She mopped her eyes and looked at him with interest. It was jean trousers, she had told him, that she had been attempting to make ever since she had been a breadwinner. But the factories from which she had taken work to be done at home had been so exacting, "docking" her for every mis-stitch, and every mistake in hemming so that there was always very little money coming to her when she finally brought her work back.

Paul surmised as much but had already thought out a plan to meet the situation. He would put her directly under the seamstress in charge, for supervision and instruction. And so, at length, Mlle. 'Tasie was installed into the business of her former slave. Her backwardness in learning to do the work set before her was, at first, disheartening. But for the sake of "Auld Lang Syne," Paul nerved himself into forbearance. When, at last, she gave evidence of beginning to "get the hang" of it, so to speak, she caught a dreadful cold at the Creole Mardi Gras ball.

For Mlle. 'Tasie was still young enough to long for pleasure with something of the ardor of her happier days. She was no "spring chicken" she confessed to herself sadly; she was thirty-seven "come nex' h-All Saints Day," but that did not prevent her from wanting to "h-enjoy herse'f, yes, once een a w'ile h-any 'ow." Since Mardi Gras comes but once a year, she decided to forget everything and got to the ball. Closing her eyes at the horror of the thing—the laying aside of the mourning which she had worn for the past year for an aunt whom she had never seen—she went down into her trunk and pulled out an ancient blue organdy and a thin, white scarf. It had been years since she had seen these things, for some distant relative of Mlle. 'Tasie was always passing away, and custom compelled her to remember them during a long period of mourning.

Perhaps it was her act of rebellion against this custom, she kept telling herself, that had brought such disaster to her health. Oh, if she only had to do it again, how differently would she act. It had meant the almost giving up of her work at Paul Donseigneur's store, for most of her time was now spent at home trying to get well.

Calling one day to ascertain for himself the cause of these frequent absences, Paul became much disturbed at her appearance. She looked more frail than he had ever seen her. Certainly work, he decided, was not what she wanted now, but care and attention. She had already refused from him, in her foolish pride, everything but what she strictly earned by the sweat of her brow. How to help her now in this new extremity was indeed a problem. He must think it out. And Paul left her more perplexed than he had been before.

As he was about to enter his clothing store, he was stopped by a traveling salesman, Titus Johnson, from whom he bought most of the cottonade that he used. Titus was large and black, well-fed and prosperous-looking, with a fat cigar forever in his mouth and a shiny watch-chain forever dangling from his vest. Titus was the idol of his associates, likewise the idol of the "cook-shop" where he ate, for besides ordering the largest and most expensive steaks they carried, together with hot biscuits, rice, French fried potatoes, buck-wheat cakes and coffee, he tipped the waiter lavishly and treated him to a cigar besides. Not only generous, but full of good cheer was Titus, his hearty laugh resounding from one end of the street to the other. Especially so after he had told one of his characteristic jokes, which invariably brought as great a laugh from himself as from his listeners. Simple, whole-hearted and kindly, Titus Johnson met the world with a beaming face and received much of its goodwill in return.

"Hey dere, boss," he shouted to Paul from across the narrow street, as the latter stood upon the sill of his odd-looking suit-store. "I ben waitin' for you. W'at kep' you?" In a stride or two he was at Paul's side. "I hope you ain't gotten so prosperous," he continued, "dat you dodgin' us black folks and fixin' ter pass for white. Hya! Hya! Hya! Hya!'" His great voice sounded to the end of the block.

"No danger," smiled back Paul, whose physiognomy forbade any such intention. "I been visitin' de sick. An'"—

"De sick? Whose sick?" Titus' face bespoke concern.

"Mlle. 'Tasie," replied Paul, "De lil' lady who use to sit at dat machine dere by de winda."

"Sho' nuf?" Titus knitted his brow. "I knows her. Leastwise, I mean, I seen her time and time agin.—An' you say she's sick?—Very sick? You know, I useter lak ter look at dat lil' body. 'Pere lak dere wuz somepun' so pitiful lak, about her."

"Pitiful," reiterated Paul, his face again wearing its troubled look, "Mais, it is worse yet. It is trageec."

"You doan say!—She ain' goin' die, is she?"

"Ah, I hope not dat, me.—All de same, she need right now plenty of care, yes. An'—you know, some one to see after her—right." He led the way thru a disordered room where women of various shades of color were bending over their work, some at machines, others at long cutting tables. When at length he reached his crowded little office in another wing of the building, he sank heavily into a chair, and motioned Titus to be seated also.

Why talk of business now, he mused, when his mind was so full of Mlle. 'Tasie, and her problems? She was downright troublesome, to say the least, he decided. Why had she let herself get into that weakened condition, just when she was beginning to earn enough to support herself decently? And she was so foolishly proud! It was absurd, it was ridiculous.

Before he knew it, Paul found himself telling the whole story to Titus Johnson—the history of Mlle. 'Tasie and of her remarkable family. Titus was astounded. He had heard that before the Civil War, New Orleans had held a number of men of his race who had not only been free themselves, but had owned a large number of slaves, but he had thought it only a myth. But here, according to Paul, was a representative of that class. He longed to meet her; to really be able, as he expressed it to Paul, to give her "his compliments." Never had he felt so much interest in any one before. When she got better, if Paul would arrange a meeting between them, he would be glad to take her some evening to the Spanish Fort—the great, white way of New Orleans—or to see the Minstrel—some place where she could laugh and forget her troubles.

Titus, like most English-speaking Negroes, felt no inferiority to the better-born of his race, like Mlle. 'Tasie. Had anyone suggested it, he would have scoffed at the possibility of her looking down upon him. For was she not also a Negro? However low his origin, she could never get any higher than he. Her status had been fixed with his by the highest authority.

Paul pondered Titus' proposition. He knew Mlle. 'Tasie's prejudice to color, but he refrained from mentioning it. She was in great extremity and Titus was both prosperous and big-hearted. Suppose a match could be arranged between them in spite of her prejudices. Stranger things than that had happened. Paul was an old man, and had seen women, bigger than Mlle. 'Tasie let go their prejudices under economic stress. When insistently the stomach growls, he mused, and the shoe pinches, women cease to discriminate and take the relief at hand. The thing was worth trying.

Looking up into the eager face of Titus Johnson, Paul promised to arrange a meeting between him and Mlle. 'Tasie at the first possible opportunity. Titus went away highly pleased. Although he would not have named it so the thing promised an adventure; and, approaching forty tho he was, it was nevertheless very pleasing to contemplate. As for Paul, that man realized with misgiving that there was much preparatory work to be done on Mlle. 'Tasie before the meeting could even be mentioned to her. He, therefore, planned to set about doing so without delay.

But strange to say, when he approached her on the subject, Mlle. 'Tasie was more tractable than he dared hope for. Undoubtedly she had been doing some serious thinking for herself. Here she was, she told herself, rapidly approaching forty, her health broken down, and no help in the way of a husband anywhere in sight. How different it was from what she had dreamed. Long before this, she had thought the "right one" would have turned up—and she would have been settled down for life. But alas! the men she had wanted, had all gone to handsomer and younger women. She had been too discriminating, too exacting. That was her trouble. But all that must stop now. She must feel herself blessed if some well-to-do man, even tho he met but half her requirements, should come along and propose to her.

And so when Paul, after dilating upon the prosperity and big-heartedness of the black "Americain," advised in the most persuasive of language that she permit him to call, instead of flaring up, as he had been sure she would do, she heard him out quietly and consented after a moment or two of sad reflection. Surprised beyond measure at the ready acquiescence, he sat looking at her for a full second in open-mouthed wonderment. Then he congratulated her on her good, common sense; shook hands with her heartily and left, promising to bring Titus as soon as he returned to New Orleans.

But Mlle. 'Tasie's cheerfulness after that seemed to have deserted her. Her health, tho far from being completely restored, enabled her, before long, to resume her duties at the store. And there she sat at her machine, perplexed and miserable, a dumb spectacle of defeat. Since necessity compelled an abandonment of her prejudices, she reflected, if only she could leave the neighborhood before this black man called, so that those who knew her sentiments might not have the pleasure of laughing in her face. But to be compelled to remain right there and receive with a pretense of welcome before a group of peeping, grinning back-biters, the very kind of "Negre aux grosses oreilles" whom she had been known to look down upon—Mon Dieu!—how could one be cheerful after that?

Yet in spite of this dread, the time came at last, when Titus, traveling agent that he was, again arrived in New Orleans. To say that he was eager to meet Mlle. 'Tasie, is far, very far, from the mark, for he fairly lived in the expectation. But Titus was a natural psychologist. On the day of his arrival, contrary to his usual custom, he remained away from Paul's store during the hours that he knew Mlle. 'Tasie was in it, although he saw to it that Paul got a message that he had not only arrived in town, but would call on Mlle. 'Tasie that evening. For an adventure such as this must not be spoiled thru haste or lack of preparation.

"Ef you wants a lady to 'preciate you," Titus mused, "you must fust have de proper settin'; 'cause settin's everything. You mustn't on'y fix to 'self up for her, but you must git her all worked up fixin' up for you. Den w'en you comes in swaggerin' on yo' cane, a half hour or a hour after she expected you to come, you got her jes' as anxious to meet you, as you is her. All de rest den is clare sailin'."

Arriving in the morning, Titus spent the day shopping. Nothing but the newest apparel must meet her eye when first she beheld him. When Paul, therefore, rather falteringly presented him in the evening after having apprised Mlle. 'Tasie much earlier of his expected visit, Titus was resplendent in brand new "malakoff"–bottom trousers, well creased in the middle, a "coffin-back" shaped coat to match, creaking red brogues, lemon colored tie, and a deep red Camellia in the buttonhole of his coat.

To a man, less self-conscious than Titus was at the moment, the meeting would have been a dismal failure. For there was nothing of cordiality in Mlle. 'Tasie's subdued and rather mournful greeting. Paul was so impressed by the chilliness of it, that he beat a hasty retreat, leaving Romeo to the winning of his Juliet unaided. And Titus proved that he was not unequal to the task, for he soon had Mlle. 'Tasie's interest in spite of herself. He told her of his travels up and down the State, described the dreary islands of Barataria with their secret passages, where smugglers and robbers nearly a hundred years before had hidden their ill-gotten gains. And had a world of news about the folks of Opoulousas and Point Coupee, places she had not visited since she was a girl. When at length he rose to go, she felt something very much like regret, and before she knew it, entirely forgetful of his color, she had invited him to call again.

Not only was Titus' "gift of gab" an asset to his courting but his frequent absences from town as well. For Mlle. 'Tasie could not help but feel the contrast between the quiet, uneventful evenings without him, and the cheer, the jokes, the kindly gossip that filled the hours when he was there. If only she had not to face the "pryers" with explanations as to why she had become suddenly so "cosmopel" as to bring into her home an American of his complexion. Relatives whom she hadn't seen for months hearing of the strangeness of her conduct, came way from Bayou Rouge and Elysian Fields Street to beg her with tears in their eyes not to disgrace them by allying herself with an American "Negre aux grosses oreilles."

Mlle. 'Tasie became distracted. The opinion of these people meant much to her; but after long thinking she realized that the protection and assistance of a husband would mean vastly more. So she nerved herself to defiance. When at length, Titus proposed marriage to her, she accepted him, not with any feeling stronger than liking, it is true, but with a sense of great satisfaction that now she was for a truth, to have a protector at last.

But now that the marriage day had arrived she felt all the old hesitancy, the repugnance, the sensitiveness because of what the others had been saying, come back upon her, with painful intensity. Yet, nevertheless, she bravely prepared for the event. When, at length, evening came and her shabby, little parlor where the ceremony took place became enlivened by the cheery presence of Titus and the only two invited guests—Paul and the owner of the "cookshop" where Titus ate—Mlle. 'Tasie felt herself grow calmer.

After partaking lavishly of her "wine sangeree" and her carefully-prepared teacakes, the guests finally took their departure, Titus went up to her and putting both his fat hands upon her shoulders, smiled reassuringly into her eyes. "Well, ole' woman," he said, "you an' me goin' ter make it fine! It's me an' you 'ginst de whole worl', you heah me? You po' lil' critter! You needs somebody ter take care o' you, an' Titus Johnson is de one ter take de job." Then Mlle. 'Tasie felt a sort of peace steal over her, the harbinger, she hoped, of happier days.

[*Opportunity* 3.33 (September 1925): 272–276]

JOHN REDDING GOES TO SEA

by Zora Neale Hurston

The villagers said that John Redding was a queer child. His mother thought he was too. She would shake her head sadly, and observe to John's father: "Alf, it's too bad our boy's got a spell on 'im."

The father always met this lament with indifference, if not impatience.

"Aw, woman, stop dat talk 'bout conjure. Tain't so nohow. Ah doan want Jawn tuh git dat foolishness in *him*."

"Cose you allus tries tuh know mo' than me, but Ah ain't so ign'rant. Ah knows a heap mahself. Many and manys the people been drove outa their senses by conjuration, or rid tuh deat' by witches."

"Ah keep on telling yuh, woman, tain's so. B'lieve it all you wants tuh, but dontcha tell mah son none of it."

Perhaps ten-year old John *was* puzzling to the simple folk there in the Florida woods for he was an imaginative child and fond of day-dreams. The St. John River flowed a scarce three hundred feet from his back door. On its banks at this point grew numerous palms, luxuriant magnolias and bay trees with a dense undergrowth of ferns, cat-tails and ropegrass. On the bosom of the stream float millions of delicately colored hyacinths. The little brown boy loved to wander down to the waters edge, and, casting in dry twigs, watch them sail away down stream to Jacksonville, the sea, the wide world and John Redding wanted to follow them.

Sometimes in his dreams he was a prince, riding away in a gorgeous carriage. Often he was a knight bestride a fiery charger prancing down the white shell road that led to distant lands. At other times he was a steamboat captain piloting his craft down the St. John River to where the sky seemed to touch the water. No matter what he dreamed or who he fancied himself to be, he always ended by riding away to the horizon; for in his childish ignorance he thought this to be farthest land.

But these twigs, which John called his ships, did not always sail away. Sometimes they would be swept in among the weeds growing in the shallow water, and be held there. One day his father came upon him scolding the weeds for stopping his sea-going vessels.

"Let go mah ships! You ole mean weeds you!" John screamed and stamped impotently. "They wants tuh go 'way. You let 'em go on!"

Alfred laid his hand on his son's head lovingly. "What's mattah, son?"

"Mah ships, pa," the child answered weeping. "Ah throwed 'em in to go way off an' them ole weeds won't let 'em."

"Well, well, doan cry. Ah thought youse uh grown up man. Men doan cry lak babies. You musn't take it too hard 'bout yo' ships. You gotta git uster things gittin' tied up. They's lotser folks that 'ud go on off too ef somethin' didn' ketch 'em en' hol 'em!"

Alfred Redding's brown face grew wistful for a moment, and the child noticing it, asked quickly: "Do weed tangle up folks too, pa?"

"Now, no, chile, doan be takin' too much stock of what Ah say. Ah talks in parables sometimes. Come on, les go on tuh supper."

Alf took his son's hand, and started slowly toward the house. Soon John broke the silence.

"Pa, when Ah gets as big as you Ah'm goin' farther than them ships. Ah'm goin' to where the sky touches the ground."

"Well, son, when Ah wuz a boy Ah said Ah wuz goin' too, but heah Ah am. Ah hopes you have bettah luck than me."

"Pa, Ah betcha Ah seen somethin' in th' wood-lot you ain't seen!"

"Whut?"

"See dat tallest pine tree ovah dere how it looks like a skull wid a crown on?"

"Yes, indeed!" said the father looking toward the tree designated. "It do look lak a skull since you call mah 'tention to it. You 'magine lotser things nobody else evah did, son!"

"Sometimes, Pa dat ole tree waves at me just aftah the sun does down, an' makes me sad an' skeered, too."

"Ah specks youse skeered of de dahk, thas all, sonny. When you gits biggah you won't think of sich."

Hand in hand the two trudged across the plowed land and up to the house, the child dreaming of the days when he should wander to far countries, and the man of the days when he might have—and thus they entered the kitchen.

Matty Redding, John's mother, was setting the table for supper. She was a small wiry woman with large eyes that might have been beautiful when she was young, but too much weeping had left them watery and weak.

"Matty," Alf began as he took his place at the table, "Dontcha know our boy is different from any othah chile roun' heah. He 'lows he's goin' to sea when he gits grown, en' Alf reckon Ah'll let 'im."

The woman turned from the stove, skillet in hand. "Alf, you ain't gone crazy, is you? John kain't help wantin' tuh stray off, cause he's got a spell on 'im; but *you* oughter be shamed to he encouragin' him."

"Ain't Ah done tol' you forty times not tuh tahk dat low-life mess in front of mah boy?"

"Well, ef tain't no conjure in de world, how come Mitch Potts been layin' on his back six mont's an' de doctah kain't do 'im no good? Answer me dat. The very night John wuz bawn, Granny seed ole Witch Judy Davis creepin outer dis yahd. You know she had swore tuh fix me fuh maryin' you, 'way from her darter Edna. She put travel dust down fuh mah chile, dat's whut she done, tuh make him walk 'way fum me. An' evuh sence he's been able tuh crawl, he's been tryin tuh go."

"Matty, a man doan need no travel dust tuh make 'im wanter hit de road. It jes' comes natcheral fuh er man tuh travel. Dey all wants tuh go at time or other but they kain't all get away. Ah wants mah John tuh go an' see cause Ah wanted to go mah self. When he comes back Ah kin see them furrin places wid his eyes. He kain't help wantin' tuh go cause he's a man chile!"

Mrs. Redding promptly went off into a fit of weeping but the man and boy ate supper unmoved. Twelve years of married life had taught Alfred that far from being miserable when she wept, his wife was enjoying a bit of self-pity.

Thus John Redding grew to manhood, playing, studying and dreaming. He attended the village school as did most of the youth about him, but he also went to high school at the county seat where none of the villagers went. His father shared his dreams and ambitions, but his mother could not understand why he should wish to go strange places where neither she nor his father had been. No one of their community had ever been farther away than Jacksonville. Few indeed had even been there. Their own gardens, general store, and occasional trips to the county seat—seven miles away—sufficed for all their needs. Life was simple indeed with these folk.

John was the subject of much discussion among the country folk. Why didn't he teach school instead of thinking about strange places and people? Did he think himself better than any of the "gals" there about that he would not go a-courting any of them? He must be "fixed" as his mother claimed, else where did his queer notions come from? Well, he was always queer, and one could not expect the man to be different from the child. They never failed to stop work at the approach of Alfred in order to be at the fence and inquire after John's health and ask when he expected to leave.

"Oh," Alfred would answer, "jes' as soon as his mah gits reconciled to th' notion. He's a mighty dutiful boy, mah John is. He doan wanna hurt her feelings."

The boy had on several occasions attempted to reconcile his mother to the notion, but found it a difficult task. Matty always took refuge in self-pity and tears. Her son's desires were incomprehensible to her, that was all. She did not want to hurt him. It was love, mother love, that made her cling so desperately to John.

"Lawd knows," she would sigh, "Ah nevah wuz happy an' nevah specks tuh be."

"An' from yo' actions," put in Alfred hotly, "You's determined *not* to be."

"Thas right, Alfred, go on an' 'buse me. You allus does. Ah knows Ah'm ign'rant an' all dat, but dis is mah son. Ah bred an' born 'im. He kain't help from wantin' to go rovin' cause travel dust been put down fuh him. But mebbe we kin cure 'im by discouragin' the idee."

"Well, Ah wants mah son tuh go; an' he wants tub go too. He's a man now, Matty. An' we mus' let John hoe his own row. If it's travelin' twon't be foh long. He'll come back to us bettah than when he went off. What do you say, son?"

"Mamma," John began slowly, "It hurts me to see you so troubled over my going away; but I feel that I must go. I'm stagnating here. This indolent atmosphere will stifle every bit of ambition that's in me. Let me go mamma, please. What is there here for me? Why, sometimes I get to feeling just like a lump of dirt turned over by the plow—just where it falls there's where it lies—no thought or movement or nothing. I wanter make myself somethin—not just stay where I was born."

"Naw, John, it's bettah for you to stay heah and take over the school. Why don't you marry and settle down?"

"I don't *want* to, mamma. I want to go away."

"Well," said Mrs. Redding, pursing her mouth tightly, "You ainta goin' wid *mah* consent!"

"I'm sorry mamma, that you won't consent. I am going nevertheless."

"John, John, mah baby! You wouldn't kill yo' po' ole mamma, would you? Come, kiss me, son."

The boy flung his arms about his mother and held her closely while she sobbed on his breast. To all of her pleas, however, he answered that he must go.

"I'll stay at home this year, mamma, then I'll go for a while, but it won't be long. I'll come back and make you and papa oh so happy. Do you agree, mama dear?"

"Ah reckon tain' nothin' tall fuh me to do else."

Things went on very well around the Redding home for some time. During the day John helped his father about the farm and read a great deal at night.

Then the unexpected happened. John married Stella Kanty, a neighbor's daughter. The courtship was brief but ardent—on John's part at least. He danced with Stella at a candy-pulling, walked with her home and in three weeks had declared himself. Mrs. Redding declared that she was happier than she had ever been in her life. She therefore indulged in a whole afternoon of weeping. John's change was occasioned possibly by the fact that Stella was really beautiful; he was young and red-blooded, and the time was spring.

Spring-time in Florida is not a matter of peeping violets or bursting buds merely. It is a riot of color in nature—glistening green leaves, pink, blue, purple, yellow blossoms that fairly stagger the visitor from the north. The miles of hyacinths lie like an undulating carpet on the surface of the river and divide reluctantly when the slow-moving alligators push their way log-like across. The nights are white nights for the moon shines with dazzling splendor, or in the absence of that goddess, the soft darkness creeps down laden with innumerable scents. The heavy fragrance of magnolias mingled with the delicate sweetness of jasmine and wild roses.

If time and propinquity conquered John, what then? These forces have overcome older men.

The raptures of the first few weeks over, John began to saunter out to the gate to gaze wistfully down the white dusty road; or to wander again to the river as he had done in childhood. To be sure he did not send forth twig-ships any longer, but his thoughts would in spite of himself, stray down river to Jacksonville, the sea, the wide world—and poor home-tied John Redding wanted to follow them.

He grew silent and pensive. Matty accounted for this by her ever-ready explanation of "conjuration." Alfred said nothing but smoked and puttered about the barn more than ever. Stella accused her husband of indifference and made his life miserable with tears, accusations and pouting. At last John decided to bring matters to a head and broached the subject to his wife.

"Stella, dear, I want to go roving about the world for a spell. Would you stay here with papa and mama and wait for me to come back?"

"John, is you crazy sho' nuff? If you don't want me, say so an' I kin go home to mah folks."

"Stella, darling, I do want you, but I want to go away too. I can have both if you'll let me. We'll be *so* happy when I return...."

"Naw, John, you cain't rush me off one side like that. You didn't hafta marry me. There's a plenty othahs that would have been glad enuff tuh get me; you know Ah wan't educated befo' han'."

"Don't make me too conscious of my weakness, Stella. I know I should never have married with my inclinations, but it's done now, no use to talk about what is past. I love you and want to keep you, but I can't stifle that longing for the open road, rolling seas, for peoples and countries I have never seen. I'm suffering too, Stella, I'm paying for my rashness in marrying before I was ready. I'm not trying to shirk my duty—you'll be well taken care of in the meanwhile."

"John, folks allus said youse queer and tol' me not to marry yuh, but Ah jes' loved yuh so Ah couldn't help it, an' now to think you wants tuh sneak off an' leave me."

"But I'm coming back, darling ... listen Stella."

But the girl would not. Matty came in and Stella fell into her arms weeping. John's mother immediately took up arms against him. The two women carried on such an effective war against him for the next few days that finally Alfred was forced to take his son's part.

"Matty, let dat boy alone, Ah tell you! Ef he wuz uh home-buddy he'd be drove 'way by you all's racket."

"Well, Alf, dat's all we po' wimmen kin do. We wants our husbands an' our sons. John's got uh wife now, an' he ain't got no business to be talkin' 'bout goin' nowheres. I lowed dat marrin' Stella would settle him."

"Yas, dat's all you wimmen study 'bout—settlin' some man. You takes all de get-up out of 'em. Jes' let uh fellah mak uh motion lak gettin' somewhere, an' some 'oman'll begin tuh hollah 'Stop theah! where's you goin'? Don't fuhgit you belongs tuh me.'"

"My Gawd! Alf! Whut you reckon Stella's gwine do? Let John walk off an' leave huh?"

"Naw, git outer huh foolishness an' go 'long wid him. He'd take huh."

"Stella ain't got no call tah go crazy 'cause John is. She ain't no woman tuh be floppin' roun' from place tuh place lak some uh dese reps follerin' uh section gang."

The man turned abruptly from his wife and stood in the kitchen door. A blue haze hung over the river and Alfred's attention seemed fixed upon this. In reality his thoughts were turned inward. He was thinking of the numerous occasions upon which he and his son had sat on the fallen log at the edge of the water and talked of John's proposed travels. He had encouraged his son, given him every advantage his own poor circumstances would permit. And now John was home-tied.

The young man suddenly turned the corner of the house and approached his father.

"Hello, papa."

"'Lo, son."

"Where's mama and Stella?"

The older man merely jerked his thumb toward the interior of the house and once more gazed pensively toward the river. John entered the kitchen and kissed his mother fondly.

"Great news, mamma."

"What now?"

"Got a chance to join the Navy, mama, and go all around the world. Ain't that grand?"

"John, you shorely ain't gointer leave me an' Stella, is yuh?"

"Yes, I think I am. I know how both of you feel, but I know how *I* feel, also. You preach to me the gospel of self-sacrifice for the happiness of others, but you are unwilling to practice any of it yourself. Stella can stay here—I am going to support her and spend all the time I can with her. I am going—that's settled, but I want to go with your good will. I want to do something worthy of a strong man. I have done nothing so far but look to you and papa for everything. Let me learn to strive and think—in short, be a man."

"Naw, John, Ah'll nevah give mah consent. I know yous hard-headed jes' l-ak yo' paw; but if you leave dis place ovah mah head, Ah nevah wants you toh come back heah no moh. Ef Ah wuz laid on de coolin' board, Ah doall want yuh standin' ovah me, young man. Doan even come neah mah grave, you ongrateful wretch!"

Mrs. Redding arose and flung out of the room. For once, she was too incensed to cry. John stood in his tracks, gone cold and numb at his mother's pronouncement. Alfred, too, was moved. Mrs. Redding banged the bed-room door violently and startled John slightly. Alfred took his son's arm, saying softly: "Come, son, let's go down to the river."

At the water's edge they halted for a short space before seating themselves on the log. The sun was setting in a purple cloud. Hundreds of mosquito hawks darted here and there, catching gnats and being themselves caught by the lightning-swift bullbats. John abstractly snapped in two the stalk of a slender young bamboo. Taking no note of what he was doing, he broke it into short lengths and tossed them singly into the stream. The old man watched him silently for a while, but finally he said: "Oh, yes, my boy, some ships get tangled in the weeds."

"Yes papa they certainly do. I guess I'm beaten—might as well surrender."

"Nevah say die. Yuh nevah kin tell what will happen."

"What *can* happen? I have courage enough to make things happen; but what can

I do against mamma! What man wants to go on a long journey with his mother's curses ringing in his ears? She doesn't understand. I'll wait another year, but I am going because I must."

Alfred threw an arm about his son's neck and drew him nearer but quickly removed it. Both men instantly drew apart, ashamed for having been so demonstrative. The father looked off to the wood-lot and asked with a reminiscent smile: "Son, do you remember showin' me the tree dat looked lak a sekelton head?"

"Yes, I do. It's there still. I look at it sometimes when things have become too painful for me at the house, and I run down there to cool off and think. And every time I look at it, papa, it laughs at me like it had some grim joke up its sleeve."

"Yuh wuz always imagin' things, John; things that nobody else evah thought on!"

"You know, papa, sometimes—I reckon my longing to get away makes me feel this way.... I feel that I am just earth, *soil* lying helpless to move myself, but *thinking*. I seem to hear herds of big beasts like horses and cows thundering over me, and rains beating down; and winds sweeping furiously over—all acting upon me, but me, well, just soil, *feeling* but not able to take part in it all. Then a soft wind like love passes over and warms me, and a summer rain comes down like understanding and softens me, and I push a blade of grass or a flower, or maybe a pine tree—that's the ground thinking. Plants are ground thoughts, because the soil can't move itself. Whenever I see little whirls of dust sailing down the road I always step aside—I don't want to stop 'em 'cause they're on their shining way—moving! Oh, yes, I'm a dreamer.... I have such wonderfully complete dreams, papa. They never come true. But even as my dreams fade I have others."

"Yas, son, Ah have them same feelings exactly, but Ah can't find no words lak you do. It seems lak you an' me see wid de same eyes, hear wid de same ears an' even feel de same inside. Only thing you kin talk it an' Ah can't. But anyhow you speaks for me, so whut's the difference?"

The men arose without more conversation. Possibly they feared to trust themselves to speech. As they walked leisurely toward the house Alfred remarked the freshness of the breeze.

"It's about time the rains set in," added his son. "The year is wearin' on."

After a gloomy supper John strolled out into the spacious front yard and seated himself beneath a China-berry tree. The breeze had grown a trifle stronger since sunset and continued from the southeast. Matty and Stella sat on the deep front porch, but Alfred joined John under the tree. The family was divided into two armed camps and the hostilities had reached that stage where no quarter could be asked or given.

About nine o'clock an automobile came flying down the dusty white road and halted at the gate. A white man slammed the gate and hurried up the walk toward the house, but stopped abruptly before the men beneath the China-berry. It was Mr. Hill, the builder of the new bridge that was to span the river.

"Howdy John, Howdy Alf: I'm mighty glad I found you. I am in trouble."

"Well now, Mist' Hill," answered Alfred slowly but pleasantly. "We'se glad you foun' us too. What trouble could *you* be having now?"

"It's the bridge. The weather bureau says that the rains will be upon me forty-eighty hours. If it catches the bridge as it is now, I'm afraid all my work of the past five months will be swept away, to say nothing of a quarter of a million dollars worth of labor and material. I've got all my men at work now and I thought to get as many extra hands as I could to help out tonight and tomorrow. We can make her weather tight in that time if I can get about twenty more."

"I'll go, Mister Hill," said John with a great deal of energy. "I don't want papa out on that bridge—too dangerous."

"Good for you, John!" cried the white man. "Now if I had a few more men of your brawn and brain, I could build an entirely new bridge in forty-eight hours. Come on and jump into the car. I am taking the men on down as I find them."

"Wait a minute. I must put on my blue jeans. I won't be long."

John arose and strode to the house. He knew that his mother and wife had overheard everything, but he paused for a moment to speak to them.

"Mamma, I am going to work all night on the bridge."

There was no answer. He turned to his wife.

"Stella, don't be lonesome. I will he home at day-break."

His wife was as silent as his mother. John stood for a moment on the steps, then resolutely strode past the women and into the house. A few minutes later he emerged clad in his blue overalls and brogans. This time he said nothing to the silent figures rocking back and forth on the porch. But when he was a few feet from the steps he called back: "Bye, mamma; bye, Stella," and he hurried on down the walk to where his father sat.

"So long, papa. I'll be home around seven."

Alfred roused himself and stood. Placing both hands upon his son's broad shoulders he said softly: "Be keerfull son, don't fall or nothin'."

"I will, papa. Don't *you* get into a quarrel on my account."

John hurried on to the waiting car and was whirled away.

Alfred sat for a long time beneath the tree where his son had left him and smoked on. The women soon went indoors. On the night breeze were borne numerous scents: of jasmine, of roses, of damp earth of the river, of the pine forest near by. A solitary whip-poor-will sent forth his plaintive call from the nearby shrubbery. A giant owl roared and boomed from the wood lot. The calf confined in the barn would bleat and be answered by his mother's sympathetic "moo" from the pen. Away down in Lake Howell Creek the basso profundo of the alligators boomed and died, boomed and died.

Around ten o'clock the breeze freshened, growing stiffer until midnight when it became a gale. Alfred fastened the doors and bolted the wooden shutters at the windows. The three persons sat about a round deal table in the kitchen upon which stood a bulky kerosene lamp, flickering and sputtering in the wind that came in through the numerous cracks in the walls. The wind rushed down the chimney blowing puffs of ashes about the room. It banged the cooking utensils on the walls. The drinking gourd hanging outside by the door played a weird tattoo, hollow and unearthly, against the thin wooden wall.

The man and the women sat silently. Even if there had been no storm they would not have talked. They could not go to bed because the women were afraid to retire during a storm and the man wished to stay awake and think with his son. Thus they sat: the women hot with resentment toward the man and terrified by the storm; the man hardly mindful of the tempest but eating his heart out in pity for his boy. Time wore heavily on.

And now a new element of terror was added. A screech-owl alighted on the roof and shivered forth his doleful cry. Possibly he had been blown out of his nest by the wind. Matty started up at the sound but fell back in her chair, pale and trembling: "My Gawd!" she gasped, "dat's a sho' sign uh death."

Stella hurriedly thrust her hand into the salt-jar and threw some into the chimney of the lamp. The color of the flame changed from yellow to blue-green but this burning of salt did not have the desired effect—to drive away the bird from the roof. Matty slipped out of her blue calico wrapper and turned it wrong side out before replacing it. Even Alfred turned one sock.

"Alf," said Matty, "What do you reckon's gonna happen from this?"

"How do Ah know, Matty?"

"Ah wisht John hadn't went away from heah tuh night."

"Humh."

Outside the tempest raged. The palms rattled dryly and the giant pines groaned and sighed in the grip of the wind. Flying leaves and pine-mast filled the air. Now and then a brilliant flash of lightning disclosed a bird being blown here and there with the wind. The prodigious roar of the thunder seemed to rock the earth. Black clouds hung so low that the tops of the pines were among them moving slowly before the wind and made the darkness awful. The screech owl continued his tremulous cry.

After three o'clock the wind ceased and the rain commenced. Huge drops clattered down upon the shingle roof like buckshot and ran from the eaves in torrents. It entered the house through the cracks in the walls and under the doors. It was a deluge in volume and force but subsided before morning.

The sun came up brightly on the havoc of the wind and rain calling forth millions of feathered creatures. The white sand everywhere was full of tiny cups dug out by the force of the falling raindrops. The rims of the little depressions crunched noisily underfoot.

At daybreak Mr. Redding set out for the bridge. He was uneasy. On arriving he found that the river had risen twelve feet during the cloudburst and was still rising. The slow St. Johns was swollen far beyond its banks and rushing on to sea like a mountain stream, sweeping away houses, great blocks of earth, cattle, trees—in short anything that came within its grasp. Even the steel framework of the new bridge was gone!

The siren of the fiber factory was died down for half an hour, announcing the disaster to the country side. When Alfred arrived therefore he found nearly all the men of the district there.

The river, red and swollen, was full of floating debris. Huge trees were swept along as relentlessly as chicken coops and fence rails. Some steel piles were all that was left of the bridge.

Alfred went down to a group of men who were fishing members of the ill-fated construction gang out of the water. Many were able to swim ashore unassisted. Wagons backed up and were hurriedly driven away loaded with wet shivering men. Two men had been killed outright, others seriously wounded. Three men had been drowned. At last all had been accounted for except John Redding. His father ran here and there asking for him, or calling him. No one knew where he was. No one remembered seeing him since daybreak.

Dozens of women had arrived at the scene of the disaster by this time. Matty and Stella, wrapped in woolen shawls, were among them. They rushed to Alfred in alarm and asked where was John.

"Ah doan know," answered Alfred impatiently. "That's what Ah'm trying to fin' out now."

"Do you reckon he's run away?" asked Stella thoughtlessly.

Matty bristled instantly.

"Naw," she answered sternly, "he ain't no sneak."

The father turned to Fred Mimms, one of the survivors and asked him where John was and how had the bridge been destroyed.

"Yuh see," said Mimms, "when dat turrible win' come up we wuz out 'bout de middle of de river. Some of us wuz on de bridge, some on de derrick. De win' blowed so hahd we could skeercely stan' and Mist' Hill tol' us tuh set down fuh a spell. He's 'fraid some of us mought go overboard. Den all of a sudden de lights went out—guess de wires wuz blowed down. We uoz all sheered tuh move for slippin' overboard. Den dat rain commenced—an' Ah nevah seed such a downpour since de flood. We set dere and someone begins tuh pray. Lawd how we did pray tuh be spared! Den somebody raised a song an' we sung, you hear me, we sung from de bottom of our hearts till daybreak. When the first light come we couldn't see nothin' but fog everywhere. You couldn't tell which wuz water an' which wuz lan'. But when de sun come up de fog begin to liff, an' we could see de water. Dat fog wuz so thick an' heavy dat it wuz huggin' dat river lak a windin' sheet. And when it rose we saw dat de river had rose way up durin' the rain. My Gawd, Alf! it wuz runnin' high—so high it nearly touched de span of de bridge—an' red as blood! So much clay, you know from lan' she done overflowed. Comin' down stream, as fas' as 'press train wuz three big pine trees. De first one wuzn't fohty feet from us and there wasn't no chance to do nothin' but pray. De fust one struck us and shook de whole works an' befo' it could stop shakin' the other two hit us an' down we went. Ah thought Ah'd never see home again."

"But, Mimms, where's John?"

"Ah ain't seen him, Alf, since de logs struck us. Mebbe he's swum ashore, mebbe dey picked him up What's dat floatin' way out dere in de water?"

Alfred shaded his eyes with his gnarled brown hand and gazed out into the stream. Sure enough there was a man floating on a piece of timber. He lay prone upon his back. His arms were outstretched, and the water washed over his brogans but his feet were lifted out of the water whenever the timber was buoyed up by the stream. His blue overalls were nearly torn from his body. A heavy piece of steel or timber had struck him in falling for his left side was laid open by the thrust. A great jagged hole wherein the double fists of a man might be thrust, could plainly be seen from the shore. The man was John Redding.

Everyone seemed to see him at once. Stella fell to the wet earth in a faint. Matty clung to her husband's arm, weeping hysterically. Alfred stood very erect with his wife clinging tearfully to him, but he said nothing. A single tear hung on his lashes for a time then trickled slowly down his wrinkled brown cheek.

"Alf! Alf!" screamed Matty, "Dere's our son. Ah knowed when Ah heard dat owl las' night...."

"All see 'im, Matty," returned her husband softly.

"Why is yuh standin' heah? Go git mah boy."

The men were manning a boat to rescue the remains of John Redding when Alfred spoke again.

"Mah po' boy, his dreams never come true."

"Alf," complained Matty, "Why doancher hurry an' git my boy—doantcher see he's floatin' on off?"

Her husband paid her no attention but addressed himself to the rescue-party.

"You all stop! Leave my boy go on. Doan stop 'im. Doan' bring 'im back for dat ole tree to grin at. Leave him g'wan. He wants tuh go. Ah'm happy 'cause dis mawnin' mah boy is goin' tall sea, *he's goin' tuh sea.*"

Out on the bosom of the river, bobbing up and down as if waving good bye, piloting his little craft on the shining river road, John Redding floated away toward Jacksonville, the sea, the wide world—at last. [*Opportunity* 4.37 (January 1926): 16–21]

THE LEGEND OF NGURANGURANE (THE SON OF THE CROCODILE)

by Violette de Mazia*

There was in the olden times—it is a long time since that, quite a long time—a very great magician, and it was Ngurangurane, the son of the Crocodile.

And here is how he was born, that is the first thing: what he did and how he died, that is the second. To tell all his actions it is impossible, and, besides, who would remember them?

Here is how he was born, that is the first thing.

At that time, the Fangs were living on the bank of a large river, large, so large that one could not see the other side; they used to fish from the border. But they did not go on the river; no one yet had taught them how to build canoes: he who taught it to them, it was Ngurangurane. Ngurangurane taught this art to the men of his family, and, his family, they were the men, they were the Fangs.

In the river lived an enormous crocodile, the master crocodile; his head was longer than this cabin, his eyes were bigger than a whole kid, his teeth could cut a man in two as I cut a banana, criss! He was covered with enormous scales: a man could strike him with his javelins, tō, toō, but pfat, the javelin fell back; and he who did thus he could be the most robust man; pfut, the javelin fell back. It was a terrible animal.

Now, one day, he came into the village of Ngurangurane; but this one was not yet born. And the one who was commanding the Fangs was a great chief, and he commanded many men. He commanded the Fangs and others besides. Ngan Esa, the

Translated from Blaise Cenrars "Anthologie Negre"

master crocodile, came then one day into the village of the Fangs and he calls the chief:—"Chief, I call you."

The chief hastens at once. And the crocodile-chief said to the man-chief:—"Listen attentively."

And the man-chief answered:—"Ears" (that is to say, I listen well).

"What you shall do from to-day on, this is it. Each day I am hungry, and I think that the flesh of the man is better for me than the flesh of the fish. Each day, you shall bind a slave and you shall bring it for me on the bank of the river, a man one day, a woman the next day, and, on the first day of each moon, a young girl well painted with baza and all shining with grease. You shall do thus. If you dare to disobey me, I shall eat your whole village. There! This is ended. Speak not."

And the crocodile-chief, without adding a word, returned to the river. And in the village, they began mournful lamentations. And each one said: "I am dead." Each one said it, the chief, the men, the women. The next day, in the morning, when the sun rose, the crocodile-chief was on the bank of the river. "Wah! Wah!" his mouth was enormous, longer than this cabin, his eyes were large like a whole kid. The crocodiles that you see to-day are not crocodiles any more! And they hastened to bring to the crocodile-chief that which he had asked, a man one day a woman the next day and, on the first day of each moon, a young girl painted with red and all shining with grease. They did that which the crocodile-chief had ordered, and none dared disobey, for he had everywhere his warriors, the other crocodiles.

And the name of this crocodile, it was Ombure: the waters were obeying Ombure, the forests were obeying Ombure, his "men" were everywhere, he was master of the forest, but he was above all master of the water. And, each day, he ate either a man, or a woman, and he was very pleased and very friendly to the Fangs. But these, finally, had given all their slaves and, to buy some, the chief had handed over all his riches. He had not one coffer left, not one elephant tooth! He had to give a man, a Fang man! And the chief of the Fangs gathered all his people in the common cabin; he spoke to them a long, long time, and after him, the other warriors spoke also a long time. When the conference was ended, everyone agreed and thought with one heart that they should depart. The chief then said:—"Now this question of departure is settled: we shall go far, far from here, beyond the mountains. When we shall be far, very far from the river, beyond the mountains, Ombure will not be able to reach us, and we shall be happy." And it was decided that they would not renew the plantings, and that at the end of the season the whole tribe would leave the banks of the river. And thus it was done.

At the beginning of the dry season, when the waters are low, and traveling is good, the tribe started to march. The first day, they went quickly, quickly, as quickly as they could go. Each man hurried his women, and the women quickening their pace, marched in silence, bending under the load of the provisions and the household utensils, because they were carrying away everything, pots, dishes, pestles, baskets, swords and hoes, everything; each woman had her load and she had it heavy. She had it heavy because, with all that, they had also dried some monioc and carried it away. She had it heavy, because she had also to carry the children, the little ones who could not walk and those who were beginning to walk.

And they had to be silent: the men were silent, the women were silent, and the children were crying, but the mothers said:—"be quiet." The great chief was at the head: he led the march, for it was he who knew the country the best: he often had been hunting, and around his neck he wore a necklace of a big monkey's teeth.

He was indeed a great hunter.

On the first day, many looked behind them, they thought they heard the crocodile: Wah! Wah! And he who was at the end felt cold in his heart! But they heard nothing. And on the second day, the march was the same, and they heard nothing. And on the third day, the march was the same, and they heard nothing.

On the first day, however, the crocodile-chief had come out of the water, according to his habit, in order to come to the place where he used to find the slave who had been destined to him. He comes: "Wah! Wah!" Nothing. What is this? He takes at once the road to the village.

"Chief of the men, I call you."

Nothing! He hears no noise; he enters, all the cabins are abandoned; he goes to the plantations, the plantations are abandoned: "Wah! Wah!" he goes through all the villages, all the villages are abandoned; he goes through all the plantations, all the plantations are abandoned.

Ombure then flies into a terrible rage and dives again into the river to consult his fetish, and he sings:

"You who command to the waters, spirits of the waters,
All you who obey me, it is I who calls to you,
Come, come to the call of your master,
Answer without delay, answer immediately
I shall send the lightning which flashes through the sky,
I shall send the thunder which breaks all on his path,
I shall send the wind of the tempest that tears down the banana tress.
I shall send the storm which falls from the clouds and sweeps everything in front of him.
And all will answer to the voice of their master.
All you who obey me, show me the road,
The road which those who have fled have taken.
Spirits of the waters, answer."

But to his great surprise, the spirits of the waters do not answer, not a single one answers!

What then had happened? This. Before leaving his village, the chief of the men had offered great sacrifices. He had offered a great sacrifice to the spirits of the waters, asking them to remain mute and they had promised. They had promised: "We will say nothing."

Ombure begins again a conjuration, a stronger one still:

"You who command to the waters, spirits of the waters,
All you who obey me, it is I who calls you...."

And the spirits of the waters, forced to obey, appear before Ombure:—"Where are the men, have they used your roads?" "We have seen nothing, they have not used our roads." (And Ombure says: "They have not used the roads of the waters: the spirits of the waters could not disobey me).

And he called the spirits of the forests:

"You who command to the forests, spirits of the forests,
All you who obey me, it is I who calls to you,
Come, come to the call of your master,
Answer without delay, answer immediately.

> I shall send the lightning that flashes through the sky,
> I shall sent the thunder which breaks all on his path,
> I shall sent the wind of the tempest which tears down the banana trees,
> I shall sent the storm which falls from the clouds and sweeps everything in front of him
> And all will answer to the voice of their master.
> All you who obey me, show me the road,
> The road which those who have fled have taken,
> Spirits of the forests, answer."

But, to his great surprise, of all the spirits of the forests, not one spirit answers, all are silent.

What, then had happened? This. Before leaving his village, the chief of the men had offered great sacrifices. He had offered a great sacrifice to the spirits of the forests, asking them to remain mute, and they had promised: "We will say nothing."

Ombure began again a conjuration, a stronger one still:

> "You who command to the forests, spirits of the forests,
> All you who obey me, it is I who calls you."

And the spirits of the forests, forced to obey, appear before Ombure.—"Where are the men, have they passed through your roads?" And the spirits of the forests answer: "They have passed through our roads."

And, successively, Ombure calls the spirits of the day, the spirits of the night, and, thanks to them, he knows the road which the Fangs have taken.

They have told him the news!

And when Ombure had ended his enchantment, he knew the road which the fugitive Fangs had taken. These had concealed their path in vain. Ombure knew their road. Who had told it to him? The Lightning, the Wind, the Storm had told it to him; the Lightning, the Wind and the Storm.

The Fangs continued their march for a long time, a very long time.. They crossed the mountains and the great chief consulted his fetish:—"Shall we stop here?" and the fetish, who, since a long time, since the first day, was obeying the orders of Ombure (but this the chief did not know), the fetish answered:—"No, you shall not stop here, this is not a good place."

They crossed the plains, and when they had crossed the plains and had found again the great forest, the forest that never ends, the great chief consulted his fetish:—"Shall we stop here?" And the fetish, once more, answered:—"Further yet."

They arrived finally in a great plain, in front of a great lake which closed all passage, and the great chief consulted his fetish:—"Shall we stop here?" And the fetish who obeyed Ombure answered: "Yes, you shall stop here."

And the Fangs had walked many days and many moons: the little children had become youths, the youths had become young warriors and the young warriors, matured men. They had walked many days and many moons. They stopped on the banks of the lake. They built new villages, plantings were made and everywhere the corn gave its new yield. The chief then gathered his men in order to give a name to the village, and they called it: Akurengan (Deliverance-from-the-Crocodile.)

But, that very night, towards midnight, a great noise is heard and a voice cries:—"Oh! come, come here." And all go out, very scared. What do they see? (The moon was very bright.) Ombure was in the middle of the village. He was in front of the great chief's cabin. What is to be done? Where to can one run? Where can one hide? No one dared to think about it! And when the great chief came out to see what was happening, "You," he was the first one to be taken! With a single bite, Ombure cut him in two! "Kro, Kro, Kwas!"—"There! Akurengan," he said.

And he returned towards the lake.

The trembling warriors chose at once another chief, the brother of the last one, according to the law; and, in the morning, they took the wife of the last chief and they bound her on the bank of the lake, as an offering to Ombure. And he came; and the woman was crying. "Kro, Kro!" he ate her. But, in the evening, he came back to the village and called the chief:

—"Chief, I call you."

And this one, trembling, answered:—"I listen."

—"This is what I command to you, I, Ombure, and you shall do it. Every day, you shall bring two men, one man in the morning, one man in the evening, and the next day, you shall bring me two women, one woman in the morning, one woman in the evening. And on the first day of each moon, two young girls painted with red and shining with oil. Go, this is I, Ombure, the King of the forest, this is I, Ombure, the King of the Waters.

And thus they did during many years. Each morning, each evening, Ombure had his meal: two men one day, two women the next day two and young girls on the first day of the month. Thus it happened for a long time. In order to pay Ombure, the Fangs made war far, far away. And everywhere they were the victors, because Ombure, the crocodile-chief, protected them, and they became great warriors.

But the years passed, one after the other, and for a long time the Fangs had renewed their plantings. And they were tired of Ombure. How he had caught them in their flight, that, they had forgotten. And they were very tired of Ombure.

And they had forgotten. And the young men said: "We are tired, let us leave." And the young men left in front, the warriors followed, and the women carried the bundles after the warriors.

The next morning Ombure came on the bank of the lake to seek his daily food, as was his habit. He looks, he searches. Nothing. He comes to the village. Nothing. What does he do? He takes his fetish and calls at once the spirits of the forest. "This is what commands to you, Ombure, your master," he says to them. "My slaves have fled, they are in your domain, let all passages close in front of them. Wind of the storm, break the trees in front of them; spirit of the thunder, spirit of the lightning, blind their eyes! Go, it is Ombure who commands you."

And they go. The roads close in front of the Fangs, the big trees fall, darkness invades everything. In despair, they have to return to the lake, and there Ombure awaits them. But Ombure is old, instead of two men, he now demands: "You shall give me each day two young girls as a sacrifice."

And the Fangs had to obey and each day had to bring two young girls to Ombure, two young girls painted with red and shining and rubbed with oil. It is their Wedding festival.

They cry and mourn, the daughters of the Fangs; they cry and mourn: it is the festival of the sad betrothing.

They cry and mourn in the evening; in the morning, they do not cry nor do they mourn: their mothers do not hear from them any more: they are at the bottom of the lake, in the grotto where Ombure lives: they serve him, and he makes his food of them.

But one day, there happened this: the young girl who had to be taken to the bank of the river that evening; the young girl whose turn had come, it was Alena-Kiri, the child of the chief. She was young and she was beautiful. And, in the evening, she was bound on the bank of the lake, with her companion. The companion did not return, but the next day, when daylight appeared again, the chief's daughter was still there. Ombure had spared her.

Therefore they called her: "Dawn has come."

But nine months later, the chief's daughter had a child, she had a son. In remembrance of his birth, this boy was named Ngurangurane, the son of the crocodile.

Ngurangurane was then the son of Ombure, the crocodile-chief: this is the first story. Ngurangurane was thus born.

Here is the second story: the death of Ombure.

Ngurangurane, the child of the crocodile Ombure and the chief's daughter, grew, grew, grew, each day. From a child, he became a youth, from a youth he became a young man. He is then the chief of his people. He is a powerful chief and a very learned magician. In his heart he had two desires: to avenge the death of the chief of this his race, his mother's father, and to free his people from the tribute which the crocodile exacted.

To attain this end, here is what he did:

In the forest there is a sacred tree, this you know; and this tree they call it "palm-tree." Cut a palm-tree: the sap flows, flows abundantly, and if you wait two or three days, after having enclosed it in earthen vessels, you will have the dzan, the drink that makes the heart happy. This, we know it now, but our fathers did not know it. He who taught it to them, it was Ngurangurane, and the first one who drank the dzan it is Ombure, the crocodile chief. Who taught Ngurangurane about the dzan? It was Ngonomane, the fetish stone which his mother had given him.

Now, following Ngonomane's advice, Ngurangurane did thus:

"Take all the earthen vessels that you possess, all of them, bring them into my cabin." He said that to the women: they brought then all the earthen vessels they possessed, and there were many and many of them. "Go, all, into the forest," he said to them again, "near the brook with the clay and make more vessels yet." And they went to the brook with the clay and made some vessels, many of them.

"Let us go into the forest," he said to the men, "Let us go and you will cut the trees that I shall show to you." And they went, all together, with hatchets and with knives, and they cut the trees which Nguranguane showed them. These trees, they were palm trees. And when they were all cut, they collected the sap which was flowing abundantly from the wounds. The vessels were brought (the women did that), the old vessels and the new ones, and when all were there they filled them with the dzan, and the women carried them back to the village. Every day, Ngurangurane tasted the liquor, the men wanted to do like him, but this he forbid them by a great eki. A man said: "Since Ngurangurane drinks of it, I shall drink of it." And he drank of it, but in secret, and it went to his head. Nguranguane came near him and killed him with a gun shot.

Three days later, Ngurangurane gathered his men, the men and the women, and said to them: "This is the time, take the vessels and come with me to the bank, near the lake. They took the vessels and went with him. When they were on the bank of the lake, Ngurangurane ordered this to his men: "Bring on the bank all the vessels." And they did it. "Bring the clay for which I sent you," he said to the women, and thus they did. And, on the bank of the lake, with the soft clay they built two large basins, carefully beaten with the feet, carefully smoothed with the palm of the hands. Then, into the two basins, they pour all the dzan that was contained in the vessels, without leaving one drop; Ngurangurane begins a great fetish, and they break then all the vessels, and they throw them into the lake. They bind the two captives near the basins and everyone goes back to the village.

Nguranguane stays alone, hidden near the basins.

At the usual hour, the crocodile comes out of the water. He goes towards the captives who were trembling with fear; but, first of all:

"What is this?" he says as he comes near the basins. "What is this?" He tastes a little of the liquid. The liquor seems good to him and he cries aloud: "This is good: from tomorrow on I shall order to the Fangs to give me some of it every day."

And Ombure, the crocodile, drank the dzan. He drank it to the last drop, forgetting the captives. When he had finished, he sang:

"I have drunk the dzan, the liquor which bring joy to the heart;
"I have drunk the dzan,
"I have drunk the dzan, my heart is rejoicing,
"I have drunk the dzan.
"The master whom all obey, it is I,
"I, the great chief, I, Ombure.
"It is I, Ngan, I am the master.
"Ombure is master of the waters,
"Ombure is master of the forests.
"It is I, the master whom all obey.
"I am the master.
"I have drunk the dzan, the liquor which brings joy to the heart;
"I have drunk the dzan.
"I have drunk the dzan, my heart rejoices;
"I have drunk the dzan."

He sings, and on the sand, forgetting the captives, he falls asleep, joy in his heart.

Ngurangurane at once comes near Ombure asleep; with a strong rope, and helped by the captives, he binds him to the post, then brandishing with force his javelin, he strikes the sleeping animal: on the thick scales, the javelin bounces back without touching the crocodile, and this one, still asleep, shakes himself and says: "What is this a mosquito has bitten me."

Ngurangurane takes his hatchet, his strong stone hatchet; with an immense blow he strikes the sleeping animal; the hatchet bounces back without wounding the animal; this one begins to move: the two captives, terrified, run away. Ngurangurane makes then a powerful fetish: "Thunder," he ways, "thunder, it is you whom I call, bring me your arrows."

And the lightning came. But when he learns that he must kill Ombure: "It is your father," he cries, "and it is my master." And, frightened, he went away. But Alena Kiri comes to help her son, and she brings Ngonomane, the fetish stone. And in the name of Ngonomane, Ngurangurane says: "Lightning, I command you to strike."

And the lightning strikes, for he could not disobey. On the head, between the eyes, he strikes Ombure, and Ombure remains immobile, thunderstruck, dead. He who has killed him, it is Ngurangurane, but Ngurangurane killed him with the help of Ngonomane.

And the end of this story, here it is:

Ngurangurane hastens back to the village, "All you, men of the village," he says, "all you, come." And they all come on the bank of the lake. Ombure is there, lying dead, immense. "He who has killed Ombure, the crocodile, it is I, Ngurangurane. He who has avenged the chief of his race, it is I; he who has freed you, it is I, Ngurangurane.

All rejoiced and, around the corpse, they danced the fanki, the great funeral dance; they danced the fanki for the spirit of Ombure must be appeased.

And this is the end of Ombure. [*Opportunity* 4.41 (May 1926): 153–155, 170]

THE TYPEWRITER

by Dorothy West

It occurred to him, as he eased past the bulging knees of an Irish wash lady and forced an apologetic passage down the aisle of the crowded car, that more than anything in all the world he wanted not to go home. He began to wish passionately that he had never been born, that he had never been married, that he had never been the means of life's coming into the world. He knew quite suddenly that he hated his flat and his family and his friends. And most of all the incessant thing that would "clatter clatter" until every nerve screamed aloud, and the words of the evening paper danced crazily before him, and the insane desire to crush and kill set his finger twitching.

He shuffled down the street, an abject little man of fifty-odd years, in an ageless overcoat that flapped in the wind. He was cold, and he hated the North, and particularly Boston, and saw suddenly a barefoot pickaninny sitting on a fence in the hot, southern sun with a piece of steaming corn bread and a piece of fried salt pork in either grimy hand.

He was tired, and he wanted his supper, but he didn't want the beans, and frankfurters, and light bread that Net would undoubtedly have. That Net had had every Monday night since that regrettable moment fifteen years before when he had told her—innocently—that such a supper tasted "right nice. Kinda change from what we always has."

He mounted the four brick steps leading to his door and pulled at the bell; but there was no answering ring. It was broken again, and in a mental flash he saw himself with a multitude of tools and a box of matches shivering in the vestibule after supper. He began to pound lustily on the door and wondered vaguely if his hand would bleed if he smashed the glass. He hated the sight of blood. It sickened him.

Someone was running down the stairs. Daisy probably. Millie would be at that infernal thing, pounding, pounding.... He entered. The chill of the house swept him. His child was wrapped in a coat. She whispered solemnly, "Poppa, Miz Hicks an' Miz

Berry's orful mad. They gointa move if they can't get more heat. The furnace's bin out all day. Mama couldn't fix it." He said hurriedly, "I'll go right down. I'll go right down." He hoped Mrs. Hicks wouldn't pull open her door and glare at him. She was large and domineering, and her husband was a bully. If her husband ever struck him it would kill him. He hated life, but he didn't want to die. He was afraid of God, and in his wildest flights of fancy couldn't imagine himself an angel. He went softly down the stairs.

He began to shake the furnace fiercely. And he shook into it every wrong, mumbling softly under his breath. He began to think back over his uneventful years, and it came to him as rather a shock that he had never sworn in all his life. He wondered uneasily if he dared say "damn." It was taken for granted that a man swore when he tended a stubborn furnace. And his strongest interjection was "Great balls of fire!"

The cellar began to warm, and he took off his inadequate overcoat that was streaked with dirt. Well, Net would have to clean that. He'd be damned—! It frightened him and thrilled him. He wanted suddenly to rush upstairs and tell Mrs. Hicks if she didn't like the way he was running things, she could get out. But he heaped another shovelful of coal on the fire and sighed. He would never be able to get away from himself and the routine of years.

He thought of that eager Negro lad of seventeen who had come North to seek his fortune. He had walked jauntily down Boylston Street, and even his own kind had laughed at the incongruity of him. But he had thrown up his head and promised himself: "You'll have an office here some day. With plate-glass windows and a real mahogany desk." But, though he didn't know it then, he was not the progressive type. And he became successively, in the years, bell boy, porter, waiter, cook, and finally janitor in a down town office building.

He had married Net when he was thirty-three and a waiter. He had married her partly because—though he might not have admitted it—there was no one to eat the expensive delicacies the generous cook gave him every night to bring home. And partly because he dared hope there might be a son to fulfill his dreams. But Millie had come, and after her twin girls who had died within two weeks, then Daisy, and it was tacitly understood that Net was done with child-bearing.

Life, though flowing monotonously, had flowed peacefully enough until that sucker of sanity became a sitting-room fixture. Intuitively at the very first he had felt its undesirability. He had suggested hesitatingly that they couldn't afford it. Three dollars the eighth of every month. Three dollars: food and fuel. Times were hard, and the twenty dollars apiece the respective husbands of Miz Hicks and Miz Berry irregularly paid was only five dollars more than the thirty-five a month he paid his own Hebraic landlord. And the Lord knew his salary was little enough. At which point Net spoke her piece, her voice rising shrill. "God knows I never complain 'bout nothin'. Ain't no other woman got less than me. I bin wearin' this same dress here five years, an' I'll wear it another five. But I don't want nothin'. I ain't never wanted nothin'. An' when I does as', it's only for my children. You're a poor sort of father if you can't give that child jes' three dollars a month to rent that typewriter. Ain't 'nother girl in school ain't got one. An' mos' of 'ems bought an' paid for. You know yourself how Millie is. She wouldn't as' me for it till she had to. An' I ain't going to disappoint her. She's goin' to get that typewriter Saturday, mark my words."

On a Monday then it had been installed. And in the months that followed, night after night he listened to the murderous "tack, tack, tack" that was like a vampire slowly drinking his blood. If only he could escape. Bar a door against the sound of it. But tied hand and foot by the economic fact that "Lord knows we can't afford to have fires burnin' an' lights lit all over the flat. You'all gotta set in one room. An' when y'get tired settin' y'c'n go to bed. Gas bill was somep'n scandalous last' month."

He heaped a final shovelful of coal on the fire and watched the first blue flames. Then, his overcoat under his arm, he mounted the cellar stairs. Mrs. Hicks was standing in her kitchen door, arms akimbo. "It's warmin'," she volunteered.

"Yeh," he was conscious of his grime-streaked face and hands, "it's warmin'. I'm sorry 'bout all day."

She folded her arms across her ample bosom. "Tending a furnace ain't a woman's work. I don't blame your wife none 'tall."

Unsuspecting he was grateful. "Yeh, it's pretty hard for a woman. I always look after it 'fore I goes to work, but some days it jes' ac's up."

"Y'oughta have a janitor, that's what y'ought," she flung at him. "The same cullud man that tends them apartments would be willin'. Mr. Taylor has him. It takes a man to run a furnace, and when the man's away all day—"

"I know," he interrupted, embarrassed and hurt, "I know. Tha's right, Miz. Hicks tha's right. But I ain't in a position to make no improvements. Times is hard."

She surveyed him critically. "Your wife called down 'bout three times while you was in the cellar. I reckon she wants you for supper."

"Thanks," he mumbled and escaped up the back stairs.

He hung up his overcoat in the closet, telling himself, a little lamely, that it wouldn't take him more'n a minute to clean it up himself after supper. After all Net was tired and prob'bly worried what with Miz Hicks and all. And he hated men who made slaves of their women folk. Good old Net.

He tidied up in the bathroom, washing his face and hands carefully and cleanly so as to leave no—or very little—stain on the roller towel. It was hard enough for Net, God knew.

He entered the kitchen. The last spirals of steam were rising from his supper. One thing about Net she served a full plate. He smiled appreciatively at her unresponsive back, bent over the kitchen sink. There was no one could bake beans just like Net's. And no one who could find a market with frankfurters quite so fat.

He sank down at his place. "Evenin', hon."

He sees her back stiffen. "If your supper's cold, 'tain't my fault. I called and called."

He said hastily, "It's fine, Net, fine. Piping."

She was the usual tired housewife. "Y'oughta et your supper 'fore you fooled with that furnace. I ain't bothered 'bout them niggers. I got all my dishes washed 'cept yours. An' I hate to mess up my kitchen after I once get it straightened up."

He was humble. "I'll give that old furnace an extra lookin' after in the mornin'. It'll las' all day to-morrow, hon."

"An' on top of that," she continued, unheeding him and giving a final wrench to her dish towel, "that confounded bell don't ring. An'—"

"I'll fix it after supper," he interposed hastily.

She hung up her dish towel and came to stand before him looming large and yellow. "An' that old Miz Berry, she claim she was expectin' comp'ny. An' she knows they must 'a' come an' gone while she was in her kitchen an' couldn't be at her winder to watch for 'em. Old liar," she brushed back a lock of naturally straight hair. "She wasn't expectin' nobody."

"Well, you know how some folks are—"

"Fools! Half the world," was her vehement answer. "I'm goin' in the front room an' set down a spell. I bin on my feet all day. Leave them dishes on the table. God knows I'm tired, but I'll come back an' wash 'em." But they both knew, of course, that he, very clumsily, would.

At precisely quarter past nine when he, strained at last to the breaking point, uttering an inhuman, strangled cry, flung down his paper, clutched at his throat and sprang to his feet, Millie's surprised young voice, shocking him to normalcy, heralded the first of that series of great moments that every humble little middle-class man eventually experiences.

"What's the matter, poppa? You sick? I wanted you to help me."

He drew out his handkerchief and wiped his hot hands. "I declare I must 'a' fallen asleep an' had a nightmare. No, I ain't sick. What you want, hon?"

"Dictate me a letter, poppa. I c'd do sixty words a minute.—You know, like a business letter. You know, like those men in your building dictate to their stenographers. Don't you hear 'em sometimes?"

"Oh, sure, I know, hon. Poppa'll help you. Sure. I hear that Mr. Browning—Sure."

Net rose. "Guess I'll put this child to bed. Come on now, Daisy, without no fuss.—Then I'll run up to pa's. He ain't bin well all week."

When the door closed behind them, he crossed to his daughter, conjured the image of Mr. Browning in the process of dictating, so arranged himself, and coughed importantly.

"Well, Millie—"

"Oh, poppa, is that what you'd call your stenographer?" she teased. "And anyway pretend I'm really one—and you're really my boss, and this letter's real important."

A light crept into his dull eyes. Vigor through his thin blood. In a brief moment the weight of years fell from him like a cloak. Tired, bent, little old man that he was, he smiled, straightened, tapped impressively against his teeth with a toil-stained finger, and became that enviable emblem of American life: a business man.

"You be Miz Hicks, huh, honey? Course we can't both use the same name. I'll be J. Lucius Jones. J. Lucius. All them real big doin' men use their middle names. Jus' kinda looks big doin', doncha think, hon? Looks like money, huh? J. Lucius." He uttered a sound that was like the proud cluck of a strutting hen. "J. Lucius." It rolled like oil from his tongue.

His daughter twisted impatiently. "Now, poppa—I mean Mr. Jones, sir—please begin. I am ready for dictation, sir."

He was in that office on Boylston Street, looking with visioning eyes through its plate-glass windows, tapping with impatient fingers on its real mahogany desk.

"Ah—Beaker Brothers, Park Square Building, Boston, Mass. Ah—Gentlemen: In reply to yours of the seventh instant would state—"

Every night thereafter in the weeks that followed, with Daisy packed off to bed, and Net "gone up to pa's" or nodding inobtrusively in her corner, there was the chameleon change of a Court Street janitor to J. Lucius Jones, dealer in stocks and bonds. He would stand, posturing, importantly flicking imaginary dust from his coat lapel, or, his hands locked behind his back, he would stride up and down, earnestly and seriously debating the advisability of buying copper with the market in such a fluctuating state. Once a week, too, he stopped in at Jerry's, and after a preliminary purchase of cheap cigars, bought the latest trade papers, mumbling an embarrassed explanation: "I got a little money. Think I'll invest it in reliable stock."

The letters Millie typed and subsequently discarded, he rummaged for later, and under cover of writing to his brother in the South, laboriously, with a great many fancy flourishes, signed each neatly typed sheet with the exalted J. Lucius Jones.

Later, when he mustered the courage, he suggested tentatively to Millie that it might be fun—just fun, of course!—to answer his letters. One night—he laughed a good deal louder and longer than necessary—he'd be J. Lucius Jones, and the next night—here he swallowed hard and looked a little frightened—Rockefeller or Vanderbilt or Morgan—just for fun, y' understand! To which Millie gave consent. It mattered little to her one way or the other. It was practice, and that was that she needed. Very soon now she'd be in the hundred class. Then maybe she could get a job!

He was growing very careful of his English. Occasionally—and it must be admitted, ashamedly—he made surreptitious ventures into the dictionary. He had to, of course. J. Lucius Jones would never say "Y'got to" when he meant "It is expedient." And, old brain though he was, he learned quickly and easily, juggling words with amazing facility.

Eventually he bought stamps and envelopes—long, important-looking envelopes—and stammered apologetically to Millie, "Honey, poppa thought it'd help you if you learned to type envelopes, too. Reckon you'll have to do that, too, when y' get a job. Poor old man," he swallowed painfully, "came round selling these envelopes. You know how 'tis. So I had to buy 'em." Which was satisfactory to Millie. If she saw through her father, she gave no sign. After all, it was practice, and Mr. Hennessey had promised the smartest girl in the class a position in the very near future. And she, of course, was smart as a steel trap. Even Mr. Hennessey had said that—though not in just those words.

He had got in the habit of carrying those self-addressed envelopes in his inner pocket where they bulged impressively. And occasionally he would take them out—on the car usually—and smile upon them. This one might be from J. P. Morgan. This one from Henry Ford. And a million-dollar deal involved in each. That narrow, little spinster, who, upon his sitting down, had drawn herself away from his contact, was shunning J. Lucius Jones!

Once, led by some sudden, strange impulse, as an outgoing car rumbled up out of the subway, he got out a letter, darted a quick, shamed glance about him, dropped it in an adjacent box, and swung aboard the car, feeling, dazedly, as if he had committed a crime. And the next night he sat in the sitting-room quite on edge until Net said suddenly, "Look here, a real important letter come to-day for you, pa. Here 'tis. What you s'pse it says," and he reached out a hand that trembled. He made brief explanation. "Advertisement, hon. Thassal."

They came quite frequently after that, and despite the fact that he knew them by heart, he read them slowly and carefully, rustling the sheet, and making inaudible, intelligent comments. He was in these moments, pathetically earnest.

Monday, as he went about his janitor's duties, he composed in his mind the final letter from J. P. Morgan that would consummate a big business deal. For days now letters had passed between them. J. P. had been at first quite frankly uninterested. He had written tersely and briefly. Which was meat to J. Lucius. The compositions of his brain were really the work of an artist. He wrote glowingly of the advantages of a pact between them. Daringly he argued in terms of billions. And at last J. P. had written his next letter would be dedecisive. Which next letter, this Monday, as he trailed about the office building, was writing itself on his brain.

That night Millie opened the door for him. Her plain face was transformed. "Poppa—poppa, I got a job! Twelve dollars a week to start with! Isn't that *swell*!"

He was genuinely pleased. "Honey, I'm glad. Right glad," and went up the stairs, unsuspecting.

He ate his supper hastily, went down into the cellar to see about his fire, returned and carefully tidied up, informing his reflection in the bathroom mirror, "Well, Lucius, you c'n expect that final letter any day now."

He entered the sitting-room. The phonograph was playing. Daisy was singing lustily. Strange. Net was talking animatedly to—Millie, busy with needle and thread over a neat, little frock. His wild glance darted to the table. The pretty, little centerpiece, the bowl and wax flowers all neatly arranged: the typewriter gone from its accustomed place. It seemed an hour before he could speak. He felt himself trembling. Went hot and cold.

"Millie—your typewriter's—gone!"

She made a deft little in and out movement with her needle. "It's the eighth, you know. When the man came to-day for the money, I sent it back. I won't need it no more—now!—The money's on the mantle-piece, poppa."

"Yeh," he muttered. "All right."

He sank down in his chair, fumbled for the paper, found it.

Net said, "Your poppa wants to read. Stop your noise, Daisy."

She obediently stopped both her noise and the phonograph, took up her book, and became absorbed. Millie went on with her sewing in placid anticipation of the morrow. Net immediately began to nod, gave a curious snort, slept.

Silence. That crowded in on him, engulfed him. That blurred his vision, dulled his brain. Vast, white, impenetrable.... His ears strained for the old, familiar sound. And silence beat upon them.... The words of the evening paper jumbled together. He read: J.P. Morgan goes—

It burst upon him. Blinded him. His hands groped for the bulge beneath his coat. Why this—this was the end! The end of those great moments—the end of everything! Bewildering pain tore through him. He clutched at his heart and felt, almost, the jagged edges drive into his hand. A lethargy swept down upon him. He could not move, nor utter sound. He could not pray, nor curse.

Against the wall of that silence J. Lucius Jones crashed and died.

[*Opportunity* 4.43 (July 1926): 220–222, 233–234]

MUTTSY

by Zora Neale Hurston

The piano in Ma Turner's back parlor stuttered and wailed. The pianist kept time with his heel and informed an imaginary deserter that "she might leave and go to Halimufack, but his slow-drag would bring her back," mournfully with a memory of tom-toms running rhythm through the plaint.

Fewclothes burst through the portieres, a brown chrysalis from a dingy red cocoon, and touched the player on the shoulder.

"Say, Muttsy," he stage whispered. "Ma's got a new lil' biddy in there—just come. And say—her foot would make all of dese Harlem babies a Sunday face."

"Whut she look like?" Mutsy drawled, trying to maintain his characteristic pose of indifference to the female.

"Brown skin, patent leather grass on her knob, kinder tallish. She's a lil' skinny, "he added apologetically, "but ah'm willing to buy corn for that lil' chicken."

Muttsy lifted his six feet from the piano bench as slowly as his curiosity would let him and sauntered to the portieres for a peep:

The sight was as pleasing as Fewclothes had stated—only more so. He went on in the room which Ma always kept empty. It was her receiving room—her "front."

From Ma's manner it was evident that she was very glad to see the girl. She could see that the girl was not overjoyed in her presence, but attributed that to southern greenness.

"Who you say sentcher heah, dearie?" Ma asked, her face trying to beam, but looking harder and more forbidding.

"Uh-a-a man down at the boat landing where I got off—North River. I jus' come in on the boat."

Ma's husband from his corner spoke up. "Musta been Bluefront."

"Yeah, musta been him," Muttsy agreed.

"Oh, it's all right, honey, we New Yorkers likes to know who we'se takin' in, dearie. We has to be keerful. Whut did you say yo' name was?"

"Pinkie, yes, mam, Pinkie Jones."

Ma stared hard at the little old battered reticule that the girl carried for luggage—not many clothes if that was all—she reflected. But Pinkie had everything she needed in her face—many many trunks full. Several of them for Ma. She noticed the cold-reddened knuckles of her bare hands too.

"Come on upstairs to yo' room—thass all right 'bout the price—we'll come to some 'greement tomorrow. Jes' go up an take off yo' things."

Pinkie put back the little rosy leather purse of another generation and followed Ma. She didn't like Ma—her smile resembled the smile of the Wolf in Red Riding Hood. Anyway back in Eatonville, Florida, "ladies," especially old ones, didn't put powder and paint on the face.

"Forty-dollars-Kate sure landed a pippin' dis time," said Mutsy, sotto voce, to Fewclothes back at the piano. "If she ain't, then there ain't a hound dawk in Georgy. Ah'm goin' home an' dress."

No one else in the crowded back parlor let alone the house knew of Pinkie's coming. They danced on, played on, sang their "blues" and lived on hotly their intense lives. The two men who had seen her—no one counted ole man Turner—went on playing too, but kept an ear cocked for her coming.

She followed Ma downstairs and seated herself in the parlor with the old man. He sat in a big rocker before a copper-lined gas stove, indolence in every gesture.

"Ah'm Ma's husband," he announced by way of making conversation.

"Now you jus' shut up!" Ma commanded severely. "You gointer git yo' teeth knocked down yo' throat yit for runnin' yo' tongue. Lemme talk to dis gal—dis is *mah* house. You sets on the stool un do nothin' too much tuh have anything tuh talk over!"

"Oh, Lawd," groaned the old man feeling a knee that always pained him at the mention of work. "Oh, Lawd, will you sen' yo' fiery chariot an' take me 'way from heah?"

"Aw shet up!" the woman spit out. "Lawd don't wantcher—devil shouldn't have yuh." She peered into the girl's's face and leaned back satisfied.

"Well, girlie, you kin be a lotta help tuh me 'round dis house if you takes un intrus' in things—oh Lawd!" She leaped up from her seat. "That's mah bread ah smell burnin!..."

No sooner had Ma's feet cleared the room than the old man came to life again. He peered furtively after the broad back of his wife.

"Know who she is," he asked Pinkie in an awed whisper. She shook her head. "You don't ? Dat's Forty-dollars-Kate!"

"Forty-dollars-Kate?" Pinkie repeated open eyed. "Naw, I don't know nothin' 'bout her."

"Sh-h," cautioned the old man. "Course you don't. I fughits you ain't nothin' tall but a young 'un. Twenty-five years ago they all called her dat 'cause she *wuz* 'Forty-dollars-Kate.' She sho' wuz some p'uty 'oman—great big robu' lookin' gal. Men wuz glad 'nough to spend forty dollars on her if dey had it. She didn't lose no time wid dem dat didn't have it."

He grinned ingratiatingly at Pinkie and leaned nearer.

"But you'se better lookin' than she ever wuz, you might—taint no tellin' whut you might do ef you git some sense. I'm a gointer teach you, hear?"

"Yessuh," the girl managed to answer with an almost paralyzed tongue.

"Thass a good girl. You jus' lissen to me an' you'll pull thew alright."

He glanced at the girl sitting timidly upon the edge of the chair and scolded.

"Don't set dataway," he ejaculated. "Yo' back bone ain't no ram rod. Kinda scooch down on the for'ard edge uh de chear lak dis." (He demonstrated by "scooching" forward so far that he was almost sitting on his shoulder-blades.) The girl slumped a trifle.

"Is you got a job yit?"

"Nawsuh," she answered slowly, "but I reckon I'll have one soon. Ain't been in town a day yet."

"You looks kinda young—kinda little biddy. Is you been to school much?"

"Yessuh, went thew eight reader. I'm goin' again when I get a chance."

"Dat so? Well ah reckon ah kin talk some Latin tuh yuh den." He cleared his throat loudly. "Whut's you entitlum?"

"I don't know," said the girl in confusion.

"Well, den, whut's you entrimmins," he queried with a bit of braggadocio in his voice.

"I don't know," from the girl, after a long awkward pause.

"You chillun don't learn nothin' in school dese days. Is you got to 'goes into' yit?"

"You mean long division?"

"Ain't askin' 'bout de longness of it, dat don't make no difference," he retorted. "Sence you goin' to stay heah ah'll edgecate yuh—do yuh know how to eat a fish—uh nice brown fired fish?"

"Yessuh," she answered quickly, looking about for the fish.

"How?"

"Why, you jus' eat it with corn bread," she said, a bit disappointed at the non-appearance of the fish.

"Well, ah'll tell yuh," he patronized. "You starts at de tail an liffs de meat off de bones sorter gentle and eats him clear tuh de head on dat side; den you turn 'im ovah an' commence at de tail again an deat right up tuh de head; den you push *dem* bones way tuh one side an' takes another fish an' so on 'till de end—well, 'till der ain't no mo'!"

He mentally digested the fish and went on. "See," he pointed accusingly at her feet, "you don't even know how tuh warm yoself! You settin' dere wid yo' feet ev'y which a way. Dat ain't de way tuh git wahm. Now look at *mah* feet. Dass right put bofe big toes right togethah—now shove 'em close up tuh de fiah; now lean back so! Dass de way. Ah knows uh heap uh things tuh teach yuh sense you gointer live heah—ah learns alll of 'em while de ole lady is paddlin' roun' out dere in de yard."

Ma appeared at the door an the old man withdrew so far into his rags that he all but disappeared. They went to supper where there was fried fish but forgot all rules for eating it and just ate heartily. She helped with the dishes and returned to the parlor. A little later some more men and women knocked and were admitted after the same furtive peering out through the nearest crack of the door. Ma carried them all back to the kitchen and Pinkie heard the clink of glasses and much loud laughter.

Women came in by ones and twos, some in shabby coats turned up about the ears, and with various cheap but showy hats crushed down over unkempt hair. More men, more women, more trips to the kitchen with loud laughter.

Pinkie grew uneasy. Both men and women stared at her. She kept strictly to her place. Ma came in and tried to make her join the others.

"Come on in, honey, a lil' toddy ain't gointer hurt nobody. Evebody know *me*, ah wouldn't touch a hair on yo' head. Come on in, dearie, all the' men wants tuh meethcer."

Pinkie smelt the liquor on Ma's breath and felt contaminated at her touch. She wished herself back home again even with the ill treatment and squalor. She thought of the three dollars she had secreted in her shoe—she had been warned against pickpockets—and flight but where? Nowhere. For there was no home to which *she* could return, nor any place else she knew of. But when she got a job, she'd scrape herself clear of people who took toddies.

A very black man sat on the piano stool playing as only a Negro can with hands, stamping with his feet and the rest of his body keeping time.

> *Ahm gointer make me a graveyard of mah own*
> *Ahm gointer make me a graveyard of mah own*
> *Carried me down on de smoky Road—*

Pinkie, weary of Ma's maudlin coaxing caught these lines as she was being pulled and coaxed into the kitchen. Everyone in there was shaking shimmies to music, rolling eyes heavenward as they picked imaginary grapes out of the air, or drinking. "Folkes," shouted Ma, "look a heah! Shut up dis racket! Ah wantcher tuh meet Pinkie Jones. She's de bes' frien' ah got." Ma flopped into a chair and began to cry into her whiskey glass.

"Mah comperments!" The men almost shouted. The women were less, much less enthusiastic.

"Dass de las' run uh shad," laughed a woman called Ada, pointing to Pinkie's slenderness.

"Jes' lak a bar uh soap aftah uh hard week's wash," Bertha chimed in and laughed uproariously. The men didn't help.

"Oh, Miss Pinkie," said Bluefront, removing his Stetson for the first time, "Ma'am, also Ma'am, ef you wuz tuh see me settin' straddle of ud Mud-cat leadin' a minner whut ud you think?"

"I-er, oh, I don't know, suh. I didn't know you-er anybody could ride uh fish."

"Stick uh roun' me, baby, an' you'll wear diamon's" Bluefront swaggered. "Lok heah, lil' Pigmeat, youse *some* sharp! If you didn't had but one eye ah'd hink you wuz a needle—thass how sharp you looks to me. Say, mah right foot is itchin'. Do dat mean ah'm gointer walk on some strange ground wid you?"

"Naw, indeedy," cut in Fewclothes. "It jes' means you feet needs to walk in some strange water—wid a lil' red seal lye thowed in."

But he was not to have a monopoly. Fewclothes and Shorty joined the chase and poor Pinkie found it impossible to retreat to her place beside the old man. She hung her head, embarrassed that she did not understand their mode of speech; she felt the unfriendly eyes of the women, and she loathed the smell of liquor that filled the house now. The piano still rumbled and wailed that same song—

> *Carried me down on de Smoky Road*
> *Brought me back on de coolin' board*
> *Ahm gointer make me a graveyard of mah own.*

A surge of cold, fresh air from the outside stirred the smoke and liquor fumes and Pinkie knew that the front door was open. She turned her eyes that way and thought of flight to the clean outside. The door stood wide open and a tall figure in an overcoat with a fur collar stood there.

"Good Gawd, Mutsy! Shet' at do'." cried Shorty. "Dass a pure razor blowing out dere tonight. Ah didn't know you wuz outa here nohow."

> *Carried me down on de Smoky Road*
> *Brought me back on de coolin' board*
> *Ahm gointer make me a graveyard of mah own.*

sang Muttsy, looking as if he sought someone and banged the door shut on the last words. He strode on in without removing hat or coat.

Pinkie saw in this short space that all the men deferred to him, that all the women sought his notice. She tried timidly to squeeze between two of the men and return to the quiet place beside old man Turner, thinking that Muttsy would hold the attention of her captors until she had escaped. But Muttsy spied her through the men about her and joined them. By this time her exasperation and embarrassment had her on the point of tears.

"Well, whadda yuh know about dis!" He exclaimed, "A real lil' pullet."

"Look out dere, Muttsy," drawled Dramsleg with objection, catching Pinkie by the arm and trying to draw her toward him. "Lemme tell dis lil' Pink Mama how crazy ah is 'bout her mahself. Ah ain't got no lady atall an'—"

"Aw, shut up Drams," Muttsy said sternly, "put yo' pocketbook where yo' mouf is, an' somebody will lissen. Ah'm a heavy-sugar papa. Ah eats fried chicken when the rest of you niggers is drinking rain water."

He thrust some of the others aside and stood squarely before her. With her downcast eyes, she saw his well polished shoes, creased trousers, gloved hands and at last timidly raised her eyes to his face.

"Look a heah!" he frowned, "you roughnecks done got dis baby ready tuh cry."

He put his forefinger under her chin and made her look at him. And for some reason he removed his hat.

"Come on in the sitten' room an' le's talk. Come on befo' some uh dese niggers sprinkle some salt on yuh and eat yuh clean up lak uh radish." Dramsleg looked after Muttsy and the girl as they swam through the smoke into the front room. He beckoned to Bluefront.

"Hey, Bluefront! Ain't you mah fren'?"

"Yep," answered Bluefront.

"Well, then why cain't you help me? Muttsy done done me dirt wid the lil' pigmeat—throw a louse on 'im."

Pinkie's hair was slipping down. She felt it, but her self-consciousness prevented her catching it and down it fell in a heavy roll that spread out and covered her nearly to the waist. She followed Muttsy into the front room and again sat shrinking in the corner. She did not wish to talk to Muttsy nor anyone else in the house, but here were fewer people in this room.

"Phew!" cried Bluefront, "dat baby sho got some righteous moss on her keg—dass reg'lar 'nearrow mah Lawd tuh thee' stuff." He made a lengthy gesture with his arms as if combing out long, silky hair.

"Shux," sneered Ada in a moist, alcoholic voice. "Dat ain't nothin.' Mah haih useter be so's ah could set on it."

There was general laughter from the men.

Yas, ah know it's de truth!" shouted Shorty. "It's jus' ez close tuh yo' head *now* ez ninety-nine is tuh uh hund'ed."

"Ah'll call Muttsy tuh you," Ada threatened.

"Oh, 'oman, Muttsy ain't got you tuh study 'bout no mo' cause he's parkin' his heart wid dat lil' chicken wid white-folks' haih. Why, dat lil' chicken's foot would make you a Sunday face."

General laughter again. Ada dashed the whiskey glass upon the floor with the determined stalk of an angry tiger and arose and started forward.

"Muttsy Owens, uh nobody else ain't to gointer make no fool outer *me*. Dat lil' kack girl ain't gointer put *me* on de bricks—not much."

Perhaps Muttsy heard her, perhaps he saw her out of the corner of his eye and read her mood. But knowing the woman as he did he might have known what she would do under such circumstances. At any rate he got to his feet as she entered the room where he sat with Pinkie.

"Ah know you ain't lost yo' head sho' 'nuff, 'oman. 'Deed, Gawd knows you betah go 'way f'um me." He said this in a low, steady voice. The music stopped, the talking stopped and even the drinkers paused. Nothing happened, for Ada looked straight into Muttsy's eyes and went on outside.

"Miss Pinkie, Ah votes you g'wan tuh bed," Muttsy said suddenly to the girl.

"Yes-suh."

"An' don't you worry 'bout no job. Ah knows where you kin git a good one. Ah'll go see em first an' tell yuh tomorrow night."

She went off to bed upstairs. The rich baritone of the piano-player came up to her as did laughter and shouting. But she was tired and slept soundly.

Ma shuffled in after eight the next morning. "Darlin', ain't you got 'nuff sleep yit?"

Pinkie opened her eyes a trifle. "Ain't you the puttiest lil' trick! An' Muttsy done gone crazy 'bout yuh! Chile, he's lousy wid money an' diamon's an' everything—Yuh better grab him quick. Some folks has all de luck. Heah ah is—got uh man dat hates work lake de devil hates holy water. Ah gotta make dis house pay!"

Pinkie's eyes opened wide. "What does Mr. Muttsy do?"

"Mah Gawd, chile! He's de bes' gambler in three states, cards, craps un hawses. He could be a boss stevedore if he so wanted. The big boss down on de dock would give him a fat job—just begs him to take it cause he can manage the men. He's the biggest hero they got since Harry Wills left the waterfront. But he won't take it cause he makes so much wid the games."

"He's awful good-lookin," Pinkie agreed, "An' he been mighty nice tuh me—but I like men to work. I wish he would. Gamlin' ain't nice."

"Yeah, 'tis, ef you makes money lak Muttsy. Maybe yo ain't noticed dat diamon' set in his tooth. He picks women up when he wants tuh an' puts 'em down when he choose."

Pinkie turned her face to the wall and shuddered. Ma paid no attention.

"You doan hafta git up till you git good an' ready, Muttsy says. Ah mean you kin stay roun' the house 'till you come to, sorter."

Another day passed. Its darkness woke up the land east of Lenox—all that land between the railroad tracks and the river. It was very ugly by day, and night kindly hid some of its sordid homeliness. Yes, nighttime gave it life.

The same women, or others just like them, came to Ma Turner's. The same men, or men just like them, came also and treated them to liquor or mistreated them with fists or cruel jibes. Ma got half drunk as usual and cried over everyone who would let her.

Muttsy came alone and went straight to Pinkie where she was trying to shrink into the wall. She had feared that he would not come.

"Howdy do, Miss Pinkie."

"How'do do, Mistah Owens," she actually achieved a smile. "Did you see bout m'job?"

"Well, yeah—but the lady says she won't needya fuh uh week yet. Doan' worry. Ma ain't gointer push yuh foh room rent. Mah wrist ain't got no cramps."

Pinkie half sobbed: "Ah wantsa job now!"

"Didn't ah say dass alright? Well, Muttsy doan lie. Shux! Ah might jes' es well tell yuh—ahm crazy 'bout yuh—money no objeck."

It was the girl herself who first mentioned "bed" this night. He suffered her to go without protest.

The next night she did not come into the sitting room. She went to bed as soon as the dinner things had been cleared. Ma begged and cried, but Pinkie pretended illness and kept to her bed. This she repeated the next night and the next. Every night Muttsy came and every night he added to his sartorial splendor; but each night he went away, disappointed, more evidently crestfallen than before.

But the insistence for escape from her strange surroundings grew on the girl. When Ma was busy elsewhere, she would take out the three one dollar bills from her shoe and reconsider her limitations. If that job would only come on! She felt shut in, imprisoned, walled in with these women who talked of nothing but men and the numbers and drink, and men who talked of nothing but the numbers and drink and women. And desperation took her.

One night she was still waiting for the job—Ma's alcoholic tears prevailed. Pinkie took a drink. She drank the stuff mixed with sugar and water and crept to bed even as the dizziness came on. She would not wake tonight. Tomorrow, maybe, the job would come and freedom.

The piano thumped but Pinkie did not hear; the shouts, laughter and cried did not reach her that night. Downstairs Muttsy pushed Ma into a corner.

"Looky heah, Ma. Dat girl done played me long enough. Ah pas her room rent, ah pays her boahd an' all ah gets is uh hunk of ice. Now you said you wuz gointer fix things—you tole me so las' night an' heah she done gone tuh bed on me agin."

"Deed, ah caint do nothin' wid huh. She's thinkin' sho' nuf you gon' git her uh job and she fret so cause tain't come, dat she drunk uh toddy un hits knocked her down jes lak uh log."

"Ada an' all uh them laffin—they say ah done crapped." He felt injured. "Caint ah go talk to her?"

"Lawdy, Muttsy, dat gal dead drunk an' sleepin' lak she's buried."

"Well, cain't ah go up an'—an' speak tuh her jus' the same." A yellow backed bill from Muttsy's roll found itself in Ma's hand and put her in such good humor that she let old man Turner talk all he wanted for the rest of the night.

"Yas, Muttsy, gwan in. Youse *mah* frien'."

Muttsy hurried up to the room indicated. He felt shaky inside there with Pinkie, somehow, but he approached the bed and stood for awhile looking down upon her. Her hair in confusion about her face and swinging off the bedside; the brown arms revealed and the soft lips. He blew out the match he had struck and kissed her full in the mouth, kissed her several times and passed his hand over her neck and throat and then hungrily down upon her breast. But here he drew back.

"Naw," he said sternly to himself, "ah ain't goin' ter play her wid no loaded dice." Then quickly he covered her with the blanket to her chin, kissed her again upon the lips and tipped down into the darkness of the vestibule.

"Ah reckon ah bettah git married." He soliloquized. "B'lieve me, ah will, an' go uptown wid dicties."

He lit a cigar and stood there on the steps puffing and thinking for some time.

His name was called inside the sitting room several times but he pretended not to hear. At last he stole back into the room where slept the girl who unwittingly and unwillingly was making him do queer things. He tipped up to the bed again and knelt there holding her hands so fiercely that she groaned without waking. He watched her and he wanted her so that he wished to crush her in his love; crush and crush and hurt her against himself, but somehow he resisted the impulse and merely kissed her lips again, kissed her hands back and front, removed the largest diamond ring from his hand and slipped it on her engagement finger. It was much too large so he closed her hand and tucked it securely beneath the covers.

"She's *mine*!" He said triumphantly. "All mine!"

He switched off the light and softly closed the door as he went out again to the steps. He had gone up to the bed room from the sitting room boldly, caring not who knew that Muttsy Owens took what he wanted. He was stealing forth afraid that someone might *suspect* that he had been there. There is no secret love in those barrens; it is a thing to be approached boisterously and without delay or dalliance. One loves when one wills, and ceases when it palls. There is nothing sacred or hidden—all subject to coarse jokes. So Mutsy re-entered the sitting room from the steps as if he had been into the street.

"Where you been Muttsy?" whined Ada with an awkward attempt at coyness.

"What *you* wanta know for?" he asked roughly.

"Now, Muttsy you know you ain't treatin' me right, honey. How come you runnin' de hawg ovah me lak you do?"

"Git outa mah face 'oman. Keep yo' han's offa me." He clapped on his hat and strode from the house.

Pinkie awoke with a griping stomach and thumping head.

Ma bustled in. "How yuh feelin' darlin'? Youse jes lak a li'l doll baby."

"I got a headache, terrible from that ole whiskey. Thass mah first und las' drink long as I live." She felt the ring.

"Whut's this?" she asked and drew her hand out to the light.

"Dat's Muttsy' ring. Ah seen him wid it fuh two years. How'd y'al make out? He sho is one thur'bred."

"Muttsy? When? I didn't see no Muttsy."

"Dearie, you doan' hafta tell yo' bizness ef you dan wanta. Ahm a hush-mouf. Thass all right, keep yo' bizness to yo' self." Ma bleared her eyes wisely. "But ah know Muttsy wuz up heah tuh see yuh las' night. Doan' mine *me* honey, gwan wid 'im. He'll treat right. Ah *knows* he's crazy 'bout yuh. An' all de women is crazy 'bout *im*. Lawd! lookit dat ring!" Ma regarded it greedily for a long time, but she turned and walked toward the door at last. "Git up darlin'. Ah got fried chicking fuh breckfus' un mush melon."

She went on to the kitchen. Ma's revelation sunk deeper, then there was the ring. Pinkie hurled the ring across the room and leaped out of bed.

"He ain't goin' to make *me* none of his women—I'll die first! I'm goin' outa this house if I starve, lemme starve!"

She got up and plunged her face into the cold water on the washstand in the corner and hurled herself into the shabby clothes, thrust the three dollars which she had never had occasion to spend, under the pillow where Ma would be sure to find them and slipped noiselessly out of the house and fled down Fifth Avenue toward the Park that marked the beginning of the Barrens. She did not know where she was going, and cared little so long as she removed herself as far as possible from the house where the great evil threatened her.

At ten o'clock that same morning, Muttsy Owens dressed his flashiest best, drove up to Ma's door in a cab, the most luxurious that could be hired. He had gone so far as to stick two one hundred dollar notes to the inside of the windshield. Ma was overcome.

"Muttsy, dearie, what you doin' heah so soon? Pinkie sho has got you goin'. Un in a swell cab too—gee!"

"Ahm gointer git mah'reid tuh de doll baby, thass how come. An' ahm gointer treat her white too."

"Umhumh! Thass how come de ring! You oughtn't never fuhgit me, Muttsy, fuh puttin' y'all together. But ah never thought you'd mah'ry *nobody*—you allus said you wouldn't."

"An' ah wouldn't neither ef ah hadn't of seen *her*. Where she is?"

"In de room dressin'. She never tole me nothin' 'bout dis."

"She doan know. She wuz sleep when ah made up mah mind an' slipped on de ring. But ah never miss no girl ah wants, you knows me."

"Everybody in this man's town knows you gets whut you wants."

"Naw, ah come tuh take her to brek'fus' 'fo we goes tuh de cote-house."

"An' y'all stay heah and eat wid me. You go call her whilst ah set de grub on table."

Muttsy, with a lordly stride, went up to Pinkie's door and rapped and waited and rapped and waited three times. Growing impatient or thinking her still asleep, he flung upon the door and entered.

The first thing that struck him was the empty bed; the next was the glitter of his diamond ring upon the floor. He stumbled out to Ma. She was gone, no doubt of that.

"She looked awful funny when ah tole her you wuz in heah, but ah thought she wuz puttin' on airs," Ma declared finally.

"She thinks ah played her wid a marked deck, but ah didn't. Ef ah could see her she'd love me. Ah know she would. 'Cause ah'd make her," Muttsy lamented.

"I don't know, Muttsy. She ain't no New Yorker, and she thinks gamblin' is awful."

"Zat all she got against me? Ah'll fix that up in a minute. You help me find her and ah'll do anything she says jus' so she marries me." He laughed ruefully. "Looks like ah crapped this time, don't it, ma?"

The next day Muttsy was foreman of two hundred stevedores. How he did make them work. But oh how cheerfully they did their best for him. The company begrudged not one cent of his pay. He searched diligently, paid money to other searchers, went every night to Ma's to see if by chance the girl had returned or if any clues had turned up.

Two weeks passed this way. Black empty days for Muttsy.

Then he found her. He was coming home from work. When crossing Seventh Avenue at 135th Street they almost collided. He seized her and began pleading before she even had time to recognize him.

He turned and followed her; took the employment office slip from her hand and destroyed it, took her arm and held it. He must have been very convincing for at 125th

Street they entered a taxi that headed uptown again. Muttsy was smiling amiably upon the whole round world.

A month later, as Mutsy stood on the dock hustling his men to greater endeavor, Bluefront flashed past with his truck. "Say, Muttsy, you don't know what you missin' since you quit de game. Ah cleaned out de whole bunch las' night." He flashed a roll and laughed. "It don't seem like a month ago you wuz king uh de bones in Harlem." He vanished down the gangplank into the ship's hold.

As he raced back up the gangplank with his loaded truck Muttsy answered him. "An now, I'm King of the Boneheads—which being interpreted means stevedores. Come on over behind dis crate wid yo' roll. Mah wrist ain't got no cramp 'cause ah'm married. You'se gettin' too sassy."

"Thought you wuzn't gointer shoot no mo'!" Bluefront temporized.

"Aw Hell! Come on back heah," he said impatiently. "Ah'll shoot you any way you wants to—hard or soft roll—you'se trying to stall. You know ah don't crap neither. Come on, mah Pinkie needs a fur coat and you stevedores is got to buy it."

He was on his knees with Bluefront. There was a quick movement of Muttsy's wrist, and the cubes flew out on a piece of burlap spread for the purpose—a perfect seven.

"Hot dog!" he exulted. "Look at dem babies gallop!" His wrist quivered again. "Nine for point!" he gloated. "Hah!" There was another quick shake and nine turned up again. "Shove in, Bluefront, shove in dat roll, dese babies is crying fuh it."

Bluefront laid down two dollars grudgingly. "You said you wuzn't gointer roll no mo' dice after you got married," he grumbled.

But Muttsy had tasted blood. His flexible wrist was already in the midst of the next play.

"Come on, Bluefront, stop bellyachin'. Ah shoots huy for de roll!" He reached for his own pocket and laid down a roll of yellow bills beside Bluefront's. His hand quivered and the cubes skipped out again. "Nine!" He snapped his fingers like a trap-drum and gathered in the money.

"Doxology, Bluefront. Git back in de line wid yo' truck an' send de others roun' heah one by one. What man can't keep one li'l wife an' two li'l bones? Hurry 'em up, Blue!"

[*Opportunity* 4.44 (August 1926): 246–250, 267]

THE PINK HAT

by Caroline Bond Day

This hat has become to me a symbol. It represents the respective advantages and disadvantages of my life here. It is at once my magic-carpet, my enchanted cloak, my Aladdin's lamp. Yet it is a plain, rough, straw hat, "pour le sport," as was the recently famous green one.

(Day) The Pink Hat

Before its purchase, life was wont to become periodically flat for me. Teaching is an exhausting profession unless there are wells to draw from, and the soil of my world seems hard and dry. One needs adventure and touch with the main current of human life, and contact with many of one's kind to keep from "going stale on the job." I had not had these things and heretofore had passed back and forth from the town a more or less drab figure eliciting no attention.

Then suddenly one day with the self-confidence bred of a becoming hat, careful grooming, and satisfactory clothes I stepped on to a street car, and lo! the world was reversed. A portly gentleman of obvious rank arose and offered me a seat. Shortly afterwards as I alighted a comely young lad jumped to rescue my gloves. Walking on into the store where I always shopped, I was startled to hear the salesgirl sweetly drawl, "Miss or Mrs.?" as I have the customary initials. I heard myself answering reassuringly "Mrs." Was this myself? I, who was frequently addressed as "Sarah." For you see this is south of the Mason and Dixon line, and I am a Negro woman of mixed blood unaccustomed to these respectable prefixes.

I had been mistaken for other than a Negro, yet I look like hundreds of other colored women—yellow-skinned and slightly heavy featured, with frizzy brown hair. My maternal grand-parents were Scotch-Irish and English quadroons; paternal grand-parents Cherokee Indian and full blooded Negro; but the ruddy pigment of the Scotch-Irish ancestry is in my inheritance, and it is this which shows through my yellow skin, and in the reflections of my pink hat glows pink. Loosely speaking, I should be called a mulatto—anthropologically speaking, I am a dominant of the white type of the F3 generation of secondary crossings. There is a tendency known to the initiated persons of mixed Negro blood in this climate to "breed white" as we say, propagandists to the contrary notwithstanding. In this sense the Proud Race is, as it were, really dominant. The cause? I'll save that for another time.

Coming back to the hat—when I realized what had made me the recipient of those unlooked for, yet common courtesies, I decided to experiment further.

So I wore it to town again one day when visiting an art store looking for prints for my school room. Here, where formerly I had met with indifference and poor service, I encountered a new girl today who was the essence of courtesy. She pulled out drawer after drawer of prints as we talked and compared from Gritto to Sargent. Yet she agreed that Giorgione had a sweet, worldly taste, that he was not sufficiently appreciated, that Titian did was not sufficiently appreciated, that Titian did overshadow him. We went back to Velasquez as the master technician and had about decided on "The Forge of Vulcan" as appropriate for my needs when suddenly she asked, "but where do you teach?" I answered, and she recognized the name of a Negro university. Well—I felt sorry for her. She had blundered. She had been chatting familiarly, almost intimately with a Negro woman. I spared her by leaving quickly, and murmured that I would send for the package.

My mood forced me to walk—and I walked on and on until I stood at the "curbmarket." I do love markets, and at this one they sell flowers as well as vegetables. A feeble old man came up beside me. I noticed that he was near-sighted. "Lady," he began, "would you tell me—is them dahlias or peernies up there?" Then, "market smells so good—don't it?"

I recognized a kindred spirit. He sniffed about among the flowers, and was about to say more—a nice old man—I should have liked to stop and talk with him after the leisurely southern fashion, but he was a white old man—and I moved on hastily.

I walked home the long way and in doing so passed the city library. I thought of my far away Boston—no Abbey nor Puvis de Chauvannes here, no marble stairs, no spirit of studiousness of which I might become a part. Then I saw a notice of a lecture by Drinkwater at the woman's club—I was starved for something good—and starvation of body or soul sometimes breeds criminals.

So then I deliberately set out to deceive. Now, I decided, I would enjoy all that had previously been impossible. When necessary I would add a bit of rouge and the frizzy hair (thanks to the marcel) could be crimped into smoothness. I supposed also that a well-modulated voice and assurance of manner would be assets.

So thus disguised, for a brief space of time, I enjoyed everything from the attentions of an expert Chiropodist to grand opera, avoiding only the restaurants—I could not have borne the questioning eyes of the colored waiters.

I would press on my Aladdin's lamp and presto, I could be comforted with a hot drink at the same soda-fountain where ordinarily I should have been hissed at. I could pull my hat down a bit and buy a ticket to see my favorite movie star while the play was still new.

I could wrap my enchanted cloak about me and have the decent comfort of ladies' rest-rooms. I could have my shoes fitted in the best shops, and be shown the best values in all of the stores—not the common styles "which all the darkies buy, you know." At one of these times a policeman helped me across the street. A sales-girl in the most human way once said, "I wouldn't get that, Sweetie, you and me is the same style and I know." How warming to be like the rest of the world, albeit a slangy and gum-chewing world!

But it was best of all of an afternoon when it was impossible to correct any more papers or to look longer at my own Lares and Penates, to sit upon my magic-carpet and be transported into the midst of a local art exhibit, to enjoy the freshness of George Inness and the vague charm of Brangwyn, and to see white-folk enjoying Tanner—really nice, likable, folk too, when they don't know one. Again it was good to be transported into the midst of a great expectant throng, awaiting the pealing of the Christmas carols at the Municipal Pageant. One could not enjoy this without compunction however, for there was not a dark face to be seen among all of those thousands of people, and my two hundred bright-eyed youngsters should have been there.

Finally—and the last time that I dared upon my carpet, was to answer the call of a Greek play to be given on the lawn of a State University. I drank it all in. Marvelous beauty! Perfection of speech and gesture on a velvet greensward, music, color, life!

Then a crash came. I suppose I was nervous—one does have "horrible imaginings and present fears" down here, sub-conscious pictures of hooded figures and burning crosses. Anyway in hurrying out to avoid the crowd, I fell and broke an anklebone.

Someone took me home. My doctor talked plaster-casts. "No," I said, "I'll try osteopathy," but there was no chance for magic now. I was home in bed with my family—a colored family—and in a colored section of the town. A friend interceded with the doctor whom I had named. "No," he said, "it is against the rules of the osteopathic association to serve Negroes."

I waited a day—perhaps my foot would be better—then they talked bone-surgery. I am afraid of doctors. Three operations have been enough for me. Then a friend said, "try Christian Science." Perhaps I had been taking matters too much in my own hands, I thought. Yes, that would be the thing . Would she find a practitioner for me?

Dear, loyal daughter of New England—as loyal to the Freedmen's children as she had been to them. She tried to spare me. "They will give you absent treatments and when you are better we will go down." I regret now having said, "Where, to the back door?" What was the need of wounding my friend?

Besides, I have recovered some now—I am only a wee bit lame now. And mirabili dictu! My spirit has knit together as well as my bones. My hat has grown useless. I am so glad to be well again, and back at my desk. My brown boys and girls have become reservoirs of interest. One is attending Radcliffe this year. My neighborly friend needs me now to while away the hours for her. We've gone back to Chaucer and dug out forgotten romances to be read aloud. The little boy next door has a new family of Belgian hares with which we play wonderful games. And the man and I have ordered seed catalogues for spring.

Health, a job, young minds and souls to touch, a friend, some books, a child, a garden, Spring! Who'd want a hat? [*Opportunity* 4.48 (December 1926): 379–380]

MASKS: A STORY

by Eloise Bibb Thompson

Paupet, an octoroon and born free, was a man of considerable insight. That was because, having brains, he used them. The cause of Julie's, his wife's, trouble was no secret to him. Although it never dawned upon him fully until after she died. Then he dictated the words to be placed upon her tombstone. The inscription proved to be unique, but not more than the cemeteries themselves of old New Orleans. The motto written in 1832 read as follows: "Because she saw with the eyes of her grandfather, she died at the sight of her babe's face."

This grandfather, Aristile Blanchard, had been an enigma to the whole Quadroon Quarter of New Orleans. But he was no enigma to Paupet although he had never lain eyes upon him. Seeing him had not been necessary for Paupet had heard his whole life's history from Paul, Julie's brother, whom he met in Mobile before he had known Julie. Paul, although a ne'er do well who had left the homefires early, admired his grandfather immensely. Hence he had found delight even as youth in securing from the old man those facts of his life which had proved so interesting to Paupet.

Now Paupet, among other things, was a natural psychologist albeit an unconscious one. He was accustomed to ponder the motives of men, their peculiar mental traits and their similarity to those of their parents whom he happened to know. No one was more interesting to Paupet than Julie, his wife. So of course he gave much thought to her. But the occasion is always necessary for the knowledge of a soul, and the opportunity for really knowing Julie came only when she was expecting her offspring. But even then Paupet would not have known where to place the blame for her peculiarity had he not known, as we have said, all there was to know about old Aristile Blanchard.

That Aristile was a man to be pitied Paupet felt there was no question. For what man does not deserve pity who sees his fondest dream fall with the swiftness of a rocket from a starlit sky to the darkness of midnight? No wonder that hallucination then seized him. With such a nature as his that was to be expected. But that the influence of such a delusion should have blighted Julie's young life was the thing of which Paupet most bitterly complained.

Aristile, Paul told Paupet, had been a native of Hayti. Coming to New Orleans in 1795 when the slave insurrection was hottest, he had set up an atmosphere of revolt as forceful as the one he had left behind him. Of course when Julie entered the world, the revolution had long been over; Toussaint L'Ouverture had demonstrated his fitness to rule, had eventually been thrown in an ignominious dungeon and been mouldering in the grave some five years or more. But the fact that distressed Paupet was that Aristile lived on to throw his baneful influence over the granddaughter entrusted by a dying mother to his care.

Of all the free men of color in Hayti at the time none were more favored than Aristile. A quadroon of prepossessing appearance with some capital at hand, he had been sent to Bordeaux, France, by a doting mother to study the arts for which he was thought to show marked predilection. In reality he was but a dabbler in the arts, returning at length to his native land with some acquaintance with most of them, as for instance sculptor, painting, woodcarving and the like but with no very comprehensive knowledge of any one of them. There was one thing, however, that did not escape him—being there at the time when France was a hotbed of that revolt which finally stormed the Bastille—and that was the spirit of liberty. "Liberty, Fraternity, Equality" was in the very air he breathed. He returned from France with revolutionary tendencies far in advance of any free man in the island, tendencies that waited but the opportunity to blossom into the strongest sort of heroism.

Although he burned to be of service to his race on returning to his native land he forced himself to resume his usual tenor of life. He sought apprenticeship to an Oriental mask-maker, a rare genius in his line where the rich French planters were wont to go in preparation for their masquerades and feast-day festivities. Masks had always had a strange fascination for Aristile. He would often sit lost in thought beside their maker, his mind full of conflicting emotions. But when the French slaveowners assembled at Cape Haitien to formulate measures against the free men of color to whom the National Assembly in France had decreed full citizenship, he forgot everything and throwing down his tools immediately headed the revolt that followed.

With Rigaud, the mulatto captain of the slaves, he gave himself to the cause of France, offering at the risk of his life to spy upon the English when they came to the support of the native French planters bent upon re-establishing slavery upon the island.

Making up as a white man as best he could, he boldly entered the port of Jeremie where the English had but recently landed. His ruse would have succeeded had it not been for a native white planter all too familiar with his African earmarks, who standing by at the time readily spotted him out. Without warning, Aristile was seized, flogged unmercifully and thrown into a dungeon to die. But he was rescued after a time by a good angel in the form of an octoroon planter identified with whites all his life because of a face that defied detection; not only rescued but shipped with his daughter in safety to New Orleans. Then the octoroon rescuer took up the work of spy upon the English which Aristile had been forced to relinquish. That he was successful is manifested in the subsequent work of Toussaint L'Ouverture who because of him was able before very long to drive in all the troops of the English, to invest their strongholds, to assault their forts, and ultimately to destroy them totally.

This incident had a lifelong effect upon Aristile. Full of despondency, disappointment over his failure in the work he had set himself to do with the enthusiasm and glow of a martyr, his mind dwelt wholly upon the facial lineaments that had brought about his defeat. "Cheated!" he would exclaim bitterly. "Cheated out of the opportunity of doing the highest service because of a face four degrees from the pattern prescribed for success. Fate has been against me.—Nature has been against me. It was never meant that I should do the thing I burned to do.—O, why did not Nature give me the face of my father?—Then all things would have been possible to me. Other quadroons have been so blessed. Hundreds of them—thousands of them! Save for a slight sallowness of the skin there was absolutely nothing to show their African linage. But Nature in projecting my lips and expanding my nose has set me apart for the contumely of the world.—The ancients lied when they said the gods made man's face from the nose upwards, leaving their lower portion for him to make himself. Try as I may I will never be able to change the mask that Nature has imposed upon me."

Day and night these thoughts were with him. Paul described this state to Paupet declaring that his mother had feared for Aristile's mind. At length this mood suddenly changed to one of exultation and he rose from his bed a new man.

"I have found the formula for greatness!" he told those about him, "It reads, Thou shalt be seen wearing a white man's face.—But only a fraction being able to carry out this prescription it is left for me to create a symbol so perfect in its imitation of Nature that the remainder of mankind may likewise receive a place in the sun. My brothers and I shall no longer be marked for defeat. I shall make a mask that will defy Nature herself. There shall be no more distinct and unmistakable signs that will determine whether a man shall be master or slave. All men in future shall have the privilege of being what they will."

With this end in view he repaired to the Quadroon Quarter of New Orleans and set up a workshop that soon became the talk of the district because of the strange-looking objects it contained. Paupet could vouch for their strangeness for they were still in existence when he came to the place. Upon the walls of this room hung many attempts of the thing Aristile had set himself to do. There were masks of paper patiently glued in small bits together in a brave effort to imitate Nature in the making of a white man's face. Likewise masks of wood, of papier mache and of some soft, clinging, leaflike material which it is very likely he discovered in Louisiana's wondrous woods. Interesting-looking objects they were, everyone of them, most of them, however, were far from the goal; but a few in their skin-like possibility of stretching over a man's face might have been made perfect—who knows—greater marvels have been seen—had their completion not been suddenly broken off. There was about the whole of this room an unmistakable depression, an atmosphere of shattered hope as if the maker of these objects had set out with high purpose toward their completion then suddenly been chilled by some unforeseen happening that filled him with despair. And so it really had been. While Negro supremacy existed in his beloved country Aristile worked with ever-increasing enthusiasm toward his cherished dream. He had been unable, he told himself, to assist his brothers as a soldier because of the lineaments that Nature had imposed. But he would present them with a talisman like unto Aladdin's lamp that would work wonders for them in a world where to be blessed was to be white. But when the news reached him that Toussaint, the savior of his race had been tricked and thrown into a French prison to die, he was plunged into the deepest sorrow and turned from his purpose in despair. Laying aside his implements, for a long time he could not be induced to take interest in anything. At length when his funds began to dwindle, it was bourne in upon him that men must work if they would live. Then he turned to the making of those limp figures in sweeping gowns that when Paupet saw them were no doubt of his own distorted mind, designed for standing in the farthest corner of the room—grotesque figures wearing hideous masks, the reflection, clown and actors of the comic stage.

It was not very long before the place began to be frequented by patrons of the Quadroon Masques and of those open-air African dances and debaucheries known as "Voodoo Carousals" held in the Congo Square. Later actors from the French Opera looked in upon him. Then he conceived the idea of having Clotile, his daughter, already an expert with the needle, prepare for his patrons of the masque and stage to be rented at a nominal fee, those gowns and wraps that were now fading behind the glass doors of yonder cabinets. But though he worked continuously it had no power, apparently, to change his usual course of thought. His mind ever dwelt upon the disaster that had blighted his life.

And then came Julie in this atmosphere of depression to take up in time the work which fate decreed Clotile should lay down. As apt with the needle as her dead mother had been she was able, when her grandfather through age and ill-health became enfeebled, to maintain them both. And those were formative years for the young Julie, obliged to listen to her grandfather's half-crazed tirade against Nature's way of fixing a man to his clan through the color of his skin. Unaccustomed to thinking independently she, however, could see something of the disastrousness of it all because of the stringent laws confronting her in New Orleans. As much as she longed to do so, for instance, she dared not wear any of the head-gear of the times, although much of it was made by her own fingers, because of the law forbidding it; a bandana handkerchief being decreed to all free women of color so that they might easily be distinguished from white ladies. And that was only one of the minor laws. There were others graver and more disastrous by far. So these conditions forced her to realize early that her grandfather had good reason for his lament. She too deplored the failure of his design—the making of a mask that would open the barred and bolted doors of privilege for those who knocked thereon. Without anything like bitterness for these conditions, she began to reason that color and not mental endowment or loftiness of character determined the caliber of a man. For did not color determine his destiny? He was rich or poor, happy or unhappy according to his complexion and not according to his efforts at all. And so the words superior and inferior were invariably dependent upon the color of his skin. She, a brunette-like quadroon, the counterpart of her grandfather, was far superior to the black slave-peddlers who sometimes came into the Quadroon Quarter begging a place to rest. And that was why the Quarter guarded the section so jealously from all black dwellers, however free they might be because they wanted only superior people in their midst.

One morning some months after her grandfather's death she awoke trembling with a great discovery, for years she reflected in wonderment her revered relative had tried to make a mask that when fitted to a man's face would change his entire future and had failed. And lo! the secret had just been whispered to her. "To me," she whispered to herself ecstatically, "to po' lil' me. An' I know it ees tr-rue, yes. It got to be tr-rue. 'Cause madda Nature, she will help in de work, an' w'at else you want?" For the life-mate she would choose for herself would be an octoroon, as fair as a lily. With her complexion and his she knew that she would be able to give to her children the mask which her grandfather had yearned. She saw now why he had failed. No doubt it was never meant for men to know anything about it at all. It must be in the keepings of mothers alone. "Now we will see," she told herself exultantly. "Ef my daughter got to wear a head handgcher lak me. Fo' me it ees notting. I cannot help. But jes' de same a son of mine goin' be king of some Carnival yet. You watch out fo' me."

And so when Paupet, the whitest octoroon that she had ever seen, came to the Quarter, she showed her preference for him at once. When, after their marriage, in the course of time their first born was expected she was like an experimentalist in the mating of cross-breeds, painfully nervous and full of the greatest anxiety over the outcome of a situation that she had been planning so long. What preparations she made! She fitted up a room especially for the event. She was extravagance itself in the selection of the garments, buying enough material to clothe half a dozen infants. She literally covered the fly leaves of the Bible with male and female names in preparation for the Christening: and made so many trips to town for all sorts of purchases that Paupet became full of anxiety for the outcome of it all.

To him she talked very freely now of her readiness in marrying him—it was really for the good of the child that was about to come to them. Her trials would not be her infant's. She had seen to that. He would look like Paupet, and could therefore choose his own way in life unhampered by custom or law.

To the midwife too she communicated her hopes and expectations, dwelling at great length upon the future of the child the whiteness of whose face would be a charm against every prevailing ill. Such optimism augured ill to the midwife who rarely vouchsafed her a word. When at length the child was born, the midwife tarried a long time before placing it into Julie's arms. It was sympathy upon her part that caused the delay. But Julie could not understand it. In the midst of her great sufferings she marveled at it, until at length she caught a glimpse of her child's face. Then she screamed. With horror she saw that it was identical with the one in the locket about her neck. I was the image of her chocolate-colored mother. [*Opportunity* 5.10 (October 1927): 300–302]

BLACK

by Nellie R. Bright

Have you ever longed to go to Hankow, or Nice, or Scheveningen, but you never went because your shekels were too few? That often happens to me, but last summer I went to Scheveningen on the North Sea.

Getting passage is quite an adventure.

As I wanted to get accommodations in the tourist third cabin, I went to the steamship office six months before sailing. The clerks looked at me in great amazement over the shining black counter. Then, they looked at each other. As I continued to stand, one arose and came to me. "What can I do for you?" he asked doubtfully.

"I should like to get passage on one of your steamers carrying tourist third accommodations."

"They're all booked," he said, eyeing me in a strange way.

"But this is February and I don't want to sail until July. Are you sure there's nothing left?"

At this unexpected sally, another clerk came to his assistance. "You see," he began suavely, "this is one of the oldest and most popular lines and we book early. We really have nothing left."

"Thank you," I breathed, and headed for an office on the opposite corner. The force must have seen me enter the rival office, for as I went in every clerk was on his feet. One stood expectantly looking in my direction. In my handbag was an advertisement that I had cut from the morning paper. "Now you are permitted more than a dream of the old fame of Europe." Go the "new way," by "tourist third." "In the first place, of course, it is really intended for students and teachers, writers, artists, and people of this class on both East-bound and West-bound sailings."

This was just what I wanted. As I turned from closing the door, a clerk said, "Well—?"

I repeated my query as to accommodations on their tourist third to Europe. "We haven't any tourist third. I suppose that we're the only line that doesn't have it."

"But," I began, taking the ad from my bag, "here is your announcement giving dates for these accommodations."

"Some mistake. We don't—" I waited to hear no more.

That morning I went to five steamship offices, making the same request, and was looked at in great consternation, answered glibly or curtly, but always with the flat denial that there were any bookings left. I had no idea what a tremendous business steamship offices carried on six months before sailings!

Perhaps the —Line had a berth left. When I entered, all of the clerks became so suddenly entranced with their typing or 'phoning that none saw me. I waited, the blood pounding at my temples, my heart beating at such a pace that when a little boy was sent to ask me what I wanted, I could only gasp.

"The manager wants to know why you're waiting in here."

"I'm waiting here to get information concerning your bookings to France," I answered loudly enough to be heard by the office force and the clerk at the rear behind a screen.

No one lifted his eyes from his work. There was a stillness as if fingers had suddenly forgotten the keys of the typewriters. After a brief conference, during which I heard the rasping voice of the manager, and saw the screen move, then return to its former position, the boy came to me and said, "We don't sell tourist third to Negroes."

"Sacre bleu!"

* * *

Then, that was it. It wasn't that it was a curse to be poor, but in my case it was a curse to be a Negro. My skin was brown. In my excitement in planning for the adventure, I had committed a new crime. I had forgotten that I was a brown girl. Now, I saw clearly how foolish I had appeared to those Nordic clerks. I was too eager to be "permitted more than a dream of the old fame of Europe." I was a "student," but brown. A brown "student," a brown "teacher" should not "wish to make a trip to Europe at moderate cost, in comfort, and with a minimum expenditure for the ocean passage." God!

I had always wanted to go to Europe. When a few years old I had gone with my father and mother. As I grew, I never wearied of retraversing the scenes dear to my father, as he described our first service in Westminster, or a sail down the Thames, as he told of the ivy-covered walls of Christ Church, or a jaunt to the island of Marken. I must go to the "Cheshire Cheese," to Anne Hathaway's cottage, to the Louvre.

Then, in those years I had become a student. I was even now engaged in writing a thesis and I must go to Bodley and to the British Museum to search out old manuscripts for myself. I, a brown girl, would reveal to the world of literature knowledge that has lain secret for centuries. But, since they did not want to give me passage, I wondered if, after all, the trip would be worth the effort. Wouldn't I be meeting Nordics everywhere? I was going to the north of Europe. Wouldn't the American students tell the librarians what a despicable creature I was because my skin was brown, and would they, because of this, say, "We can't register any more students to search records. You see 'this is one of the oldest and most popular' libraries, and we 'register' 'early'."

And, when I went to Bodley, would the keeper of the manuscripts look at me queerly when I asked to see the original "Roland," which I had translated the year before from photostats, and say, "You are permitted no more than a dream of the old fame of the 'Roland.' We don't expose it to the gaze of Negroes?" And, when I stood at the end of that long corridor in the Louvre with the vision of the Venus de Milo luring me from the velvety shadows, would an attendant come silently to me and say, "You must go no nearer; you see the Venus is dazzling white, and her beauty would be marred by the blackness of your visage. We must protect our masterpieces for the white men of the earth." And, being so near, would I withdraw in confusion without steeping my soul in the loveliness of that statue, because I was black?

Thus debating the question, I threaded my way thru the traffic like one bearing a life apart, and entered another steamship office. How alert they were in that last output, and how busy. They must be too busy to see me, I thought. But, after waiting five minutes, a woman came forward and asked, "What do you want?"

"I should like to book passage on your tourist third for Liverpool," I ventured. Without a word, she turned and called to Mr. Johns, who evidently did the booking. I told him my errand and he proceeded to take out a huge book. As he turned the leaves, he shook his head. Before he could say, "We're full," I asked him for two dates and told him that I could make the first payment immediately. "Have a seat and I'll tell you in a few minutes."

Mr. Johns consulted three other clerks then, "Here's something that will suit you," he said. We settled the dates and the first payment. He took my name and address. This surely looked as if I were going to Europe. But I was weary with their subterfuges and thot as soon as I was out of the office, "That's only a bluff, too. I suppose he took my address so as to be able to identify that audacious person who wanted to go on a holiday with the "best youth of America."

I had seen enough of American youth in the schools and at the University. I knew only too well how the "best" would smile with their faces and draw their skirts aside at my coming. What I wanted was the cleanliness, the wholesome food, deck space, comforts that I would not get in the steerage. While the American youths smirked and smoked and babbled of Freud and Ford, I should be wrapped in my blanket, my thots racing with the waves.

* * *

Sailing day came! I was rushed down, down, down into the hold of the ship. My father, who knows ships, would not look at me. He did not want me to see the hurt in his eyes. I didn't have tourist accommodations after all. This ship didn't carry student tours. Black! What did it matter?

That night I sat upon a coil of hawsers. There were no chairs for steerage passengers. At my back, the winches black with shining grease. The soft night wind caressed my cheek and my breath came quickly as I watched for the first star. I had eaten no supper. When I emerged from my stateroom in the hold of the ship, I felt that I would never eat again, so choked was I with the echoes of the voices of lily white liars in steamship offices.

Gradually, my fellow passengers came up from the dining saloon. There was the ruddy-cheeked, black-haired woman who had embarked so stylishly dressed with her husband and two boys. She now wore a loose sweater over an ill-fitting blue dress. She sat moodily, her family near her. The red-lipped girl whom I had fancied a Paquin model came on deck, her raven locks hidden beneath a somber scarf. The Welsh woman who had put her babies to bed chatted with the old Spaniard. He had come aboard in a dapper blue suit and yellow shoes but now had a red kerchief knitted at his throat and his feet encased in knitted bedroom slippers.

An elderly man, graying hair at his temples, sat beside me. I kept my gaze fixed upon the deepening sky for should he see even in the dusk the black of my face he might leap away. And I was too lonely to have a fellow creature shun me just then.

Voices babbled incessantly. Everybody talked but me. They were talking about themselves. Two English boys, having made a fortune, were returning to care for their mother. I heard the Irish girl say that she was being deported because she had no wealth save her fur coat.

Presently, a voice beside me asked, "And what of you, lass?" Are you going home too?"

"No," I answered, "America is my home." The muscles of my throat tightened. "I'm off on a holiday." At the mention of holiday, several forms loitered nearer. Some had never had a holiday. What a joyful thing it must be to go just where one wanted and to do the things one liked best. The Englishman became eloquent. "You must go to the cheese market at Shrewsbury. Shop in 'petticoat alley' on a Sunday morning. Don't miss the changing of the horse guard at Whitehall. Go to Kew and to the Tower. I'll make a list of the places that you must visit."

"You're very kind," I murmured, skeptical at his enthusiasm. He surely hadn't seen my face. How could he know that the word "holiday" had made my voice husky, that my holidays were honey drained from crystal cups with jagged edges?

As we talked, the lights came on. They looked full upon my face. I looked straight at them, a challenge in my eye. None even winced. Then, they knew—and didn't care? I pondered this while they chatted.

The Spaniard, his face gashed with wrinkles, wondered if his family in Madrid would recognize him after forty years. He was darker than I. Perhaps they talked to me because they thot me a Spaniard, too. Odd! Anything but a Negro.

One day, the social worker (she knew) came to me, her eyes wet. "Do go over and talk to that poor boy by the railing. He's a Nigerian and was brought to America by missionaries. But he seems so depressed and he won't tell me what troubles him. Perhaps he'll tell you."

"I didn't know that such a person was on board," I replied. "Where has he been all this time?"

"They've had him locked in his cabin for fear that he would injure himself," she explained. "But, go to him, now."

The boy, a youth of eighteen, stood gazing fixedly at the horizon, much as I had done that first night at sea. Already, I knew his sorrow, I thot. He is suffering as I did. I stood near him for a moment, then made a casual remark about the speed of the vessel as is the way with fellow passengers.

"It can't fly too swiftly for me," replied Oojoula, looking at me almost fiercely.

"Where are you going?" I asked.

"To my home, five hundred miles from the Gold Coast, where my father is chief and where the white man has never set foot."

"How long were you in America?"

"Four long years."

"Where you in school?"

"Yes, civilized, educated, Christianized. They made me a Christian. Think of it— a Christian! I was but a child then. I even believed in their Christ until I felt their hatred for us. My people are more loyal to their gods than Christ's followers to Him. I would have killed myself, but I must go back to the jungle. I go to my people. I shall warn them against the white man. I would record their history. It is necessary. The world must know how noble black men are."

Oojoula turned his eyes from mine. I was forgotten.

How could I help him? This poor, disillusioned boy? He hadn't grown up with them as I had. He didn't know that equal opportunity for us meant denial of opportunity, or a struggle for opportunity that is so bitter that, when the end is realized, our strength and enthusiasm are spent. How was he to know that these people whom he hated with an intensity greater than the blackness of his skin, felt it their duty to prevent a Negro from enjoying the simplest of pleasures, from having the barest comforts. I could never make him understand.

We were too different. He had lost his faith in man suddenly. I had been losing mind all thru my childhood, all thru my time of dreams, all thru my college days. It was simply this: I had been born in a county where a man was good or evil according to the color of his skin. Oojoula had not.

When the ship's orchestra dropped down the ladders from the second class deck to entertain us that afternoon, the first and second class passengers crowded the rail. To look down upon the steerage passengers was quite a diversion. Oojoula, unable to bear the amused stare of the "superior" group, pointed out to me the priest and his wife who were taking him back to Africa. Then he locked himself in his cabin.

That night, while the ship's orchestra played in the first class saloon, a fiddler from Lisconnel, perched himself upon a capstan and drew his bow across the strings. Forms rose from the shadows, swaying. There was the click of heels, the clap of hands. They were "stacking the barley." A rollicking dance. One of the English lads held out his hands to mine. "Come, jig with me," he urged, his feet beating a tattoo to the rhythm. The blood tingled in my veins. I drew away. How could I, a brown girl, dance with him? I loved to dance—but—with an English lad! He must be joking. I was a Negro. I had only danced with boys of my own race. All the inhibitions that had grown up with me forbade me to put my hand into his and swing with him in the sheer enjoyment of the dance.

"No," I said, by heart contracted with fear—the fear that he had chosen me to play the fool because I was black.

"No?" he repeated; "I don't take 'no' for an answer. I just know that you dance. You're like a willow. Won't you try it? Look, it goes like this." He showed me the steps. He was in earnest. I mustn't be rude. He was simply being kind. But, why? Wasn't he white and I—? Queer!

He insisted. What could I say? I was confused. "I do dance," I stammered, "but not the Irish folk dances, so you'll have to get another partner."

"No, I don't," he persisted. "I'll teach you the 'stack the barley' in a trice. Come!" He seized both my hands in a firm grip, drawing me to my feet. My body, singing with the music, danced one round. As the fiddler laid by his bow, I fled to my cabin.

What had I done? I had danced, a joyful thing in itself, but I had degraded myself by dancing with a Nordic.

As I lay in my berth, I marveled at many things. I thot of what I had done, of Oojoula, of my fellow passengers. They were Nordics, to be sure, but they had seemed kind. They had treated me as a human being. But, perhaps, that was only the camaradie of the traveler. We would soon land in old England. Would they perchance know me if they spied me on the pier? If we should pass each other in Piccadilly, would they see me?

At times as I sat silent in black isolation for fear of inviting insult, they had come to me and chatted of the merits of farming in Poland, or of Yeats' poetry, or of their families. Sometimes I found myself holding the Portuguese baby while its mother took her turn about the deck. Again, I was the center of a group swapping yarns. They hadn't seemed to notice. Perhaps, after all these people were different from Americans in that they did not despise my color. My doubts would soon be quelled for we were nearing Queenstown, our first stop; then England, Belgium and France.

The next day there was a perceptible restlessness among the passengers and crew. Gulls began to follow the ship. As sailors walked the deck they would stop, lean far over the port rail and peer toward the horizon. Toward sunset, I discerned an opalescent mist low in the sky. Knots of passengers began to watch the cloud. Field glasses were eagerly borrowed. The mist remained, began to take definite shape. The mist remained, began against the sky. This was no cloud. Land! The wild, rocky coast of Ireland. There was a cry of joy that thrilled from every deck. There came a shout, and a song of Erin floated across the waves to Killarney.

The people with whom I had lived for eleven days embraced each other and some wept for joy. They rushed below and returned, dressed in their stylish American clothes. Once more they saw their beloved Ireland. They were going home. I rejoiced with them. Oojoula looked on from his cabin. He, too, was going home. He was thinking of the kindly black faces that would greet him.

At eleven o'clock that night, we set off two flares. In the wavering ribbon of light picking out a path of quicksilver from Queenstown to our steamer, glided the pilot's tiny boat. I drew my coat close against the cold. There was the roar of the propeller as we swung round toward the city. There was the tang of green hills in the air. Shrill cries and deep laughter mingled with the clanking of chairs and the bustle of passengers. Two tenders chugged along side. My fellow passengers beamed upon me. As soon as the mail had been taken off, they would go. As they went across the bridge to the second class deck, I went with them. Irish women who had just come on board with huge baskets were selling lace and shawls of soft silk. I stooped to look, then fled down the deck as the order came, "Steerage passengers not debarking, go below."

I must bid my friends goodbye as they went down the gangplank to the waiting tender. It began to rain, a sharp, drenching shower. Lights flowed from the city across the harbor to us. Those that were leaving wrung my hands, smiled wistfully, and were gone. I followed with my eyes and smiled as the steamer was lost in the thick night. I was weeping.

Was it because I should never see those kindly faces again, or because I had thot them kind when they only thot of me as black? [*Opportunity* 5.11 (November 1927): 331–334]

HIGH FALUTIN'

by Pearl Fisher

Lew Haskins, porter and soda fountain attendant in Greene & Scott's Pharmacy, was in his glory. Both Doctor Greene and Doctor Scott were out, the errand boy was off for the afternoon, and Lew was in charge. He looked around the store. Yes, everything was in order. The cases had been dusted, the fountain was spotless, the chairs and tables were arranged with geometric precision. Assuring himself that nothing was amiss, he turned to survey his own lordly person in the mirror.

He liked himself hugely, did Lew. His white coat was exactly like Dr. Greene's. Yes, it was quite possible that customers might mistake him for the proprietor, or at any rate for the chief clerk. He was certain that none would suspect him of being merely a porter. He almost made himself believe that he was in fact the chief clerk helping out at the fountain in an emergency. With the thought, he straightened his narrow sloping shoulders, and smiled approvingly at the reflection of his yellow-brown, heavy-featured face topped with a mass of crinkly black hair stocking-capped into a semblance of a brush back.

The entrance of two white men interrupted Lew's self-admiration. They asked for the proprietor. With a skill born of experience he classified them as salesmen and, in his most proprietary manner, invited them to wait, whereupon the men ordered refreshments and seated themselves at a rear table. Having served them condescendingly, Lew was again left free to muse on his own sartorial impeccability.

"Hello, Lew!"

Lew wheeled, his slouching figure suddenly rigid, eager—

"Hello, Ossie! When did you get back?"

"Oh, the other day."

Osceola Pitts, known as Ossie, tall, white-skinned, blue-eyed, and blonde, insinuated herself on a high stool before the fountain. She was distinctly personable and knew it. Her silk frock fitted her with an air of careless, expensive elegance. True, her crossed legs displayed an undue amount of silken hosiery, her nails were rather too sharply pointed and too highly polished, and perhaps a trifle less rouge might have been used with better effect, but Lew saw in all this nothing to condemn. He saw only perfection—a perfection that he desired above all else to possess.

"What's it to be this time?"

"Oh, per usual."

Lew proceeded to make the sundae, piling in a double portion of ice-cream and serving the final concoction with elaborate care. He leaned over the counter towards the girl.

"Missed you while you was away."

"That so?"

"Yeah. Be home this evening?"

"Got a date."

"To-morrow, then?"

"Sorry Lew."

"When, Sunday?"

"Can't say, Lew. I'm kinder busy these days and I'm always away over the week-ends," parried Ossie.

"Oh, that's what you always tell me here lately."

Lew became conscious of the fact that the two white men at the table in the rear were watching him. Certain that they couldn't hear, he smiled broadly, glad of the effect that his familiarity with the girl was producing.

Ossie finished her sundae, but Lew held her in conversation, trying to inveigle from her an open date. Laughing, the girl evaded, backing slowly toward the door. Suddenly, by some telepathic medium she became aware of eyes upon her. Other eyes—

not Lew's. Suddenly found herself staring into a tense, tight-lipped face with eyes hard as spear points and as sharp—eyes that seemed to pierce through the present to some well remembered past. Eyes that questioned while they defied her to deny. A moment, speechless, confused, she stared back, then turned and hurried into the street.

Lew, puzzled, watched her out of sight then slowly began putting the counter to rights.

"I wonder," he muttered under his breath. The men arose and approached Lew.

"Sorry we can't wait any longer," said one. We'll be back some other time."

Still he hesitated. Leisurely he lighted a cigarette and flicked the match away.

"Who's the beautiful blonde?" he began trying to seem casual. Lew was instantly on the alert.

"Huh?"

"Who's the blonde beauty who just left?"

"Oh, a customer."

"You seem to know her pretty well."

"Oh, I know 'em all. They all kid with me."

"White?"

"Huh?"

"White or colored?"

"How do I know?"

"You know damn well."

Lew noted the loss of self-control and dared.

"How do I know what she is or anybody? What are you? How do I know? I only know what you look like. Same with her."

Off his guard, the speaker blurted out, "Damn your insolence. But I'm hanged if I wouldn't like to know."

"Why you so interested?"

"Because I hate my best friend to have a raw deal put over on him, even if he is—. If she's a—. Well." He left off short and followed his companion out of the store.

Lew stood still a long time.

"I wonder," he said again.

Two hours later, Lew still pondering on Ossie's hasty retreat, saw her come in and enter the telephone booth.

Stealthily he slid behind the counter and up near the booth. She had not closed the door entirely. He heard her give the number, Calvert 4683. He moved away and busied himself ostensibly about the shelves.

Ossie came out of the booth and stood before him.

"Say Lew."—

"Oh, 's that you Ossie?"

Ossie gave a nervous laugh.

"Lew, er, did you see that ofay in here this afternoon?"

"Huh?"

"You know—when I was in here. He was sittin' back there."

"Oh, yeah."

"Did he—did he say anything about—ask anything about me?"

"No," lied Lew. "What would he be askin' me 'bout you?"

"Oh nothin'. I thought maybe—that is he looked at me so hard—I thought maybe he took me for somebody else. He didn't say nothin'?"

"Nothin' 'tall."

Ossie looked relieved.

"So long, Lew!"

"S' long Ossie."

At nine o'clock Lew changed the white coat for a dark one, straightened his polka dot tie, put on his hat, and swaggered into the street, trying to stroll with the air of a gentleman of leisure out taking the air.

Lew always walked the length of the Avenue before going home. The street was lined with rows of tall, red brick houses still retaining some remnants of a former glory. Houses once the abode of aristocrats, now become the dwelling place of their servitors. People sat on the low, white stone door steps, making the most of the occasional breezes that sifted through the sultry air. People sauntered along talking, laughing, whistling snatches of popular tunes. Lew was enjoying himself immensely. He idled on his way, peering at the strollers so as not to miss a chance of speaking. He liked to appear to know everybody, and was in no way disturbed that some to whom he bowed responded coldly and others not at all.

From a house a short distance ahead came fragments of syncopation, the wail of a saxophone, the strumming of mandolins, the thumping of a piano—

"Everybody loves mah baby,
But mah baby don't love nobody but me,"

sang a husky voice above the instruments.

Lew noted the house where the party was in progress, and stopped to glance through the open windows at the dancers clasped tight in each other's arms, their bodies scarcely moving, their feet keeping up a rhythmic shuffle on the bare floor. None of the faces inside was sufficiently familiar for Lew to risk "breaking in" on the party. Disappointed, he was about to pass on, when a man and a woman mounted the steps and rang.

The door opened, and a wedge of light split the darkness. The man and woman were clearly visible to the watching Lew before they passed inside. His face hardened. He dug his nails into his palms.

"Had a date, eh?" he muttered. "A date with that damn black Matt Hicks. I ain't good enuf fo' you any mo' since you got to wearin' good clothes and goin' roun' with the high flyers. Matt Hicks eh! Who's Matt Hicks any mor'n me? Nothin' but a railroad porter crazy 'bout every good lookin' high yaller he sees. And they fall for him cause he's good lookin' and wears swell clothes and spends dough on 'em." Even in his jealous rage Lew remembered with envy the stalwart figure, the broad shoulders, the air of easy grace and poise that made Matt Hicks so popular with the women in spite of vague unsavory rumors concerning his amorous exploits.

"Turned me down for Matt Hicks," he muttered.

Lew continued his way up the Avenue but he no longer smiled nor bowed.

* * *

Saturday morning found Lew on hand at the store a half hour earlier than usual. He set to work at once, and before anybody else arrived he had finished his morning chores. He changed his blue porter's apron for the white coat, and taking the telephone directory began laboriously scanning its pages, all the while mumbling a number over and over. But there were frequent interruptions, and it was past noon before his search was rewarded. Taking a worn memorandum from his vest pocket he wrote—

>Hugh Middleton,
>>The Wellington Arms,
>>>Charles Street.

Then he waited his chance. When the store was empty he slipped into the telephone booth. Nervously he gave the number, Calvert 4683, and waited. A woman's voice answered. Lew's heart pounded at the familiar sound. He couldn't be wrong. That smoky softness was rather uncommon.

In a high falsetto he asked for Mrs. Middleton.

"Mrs. Middleton speaking," came the response.

Lew's story was ready. All day he had rehearsed what he would say. Hurriedly he went on. Would Mrs. Middleton care to look at a group of imported gowns that he was showing only to a few customers who had been recommended? His supply was limited. He'd like her to see them before the choice ones had been sold.

The soft smoky voice was answering. If he came at seven o'clock she would be in. She was going out at eight. She'd be glad to look at the gowns.

Lew hung up and mopped the perspiration from his face and neck. There was a malicious glint in the black eyes as he returned to his place at the fountain.

When the errand boy started out, Lew handed him an envelope. "Leave this while you're out," he directed. The envelope was addressed to Mr. Matthew Hicks.

But the boy had barely gotten out of sight when Lew began to have misgivings. He wished he hadn't sent the note. Suppose he had been mistaken? He had worked on such a slight clue. He had heard her call a number, had spent hours searching for that number, until he had located it and the name under which it was listed. He could think of no reason why Ossie should be calling an exclusive white apartment house— no reason except—. He had taken a chance on calling up the number and she had answered. Ossie had answered. He had been sure at the time that it was she, but suppose he was wrong! That note. True it was unsigned and the handwriting disguised—.

"If you want to know where your high falutin' high yaller gets her swell clothes and where she spends her week-ends go to The Wellington Arms, Charles Street at 8 o'clock," he had written.

Lew knew Matt's boast that no nigger could get a woman away from him. Well, let Matt see her with an ofay. She would be going out about eight she had said. Lew knew Matt would follow the clue—would try to find out what it meant. Well let him feel what he, Lew, had felt. Matt was such a smart guy. He wouldn't fly so high after he knew. And Ossie,—maybe, with Matt out of the running, Ossie might not be so uppish with a drug store porter.

Evening came. Greene & Scott's Pharmacy always did a rushing business on Saturday night. Refreshments were not much in demand, and Lew was pressed into service to cater to the wants of the stream of customers that came in search of means for improving either health or pulchritude. They asked for every known tonic and pill; every cream, lotion, powder, pomade, and perfume on the market, and some that weren't. Lew usually enjoyed his Saturday prestige, but tonight he was ill at ease. How the time lagged! Nervously he watched the door and the clock longing for closing time.

Then, vaguely into the penumbra of his consciousness, was born the sense of a commotion outside. A woman screamed. People went running in the direction of the sound. Lew strode to the door. Half-way down the block a taxi had stopped. People crowded around it. Lew, straining eyes and ears to catch the meaning of it all, dimly saw a form being carried into a house. At length the bystanders began to move away. Stray snatches of comment floated to him.

"Oh boy!"
"Tell you 'bout cheat'n!"
"Kinder bowled the old lady over."
"Wonder how bad she's hurt?"
"Old Matt sho' did get her."
"Did he make a get-a-way?"
"He didn't miss."
The errand boy emerged from the crowd. Lew grabbed him by the shoulders.
"What's the matter down the street?"
"Miss Ossie Pitts is been hurt and old lady Pitts is tryin' to die."
"Hurt? Miss Ossie?" Lew's throat was dry. "Hurt? How?"
"Some guy saw her out walkin' with an ofay and slashed her with a razor."
"Slashed Ossie Pitts?"
"Uh huh."
"Bad?" Lew tried to hide his agitation.
"Oh, they say she ain't hurt bad, but she's sho marked for life. He got her right across the face. They give her treatment at the hospital but when they found she was colored they sends her home. When her Maw sees 'em bringing' er in all bandaged up she yells blue murder."

Lew's hands fell heavily from the boy's shoulders. Slowly he shambled out of the door and down the street. Only a few people now stood looking curiously at the Pitt's house. From inside came a woman's sobs. Lew slouched against a lamp post, staring blankly at the lighted second story windows, oblivious of the presence of the by-standers—of their abortive attempt at humorous comment on the fracas. Ossie—marked for life—he hadn't thought—he hadn't meant—God! His face worked painfully.

The sobbing ceased. The lighted windows grew dark. Inside all was quiet . Outside only Lew kept watch. The Avenue had forgotten.

[*Opportunity* 6.10 (October 1928): 301–303]

A Slave for Life:
A Story of the Long Ago

by Coralie Franklin Cook

Night had settled down upon the big plantation. All was darkness and stillness. No horse was neighing in the stables, no dog barking in the kennels. One lone light shone, as was the custom, in the lower hall of the great house. Elsewhere the darkness was so dense that the man had to grope his way along the path to the bay. When nearly there he turned aside and, still groping his way, crept into a thick shrubbery. Suddenly kneeling, he brushed away some leaves and moss, evidently familiar to his touch, and arose holding a bundle. It was enveloped in a piece of sacking and it contained all his earthly possessions. Attaching it to a stout stick, previously provided, he turned back to the path and with quickening steps reached the water's edge.

Once there, he stopped and, peering about in the black darkness, bent his head, first in one direction then in another, as if listening intently. Apparently satisfied, he waded out into the stream and loosened from its moorings a row boat into which he sprang as lightly as if he had been working in broad daylight.

Ephraim had been wise in his selection of time and tide. Had there been a patrol near, his figure would scarcely have been discernible, so deep was the gloom, and he had no need yet to dip his oars, for the tide was taking the boat out in the very direction he wanted it to go.

When he had drifted far enough away from shore to be satisfied that his departure had not been noted, he rose from his crouching attitude, fitted the oars into their locks and began making strong, swift strokes that sent has bark steadily forward.

The night afforded no friendly North star to guide this solitary boatman, and he was too intelligent not to be conscious of his danger. Even in the darkness some belated vessel might run him down, overhaul and capture him; yet there was in his heart more fear of what lay behind than of what might await him ahead.

From childhood Ephraim had been familiar with the waters of "old" Chesapeake, and in the ship yards of Baltimore, working for six long years at his trade of caulking, he had learned so much of their art from sailors that he was far from being a novice in the *role* of seaman.

His plan was to go ahead as rapidly as possible, all the time keeping near enough to shore to be able to make a quick landing in case of need. By daybreak he must be at least twenty miles from the place of starting.

He must land where he could hide during the day and resume his journey at night fall.

His capable mind worked clearly and rapidly and, as the blackness changed to gray on sky and water, his muscular arms bent to their task with unflagging energy. Several times he stood up and, balancing himself in the small craft, sought to get his bearings. His whole being pulsed with joy at the certainly that he had made good time. He felt his muscles strong as tempered steel. "All my life," he murmured, "they've been working for others, now they're working for me." How he loathed the thought of that slavery to which he was still bound!

Listening to the swish of the waters, they seemed to him to follow the stroke of the oars with words like these, on the one side, "A slave!" and on the other, "for life"! The repetition kept up—"A slave!—for life!" "A slave!—for life!" What a horrible nightmare it was! He must shake it off and push ahead.

Already it was time to think of landing, for day was breaking—a new day indeed for the man in the boat! His keen eyes watched the dim outline of shore.

There were numerous landing-places, and selecting one which seemed best suited to his purpose, the boatman beached his craft and, with bundle and stick, set forth upon land.

Who can fathom the depth of the conflicting emotions in this free-born soul seeking liberty for its fettered body? Fearful but determined and shunning danger, Ephraim pushed cautiously on. He was well aware that, had he stayed on the water, with the coming of day he was almost certain to be captured, if not by those directly in pursuit of him, then by others of that scarcely human element who made their living by lying in wait for runaway slaves and securing the prize money awarded when the poor creatures were returned to their masters.

After walking some little distance the wanderer knew himself to be about twenty-five miles from home. Not wholly unfamiliar with the neighborhood, he felt sure of finding some shelter where he might hide until, under cover of darkness, he could again resume his flight.

Stealthily he set out to find the highway. Before reaching it, however, he came up against a rail fence and there, as if especially provided, beheld, with joy, a great straw stack, fresh and sweet and clean. Some distance away and separated by another fence cattle were grazing. It was reasonable to conclude that he was near some habitation. Daylight was dangerously near and he knew the habits of overseers too well to take any risk. He must quickly worm his way into that straw stack so providentially at hand.

Look at him, poor fugitive, before he conceals himself! His physical match would be hard to find. More than six feet tall, his body and limbs are so well proportioned that he does not seem of undue height. A head, noble in outline, is covered with a mass of dark, curly hair. His skin is of that peculiar, golden tint—the legacy of one born of a black mother and white father. His eyes, big, dark and usually keen, are now full of apprehension and sadness. Running from the accursed soil of slavery he senses all the meaning of liberty and once on the way his mind is made up never to be taken alive.

Making several irregular openings near the bottom of the stack and strewing a few handfuls of straw about the ground to simulate the appearance due to the depredations of passing cattle, Ephraim was not long in selecting a place of entrance and, after taking one long, searching survey of his surroundings, bowed his head and, working his way with shoulders, hands and feet, burrowed far into the stack of straw.

His last thought was to reach out one hand and pull a heavy rail across the very place where he had entered. Half sitting, half lying down and in a decidedly cramped position, the poor fellow settled himself for the long hours of waiting.

After all the place was not so stifling as he had expected, for the straw had been stacked so as to let rain, sunlight and air filter through, and even in his great extremity Ephraim breathed a prayer of thankfulness for the good fortune that had so far attended him.

Lying there, he began to think over his great adventure. How long he had been planning to get away! He could hardly remember a time when the thing had been out of his mind. All his past came before him. Once more he was a little boy tumbling about his "gran' mammy's" door in company with other slave children. Thoughts of her brought memories of the ash cake she used to make, and all at once her runaway grandson became ravenously hungry. Drawing some bread and meat from his pocket he began to eat in considerable discomfort, which was in no sense alleviated by a great thirst that made his throat ache and burn. Reviling the stupidity which had let him forget to provide himself a flask of water, he once more fell into a train of thought.

This time it was his mother who came into his mind. He had seen her so seldom and knew so little about her. She had been a field hand and had visited him mostly at night; but how tender she was, and what happiness it had been to climb into her lap and forget cold and hunger, loneliness and every childish grief, as she crooned over him and told him those funny stories about "brer" fox and "brer" rabbit. In a childhood so destitute of those things dear to all children, that mother love made the one green spot in the desert of bondage. Tenderly, reverently, he thought of that mother who now lay in a lonely grave on the old plantation.

Ephraim recalled at what an early age he had discovered his social status, and with what deep mortifications and sense of injustice he had found himself to be a slave, and not only a slave, but, *a slave for life!* with no way out.

Once more he was going up to the great house to be outfitted for work. He was a big boy now. Hitherto his garb had been of the simplest sort—a tow linen shirt falling just below the knees. He had long been ashamed to be seen in it and had kept out of folks' way as much as possible. Now he came into possession of two pairs of coarse cotton pants, the same number of "hickory" shirts and one pair of heavy shoes. Such continued to be the annual supply of his wardrobe until he had succeeded in hiring his time and had bought clothes of his own choosing. Thus memories of the past surged through his active mind.

He felt glad he had learned to read and write, he laughed even, as there rose before him sidewalks which had stood for him in lieu of blackboards, and the sign boards, bits of newspaper and barrel heads that had been his teachers.

Again returned the weary days in cotton and corn field, the welcome change from country to city life when he had worked in the great shipping yards, the savage unrest that had made him long for liberty, and, at last, the determination to escape.

One by one, faces of the old slaves he had known, came before him. "Broke-back Mimy," who bore the appellation because she went about terribly bent over, and whose back actually had been broken by a fence rail in the hands of an angry overseer; "Unc Lem," who had but one eye, having lost the other in a fight with his young master. Ephraim shuddered and tried to banish thoughts of his unfortunate old fellow-servant. It had been because of "young mahstah's" unwelcome attentions to the slave's comely wife that the fight had been so bitter and the punishment so terrible, for poor Lem had come out worsted.

These and similar episodes had made deep and lasting impressions upon Ephraim and had caused him to swear, while yet a stripling, that he would never marry unless he became free, never be the father of a child. Now, saddest of all the sad thoughts that filled his mind was the memory of Nan, whom he had left behind. He loved Nan. He had not even told her goodbye, trusting her intuition to tell her why. Would she, perhaps, bear a child to some other man, husband or no? True, she was a free woman, but how many free women escaped the slime of the slavery cursed country? Afflicted by all these torturing thoughts, apprehensive concerning the outcome of his attempt to escape, the fugitive's weary body crumpled up and he gave himself to utter misery.

At last he fell asleep and for hours slept as only the healthy, yet worn and weary, can sleep.

Aroused at last by the sound of loud and angry voices, he instantly became alert. Heavy footsteps were close to his hiding-place. Sticks were being thrust into the stack. Merciful God! Was he to be captured like a rat in a hole? Great tremors ran through his body. He broke into a heavy sweat, his very flesh seemed crawling. What was it they were saying? "No use looking for the d— nigger in here. He's either on the road or on the water."

Ephraim knew that voice only too well. It belonged to his master's overseer, a man given to oaths, to whiskey, to the cowhide and shotgun. He held his breath. Evidently the words had been heeded, for after some further cursing and kicking, footsteps and voices ceased to be heard. Ephraim, however, was thoroughly alarmed. He must think, *think* what it was best to do. The going off might be only a trick to lure him out; in that case he would be perfectly still and give them a game of waiting. So for a long time he remained in his cramped position, not daring to move and breathing softly.

Finally he concluded that the searching party had gone, but for some reason he could not shake off the impression that they would return—and soon. This foreboding became unbearable. It was impossible to stay there longer. He must get away.

Brushing aside the straw, he peered cautiously out; not a creature was to be seen. Looking skyward he was amazed to read by the sun's slanting rays that it was late afternoon. Crawling out from the stack he lay for a short time prone on the ground. He thought of his boat but was too shrewd to go in search of it.

At right angles to the road by which he had approached the stack of straw lay a dense wood. Poplars, maples, oak and the thick shade of the horse chestnut all were there. Less than a quarter of a mile from where he lay he could safely hide in one of those trees. His pursuers would hardly think to look for him there, at any rate it seemed the only present means of escape and he would try it.

Taking from his pocket a small tin box, he dipped from it a quantity of tar with which he smeared liberally, the soles of his feet and, after making sure that there was no one in sight, he crept away, at first on hands and knees until some yards from the stack, then rising, he fled in great leaps and bounds to the shelter of the woods.

Selecting a big tree whose branches were covered with broad and thick leaves, Ephraim lost no time in disposing of himself as he had been wont to do when a boy at play and when, as he now remembered hopefully, none of his mates had ever been able to "smoke" him out. Nor was he settled a minute too soon. Whether some divine prescience or the "root" given him by "conjurah" Sam had guided him, he was not at all certain, but the baying of hounds fell upon his ear and, as cold chills ran up and down his spinal column, sounds of threats and curses mingled with the yelping of the bloodthirsty beasts that had been brought to trail him. To add to his horror a great blaze of light warned him that the slave hunters had set fire to his late hiding-place. The stack had been a big one and even in the shelter of the tree Ephraim began to fear that the brilliant light might reveal his presence should the searchers come into the woods. With anxious heart he waited but they never turned in his direction.

What was it that had prompted him to bring the tar? By means of it the hounds had lost scent and his pursuers had been baffled. Was it God? He believed so, and as the sound of horse's feet was lost in the distance and the noise of beasts and men ceased to beat upon his listening ears he was overcome by a strange ecstasy. Instead of feeling scared and despondent as he had in the straw stack he now rejoiced in the belief that he was destined to escape. Had not the waters of the Red Sea divided for the children of Israel? Were not the three Hebrew children protected from the flames of the fiery furnace? Was not he, Ephraim, in the care of the same Jehovah who had guarded them? With thoughts like these, the lone wayfarer kept his place in the crotch of the oak until darkness had fallen, and stiff and sore he let himself down from his place of sanctuary.

His throat was parched and dry. He could no longer do without water, and in the falling darkness with a woodman's instinct he hunted for a spring. He failed to find one, but a brook was coursing through the woods, and stretched at full length he drank and drank and felt so refreshed that he began, in his sanguine way, to wonder whether these might not be healing waters given him by the "God of Moses."

Not long, however, did Ephraim indulge in fancy. Very cautiously, for there was still a bit of lingering daylight, he made his way to the open road. Every fence rail must be watched; every tree trunk. The slightest sound, even the fall of a dead leaf, staid his eager footsteps. Were the shadows peopled? To his tense imagination they sometimes were.

With the settling down of night the wayfarer kept steadily on. Presently he came to a cross road which he recognized with glad surprise, for it meant that he was miles from home and not far from the town of H—, where, if he could reach it before day, he was sure of finding shelter among friends.

At thought of friends his heart kindled, for the burning straw stack, the sickening bay of the bloodhounds and the vigil in the tree top had taken toll of his strong nerves, and he felt a choking in his throat and held back unbidden tears.

It was about four o'clock in the morning when, foot-sore and weary, Ephraim entered the little town of H—, at the mouth of the Susquehannah river. Folks were not up yet and he made his way toward the familiar out of the way spot where his friends lived.

No sound of man or beast broke the quiet. The choking pain that had, for a while, affected him was gone, and breathing far more freely he hurried on. A turn of a corner and poor Ephraim found himself facing a gun! "Halt, nigger!" came the challenge. He obeyed instantly. "Wha's yo' pass?" With apparent coolness Ephraim produced one which he himself had written. Swinging his lantern close to the paper the patrol took a long time to look it over. He belonged to the class known as "crackers" and his knowledge of letters was probably less than Ephraim's own. Finally he grunted out, "Papah seems ter be all right, but what yer doin' heah?" "I've been 'lowed time off t' visit some friends," with a show of confidence. "Wal, yer kin go on." The stricture in Ephraim's throat began to relax. He had barely taken two steps forward, however, when the watchman was once more close behind him. "I dunno as I orter let yer go on; yer don't look ner talk like a' eastern sho' darkey; but nevah min', go erlong, I kin soon ketch yer if yer up ter any tricks." "Oh, I'm all right, sir," was the shrewd rejoinder, and Ephraim trudged on.

Silas Jones was a slave who hired his own time. His wife was a free woman and in a tiny house in a back street they lived and toiled.

Ephraim was made heartily welcome. He was permitted to take a warm bath, to eat a substantial meal and to sleep while Silas and Nancy kept watch. At midnight Silas awakened him and he set forth upon the last lap of his journey.

To the watchman at the bridge he presented an entirely different pass, with a different name from the one given the patrol whom he had met in the early morning, and was permitted to proceed without question.

Having crossed the bridge, and feeling much better as a result of the kindly ministrations of his humble friends, Ephraim set out almost light heartedly. Silas, who was a teamster, and familiar with all the roads, had given him careful directions and he knew he was not far from the Pennsylvania line—and Freedom! That thought which had haunted him for so long, that he was a slave for life, had fallen into a mental background and in its stead dreams of liberty were shaping themselves—reunion with Nan, a home and—What was that? A footstep in the dark? A falling twig? Which? "It's late for me to be getting scared now," he thought, as he started to cross a field in order to skirt a village where lights were still burning. Once more he stopped, assured now that he was being followed. Turning around abruptly he encountered, not a patrol as he had feared, but a Negro who advanced toward him and in a friendly voice said, "Howdy, man, what's yo' hurry?" The voice and words were reassuring, and with the utmost relief Ephraim answered in an easy way, "Well, it's late, ain't it, to be on the road? Time all honest folks was in bed, eh?" "Oh, I dunno," laughed the newcomer, "I'm heah an' I peahs t' be hones', doesn't I? I jes come this way fo' a sho't cut. I lives on the' aidge o' town an' this brings me out right neah muh stoppin place. Is yo' goin fuh, may I ax?"

Thrown completely off guard by the friendly bearing of the fellow, poor Ephraim forgot to be cautious and admitted, "Yes, I've got a good bit further to go."

The two chatted amicably, and, leaving the field, after a time, struck back again into the road.

When they had trudged along for about a mile the man halted. "Well, stranjah," he said, "heah we pahts company, I reck'n, lessen you'll cept o' sheltah wiv me fo' the' night." Ephraim was not ungrateful for the offer, but too eager to push on to be temped by it, so, reaching out a hand, he was about to say a cheery goodbye when his new acquaintance uttered so loud a guffaw that it caused him to hesitate. That was no genuine laugh. It seemed like a signal.

Accustomed to the tricks to which slaves often resorted to secure secrecy or give warning, he braced himself for he knew not what.

It flashed through his mind how that officer at the bridge had let him cross without a word. Why had he not thought of it sooner? Anyway he had been betrayed. Before he had time to realize what was happening a horseman had come upon them, and flashing a lantern in their faces, demanded to know that they were doing there at that time of night. Ephraim recognized in the horseman, who had now dismounted, a white man of low grade, probably a "nigger trader," and as he bent to scrutinize the face of his late friendly companion he was at once convinced that he had been fooled and betrayed by that lowest and meanest of human beings—a Negro kidnapper of runaway slaves, working in collusion with a poor white.

Righteous indignation gave strength to the poor, hunted creature. He knew himself too near his goal to give up until he had exhausted his every means of self-preservation. Moreover, he did not doubt his ability to match both the men in a fair fight.

No sooner was he aware that the white man was leveling a pistol at him than he sprang forward with the agility of a panther, knocked the weapon from the threatening hand and, before his would-be captor could recover from his surprise, pinioned both his arms and bore him to the ground, where he beat him almost into insensibility.

What, in the meantime, had become of the Negro, coward that he was? Afraid to openly desert his confederate, though he offered no assistance, he was now cowering before the angry giant who had exhibited such rare courage in assailing one of the master class. Weakly, but mistakenly, he essayed to keep up the *role* of friend, for Ephraim, enraged by the fellow's treachery and smarting under the humiliation of having permitted himself to be so easily trapped, turned on the black kidnapper with terrible wrath. "You scoundrel!" he cried, heedless of the possibility of being heard, "I've a mind to break every bone in your cursed little body. Don't open your mouth or I'll kill you. Take the rope from the horse's saddle," he commanded, as, at the same time he got possession of the fallen pistol. Compelling the black traitor to cross his hands behind him, he fastened them securely, did the same for his feet, and then gagged him in the most approved fashion.

As the first victim of his physical prowess began to give signs of returning sense, Ephraim lost no time in attending to his needs, omitting the gagging.

"I'll leave you two to keep one another company, and if it wasn't that I have fear of Almighty God I'd have sent you both to the hell where you belong."

Afterward when he remembered his fury and his profanity, Ephraim was at a loss to account for the latter. Never before had he been half so profane! Accustomed as he was to hear cursing and blasphemy, he had always scorned their use, but on this occasion he seemed not to be able to speak enough of strong and bitter words.

Free now to continue his journey, he felt a sickening sensation come over him, and found himself trembling in every limb.

Great God! Was he to give up now, now so near to freedom? Summoning all his strength, he stumbled along. But it was a stumble, no longer the steady tramp, tramp that was taking him to a "Promised Land." Still he kept on. Once he went straight through a village, making no attempt not to be seen. In a measure dazed, he was conscious of but one thought—On! on! he must keep on! All at once he began to run, slowly at first, then faster and faster. Was it a race? It seemed so to him and that he, Ephraim, was ordained to be the winner. Faster! faster! Harder! harder! Were his lungs bursting? Was he going blind? There was no longer any time, any world, anything, only the race, until finally he tottered and fell.

There he lay, poor, hunting fugitive, pitiful yet noble slave, who had willed to barter life itself in quest of liberty!

When he came to himself day had broken. A figure was bending over him. A tall, slightly built man of middle age, wearing a drab suit and broad rimmed hat of the same color was shaking him gently and demanding to know if he were ill.

Where was he? What had happened? For a minute or two everything was blank, then it all came back to him—the Negro who had betrayed him, the fight and flight.

He bethought him of the sorry picture he must make, and rose to his feet while the Quaker who had stopped to befriend him took account of his towering height, his breadth of shoulder and his great dark eyes, full of sadness and mystery. "I have lost my way," he faltered, "and I must have fallen asleep." "Thee must be very tired. Get into my wagon and I will give thee a lift."

At these words Ephraim saw for the first time a small spring wagon in the road, from which the stranger had evidently alighted. Slowly he fixed his gaze upon this good Samaritan. The answering look, honest, serene, friendly, sent great waves of confidence and cheer through all his stricken spirit. He asked no questions, felt no fear, but with the faith of a little child seated himself beside this angel of his deliverance.

Was it chance or was it God? The man in drab was one of the most vigilant and untiring "conductors" on the "Under Ground Railroad."

By nine o'clock that August morning, the two were well across the Pennsylvania state line.

In Ephraim's heart a great joy was upspringing and in place of the dirge, "A slave!—for life!" a new song was singing itself though all his being—the Song of Freedom!

[*Opportunity* 7.6 (June 1929): 183–187]

Dark Laughter

by Ethel Riley*

"Here comes the circus parade!"

Magic words of American childhood! In order that the pupils might witness the eventful pageantry, both the white and colored schools of Lodar, county seat in Mississippi, had dismissed classes for the day. Central Avenue was aflutter with whites, near-whites, browns and blacks, all children of God for one fleeting hour.

Chloreta Collins, better known as Rita, skillfully wormed her way through a group of scattered onlookers until she secured a clear site for her class of some fifteen children. Having ascertained for the fortieth (or was it the fiftieth?) time that her brood was still intact, she gave herself to the affair of the moment. Laughter and good natured banter on every side. Claws of racial animosity smugly folded under for the time being.

"O, lookut, Miss Rita! See that horse! Golly, don' he cut up!"

"An' jes' lookut them Injuns? Be they honest-tuh-goodness Injuns, Miss Rita?"

"An' O, Miss Rita! Looked that big thing what looks lak a cat! What'd y'all tell us that'n is?"

*With apologies to Sherwood Anderson

Her patience was unlimited but her interest negative.

"Ah-h-h!"

The children looked their surprise at her sudden ejaculation. The sound had the peculiar quality of wind hissing in treetops. Her eyes, usually calm and of a piercing blackness, were eagerly riveted on a passing wagon cage. The children followed the glance and beheld that spine-thrilling headliner, the beautiful snake charmer.

This one held a python, twelve or fourteen feet long, passively wrapped about her. Instinctively the children huddled close to Rita, but Rita had eyes and attention for the snake charmer only. A hand touched her lightly on the arm. Turning, she looked into the mysterious, compelling eyes of a gaunt black woman. No word passed but two pairs of kindled black eyes feverishly followed the wake of the snake charmer, until the cage was lost to sight.

When the last elephant had passed Rita turned to address her silent companion. The woman had disappeared as abruptly as she had come. Instead, the teacher looked into the leering face of a half drunken white.

"Howdy, Rita!"

Tobacco juice rimmed the loose, sensual lips. Subconsciously she noted the similarity in texture between the skin of his neck and that of the elephants that had just passed.

Carnally, he appraised her.

"Lookin' powerful good this evenin'!"

No answer.

"See heah, you! You ain't got no call tuh put on airs with me. Ah'm gettin' damn tired o' y'all's foolishness an' Ah don' aim tuh stan' it no longer. Ah done picked y'all fo' mah wench an' damit Ah'm a-goin' a have yuh!"

A fiery wad of tobacco juice spewed forth.

She had shooed the children on ahead and the man was walking at a discreet distance behind her.

"Reckon y'all got some niggah bastud, huh?"

Still no answer save two cheeks of crimson shame.

"Ah'll be at y'all's house directly aftah sundown tomorrer evenin'. You be thar an' be thar alone! Heah me!"

The tone augmented the open threat.

He was gone and she walked mechanically on without so much as a backward glance.

By this time the children had scattered, singly and in groups, to their several homes, still chattering excitedly of the many circus wonders. Rita neither saw nor heard them. She greeted this acquaintance and that in her habitual way but her smile was a contraction of facial muscles only.

She unlatched the gate of a flower-filled front yard. Here bloomed bachelor's-buttons, sweet alyssum, candytuft, four-o-clock and hollyhock in riotous profusion. In a sheltered corner the dainty Marechal Neil rose showered its soft, friendly beauty on all who chanced to look that way. The traditional front porch of the humble one-story cottage in the rear was effectually screened with a thick and redolent lattice of hardy honeysuckle and fragrant morning-glory.

Walking stolidly on to the rear of the house, Rita entered by way of a back porch into a full length hall which gave access to the three parallel rooms. She entered her own. Those piercing eyes of black now gave back a cold, hard glitter but the body moved rhythmically on, its tempo unchanged.

The most pretentious article of furniture in the room was a bird's eye maple dresser with beveled glass of narrow dimensions. Having changed her clothes she walked over to the dresser, leaned forward until her face was scarcely an inch from the surface of the mirror and gazed unblinkingly at her reflection. Hate glowed furiously there.

Abruptly she laughed, a laugh as cruel and hard as her eyes. Then she went out into the backyard and on into the woodhouse, whence she presently emerged with a small empty barrel and an improvised tool kit which she carried into the detached kitchen.

Placing the barrel in a corner, she walked over to the opposite doorway where sat a gaunt black woman picking over collard greens, the while she smoked a strong corncob pipe. Rita seated her.

The old woman's ferreting eyes continued to wander back and forth from the barrel to Rita. At length the eyes of black grandmother and quadroon granddaughter met. A searching glance and then cold, mirthless laughter.

The task finished, Rita arose to wash the greens and put them to cook in the pot with the fat meat. The gaunt black woman locked her hard, worn-out hands and relentlessly looked off into memory. Her clear mind again conjured up the oft-told tale of her dead father. In vivid imagination she re-lived the familiar graphic scene.

Code drum beats! The krajio's prophecy was being fulfilled! In the brooding hush of the oppressively still, equatorial noon, the portentous, replayed omen startled the sleeping natives into instant, disorganizing activity, for the prophecy had also predicted subjection, annihilation, for this much warred-against black tribe of the African bush.

Her father, the only child of the chief, was then a boy of nine. True to family tradition, he had been faithfully taught the art of the krajio, apprenticing from the time he was able to walk and to talk.

That afternoon the invading tribe pounced upon the village and savagely fulfilled the witch-doctor's prediction. Of all the men the chief, her grandfather, alone was spared because of his superior cash value. Together with the woman and children he and his little son were marched to the coast. There, with seven hundred other captives, they were sold into the bowels of a slave hell-ship bound for young America.

The proud old chief took ill on the voyage and died soon after reaching land, but the son remembered his teachings and practiced them secretly. When in after years a daughter was born to him, he piously passed the knowledge on to her.

"An' it nevah been fail me yet," she muttered.

Captivity and arduous toil had curtailed the opportunity for highest development of the art. Superstition the white folks called it. Telepathy and hypnotism are the names they should have applied to it.

Again she lived the agony of the auction black. Her mother ruthlessly torn from her by the yelping, bullying auctioneer and dragged away by her newest purchasers. Herself tossed inconsequentially into a group of five or six male slaves and driven like cattle before the lash to the plantation that became home. She had neither seen her nor heard of her mother since.

Her toilworn body began to rock and her resonant voice kept time with the majestic, age-old slave plaint:

"Go down, Moses.
Way down in Egyp' lan'.
Tell ole Phar'oh,
Let mah people go!"

The song died away but the body continued its rhythmic swing, the vein-knotted hands hard-locked.

Having finished the preparations for supper, Rita resumed her place on the doorstep. The gaunt black woman shifted the pipe to the opposite corner of her mouth.

"When he say?"

"Tomorra, come sundown."

The two women looked at each other with an all-knowing, voluble glance. Then hollow, deadly laughter.

Rita stood up abruptly as though suddenly remembering something. She crossed quickly to where the small barrel stood in its corner and lifted off the close-fitting cover. Next, she searched in the depths of the homely took box until she found a bit and brace. For the next half hour she occupied herself with boring holes in the wooden head and a single one on either side of the barrel near the top and directly opposite each other.

This task finished, she extricated from the kit a heavy steel wire of medium length and proceeded, with aid of pliers, to fasten the ends of the wire into the two holes on either side of the barrel. Silently the gaunt black woman watched. Awkwardly but surely Rita toiled and soon had the wire so adjusted that by giving a strong, quick pull the fastening bolted from its mooring and left the cover free.

Three times she experimented with it. Apparently satisfied, she disappeared into the dusk of the back yard with the covered barrel. A few minutes more and the clank of a horse's harness punctuated the solemn stillness. Staid hoof-beats and the accompanying cadence of revolving wagon wheels soon followed. The gaunt black woman rocked, sang and chuckled. The stride that carried her to her room a few minutes later was born in the wilds of the African jungle.

On bended knees she sent up a wild, impassioned prayer to her Christian God, then standing stiffly erect began a series of magic incantations of witchcraft lore. This continued for about a half hour. At the end of that time she succinctly muttered three unintelligible words and crawled slowly into bed. Her piercing eyes burned with a mystic light.

She lay awake until even hoofbeats and crunching wheels passing her window, announced Rita's return. A little later a reverberating sound followed the placing of a heavy article on the kitchen floor. A faint, weary laugh resounded. The old woman echoed it and dropped placidly off to sleep.

The next morning was as other mornings. The grandmother prepared the breakfast of hominy grits and fried fat meat, coffee and feathery biscuits while Rita fed the chickens and Ben, the old brown horse.

The gaunt black woman was devoted to Ben. As a young woman she had been an Amazon, equaling many of the male slaves in physical strength. The overseer had used her regularly to follow the plow and in emergencies to walk before it, yoked to a male companion. Old age now demanded its toll of an outraged body and whenever any distance greater than a block was involved, the faithful Ben and a clattering old farm wagon supplied the means of locomotion.

On entering the kitchen Rita walked over to the barrel, now returned to its corner and after bending intently above it for some seconds, gently released the steel fastening.

As the two women seated themselves at the oil-cloth-covered breakfast table, the barrel cover was pushed off and the ugly head of a spotted brown-black python slowly lifted itself from within and by means of graceful waves and ripples guided its body into the middle of the room, stopped, then glided noiselessly on to the side opposite the two women.

Neither of them appeared to notice him but a careful observer would have seen the hypnotic glare which the old woman fastened on the girl. Finally he crawled up on the central kitchen beam by way of the unsealed wall. From his lofty perch he continued to regard them with his small, beady eyes.

Breakfast over, the grandmother seated herself in a rocking chair near the open doorway. Taking a plain white bowl from the cupboard, Rita poured into it as much milk as it would hold and placed it in the middle of the floor. Then she sat down in the same chair she had occupied at the breakfast table.

Minutes passed and no one moved. At last slowly and with infinite grace the long, brown reptile lowered itself from the beam to the floor, landing within a few inches of the bowl. Greedily he consumed the milk. The glittering eyes of both women were steadily centered on him. Slowly he began to glide about the room. After several twistings and turnings he brought up in the middle of the floor.

Raising his head little by little, higher and higher, he began to sway from side to side, the two seeming poles of attraction being the watchers. The grandmother shifted her gaze to the window. Slowly, very slowly, the python began to glide toward Rita. Her eyes remained unblinkingly fixed upon him. Up the right leg of her chair and into her lap he climbed, then up and around her neck, knapsack fashion.

She allowed him to remain so a moment, then almost imperceptibility extended both arms until they were on a perpendicular level with her shoulders. Slowly he unwound himself onto the length of the extended arms. Carefully she placed her right hand beneath his neck while with her left she gently stoked his body. Rising, she gradually raised her arms aloft until they were uplifted full length, supporting the huge reptile. The lips of the gaunt black woman moved as in prayer but her rapt gaze never left the window.

Moving over to the corner Rita deposited her load, tail first, within the barrel, put the perforated head back on and fastened it securely. She crossed to where the Grandmother sat in bent-over posture, now softly crooning a weird, triumphant chant, as she kept time with her feet. Rita stooped quickly and gratefully kissed the wrinkled forehead. With an aroused consciousness of time she darted off to her room and soon returned, fully dressed for school.

The routine of the classroom seemed endless and the circus chatter of the children distracting. Would they never stop shouting their foolish fear each time someone stupidly suggested the possibility of the secret presence of the much-advertised, escaped python? Yet she had no feeling of joy as she passed out of the rickety frame firetrap, known as the Prince Hall School, at the close of the day's duties. When she reached home the hand that unlatched the gate to the flower-filled front yard distinctly trembled.

This time she went straight to the kitchen first. The gaunt black woman sat in the same doorway as of yesterday, idly smoking her pipe but dressed in fresh, crisp, calico. Neither greeted the other though the grandmother nodded in answer to an unspoken query in Rita's eyes. The girl went directly to the make-shift stable and harnessed old Ben to the ancient wagon.

Her head beturbaned in spotless white and with a small, old fashioned shawl hung round her shoulders, the grandmother came forth and laboriously mounted the wagon seat. She gathered up the reins and clucked to old Ben who responded with a slow amble. Rita watched until they turned into the street then hurried to her room.

She put on a simple gingham housedress, patted her stringy brown hair into place and went back into the kitchen. Struggling valiantly with the heavy barrel she carried it from the kitchen to her room, placing it by the wall directly between the door and the bed. Then she drew a chair beside the barrel and sat down to watch its occupant through the holes. The little beady eyes returned her gaze.

The last rays of the blood-red sun suddenly wrapped the room in cloth of gold and vermilion. Rita got to her feet and lighted the coal oil lamp, turning it low. Leaving her room door open she went to sit on the back porch steps.

The first shadows of evening were falling when she became acutely conscious of stealthy footsteps on the cinder path. Pretending not to have heard, she rose and entered the dark hall. Bold footsteps mounted the three short steps and followed her in to the hall.

"Howdy, Rita!"

"Howdy."

"Ain't y'all got a kiss fo' a fellah?"

She evaded his clumsy grasp and escaped into her room, turning up the light. Quickly he followed her and closed the door.

He regarded her with a rakish grin.

"Ah allus knowed y'all'd take tuh me. Jus' been kiddin' me, ain't yuh, gal?"

He sidled over to where she sat on the farther side of the bed. Before he could reach her she vaulted nimbly to the opposite side.

"Lije Bonner. Ah'm a-warnin' yuh! Don't you touch me! Don't y'all come near me! Keep back. Ah say! It's dangerous. Ah tell yuh! You old fool! Keep back. Ah say!"

Ice and smoldering flames and pointed steel were in her voice. Her eyes championed every word.

Forestalling her next move he made an angry dash toward the only exit. There was a key in the door. The lock clicked and he put the key in his pocket.

The chase started again. Much pushing and pulling had drawn the frail iron bed into the middle of the room. Around and over it they went, the while the man grew audibly angrier and more profane. Watching his chance he pinioned her between the side of the bed and the door.

The struggle began.

The girl was no match against his demoniacal strength. Gradually he forced her down on the bed. She writhed and struggled until they both fell to the floor, directly beside the barrel. Planting one knee on her chest he impatiently pulled off his coat, revealing a sweat-stained shirt of indefinite color, open at the throat. As he turned to toss the coat on the bed, she desperately released the single fastening that held the barrel head.

As the man again attacked her, the huge, ugly head of the python shot from the barrel and fastened its teeth on the exposed chest of the man. Fourteen feet of swift brown spiral wrapped his body in a press of living steel. The acute sense of smell of the reptile had warned him of the turbulent presence of an enemy. Released, he made straight for that enemy.

Rita grabbed the snake by its neck and gently stroked it. By degrees the taut muscles relaxed and fell away from the crushed body. The body crumpled over and was silent.

The panting girl placed her heavy protector back in the barrel, fastening the top securely. From her closet she dragged forth a rusty-looking, moth-eaten blanket. Stoically she wrapped the lifeless form in it, then went outside on the porch steps to wait.

Nor did she wait long. Soon old Ben hove in sight with his single sphinx-like passenger. On seeing Rita the old woman drew up short and her eyes burrowed Rita's. The girl gave a slight nod and walked into the house. The gaunt black woman continued to sit on her lofty perch. Nor did she move when Rita returned dragging a long, blanket-enveloped weight which she pushed, tugged, and shouldered into the body of the ancient vehicle. Returning to the house again she next staggered out with the barrel.

Then and then only did the stolid figure descend from its post. Together they lifted the barrel into the wagon. Coatless and hatless, Rita helped her grandmother aloft. When Ben again headed for the highway the reins were in the urging hands of Rita. Jogging, trotting, poking, they rode until the outskirts of the next town were reached. The sudden panorama of circus tents became faintly visible. Nearer and nearer they rode until the animated outlines of the busy work-crew were clearly discernible.

Without pulling to one side Rita brought old Ben to a welcome halt and jumped to the ground. With all possible speed and concealment she unloaded her gruesome cargo and placed the two objects side by side on the ground. From within her blouse she drew forth a square-cut piece of red flannel and tied it to the wire fastening on one side of the barrel as a danger signal.

Next she reached into to the wagon for an old hand rake and painstakingly effaced all traces of her footprints and labor. Vaulting aloft by way of the hub, she urged old Ben into a trot, returning home by an entirely different route.

Still far outside of their home town, a gaunt black grandmother and a young quadroon granddaughter suddenly embraced each other and four avenged generations broke forth into a bitter laugh, mocked by accompanying tears.

[*Opportunity* 7.8 (August 1929): 250–253]

BEYOND THE YEARS

by Mary Etta Spencer

It is May. The sun is shining. Through the open windows the wind wafts the bitter sweet fragrance of the blossoming peach trees and the aromatic odors of the honeysuckle. The birds and the bees move here and there. The bees stopping to drink the nectar from the blossoms; the birds swelling their throats with songs. Out on the velvety green lawn, the dandelions lift their heads with impertinent pride. Beyond the lawn are fields of growing wheat whose lithe green bodies are tossed by the gentle breezes as the billows of the ocean. Without there is serene sublimity. Within restlessness.

Jennie Rice walked the floor. She was nonplussed. It was the first time during her period of teaching that she was ever so. In spite of her rigid discipline, she was losing absolute control of her pupils.

More than twenty years ago, Jennie Rice, then barely seventeen years old, accepted the position to teach at the little one room school in Rich Neck, a rural district in Queen Anne County, Maryland. She was compelled to accept this proposition before completing normal school, to support an invalid mother. She gave up the desire to go to college.

She taught two years, then closed the school with an afternoon May–day party for the children and their parents, with a firm decision never to enter its doors again. But she did. No one was ever able to learn the true reason. There were two rumors: one, she was not capable of teaching in the city schools, the other, she was in love with the son of a successful farmer. She boarded with his parents. Anyway she had come back so long ago that no attention was paid to anything that was said about her staying away.

Jennie turned her thoughts to her pupils. A restless mass of humanity.

"Less noise, less noise, please," she reiterated.

She ran her fingers through her affluent black hair. She glanced at the old hickory switch which had been ruled out of service, and now hung upon the side of the yellow painted two door bookcase, like some, pensioned, knighted veteran. She longed for the privilege of its usage once more. With it she could at least appease her own temper. The most she could do was to threaten its use. Anything more would have meant a mothers' day, even in the remote countryside.

She looked at her watch meditatively; two hours more before closing time. She would let them out for a few minutes to expel some of the excess energy, but one of the members of the school board lived near. He had no children. He had enforced a one recess law upon the school—that was at noon. His theory was "children are sent to school to learn—not to play." Jennie could think of no way out. She had asked each child to commit to memory a short verse from the Bible.

She thought that it would be a good time to hear them recite, but when each child, thirty of them, recited the eleventh chapter, the thirty-fifth verse of St. John, "Jesus wept," she went to the board and began to write.

A bright light flashed around the room. Jennie turned just enough to see Johny Maze busy with a piece of mirror. He was having difficulty to hold it so he could see down Leman Morgan's throat. He finally succeeded. Several others submitted themselves to the same test.

"All of you have two tongues and one of them will have to come out," he whispered.

Charles Higgins took two rulers and began giving an imaginary violin recital. Jim Taylor made funny faces and the children strove heroically to repress laughter. William Nickerson and Frank Saunders were interested in a picture of western harvesters in a geography. Jane Miller platted and unplatted Theresa Hinson's hair, until Jennie wondered that the child did not scream for mercy. Thomas Lee drew sketches of houses upon the top of his desk, until not an inch of space remained. He proceeded to do the sides. Clarence Wilson left his desk and stood looking at a hole in the ceiling with grave seriousness. Percy Hall stole across the room where the lunch baskets and buckets were and began eating everything that he could get. Stella Gould was talking so fast that Jennie wished she would choke, but she did not choke, and she was holding the attention of others too. Ned Nicholas measured Tete Sparks more than a dozen times. He was looking for a longer string. Norman Fassit crawled along the floor taking all the pencils that he could find in the desks. Mary Brown helped the twins, Bessie and Tressa Ferrel, to do their work. Here, and only here, did Jennie's heart soften. The twins were orphans. She tried hard to convince Mary that they must do their own work. William Adderson examined minutely a Sunday–school card. It contained the picture of the Apostle Paul.

"See!" William whispered to Thomas Gibbs, "He says he has finished his work."

Thomas eyed the card with vague indifference. He twisted his mouth to the side and whispered back, "Don't s'pose he had much to do." The thing that was uppermost in Thomas Gibbs' mind was the filling of the big wood box behind the stove before he could have his supper. The wood had to be cut.

Fred Wallace tried his fist on every boy within reach. Mattie Green seemed to think that no one was completely dressed without her help. And there were others that sat staring blankly into space. These annoyed Jennie more that the mischievous ones.

Staccatoed giggles resounded throughout the room. Jennie saw Joe Hinson making a desperate effort to seize a piece of paper that was being displayed by John Harrison, but not before she had seen an exact caricature of herself. Beneath the sketch was printed in large letters, "who would want this for a mom' don't understand nothing."

All sat nearly paralyzed with fright and ready for a severe scolding. They were not half as astonished as Jennie herself was when she commanded mildly and judiciously, "All pack books please."

As if in appreciation for the withheld reprimand, the children packed their books almost without a sound. Jennie tapped the bell. They stood. She tapped it again. They marched out. When the last one had left the door, Jennie sank into the chair and rested her head upon the desk. She made no effort to stifle the feeling of desperation.

"Oh, this dreary life. It is so terrible. I wish I could die. I am so tired of it all!"

She put on her things and went out. She locked the door and stood with her hand upon the knob. Some indefinable power seemed to possess her.

From over the roads came the voices of the departing youngsters. There was Edgar Burns' soft tenor voice,

> "Jesus lover of my soul,
> Let me climb the telegraph pole
> When that pole begins to shake,
> Take me down for Jesus sake."

Intermingled with it was Joe Green's melodious baritone,

> "Possum up dat 'simmon tree"

And like the drone of the king bee, floated Leman Morgan's resonant bass,

"Said the ant to the elephant, 'Look out, sir, who're you shov-ing!'"

Not one of the songs, the expression of adolescent youth, brought a single smile to Jennie's lips. To her they were so vulgar and so absurd.

She was aroused out of the reflectory stupor by the familiar voice of Uncle John Wright, who was renowned for his singing of camp-meeting spirituals. He could be heard distinctly at a distance of three or four miles.

He was returning from a cross county trip, with a load of phosphate. He was driving Joe and Pete, the only remaining team of oxen in the county. He was singing, "Don't call de roll till I git dere." Jennie turned her head in disgust and started on the three-mile walk to her boarding place, with disillusion emblazoned upon her heart.

* * *

It is May. The sun is shining. Through the open windows comes the perfume of the blossoming trees. The birds are singing, the bees are flying here and there. Without there is serene sublimity, within—

A woman trudges slowly along the country road.

"Hello there, Miss Jen, calls Uncle Nat Hinson as he stops his team of bays, panting and steaming like so much brown velvet. "Aint seen you 'round here for many a day. How far are you going?"

"Out to the school," answered Jennie almost derisively.

Uncle Nat opened wide his eyes. "By golly, had Jennie Rice come back to teach again?" She divined his thoughts.

"Oh, I'm like the black cat. I always come back." There was a twinkle in her dim eyes. "We are having a reunion," she added.

"Better hop in."

"No, I want to walk."

"But its over a mile to the school yet, Miss Jen."

"I know it. I know every inch of the road. But I want to walk. I'll go along slowly—I guess that's the only way I can walk now," she chuckled heartily. She held up a stout cane.

"This will help some," she smiled again.

After many protests the bewildered old man drove on. He was at his wits end, trying to find a cause that had brought about such a miraculous change in Jennie Rice. He arrived at but one conclusion; he was a widower.

As Jennie neared the school, she thought of a camp meeting spiritual that she had often heard the country folks sing. "Oh, what a change down here, things I used to see I don't see any more."

In the large orchards, where used to bloom the peach trees, rows and rows of tomato plants now lifted their yellow buds. The bleating of the sheep and the childlike cry of the lambs were hushed. They were replaced by herds of Jersey Reds, which moved slowly, almost gracefully as they nipped mouthfuls of clover. There also was strange vegetation growing in many of the fields where used to flourish the sturdy corn.

The pretty green thorn hedges, and the zigzag rail fences were replaced by wire fences of many descriptions.

Jennie was not sure she welcomed but one change, and that was the beautiful, smooth asphalt roads. They were a God sent blessing to the rural people.

Jennie was very tired when she entered the schoolroom. A stupendous welcome greeted her—silence.

Chairs and desks of modern style were arranged around the sides of the room. Lanterns were hung. Everywhere there were jars and jars of roses, roses that would have cost a small fortune in Baltimore, from which she came.

She walked to the desk and lifted its top. With trembling hands she brought forth the old roll book, wrapped in newspaper, now yellow with age, and the old bell. They had not been used for nearly thirty years. She laid them carefully upon the top of the desk. As she did her eyes encountered a volume of Paul Laurence Dunbar's complete works, left there by mistake, or perhaps, placed there on purpose. She took the book and glanced hastily through its pages. A poem on page one-hundred sixty-two interested her. She read the second stanza.

> "Beyond the years the prayer for rest
> Shall never more beat upon thy breast
>   The darkness clears,
> And morn perched upon the mountain's crest
>   Her form uprears—
> The day that is to come is best,
>   Beyond the years."

The silence was broken by the shrill whistle of an approaching car. She brushed back a stray lock of hair, and straightened her collar.

Leman Morgan entered. "Hello there, Miss Jen," his heavy voice resounding through the room. They clasped hands as only they do who are truly glad to meet.

An hour more and they were all there.

Jennie tapped the bell. They stood, and with bowed heads repeated the twenty-third Psalm. Jennie's hair, white almost to a strand, blended beautifully with the graying hair of her ex-pupils.

She lifted the roll book closer and with unsteady voice began calling the roll.

"Johnny Maze."

"Present—Throat specialist."

"Aaron Green."

There was silence. All bowed heads as Jennie said "Absent."

"William Nickerson."

"Present—Farmer."

Frank Saunders."

"Present—Farmer."

Jennie stopped. She stared. It seemed that a curtain was lifted and she was looking into the great blue ether. Before her was a mass of wiggling, scurrying, shapeless things.

"Jane Miller."

Present—Hair dresser."

"Leman Morgan."

"Present—Concert singer, bass."

Those shapeless things were taking form. The room was filled with—she looked closer. They were children, effervescent with the spirit of youth.

"Clarence Wilson."
"Present—Plasterer."
"Percy Hall."
"Present—Proprietor of a lunch room."
"Thomas Gibbs."
There was no answer. All bowed heads.
"Stella Golds."
"Present—Actress."
"Ned Nicholas."
"Present—Tailor."
"Norman Fassit."
"Sentenced to penitentiary for stealing," answered one of them.

Jennie nearly collapsed. Leman brought her a chair. "Better sit a while Miss Jen, I'm afraid you are a little tired."

She shook her head "no." Tears trembled on her long lashes.

"Mary Brown."
"Present—Founder of home for orphans."
"William Adderson—Minister—she was again at the board. She was writing, and they—
"Fred Wallace."
"Present—Prize fighter."

Children—children—she hears them calling her; she is going slowly down the aisle. Yes, dears, I'm coming. "How helpless they are," she thought. Each child is telling her of his future hopes—

"And when you come back," they whisper.

"No, I will not be back again. It is my last term."

"You can't fool us Miss Jen," they venture timidly, with mischievous glances toward each other.

She smiles—"Now they are ready to go, it is impossible to hold their attention longer—their thoughts are so abstract, and they are eager to be off—out there. If they would only stay and get wisdom and knowledge and understanding far out there—Ah, well they will go, it will be useless to try to keep them." She taps the bell. They stand—"How restless and impatient they are." She makes them wait, one tiny second, to them it is an eternity—she taps the bell again—they are gone.

Again she stands with her hand upon the door knob. Again some strange power seems to possess her. She lifts her head and through her dilated nostrils breathes in the balmy air.

"How beautiful is the handiwork of God—everywhere is manifestation of his greatness—earth and sea and—"

She smiles. "How funny are the songs of the departing youngsters. If they could only be children always. They are so happy and care-free." Tears stream down her face. She is walking—slowly—She stops to look at the western horizon, now crimson with the rays of the setting sun.

She smiles again. Before her is the scene of the boys making a dash after the sketch that they had drawn of her. How she had surprised herself more than them by not scolding. "They were right." She did not—the shades of night are gathering fast—ah, the echo of a voice, a voice tired; but full of happiness and submission. "Don't call de roll till I get there"—How often had that voice rung out in the early morns in bygone years—Did she hear the creaking of the heavy loaded two-wheel cart? There is a pause in the singing. He is urging Joe and Pete on. How faithful are the beasts of burden. How tender the driver—silence. They are crossing the stream. He will cross on the old bridge—no, there is a new bridge. The oxen will wade through the water. It will help the wheels and they will drink. Now they are ready for the heavy pull up the long hill. Half way up the hill Joe and Pete will rest on their knees. They will need no urging to go. How like a pilgrim traveler. At the top of the hill Uncle John will take his old blue handkerchief and wipe the lathery sweat from the heavy yoke. Then he will crack that heavy whip. No, no, not on the bodies of Joe and Pete; they have never felt the sting of the whip from him. The old cart is rumbling on. Uncle John will hum a few minutes. Then—Yes there it is ringing so clear. How beautiful is the rhythm and the words of that spiritual, "Sometimes up and sometimes down. Still my soul is Heavenward bound. Don't call de roll till I get dere." She is singing. But she is so tired. She will rest. No—she will go on. The twilight, so tranquil and soothing to the nerves. But the night is gathering fast—and she is so tired. She will rest just for a moment. How faint is Uncle John's voice. He must be nearing the end of his journey. There is silence.

Uncle Nat Hinson summons a passing farmer. They lift her into the wagon. On page one-hundred and sixty-two a handkerchief was placed directly on the poem. "Beyond the Years." The last two lines of the second stanza:

> "The day that is to come is best
> Beyond the years"

were marked.

Beyond the years Jennie Rice had understood.

[*Opportunity* 7.10 (October 1929): 311–313]

RECOMPENSE

by Lilith Shell

Old Alec Ferree lounged heavily in his chair and lifted the puffy lids from his bloodshot eyes. He stared dazedly about him, the furniture of the room appearing vague and distorted to his muddled vision. He raised one fat shaky hand and regarded the ragged nails of his fingers; he stretched out his big feet, encased in carpet slippers, and regarded them disgustedly, then planting them squarely upon the floor he essayed to rise, heaving himself unsteadily upward with the assistance of his hands upon the arms of his chair. Standing was a precarious undertaking and before he was able to balance himself sufficiently to take a step forward a horrible nausea seized him and he fell limply back into his chair, his head lolling miserably upon his shoulders. After a few minutes of semi-comitosity he again pulled himself together and reaching a small chair near him he banged upon the floor with it until it brought a response. The door of the room opened slightly and a dubious black face was thrust tentatively around its edge, plainly reconnoitering the situation before venturing in.

"Come on in, you damned old fool. What you hanging out there for? Nobody's going to kill you."

Alec mumbled his words thickly and a thin old woman evidently assured by them, slipped inside, softly closing the door behind her. Her attitude was one of respectful discretion and she kept silent and safely distant from the brutal old man in the chair.

"Get me some water, you Moll, and hustle up with it. My insides are on fire," he mouthed.

The woman disappeared and soon returned with a pitcher of ice water. Deftly adjusting the clutter of bottles and glasses on a small table she lifted it to a position easily accessible to Alec's shaking fingers and stood by while he gulped down the water, her hands upon her bony old hips. He drank long and deeply, giving lustily gratified grunts between draughts.

"Now fill me this bottle out of the demijohn in that corner cupboard," he ordered.

Moll moved with alacrity to the cupboard and lifting down the demijohn bore it toward the table.

"Doan seem t' be no likker in 'er, Marse Alec. Ah spec's y'all done drunk 'er all up, huh?" she said.

"Hold your tongue, you old fool. A man couldn't drink that jug full of liquor in six months," Alec snarled.

"Ah reck'n y'all c'd drink 'er soonah'n dat, Marse Alec," responded the old Negress as she rested the mouth of the jug upon that of the bottle. Vainly she tipped the great jug higher and higher. "She'm all gone, anyhow," she announced.

Alec regarded her suspiciously out of his swollen eyes but she remained well out of his reach and her wrinkled and leathery old face was inscrutable.

"I guess you have company of our own off and on, Moll, but I don't remember giving you permission to treat 'em out of my demijohn. Did I?" Alec demanded dourly.

"Nossah, yo' sho' nevah did do dat, Marse Alec," Moll answered meekly.

Alec shifted his gaze from Moll's black mask and drummed heavily on the arms of his chair with his dirty fingers, the woman standing by with the empty demijohn hanging by her side, her long forefinger thrust through the handle.

"Moll, how long have I been in here?" he asked at last.

"Evah sense Choosd'y, Marse Alec."

"Why don't you answer what I ask you?" Alec growled. "Tuesday? Well what day is this, Wednesday or Sunday?"

"'Tain't nuther one, Marse Alec. 'Tain't on'y but Satd'y."

"That long? I guess I've been a pretty sick man this time, eh Moll?"

"Yassah, Marse Alec, yo' sho' am dis time. Yo' bin a li'l mite sickah'n Ah evah seen yo' afo.' Ah's mighty 'feah'd y'all's gwine die dis time, sho.'"

"Oh, you were, were you? Well, I fooled you again, didn't I?"

"Ah 'low 'bout nex' time y'all ain't gwine fool me so big, Marse Alec. Ah 'low y'all cain't stan' moah'n 'bout one mo' dese yere spells o' deler'us trembuls."

"Oh well, we'll see about that. I guess Stanfield was down, was he?"

"Oh, yassah, he was down."

"Pretty warm, I guess?"

"Oh, yassah, he was a bilin.'"

"Well, don't bother to tell me what he said. The whole outfit'll be glad when I'm gone. About the best thing that could happen, too, I s'pose, for them as well as for me. Say Moll," he added after a pause and his voice carried a malicious note, "did you ever think what you'll do after I check in?"

"Nossah, Marse Alec, Ah ain't bin a figgah'n enny on dat circumstance but what *Ah* ben a considah'n 's what *y'all* gwine do ef de Lawd calls me fust. Yo' bin a thinkin' enny 'bout *dat*, Marse Alec?"

"Oh, no, Moll, there's twenty years more in your tough old hulk. There's plenty of skinny niggers like you live to be a hundred."

"Wal, de Lawd on'y knows. I reck'n Ah fotch y'all a li'l pench o' braffus, Marse Alec," and the old woman vanished.

II

When Alec Ferree was born into the pretentious old southern home Moll was a pickaninny of five running about the Negro huts in a single scant garment. She had grinned with delight when she had been allowed to see the "young Marse," her devotion to him beginning with that first sight of his pudgy face and batting hands. She had grown up a little ahead of him always willingly subject to him, submitting to the blows of his tiny fists at first and later to those of his heavier hands. She had seen and shared the pride and grief of his family when the gallant young son went to the war; she had howled as disconsolately as a devoted dog when news of a wounded Alec was brought home; she had rejoiced and sorrowed with the family when the end of the war brought him home and left them penniless and slaveless. Moll was the only one of the young Negroes who was willing to remain with her mistress, and this she did willingly and without pay until the old lady's death. Then at Alec's marriage to pretty Fanny Disborough she became a servant in his house and had remained so ever since. She had delighted in the dainty beauty of Fanny even before Alec had ever shown any preference for her and now when opportunity offered to serve them both together Moll's cup of satisfaction was full. She was by when the children were born, six of them in as many years, and it was her hard black hands that composed the body of the weary little wife when, in bearing the last child, the struggle had been too much and her life had gone out. With silent sympathy Moll had witnessed Alec's dumb grief and had watched him with apprehension as he tried to assuage it with a deluge of drink. She attended him faithfully in his shameful debauches. Later when contagion invaded the unguarded household, Moll carried on bravely, ignorantly fighting for the lives of the children, losing four in the unequal battle.

Then Alec married again—Nancy Humphrey, a woman still young and good looking but without the dainty grace of Fanny Disborough. Again came children in swift succession, seven—eight—ten of them. Then after twenty years Nancy, too, long since old and disillusioned, was carried up the hill to the cemetery but she was not laid beside Fanny for seven of her ten children had preceded her there and one by one had been laid beside Fanny's four until by the time Nancy went to claim a place eleven small graves separated the two wives. When the people had gone away the day Nancy was buried Moll lingered about the graves for a while and as she went sadly down the hill she took account of Alec's family, living and dead.

"Ah b'leeves Marse Alec got mo' ob um lyin' heah dan he got a libbin,'" she muttered and began to name those living, counting them off on her fingers and finding that she had named them all on the fingers of one hand.

III

As the years went along from the time of Alec's first marriage fortune had smiled upon him. He established a line of five flour mills along the banks of the brisk Swan River and as time mercifully carried the country farther from the consequences of the war business thrived and by the time Alec stood by the grave of his second wife he was a wealthy man. But with her death he threw all restraint to the winds. Always loose in his life he now cast aside every semblance of restraint and gave full sway to his inherent passions.

"But Marse Alec, dars dem chillum," Moll had remonstrated at first. "Ain't y'all gwine be no pap to um? Whar y'll reck'n um all gwine en' up at? Ah 'lows day all gwine go t' de pen soon's as dey's ol' 'nough ef dey doan' do it afo.'" But these remonstrances lost point when for lack of some more attractive woman, black or white, Alec unhesitatingly demanded and received Moll's body for his gratification.

In some mysterious way, however, through the influence left with them by their mothers, through the effect of the association with other children whose mothers were scandalized by Alec's demoralized life and who were keenly sympathetic for the young ones, in some way, I say, I do not know how—God my have had a hand in it—the children grew up to respectable man and womanhood, all despising their disreputable old father, all holding in horror the thirteen graves on the hill, to them shameful evidence of their father's bestiality and cruelty. The time came when not one of them except Stanfield, Fanny Disborough's oldest child—the one child of them all who was born of love—regarded him with any toleration at all, and neither that dignified gentleman nor anyone else understood that the strange feeling of attachment which he felt for the old man was the divine spark planted in his life by that love between his father and mother.

But now they were all gone from Alec's home. When Dessa married she took little Ethel with her and for ten years Old Alec had lived alone in the big house with Moll, alone, except for the wild disreputable companions each chose to entertain. The very house had become anathema to the town.

As the years crept upon them and Moll saw the evidence of old age lay heavier and heavier upon Alec her own old heart became troubled and she trembled with one excessive fear—that the time would come when she would be called to leave Alec.

"Marse Gawd," she prayed, "jes' y'all lemme lib ontwel Marse Alec done gawn. Ain't nobody but me t' take cyar o' him, ugly an' contrairy like him got t' be now. Ah ain't complainin' none w'en he ain't good to' me, Lawd, me wot nussed him w'en him 's a baby. Ah c'n git 'long, anyhow. Jes' y'all lemme lib,' Lawd, jes' a li'l longah'n him's all Ahm axin.'"

But this poignant selfless plea of the black woman was not answered according to her will. In spite of her desire to remain the grim reaper came in the stillness of the night and cut down the withered stalk of her life and she was laid in the little weed-grown graveyard of her own race and kindred far from the thirteen graves on the hill.

Alec was now alone indeed. He was able to secure two young Negro girls to cook his meals and look after the house in a haphazard, slovenly way during the day but they could not be prevailed upon to remain in the house at night. Stanfield Ferree tried conscientiously to persuade them to do so but was unable to offer sufficient inducement. To the failing old man the days were bearable but he looked forward to the evenings and nights with dread. Drink failed to bring peace to him or the oblivion it had once afforded. Gradually he began to mumble aloud to himself and if there had been anyone to listen strange, foolish and sometimes fearful words might have been hard from the old man's coarse lips as he sat before his fire at night.

One night as he poured out a glass of liquor and as the spirit of loneliness was unusually heavy upon him a sense of companionship suddenly pervaded the place and without knowing just how or when it came about he was aware that Moll was standing at the opposite side of the fireplace. He felt no surprise, no shock; just an immense relief from his burden of loneliness. She was there for a time and he did not notice when she went away but when he again found himself alone he dragged himself up from his chair and went to bed, sodden and numbed with drink. Moll did not come to him every night. Sometimes he was in a perfect hell of loneliness, a perfect desolation of dread. He longed for her commonplace presence there on the other side of the fire and that in spite of the fact that there was something sinister about that presence.

Then one night he noticed about the old black woman some strange quality of diffidence which he knew was not directed toward himself. She seemed less sinister than usual but at the same time more remote, more aloof from him than she had ever appeared; there was some very definite and tangible barrier between them, but what this barrier was his chaotic mind could not determine. Once when he glanced at her standing across the hearth from him she seemed not at all concerned with himself but with someone at her side; she stooped low as if over someone sitting and her face was very kind and compassionate. Alec noted this attitude but vaguely, making no attempt to analyze it.

Some time later, perhaps the next night, perhaps a week after—Alec had never been able to keep any account of these duly perplexing nights—he *knew* that someone other than Moll was in the room with him. He suddenly understood that Moll's deferential attitude was true to its appearance. She *was* stooping over a sitting figure and no sooner had he discovered the actuality of this then, as if at a spoken command from himself, she moved aside and he saw Fanny sitting there in the low chair where she had always sat when she was first down stairs after the numerous births. Sweet, she looked; he had always been so glad to have her about the house again after the lyings-in. He scrambled up and staggered across the hearth to her side but she shrank away from him, a sort of pitiful aversion written plainly upon her face and Moll quickly stepped in front of her, warning him away with an imperative gesture. For a moment he was angry at the antipathy of the one and the presumption of the other but his anger was soon dissipated for lack of the will to sustain it and he sank down upon the hearth moaning, the maudlin tears wetting his face. When he looked up again he was alone.

The two black wenches who worked and loafed about the house during the day carried away grim tales of signs and sounds about the old house. Shivering with fear they left the place at the first approach of darkness and did not return until day was abroad in the earth. The town people, always alert to old Alec's doings, noticed that he was getting more dotty every day. Stanfield Ferree from his respectable house at the other end of town came frequently now to his father's house, not remonstrating any more, only silently enduring the disgrace until his father should "break up" as he smoothly referred to the death which seemed hovering upon the old man's heels.

When Alec could get a listener he talked incessantly out of very relief from the silence he endured at home but of his ghostly visitors he said nothing, neither to his son nor to anyone else, but both the women were constantly present in his consciousness filling his days with apprehension and his nights with fear and dread.

On a chill November morning with his befuddled brain a little clearer than usual Alec went to the mill nearest his house with the long deferred intention of holding what he considered a conference with his superintendent. Arrived there and having secured the attention of the man he laid before him certain plans for carrying forward the work of the mills—lucid, workable plans they were but plans which at his own suggestion had been in effect in the mills for years. The superintendent listening respectfully, agreeing on all points, declaring himself ready to undertake whatever thing Alec might recommend, smiled sadly at the wreck of a man before him. All that day Alec went about more alert than he had been for many weeks, greeting old cronies and recounting oft told tales to whomever could be induced to listen. He went across town to Stanfields's house in mid-afternoon, shattering the composure of his daughter-in-law by walking into her drawing room while she poured tea for her guests. He passed by the house of his daughter Rena but the dragging old feet felt no pull to turn in there. Indeed between Alec and his children, with the one exception of Stanfield, there was no link of kinship except the physical one and every one of them would gladly have broken that if it had been possible.

After this day of tramping about, touching his affairs here and there with a helpless hand, Alec went reluctantly back to the old house as the early twilight was falling. The Negro girls, glancing fearfully at him, were just leaving as he entered. He found his dinner ready upon the table and laying aside his coat he stumbled into his chair and ate heavily of the meal, then rose and moved toward the living room. But as he stood on the threshold a figure more sinister than that of Moll, more accusing than Fanny had been, for upon her face was that look of compassion, met him threateningly; not with any threat of violence, indeed, but with an attitude wholly condemnatory. Before this one his face fell guiltily and his knees became week and smote together. Here was Nancy Humphrey, not the glum and brooding Nancy who had been his wife, but an avenging Nancy, a just Nancy, demanding payment for the indignities he had heaped upon her womanhood—demanding recompense for the lives she had borne and lost.

Grimly she laid her hand upon Alec's shoulder and turned him toward the outer door. There he saw Moll holding the door open and she was crying—the old black fool, his thoughts ran, actually sniffing aloud with the tears running down over her wrinkled old hide. He looked about for Fanny; there she was near Moll. He stretched his hands toward her but even as she shrank away from his touch Nancy's hand upon his arm impelled him through the door and he felt the bleak wind upon his face. He shivered and reached to draw his coat more closely about him but remembered that he had laid it off before he ate his dinner. So, with the wind cutting about him like a cold steel knife blade he was hurried along over the rough ground. Now Moll's hands were upon him, too, urging him on, on,—on—

"Let's go, Moll, you old fool," he chattered. "Let me alone, can't you? What do you mean?" But with averted face Moll rushed on, hurrying him along with her.

They passed through the familiar streets of the town, past Rena's dark house, past Stanfield's and across the icy little stream. Alec was now numbed with the cold but the black hands on one side and the white ones on the other had no mercy. They pressed him inexorably onward after he felt that there was no longer any possibility of motion in his body. And somewhere about he knew Fanny was there, consenting to all this indignity. He thought he would ask them where they were taking him but his jaw was so stiff and his tongue so thick that he could not speak.

And then when the cold was almost unbearable they slowed down and stopped. He had almost lost consciousness during the last few moments and at first did not see where they had stopped. But as he slowly looked about him he saw that they were in the graveyard. A moment more and he saw the stones of the graves of his own dead looming before him. Then as if from a great distance Moll's voice penetrated his dulled intelligence.

"Marse Alec," it said, "dese is dem y'all done wrong. Ah reck'n y'all 'membahs mos' ob 'um. Op'n yo' eyes, Marse Alec, an' look at um," she insisted, emphasizing her command with a tighter grip of her cold fingers upon his arm for he was closing his eyes and would gladly have fallen asleep and shut out the sight.

About him clustered a group of small figures. Some were tiny baby forms with innocent, vacant little baby faces; some were larger, their faces bright with the cunning knowingness of the older baby. They were all vaguely familiar to Alec. As he looked at them his head drooped again upon his breast and he fain would have refused to see, but again Moll prodded him into more alert consciousness.

"Y'all ain't seed um all yit, Marse Alec," and her long black finger indicated two figures standing a little farther back. He looked indifferently where she pointed, hoping soon to be done with this torture.

"Why—why—well—? Well?"—he mumbled. "B—Benny and Martin!" and he moved stiffly toward them. But upon his arms closed Moll's black fingers and Nancy's white ones, dragging him back and at the first motion forward the little boys shrank into the darkness.

He shivered violently. The bitter cold was eating its way into his very marrow. Just when his legs would no longer support him and he knew that he must give way in spite of those hands upon his arms he felt himself pushed vigorously forward and he fell, sprawling stiffly upon the ground, his benumbed fingers clutching at the frozen earth. Just as the last vague consciousness was slipping away from him he heard bitter sobbing and pitiful crying all about him and through the black obscurity closing about him, a cruel, sardonic laugh, a woman's laugh—Nancy's, forced its harrowing bitterness into his brain.

The next morning the two Negro girls found the house door open, the house itself empty and cold. Not until two days later was Alec's stark body found sprawling among the thirteen graves upon the hill. [*Opportunity* 8.2 (February 1930): 52–55]

CROSS CROSSINGS CAUTIOUSLY

by Anita Scott Coleman

Sam Timons rarely thought in the abstract. His thoughts as were his affections were marshalled concretely. His affections were rolled into a compact and unbreakable ball which encircled his wife Lettie and his young son Sammy. His thoughts—he did not think much—but such as his thoughts were, they involved this, if he did a good turn for somebody, somebody else would quite naturally do him or his a good turn also.

Usually Sam was a cheerful creature. Work and love; love and work, that, boiled down to brass tacks is the gist of all life, and Sam possessed both. Even though, at present, he was out of a job.

He walked along the shady road stirring up miniature dust clouds with every step for his heavy feet shuffled wearily with the burden of his dejected body.

He felt down and out. He was at the end of his rope. One dollar in his pocket. He gripped it in his fingers. All he had. But he could not give up. The ball of this affection, as it were, trundled along before him luring him on. He was "hoofing it" to another town to try again.

"Saw wood ... clean house, paint barns, chop weeds ... plow, anything, suh.... Just so it's work so's I can earn somethin.' I'm a welder by trade, but they don't hire culled."

Behind him stretched the long, dusty way he had come. Before him a railroad zigzagged his path. As his feet lifted to the incline, he raised his eyes, and met advice from a railroad crossing sign:

CROSS CROSSINGS CAUTIOUSLY

He paused to spell out the words, repeating them painstakingly. Then he went on. A little beyond and across the tracks another huge sign caught his attention.

Soon, he had halted beside this one, letting his eyes sidle up and down and over the gaily painted board. Now he was staring open-mouthed at the glaring yellow lion who crouched to spring, now, at the flashy blond lady pirouetting on a snow white mount. He stood quite still thinking. Wouldn't Lettie and little Sam be wild to see such a show.

* * *

"'Lo Mister."

Sam swung around like a heavy plummet loosed from its mooring.

"Gee ... Mister, you 'fraid of me?"

A little girl hardly more than a baby addressed him. She was regarding him with the straight unabashed gaze of the very innocent and of the very wise.

"I want you to carry me to the circus, she announced, when their mutual survey of one another seemed to her enough.

Sam's eyes were fixed on the web-fine, golden hair escaping from two torn places in the child's hat. Already he had seen that the eyes searching his were blue.... He fidgeted. He made a move to go.

"Oh, don't, don't go," beseeched the child. "Mother has to 'tend a meeting, and father is always busy. There is no one else. Mother said I might if only somebody'd take me. See." She thrust out a little smudgy fist—and opening it, revealed a shiny new fifty-cent piece. "This is mine," she said plaintively, "Can't we go?"

* * *

Mrs. Maximus McMarr was a busy woman. She managed to attend fourteen clubs each week, but that excluded any time to manage Claudia, her five-year-old daughter. Claudia's father considered children woman's responsibility. One advantage or disadvantage this sort of bringing up gave Claudia, she always got what she wanted.

Something about her made Sam do her bidding now.

They were half way between the McMarr place and the circus grounds before he thought about what he was doing. He clutched at the dollar in his pocket. He wanted to laugh, guessed he was nervous. Suddenly, he stopped abruptly—there was another of those signs where the train's right-of-way intersected another dusty country road.

CROSS CROSSINGS CAUTIOUSLY

"Oh do come on," urged the child jerking his hand in an ecstasy of delight and impatience.

Further on a half-grown lad passed them, but stopped and turned to watch them down the road. As the man and the little girl drew out of sight, he faced about and pelted up the road.

The noise of the circus leapt up to meet and welcome Sam and Claudia. The music of the band was sweet to their ears. Sam reveled in it and Claudia's little feet danced over the road. Even the bellowing and roars of the wild animals left them undismayed. It was circus day.

Mrs. McMarr had alighted from a friend's car and remained standing beside it, to talk. Both women observed the runner at the same time. Mrs. McMarr felt her heart skid upward into her throat. Claudia had not appeared. She divined that the messenger tended evil for no other than her precious baby. She made up her mind to swoon even before she received the tidings.

The friend went in search of McMarr who for once allowed himself an interruption. Close–lipped, he tumbled off his harvester and rushed pell-mell across his field.

* * *

All afternoon, Claudia had been surfeited with care. One after another had tendered and petted and caressed her. Even her father had been solicitous. She curled up, drowsy and very tired, in the big arm chair.

The rain that had threatened to fall all day suddenly commenced like the tat-a-rat-tat of far-off drums. Claudia was wide awake. She sat up. Remembering. The circus band! The monkeys in their little red coats! Her circus man! Something had happened. What?

The impulse to know surmounted the fear she harbored of her father. She slipped over to his chair. He had been very kind today. Perhaps ... he wouldn't mind telling her... Where her circus-man was? [*Opportunity* 8.6 (June 1930) 177; 189]

PRODIGAL

by Laura D. Nichols

A sudden hush fell on the congregation, and the faces of the listeners assumed the leaden stillness of masks. Only the startled black eyes that stared out from the vari-colored wall of faces told the earnest, young preacher that his people were listening as never before. A child cried, and its mother dropped a full, golden breast into its mouth, not once moving her eyes from the preacher's face.

Unperturbed by this unwonted stillness that held a people usually so ready to respond with "Amen" and "Tell the truth, brother," the minister went on in his cool, even voice, "And God holds us to this commandment as it is written, 'Thou shalt not commit adultery.' Inquire into your own lives, my brothers, my sisters. Too many of you are living in a way to shame your church and your profession as Christians."

"Do that young fool know what he's sayin'? Don't he know he's hittin' some of the best givers in the church? Who he hittin' at anyhow?" Deacon Jones shook his head and sighed. He knew what this sermon would mean to the collection. And the responsibility of raising the preacher's salary rested heavily upon the shoulders of Deacon Jones.

"Thang God it don't hit me." Mama Jane shifted her snuff to the other side of her mouth, and managed a muffled "Amen." Mama Jane did not know her age, but she was "a good-sized gal in time of Abraham Lincoln's war." She had come north with her children and grand-children during the industrial boom that had followed the World War, and had aided in establishing this little church. The migrant Negro did not often find the established churches of the North to his liking, and so began his own. Mama Jane continued to mutter to herself, "Old as I is, do', and many preachers as I'se heard in my time, I ain't never hear one ain't got no mo' sense dan to badaciously insult de people wha' he got to git his bread and butter f'om."

Her mumbling did not stop the preacher. Indeed, he must have taken it for sanction, for sharper, more trenchant words fell from his lips, and hung like small, glittering blades in the air. His voice rang out once more, "The wages of sin is death, but the gift of God is eternal life."

The service was over, and the people swarmed out to the lawn surrounding the pretty little church, to give vent to feeling that this morning had not found the usual emotional outlet. An odd picture they made, these transplanted human beings, pulled up from their rural homes in the Southland and dropped in the heart of an eastern industrial city. The problems of adjustment were often disconcerting, but they had kept their religious life entirely apart from the changes. There was to be a lodge funeral this afternoon, and many of these people must "turn out." While they waited, they fell into groups on the ill-kept green to discuss the sermon.

"Ef I had only known that was wha' he was goin' to talk about, I'd a' sho' stayed home and baked my rolls dis mornin'. Spec dey riz all out de pan by now." Sister

Mary was plainly peeved. She had on a good-as-new black straw hat her "Tuesday Lady" had given her. And not the least excuse to shout. Sister Mary was an expert shouter. She always circled the church before the 'spirit' departed from her. She sometimes embraced happy fellow Christians, but she never committed the blunder of hugging comely Anna Brown. Not since Big Lige Pierce had taken up with Anna over a year ago.

Partly hidden by the fragrant, feathery beauty of a lilac in full bloom, a group of men, strong, black and young, passed a bottle from hand to hand, and shakily condemned the sermon and the preacher. "Better learn to tend to his own business ef he wants to stay here."—"How come you so touchy, big boy? Eve'y body know Anna Brown' husband ain't dead. Wouldn' I love to see him walk up someday when you 'busin some o' his children! Preacher sho' have one mo' sermon to preach. Fesser Brown plumb crazy 'bout his lil yaller children." Big Lige made no answer to this.

On the steps a group of deacons and other officers of the church smoked and spat and studied. Deacon Jones grumbled, "Collection was powerful small this mornin.' That man go' ruin hisself yet. Better be studyin' bout them hongry children o' his'n, stead o' insultin' some o' his best payin' members." The old man spat viciously into space.

Apart from these various groups, Anna Brown and her three attractive children laughed and talked happily together. The sermon was not mentioned. Anna was by far the best-looking woman in the congregation and by the same token, one of the least popular. Though rather given to plumpness, she was both neatly and becomingly dressed. Her small bright eyes twinkled in a yellowish brown face, like stars peeping thru a sunset sky and laughing because they shouldn't be there. She was the sort of woman who says little soft, kind things to people when she might just as well say nothing at all. Mama Jane, who took care of the children while Anna went out to sew by the day, often said of her, "Poor chile, she don' do nobody no harm, only wha' she do to herself." Though for the life of her, Mama Jane couldn't see what Anna wanted of that big, rough Lige Pierce hanging around, and her husband a school teacher in the South, and as nice a boy as ever drew breath. She could never understand why Anna and Hal had separated, for Anna was a close-mouthed woman, for all her gentle, smiling ways. Her lips could close in a hard, straight line, and the warm twinkle in her eyes change to the cold gleam of burnished steel.

The people began to move quietly toward the church door, as the funeral cars approached. From hidden recesses in bags and purses, quaint little black and purple bonnets appeared, along with big, bright badges. Hands slipped awkwardly into white gloves, and the order formed in solemn procession behind the bier and followed it into the church.

Lige Pierce sauntered over toward the little group that remained outside, for Anna did not belong to the order, and had only tarried because the children wanted to see the order turn out. Lige's hungry eyes rested, not on the familiar form of the woman, but on the slim, brown girl at her side. Esther, still unconscious of the charm of youth's first rounding out, felt his look, and flinched. Anna saw it with her smiling eyes, and the glint of steel veiled the smile. The words of the preacher fell again on her heart and cut like small, sharp blades. "The wages of sin is death." Death, yes; but that caressing look at her girl meant hell itself.

All the sorry memories of these past three years came to her as she walked slowly to the car line with her children. Lige was a few paces behind, and her heavy heart told her where his eyes rested now and again. Hal's voice rose in her ears as on the day he left to go back South to his schoolroom: "I cannot do the rough railroad yard work which is all our men find to do here now that the boom is over. We can make it at home on my salary, and send the children away to school later on." And her own voice, "Never. I'd rather wash and iron and be free than to have my children grow up on the South." Hal had gone, and Lige had drifted into her life. Hal's letters always begged her to return, but without avail. She could think of no reason why she should.

Until today.

When the little party stopped in town to transfer, Anna slipped around the corner and sent Hal the following terse message: "Home next Sunday." She would need a few days to get the children ready.

And on the next Sunday, all the pent-up emotion of the worshippers burst forth when the earnest young minister thanked God that his words had borne fruit in one heart. Sister Mary gave two or three quick, frog-like jumps, and let the 'spirit' have full sway. She circled the church three times and fell exhausted in her seat. Mama Jane, too old for active shouting, fanned her vigorously and murmured, "God do move in a musterious way. Bless his name."

In a little southern city, Hal Brown welcomed his loved family home, and thanked God piously that his prayers had at last been answered.

And Anna held her peace and smiled her quiet smile.

[*Opportunity* 8.12 (December 1930): 364–365]

Faith: A Story

by Thelma T. Clement

Jefferson Davis Johnson chuckled contentedly as he gazed at the torn page of the "Daily News." For a moment—and just a moment—his grin faded and he groaned as he drew one leg under him. That leg felt dead, for Jefferson Davis Johnson had been stretched out on this cold floor—cold even in August—for four nights and four days. He twisted himself around on the floor so that the light from the one window with the bars in front shone directly on his paper, then he stretched himself. His foot touched a wall and his outstretched arm touched the opposite wall. Not a tall man either, just five feet five inches to be exact. Scanning the page carefully, he found the place where he had stopped reading, then began again, pronouncing aloud syllable by syllable in a harsh but steady voice the words he understood, often omitting words necessary to the intelligibility of the sentence.

Jefferson Davis Johnson was pleased—why shouldn't he be? The largest white paper in town and there was his picture—the one he had taken at the last fair. Looked like an immense ink blot on the gray white paper, but it was he himself—and his derby and his grin! Then the headlines. That was what pleased him most.

"Johnson, Negro to Hang Thursday."

He laughed hysterically and sat up on the floor.

The paper had the facts down just as he had told them, the robbery, the shooting, and the escape. Only one thing hurt him; there was another article in the paper that attributed other crimes to him. He did not mind bearing guilt for his Cap'n, but he objected to bearing it for anyone else.

"Johnson, Negro to Hang Thursday." The Negro thoughtfully stroked his unshaven chin. Thursday! This was Tuesday. Must be about five o'clock in the morning, for it had just become light enough for him to read the pages that someone had thrust in his cell during the night while he slept peacefully. Two more days for his Cap'n to make the police the laugh of the country! Why, Thursday he'd be in South America! Hadn't Cap'n Jim told him so? Jefferson Davis Johnson laughed again—a hollow voice that echoed and reechoed in his dismal dungeon. Funny. He—the most harmless man in his community and a deacon of the Ebenezer Baptist Church—in jail for killing a man. A white man! Reminded him of Bible stories—Jesus suffering for his brothers' sins. A martyr.

But not for long. Hadn't Cap'n Jim told him so?

Jefferson Davis Johnson thanked God that he was a Christian and that because he was a Christian and recognized duty, he had not feared to stick to this man to whom he owed so much. Fearlessly he had followed and fearlessly he had done just as he had been told to do. He had wondered many times since then just why the Cap'n should want any one killed—but it was white folks' business and not for a nigger to meddle in. Of course he'd heard whispers—about a quarrel between the Cap'n and this man over the Cap'n's wife, but that was *none of his business*. Hadn't the Cap'n let him live in one of his houses without paying for it? Hadn't the Cap'n given him clothes and food and a job when he needed them? At first he'd refused but the Cap'n had shown him the path of Duty.

And everything was all right; everything had happened just as Cap'n Jim had said it would—the capture and all. A smile again appeared on his solemn face. He was thinking of yesterday, his first time in a court room. Cap'n Jim was on the jury. If the Negro had had any misgivings, they had all left him when the Cap'n had winked at him once during the trial, and when he had put his arm around his shoulders after the trial and whispered that everything was all right. These things had reassured him of his master's power.

He had confessed and been sentenced to hang Thursday. What fools those officials were! Tonight, yes, Tuesday night, Cap'n Jim was going to take him to New Orleans and send him on to South America where his young wife and child were perhaps already waiting for him. Cap'n Jim said he'd send them earlier. How he longed to see them! Two weeks since he left that night—two long weeks away from them. For the first time this man seemed weak. He swayed, and again stretching himself on the floor, he pressed his forehead against the coldness of it and wept aloud.

II

Jefferson Davis Johnson lay still as death. Suddenly he raised himself on his elbow and held his head. "My Gawd," he mumbled, "it's dark—mus' be night." He felt a quick cold draft of air, and as his vision cleared he saw a man's leg just at his head. Without looking up he threw both arms around the legs and holding them tightly whispered huskily:

"Ready, Cap'n. So glad—so tired—"

"Cap'n Hell!" a voice rasped in a fierce undertone, and wrenching free one leg, the man kicked the Negro against the wall.

One arm supporting his body and the other shielding his face, the Negro queried pathetically:

"What ya want, Master?"

With a triumphant grin the man leaned above Jefferson Davis Johnson and said slowly and emphatically, "Yuh gonna hang now, Nigguh—now! Damn yuh!"

"But the Cap'n—Thursday—de jury—de papers—wait—heah 'tis"—reaching for the paper.

"Thursday Hell!" and dragging him to the cell door—"See anybody in that there hall?"

"No, suh—"

"Ain't there and won't be soon—c'mon damn yuh! Lose my bet if I don't show yuh in ten minutes!"

Everything went black to the Negro as he felt his way down the corridor—prodded from behind by the man—too weak and frightened to resist. He tried to pray, and once he said aloud, almost prayerfully, "Cap'n Jim, O Gawd, Cap'n Jim. Come quick—don't let 'em hang me!"

The rest was lost in the noise of a thousand bloodthirsty voices as captor and captive appeared in the doorway.

The Negro was lifted and thrown in a wagon where he lay limp and senseless—and was taken miles—thousands of them it seemed to him. In the midst of a forest where even the starlight was hidden by spreading branches, a thousand savage men who had left their civilization behind them, lost themselves in utter abandon. There was darkness there so thick that the first red flicker on a distant tree seemed to shatter it into atoms. The flicker rose, a giant candle lighted the forest and the demoniacal faces of those thousand men whose shrill voices rose in a thousand discordant yells.

Jefferson Davis Johnson had not resisted. Dazed since he had been taken from the jail, he had no thought or feeling. He had not even felt the rope tighten about his wrists as they were fastened to two branches of a tree, and he did not now feel the red ribbons of flame as they encircled his body. As the forest grew lighter he seemed to be searching, intently searching the crowd. Finally his face glowed with a light that was not of the flames. A light that seemed to come from within—he had found that for which he had been searching, a familiar face, almost close enough for him to touch had he been able. He did not notice that the face was a leering mask of contempt and deceit—he only saw behind that mask the features he loved so well.

"Thank Gawd," he whispered, "I knew yuh'd come, Cap'n."

A screen of red and blue flame hid his Cap'n from him forever.

[*Opportunity* 9.5 (May 1931): 140–141]

THE ETERNAL QUEST

by Anita Scott Coleman

When Evan Given gave up his wife to that grim reaper who holds a mortgage on every man's house and forecloses with or without notice, he turned with a stolid, white-hot passion to his baby, a year-old daughter, for what little comfort he cold squeeze from life. The love that he severed with such visible effort from the mother to bestow upon the offspring doubled and trebled in the years during which Polly Given grew up.

At eighteen, she was a sweet flower of a girl. Then, as stealthily as comes the dew at eventide, the Reaper struck again, deftly, swiftly, and Polly sped forth into the unknown whither Evan dared not follow. And the reason that he dared not was because of a tiny spark that glowed in the very depth of his being—his faith. He believed in life after death, and that the self-destroyer forfeited much if not all of the future existence.

Because Evan Given was one of the foremost surgeons of his day, and dabbled in science as a side-line, it was not altogether incredible, after his burdensome grief, that he elected to give up the one in which he had won fame and fortune for the other, the lesser as a buffer for his sorrow. Quietly, and with no more ado than is usual for a man changing his barber, he dropped all else, and took up the study of science—the science of faith. He closed his house, the palatial dwelling, he had erected for his daughter; cut his London connections, and set himself adrift, as much as it was possible for a man of his standing to do.

What is the thing, faith.... Why does it suffice for some.... Why is it insufficient for others.... Why believing as I do that God is the giver, and therefore has a Divine right to take when and as He wills, am I rebellious because he has bereft me of mine? These were the questions Evan Given sought to solve.

* * *

No. 60 in ward 400 was one of the strangest cases ever admitted to the county hospital. His was a unique malady and of a far-reaching scope. Plainly it came under the category of cases wherein the great Evan Given had labored so magnificently. It was known that the famous English surgeon was sojourning in the American city. If he could be prevailed upon to grant but an hour of his time, if for no more than a consultation, if only for an observation, anything he might choose to do would be a priceless gift to the medical profession.

At last, when all arguments had failed, someone mentioned that, which seemed to him, the strangest phase of the case in question, that this great hulking giant of a fellow—No. 60 was well over forty—should lay day after day, calling for his mother.

"That," said Evan Given, instantly, "is faith. Wait. I will come."

The span of No. 60's shoulders came near to over-taxing the width of the white iron cot. His massive head pressed against the head post. His feet protruded through the foot rails. He was easily six foot, ten, and he was delirious when Evan Given saw him first. He was strapped, but yet the strong thongs were proving inadequate, the motions of the man lifted the cot until it tossed about like a frail craft on a windy sea. And always, he screeched the one word, "mom-mer."

"Too late .... Nothing can be done!" proclaimed the great man. At least, he can be made comfortable. Send for his mother!"

"There can be no visitors." Head Nurse of ward 400 voiced a protest, that was curbed at a glance from the Surgeon.

No. 60's mother arrived when he was at his worst. It was the crucial hour. He was seeking with maniacal strength to break his bonds, and screaming fiendishly. The mother, after a brief period with the great London physician, hurried to her son's bedside.

She was a small woman, a tightly, shriveled hard little person, not unlike a black walnut.... Her timidity fell from her, as she drew near the bed. She became no longer an uneasy visitor among countless strangers, but a mother with her only son, and it was he and she against the world.

The great Evan Given was a close observer of all that passed. This was a pregnant moment to him, in his study of faith.

The mother said quickly and a little shrilly, "Lie down 'dar." Then in firmer tones, and quieter: "Be still. Didn't ah tells you!"

Magically, the huge form upon the bed grew calm.

"What's you a-laying here fo', disturbin' these yere folks, ain't yo mammy done taught yo better'n 'at...." Her voice was crooning. "Ain't yo' shame yo'self. Here's yo mammy done come this long ways to see yo, and yo is lying here yellin' like yo is possessed."

"Mommer."...

To the amazement of those watching, the man on the bed was muttering in his turn to the old woman. The mother down on her knees bent her head to hear. Quickly, she stood erect, and called loudly.

"Nurse ... Doctor ... somebody come quick and take off dese bindings. My boy wants to die free.... Come quick, somebody, quick."

Evan Given came—interns and nurses together removed the straps. No. 60 heaved a great sigh of relief. His head jerked back convulsively, and his eyes rolled wildly towards his mother. "De Lord's done come," he intoned majestically, and fell into his final sleep, peacefully as a babe.

"Faith," jotted Given, mentally.

The old woman sat beside the cot with folded hands. Evan cleared his throat. Surely this was a strange manner in which to meet death, not a tear, in no wise, did she betray regret. "Why-er—why-er," began Evan.

"Blessed lamb.... Sweet Jesus, done come and set my po' suff'ring boy, free," chanted the old woman, almost gaily.

"Faith," tabulated Given in his scientific mind.

"What will you do?" he inquired curiously, and not unkindly.

"Do heah this man," exclaimed No. 60's mother, "I's goin'er do muy wo'k." As an afterthought, "I'se got 'er wo'k for sho' now, 'cause dis boy a-lying heah is my sole suppo't. But de Lord will provide."

"Faith," said Evan Given audibly in the voice of a man who talks often to himself. "I must find it."

EBONY—A STORY

by Isabel M. Thompson

If you maintain a "purely healthy" attitude toward mediums and their predictions—if you have always sneered at superstition—if that tiny spark of intuition in your soul has never flared up—then you can very easily place yourself in Lizzie's position on that particular morning in October. There she was, standing in the doorway to Madame Faro's studio—but she was not sneering (not even mentally).

For several months, she had known "The Ebony Seeress," but had only encountered her outside her profession. To Lizzie, Madame Faro was merely a very pleasant, middle-aged neighbor, and her "fortune-telling business" was—well, just a means of earning a living and, incidentally, fooling the public. The young girl had run over to borrow a cup of sugar and have a little chat. And this is what she saw this morning....

Madame Faro, a large, loosely-built brown-skinned woman, was staring intently at a small black oblong lying on the table in front of her. The table—a very unusual one—was covered with an obviously expensive scarf and also held a beautiful crystal ball.

After standing in awe-stricken silence for exactly three minutes and forty seconds, Lizzie became impatient and scraped her left foot lightly on the floor.... The spell was broken; and Madame exclaimed, "Oh, it's you, Lizzie!" as if she were at once glad and disappointed to see her.

"Why, of course, Madame! Who'd you expect? Your beau?" But she immediately recognized a faux pas, for there was no mistaking the spasm of pain that flashed in the bright, gimlet-like eyes that faced her. What was the matter with her friend today? Lizzie was seriously considering a phone call to a doctor. Then, quite suddenly, Madame said, "Come heah, chile."

Lizzie hesitated. These was something about that room that repelled her. There was something that dampened her "sunshiny" nature.... There was encompassing mystery.

"Well, what ails you?" the medium snapped out.

Lizzie, as she would have expressed it in her lighter moments, snapped into action, and took the seat offered her in the studio.... Strange how an atmosphere can affect you. Lizzie dropped her healthy-mindedness and flippant manner, as if they were cumbersome garments. To her, the studio lost the semblance of a room. It became a sanctum where suspicions and hopes were born side by side; where faith might be created or immediately destroyed; where whole dream futures were built. In other words, she felt just what every patron experienced upon entering Madame Faro's studio. What caused this? Were the heavily elaborate furnishings to blame? Was it the mysterious absence of daylight? No—none of these was responsible. It was the personality of the strange woman who now presided behind the crystal ball—a personality that kept a steady stream of persons, many of whom were very wealthy, coming to her for advice and counsel.

The Ebony Seeress now extended the palm of her right hand in which lay the small black oblong. "This heah," she said, in a clear voice, "is ebony—my lucky piece, Lizzie. I give a little piece of it to every one of my patrons—an' they always has good luck." After an almost imperceptible pause, she continued, "It's black—that's why!" This last statement appeared to be challenging some opposing element. Or was it merely because Lizzie had raised her eyebrows?

As rapidly as the medium's visitor was becoming accustomed to surprises, yet she was wholly unprepared for the torrent of words that suddenly swept over her, plunging her into the story of Madame Faro's early life... .The Ebony Seeress forgot herself—forgot the "correct grammar" she had studied so painstakingly in No'thun schools—and allowed her speech to lapse into a more decided dialect.

"But it ain't always been like that. No, suh! Time was when I wushupped 'white.' De whites' clothes was always de cleanes'. My white dress was foh bes'. De white folks always knew what was right—an' didn' de good Lawd Hisself wear a long white robe? My ole ma tole me that I was wrong—an' tried huh bes' to change my min', but I was dead set agin black, an' thought I knowed evahthing! Ma said, "Why, chile, cain't you see dat de groun' dat grows de pretties' flowahs is de blackes', an' dat ole Aunt Sue an' Uncle Jim is de kindes' souls on de plantation? Hattie, honey, is you blin'?"

But young Hattie had burst out in anger, and replied triumphantly that the Lord knew best, because he made every human being shut his eyes at night when the "whole worl's black."

Ma had suffered greatly from a sense of frustration after this encounter with her only child ... for the old lady had possessed a peculiarly accurate sense of values. She was not one to be blinded by the gleam of alabaster, or deafened by the blare of brass bands. She had faith in the durability of ebony and the serenity of still waters.

"Oh! hits true," said Madame, "dat she'd string de white folks along—same as I do now. Made 'em think they was gods sittin' on marble thrones. Why, they'd go clean out o' they way to do a little favor for Ma Haney. An' I'd be so tickled, an' say, 'Ma, ain't white folks jes' gran'?" She'd jes' puff away on her ole cob pipe, an' say, 'Honey, hit's all de same—black or white—ef folks is good, dey's good, an' ef dey's bad, dey's bad. Haint no diffunce.'"

Seemingly, the whites as well as the blacks perceived a superior individuality in Ma's attitude toward life, for her opinions were greatly respected. They came to her with their sorrows and received consolation; they came with their perplexities and left with the burdens lifted. And, too, they brought their joys, their successes, their triumphs—large and small—and shared them with Ma Haney.

The weaving of this narrative was suspended for several minutes, while the medium sat with closed eyes, obviously re-living former days and incidents. For Lizzie—the studio walls crumbled, elegant furnishings were swept out, even the crisp Northern atmosphere gave way to the genial warmth of the South. Ma Haney sat just outside her cabin door, and smiled beautifully as she comforted a world-weary soul; and then, unconsciously assumed a knowing attitude, as she gave a bit of advice to a wayward youth. Her powerful personality influenced everyone around her. And Lizzie was approaching—to pour out the tale of her disillusions, her restlessness and discontent. Surely she would find solace here ... everything would be right again. But—though approaching, she came no nearer—her feet would not move, her voice was silenced.... Had she snored very loud?... Once more, reality faced her.

Madame Faro resumed. "And then, when I was about seventeen, *he* come my way—!" and broke off on a sobbing note. "Oh, Lizzie—I haint nevah tole nobody up heah about it! I been keepin' it put away—but, now it caint stay in my heart no longah—it's gotta come out! Ain't it bettah to do that, some time?" she appealed to the young girl.

"Why, certainly it is," Lizzie assured her, and admired the courage of a woman who had so successfully suppressed emotion for many years.

"From the first moment I seen him, I was done for. To me, he was the bes'-lookin' thing the Lawd evah made. Natchelly—he was light. Why, Lizzie, you could hardly tell him from a white man—or a furriner at least. His hair was kinda crinkledly—not much though.

"All the folks was talkin' 'bout him—wondrin' where he come from, an' what he was doin' aroun' there an' all sich stuff. Ole Aunt Sue asked me if I'd found out anything, and 'thout waitin' for me to say, she says, 'I heerd tell he's a young *Liyar* f'm up No'th!' an' stopped to cackle, like that was somethin' funny. She looked at me, an' I tried to say somethin', but the words jes' stuck and they was a big lump in my throat. Aunt Sue said, 'Hattie, I b'lieves to my soul you is took up wid dat man.' I jes' giggled kinda silly an' walked away."

"She was right. I had took up wid him, and he seemed to like me right smaht, too.... An' I mean he sho had swell callin' cahds."

But the rest of the community did not seem to share Hattie's opinion of "S. Lemuel Jonson, Atty.-at-Law from Duluth, Minnesota." Although they were courteous enough to him, he could easily feel that distrust underlay their politeness. One disapproved of his shifty eye, another of his flashy dress, and still others frowned on the obviously pseudo-smile that was unceasingly slapped on his countenance.

"As fer Ma—she jes' hated the very groun' he walked on. She tried her bes' to hide if from me, 'count o' me bein' sich a hahd-head, but I could tell."

"Him an' me sho had swell times—an' I says to myself—'Hattie Thomas, I jes' caint believe hevvun's any bettah than this! Naw suah!'"

"Then one day, he says, 'Hattie, darling, I'd like to have a private conference with your mother about some very pressing legal matters'—jes' like that."

"I blinked my eyes and says, 'Yas, honey—but what is legal mattahs?' An' don't you think I warn't proud when he rares back and says with sich good grace that he 'forgot that I was unacquainted with the termologies of law and equity' or somethin' like that. Aunt Sue was jus' machin' by, an' she stopped dead still to listen at sich a educated man talk. An' when she walked away real fas,' I knew she'd be sho an' tell evahbody how Lem done showed out."

"Lizzie—You should a seen 'im—han'some ain't the word for it! Jes' so tall an' broad-shouldahed. You see, I couln' nevah tolerate no little men—they jes' didn' 'peal to me somehow.... Always dressed so becomin,' he was ... in a dif'runt suit mos' ev'ry othah day. But no mattah what clothes he wore, they was always a real swell ruby stickpin in his tie. Many's the time I heerd Ma say that they was somethin' wrong wid a man dat looked good all de time. She says, 'A honest man ain't nevah feered o' soilin' his han's nor his clothes neithah, for that mattah.' But, I says to myself, ef she heered him talk some o' them big words, who she could see that he warn't like them othah common roustabouts on de plantation. So, after me pleadin' with ma, she says yes, he could come ovah to the cabin an' talk to her."

However, it was soon evident that Jonson did not impress Ma Haney so favorably; for, after they had been talking for several minutes, she flung open her cabin door, stood there with blazing eyes, and told him, in unquestionably sharp tones, to "get out o' town an' nevah come back!" And Hattie overheard her mother mumbling, "Dat skunk ain't nevah gwine git mah money! Nevah!" But, beyond that, no additional information came her way.

"Cose I pouted 'roun the house, but me an' Lem kep' meetin' on the sly. An' one day, when I come in, Ma says, 'Come heah to me, Hattie.' I sho was skeered, an' shamed o' myself, too. But Ma tole me to set down—an' she pulled me close to her an' I laid my head in huh lap an' cried like a baby. 'Ma jes' wants to do de bes' by huh baby—you know dat—don't you, honey?'" And with a peculiar gleam in her eyes, Ma Haney had bent over and scooped up a handful of the white sand, often found on top of the rich river-bottom land. She had sifted it through her fingers and said to her daughter—"This heah san' is white, honey, but hit's might shifty—hit ain't tuh be depended on." While Hattie followed her movements with fascinated eyes, she pulled a piece of ebony out of her apron pocket, and said—"But this heah ebony is black—an' hit's strong. Why, chile, Marse Robert gimme this when he come back fum dat trip to India. I warn't nothin' but a little thing then. All this time... I has kep' it—dropped it sometime—stepped on it—hit won't break. Hattie—hit's solid stuff."

Madame Faro wiped her eyes, and spoke again in the peculiar mixture of dialect and correct grammar, "An! heah in my hand, is that same piece of ebony, my good luck chahm. Without it, I'd prob'ly been daid or worse than daid, now. But, thirty years have come and gone. I am another woman—much richer in experience ... and dollars too. Even my South'n dialect fades away at times. But this little piece of black wood stays the same. I love it—just like I love everything black.... God! when I think of that low-down yellow cur ... ran out o' town, an' lef' me with my baby comin'! Yes ... she's livin' in Chicago now. I sent her away ... she looked too much like 'im. I couldn't stand it!"

The little bell tinkled. Madame and Lizzie arose simultaneously—the seeress to receive her patron—the young girl to return home with her cup of sugar. As Lizzie turned toward the kitchen, there was a peculiar sound behind her, as Hattie cried out—"Lem!... Oh, Lem, honey—is you come back *foh good*?"

Lizzie wheeled around to confront a tall gentleman wearing a large ruby pin stuck in a bright blue tie!   [*Opportunity* 9.10 (October 1931): 312–314]

THE NOOSE

by Octavia B. Wynbush

The Louisiana moon, riding high in the sky, made a rippling path of light across the slow-moving waters of the Mississippi River. A boat rounding the bend in the river at this point, slid into the shadows cast by the high bank which sloped gently down to the water's edge. As the clumsy craft came silently and carefully to rest in the shadows, a man who had sat bunched at the oars leaped quickly ashore and dragged the boat to a sheltered spot. Without a backward glance he began climbing a narrow, shadowy path leading to the top of the high embankment.

At the top of the ascent the path lost itself between two lines of massive, wide-sweeping live-oaks. The mighty mosscovered arms of these trees swept upward and met in an arch which the light of sun and moon barely penetrated. Only an occasional ghost of a moonbeam shone now through the foliage, as the man, with the step of one long accustomed to treading this way, plunged into the path between these giants. He had not gone far, however, when a sudden rustle in the pathway turned him into a statue of attention.

"King?" A woman's voice breathed the word. "It's me, King, it's Leora."

"Leora? What you doin' here dis time o night?"

In the dark a slim hand, young but coarsened by toil, touched him timidly, sliding down his shoulder, down his arm, and finally coming to rest in his own toil-roughened hand.

"I—I couldn't sleep, King. Nobody could sleep. Dey's all talkin' and speculatin' 'bout—'bout—"

"'Bout him?"

"Yes. Is—is—it—"

"Yes, it's all over." There was an unmistakable satisfaction in his whispered response.

A sharp intake of breath from the girl. "O, King, he done daid?"

"Dat's it. Twelve o'clock sharp, de trap was sprung.—He died—in a few minutes."

They were walking hand in hand through the tunnel of oaks. A few moments of slow, silent walking brought them to the end of the lane, and into a semi-circular clearing. They stood in silence, looking at the scene about them.

The black, indistinct silhouettes that formed the background of the cleared semicircle were by day the oaks, pines, magnolias and pecan trees that with vines and ferns made up mysterious Devil's Swamp. Across the clearing, so close to the trees that the arms of some of them reached over and caressed its rotten roof, stood a cabin—King's cabin. The cleared space around it was what remained of a once-lovely flower garden—a garden that had been beautiful with jasmine, roses, and old-fashioned sweet William and honeysuckle when Nomia used to move among them.

King's face twitched suddenly at the picture that rose in his mind. Leora, womanlike, sensed his thoughts and squeezed his hand. A strangely contrasting pair they were, as they stood in the moonlight. Tall, magnificently proportioned, ebony black was the man. Strength, brute force rippled in the muscles of his body. His face, lined heavily had the sere look of a leaf shriveled not so much by the chill of winter, as withered prematurely by a drought, or the searing heat of a forest fire. His hair lay in a mat half tangled, half kink, over his head, suggesting some admixture of blood. His eyes were murky pools.

The girl, slender and yellow-brown, her large dark eyes filling with tears that quivered down her hollow cheeks, squeezed King's hand once more.

"King?"

"What you want, chile?"

"Did—did—he do it? Did he kill Jeems?"

"A jedge and twelve jurymens said he done it."

"Yes, but dat don't mean nothin'. It could of been—"

"It could of been who?" The question was shot at her with the force of a pistol report.

"Anybody. He done say all time, he don' be guilty."

"He was guilty as hell! What did he do to you an' me, gal? Didn't he stole my wife and break yo' mammy's heaht 'cause she done took so much pains to raise you gals so you kin hol' yo' haids up wid de best?"

"I—I—know dat, too. But dat don' say he killed a man."

"Go home, gal! A man dat'll stole another man's wife will do any thing else. Go home!" He gave her a little push toward an opening in the trees, an opening leading to her own home, where slept her father, unconscious of his daughter's nocturnal adventure.

Leora walked off a few paces, turned and looked around. King was striding toward his cabin. Leora stopped.

"King," she called softly.

"Huh?" Impatience had succeeded the anger in his last speech. He stopped in the shadow of the cabin, his hand on the latch.

"Do you know what he done tol' de preacher what seed him last?"

"What?"

"He done say he ain't guilty."

"You done tole me dat befo.'"

"An' he say—dat—whoever be guilty—he comin' back an' tie dat same noose aroun' his neck."

King threw back his head and laughed, a silent laugh, but hearty, and stepped into the moonlight.

"Git to bed, gal! Don' you know dere ain't no ghosts? Don' you know when a man goes to Hebben he don' wanna come back, an' when he to hell de debbil ain' let im come back? Stop fearin' de daid, gal, an' fear de livin.'"

"I do." The penetrating glance from the girl's shrewd young eyes lingered a moment on the man's face, and she had turned to run away home.

King watched her out of sight, a startled, puzzled look on his face. There was something in Leora's tone which had started a question in his mind. What did she mean? What did she know? With a sudden shrug he turned toward his home again.

Unlatching the door, he entered the darkness. Taking a match from his pocket he made a light and applied it to the jagged wick of an oil lamp on a dirty, cluttered table. Through the cracked chimney a few straggles of yellow light made their way.

The unplaned planks in the flooring emerged from one shadowed end of the room, spread for a brief while in the dim light and vanished into the shadows at the other end before an open fireplace, cold and black now, in the heat of summer. On one side of the fire place tilted a rickety cane bottomed chair. On the other side stretched a crude bunk nailed to the wall. A few rags of dirty bed-covering were thrown across it. One or two boxes, a few traps piled in the corner, constituted the remaining furnishings of the room. Clothing in all states of use and disuse hung from nails driven into the walls. From the rafters of the cob-webby ceiling dangled bunches of red peppers, stuffed sausages and onions.

King fastened the door, made his way to the bunk and sat down. His head sank wearily into his hands, and his mind moved swiftly back into the past, bringing picture after picture into the dim, cheerless room.

There was Nomia, first, Nomia, slender, undersized with her sharp, yellow features, brown eyes and abundant brown hair never tidily arranged, never becomingly dressed for her face. She had not the adeptness of her sister Leora in making her cheap clothes look becoming, yet he had loved her. The witchery of Nomia for him had been the witchery of youth, for she was twenty-one and he was forty. She danced before him now, singing in the liquid, untrained soprano that to him had seemed a miracle coming from a throat so slim. Tantalizing, laughing and deceiving, twisting him about her fingers with the lure of her youth, she stood before him.

The knuckles of King's huge fingers stood out sharply as he balled his hands into fists at another image. Jed—Jed who had been hanged that afternoon—floated boldly, arrogantly into his vision. A rascal from the city, whose summers spent in Chicago hotels had given him a patronizing, counterfeit "gentlemen's air" as Nomia had called it. Jed's conquest of Nomia had been easy. His flattery, his oily compliments had sunk deep into her unstable, impressionable consciousness.

King groaned as he lived again through scenes which time had not erased for him. Jed's first long compliments to him on having a wife who could "sing like a mocking bird;" his long visits to the then cheerful cabin, ostensibly to see the husband; the chattering of the plantation women—chattering that, when King approached a group; give place to meaningful signs, sly looks and nudges; the shock of coming home one day to an empty cabin, to a note from Nomia, stating she had gone away with Jed.

King felt again the days of black despair, the days when the opening magnolia blossoms and the scent of roses and jasmine Nomia's hands had planted, were to him as instruments of torture, squeezing closer and ever closer his soul, bursting his heart and draining it of life. He lived through the night of blackness his soul had touched and found to be an impregnable wall closing him from the light.

The great passion passed; the scene changed once more. Five years dragged across his life—five years of silence, hurt pride, withdrawal from his fellows except Nomia's sister and father. Then, one day, Jed returned to a neighboring plantation. Nomia had died during one of the cruel winters in the North. King recalled with a bitter smile the open, crude hints that had come to him from time to time to "kill that rascal like a dog." But he had made no move. He preferred to suffer the scorn of those from whom he had practically withdrawn himself. He bided his time. Fate would devise a more subtle plan.

And fate did. King's smile became a sneer as there came before his mind the form of James Holloway. He heard again the searing, slurring obscenity James had uttered at the general store one evening after the flight of Nomia and Jed. He remembered the blind rage that had swept over him at the ribald jest. He lived through the fight, the heavy blows he had rained on the speaker. He remembered how, panting with rage, he had finally been dragged from the prostrate figure and shoved out of the store. Never again had King entered that store; not one word did he utter to anyone concerning his encounter with James, but a purpose was born in his mind.

Then, one night after Jed's return, Jed and James had come to blows over a card game. There had been threats and recriminations, with a threat on Jed's part to "settle later." A few nights after that Holloway was found dead, shot through the heart. No weapon was found, but the fact that James was killed with a rifle of the same bore of one Jed owned, together with the fact that Jed's rifle had mysteriously disappeared, although he had been hunting with it the day before the killing, turned suspicion on him. Despite his frantic declarations of innocence, he had paid the debt.

"Dey ain't think I might know who killed Jeems, an' who hide Jed's gun," King chuckled. Then he thought of Leora's last remark and her strange, shrewd glance. Had she, in some uncanny fashion, guessed the truth?

With a yawn he rose from his bunk. It was high time to be in bed. Stretching in sheer weariness, he threw back his head. A sudden shiver ran through his body; his arms dropped sharply to his side. His shadow, huge, distorted, lay along the wall and partly across the ceiling. The head emerged from a noose, one end of which sprang upward as if attached to a beam out of sight. In a moment King recovered himself, and his agitation gave place to relief. The shadow of a coil of rope dangling from one of the rafters crossed his shadow so as to give the illusion of being around the neck of the huge, sprawling figure.

With shaking hands and a muttered oath he stepped to the table and blew out the light. What a fool he was getting to be! Leora's words about Jed's threat—had they taken such hold on him? Didn't he know that such talk was nonsense? What sensible man would take stock in such nonsense? Time for a man to be in bed when his nerves began jumping at his shadow. Leora had been brought up on tales—

Tales! A thousand plantation ghost stories of his boyhood rushed into his mind. Barred doors opening, and no hand seen opening them—wronged spirits coming back—the man murdered in his sleep by the ghost of a man he had murdered. He swore under his breath, as he kicked his boots across the room, and plunged into the tumbled bunk to sleep. It would not be long before daylight. Things always cleared up in the day.

Sleep came at last, fitful, broken with mutterings and dreams; Leora waiting at the end of the lane of trees; Nomia's face, mocking, smiling, teasing; James dropping like a log in the grass, dying without a sound; himself slinking down the path to the river, and dropping the gun into the swiftest part of the current; Jed's gray, agonized face, as he was half-carried from the courtroom after pronouncement of sentence; the crowd outside the prison walls; noon whistles shrieking the last moments of the condemned man's life.

The night had given way to the blackness of early morning when King was suddenly shocked into wakefulness. Something sinuous, like a thread was passing slowly across his throat. A cry of fear came from the awakened man's lips. What was it?

What was this thing? He put up his hand to tear it away. He shrieked out again. It was a rope, a noosed rope tightening around his throat.

"Good God!" His hand crept fearfully to his throat again, striving desperately to summon strength to tear the thing away. Another cry. The cords were growing—growing thicker and tighter.

"Help! God have mercy!" King made a lunge toward the floor. He was jerked to his knees on the edge of the bunk. Fearfully, her raised his eyes. A scream of agony broke through his burning lips:

"Jed! Jed! Don' do dat! Don'—Have mercy! God have—" His voice broke in a gurgling sob. His body sagged limply on the bunk. Outside the early breeze of morning passed in a shuddering sigh through the lane of trees, in the first faint streaks of morning.

When, after a day, King failed to appear among his fellows, four men, under the guidance of Leora, broke into the cabin. On the bed they found him, his body rigid, his face set in its mask of mortal terror. Over his face and around his neck were the broken filaments of a spider web. [*Opportunity* 9.12 (December 1931): 369–371]

THERE WERE THREE

by Marita O. Bonner

Foreword

Now, walking along Frye Street, you sniff first the rust tangy odor that comes from a river too near a city; walk aside so that Jewish babies will not trip you up; you pause to flatten your nose against discreet windows of Chinese merchants; marvel at the beauty and tragic old age in the faces of the young Italian women; puzzle whether the muscular blond people are Swedes or Danes or both; pronounce odd consonant names in Greek characters on shops; wonder whether Russians are Jews, or Jews, Russians—and finally you will wonder how the Negroes there manage to look like all men of every other race and then have something left over for their own distinctive black-browns.

There is only one Frye Street. It runs from the river to Grand Avenue where the El is.

All the World is there.

It runs from the safe solidity of honorable marriage to all of the amazing varieties of harlotry—from replicas of Old World living to the obscenities of latter decadence—from Heaven to Hell.

All the World is there.

There were three of them.

There was Lucille, there was Little Lou, there was Robbie.

Lucille was the mother of Little Lou and Robbie. She was fat, but most certainly shapely and she was a violet-eyed dazzling blonde. But something in the curve of her bosom, in the swell of her hips, in the red fullness of her lips, made you know that underneath this creamy flesh and golden waviness, there lay a black man—a black woman.

Little Lou and Robbie had a touch of their mother's blondness matched with an ivory tinted flesh in the girl and shaded to a bronze brownness in the boy.

Lots of the women of Frye Street, the colored women—the white women—looked at Robbie's lithe slenderness, small features, and black eyes, with a measuring, waiting, stalking look. Robbie was but sixteen.

"Ku Kaing told me I was the prettiest girl on Frye Street!" Little Lou told Lucille once with the bubbling vanity of flattered fourteen. "And Mr. Davy, that funny Scotchman who keeps the grocery store, said I could be his cashier when I grow up! and Sam Taylor ..."

"Don't tell me nothing that feather-bed said!" Lucille had screamed. Then she shot out at Robbie, "Why the hell can't you keep care of your sister when I am out working all night?"

Things were like that at Number 12 Frye Street where they lived. There were silk sheets on the beds, there was silk underwear in abundance in the bureau drawers, there were toilet waters, perfumes and flashy clothes. But sometimes there was no dinner or no breakfast. And unless Robbie or Little Lou took up the broom, the house was always unswept. Moreover, you continually ran the possibility of sitting down on anybody's hat.

A father?

Nobody gave a thought to such a person. "You're all mine the both of you!" Lucille had told them once, and neither one of them had ever pushed in behind this for more.

Every night at six thirty Lucille made Little Lou run the bath tub full of warm water.

"Put in half a cup of bath-salts, baby!" Lucille would call from her bedroom while she was undressing.

Little Lou would search out a bottle of heliotrope, jasmine or rose-verbena and drop the crystals daintily in. She would lean way over the steamy tub and sniff with a hungriness at the warm scent as it swept up.

After she had splashed, powdered and partly dressed, Lucille always called the other two into her room to talk. They knew at the call that their mother had put on her dress and was doing her nails and finishing her face.

"You all keep in the house and off the streets while I'm at work, you hear?" she usually began.

"Yes, mama," they never failed to reply readily.

But Robbie stayed out on the corner of Grand Avenue up by the "Toot Sweet Music Shop" with as much of his gang as was not working, until 11 o'clock.

Little Lou went on visits up and down Frye Street, with this girl—with that. But they never left the house until Lucille had finally cocked her hat, settled her complexion to a suitable finality, and silked out to her taxi—to go to work.

"What kind of woman got to go to work dressed better than Sheba when she visited King Solomon and ridin' in a taxi?" Mrs. Lillie Brown who lived at number 14 often asked her husband.

The question was purely rhetorical. The women like Mrs. Brown who waddled wearily beneath a burden of too much of what was not needed in Life—and did not know how to escape it—had already settled the answer among them. To them, Lucille was that flamboyant symbol of uncleanness that always sets the psalm-singers of all earth into rhapsodies.

But Lucille taxied out of Frye Street every night and remained within doors and in bed of a day, so that neither the full chorus nor the free-tones and embellishments of the rhapsodies ever reached her.

It was one of those evenings in April when even a city river tries to smell of spring. The three were shut up in Lucille's room.

"—And you two stay in the house!" Lucille had finished as usual, but she was looking at her buffer when she spoke.

Little Lou and Robbie stared at each other.

"I wish I could go up-town and hop bells with Sammy Jackson at the Sumner!" Robbie remarked after a while.

"You stay down here and stay out of hotels!" Lucille blazed. She hurled the buffer back on her dressing table. "I don't want you 'round no hotel! White women are the devil! Ruin you!"

"They haven't ruined Sammy!" protested Robbie.

"No! the colored women done that for him, 'fore he left Frye Street," retorted his mother.

"Sammy doesn't chase after girls Ma! He always hangs with the gang up to the music store."

"Stay in here and let Sammy alone!" his mother fired. "You hear me?"

"Yes!" Robbie lowered his eyes as he answered.

Before either one of them could speak again, Lucille's taxi tooted, and with a kiss for Little Lou, the mother went to her work.

Little Lou leaned on the bureau gazing absently in the mirror listening to the diminishing coughs of the taxi.

"You going?" she turned to Robbie with the question when the last sound had been lost in the roar of the El.

"You bet!" answered her brother. He swung his leg down from the trunk where he had been sitting. "I got Sammy to ast the man if I could work in a guy's place tonight and believe me I'm going. Get swell tips!"

"Bring me some strawberry ice-cream!" Little Lou begged.

"Sure! I am gonna make two dollars tips!" Robbie expanded.

"We can go to the show!"

"You mean I can!"

"I'll tell if you don't give me some money!"

"Go ahead!"

Robbie swaggered off and out of the house with that, but both of them knew that Little Lou would get a part of the money.

* * *

It was a happy Robbie that perched in the midst of the bell-hops at the Sumner two hours later. By that time he had carried two bags, made fifty cents, cursed a little with the boys and already promised the captain that he would gamble below stairs with the bunch when the night was finally over. Robbie felt as smart as his cerise uniform.

"You kin make the next run up-stairs kid!" the captain had offered in a glow of approval.

This new kid was promising. Gave signs of being a good fellow.

Robbie kept an eager eye on the little black register above their seat. When number 740 showed a sudden white eye, Robbie was on this feet before the little plunger had been pushed up to make the board black again.

"Two Silver Sprays for 740!" ordered the captain from his 'phone.

Robbie nodded and flew out into the kitchen to get the tray and the bottles.

"Where you going boy!" the elevator man queried as he closed the doors behind Robbie.

"740!"

"Aw that's a regular souser, that dame! She always gets her sweeties to start the evening by letting her swim in liquor! That's about the sixth bottle of Silver Spray I see go up there tonight!"

"Hot night!" observed Robbie as he stepped off.

"For some folks!" the other called after him and shot the car down again.

In his little flurry of excitement, Robbie found himself following the numbers of the rooms in the wrong direction at first. He reversed his march and stopped to catch his breath before he knocked on 740.

"Come in!" called a woman's voice.

Steadying the tray against the door, Robbie slid into the room.

"Over here by the bed!" the woman spoke again.

Robbie closed the door with his foot and kept his eyes on his bottles as he headed in the general direction of the voice.

He had almost reached the table when the bed came within his range of vision. It sort of swam up between the bottles he was watching so closely.

A pair of plump bare legs protruded between a pink comforter and the sheet. A broad creamy thigh showed through a black satin negligee. Robbie halted.

The door which led into the bath flung open quickly.

"How much boy?" demanded the man who stepped forth.

Robbie sat down his tray. "A dollar and a half, sir," he replied turning around.

"Wait'll I get my trousers!" the man ordered and walked across the room.

Robbie saw that he must have just bathed for he wore only a silk bathrobe. Even his slippers were lacking.

Robbie stole another look toward the bed.

The woman there had been lying on her side with her back toward the boy, but now she began to stir and finally turned over on her back, drawing the comforter up well all around her.

Her movements among the covers drew the boy's eyes once more.

A pair of violet eyes peering sleepily through tangled blond hair, met his.

Perspiration prickled out all over Robbie.

"Mama!" he whispered hoarsely. "Mama."

"Oh! Jesus!" cried the woman in the bed loudly.

"Mama? Mama!" Robbie began shouting. He tore at the bed clothes. "Mama!!!"

There was a rush of feet across the room.

"Here! what the hell do you mean, you little nigger!" shouted the man as he ran.

Now Robbie was by the window.

It was April.

Even a city river opens up to Spring.

The window tried to draw Spring in, opened as it was, seven stories above the city pavement.

The man rushed up behind Robbie.

The man struck Robbie to knock him down.

The window was open.

... A woman on the third floor said that the boy was screaming for his mother as his body hurtled through the air.

But it was an accident.

It was an accident that could not possibly find its way into the daily papers.

There was a note, though, that a bell boy had lost his balance and fallen to his death while opening a window in the Sumner. There was further note that no parents had yet come to claim the body.

That was all to that.

But—there were three.

Now, up at McNeil Institute where those people stay whose wealthy connections can prevent them from being assigned to an ordinary asylum, there is a stout blonde woman patient with violet eyes.

Sometimes she screams: "Take your yellow hands off! Off! Off!"

Again she cries: "Don't smother me—don't smother me—black feather bed!"

Or even: "Take your dirty white hands off! Off! Off!"

Nobody knows what she means.

It's a color fixation, some people say.

But—there were three you see.

Sometimes I wonder which door opened for that third.

[*Opportunity* 11.7 (July 1933): 205–207]

OF JIMMIE HARRIS

by Marita O. Bonner

Jimmy Harris was dying.

"Can't believe it!" said the "boys."

... Every night the "boys" gathered in the Valet de Luxe tailor shop. A day was not completed properly unless the colored men of Frye Street—those who were through with the fleshpots up-town and just as through with wives with whom they had lived some several years—did not gather in Jimmy's shop from eight until ten. They call themselves the "Boys," but every single one of them was well beyond thirty-five. Indeed, Pop Gentry, the one who told the nastiest jokes, strutted the most vibrant impromptu dances, drank the most, cursed the loudest, was sixty.

Rain, sleet, wind, family wars, could not keep one of the "boys" away from the De Luxe.

Of a night—except Sundays—every chair and piece of chair, every box, and even the cutting tables were filled with colored men of all sizes and varieties. Some of these temporarily devoid of funds, stood around half-dressed and pressed their own trousers while they guffawed and bantered.

Jimmy Harris had a seal-smooth skin coupled with the straight cast features and hair of a nature smooth waviness that constitutes "a good-looking brown." The clothes which he made for himself sat his medium-sized figure neatly. He was usually amiable, knew how to listen when the gang wanted to do the talking, had a bad reputation for good living and money, and minded his business.

Everybody liked Jimmy.

He always sat cross legged on one of the big black tables, stitching,—stitching—stitching—while the others talked.

"Nigger! don't you never lay off workin'?" Pop Gentry asked this more than once. "Them pantsies and coatsies'll all be 'round here waiting for somebody to wear and yo'll be with de worms and daisies, boy! How 'm I talkin'!" he would end in a shout of laughter, and slap Jimmy on the back or any handy portion of his anatomy before he sat down.

Usually Jimmy would smile and murmur, "That's right," before he lapsed into silence and went on stitching—stitching—stitching.

It was Pop Gentry who had carried Jimmy's head and shoulders when he pitched head first off of his table one night and laid quiet on the floor in their midst.

"My God! the boy got a stroke!" somebody had chattered after the first dazed moment of speechless surprise.

"It's his liquor maybe!" someone else had suggested.

"Jimmy can carry his 'thout laying on the floor and pavements!"

"Git a doctor!" Pop had shouted.

"Cerebral hemorrhage! Put him in bed at once!" the doctor had ordered.

"No hope, I am afraid!" he added.

* * *

... "Can't believe it," sobbed his mother adjusting an ice bag over Jimmy's temples. "I can't believe God's goin' take my boy home yet! He's not but thirty-eight!"

She wiped her eyes on a huck towel which she had in her hand. Then she walked to the window. Seemed as if there could be a little less light in the room.

Would it be all right to lower the lace-edged window shades a few fractions of an inch?

That Louise—Jimmy's wife—was such a durn fool about her house.

"Don't break my John Haviland china!" "Use the jelly glasses to drink out of!

You'll chip my hand-etched goblet! Don't take an ice pick to get the ice cubes out of the Frigidaire! If you slam that oven door, you'll upset my thermostat!" she made Jimmy's mother sweat blood for every hour spent visiting at his house.

"Marm Harris" would have preferred to remain in Luray, Virginia, in her own modest five rooms where a body could feel at home and eat with elbows on the table dressed only in a cotton kimono if the urge seized her.

But she never felt easy about Jimmy.

She never felt easy about Jimmy up in the big city on Frye Street with a tailor shop and a blonde wife who said she was colored—and Mary Linn, staying single all the fifteen years that had elapsed since Jimmy forgot her for Louise.

And though she hated Frye Street, hated Louise, hated the smoothness of Jimmy's home, Marm would bundle up herself every year and go north to Jimmy's.

One night in the dark solitude of their bedchamber, Louise had tried a plaintive air of long suffering affliction.

"Does your mother have to visit you this year again?" she had asked.

"My mother can come any time she wants and stay as long as she wants! The other bedroom is for her!"

"Oh, oh! I did not know that!" Louise had retorted stiffly. "I thought that was the spare-chamber!"

"Spare hell! It's Ma's!"

Louise had been surprised into silence at the violence of Jimmy's retort. She usually swung the reins of their life together skillfully in one hand. Jimmy had never balked before.

It would not do to carry things to open battle. Sniping is more annoying than straight line firing.

The old lady would find her visit "spare hell."

But Marm came and came again and came when Jimmy was sick and Louise had wired that she herself was unable to take care of him.

* * *

"I can't believe Jimmy is dying!" Louise cried to Doctor Whetbone. She sat well in the center of the green satin love-seat which made some visitors unwelcome to her parlor.

"Well, dear lady, I am very sorry but I can offer no hope!" Doctor Whetbone repeated.

"Gosh! A lanky bronze colored man with deep set gray eyes is a heart ache, believe me!" thought Louise watching the doctor.

Whetbone leaned easily against the mantle.

He was one of those tall men who never sat down unless it was absolutely necessary. Some people said that he stood up so you could see how well his suit fitted him across the shoulders, how well his shoes fitted his feet, how well he himself fitted into any surroundings under any circumstances—in short—what a patrician he was.

That was what some people said.

People say a lot of things about a reasonably decent looking man who can earn a comfortable living and is still single at 34.

Louise widened her eyes until water flowed into them. "What'll I do?" she lifted her voice and her eyes piteously to Dr. Whetbone.

"Now—now," countered the physician. "Just try to realize that you have done your best for him—kept your home beautifully for him!" he made a sweeping gesture of the room.

"Oh, yes," murmured Louise.

"You tried to make him take more rest and better care of himself!" continued Whetbone soothingly.

"Yes, I made him put in oil-heat so he would not have to shovel coal and buy a car so we could go out for nice rides in the evenings together, and buy an electric refrigerator so I could always keep milk and vegetables fresh for him!"

"Yes, yes!" finished the Doctor. "Let's run upstairs and take a look at him."

And Jimmy, fastened inside of his body by a tongue that could no longer speak, saw Louise standing close beside the doctor at his bedside.

Saw her lift and lower her eyes as she talked to him.

Why were they smiling at each other?

He watched them.

The doctor left the room presently.

Louise went to the bureau and smiled into the mirror at herself pinching first her arm, then her cheek, fluffing out her hair, smoothing down her black satin dress.

Then she went out of the room too.

She did not look toward the bed again.

* * *

"Oh I can't believe it! Jimmy can't be dying!" a tall thin brown woman cried aloud.

She was walking up a country road in Luray.

"God don't take him! Oh God!!" she stopped and knelt on a bank that was tangled with rose vines and dead leaves.

But she had stopped and cried and prayed on rose banks for fifteen years—and Jimmy had married Louise and stayed up north on Frye Street and waxed and prospered—though he had no children.

Presently she arose from the rose-vines and went walking on crying and praying.

But God must despise a sniveler.

She had cried and prayed for fifteen years.

Jimmy Harris was dying.

* * *

Pain thundered down across Jimmy Harris.

Back and forth it avalanched, dragging him down, sucking him deeply under.

Once he fought through, came up out of the thundering to find himself in his own bed—in his own room. The lavender electric clock on the bureau was flanked by the lavender and green figurines that supported Louise's boudoir lamps there. But everything looked new, distant.

"God!! I've been sick!! Sick!!" Jimmy told himself.

He sent his thoughts here, there, into himself to seek out the sick spot, the weak spot.

But before he had found it, pain tumbled back angrily, smotheringly, sucked him under, dragged him down, pulled,—pulled—pulled—.

"I can't fight back! I can't get up over this pain mountain over me!" Jimmy cried within.

He began to sink straightway.

That is what they call being reconciled to die. They call it reconciled when pain has strummed a symphony of suffering back and forth across you, up and down, round and round you until each little fiber is worn tissue-thin with aching. And when you are lying beaten, and buffeted, battered and broken—pain goes out, joins hands with Death and comes back to dance, dance, dance, stamp, stamp, stamp down on you until you give up.

"I can't believe it!" Jimmy cried to himself—and all of the time the Two were dancing, dancing, stamping, stamping.

"I can't believe it! I'll get up! Go out! Go to work! Finish! Finish! Stitch! Stitch!"

—What was that uprooting like a tree in a windstorm?

—What was that bright glowing in his eyes?

—What was that loosing—tearing loose—uprooting—shedding—?

"He's gone!" exclaimed Dr. Whetbone walking to the bed.

"Gone!" sobbed Marm, kneeling beside the bed.

Louise sat on the steps outside of the room. She had not been able to stay in the room while Jimmy Harris had been breathing, breathing, breathing so that it sounded as if the room were filled with many tubs of water draining off with that gurgling of water settling to waste.

Jimmy Harris was dead.

I guess he'd been happy, though.

He had had his hands on what he wanted.   [Opportunity 11.8 (August 1933): 242–244]

CORNER STORE

by Marita O. Bonner

"Some more lachs, Anton? A little matzos and wine? A pickled tomato?" A quiver of appeal, entirely too searing for so simple a thing as an invitation to dally with more food, ran through Esther Steinberg's voice.

Anton Steinberg shook his head vigorously in denial. His hands and mouth were full of lebkuchen. He shook his head because he did not wish more food, nor did he wish to recognize the seeking in Esther's tone. He lowered his eyes so that he would not have to see his wife.

Her flabby body, slouched in faded grey house dress and muffled in ragged black sweater, was as dismal as the pallor of her flaccid face. Esther's only beauty had been a head of black hair that seemed to spring in aliveness in each curl.

Working from dawn until midnight for seven years behind the counter of Steinberg's Grocery-Market on Frye Street, had made an old woman of Esther at thirty-nine.

Anton crammed crumbs of gingerbread hastily into his mouth, wiped his hands on the apron which he never removed for the noon lunch served in this kitchen in back of their store, and rushed out as the bell tinkled in the shop.

As soon as she was alone, Esther drew a sibilant sobbing sigh and covered her face with both hands.

"Teach me what I should do, Gott!" she prayed in a hoarse whisper.

"Say something, ma?" called a girl's voice suddenly from a room within.

Esther snatched down her hands and crouched lower in her chair. She said nothing.

A sound of yawning came now from within, then all at once, pushing aside the gunny-sacking which served as a drapery between the two rooms, Meta, daughter of Esther and Anton, stood in the door. She rubbed her eyes and stretched with the elastic abandon of seventeen years.

"Who are you talking to, ma?" she queried again.

Esther shook her head. "Nobody. I—I was—I was wishing I was back in the old country. In the ghetto," she finished timidly with a swift look at her daughter's face.

Meta made a rapid gesture, shrugged her shoulders and shaking her black hair out around her, began combing it with quick strokes.

"Oh for God's sake, ma! What do you want to be back in that old mud hole for with nothing but Jews, Jews, before you, behind you and beside you? You ought to be glad to get to a free country, for heaven's sake!"

Esther looked first at Meta's high-heeled patent-leather pumps, then at her gun-metal chiffon stockings drawn over nicely-turned legs. Her red flannel dress caught her snugly across the bosom and at the hips, but its vivid color brought out the blackness of her curly bob the rich red of her lips and the soft moulding of her delicate, oval face. Jewish girls in the Old World did not dress this way.

"You ashamed to be a Jew?" Esther demanded harshly.

"No, ma! but for pete's sake, I should think you'd be glad papa is making good money and spending it here like you never could back there!"

"I want to be near a nice Schule and have nice Jewish neighbors!" persisted the mother with a sort of stubborn sullenness.

"Then you don't want the new auto and the fur coat and the flats that we own on the West Side?"

Esther made an exclamation like a cat when it spits. "Tcha! We got just as good in the old country—!"

"Like fun! Don't you think I remember those odd cold stone houses with no heat and nothing else in them! Why do you want to go back to a place where dirty German kids wait around to throw mud on you when you go out? No! Give me Frye Street!"

Meta dropped down to the table and helped herself to some of the smoked salmon. Her mother drew back into her corner—drew back into herself.

Anton's heavy step sounded in the little hall outside the kitchen. He scowled as soon as he saw his daughter.

"You up, you Meta! What for do you sleep all the day when I want that you should help me with the Saturday rush?"

Meta wiped her fingers on a piece of wax paper and licked one daintily. "Don't you think I go to sleep, maybe?"

"Why don't you sleep nights instead of racing the streets? That's what I want to know!"

An angry flush swept the girl's face. "Yah!" she mocked. "Why don't I go to the Schule at night—Monday—Tuesday—Thursday again like you! You!! At the Schule—"

Her pertness trailed off into a frightened silence. The vein in Anton's left temple was standing out like a rope. His face was swollen a dark purple.

"Du—du—!" he choked and lifted his hand.

"Anton! Anton!" shrilled Esther. "Strafe nicht!"

Meta stared back at her father. But she did not flinch.

The bell on the door of the shop jangled.

No one moved.

"One comes to buy!" Esther urged in Jewish.

"A customer comes, Anton!" she repeated as he did not move.

Her husband hung an instant on the threshold, then with a snort that was almost a snarl, he went back up the passage to the store.

"Gott! Was fur ein' Mann!" Esther chattered in an agony of fear. "Ever since we got to this place he becomes more cold to me! Now he wants to hit you, Liebschen!"

"If he hits me I'll run off to get married, right away." Meta burst forth passionately.

"Ja! David Sorbenstein is one nice boy. Me and papa chose him for you ourselves! Goes to the Schule every week and stays bei the shop of his Vater." Esther garbled Jewish and such English as she knew. "Ach solche ein' Knabe!"

"David Sorbenstein is a fat greasy slob! A dumbell! He makes me sick! I wouldn't marry that guy!"

"Meta! he'd make such a goot husband ! Such an industry—"

But Meta shook her shoulders impatiently and switched David's virtues to scorn as fast as Esther could tell them off.

"I'd run off to marry Abe Brown," Meta declared.

"A goy—a Gentile?" Esther could not believe herself.

Meta nodded. "He isn't all goy. His grandfather is a Jew and his mother is colored. Schwartze!"

"Ein' Schwartze! Du mein' lieber Gott!" Esther laid her face on her arm and wept aloud and loudly.

Anton came running back again. "Was ist geschied'? Na! Na, Esther," he cried as he came.

He rubbed his hands soothingly across his wife's hair.

"Du!" he glowered at Meta across Esther's bowed head.

"Ein' Schwartze! Meta!" screamed Esther.

Anton's eyes hung in Meta's. "Du?" the word was a gasp.

His face whitened.

Meta shook her head. "Only Abe," she whispered.

Something desperate oozed out of Anton's face. Vast relief grew there.

"Na na! Esther!" he began again. "Nichts! Nichts! Es gibt nichts! Du musst dass nicht! Meta don't mean nothing! She wouldn't marry no Gentile. She wouldn't marry no Schwartze!"

The bell on the shop rang loudly.

"I'll go!" Anton announced briskly, and he was out and back by the time Esther's wails had subsided to an incessant hiccoughing.

"Now mama! Now mama! Our little girl will make bei Yom Kipper mit Sorbenstein's boy a nice marriage!"

"I won't!" Meta shouted.

"Aah—aah!" began Esther in a rising tone of lamentation.

The shop bell rang.

"You go mama! Wait on the custom! Papa will talk to Meta!" Anton ordered.

Esther moved on heavy feet forward to the store. Early twilight was falling thickly over everything. Esther turned back to fumble for the switch box.

"Anton! Anton?" called a woman's voice softly from somewhere near the door.

Esther's hand froze uplifted as it reached the switch. Who was this woman who dared to stand in her store calling Anton by his name with that soft, urgent, intimate lift of the voice?

Esther shot on all of the lights and stepped out on to the floor.

Standing by the butcher block, was a woman. Her limbs curved heavily beneath a pink cotton house dress. Her black hair shone in a series of braids coiled high around a lovely head. On first glance, she was Semitic. It was not until Esther was upon her that she saw that she was a colored woman.

"You want something?" demanded Esther brusquely.

"No—" the other replied hesitatingly.

Heavy steps padded from the rear. I'll attend the custom, mama!" Anton nearly shouted as he bounded forward.

"Mama—mama!" he gabbled. "Meta wants that you should come there. She will tell you something.

"Noch der schwartze? (Is it still to be the black man)" his wife queried.

"Moglich! We must be patient, though after a little—verleicht—David Sorbenstein! We'll see! Nun!"

Esther sped along the hall to the kitchen but Meta was back in the inner room talking on the telephone.

—"So listen, Abe darling,—I just told him that you were Ella's nephew and that you knew already about his going to the "Schule"—ha! ha!—every night. And he says to me, 'Well, maybe then I'll talk to mama and tell her to wait a little, but don't you do nothing about marrying, yet awhile!'—What? Sure! He's crazy about her! She's out there now! Ella's out in the store talking to him now—What? Sure! Makes a swell whip to hold over papa!"

Standing in the kitchen, Esther stared slowly around her, listening. As the words bore into her, she began to stare wildly, shaking her head from side to side—side to side.

This wasn't Meta talking!

That was not Anton outside!

This room was not home. Only stone houses in ghettoes are homes.

The narrow kitchen with its barren huddled air was closing her in.

—"She's out there now! Yah! Ella!!"—

—"Anton?" a woman's voice had called softly with a caress in it that searched like a gentle hand seeking to find something loved in a dark place....

Esther tore back up the hall toward the store.

Anton stood beside his block, a cleaver trailing idly from one hand talking, talking, looking down into the woman's face.

There they stood.

Close together.

Her head tilted back, her eyes veiling, then lifting.

Esther rushed back and standing in the hall between the shop and the kitchen—she lifted up her voice and screamed and screamed.

She caught hold of the sacking. It tore down from its place between the doors. She fell as it ripped and lay prone on the floor, the sack cloth around her and screamed and screamed.

"Like a wild thing in a forest, you holler!" Anton came running to swear at her.

"Like one who moans for Israel!" replied! Esther—and lay and sobbed in her sack cloth.

THE BLACK DRESS: A SHORT SHORT STORY

by Dorothy West

They sent me word that morning that old Mr. Johnson had died in the night. It was not really a surprise to me. I knew he had been lingering for weeks.

That was my chiefest reason for writing to Margaret. Deep in his heart old Johnson, her father, loved her very much. It would not be so hard for him to go with her hand in his. Margaret I knew had forgiven him his early injustice. I felt she would be glad to brighten his last pain-black days. They would not be many. He could not live beyond the year, and it was Christmas week when I wrote her to come.

I did not mention her father's hopeless illness. I simply asked her, for old time's sake, to come and hang up her stocking with mine, as we had done when we were very young.

Her acceptance came in a day or two. She was between shows and husbands. It would be good to see me again after twelve long years. Did I still have dimples? Would I find her changed? For better, for worse?

I wondered. Margaret and I had been like sisters all our growing years. I suppose she loved me more than she loved anyone else. She had only an impatient tolerance for her bigoted father. But the years had probably softened this into something nearer affection. After all, he was her only living relative.

To my knowledge she never wrote him. Nor did she write me. Occasionally I would get a telegram of extravagant endearment, and very often a generous check. My babies, who had never seen her, spoke of her as Aunt Margaret.

I wrote her regularly. She had always seemed hard to the home folks, but I felt I understood her. She was not hard. She was simply unsentimental. She had one goal, the stage. She had had to fight the whole community, beginning with her father, to make them accept the theatre as a legitimate profession. The fight with her father had been long and bitter. The neighbors had taken his side. Naturally that did something to her spirit. When she left home at eighteen, it was not a girl but a bitter woman who said good-by to me, the only one to bid her good-by and God-speed.

I hoped the years had taken the edge off her bitterness. I always mentioned her father in my letters.

Toward the last I would say he sent love. For old Johnson did love Margaret. And I am sure, on the lonely nights, he wished very much he could unsay the things that had sent her from him. Well, while there is life, it is not too late. At least he could say he was sorry he had said them. That was in my mind, knowing the time, his time, was so short, when I wrote to Margaret.

The hospital called me the morning of Christmas eve. They asked me the address of old Johnson's nearest of kin. I gave them Margaret's before I realized she would be in town that evening. After I hung up I hoped she had already left. For I could tell her more tenderly than a cold telegram.

Someone rang my bell. It was the boy with the tree my husband had bought on his way to work. The children were wild. And when I saw their excited faces, I suddenly and selfishly decided that I could not bring death into my house to mar the happiest day of their year.

No, Margaret must wait until tomorrow evening to be told. I would tell her after the last tired child had been tucked into bed. In the meantime I would make some arrangements with an undertaker.

I knew this was the most wicked thing I would ever do in my life. But, oh, she would understand when we stood and smiled down at the sleeping children that it would have been cruel to spoil their day with our grown-up grief.

Early that evening a taxi rolled up. A woman got out. I flew downstairs to open my door with words of gay greeting or solemn condolence ready on my lips. Margaret's dear familiar face was radiant. She did not know. I held her fast in my arms.

I shall never forget our happy evening. She was like a sprite, never still. She fell in love with small Margaret. Once she said fiercely to the shining faces, "Be happy. Let nothing stand in the way of your being happy." I thought, How hard her beautiful face is. It is only I who know she is not hard.

We were tired at last. Sentimentally we were going to sleep together. My husband was banished to a cot in the dining room, and sometime during the night he would fill our stockings.

Margaret and I were in my room together. She opened her bag to fetch out the stocking. On the top lay a black dress, looking as if it had been stuffed in hastily. I caught my breath sharply. She followed my glance.

She said indifferently, "This went in at the last moment. It'll have to be pressed before I wear it."

My throat went dry. For the first time in my life I was going to sleep with a stranger.

Tin Can

by Marita Bonner Occomy

> "For my people have committed two evils: they have forsaken me, the fountain of living waters—and hewed them out cisterns, broken cisterns, that can hold no water."
> —Jeremiah

Take an empty tin can.
Stand it up.
Drop two or three hard jagged pebbles in it.
Knock the tin can down. The pebbles will rattle-rattle-rattle. You can hear each little rock pattering its own little rattle, its hollow rattle, when the can is shaken and knocked down.
You can hear each hard rattling—like undigested thoughts—hollow.
Hollow.

* * *

Jimmie Joe was dancing. There are no words in any language under the sun rich enough in color, movement and sound to make you see a young black boy lilting a slim seventeen-year old body through a dance.

Right now, Little Brother sat hunched up on his own cot watching. The holes in his cotton union suit were as wide as his mouth as his eyes danced with Jimmy Joe.

"Yappy-titty yap-yap! Skee-dad-dad!" chanted Jimmie Joe. He slid a neat step up into the corner between his own bed and the bureau and began "falling-off-the-log" to get out again when the sound they had both been praying would not come before the dance had finished—tore from below stairs.

"You, Jimmy-Joe! You, Little Brother!" It was Ma, standing at the foot of the stairs. "You all stop that racket and get them clothes on and get down here 'fore I comes up there!"

"Unh-unh!" exclaimed Little Brother on two tones. He dropped his knees at once and began to wiggle his black-brown feet into stockings and shoes.

With the dance rhythm on him, Jimmie Joe had to tap his mood out to a finish. He circled the some barnyard fowl, his arms moving in an exaggerated flapping.

Little Brother tore his eyes from his square toed scuffed boots long enough to take in Jimmy Joe's neat black suede oxfords, black trousers black belt, white sweater and white shirt with its black bow tie.

"You all right, boy!" he worshipped in an awed tone. "Jes wait'll ma let's me git to them Sunday night dances! I'll show you some steps every Monday, too!"

Panting a little, Jimmie Joe stopped in front of the mirror to straighten the bow tie. "She aint *lettin'* me git there yet! I jes goes on my hardness, boy!"

Little Brother hoisted his garnet corduroy slacks on over his chunky body. "You all right, boy!" he breathed again.

"Y'all want me to come up there with this clothes stick?" Ma's voice had a real edge on it now.

That meant it was near seven then and that Ma was fidgety to get breakfast on the table and get out so that she could get the eight o'clock car to go to work.

That edge in Ma's voice pried Little Brother up from his seat on the side of the cot and even unfastened Jimmie Joe from his place, glued as he was in a close gazing at himself before the mirror.

Ma got up at half past five every morning and made the fire in the kitchen and cooked breakfast and cleaned up as much of the house as she could get at at that time in the morning.

"I always believes in leavin' my house clean every day!" she told Jimmie Joe and Little Brother many a time. "You never know what day somebody's gonna bring you back home from a accident! And what'd I feel like if the house was dirty and the beds not clean and me not clean underneath my clothes!"

Ma worked from five-thirty to seven, thus. Then she gave the boys their breakfast and ate her own—usually walking back and forth from her bedroom to the kitchen as she ate—dressing so she could catch the eight o'clock car and go and do her day's work.

She would be at work when the boys came back from school. She would be at work when they came home to supper. Ma never came back from her "Rich white folks"—as Little Brother called them—until well after eight o'clock.

And though her steps would usually be slow by then and her breathing hard, she always washed and ironed and mended and cleaned up some more.

The only time Jimmie Joe and Little Brother saw her to talk to her on week days was the time in the morning when she was walking back and forth, drinking a sip of tea, putting her dress on, eating a fork full of grits, putting her hat on—gnawing a piece of bread and telling Jimmie Joe how much to spend for dinner and how to fix it—all at the same time.

"You, Jimmie Joe!" Ma yelled this morning as soon as the two reached the kitchen door. "How come you can't never bring no coal in like I done tole you so's I can fix the fire every morning?"

"Unh-unh!" bleated Little Brother. He scurried to a seat at the table and sat back mentally to watch Jimmie Joe wiggle out of a tight place.

Nobody could ever corner *his* brother!

"I tol' Little Brother to git the coal last night, Ma!" Jimmie Joe yelled back as loudly as his mother had spoken.

"Heah! Don't you holler at me, boy!" Ma snatched up the coal shovel and held it, batwise, pressed against her left shoulder.

Little Brother breathed noisily.

Jimmie Joe did not flinch. "Little Brother didn't bring it in, Ma! I tole him to do it while I was at Lucas's last night—studyin'!" Jimmie Joe repeated as if the shovel had not been there.

"Dat boy kin sure lie!" Little Brother marveled to himself. "I aint heard you!" he apologized aloud on a whining note to Jimmie Joe.

Ma said nothing to this. Jimmie Joe slid into a chair, kicked Little Brother slyly under the table, and began to shovel up hominy grits and gravy.

"Don't forgit to thank God for them vittles!" Ma exploded next. "I 'clare you is going to the devil fas' as you kin make it, Jimmie Joe!"

Jimmie Joe lowered his head over the plate an instant, then raised his head and voice in his own defense.

"I always says my blessing, Ma! You just come jumping on me this morning 'fore I got in here good 'bout something Little Brother didn't do and made me fergit! Aint I been going to church every Sunday like you tole me?"

"You aint been there no Sunday nights! You better not be hanging 'round no dance halls on Sunday nights like Anna Lucas's boy. I bet I'll take the hide off you ef I hears you been there!"

Jimmie Joe eeled into another tangent.

"I got to get another book today for English, Ma!"

"What the name of God you got to buy so many books for? Ain't I given you money to buy six English books this year and this ain't but March? What them teachers think I is?"

Jimmie Joe slid into a closer position. "But I got to have it or Miss Thomas 'll flunk me and you know Pa says he'll take me out of school if I flunk English again!"

That silenced Ma. She and Pa fought a constant war over the fact that Jimmie Joe and Little Brother went to school. Pa maintained a colored boy did not need high school—like Jimmie Joe was getting—nor even junior high school—where Little Brother was—to do the kind of work a colored man could get to do. All you needed was a little reading so you could find a "Help Wanted" sign and get on the right street cars and a little numbering "so's these sheenies" could not cheat you in the stores! And you could get that much—while you had your diapers on!

But Ma—like all women—had her ear tuned to the melody that might be someday, somewhere.

"Them boys may be big Negroes someday! Can't never tell!" she'd always countered.

So Jimmy Joe knew which note to sound.

"That boy sure kin lie! He aint got to get no book." Little Brother kept telling himself. His thoughts wriggled through him so rapidly that he began to gobble his food.

"Little Brother! You chew that food 'fore you chokes to death!" Ma ordered.

"Yas'm!" Little Brother was meek.

"He sure God is dumb!" sneered Jimmie Joe to himself. He studied Little Brother's round blobby face in contempt. "No stuff in him! That guy will never be smart!"

"The book'll be six bits, Ma!" Jimmie offered next, his eye on the clock.

"Six bits! You mean seventy-five cents! What kinder book you got to get now?"

This was a crack that could be widened. Jimmie Joe began to work on the opening. "Shakespeare!"

"Ain't that what you got the las' time?"

"Aw yes, Ma! But that guy wrote a whole lot of stuff! You gotta read some this year and some next year too!"

"Well you gotta *earn* some of the money yourself this year and next year too! I 'clare I aint got no seventy-five cents for no book this day!"

Ma flung her tea-cup from her to the ledge on the back of the stove, gave a hurried glance at the clock which was indicating quarter of eight and fled to the bedroom for her hat and coat.

Little Brother laid his fork down to watch Jimmie Joe. Would he be defeated?

Ma came charging out of the bedroom. "Aw, I aint got no time to argue with you," she called back to Pa—who was still in bed. She snatched up her pocket-book from the place where it had been hanging on the knob of the sideboard door.

"You, Little Brother! You bring that coal in tonight!"

"Amen!" chanted Jimmie Joe, sotto voce.

"Shut up!" Ma stopped for a momentary battle of eyes. "And, Little Brother, you put them sugar loaf cabbages to soak in salt and water, when you get home! Don' cook 'em for an hour! Jes let 'em soak so's the bugs and worms will die out of them! Then put it in that water what I cooked the ham knuck in yestiddy!"

"Yas'm!"

"Y'all behave in school!"

"Yas'm!" in chorus.

"And you come in the house at five—both of you!"

"Yas'm!" final chorus!

"Bye!"

"Bye!"

And Ma was gone.

Ma hurried up Tenth Street, around the corner and stood under the "El" waiting for a cross town surface car. Through the city streets flecky, dirty mounds of snow Spring had forwarded a subtle something into the morning air.

Ma looked in a shop window at herself. "I 'clare I gets fatter every year! Who'd think I weighed jes' ninety-seven when I married Pa! I ought to git me one of those new satin hats this week. This thing is a mess!"

She passed on a little farther.

Krönen's Swedish Bakery, fresh in a coat of light blue paint on the woodwork and bedecked inside with pink crepe paper napkins—had a pyramid of pink and yellow cakes in the window.

Ma stopped short.

Believe I'll git me one of them cakes for lunch today!" she decided, suddenly reckless, and she went in.

"Nice day!" grinned Mrs. Krönen as she drew the cake in from the window. "Anything else?" she seemed to beg it as she started wrapping the cake.

"No!" Ma grinned back. She opened her pocketbook.

One lone nickel and three pennies rolled in there as she shook it.

Where was the ninety cents that she had put back in there after she had put a dime in church last night? She had broken a dollar!

Her mind made a frantic hurdle forward. Where would Tuesday's and Wednesday's dinner come from if she had no money?

Maybe the ham knuck would hold out if they ate fried potatoes and onions with it.

Then her mind hurdled distractedly back.

She couldn't give the woman five cents for a cake and then walk to work. She'd never get there!

She jangled coins fiercely again, trying to concoct ninety cents out of a nickel and three pennies.

—"Ma! I gotta get a book this morning! Six bits!"

Jimmie Joe had it.

Mrs. Krönen held out the cake.

Sweat hung in huge beads on Ma's face and neck, itched along her body.

Jimmie Joe stole!

"I guess I can't take the cake!" Ma panted.

Mrs. Krönen's smile froze and faded.

Ma stumbled out, slamming the door behind her.

Jimmie Joe was a thief.

* * *

In the meantime scrocking his heel plates grandly in the midst of his gang, Jimmie Joe was advancing on the High School.

Situated as it was in the middle of the Black Belt of that big northern city, nobody called the school the colored high school but every thing in it from top to bottom, from janitor to principal was some one of the varieties of Negro. The School Board sent all the colored children from every district there. The School Board appointed colored teachers with the proper qualifications to this one high school.

By licking the boots of those above him and kicking the backs of those below, and by never walking upright where it would gain him a point to crook his spine physically and morally, the black principal gained and held his job.

It was of him Jimmie Joe and his gang talked that morning.

"Wonder what tune that old Black Bass Drum is going to be playing in assembly this mornin.'"

Three boys sang aloud in derision, "The Character building program! Blah! Bloo! Wah!"

"Aw—!" One scraped his feet and cursed.

You have seen Jimmie Joe s gang in every Negro section of every city of any size in the world. They range from sixteen to nineteen—they range from coal black to it-takes-a-second glance-to-tell light. They are all neat and well dressed after their own particular pattern of heel-plated oxfords, wide trousers, foppish overcoats, gay sweaters and lumberjackets and pastel-toned felt hats.

And like Jimmie Joe, most of them had sounded every note in the scale of living except the whole note of legitimate marriage. All the half-tones and chromatic inversions of indecent living they had played, until an overlay of boredom, such as might weight the jaws of a forty-year old rounder, masked the youth in their faces before they were twenty.

So—scraping their feet cursing, gibing at each other and at groups of boys and girls they passed, they reached the building just as the bell rang.

"Hell! I aint going to no home room!" exploded Jimmie Joe at the sound. "Come on, George!" He singled out one rangy fair youth who was his special confrere. "Let's grab us a smoke in the Auto Paint Shop!"

"Yeah!" asserted George, swinging off from the larger group with Jimmie Joe. "I sure don't feel like hearing that character stuff today! I get damn sick of that Black Bass Drum telling you how much manners and stuff he's got, and honest to God, when

I used to work in his office on the switchboard, I've seen that nigger plug in his 'phone so he could listen to the teachers talk when they got an outside call!"

"Aw he ain't got nuttin—!" began Jimmie Joe—but just as they swung around the next corner there met them face to face, the principal.

He skinned back his lips in what he took to be the proper degree of cordiality to students whose parents were not his social equal.

"Mawnin!" muttered George and Jimmie Joe.

The man passed on, swaying an overstuffed figure from side to side on rubber heels. What character he might have once had, had long been swallowed up in a morass of petty littleness, snobbishness and downright silly conceit. He prided himself on three things: that he was a leading Negro—that is to say, he had been placed at the head of a school—; then, he could never cease to marvel that though his own skin was jet black his children had managed to be born with tawny skins, slightly darker than their fair mother's. Finally, he could not forget that he was the first black man born in a certain college town to graduate from a famous college.

Anything that did not contribute to these conceits, simply did not exist to the Black Bass Drum.

You could not make him understand that something besides formal platform speeches should be done about the fact that there was a gang of boys in his school who stole everything from everybody. No teacher could persuade him that instead of sending on inflated reports full of empty embroidered phrases—saying absolutely nothing—to the higher ups—somebody ought to appeal to someone to stop the glowing menace of the spread of social diseases among students. He closed his eyes to the annual crop of unmarried mothers in the senior class, blamed the teachers because the general scholarship was unspeakably low—and never admitted that he had any vital part in all of these problems but to lead where his narrow soul dictated.

He was not so much a black bass drum as he was just the fool ostrich, sticking his head into a hollow hole—the height and depth of his particular brain capacity—while an overwhelming world and ocean full of a million new conditions were sweeping up on him.

Bells were ringing at regular intervals all over the building as George and Jimmie Joe took their furtive way toward the paint shop. As they passed groups of students scurrying in cockroach fashion up and down the corridors, Jimmie Joe seemed to be on a restless lookout for someone. He would cut short whatever he was saying to George to stare into this group—then that.

"This nigger sure has got a bad case of Caroline," George thought to himself—but he said nothing of what he thought, aloud. "If she jus' doesn't happen by till we get to the paint shop, we'll get a smoke!"

And then Caroline met them face to face.

There is no accounting for the Carolines of this world—not that they are all called Caroline. Their names never matter really. What does matter is that they are all compelling, all glamorous, all undeniably attractive to all men of all types and all ages.

This Caroline was not fair. She would have been just another white girl if she had been. Instead, she was a golden reddish brownish shade. She was dimpled and smooth and clear. Her eyes were black and thick-lashed and her mouth took rouge with a pouting insouciance. She dressed beautifully, neatly, smartly and daintily, though she got her clothes by the nastiest possible means.

And her love affairs—or affairs of sex—it would be far better to call them—had given her a subtle languor as well as a confident seductive dash—and a body well filled with unmentionable disease.

At the sight of her, Jimmie Joe stood stock still. So did the world, so far as he was concerned. He did not even answer George's "See you later!" as he plunged on.

"Jimmie Joe!" Caroline crescendoed on all the nearest delightful tones of the scale. "I was thinking about you," which she wasn't. "Come on and carry my books up to my locker and then walk down to the assembly hall with me!"

Dumbly Jimmie Joe swung around, dumbly Jimmie Joe went down to the assembly hall and followed his section up the aisle to their usual seats, though he had not meant to be there.

The Black Bass Drum rapped out his usual monotonous roundel of so much palaver to an audience that was only younger than he—chronologically.

"Character is everything. I never forget my fellowman! It's easier to be good than to be bad!"

There were no new arrangements of words. It was all so empty, so vacant, so useless, so futile. Nobody—nobody—nowhere by talking from a platform can make you really know things that need to be inducted gently, firmly, carefully, steadily into the essence of you every moment of your life. It's too late when fourteen years or more of haphazard, slap-dash, hit-or-miss, grab-bag living has snatched you through the lowly life of poor colored homes in black sections.

There was nothing new in it all. His audience dozed or ruminated or plotted and planned as peacefully as if they had all been seated by a placid pool, letting the ripples ruffle its surface—unheeded.

Jimmie Joe sat plunged in a daze of joy that was to cost him one F in English, the first period for inattention and two the second and third periods in General Science for staring out of the window instead of into a microscope. Caroline was going to eat lunch with Jimmie Joe at recess.

The eighty-two cents of which Ma had been relieved, was going to buy two hot-dogs, two pieces of strawberry meringue pie and two ten cent boxes of vanilla ice cream.

For the hot-dogs, pie and ice-cream, Jimmie Joe was going to have the privilege of sauntering by Caroline's side down the streets near the school as they ate.

All the gang would see him.

All the gang would know, accordingly, that Jimmie Joe had money from somewhere because no male could talk to Caroline long without a money-ed backing of some sort.

All the school would see and know straightway that Jimmie Joe was a man of parts.

Dazed back in the midst of his seat as he waited through three periods and three F's for the fourth period and recess and Caroline, Jimmie Joe's only regret was that the eighty-two cents had not been eighty-two dollars.

* * *

It was the second Sunday in April when Ma first mentioned the theft of the eighty-two cents—and that indirectly.

Ma did not go to work on Sunday.

She got up at six o'clock, took her bath in the tin wash tub in the kitchen, straightened her hair with an old knife and crimped it with a hot fork before she waked the boys to breakfast.

Sunday morning she always sat between them at the table. Pa never got up to eat unless they had breakfast nearer ten o'clock than nine.

This particular morning, though, Ma served the boys at nine.

The three were, thus, alone.

"Y'all is goin' to church with me this mornin'!" Ma announced after she had bowed her head and thanked a good Father for the victuals.

Jimmie Joe shot an oblique glance up from his plate. He was swallowing his food to clear a way to mouth his lie that would get him out of the ordeal.

Ma was ahead of him, though.

"I want you to go especial, Jimmie Joe! I ast the Reverend to speak on young liars and thieves!"

This was too much for Little Brother. He swallowed half a pancake in one whop and had to be smacked on the back.

Ma gave Little Brother a drink of coffee, but she was not through with Jimmie Joe.

"A lots of us women of the church what has no count chillun has been astin the Reverend to for God's sake do somethin' 'bout the lyin' and thievin' and nasty dirty mess they all is up to! So today he is talkin' and you all is going!"

Jimmie Joe was as meek as Little Brother after that Ma could lead them both through the extra shining up that meant Sunday dressing—down the street—round the corner to the Holy Christian Saints of the Redeemer Church.

The Holy Christian Saints of the Redeemer was a split from the Anointed Lambs of the Most High.

The Anointed Lambs poured forth their unction on the corner of First Avenue and Second Street in the store that had been King Solomon's Pawn Shop. The split had taken up the broken lease of a tailor shop across the way. There was a great deal of friendliness between the congregations, but the Reverend Mr. Shinn, who led the Lambs no longer spoke to the Reverend Cato Seneca Brown who led the Saints.

Reverend Shinn said he had brought Cato Seneca Brown up from the foothills of Georgia, put the first pair of shoes he had ever owned on his feet—put the first piece of meat he had ever tasted which was no part of a hog, into his mouth, clothed him, got him a job, let him act as assistant pastor of the Lambs when the Spirit had called this Cato from dusting the floors in Leoin's Furniture Store and given him a fair part of the Sunday collection.

But that is the point where Reverend Brown split with Reverend Shinn. He said that what he received was no fair part of the profits. Nobody but God knew how many dollars the Lambs laid into their shepherd's hand every Sunday.

And after vainly trying to find out the exact amount and after trying still more vainly to get more for himself—Reverend Brown had left Reverend Shinn.

And though only one hundred and fifty Lambs had left the fold with him—Reverend Shinn went blind whenever Reverend Brown came near him.

Ma and the boys went in to Reverend Brown.

"Been introduced to the Father, Son and Holy Ghost!
Ah cry ho—ly, unto de Lord!"

The hymn bellowed out to meet the three as they opened the door to come in. Little Brother looked more dejected at once. Jimmie Joe's face took on a leaden mask that was supposed to be poise but was a most uncomfortable pose.

Ma, more buxom and perspiring than usual in a black straw bucket hat and black satin coat strewed with monkey fur—or monkeyed furs—bowed and smiled her way up the aisle to the third row from the front.

As she reached the chairs there, she drew severely back and let her two boys file in first.

"Lord! Look at Little Brother!!" hoarse whispers chorused up as they sat down.

Little Brother shot a miserable glance backward.

Three little girls who were in his class at school were teetering and tittering in the row behind.

"Got lard and tea on his naps this morning!" giggled one.

"Got powder on too I kin smell it!"

Little Brother crumpled in his chair, bent double with steaming confusion.

Jimmie Joe unfroze to find he was looking directly on the semi-side of Caroline's head. She sat against the wall with the heavy black woman who was her mother.

A sort of pleasant haze fell on Jimmie Joe at once. He could sit there and stare at Caroline as long as he pleased.

The Reverend Brown advanced majestically from his ebony throne at the back of the platform as the hymn died out.

"My er—friends!" he began in a rumbling of awfulness. "My er—friends? I never hear that beauteous melody of that grandiose hymn floating on the air around me, but I am not reminded of my beloved, revered, honored and respected mother back in that humble cabin of ours in the foothills of Georgia!"

"Amen! Das de way!" yowled Caroline's mother.

Jimmie Joe cringed in clammy embarrassment for Caroline. But she kept her thick lashed eyes fastened on the Reverend Brown. If she heard her mother's outcry, no tremor of her body revealed the fact.

"And its to you young upstarts, you young devils, you young Jezebels—who have no respect for man, mother or God—that I want to talk this morning!"

"Yas, sir, Jesus!" sang Ma on high C.

A deafening salvo of "Amens" and "Do Mercy Father" rocked the room for the next few minutes. It took the Rev. Brown two drinks of water and a general hand shaking from the entire deacon board before he could go on to his next sentence.

And he did go on—blasting—smothering—damning.

And the hungry still were hungry.

And a heavier darkness settled on those who walked in shadows. No light was lit. No fulfillment of visions, long tarrying, was promised.

There was vengeance and the paying of an eye for an eye and the promises of superlative damnation for iniquities.

No love—no mercy—no telling of a great enfolding love that works no ill.

And Sadie Montgomery sat in the back row and shivered and shook but decided to keep up her affair with Mary Lou Jones' husband. For if Hell so certainly faced her, why not carry the memory of tenderness and gentle love down with her into the eternal fire? Why not carry the kisses and caresses that had branded her for a thousand thousand years of burning—instead of the kicks and fists of her own husband—Jake?

And Caroline, slant-eyed, looked at the preacher and thought how much money such a good talk would draw from the niggers—and how much, as a consequence she would be able to leave at the various shops on her "Will calls."

Jimmie Joe saw her. Watched her eyes lingering on the man as he panted and ranted, back and forth across the platform.

Jimmie Joe saw—and knew what it all meant.

He shivered too, and looked at Caroline and then looked at the minister.

"Old fool! Old cheater! I wish I had your drag!" Jimmie Joe cursed within himself.

And Ma sat there and screamed out, "Aw Jesus" and felt Jimmie Joe tremble. "Gawd! Let thy Spirit rest on us dis mawnin'!" she prayed aloud in contrapuntal style to the preaching.

And when she felt Jimmie Joe shiver, she thought her answer had come.

* * *

The Wild Cat Social Club was dancing. With multi-colored crepe paper streamers and hanging baskets of artificial flowers on the ceiling, a clash-banging, rocketing jazz band on the stage, and with the floor comfortably packed with smooth-stepping young Negroes, the Wild Cats were passing a pleasant Sunday evening.

Jimmie Joe and his gang were a part of the Wild Cats, but some dozen older boys who were through with school—for various reasons—and who worked, were the backbone of the club's treasury. They paid for the hall, paid for the orchestra, bought the liquor.

"Them niggers try to run everything," George had growled in a complaint more than once.

"They got the best go! They got the most dough!" Jimmie had replied.

He had never felt the claws of the older Wild Cats too sharply.

But tonight when the Wild Cats were giving their semi-annual formal—when Caroline had lushed in, in a peach colored satin that looked as if it had been poured on her figure, and had jangled her apple-green bracelets and necklaces in the face of Dan Grey, president of the Wild Cats, something deep had scratched Jimmie Joe.

Caroline had chattered with Jimmie Joe with just the proper degree of casual aloofness as she neared Dan. Then, just as the three came fully face to face, she twinkled, dimpled, and stretched out both hands to Dan.

"Hell—o!" she cooed.

"Movie stuff!" sneered Jimmie Joe as he watched her.

Caroline sidled and angled and nodded and enfolded Dan in talk, patterning her every action—as they all did—after the only examples of the niceties of living that any of them ever saw.

The movies!

Unconsciously, too, as she mimed and copied, Jimmie puffed up in the role of the offended, jealous sweetheart. He withdrew a few paces and stood, feet apart, hands in pockets, watching the dancers with a to-hell-with-you scowl.

"Unh—unh! Ole Caroline's done got Jimmie Joe's goat time they gits here!!" tittered Sammy Raines into the ear of his partner.

Sammy Raines was one of these runty black boys who have a perpetual grin and joke for Life. No one in the hall was happier just to pirouette, jazz, dip and glide in the warmth and light and amidst gay dresses and colors and folks he knew—than Sammy.

Jimmie Joe frowned and cursed within. He wanted Caroline to hurry up so they could begin to dance. The orchestra was pulsing through one of those soul disturbing rhythmics that Negro orchestras concoct.

Dan tapped Jimmie Joe suddenly on the arm. "I'll take the next dance with the little lady, bud!" Dan announced.

Jimmie Joe's rage nearly knocked him down.

She wouldn't let him walk in with her in full view of the gang and dance off, leaving him standing alone!

He looked at Dan's suave Japanesy yellow face. Then he looked into Caroline's eyes.

She would. He saw that as he looked at her.

She did.

Jimmie Joe cursed his way through the laughing dancers who had been watching this by-play.

George danced his girl to the edge of the crowd and plunged into the dressing room after Jimmie Joe.

"Hey, feller!" he greeted Jimmie Joe gravely. "Some?" He offered Jimmie Joe a drink of gin.

Jimmie Joe grabbed the flask and swallowed and swallowed. George watched him in silence. He could have knocked Caroline's face in with joy.

The gin down, Jimmie Joe began to feel worse. "What the hell you gimme that stuff for?" he swore at George.

"Aw, come off and get out on the floor!" was George's reply.

They swaggered back to the hall.

Sammy Raines was ducking past the door with a tall fair girl.

Jimmie Joe caught the rhythm of the dance, took two or three steps alone, parallel to Sammy, and then neatly pushed Sammy away and whirled the girl on without a backward look.

Sammy laughed aloud. "Well excuse me, Mr. Nigger, for livin', please!" he called and chuckled off to find another girl—any girl who could dance—just so she could dance!

Jimmie Joe found no pleasure in the gyrations of the dance. He kept glimpsing a peach satin frock on the only real form in the hall, swishing around in undulations of joy.

Jimmie cut in on another boy in the next dance.

Here, he met opposition, though.

"Here, nigger! Don't try that stuff with me!" blazed the boy. "You aint got guts enough to get your own girl. Stay away from mine!"

George and Sammy Raines separated Jimmie Joe and the lad before their clinch had blossomed into a scuffle.

"You better not start no fighting with some of these niggers, Jimmie Joe!" warned George. "Those that aint all busting out with bad liquor and knives have guns on 'em! For God sake—let 'em alone!"

Jimmie Joe drained George's flask of gin this time. "That damn fool says I aint got the guts to go git Caroline!" he was almost sobbing as he finished.

"Aw let that gal go to Hell!" George blazed.

Jimmie Joe smashed wildly at George's face.

Sammy Raines got in between them.

"Heah! Heah!!" he grunted. "You all will mess up de man's furniture. Lay off dat mess!"

George, flaming red, panted in a corner, glaring at Jimmie Joe, puffing in his.

"Whyn't you swing on Dan!" George taunted. "Ef you're so damn hot to fight—go git him!"

Jimmie Joe tore away from Sammy's clutch and shot out of the door toward the hall once more.

George's rage oozed out of him. He stared open mouthed first at the door through which Jimmie had disappeared, then at Sammy.

"God, Sammy!" George breathed presently. "He aint going after Dan, is he? Why that nigger totes a gun and a knife even when he's in bed!"

Pale now, George fled out toward the hall, with Sammy bow-legging behind.

On first glance, the dance seemed to be progressing as merrily as ever.

Up in a corner though where a peach satin dress was crushed close to Dan's navy blue figure, George and Sammy could see Jimmy Joe's head over the crowd. In silent rushes, George and Sammy threaded and waded a way around the outskirts of the hall. And they reached that far corner just when Jimmie snatched Caroline by the shoulders and wrenched her away from Dan's arms.

It was George who saw Dan's hand drawing back toward his hip.

It was George who knocked a couple down, hurdled over them as they kicked on the floor—and it was George who snatched at his own hook-shaped knife and thrust it into Jimmie Joe's right hand.

And Jimmie Joe, the gin scorching his brain, broiling with a desire for revenge, consumed with the lust to hurt, to bleed, to bruise and cut as he himself had been hurt, bled and cut—brought the knife down with this full behind it, into Dan's side.

* * *

The coroner said Dan had been stabbed *a dozen times*!

But Jimmie Joe cried out in Ma's arms that he had only brought the knife down once.

A doctor in court said that that one lunge up into Dan's side had cost him his life. "Cut the left ventricle!" he declared.

Grey-faced the "Gang" listened while the older Wild Cats told a story of Dan's superb manhood. Gene Terry, the club treasurer, broke down and wept on the stand when he swore that Dan was stabbed to death, but that he had had no knife in his own hand or on his person.

"Oh I gave Jimmie Joe the knife he had myself. He never even owned once!" mourned George as he heard. But he said nothing.

Jack Sullivan, the cop who had first reached the hall after the murder swore, too, that no gun nor knife had been on Dan's body.

The gang sat grey-faced because they knew that those older Wild Cats had taken Dan's gun and unstrapped his knife from the leather band on his wrist before they called the police.

And the younger gang said nothing. According to "Crafty Detective Stories" and the movies—the sort of things all of them lived by—the younger portion of a gang did not peach on the older heads.

The older Wild Cats meant to claw Jimmie Joe to death for robbing their ranks of the one and only Dan Grey.

When all had been told, when Caroline had had her hysterics and her fainting spell and been fanned—as she told her part in it all, the judge rose up.

"You young lawless creatures who take a life with as cool an indifference as you tear a piece of paper—must be blotted out for the good of humanity!"

The jury rose up, too, and went out.

"Aw Jesus!" Ma had screamed out once during that crucifying hour while the jury was still gone. "Ha! mercy! Ha, mercy Lawd!"

And she had cried and cried on Pa and even the bailiff had patted her shoulder to comfort and quiet her.

Her rich white folks had supplied a lawyer for Jimmie Joe. The woman of the house had said that somehow she felt responsible since Ma was in her cellar washing and ironing or around her house cleaning, instead of being at her own home to talk to Jimmie Joe all his life when he had needed someone somewhere near at hand to talk to.

The jury filed back.

"Guilty, First Degree!" They said.

Everyone felt so helpless when they said that Jimmie Joe's life must be given because he had taken a life himself.

The judge felt tangled. His own son had a way of going to the wrong places with the wrong people.

Jimmie's lawyer was not sure whether Jimmie Joe was normal. "He knows so doggone little about anything real!" the man was thinking as he gathered up the papers of the case he had lost.

Ma screamed all the way out of court as they led Jimmie Joe away. She screamed all night while Pa and Little Brother and some of the members of the Holy Christian Saints had eddied with Reverend Brown, around her bed.

"Call on God!" urged one old lady. "Das de way, Chile! He'll heah you!"

And Ma had called out into the night loudly—loudly.

They sang, too, for Ma, "Take the Name of Jesus with you!" in that sort of harmony which makes you want to fall on your knees, lay your head in the seat of your chair and shed bitter tears—tears whose bitterness could eat through the thickest armour plate scales of sophistication. Tears that would eat down to the place where the real you staggers at a world that travels under two faces, a world that teaches that the devil is the nearest possibility and God—only an impossible remoteness—

* * *

So taught, then, this God could not hear. They took Jimmie Joe, fastened him, hooded him, poured electric fire through his body until his heart burst within him.

And he had screamed all the while like a baby in a dark room. "Ma! Oh—Ma!"

They buried his burnt twisted black brown young body—

—"What could we do?" mourned the gang. "We could not squeal on the Wild Cats."

—"I gave my pal my knife when Dan was going to get him! I couldn't let him kill Jimmie Joe!" George mourned aghast.

—"Jesus? What was it I didn't do?" Ma cried in the wash-tub, dragging her mind back from the memory of a screaming cry of "Ma! Oh—Ma!" Dragging her mind back from the thought of a twisted burnt body, a body so twisted they could not straighten it, even in the coffin.

Better to scrub a million floors and plod back home on dog-tired feet to cook, clean and scrub there, if only there would be once more a slim black brown boy, dancing, jigging, joking, eating—instead of that dead empty silence that drowned everything there now. Little Brother crawled into bed every night before eight now with a scared look on his face all the time. Pa sat up in a corner with his head and shoulders—his very soul—hung down.

Pa didn't have any scrubbing or tubs or any God to help him. He could not go up and ask God—like Ma could—what it was he should have done.

—"Ma! Kin I have six bits?" he had asked.

And he had taken it.

Nobody snitched money from her now.

It lay safe in her pocket book.

—But a slim black-brown body lay twisted and burnt in its casket. It was twisted and burnt so that they could not straighten it out—even in the casket.

One morning—thinking all this—Ma turned the corner to wait for her car by Krönen's bakery.

Pink cakes pyramided in the pale blue background of the window.

And Ma—flooded with a rush of bitter sorrow—fell on the sidewalk in a faint.

"Where the devil do you 'spose these nigger women go to get drunk so early in the morning?" the driver of the patrol wagon asked the cop as they loaded Ma in to take her to the station house.

They rattled off down the street with Ma.

They rattled just like the stones in a tin can.

—Don't you wonder, sometimes, with a feeling like a knife in your heart, why Life serves up stones—hard stones—throws stones into Tin Cans so that they only rattle, rattle, with a hollow sound when the winds of Living knock them down and shake them? [*Opportunity* 12.7 (July 1934): 202–205; 12.8 (August 1934): 236–240]

PART OF THE PACK: ANOTHER VIEW OF NIGHT LIFE IN HARLEM

by Hazel V. Campbell

Steve Hall opened the door of his basement home on East 133rd Street. The wooden door cried under its labor. Sucking his teeth the tall black man bent low and stepped into the dark hallway. The door closed behind him with a bang and a lone picture hanging on the wall fell to the floor amid a bed of broken glass. The four room apartment was odorous with the smell of stale cabbage and boiled beef. Steve moistened his lips with one sweep of his tongue and walked back to the cheerless kitchen.

His wife, a tall mulatto woman, was standing over the gas stove stirring a bleak pot from which steam was issuing.

"You have been stealing again, Lu?" he asked wearily and knitting his brow.

"Sure. Where the hell you think I got this food from?" she answered indifferently, still stirring the pot.

"Aw, we've got to quit this sort of living, Lu. We've got to quit. I'm tired of eating stolen goods," and Steve's voice was strained.

"Ain't satisfied? You don't have to eat it if you don't want to," she snapped turning toward him. "That will be all the more for tomorrow," she finished.

Steve shifted on his feet. His lean face took on a hurt expression. His pride had been injured and his heart beat heavily against the ragged shirt covering his bony breast. It hurt him that he could not live up to the word of his promise to her mother, to provide for her in the proper way. Here she was now stooping to the degrading thing of stealing food so that neither he nor she might starve.

"Lu, I wish you wouldn't talk so. Why don't you talk human anymore? You do nothing but snap and snarl like a dog from morn till night." Steve spoke dully.

"Well, what if I do snap and snarl? Maybe I am a dog. I'm part of the pack ain't I, fighting for food and life against the odds," she yelled throwing a wooden spoon on the table.

"Lu, please," he coaxed raising his hands as if to quiet her.

"Please, hell!" I'm tired of please this and please that. I'm tired of this damn Yankee town anyway. I'm tired of all these damn black Yankees who do nothing but put on airs with their bellies thinking their throat is cut. Yes, look at me! You and these damn gin soaked, gun toting, razing pulling niggers," and Lu's voice rose to a scream.

"Hush, Lu. Please!" he begged raising his hand.

"Hush! hush! hush! That's why we are where are today cos it is always hush! hush! hush! I tell you I am tired. I am tired of everything from that damn jazz that beats in your ears like the tom-tom of the jungles to the false prophets who walk up and down these streets crying to have faith. Faith in what? I'm going back to the Delta. I'm going back where the music is dull and heavy and kind like the people. At least down there you won't have to fight with dogs and cats over a piece of meat," she finished, her voice growing calmer under memories of pleasant days in the Delta basin.

"It will be only for awhile, dear," he tried to say cheerfully but his voice cracked. "Only for awhile. Then there will be plenty of work. In the meantime, dear, why can't you put your pride aside and go to the Home Relief? We just can't go on like this. I hate to see you sneaking like a cat stealing food. You don't have to steal it," and Steve sat on the three legged stool and hung his head.

"Charity? Did you say charity?" she scoffed.

"Why yes. Yes, of course," he said looking up.

"Charity! Who the hell wants charity?" she screamed. "A pinch here and a pinch there, and a look of contempt written on everyone's face. Hell, who you think is going to stand for that? I'm gong back to the Delta, if I have to crawl on my hands and knees to get there."

"All right! All right!" he said, waving her aside.

"I'd rather steal than take the white man's so-called charity," she snapped.

Steve rubbed his head with both of his hands and shifted in his seat.

Some one was knocking at the door. Neither of them moved.

Again the knock. Lu looked at Steve and Steve looked at Lu.

A look of dismay passed between them. For awhile only the tick tock of the clock was heard.

"Well, what you looking at me for?" Lu spoke firmly, pressing her lips together. "You can answer the door, can't you?"

"Yes," Steve spoke slowly, rising from the seat.

"Well, answer it," she said waving her hand. "You ain't afraid are you? We've been dodging the landlord and bill collectors for the last few months, so I guess we can face the music now. If it is the landlord bring him back here so I can give him a piece of my mind. The damn cheat."

Steve walked away from her. His knees felt weak and useless under him. Suppose it was the landlord and he had come to put them out. Where would they go? No rent paid for three months and no outlook of paying any rent for the next twelve months. He could go to charity, but Lu would rather walk the streets and die from hunger. Queer woman. He opened the door slowly. A short bow-legged man was standing before him. Steve gave a deep sigh as he recognized his best friend, Bradford Hardy.

"Hi, Steve," Brad spoke warmly.

"Come in, Brad. Glad to see you," and the tone of Steve's voice was sincere.

Brad followed Steve to the rear where Lu was still standing.

She had not moved from her position. Her eyes opened in relief as Brad came toward her.

"Hi, Brad," she greeted.

"Hi, Lu."

"Did you have any luck with that job you went after?" she asked

"Hell, no," he answered shortly, and taking off his cap he placed it on the table.

"Gee, that's tough. I'm sorry, old boy," Steve said, patting Brad on the back. "I wonder just what is wrong?"

"What's wrong, man?" sneered Brad looking at Steve in contempt. "If you must know what is wrong, it is this," and Brad pointed a dirty brown finger to his face. "Just this," and taking the three legged stool he sat down.

"You ought to know just what is wrong, Steve, without asking. There is one thing I hate more than poverty and that is a dumb nigger," Lu spoke sharply. "You've been black long enough to know what is wrong. Even a baby could have guessed it was his skin," and Lu looked at him with an air of superiority.

"Not that I couldn't do the work. I've had good training in that field," and a deep frown formed in Brad's forehead. "They always have to give such lame excuses," and his voice shook. Steve caught a hint of rising anger in the tone of his friend's voice. Steve knew that anger. It was a revengeful anger, rising slowly and then suddenly bursting like an eruption. Brad was talking again. "Damn, how long you think this is going to keep up?" and Brad banged his fist on the table. "I'm damn tired of it. Damn it to hell I wish I were white—hell, no! I wish I were a yaller, bless my soul if I wouldn't cross the line and fool all these old 'ofays'. I'd get the best kind of job, and marry the best kind of them, and fool the hell out of them. Then I'd laugh."

"Would you?" Lu looked at him in amusement. "There would be that something in your blood that would call you back, and, Brad, you wouldn't be able to get away from it."

"Aw, hell!" and Brad put his head on the cupboard.

"Hungry, Brad?" Steve asked.

"Well, I'd be lying if I said no, and I don't want to lie," he laughed, looking up.

"We thought you were the landlord at first and we had made up our minds to make the best of his verdict," Lu said, going to the dish closet, taking three cracked dishes from the closet and setting them on the table. Brad moved his hat.

"If he came in my place I'm afraid I'd go in for cannibalism," Brad spoke watching the dishes on the table.

"You'd go in for what?" laughed Lu.

"Cannibalism."

"Well, as long as you have friends like Steve and I, you won't have to sink that far. Count on us sharing our meager blessings with you," Lu answered. Taking the pot from the stove she placed it on the table, and began filling each plate, giving each a generous portion. When each dish had been filled she sat down.

"I wish to hell I knew how to pray," Brad spoke mournfully.

"Well, why don't you learn?" Lu asked looking up from her plate and brushing a long strand of hair from her face.

"Then I'd pray to God from the bottom of my heart, and I'd pray and pray and pray," and Brad jumped from his seat, upsetting the food onto the floor, "and I'd pray to God to give me food, and a job, and to send a Moses to lead us to the land of milk and honey."

Neither Steve nor Lu answered him

"And I'd pray to God. God I'd pray to you," went on Brad. "God! oh God! I'd pray for justice, for fairness, and God, I'd pray. Oh hell, I wish I knew how to pray," and Brad tore at his ragged shirt and beat his bony hand against his hairy breast. "God! My god"! he said sitting down. His foot slipped on the food on the floor. He looked down. His eyes became bewildered.

"Food! God, I'm stepping on food. Good food!" and Brad bent down and picked up the dirty cabbage and beef, scraping the food in his plate. Picking out the splinters and dirt he could see he began eating again. Lu watched him thoughtfully, as she counted how many times his Adam's apple worked up and down, and his lean face twitched nervously.

When the meal was finished, Brad washed the dishes, Steve dried them, and Lu put the rest of the food on the windowsill.

Above them a woman's voice arose clear and strong.

> "It's me, it's me, it's me, oh Lord
> Standing in the need of prayer,
> It's me, it's me, it's me oh Lord,
> Standing in the need of prayer."

Lu put her hands on her hips, and looked at the ceiling.

"Listen to that damn black woman. She's been singing that song all day."

Steve and Brad wiping their hands on a soiled handkerchief. They too listened.

"Tain't mah brother
Tain't mah sister
But me, oh Lord,
Standing in the need of prayer."

"She's right. She's standing in the need of prayer. We all are," Steve said putting the dishes on the wash tub.

"Well, she doesn't have to shout it from the house tops. What if she is standing in the need of prayer, who the hell she thinks is going to pray for her. Sure, we all are standing in the need of prayer, but are we letting everyone know it? No, we're keeping our hard luck to ourselves, and if we can take it on the chin, and not cry to the whole world, that cat up there can too," Lu answered Steve.

"We can't keep it to ourselves much longer," put in Brad.

"Damn right. Damn right," Lu agreed.

Somehow or other they were glad when Brad left them. The afternoon wore on. The woman above them still sang the same song. Out on the river the boats cried and whistled. In the streets the children's laughter and cries shrilled above the noise of the traffic. The clock in the kitchen struck four. Steve paced the rooms in disgust, his wife watching him. Finally he threw himself on the bed and fell asleep. Lu walked to the window and watched with amusement two kittens tumbling over each other. Both of them fighting for supremacy, she thought. For a long time she sat by the window. Steve was snoring, and from her boredom she made a song from his snoring.

Then evening came, and the children in the streets had gone, and the woman above her had ceased her singing. Lu fell across the couch in the living room and slept. It was after nine when she was awakened by someone, knocking at the door. She sat up. She heard Steve rise from the bed and his heavy footsteps falling on the wooden, planked floor. By the tone of the voices she knew Brad had come back. She went to the front door.

"Back again?" she smiled in the dark.

Brad was out of breath.

"What's the matter? Steve asked, pulling his friend into the living room.

"Race riot," he gasped.

"What?" Lu yelled, opening her eyes wide

"Fighting down on 125th Street," he went on.

"How'd it start?" Lu asked excitedly.

Brad shrugged his shoulders. "I ran up here as fast as I could in case you all want to join in the battle. You can hear the noise clean up here."

Lu grabbed Steve's arm.

Brad tugged at the other arm of Steve's. "Come, old man."

Steve knitted his brow, and looked at Brad. "Where?"

"To the battlefield. I guess the mob is up near 130th Street by now. They were coming uptown when I came up."

Steve freed his arms, from Lu and Brad. "Who wants to fight?"

"Man alive, they are busting windows like hot cakes. The niggers have gone plumb mad. Nigger heaven has turned into a living hell now. Come on Steve, we can at least get some of the food from those stores where windows are broken. I'm not in for the fighting either, but if I can get some food and clothes without paying for it, I'm just raring," Brad finished.

"Go on, Steve. You and Brad go out and get food. Keep away from the mob as much as you can, and if you have to fight—damn it, fight. Fighting will make a man of you, Steve. A fighting man, who can snap and snarl along with the pack," Lu said, pushing him from her.

Steve did not answer. He played with the one remaining button on his shirt.

"Go on, Steve. Tain't no sin no more nohow to steal. The Lord knows we've got to eat, and if we can't get it honestly, we'll have to take matters into our own hands," Lu was coaxing.

"I'm not going," he said sharply, turning on her. "What's the sense of fighting when you don't have to."

Lu threw back her head. "Well, damn it if you don't go, I will," she shot at him. "I'll show you, you big coward. I'll be the fighter in this family. I'll get food, and I'll get clothes, and bring it back. You can stay here and nurse your petty feelings. I'll go out and fight and I'll fight like a man, and that is more than you can boast of, you— you coward," and switching past him she took a soiled coat from a nail behind the door, and together she and Brad left him standing in the dark hallway.

Steve did not know what to think. Outside he could hear the murmur of angry voices, mingled with tramping feet. He scratched his head. He wondered why he had let Lu go. She had no business out there. It was his place to fight the battles, if there was any need to fight. Lu could be a regular spit-fire when she wanted to be. She was a woman, and nice women never fought, and Lu was a nice woman. She was his wife. She was good, even though she did drink, and smoke and steal and cuss. He'd go and bring her back. Clenching his fist he slipped his overcoat on and left the house. The street was crowded. Lu and Brad were nowhere to be seen. He knew they were swallowed up in the crowd. He half walked and half ran toward Lenox Avenue, his eyes fastened on the mob ahead of him, hoping to catch a glimpse of Brad's broad shoulders or the tall figure of Lu. A woman had taken his arm. He looked down and saw that she was a gray headed woman. She grinned up at him. "We have to go with our men to war," she laughed coarsely. He could small stale gin coming from her mouth. He did not answer her. She was talking again: "Have you ever fought battles for your rights?"

"Naw," he answered with a shrug of his shoulders.

A crash of glass sounded behind him. A cry went up. "Kill him!"

"Take that 'ofay' and string him up a pole. Kill that cracker," and the cry ran down the street. Steve saw a lone white man speeding and bending low in his car trying to escape the missiles hurled at him. Steve was glad the man escaped. The street was more crowded now with men and women battling with uniformed men on foot and horse. Knives flashed, guns barked, clubs swung, fists flew and blood flowed freely in a tumult of misunderstanding and revenge.

All around was broken glass and more glass being broken rang in his ears. He found himself in the midst of the battle and he began to fight blindly, and wondered what he was fighting and why he was fighting. Something heavy struck him on the head. Blood gushed down his face ... running into his eyes ... blinding him. He felt darkness engulfing him ... his head began to swim—he could feel his legs slipping from underneath him. Wiping the blood madly from his face, he groped his way clear of the mob, and slumped in a doorway. He could hear tramping feet and angry voices far in the distance.

* * *

Lu and Brad came home long after two that morning. Their eyes were blackened and their clothes were torn to shreds, but they were happy. In their arms was food. Lots and lots of food, and more if they wanted to go through the same ordeal they just came through. No one stopped them on their way home. In fact no one would dare, for Lu and Brad would fight.

Lu stumbled in the doorway.

"Steve," she cried.

Silence.

"Steve, wake up."

Only the echo of her voice came back to her from the darkness.

"Hey, you lazy, good for nothing character, awaken yourself and see what your mamma has brought home to her baby."

Silence.

"Hey, Brad, wake that lazy nigger up," she commanded from the kitchen.

Brad tipped into the bedroom. Turning on the light he gasped in surprise.

"He ain't here," he yelled.

"Who, Steve?"

"Ain't a sign of him."

"Thank God, he went out to fight. Come in here and get me some cold water. I want to fix this eye before he comes back."

* * *

Morning came. Brad came in late bringing with him the morning paper.

"Steve ain't come home yet," she greeted him.

Brad did not answer.

"What's the matter?" she asked suddenly.

"Steve ain't coming back anymore, Lu," he said giving her the paper.

"What you mean, he ain't coming back any more?" she asked, not looking at the paper.

"He just ain't coming back," and Brad shook his head. "I took this paper from the stand," and he shook the paper so that she would take it. "Here," and Brad's voice cracked under the strain he was trying to control.

Lu looked at him, then at the paper. Tears blinded her eyes, but she blinked hard and fast. "Brad—Brad—do you mean—he—is dead. Do you mean the white people killed him? Why he can't be dead. He was here only a little while ago. Don't you remember? You do remember, Brad ... why we left him right out there in the hallway right out there—remember he was standing there all alone—and we left him just like that."

Brad said nothing. He bit his lips, and his face had become grave.

"Brad, do something," Lu screamed all at once. "Oh God! My God!! Bring Steve back to me. White papers say you are dead, but Steve, they lie, they lie, they lie," and Lu was sobbing.

* * *

Overhead a voice clear and strong was singing:

> "It's me, it's me, it's me, oh Lord
> Standing in the need of prayer."

WHITE ONLY: A STORY OF THE COLOR LINE

by Helen Faw Mull

Callie Peters walked listlessly past the drug store, and the hardware store, and the grocery. As she was passing the dry goods store, she paused to look at a hat in the second window. It was just the one to go with the new suit she was wearing. Perhaps if she had the hat, too, she might get the kind of job she wanted. She brightened momentarily in response to the thought. But bitterly she knew she was not turned down because of her appearance. Above the dark suit the fine-textured creaminess of her smooth cheek glinted softly in the window's image of her. Black hair lay in neat waves any way she combed it, giving her habitually a well-groomed trimness. Her eyes were big and dark, shadowed by long black lashes. Her figure was slim and lithe, with an aristocratic foot and ankle.

This appraisal was corroborated by the frank admiration in the stare of a man, probably some drummer, who stood picking his teeth in the doorway of the cheap, narrow restaurant next to the hat window. Out of the corner of her eye, Callie saw the restaurant's one waiter, a Hicksville boy whose family, she knew, was little better than "po' white trash," open the screen door in an effort to fan out the flies with a dish towel. The other man indicated Callie with a jerk of his head and a twist of his mouth.

"Swell-looking coon, ain't she?" observed the waiter with a careless indifference, slamming the screen.

"Gee! She a nigger?" exclaimed the transient, and ostentatiously turned his attention in the opposite direction.

Callie could not escape the import of the tone and gesture. Her eyes fell on the fly-specked sign in the dirty window of the mean little restaurant, and hot tears blurred the words it flaunted: "We Cater to White Only."

Callie drooped dispiritedly down the street. It was the noon hour and Hicksville people were going home to dinner. Although she was looking only at the sidewalk, she knew the name of everyone who passed her: Such crowds as the town boasted were never impersonal. But no one spoke to Callie, except Mr. Tom Black who said, "Howdy, Callie," without raising his hat; Callie's grandmother had belonged to his grandfather. Two girls, one who worked in the dry goods store and one who worked in the doctor's office, walking abreast, crowded Callie into the dusty grass with apparently no feeling of apology.

Just beyond the straggling business block, the girl turned off the main street and followed a hard-beaten, grass-fringed path beside deep wagon ruts to a huddle of colorless weathered cabins. Here she was greeted volubly enough. But she was dully unresponsive and disappeared directly into one of the shanties.

"Dat you, Callie?" called a mellow voice from the lean-to. "Ah knows you is hot, chile. Come git a dipperful of dis heah watah I jest drawed fresh frum de well."

Callie stepped down into the lean-to kitchen and flopped on a chair as apathetic as an unwound spring, while the older, darker woman hovered over her tenderly. "Ah can tell buh lookin' at you, honey, dat you ain't got no job yit. What did Jedge Black say?"

"No, I ain't got no job yet," flared the young girl with snapping black eyes. "And I never will get one in this place. Judge Black felt jus' the same as everybody else here does, only he didn't try to fool me wid no lies. He say he couldn't give that job to no colored girl. He say if you come roun' to his wife's Monday she's got a new washin' fuh yuh. He say I bettuh git ovah my fine notions and go home and help you." She spat out the last words as if they tasted bitter in her mouth. With the vehemence of her resentment, she had slipped unthinkingly into the soft, slurred speech of her elders.

The mother sought only to soothe and comfort. "Dere's a ledder done come fuh you dis mownin,'" she announced cheerfully. "De pos'man say its fum Lizzie Anderson. I sho do want tuh heah whut she have to say. I suttinly am curious de way she ack: her ma ain't seed huh been five yeah. She doan ne'r write to huh ma 'ceptin' tuh sin' huh money sometime. Dere her po' ole mammy lonesome all de time fer huh chile whut she done raise and work for, ter give huh mo'n whut she had; an' doan even know whar she work or whar she stay. I sho' is sorry faw 'er."

She produced the letter from a capacious apron pocket. Callie ripped open the envelope with undissembled eagerness. Her mother stood still to listen; but Callie did not read aloud.

"Whut she want?" queried her mother, with an attempt at casualness, in spite of her gnawing curiosity.

Callie took on a somewhat guarded aspect. She glanced into the other room as if she feared an unwelcome presence, perhaps an evil spirit, perhaps an eavesdropper.

"She wants me to meet her in Chattanooga this even'," she said.

"In Chattanooga," repeated the Negro woman indignantly. "Why doan she come on ovah heah and see her ma? How she gwiner splain 'erse'f?"

"She don't have to explain," declared the girl. "Won't nobody tell her mother."

Her affirmation sounded contrary to fact. But it was not a lie; it was a command. Her mother, unsubmissive, said nothing, and Callie added, "Wouldn't do no good; only make her feel bad. This is a business trip. She think she might kin git me a job in Evansville."

* * *

As Callie walked into the main waiting room late that afternoon in the railway station in Chattanooga, she saw awaiting her a modishly dressed young woman, whose pale face contrasted strikingly with the glistening jet of the eyebrows and hair. The young women greeted each other cordially, though with a certain restraint. The city girl signaled a taxi. She got out with her guest, after a brief ride, in front of a well-known hotel and inquired at the desk for mail and phone calls as she got her key. The clerk was respectful and deferential. The visitor did not speak on the way up to the room. But when the door was bolted and they were alone, they laid aside reserve with their wraps. The city girl spoke at once of what was in the minds of both.

"What do you think of the proposition I wrote you about? Won't you change your mind about coming to Evansville with me and going white? It's a chance that won't come once in every life-time. The boss is a peach of a fellow; and I would introduce you to my friends so you wouldn't have to go through the loneliness that almost sunk me."

"Lizzie," began Callie with a troubled frown, "I don't—"

"Elizabeth," corrected the other sharply. "You can't be too particular about that: you better practice calling yourself 'Catherine,' too. It makes the break easier."

"But Elizabeth," said Callie self-consciously, "I don't want to make any break. I hate white people! I despise 'em! I wouldn't mind working with them in an office. But I couldn't stand not knowing anybody else the rest of my life." All the insults, the disappointments, the smouldering antagonism of her discouraging effort to find work showed themselves in the ardor of the impetuous words.

"Oh, white folks are different when you're one of them," defended Lizzie Anderson. "I know some swell fellows."

"But you wouldn't dare marry any of them," challenged Callie acridly.

"Plenty of time to think about that when I fall in love," temporized Elizabeth. "I'm just having a good time now." After a slight pause she added, "You wouldn't have to have any children."

"No," reiterated Callie irrelevantly, "I don't want to be white. All I ask is half a chance. I'm perfectly satisfied as I am, if you just give me an equal chance in the business world. I'll get the education and the culture and the nice clothes and the beautiful home for myself. I don't ask any favors of anybody; just an equal chance."

"Well, if it's an equal chance you want," retorted Elizabeth with sophisticated flippance, "you'll die of a broken heart, my dear. For my part, I say let the preachers and the sociologists and the intellectuals and the born fighters butt their heads against race prejudice all they want to. They may help their great-grandchildren. But the only thing that's going to do you and me any good is to side-step it."

"Maybe you're right," admitted Callie stubbornly, "but think what you've given up—all your friends, and your home, and even your mother. You don't know how she misses you.... But I do. I'd rather keep on looking for a job, without trying to change my spots."

"And you'll wear out good shoe leather while you let pass the biggest opportunity you'll ever meet," concluded the other lightly, and pressed the proposition no farther.

Wearing a borrowed hat, Callie had dinner with Elizabeth in the hotel dining room. Afterwards they had good seats at a stock company's performance. Callie enjoyed for the first time in her life the homage strangers pay to a good-looking girl. She felt a tingle of pleasure over hearing herself presented as "Miss Peters" to a blond young man, an acquaintance whom Elizabeth met unexpectedly.

Next morning the separation between the girls took place two hours before the genial coming of the sunlight. Elizabeth, disappointed at losing this one friend she had hoped to retain, and chagrined at having her rare offer spurned, had to catch the early train back to her job and her adopted environment. Callie doggedly bought her ticket home, on a local train leaving forty minutes later.

Forty minutes is a long time to sit on a station bench at seven o'clock in the morning and watch a dark-skinned porter pushing a long broom over a marble-patterned floor. But train-time came at last. The great steam engine puffed importantly past Callie and came to a halt. She walked beside the track to where a conductor was putting down a step. Her ticket was in her hand. As she approached the official, she recognized Mr. Williams' oldest boy from Hicksville.

At that moment he called out, not unkindly: "How you, Callie; been to the city? Jim Crow car first one behind the engine."

Callie turned hastily, that he might not see her face. She opened her pocket-book and resentfully slipped a small piece of cardboard into it. Making her way to the Western Union booth, she took a blank note and wrote on it: "Will accept job. Meet noon train in Evansville. Signed, Catherine Peters."

STREET OF THE MORTAR AND PESTLE: A STORY OF COLOR IN THE CAPITAL

by Florence Jackson Stoddard

The concourse of the Union Station was thronged when Selma Janes arrived with her friend who was to take the 5:50 train for New York. It was late and passengers for different trains got in each other's way at the several gates, heedless of direction, confused by the dense crowd. Selma's friend continued to rush about until she found her gate then she rushed through it calling back:

"Good bye, don't try to follow me; had a grand time; so glad you could take me in and mind you don't sell your house!"

Selma did not attempt to follow her but turned slowly toward the waiting room, a despairing look in her face. Indeed she was feeling utterly hopeless and bereft; she had expected much from the visit of her rich, girlhood friend who knew so well her terrible financial distress; who could well have afforded to buy the house or pay those dreaded taxes. She had been sure this help would be offered her and thought there would be no more need to seek assistance from the Emergency Relief; no more need to sit for hours among ill-smelling, dirty, colored and foreign people or to be offered food, when there was no "job"—"Three pounds of sliced pork and a sack of potatoes" and notified that "it is imperative that unemployed persons raise as much garden truck as possible; they will be provided with seeds on application." Oh must she go through that humiliation again? Sell her home? Of course she would sell it if only a buyer could be found before she lost it, because of unpaid taxes. But not only was the sale of property anywhere next to impossible, her house, pretty and well kept up as it was, had depreciated in value with the acquisition by Negroes of nearly the whole street. They now occupied every house from the east on to her corner; her block, so far, remained to white tenants but anyone would hesitate to buy there; she even had difficulty in renting rooms although the colored people in the neighborhood were educated, refined, more quiet in manner than many of the whites on the block.

So deeply was she thinking out her problem that she did not notice a crowd of arrivals pouring into the concourse from incoming trains until her progress was hampered by jostling travelers.... Curiously she regarded these comers. Why had they come? Were they, too, seeking jobs? Didn't they know the Capital had nothing to offer them—not even sleeping places unless they had the shekels that would pay for beds? Some looked as if they had. Some gazed about eagerly as if intrigued with what they expected to find, and some looked puzzled. One white-haired woman wore an expression of dread. Selma regarded her sympathetically; like herself no longer young what was she fearing? Her clothing spoke of means. As she stared the woman's eyes turned to her; an expression of amazed joy flashed into her face; excitedly she ran forward crying, "Miss Selma, Oh Miss Selma, is it you?" A well-gloved hand grasped Selma's arm, "Oh don't you know me, Miss Selma? I'm your own 'Melia."

Then recognition was swift. "Why, bless your heart, 'Melia, where *did* you come from?"

"From the old place, Bay Shore, Miss Selma; we just got off the train." She glanced behind her and beckoned to a fine looking young man and woman following her. "Here's Stanley, you sure know Stanley, Miss Selma."

"Not my little Stanley?" holding out an eager hand.

"No other, ma'm." The young man dropped the suit cases he was carrying to give one hand to the lady and lift his hat with the other," and this is my wife Irma, Miss Selma."

The young woman came forward, gracefully, shy, taking Selma's other hand extended to her. "Have you come here to visit or live?" she asked of the trio.

'Melia spoke, "We've come to live; Stanley's been given a job in the Government; he could not leave me behind. But Oh, Miss Selma, tell us where to go now, till we find a place to live in. Stanley's a chemist; he's got a place in the Bureau of Standards so we can't—we don't want to go just *any* where. Will a hotel take us in?"

"Come in the waiting room where we can sit down and consider," Selma told the little group regarding her so earnestly. The young man and woman who had been pale of face flushed deeply but from the olive cheek of the older woman the color had drained away. They found a vacant bench and sat down. Selma between the two women, Stanley standing before them. "Now tell me," she said, her tone deeply interested, even tender, but one of command as being used to obedience.

'Melia again was the speaker. "You know Miss Selma, when you left us Stanley was entering high school, waiting on table for you mornings and evenings. After you went he got "waiting" at the hotel. There was a gentleman there liked him, found out he wanted to be a doctor, managed that Stanely went to college and then up to Boston to another college."

"Harvard," put in Stanely, "but by then I'd decided to specialize in chemistry instead of medicine so my patron helped me with that. With what I earned, and his help I went to Germany and took a degree; then to South America, Brazil, for certain investigations and taught there in the University. Now the government of my own country has brought me here," he added proudly.

"So you see, Miss Selma," 'Melia took up the tale, "We've come with a good record; we don't want to have to mix in with a low down crowd of colored. And you know we are more white than black; Colonel Mapes was my grandfather, he acknowledged my mother as his daughter, and she wasn't dark and she married a man whose father was white so I ain't but half a quarter colored. Then I married Jim Low who was half Irish and half German, and Stanley's got hardly a drop of colored blood. He's been so well thought of, how can we keep out of going back? Will we dare to live out of a Negro district? If nobody tells on us, who'll know. You wouldn't tell?"

Selma gathered the old woman's two hands in her own. "'Melia, dear 'Melia," her voice trembled, "perhaps the good Lord has thrown us together to help one another. I see a way for you if you are willing and it can be a way for me too. I must tell you that I am desperately poor; most of us in the city are now. I lost my government place when hundreds were turned out, just as President Harding died. I'd been fourteen years in office and a year more would have allowed me a tiny pension; and I had put all my savings in a house which I may now lose as I can't pay the taxes. Now even with the Recovery plan, the C.W.A. and the P.W.A. I can't get reinstated. The Departments take on new employees,—here's Stanley, one of them—but they are all young and we who have worked hard, are left out. Why? Because now we are 'middle-aged.' So I, with many others, have of late sometimes needed food. Fortunately, I still have shelter, my house, if I can keep it. If you will come to my home and share it, I will see that you are known as friends of mine just arrived; no one will suspect; none of you look your race. I believe in esteeming people for what they are, not by race, creed or color. Will you come?" She looked at each of them anxiously.

'Melia had drawn away her hands and with them covered her face; she was weeping. The young man walked to the door and stood staring out; the girl sat with frightened eyes, motionless. Selma's heart was beating suffocatingly. Her offer was a bold challenge to society, to prejudice should all become known. But if it were accepted, then the roof over her aging head would be assured. She trembled with dread of what Stanley would decide. 'Melia got up and went to him; they spoke together a few words only, then came back. Stanley spoke:

"Miss Selma, it can't do harm to try it; if it causes you any embarrassment we can take our places as your old servants, or try another way."

"I must tell you," Selma added, "that one half of my street is now in the possession of colored persons; they own or rent all the houses to the east. From my corner west it belongs to whites; but some white people refuse to live on the street because they think the colored folks will eventually get all of it."

"Then," declared Stanley, "we'll be in the most logical section we could find; perhaps it will be the mortar in which the problem will be pounded out."

* * *

Selma Janes had a good social position and many friends. Few of them knew how greatly she had been embarrassed by the depression. That she continued to live in her own house and to attend certain social functions (it was not noticed that these brought no financial obligation) prevented knowledge of her monetary state. Everybody rented rooms and when a family came as her friends and occupied the house with her they appeared as other tenants had. The young man's position in the Bureau of Standards gave him an assured reception from others in the department. He registered as formerly of Cambridge, Mass. (while at Harvard), later as of Leipzig, Germany, recently from Chicago. His credentials had contained the statements of his education, experience, ability. He was set down as son of E. L. Law, grandson of Colonel Mapes; born at Bay Shore, Mich. For it was to Bay Shore that Selma's father had removed after the Civil War had destroyed his southern home and with his family had gone 'Melia, a child accompanying her widowed mother, Mrs. Janes' maid. 'Melia, almost as fair as Selma, had gone to the public school with white children and grew up in the Janes family until she married the Irish-German grocer-boy from whom she had bought supplies for the Janes' table. As long as Selma stayed at home, 'Melia had been the ever-ready help to be called on when extra assistance was needed, and when both Selma's parents had died of the flu, in one week, 'Melia had been the devoted attendant and comforter to the younger woman. Hers had been the last familiar face seen as the train carried the desolate girl from her home town. During her first years of absence, she had written frequently and sent gifts for Stanley at holiday times. But now, for a number of years, she had not heard from them. Stanley seemed to her a stranger. His wife, they told her, was the daughter of a German-American druggist. Oh yes, she knew Stanley's ancestry; his blood, as he reminded Selma had not the proportion of African inheritance that Dumas fils had, no more than is attributed to Pushkin and even Robert Browning is said to have had a tincture "though I maintain," he declared, "that even the tincture admitted should not debar one from the right to mingle with people of equal intellectual standards. I would not demand so much for myself, Miss Selma, but for my children and children's children I seek to obliterate the stigma."

"Let us forget here that any stigma was ever felt by anyone; now you are accepted for yourself."

"As long as no one knows or suspects the 'tincture'," he said bitterly. "There are many who have the taint, but not the tint of skin that enables them to pass. I feel cowardly to ignore them though, if I acknowledge them those who are more of my blood than they will discard me. As a white man I may mingle with any class of any nation, but as a Negro, I would be debarred more in the land of my birth than anywhere else."

Selma begged him not to dwell on these facts and said it was unwise to talk of it among themselves. He acceded but as time went on she saw that he brooded.

After the newcomers had adjusted themselves to the home and city, she had little by little invited her friends to meet them. The personal charm of the young people was taking with everyone yet Selma in her heart felt she was deceiving the old friends, knowing they would not have come had they known all. Still she told herself that the prejudice was unjustifiable, mean, selfish, detestable. Nevertheless there was lurking uneasiness always in her mind.

When Stanley' wife became pregnant Selma's anxiety and apprehension grew so acute that she could hardly endure it without expressing it. Suppose, Oh suppose there should be a throw-back! The coming child's great, great grandmother had been black. To a distinguished, talented white man she had borne a daughter who became the mother of Stanley's mother; 'Melia's father, a quadroon passed for white and 'Melia though a brunette had no trace of color. Stanley's Irish father had given him the very white skin found in Ireland in black haired persons and Irma was German blond. But what could be expected of the child?

When the approaching *accouchement* made it wise to get help in the house-work which the three women had been dividing among themselves, Selma found a young farm girl, "poor white" whom she trained to certain duties; she had been unwilling to take one of the many colored maids available, to be one of the group in the home.

Stanley had been cordially received at the Bureau; more than once he had been invited to the home of his chief and he and Irma had joined the Michigan State club, attending its functions and some others though not going in for "society." Selma always felt relief if Irma accompanied her husband; unconsciously there was the thought "She, at least, is what she seems to be." Yet reflecting on what one of Great Britain's Ambassadors had said at a Washington meeting concerning a "Melting-Pot" she was grateful to Sir Auckland Geddes for having declared that England had been and was, one of the greatest, from the era of the Picts and Scots, the Danes and the Norsemen, Gauls and Celts who had overrun the island on to the present when hordes of Eastern Europeans and Orientals took it in their path westward to America, even, many stopping permanently,—she realized that "there are others" in whom blood mixtures have been and are amalgamating, and questioned, "Should we be less valiant in adjustment?"

Irma's time came at last. Both Selma and 'Melia had opposed her going to a hospital. No complications were expected; Irma's physician had declared her a remarkably healthy, normal subject. To him the reason for anxiety had not been divulged. The two older women knew each other's dread though neither spoke of it. The nurse engaged was not permitted to come until she should be summoned; they hoped the event would take place before she could arrive. And Irma quite obligingly arranged it so. Even Selma was not called until the early morning hour when 'Melia rushed into her room exclaiming "All over, Miss Selma, and all *right*; 'phone the nurse now."

Selma's excitement made it difficult for her to do the phoning coherently. Later when she stood by 'Melia who was washing a very red, very blond-headed baby boy she said chokingly, "We do thank the Lord, 'Melia, don't we?"

"He's done right well for us this time, Miss Selma, we'll hope he'll keep it up."

And Selma knew that probably there would be other times and other anxieties to go through with for the same reason.

A few days later Stanley came to her sitting room one evening saying he wanted to have a serious talk. Selma's heart quailed. Was he thinking of leaving her? He had been generous in spending his good salary and the savings he had brought to invest had not been touched; her taxes had been kept up; proper repairs had been possible; she was not making money but meeting expenses well. The peace of having this family with her had given her the security of home and objects for the affection she loved to show; perhaps it had been too wonderful to last! now would it be broken? She waited agitatedly for him to speak.

"Miss Selma," he began, "I've been thinking of the present I want to get for Irma; nothing could be good enough to match what she has given me in the boy; but I want to get her something and the best I can think of is a home; I want to buy her a home. We've been so happy here, so secure, at least as secure as we can hope to be. Will you sell me the house?"

And leave it herself—go homeless when she had just gained freedom from care? For his money couldn't buy her another real home. As though she had spoken the thought, he answered,—"Not for you to leave it, but to stay with us always—You said you'd be god-mother to little Karl."

But would she still have the ineffable sense of home feeling? Suddenly she felt desolate. But Stanely went on.

"A special reason why I want this house, Miss Selma, is that the blocks on each side are owned by my own people, to whom I am kin through generations. It would be fitting that I should rear my child among the two races he belongs to."

"How about the German-Austrian strain he gets through his mother?"

They both laughed. "To be sure and the British–Scotch-Irish he gets through my father and grandfather,—but they are all Caucasian; the hundred per cent American fetish doesn't exist," he declared.

"It might in aborigines,—the Indians."

"Not there either, for they in turn were mixtures. But to come back to the house matter. Will you sell it to me?"

But the most she would agree to was that she would make her will at once and, having no kin to leave it to she would bequeath it to Irma. Meantime—

"We are your tenants in perpetuity," he declared kissing the hand she held out to him, then by it he drew her with him to tell Irma and 'Melia and look at her godchild. She gathered the baby in her harms hiding her face aquiver with the thought, "Am I helping to solve the greatest problem of our country? In a hundred years, two hundred, will prejudice have been so pounded in the mortar of reason that it will be changed to another element?" But aloud she said.

"Oh thank Heaven, I need never go again to the Emergency Relief or be told 'You may present this order and draw three pounds of sliced pork.'"

[*Opportunity* 13.12 (December 1935): 370–373]

A Sealed Pod

by Marita Bonner

It was one fine funeral.

No matter what Frye Street might think of all the incidents that led up to it, the funeral itself—with curly plumes saluting the winds from the four corners of the white automobile hearse, two rusty black open carriages entirely buried under flowers, two perspiring doctors fanning Ma, applying smelling salts to Ma's nose—a long line of automobiles filled with crepe-hung Negroes—the funeral itself, stirred the mind, uprooted the feelings, shook the soul.

And all this was as it should be. When they were burying a girl who had been cut to death, it ought to be done so you remembered it.

"Viollette Aurora Davis was as sweet and tender as her name!" the Reverend Johnson Harris had quavered as he opened the obituary.

He had known how sweet and tender Viollette could be.

A floodtide of moans ebbed up from the packed church to second all this.

Viollette's mother—Ma—had lifted her cry above the entire assembly, "Do mercy, Jesus! Have mercy Lord! Aw Father! Aw, Jesus, Aw!"

The two doctors fanned Ma, they soothed Ma, they supported Ma between them. They had known Viollette's sweetness and tenderness, too.

Ma was alone in the world now. With Viollette gone, she had no one else except some cousins who had come in from the country for the funeral.

Frye Street (black) wept and wailed all through the obituary, the hymns, and had uttered a full symphony of lamentation when they passed around to take a last look at Viollette.

"My God, Old lady Davis'll never git over it!" one mourner had sniffed. "Jes' to think! Comin' home findin' your one and only child carved like any beef steak! Dead in her bed! My God!"

"Twarn't nobody but that Davie Jones!" Ma had screamed right out once.

That is what everybody in Frye Street agreed on.

Dave Jones it had been who killed Viollette!

Hadn't he boasted openly in Jimmie Harris's "Valet de Luxe" tailor shop—right out in front of everybody on that fatal Tuesday night—that he was going to spend a "Pleasant evening with Frye Street's Viollette!"

And when Pop Gentry had advised him to go on home to Susie, his lawful wife, hadn't Dave spat and cursed in reply, "Mind your business, ole nigger! When both my feet gits to hanging in the grave like yours is, I'll spend my nights at home!" Those men who were Pop Gentry's best friends all swore and testified to this at the inquest.

Dave was arrested—though he cried he was innocent.

Dave was convicted—though he swore he was guiltless.

Dave was hanged—crying and praying, swearing that his hands were absolutely clean of Viollette's blood.

And Susie, Davie's short, fat, square little wife, had followed him through the maze of court trials and cells—up to the very death chamber.

Then she had taken her two children and disappeared from number 15 Frye Street the day Dave died.

Some folks say she went back "Down home."

Others say she ran off uptown where the Negroes did not know her.

Pat McKeagh who drove the city refuse wagon that carried the muck of Frye Street to the river, swore he saw Susie throw her two babies in the river and then fall in herself.

But Pat was always drunk and swearing he saw things.

"Maybe she did once!" sighed Esther Weinstein, wife of Anton, who kept the Corner Store Grocery Market. She drew a breath that sobbed and touched her breast. "Maybe she did, that Susie, throw herself in the river! So much trouble! Such a heaviness! Such a stone here!" and she smote her breast many times.

"God rest her soul!" murmured Mary Sugnee and crossed herself.

"Ain't no good Christian girl like Susie Jones done no such a thing! That McKeagh's just a drunk mick! Ain't nobody what held up her church and her pastor like Susie always has—flung her soul away fur no no-count nigger man!" Ma Davis herself pronounced this—and Frye Street black, stood to a man, behind this opinion.

Christian girls didn't kill themselves.

And it was not Dave who had killed Viollette.

Dave Jones told the truth when he died, crying, "Honest to Gawd, y'all! I didn't do it!"

Frye Street, as you know, runs from Grand Avenue where the "L" is to the big river that skirts the city. It runs from Heaven to Hell (as I have already told you) with its little brick houses—too filled with every race on the earth.

Strange things can happen there.

Strange things.

For instance, black Ma Davis who lived in number nine had had a daughter, Viollette Aurora—as blonde and fair and apparently Nordic as Ma was concentratedly negroid.

Strange things can happen in Frye Street.

Ma scrubbed all night in the office buildings down town and left number nine to eighteen-year-old Viollette.

And Viollette—warmed with an odd mixture of uncontrolled passions and bloods, entertained a varied assortment of men of every race every night.

The men flowed in and out. Viollette did not care who they were or why, usually.

Only one man had she ever loved—and only this one had really loved her.

That was Joe Tamona, twenty-two-year-old Italian boy. He and Viollette made a handsome pair—he with his swarthy complexion and flashing black eyes—she, kitten-soft with the golden flesh and golden hair that marks the mixed-blood blonde.

Joe would have married Viollette in spite of the black men—and the white men—not to mention the Orientals.

But Joe had a knack of flashing a knife as quickly as he flashed his eyes. One night in a pool room, he and Andy Laughlin had an argument over a shot.

Joe's knife flashed.

Andy was dead when they picked him up.

Joe had disappeared from Frye Street that very night as completely as if he had died.

"Gone to sea"—some of the folks on Frye Street said. The police chose to believe so, too.

But Joe—after pelting wide-eyed with fear to Viollette—had borrowed some clothes from her and made her call a taxi—made her swear eternal love that would wait for his return—and then had ridden off uptown.

The police could not find Joe. He changed his name, "forgot" how to speak English and lived with a group of old country Italians on the outskirts of the city—fully forty miles from Frye Street.

Now Joe hankered for his Viollette. He could not forget the cool arrogance of her—strangely joined to the abandoned passion which could possess her.

One April night, Joe, feeling safe since twenty-two months had gone by, since he had done for Andy Laughlin—and gone scat free—went back to Frye Street.

He went back in a taxi—got out a little above number nine and started to ring the bell. However, he caught a glimpse of Ma Davis charging around in the "front" room. Joe changed his mind and drew back in a shadow to watch.

Ma was calling aloud, "You Viollette? Gal? Where de devil you put my hat! It's nigh on seven-thirty and I ain't found it yet! Where is it, I says!"

Joe could hear Viollette answering faintly from somewhere upstairs. "Here it is, Ma!"

Joe had watched the old lady go out of the room again—for the shades were up and the lamp was lit. He shrank back into the doorway of number eleven as Ma sailed by on her way to work.

Watching Ma out of sight and stepping cautiously, Joe was again approaching Viollette's door, when a man swung suddenly from the opposite direction—and leaped eagerly up the steps of number nine.

Cursing under his breath, Joe curved far out to the curb and passed on by. He sauntered a little beyond the house, doubled, and went back.

The shades at the windows were still undrawn. Peering in, Joe recognized Dave Jones as the man. His breathing altered as an overwhelming surge of desire swept over him at the sight of his Viollette.

Afraid to linger in the street, Joe decided on a bold stroke. He tried the outer door of number nine, found it open, crept in the hall, took off his shoes and passed the door of the front room which was closed. He crept upstairs to the room which he knew was Viollette's and hid himself in her closet.

That Dave Jones would be going home pretty soon, then Viollette belonged to him, Joe Tamona.

Hadn't she promised with tears in her eyes on that night nearly two years ago when he had run away—to remain truly his until such a time as he should come back to her!

Dave Jones would be going soon.

The closet was small. The closet was airless. Joe took a swig of gin and opened the door a crack.

He must have fallen asleep. Sounds and lights in Viollette's room awakened him. "Davy!" It was Viollette's voice! "Dave, darlin, why don't you let Susie go on back down South. She's too big a dumb-bell for this man's town! And you know I'm really in love with you!"

Joe leaped to his feet. A dress on a coat-hanger clattered to the floor.

"What's that?" demanded Dave.

"Aw, jes' one of them big hoss rats that bust around this place all night! Forgit it!—Say, ... listen!"

And Viollette slammed the closet door without looking in.

Joe trembled, knife in hand, ready to burst forth.

Then his brain steadied a little. He could not cut both their throats at once. The girl would scream while he was finishing Dave.

That would not do.

Knife in hand, Joe crouched down again, pulled the dresses and clothes around him and waited.

Joe sat there all night.

Joe sat there and heard Dave with his Viollette.

More gin put Joe to sleep again—but he kept his knife in his hand.

It was a scraping sound that aroused him this time. Someone was moving a chair.

"Better get home early, honey!" Joe heard Viollette cooing in a sleepy voice. "Ma'll be here soon now! It's most five o'clock! The old lady'd raise the devil if she found you!"

They laughed together—a comfortable, smug crescendo.

Joe, trembling to his knees, could hear Dave walking back and forth.

"Aren't you going to kiss your Viollette again before you go!"

Joe gripped his lips in his teeth, gripped his knife closer, braced his rubber heels against the wall to keep himself from splitting the door wide in the silence that followed.

"Come on! I'll let you out, Davie boy!" Viollette said finally. "When are you coming back? See me tonight again?"

The man laughed the tender caress tone of a man who would give you anything. "Maybe! Can't never tell!"

Their voices trailed off. Joe could hear their feet on the steps.

Now

Presently Viollette came back alone. Yawning and stretching in luxurious abandon, she perched on the side of the bed to shake off her slippers before she cuddled back for the peaceful sleep Ma always found her in every morning.

Viollette stretched, Viollette yawned, Viollette was drawing the covers up cozily when Joe burst open the door....

Ma's feet hurt her that morning. She came crawling up from the five o'clock car.

"Look heah, conductor!" she had pleaded. "No need to carry me pas' my corner! Leave me off on the wrong side this once, for God's sake! My feet's 'bout to kill me!"

The conductor knew Ma by sight, so he rang the bell for emergency stop and let the old lady off on the corner where there was no white post.

"Thank you, and thank you, Jesus!" Ma called back fervently as she climbed down.

She eased herself along the street. It was too early for many people to be out, but Ma spied Teresa Tamona as she passed number 24—black shawl on her head—her pallid face pressed against the window.

"What the name of the Lawd ails that Eye-talian dis early in the mornin'? Ever since that boy of hers been gone, she been settin' by the windows, watching out for him! Always seeing him, and 'feelin' him! and all that kinder mess!!"

Ma groaned on by. As she drew near to number nine, the sun shot a few rays up over the house opposite.

"My eyes must be gittin' worser! 'Pears like to me that gal Viollette's done left the door wide open!"

The door was open.

Ma uttered an alarmed cry. "What's the matter with that gal!"

Feet forgotten, she tore up the stairs. "Heah's Me!" she shouted, standing in the lower hall. "Git up from there, gal! What de devil you leave this front door settin' wide open for all night? I ain't got nuthin' now but I don't want nobody to steal that!"

She waited.

There was no answer.

Not a sound came from the bedroom above. Ma's anger took fire from the pain in her feet.

"You Viol—lette! You heah me!! I bet if I come up there you'll answer me!"

A blanket of complete silence covered the house.

Ma pulled herself up the stairs, strode along the hall—pushed into Viollette's room. Ma fell downstairs screaming.

Ma screamed all the way out to the sidewalk and laid down flat in the middle of the street. "Aw Jesus! Aw Gawd! Aw Jesus! Aw Gawd!" She screamed over and over.

Teresa Tamona and Anton Weinstein, who kept the grocery market, came running to Ma first.

"Du mein lieber Gott! Was ist geschien!" Anton shouted as he puffed up. ("Dear God! What has happened?")

"You seen something perhaps?" Teresa panted, her face more pale than ever.

Ma raised her head and her voice.

"My Viollette! Cut!! Cut to death!! Aw Jesus!" Ma laid back down in the mud.

"Gott!" stammered Anton who knew Viollette.

Teresa sat down on the curb. "I thought maybe you see my Joe!" she said sadly.

Others came running. The door of number 15 where Dave Jones lived with his Susie—flew open.

Dave and Susie had been having an argument.

"What the devil you got to do with where I was las' night?" Dave had cursed suddenly and struck Susie.

Screaming, Susie ran downstairs and out into the street.

She stumbled and fell and lay near where Ma Davis had fallen.

Dave heard the uproar—followed Susie—and reached the crowd just as Jimmie Harris, who owned the "De Luxe" tailor shop, came up.

"Viollette Davis been cut to death!" one Negro stammered.

Dave staggered and paled.

"Dave spent the night with Viollette—" Jimmie began loudly.

"Ain't nobody seen my Joe?" queried Teresa Tamona all at once. "Nowhere?"

That is what started all.

Dave was tried.

Dave was hanged.

Nobody—not even Teresa—saw Joe Tamona run out of number nine, down Frye Street, toward the river.

A tramp freighter with a flat end was swinging down the river when Joe reached the shore. He took a big leap—and was on it.

And everything and everybody in the case was side by side—like peas in the pod.

But the pod was sealed.

And the peas did not touch each other. [*Opportunity* 14 (March 1936): 88–91]

THE PARASITES

by Hazel Vivian Campbell

Lanny Fuller lived with his fat wife Cozie and his little son Joe on Fifth Avenue, between 134th and 135th Streets in one of those dark apartment houses where the narrow halls carry the close odor of human bodies, fried foods and strong liquors. The Fullers lived on the top floor and like most of the families in the neighborhood the Fullers were on relief. They had been on relief ever since they knew there was a relief. Lanny had quit his job for the sole purpose of being assured that his family would receive all the free food, clothing, shelter and medical attention without any effort or obligation on his part. Cozie had sanctioned his move. She patted him on his back that afternoon when he came home and told her what he had done. She told him that was the most sensible thing he had done since they had been married, for the three of them could never live off the meager earnings he was bringing home. Being on relief they could be assured of practically everything they really needed to sustain life. So the next day Lanny and Cozie had gone down to sign up as dependents on the government.

Lanny was happy in his new station in life. When evening would come he would stretch on the white iron bed that sagged in the middle and call his living fit for a king. Then he would pat his stomach which was as hard as a drum, unloose his trouser belt and sigh with deep satisfaction.

They had been on relief for two years when one evening Cozie came in from the food station with her arms laden with food. Lanny was sitting on one of the three kitchen chairs, his long legs stretched half way across the floor. He moved them a little as Cozie brushed past him. Cozie dropped the bundles on the table and took off her hat, and threw it across the room letting it fall on the floor. Neither she nor Lanny made any attempt to pick it up. He watched her walking to the stove in her half sloppy way and opening up the drafts.

Turning to him she spoke. Her voice was slow and heavy.

"Heard they aim to move us from these fire traps."

Lanny raised his head indifferently. "Oh yeah?"

"Yeah. I heard some women talking in the store today and they said they heard we were going to be moved. Us around here you know. It made me feel good."

"Guess it's near time these folks came to their senses. I'm getting tired of this place. It gives me the jitters sometimes, tho' it ain't half bad. We've been living here for near on ten years and I guess we can afford to move."

"Of course. I never did like this place no how."

Lanny raised his eyebrows. "You use to like it before we got on the Welfare. You said it was a real neat place then."

"You call a place with no bath and heat real neat?" she shot at him.

"I never said it. You said it. How come you're complaining about it now?"

"Just cos other people on the relief have more than we have. They have heat and a bath and even a big hall. We ain't got nothing a-tall."

"Oh, well, woman what difference does it make? You wouldn't use the bath anyway, and 'sides you ain't use to no heat. Down in Alabam' we ain't had no heat out there in the country, so what's the sense o' you coming up here trying to put on the dog. To tell the truth I don't care if they move us or not. We get all we want, don't we, and that's all I'm worried about." Lanny finished with a shrug of his broad shoulders.

Cozie began opening the packages on the table. Lanny kept his dark eyes fastened on Cozie's fat fingers as they moved nimbly on the white strings.

"I wish to goodness they would hurry and move us. I want to go up to Sugar Hill. Then I could sure nuff put on the dog." And Cozie twisted her kinky head proudly and a smile of expectancy came to her brown face.

"Sugar Hill! Woman, you don't want much. Why ain't no body up there gonna bother with you. Them up there is all big shots. I'm satisfied right here. All they have to give me is a mess of food. Them folks up there on Sugar Hill think they is better than God Almighty," he finished.

"They ain't thinking nothing of the kind. You know some of them up there are on relief too. They ain't no better than us. There's a woman on relief what comes from there and she is real nice. She tells me they got most everything. You know heat and a bathroom and one of those electric ice-boxes. What you call them? Got a big name to it. Oh yeah, and they have wide halls down stairs and elevators, and all that stuff," and Cozie smacked her lips together.

"They ain't got all that stuff up there? Is they sure nuff? I guess I'd like it, specially if we don't have to walk up the steps."

"Now I don't know if they get everything or not, but I do know they get food, cos this lady said so."

"Well, if they ain't gonna pay for everything ain't no sense going up there."

"I ain't sure now, but I'll ask Miss Bee when she comes around here this week."

"Gosh, looks like the government is gonna take care of everyone. I wonder if he's taking care of tax-payers too?"

"Hope not," she turned her back on him and put four large potatoes in the oven.

"Gosh, if they are gonna be taken care of too, what do you think the government is going to use to take care of us? Those nutty headed taxpayers, don't need no devilish help."

Cozie sat down and tied her brown oxford. Sitting straight again she looked at her hands. "I was thinking the same thing. We can't share food and all that stuff with them. They don't need the things we need, cos they got property. Property is money—leastways you can always get money."

"Tain't the fact they own property, but if they can afford to pay the government a heavy tax, they can afford to take care of themselves," Lanny said stretching his arms over his head.

"Sure," Cozie stood again. "I ain't feeling sorry for none of them."

"Me either. That's why I think the government should give them poor devils all the work, so that we can get a chance at life. If the taxes ain't paid, what we gonna do?"

"Did you play that number I gave you?"

"Well, don't start worrying over that now."

"Didn't have any money," and Lanny took his hands from resting on the top of his head.

"Why didn't you sell one of those iron bars you picked up on the heap? You could at least have ten cents to play with," she scolded mildly.

"Who, me walk all the way up to 145th Street with a bar of iron? Nope. Woman, you must be crazy."

"Well, how you expect to hit the numbers if you ain't got no money? I'll send Joe up there when he comes in from school tomorrow. If the man will only give us sixty cents, we can play heavy, and Greta may I win," and Cozie rubbed her two hands together. "I need new clothes and I feel so bad going back there and asking for a new dress."

"I guess you ought to be shame. I reckon you are the most hog of a woman what goes there. If you hit heavy you get your dress and I'll get a radio sure."

"A radio?" she looked at him queerly.

"We ain't supposed to have a radio, just tell me that for the millionth time. I've heard it for years and years, but anyway I'm getting one."

"Now, don't you go long and do things that is gonna get us off this relief mess. You never did make enough money for us to live off, so you just mark how you get along. 'Sides it ain't just right cheating on them."

"Aw woman, I ain't cheating anymore than they try to cheat."

"Do they cheat?"

"Show me a woman working for the government that ain't cheating."

Cozie put her hands on her sides and frowned at Lanny. "Now Lanny Fuller, tain't no sense o' talking 'bout women if you don't know just what to say 'bout them. You just keep them thick lips of yours still."

Lanny did not answer her. The two of them became suddenly quiet. Cozie reached in the drawer of the kitchen table and took out a can opener. Taking the can of veal, she proceeded to open it. The two of them listened to the crunch, crunch of the can opener. Cozie walked to the stove and tried the potatoes with a fork. Slamming the door, she walked back to the table and put the veal in a blue platter, and set it on the corner of the stove.

"What you leaving it there like that for? Ain't you gonna warm that veal?"

"Nope. It'll get warm there."

"Well, who wants to eat half warmed veal?"

She did not notice his question. She opened the oven again and took out the potatoes, throwing them on the top of the stove. One of them burst, letting a thin line of steam escape.

"How long do you think Joe should be out? He hasn't come home from school yet. You'll have to speak to him 'bout staying on these streets all hours of the night."

"Good night, Cozie, it's only seven-thirty."

"Well he ought to be in. It's dark out there."

"Joe can take care of himself. When I was Joe's age I was earning my own living."

"Well you ain't Joe, and Joe ain't you. I tend to bring up Joe a speck different than you were brought up. I tend to give him a peck of college education."

"A peck of what?"

"College education," she snorted.

Lanny grinned broadly, and even proudly. Yet he couldn't picture his son in an institution of higher learning. "What you aim to send him there with?"

"Number money."

"You'll have to do some tall hitting to let him stay there," he laughed out loud. "If you send him to school with number money you'll be wearing all that fat flesh you have there away. Why, woman, you'll worry so much and so long you'll be skinny enough to go through that there key hole," and Lanny pointed to the door with one of his long fingers.

"Never mind about me," and Cozie turned to the stove pretending she was busy, but turning her back on Lanny was sort of a protection from his critical glance.

Cozie wondered if she were really too fat. Perhaps she could get a reducing girdle from the relief, or if she hit five cents on the numbers she could get a real good one. She didn't mind being fat. In fact extra fat became her, and gave her the feeling of being prosperous, but Lanny made a crack on her fatty tissues every chance he got, so there was nothing to do but reduce. She suddenly felt as tho' he were watching her. He was searching her back, laughing and thinking of slimmer girls. The thought that he was thinking of smaller women made Cozie suddenly angry and neglected. Turning swiftly on him she spoke crossly. Lanny had hung his head and was watching his soiled shoes wondering whether or not he should get a shine. The sharpness of Cozie's voice caused him to glance up quickly, his face showing plainly his sudden surprise.

"What you sitting there looking at me for? You've been sitting in that same position ever since I came home except to put your hands on the top of that kinky head. You could at least go out and look for Joe. A lot you care for him. If he—if he was," but Cozie never finished for a wave of self-pity got the best of her and she began to cry. Lanny knitted his brow, opened his mouth, scratched his head and finished up with a frown. Pressing his lips together he said under his breath, "Well what th—."

It was a relief when Joe came in. He was a chubby, kinky headed brown boy with eyes like his father and the soft skin of his mother.

Behind Joe, sniffing at his heels was a small, half breed collie. Lanny frowned on the dog, and looked sternly at the boy. He let Joe take off his hat before he said anything to him. Pointing at the dog Lanny spoke.

"You were told not to bring that mutt in here anymore. I told you time and time again that that dog ain't nothing but a peck of hard luck. You take that mutt out of here and keep him out."

The boy opened his eyes and blinked back a sudden flow of tears. "Aw, paw, all the kids I know got dogs, and I want a dog too," and a tear fell. "'Sides he ain't a bit o' hard luck, paw." Joe spoke with that slow, heavy drag of his mother's.

"I don't care what the other kids got. You take that stray mutt out of here."

"Aw, paw, can't I keep him please? Paw you don't know how nice it is having a dog, specially if you ain't got no brothers and sisters."

"Don't argue with me. Take that dog out of here."

Cozie looked from the boy to the man and then let her eyes linger on the dog. The dog was looking at her, his brown eyes seeming to plead to her that she'd let Joe have him. Cozie read what she had so often read in the soft eyes of other dogs. Putting her hands on her hips she patted her feet, one at a time.

"What makes you think the dog is hard luck, Lanny Fuller?" she cocked her head back and looked squarely at him

"All dogs are hard luck. I've never had any luck when dogs are around. Have you ever seen a stray mutt that wasn't hard luck?"

"I never noticed," she snapped. "Besides there is no such a thing as old fool luck."

"'Sides we ain't suppose to keep dogs."

"Well, you are such a law-abiding citizen. You were going to buy a radio, weren't you?" she reminded him.

"Well that agent wasn't gonna see the radio, but that mutt can't help but be seen. The government ain't gonna take care of us and a pack of stray dogs too," he raised his voice.

"You don't have to holler at me. You're so 'fraid you'll be taken off the relief and put to work. We might not be allowed to keep that dog, but we're gonna keep him anyways."

"All right! All right! keep him then, but let me tell you a thing or two, Cozie

Fuller," Lanny sat up straight, "if they put me off the relief on account of that mutt, I'm gonna leave you two flat. Bet on it."

"I ain't gonna bet on nothing," she answered as he stood up. It was good to have had that little argument, for Cozie had a chance to throw off some of the anger she felt towards Lanny. Lanny walked from the room, and did not return for supper. She did not feel as tho' it were her duty to call him, but she did manage to call him in her mind everything from a sissy to a damn fool.

It was a little after nine the next Saturday when the investigator came. She was a handsome sort of a Negro woman with horn-rimmed glasses over the bridge of a very high nose. She came into the front room with all the dignity and grace of the world in which she lived. Taking a seat, she adjusted her glasses and looked from Cozie sitting alone on the faded davenport, to Lanny standing lazily against the side of the window. She smiled and asked after their health.

"Fine, mam," Cozie spoke up. "Our Joe is out on the playgrounds with his dog," and Cozie shot Lanny one of those contemptible looks.

"That's nice. Plenty of fresh air for young folks who want to grow up big and strong," she said taking off her glasses.

Lanny wondered why Cozie should mention the dog. It must be so that he would have to get off relief, and she had so often said that he never earned enough for their keep. He shifted his feet and frowned slightly.

The woman looked at Lanny for a second and then spoke.

"Mr. Fuller, I have some good news for you."

Lanny grinned. "I knew it. You're gonna move us from these apartments. Put us in another apartment."

"Another apartment? Why I don't understand."

"Please, mam," Cozie spoke. You see I heard that the relief was gonna move us from these fire traps and put us in decent houses, and I guess that's what Lanny is telling you about." Cozie played with the fat hands resting in her lap.

The woman looked puzzled. "Why, no," she said looking at Cozie. "There was some talk of that, but I haven't come here to tell Mr. Fuller that."

Turning to Lanny again she raised her hand and rubbed the side of her face. "Mr. Fuller the government is going to put you to work."

"What????" Lanny stood up straight and did not try to conceal the deep frown that came to his forehead.

The investigator, mistaking that frown for a well-earned surprise, smiled. Shaking her head, she went on. "Yes, Mr. Fuller, you are to be put to work. I know you think it is about time, and I am glad for your sake. I know how you all long to be independent of the government, and—"

"What kind of work?" Lanny snapped, looking first from Cozie to the visitor.

"Why, Mr. Fuller, you are not angry?"

"Well, I ain't mad, but I got to know what kind of work I've got to do." Lanny did not change his tone of voice. "I can't do everything."

"Why, of course not, Mr. Fuller, but you will try and do what will be given to you."

"Is everyone getting jobs?"

"Why—no, not everyone, but as many on the relief as can be accommodated."

"Have all the taxpayers got a job?" Cozie spoke up her voice not concealing the anger she felt towards the woman.

"Taxpayers?" the woman frowned.

"Yes, taxpayers," spoke up Lanny.

"Why taxpayers?" she asked.

"They have to work more than we do. They have to support the government, and I think they deserve all the help they can get."

"Why, yes, of course. I agree with you, but we have no taxpayers on relief, as least I don't know of any."

"They need jobs," Lanny answered her sharply.

"Mr. Fuller, I did not come here to discuss taxpayers. We are putting men to work so that the strain on the relief will be lifted. Now, Mr. Fuller—."

"How much am I gonna get?" Lanny interrupted her.

"It will all depend upon the type of work you will be doing."

"If I don't earn enough to support my family I ain't gonna work, and no one can make me," he tossed his head back a little.

"That is all taken care of, Mr. Fuller."

"How much is he gonna get, that's all I want to know," Cozie spoke again.

Turning to Cozie she raised her eyes with a look of scorn. "He'll be earning more than he has for the last two years," and her voice was cool and cut Cozie's feelings like a knife.

The investigator stayed over and hour trying to explain to the Fullers all about this new drive on jobs, almost losing her temper and good manners as she did so. Then she was gone. The two of them watched her as she descended the steps, crossed the street and became part of the crowd. Lanny turned from the window to face Cozie standing behind him.

"She has a nerve. I don't believe her," he spoke.

"She's trying to take advantage of us, cos we're poor and she ain't," and Cozie looked at the address in her hand. "Well, she ain't gonna take advantage of me," she went on with a funny toss of her head.

"Didn't I tell you that these women working for the government were a bunch of cheats? Didn't I tell you that?" Lanny said, moving from the window.

Cozie held the address toward him. "What you gonna do with this address? Are you gonna go down town?"

"No! No, woman! She didn't leave me any money to get down there and I'm not going to use my own money."

She touched his arm. "I'd go if I were you and see if she's really cheating and if she is we can get her in a peck o' trouble."

"Well, I ain't gonna take any work they give me. All those big shots down town can go jump in the lake. The government has enough money to take care of me, and it can do it."

"Of course," she agreed.

Lanny did go down town the next Monday and stayed all day. Cozie had all sorts of visions what might have happened to him, when he failed to show up after four o'clock. It was after six when he came in and brushed past Cozie as she opened the door for him. By the gait of his walk she knew he was angry. She followed him to the bedroom, where he sat dejectedly with his head resting in the palm of his hands.

"Well, what's the matter?" she asked, putting her hands on her hips.

"I feel like getting damn drunk," he answered not looking at her.

"Huh, you talk like you are drunk now."

"I should be. Those fools down town made me take a job or get off relief."

"Made you?" she spoke and the tone of her voice revealed her disbelief.

"Yes, either that or get off the relief."

"What? Lanny Fuller, they did that?"

"Yep."

"Did you tell them that you were willing to give your job to some well deserving taxpayer?"

"Didn't think of it."

"I wish that I'd been there. I'd a thought of it. What did they give you to do?"

"Digging ditches," he answered dryly.

"Digging what?"

"You heard me the first time, I said ditches."

"Did you tell them that you knew how to drive a car?"

"No. They said that I had to go on that street improving project—oh something like that."

"They got a nerve. Always trying to take advantage of people."

She looked at him for awhile. He was speaking again. Where's that dog?"

"Out," she paused. "How much they gonna give you?"

"I don't know," he looked up.

"Didn't you ask?"

"Didn't have time. I was too mad to ask."

"Lanny Fuller," she spoke disgustingly. He caught the hint of a sob in her voice.

"How long that dog been out?"

"I don't know," and Cozie unable to conceal her anger and disappointment any longer began to cry. "Now we're gonna be poor again, and we'll never get on Sugar Hill."

"Aw, woman, don't start that. If you weren't so nice and kept that mutt, we wouldn't be poor again. I told you that that mutt was hard luck, and when it comes back in here I'm gonna get rid of it, so help me Greta. I ain't gonna work for no old government no ways," and he threw himself across the bed and listened to his wife's deep sobs.

[*Opportunity* 14.9 (September 1936): 267–271]

TOO MUCH PIGMENT

by Effie Carrow

The Sunshine Special, rumbling by the gaunt old grey boarding-house beside the tracks, jerked Carmine Willard out of a deep, troubled sleep and instantly she remembered one thing. Only one.

For ten years, at exactly five-fifteen, Carmine had been rudely awakened by this noisy train. Awakened to the dreary sameness of her life—the grouchy railroad men to be fed, the constant complaining of Nora, her colored helper, the drab routine of life in a small Texas town. But this morning all these annoyances were trifles beside this other something: last night she had seen a ghost!

She had been sitting in the small section reserved for whites in a brightly lighted hall somewhere across town. She had gone there to escape the crushing, corroding depression of the present and her dark fear of a hopelessly empty future. And she had no sooner seated herself than the spectre had suddenly appeared upon the stage: a tall brown young man with drooping shoulders. Shoulders that sagged as though beneath a load.

Somehow Carmine had fought off the icy hand that clutched at her heart. Somehow she had remained in her seat. And after an eternity, she had found strength to rise and flee from the lean strong jaw, the towering brow, and the melancholy eyes upon the stage. But the ghost from the past had followed her to the drab old boarding-house, ruthlessly turning back the pages of her life to a time when she had not been Carmine Willard, a railroad boardinghouse mistress with pale cheeks and grey-streaked hair, but youthful, fresh-cheeked Carry Mae Williams, living in a little cottage close to Piney Brook. The cottage and most of its furnishings had belonged to the Ashley Lumber Company. Carry Mae and her husband—along with the other twenty-five or thirty colored families huddled about the tumbled mill yard like helpless chicks about a brooder—had belonged to the Ashley Lumber Company.

In return for being Ashley Negroes, they had been assured the pine house which kept them from freezing in winter, and which became so hot in summer that the rosin ran down its thin walls. As Ashley Negroes they had also had the privilege of ordering groceries from the Company Store. And when they had wanted a gingham dress or a pair of overalls they had gotten them, without question, "on account."

Carmine should have been happy as one of the Ashley Negroes because she had come from a tenant farm where the women and children were forced to work in the fields to help pay for their food and shelter. On the Ashley place she had merely to keep house for her family. It was only because she had chosen to do so that she had gone twice each week to wash and iron at the superintendent's home.

It was these weekly visits to the large white house, with its dark cool nooks in summer and warm cheery corners in winter, that had started the tiny spark of dissatisfaction stirring in her soul—a spark that was destined to become a cruel ungoverned flame of ambition, blinding her eyes to reality, hardening her heart against love and loyalty. It was the magazines she found at the white house—through whose pages she had glimpsed a world where white people ate from gleaming silver dishes, where cream-and-pink ladies trailed fine silk over thickly padded floors—that had awakened within her the terrible painful loathing for the sound of hard heels scuffing bare gritty floors; for beans and potatoes, spaghetti and tomatoes; and for the ready-made garments hanging limply in the Company Store. And so she had become desperately hungry for the things that apparently were made only for white people.

After twenty years, Carmine could now still feel the dreadful gnawing hunger of those days. She had been like a starving man, with the price of a loaf of bread in his pocket, gazing at a display of appetizing dishes. Now she could still hear her husband trying to stem the gulf he felt rising between them. "You jus' wait, honey, someday we'll git outta here an' I'll git paid for my work. Then things'll be better. We'll buy us a lil farm of our own."

But the hunger within Carmine's soul had demanded more than a little farm. And, wherever she went with her husband, she had reasoned, they'd still be colored people. Hadn't she heard her own mother say: "You needn't be gittin no fancy notions in yo haid, 'cause you aint no white gal. Don' make no difunce how white yo skin or how straight yo hair, you got colored blood in you and you gotta stay in yo place to git along wid these white people."

She wasn't white, but she was partly so, and a traveling salesman, with stained teeth and red flabby neck, showed her how easily she might break the slender tie that bound her to the accursed race.

So with trembling, greedy fingers, she had reached for her first gleaming opportunity to enter the magic white world. Had hugged it to her impatient heart, although it seared and scorched her conscience, until the soft fingers of an olive-skinned baby lost their grip; until the melancholy eyes and drooping shoulders of a black husband were forgotten.

But Carmine, the boarding-house mistress, now knew that there was no magic power in the white world which mysteriously made one rich and happy. She now knew that a white world could hold as much poverty as a black one. A poverty so dark with misery, so empty with loneliness she could not have envisaged it had she tried; could not have imagined the aching, futile, gnawing poverty of soul and spirit that now was slowly burning the life from her eyes.

Carmine heard soft steps entering her room. She knew it was Nora, coming to see why she had not appeared in the kitchen. She turned her face to the wall, feigning sleep. Through the mist of her troubled mind she sensed Nora bending over her; above the throbbing of her heart she heard her gasp and say: "Why, Miss Willard, you're sick. Do you want me to call a doctor?"

She lay beneath the covers for a time, not answering. Then she remembered the lie she had decided to tell.

"Naw, I'm not sick, Nora. I received bad news last night."

"Was it very bad news, Miss Willard?" Nora continued to hover over her, sympathy replacing the first fear in her voice.

"Very bad news. My sister's dead, Nora." Carmine hoped that would end the ordeal.

But Nora drew closer as though she expected more information. Carmine barely opened her eyes. She could see Nora's plump arms hanging beside her. They looked soft and smooth like black satin. Her husband's arms had looked like that, only firmer.

Nora was speaking again. "Miss Willard, is yo sister at yo native home?" She had asked the question hesitantly, and when Carmine said yes, she seemed pleased. "Well, that's good. It do you good t'go home. There ain't no tonic in th' world lak being 'mong yo own flesh an' blood sometime. I know, 'cause I thought I was serious sick last spring. I went t'see a doctor, an' took some medicine. But I didn't git well till my boy come home."

"You got children, Nora?" Surprise widened Carmine's eyes.

"Yes'm, one, a fine boy. He is at college gettin' a education, so he can git up in th' world, an' liv lak other people." Nora beamed at the door, hope and pride illuminating her simple features. Then, remembering Carmine's trouble, she added, "Yes'm, sho' do you good to be with yo own flesh an' blood sometime, Miss Willard."

Her own flesh and blood. Carmine's hands were clutching, almost tearing her cheap nightgown beneath the covers. The tall, brown young lecturer was her own flesh and blood. Tonight, she would sit again in the room with him, would hear his voice. That was all she desired: just to sit once more in the room with the ghost from her past.

"No, no, that's not all," a voice from somewhere in her being cried. She wanted to see a look of recognition in his eyes, to hear him call her mother. It seemed that all the desperate loneliness that had been slowly creeping into the very warp and woof of her being was now resolved into one burning desire. It seemed as though she could feel the fingers of her baffled heart reaching out into the damp empty void of her life, trying to contact something akin to it, something warm and friendly. A dull hard feeling filled her throat, swelled in her chest. Her head pained with the tears she could not shed.

Dressed in a cheap but neat light coat suit, Carmine soon stood at the door of her room, counting the money in her purse. There was enough. The train fare to Red Hill, Texas, was less than four dollars; and she didn't need much for room and board. Before leaving, she stopped to survey her shabby colorless room, the symbol of her life as Carmine Willard. And for an instant she recalled another time when she had recklessly run away from her life as Carry Mae Williams. She wondered, with a feeling of indifference, if she was now running away from her life as Carmine Willard. But she could not have turned back if she had desired, because today, as twenty years ago, she was moved by a power apart from her personal will. Her great desire and the hurt and loneliness in her soul were ruling supreme in her world. She moved as they willed.

The neatly dressed white woman and the grave, handsome young Negro attracted much attention as they left the train at Red Hill.

The town was just exactly what its name implied: a red hill with many narrow trails twisting through it. Above the small shack which served as a waiting room for white passengers was a large sign with Red Hill written upon it. The letter "I" in hill had been altered to an "E" by a practical joker.

The alteration could not be seen until one drew very close to the sign. There were some other things in Red Hill that could not be seen until one drew very close. The young lecturer saw them in the snarling, ruddy faces of the white men. He saw them in the cowed brown faces of the figures slinking here and there in dark-stained rags. He knew that he must choose words most carefully. But no matter what occurred, he told himself, he would not run away from these black men in rags, these remnants of the human family, whom the great movement of life had placed in a red hell.

"Red hells" had reasons for being. The inhabitants of "red hells" had reasons for being. They were all necessary to the whole. They were playing their parts in the eternal scheme of things. And he would serve them.

That night in the little church, he tried to tell the people of Red Hill that. He pleaded with them to make the best of their present life, to work hard towards pushing themselves up and out to something bigger and better, not in a distant land above the sky, but here among men.

Carmine sat in the little church listening to her boy deliver his message of wisdom and practical advice. She noted a tired, haggard look on his face and she felt concerned about him. He seemed so serious and so melancholy. She longed to take him to her room, make him a cup of hot chocolate, bathe his weary body and make him rest until he looked young and happy.

Then she saw the tired, haggard look disappear, as though it had been a mask, as the speaker's face became animated by the intensity of his message. She saw a white hot flash in his eyes, a hungry furious light, which only souls who have felt its heat can understand. It burned its message into her brain: her boy hated all the things she hated, but he had chosen to fight rather than to run. And suddenly the load that caused his shoulders to droop became visible. He was a young enthusiast with the burden of twelve million men upon his shoulders. Twelve million men who were forced to carry a load because there was too much pigment in their skin, and because this pigment had become associated with wrong attributes in the minds of white men.

His burden became her burden. She was bound to all these haggard, struggling souls by a common yoke, a yoke far more real than the physical aspects of the body. She suddenly became proud of the furious hate for the scraps of life which burned within her breast; became animated by a brave pride which made her want to stand and fight with her boy to help to lift the yoke.

The hard cold lump that was her heart began to dissolve and mingle with the hearts about her, uplifting, reviving her. A hopeful feeling crept upon her. She had come into the church a miserable, baffled, outcast woman, the present holding only defeat and misery, the future holding nothing. Now she felt warm and interested inside; the future began to stretch out before her with hope and purpose.

There wasn't much that she could do to help these weak people and their kind because she wasn't any better off than they; but she could serve them by serving her strong, capable boy. She could take care of him, make him comfortable, stand with him as he moved on with his message of encouragement.

Carmine Willard stepped from the church into the night, the hope and peace she had found enveloping and soothing her bruised soul. The wild, heavy odor of a southern spring in the country drugged her senses. A million night voices called to her on every side. She walked away from the church, forgetting everything except the tender sweetness of the night.

Before long, stepping briskly, she had passed the limits of Red Hill, and stood looking up at the tall straight bodies of many pines shooting heavenward. She sniffed their pungent odors, and was back at Piney Brook. She and her husband, and the other twenty-five or thirty colored families, huddled about the tumbled Ashley mill yard like helpless chicks about a brooder.

"No, I won't go back to that!" she said suddenly to herself. "I won't go back to that!"

It occurred to her then that the lecturer had failed to announce where he would make his next appearance. The thought made her panic stricken. He might be on a train now, or in a car, speeding away from her. And she might never find him again! She had forgotten the snarling gulf between them. She was still his mother; they belonged together.

Carmine moved as fast as she could, on her high heels, up the dirt path she had taken away from town. And in her haste, she failed to see two figures darting from tree to tree behind her.

Finally, she came again to the edge of the clearing upon the hill. She was passing the first small shanty when she noticed two figures standing beside a sagging gate. The figures separated. One left the gate, the other entered. It was a man with drooping shoulders. Shoulders that sagged beneath a heavy load.

A great surge of relief and pity swept over Carmine at the same time. Here was her boy. She hadn't lost him. He was tired and needed rest. Needed her.

She walked through the sagging gate behind the young man. He turned and stood, speechless, looking at the dark-eyed white woman with anxiety in his eyes. His face was colorless; for a second his teeth chattered together as though he had seen a ghost. Then, like a flash, an angry contemptuous light came into the melancholy eyes.

Carmine's voice whispered through stiff cold lips: "I'm your mother...."

The young man slumped upon a stone before the shanty.

After a moment he said in a quiet voice, "What do you want to do; get me killed? I don't know how long you've been following me, but I remember seeing you when I left the train this evening."

Did she want to get him killed? The thought brought memories flooding into Carmine's mind. Memories of race prejudice in all its ugly, ignorant, unreasonable forms. Memories of it as she had known it a Piney Brook.

She looked about fearfully. Then she said, "I'll leave, but please tell me this one thing: where will you go from here?"

The dark young man said, "I can't do that."

Carmine put one hand out to him. "Oh, please don' send me away from you. Really, I'm yo mother. Don' you believe me?"

"I don't know." The young man's voice was harsh. "And I don't care. My mother left me when I was a baby. My skin was too dark for her!"

There was no eloquence, no beauty in his speech now. His words were short and blunt.

"Now, will you please go? If I were seen talking with you, by even the colored people of this town, I couldn't get a place to sleep tonight."

Carmine stumbled out of the gate. She dabbed her eyes with the small handkerchief in her purse.

Back in the drab room of the only hotel the town afforded, she kicked off her tight, redstained slippers. She removed her coat and flung herself across the hard bed. The misery within her was turning to a dull ache. The hard congested feeling that had dissolved in the little church was trying to form again in her breast.

As she had walked back to the hotel, she had not noticed how noisy the streets were, partly because she had been too miserable and partly because she had forgotten how quiet a very small southern town becomes after nine o'clock. And so she lay sunk in the mire of her own soul's weariness, unaware of a greater strife gathering about her.

It started like the distant rumbling of thunder when old people look up at the lowering clouds and say, "a storm is brewing." The colored settlers of Red Hill looked out at the small knots of white men gathering about the streets and, slinking into their dark shanties, said, "hell is breaking loose."

Carmine was unconscious of it all until it came sweeping through the main street of the little town—a hungry consuming blaze. A wild senseless surge of hate sweeping up from the dark animal regions of life, demanding, ruling men, possessing them; not because they hated one man with too much pigment in his skin, nor twelve million; but because their poor uncultured souls knew better how to hate than how to love.

They were now beneath Carmine's window, spitting and swearing at each other. "Let's go get the colored fellow," someone yelled.

Carmine went to the window and looked down at the mob of men and she recalled the contemptuous light in the young man's eyes, heard him saying to her: "Do you want to get me killed?"

"No, it's not you they want; it's me!" She answered the question as though she still stood in front of the shanty talking with him.

"It's me they want!" A shaky hysterical sob was rising within her, shaking her free of the hardness that was trying to form in her breast. And yet she felt indifferent about the raving mob beneath her. She did not care whether she lived or died; that other hurt stabbed too viciously in her heart, flamed too furiously in her brain. It was the stabbing in her heart, the flaming in her brain that shook the hysterical sounds from her throat and forced tears from her eyes.

The mob struck, pushed, swore and swirled away from the hotel window: poor, uncivilized souls, caught in the angry torrent of lust for blood, swirling like an angry tornado; whirling through the main street toward a tiny shanty on the edge of town, where a figure with drooping shoulders had entered a sagging gate.

The hysterical sounds were turning to a hoarse rattle, which strained and tore at Carmine's throat. "Oh, Lord, I've killed him! Killed my baby because he couldn't follow me into this crazy world of fools who would string a boy up for talking to his own mother!"

Clammy hands were now digging into an imitation leather bag, throwing cheap underclothing about the cheap hotel room. "Lord, if I c'n only find't, I may be able to tell them fools somethin'."

The hand bag was now turned upside down. All its contents lay upon the dirty red carpet. "Lord, I gotta find't; it's my only chance. Thank God! Here is is!

"Now, jus' wait till I ketch'm; I'll tell'm somethin,' or make'm kill me t'night. Wish I hadda gun; I'd kill'm first."

Halting only to pull on her coat, she tore open the door of her room, plunged down the flight of stairs and on through the almost deserted lobby.

Before the clerk at the desk could recover from the shock of seeing her tearing madly through the lobby, she was several blocks away; running swiftly through the dimly lighted street.

Bare white feet with only thin silk hose to protect them padded down the rough dirt road; carrying a white black woman, with a piece of paper clutched in each hand, toward a shanty on the edge of town where a handful of crazed men sought to write into the pages of history another chapter of ignorance and shame; where the eyes of men who could behold the offspring of their own bodies with tenderness now blazed with death at the fruit of another man's body because their feeble minds were too small to feel the kinship of anything that appeared unlike themselves.

On and on she ran, until it seemed as though she could not breathe. Then she stopped and leaned against a tall board fence. Cold flashes leaped over the surface of her body, while there appeared to be a huge ball of fire blazing within her chest. Hot dry sobs issued through her throat and nose. But there was only one thought pondering in her brain: She must go on! Fast! Fast! Fast!

She braced herself to obey the command of her senses. But as soon as she moved away from the fence, she saw a car stop close beside her; so close she instinctively jumped away from it. Then she saw a dark form bend out of the car toward her, felt her arms being helped with a grip of steel and her body being pulled into the car. She strained with all her strength against the steel grip which pinned her arms to her sides, tried vainly to force a scream from her dry throat. Then she knew no more.

"We'll make uh example of this black buzzard! We'll learn him to stay in his place!" The mob stormed through the sagging gate—tore the flimsy door from the shanty.

"Where is he?" they hissed to the seemingly empty cave-like rooms. They threw pieces of rickety furniture through the doorway; pulled frightened old people and children from under the bed, out of the wood box, and behind the cook stove; cursed them, jerked them, abused them until the blood froze in their thin bodies. But they could find no sign of a tall figure with drooping shoulders.

When most of their vengeance had been spent on the shanty and its helpless occupants, the mob crowded out of the wrecked place. There was not much left in them now except the bitterness of defeat.

The old man whom they knocked groaning to the floor with a gash in his head had moaned: "Last I seed 'im, white folks, he went towards the church." They went to the church but it was empty. Somebody suggested that they burn it.

So while the mob got rid of the remaining heat of its anger and the bitterness of its defeat by watching hot flames lick away the only hope of a few black souls in a "red hell," a car, speeding through the darkness, left them far behind. A country school teacher sat riding at the wheel; a young lecturer with drooping shoulders and melancholy eyes huddled in the rear seat. Beside him sat a half-dressed woman with the feet of her hose torn away, and red clay made redder still by her own blood oozing between her toes. In one hand she clutched a frayed picture of a woman and an olive-skinned baby; in the other, a certificate of marriage. [*Opportunity* 16.5 (May 1937): 148–152]

THE MAKIN'S

by Marita B. Bonner

Little David remembered that he wanted ten cents when Mrs. Summers, the lady next door, tossed an empty tomato can out of her kitchen window.

The can hit the scarecrow fence that pretended to separate her yard from David's. Then it struck against David's house before it lay still.

"Teacher, she say not to throw cans and mess in the yard! She say we oughta plant grass and flowers instead! I forgot to ast Ma for my dime to git me some seeds like she said!"

He went into the kitchen. Ma was sitting on a chair between the stove and the sink. Her kinky bob stood up like a half-blown thistle pod all over her head. The dishes left from last night piled the breakfast dishes up to the shelf over the sink, where the lamps sat.

Ma was reading, "Let Me Tell All," so David had to yell to make her hear him.

"Ma! ma!! The teacher she says for all the kids to git a dime and buy seeds! She says you should pitch the cans and paper and stuff out of your back yard and plant the seeds!"

Ma grunted. "Huh–huh," and turned a page.

David waited. "Well, where's the money, Ma?" he yelled again.

Ma's book went down. "Money? What you talking 'bout, boy?"

"I told you and you said yes, Ma!"

"You done tole me what!"

"I done tole you teacher say to git a dime from your Ma and buy some seeds and plant them in your yard! And you says yes!"

"I ain't said nothin'. I ain't heard you askin' for no dime."

"You said huh-huh when I asked you!"

"Well, who the devil got any money to buy seeds? I sure God ain't goin' to buy no seeds! These teachers always got some fool notion! They ought to give you the seeds if they want you to have them! Here! Here!" Ma felt in the pocket of her pajamas and drew out a piece of paper. "Here! Take this number and this quarter down to Mr. Ed in the barber shop. Don't you lose it, neither, 'cause God knows I'd skin you if 609 was to hit today and you lost this last quarter I'm playing on it!"

David took the paper and the quarter and tried again.

"I can't git no seeds then, kin I, Ma?"

Ma always carried a cigarette behind her ear the way a clerk carries a pencil. She took her cigarette down now, reached expertly up on the lamp shelf and got a match without getting up out of her chair. She began to puff as she opened her book again.

She found her place. "I betcha you better git along out o'here," she yelled and grabbed a cup out of the dishes piled in the sink as if she meant to throw it at David.

The yell and the cup set David in motion. If he ran out of the back door again, he would be in line for a direct blow. So he curved and shot forward toward the front of the house. He heard the cup hit the kitchen door. He could already smell that sweet sickening smoke from Ma's cigarette.

"Them cigarettes sure make that gal mean!" David had heard Marm, his grandmother, say about his mother.

A burst of singing came down to him suddenly from upstairs where Marm had her room. That meant she was having a praying meeting this morning.

Maybe she'll give me a dime for some seeds," David thought, and started upstairs.

"*Glory, glory, hallelujah, when I lay this burden down!*"

Marm was leading the song. David could hear a man's voice take up a verse while the whole room answered in chorus.

"*One day, one day, I was walking along!*
(When I lay this burden down)
And de element opened and de dove came down!
(When I lay this burden down)!"

David peeked in the door.

Though Marm had on a cotton house dress and her apron, and though this was her own room, she had her hat on. Some half dozen elderly colored people were in the room with her.

Dragged north to the city by that uneasy surge of hope for better times that had fretted their children out of the South, most of them had felt poked and jibed by the strange ways of city living. They had felt alone and unwanted when they sat singly at home. Grouped together now, they counted for something and the fiery spirit of their old-time religion fused them together into a praying band that met daily.

These were not the parents of those young Negroes who can float through a white man's world balanced on some sustaining inner poise. These were those who believed everything they heard and knew that everything they saw was real. Their children seldom bothered to pray nor did they bother the old folks when they prayed.

Little David teetered on the doorsill.

Gramp Dean was beating out the time of the hymn with his cane. Aunt Susie Kiner was weeping loudly, burying her face in her apron. Old Miss Mary snatched up a song as soon as the last "When I lay dis burden down" had faded away. She began to sing loudly:

> *"I'm trampin!*
> *Trampin*
> *Tryin' to make heaven my home!*
> *(Hal–lee-loo!)"*

The room shouted joyously in response.

Marm caught sight of David in the doorway. She bustled over to him.

"What you want, boy?" she asked him and kept looking back into the room.

"I want ten cents, Marm."

Marm's head snapped around. "You want ten cents? Whyn't you Ma give it to you? She know I ain't got no ten cents."

"She ain't tole me to ask you for it!" David explained hurriedly. "I just thought maybe—"

"Well, God knows I ain't got no money. You don't need none nohow. When I was your size if I had a penny I thought I had sumtin. Y'all children in the city git so rich you wants a dime."

The hymn had ended now. Everyone was listening to Marm at the door. Marm had meant to testify to the full and rich presence of the spirit in her life.

The room was listening to her so she at once began to speak to David and everyone else at the same time.

"Y'all so rich in the city you needs a dime. Just want it for some devilment! Ain't no use no children to have so much anyhow. Got so much nowadays—ain't got no time for God!"

"Amen!" Miss Kitty Creesey cried.

Her cry oiled Marm's tongue. "What y'all needs is more God and less dealing with the devil!"

"Yassuh!" Gramp Dean shouted.

He preached the same doctrine to his son Jerry whenever he could get hold of him. Jerry ran a gambling joint and was seldom at home. His only answer to Gramp was that since he kept Gramp off of the charity rolls, surely he was a good son. And God only wanted you to be as good as you could. You couldn't be perfect. So what?

Gramp shouted "Amen! Yassuh, Jesus!" Then he shook hands with those nearest him.

David cringed back from the door. When you're eight years old, you do not want a room full of people shouting amen about you and your relations with the devil.

As David ran back down the stairs and out into the street, he wondered if the devil helped or hindered the planting of seeds in a back yard.

His father, Jack, was coming up the street. David glanced quickly at his face. Frowns creased his forehead and his mouth was in a straight line. That meant it would be better to lay low. David curved way out to the edge of the sidewalk.

"'Lo, Jack," he offered.

His father spat out in the middle of the street and said nothing.

"Ain't you working today, Jack?" a man called from the steps of the house next door.

"Hell, no!" Jack answered. "Spent my carfare to go way out to that damn place and when I git there they talk about it look like rain and we can't clean no weeds out of no lots!"

"Sure God is awful the way they take your grocery order from you and put you out workin' for a dollar a day, trashing around," the man on the steps declared.

"Jack, gimme a dime!" David could not help trying once more.

Jack turned toward him. "A dime, for what?"

"Some seeds! The teacher, she say—"

"Aw, how the hell you think I gonna give you a dime out of this damn measly dollar a day I get for you to throw away? Here! Go get me two good packages of cigarettes, and if Sam ain't got em, go somewhere's else!"

Jack began to talk to the other man again. "Been buying them a penny a piece all the time when I wasn't working, but now I'll be dogged if I'm gonna let them play me cheap anymore!"

"Damn right!" the other replied and moved up closer to Jack. Maybe he could spin on a web of talk that could hold Jack until David got back. He needed cigarettes himself. Maybe he could bum a few off of Jack.

David moved off down the street. It was four blocks to Mr. Ed's and six blocks to Sam's.

To get to Ed's, you went across Grand Avenue under the "El," passed the "Toot Sweet" Shop with its window full of steel guitars, drums and ukeleles inlaid with mother of pearl. Folks said you could play the horses as well as music in that shop.

Then David stopped and looked in at the knives and diamond rings in Sol's Pawn Palace.

But it was while he was wishing for every pink and yellow cake in the window of Kronen's bake shop that Bennie Jones caught up with him.

"Hi, David!" Bennie cried and slapped David on his shoulder. Gonna buy some of those?"

Bennie was larger than David. He might belong to that gang of older boys who stopped little children on their way to and from the stores and took their money from them.

David was cautious: "Ain't buying nuthin! No money!"

Bennie produced a quarter. "I got money!" he boasted. "I'm buying something!"

David's eye popped. "All dat yours?"

Bennie laughed scornfully. "I takin' some of it. Ma she say give it to Mr. Ed for

473! But she ain't never goin' hit nothin so I takes me some of it every day she sends me down there!"

David's breathing became noisy.

Bennie looked at him shrewdly. "Whyn't you eat up a little of your Ma's dough? Ain't she layin' out nothin today?"

David was eager. "A quarter!"

Bennie swaggered. "Come on, boy! Let me show you de way!" He laughed and swung into the bake shop.

For five cents they each got a bottle of strawberry soda. For five cents they each bought a yellow and pink cake. For five cents more they got ice cream cones.

David gobbled and gulped and looked first up the street and then down as they walked along. He was afraid.

"What you scared of?" Bennie taunted. "Your old lady's hittin' the reefers and she won't know whether the quarter reaches there or not. My Ma, she don't smoke no reefers! She says she ain't fixin' to see no snakes crawling all over her in the bed!"

David choked down a piece of cake so he could answer. "My Ma she ain't seen no snakes in bed neither! I ain't got no snakes in my house! Just roaches and stuff like that!"

Bennie tipped his strawberry soda up to his lips and took a big drink. "You sure is dumb," he told David.

A whistle blew somewhere.

"Gee–min–ity!" yelled Bennie. "Dat's quarter of twelve o'clock. Ma's number had better be in there afore twelve."

He broke into a clopping gallop. David trailed behind him.

Mr. Ed greeted them genially. "How are ya, boys?" he asked. "Come in, come in!"

He stopped to roar at a man who was going out of the door. "Going down the line, Joe? Well—tell 'em about me, boy."

"You got everything!" Joe laughed at him.

"How much your Ma send, Bennie?" Mr. Ed asked. "Only a dime? S'matter with Gert? She can't win nothin' with this chicken feed! She'd ought to play a half a dollar every day!"

David watched the sun breaking into a thousand lights on the diamond of Mr. Ed's stickpin.

"Who are you, boy?" Mr. Ed asked David suddenly.

"David Brown! My Ma she sent a dime too."

Mr. Ed looked at him sharply. "Sure she ain't sent a quarter?"

David swallowed and paled. Bennie looked wise and made a great flurry of picking up slips for David. Then he pushed him out of the door ahead of him.

"That guy must be awful rich," David told Bennie as soon as they were outside. "Did you see them sparklers?"

"Boy, he's the richest man in this town! My father say old Mr. Ed got a couple of million, he bet!" Bennie told him. I'm gonna be rich like him when I'm a man!"

"Me too! I gonna write the numbers when I get big too!" David echoed.

"You too dumb!" Bennie taunted.

"I ain't!"

"You are too. Betcha can't even swear!" To demonstrate, Bennie let loose a group of he-male curses.

David was stumped. He did not know half of that. He stuck his hands in his pockets and hung his head.

Something jingled in his right-hand pocket. Jack's thirty cents was in there.

"What ya got?" Bennie demanded. "Holding out on Mr. Ed and me?"

"Naw. I got to get my pa some cigarettes at Sam's. He's waiting for them!"

And David broke into a run that brought him up breathless to Sam's door. Then, cigarettes in hand, he trotted home.

As he stumbled through the back gate his eyes fell on the garbage, the cans, the paper and trash that littered his back yard.

"Should have bought dem seeds with some of Ma's quarter," David said to himself. "But she'd of wanted to know where I got the dime."

There was nowhere he could say he had gotten a dime for seeds. But he could pinch a little from everything she sent to Mr. Ed's every day, and eat it up.

"I'm sure gonna write numbers myself someday," he promised himself.

"You ain't tough enough!" Bennie's taunts still mocked him.

David picked up a can and threw it against another before he went into the house.

"I am, too, tough!" he yelled aloud in an imagined argument with Bennie. "You dirty ole son of a gun!"

There! He'd remembered one thing Bennie had said.

Holding the cigarettes in his hand like a gun he swaggered up the back stairs. A cat crouched on the top steps.

David aimed a kick at it. "Get the hell out of here," he roared. Then he repeated Bennie's man-sized curse.

Ma yanked the door open. "S'matter with you, boy?" she cried.

David cowered, then he swaggered. "I'm gonna be a number writer!" he told his mother.

A delighted laugh came from her. "G'long, boy! Goin' be rich, too! I have to send you down to Mr. Ed's every day. So you learn somethin!"

David brushed by her and went into the kitchen. "Hey, Jack," he called to his father. "Jack! Gotcha ciggies!... You dirty ole son of a gun," he added under his breath, to his own surprise.

His mother's laugh crackled louder. "Boy, you all right!" she screamed at him. "You *all right.*"

[*Opportunity* 17.1 (January 1939): 18–21]

Across the Line

by Grace W. Tompkins

You couldn't tell, offhand, that Dulcy Marlowe was a Negro. All the white folks, anyway, were fooled. Living in a mixed neighborhood and attending a mixed school, the question of her race was rarely brought up. Her skin was as white and her hair as silky as that of her associates; indeed, she was fairer of face and more Nordic of feature than many. And so, she "passed."

Her four years at the State University were a triumph. She joined a sorority, was nominated to the Mortar Board, served on various campus committees and maintained a straight "A" average. Her schoolmates hated to see her graduate. They sympathized with her because, for some mysterious reason, her mother could not come to the commencement, but applauded heartily when she was handed her diploma.

Armed with her sheepskin, Dulcy went home to Chicago and began to hunt a job. She visited the employment agencies and answered many advertisements.

One ad said:

> "Young woman, college graduate, smart dresser, good at meeting people. No previous experience necessary. Fair salary to start, and opportunity for advancement. Apply Room 310, Louis Building, tomorrow at 10 A.M."

Dulcy applied.

A slim, brown-haired girl in smart black presided over the reception room. A small sign on her desk bore her name, "Miss Hall."

Dulcy, wide-eyed, took in the luxurious appointments of the huge room. This would be a splendid place to work. Ten other girls were seated with her, awaiting their interviews. One by one they were called over by Miss Hall and sent into an inner office marked "Private." One by one they entered, and one by one they left with disappointed faces.

A girl had just gone in when Miss Hall beckoned suddenly to Dulcy.

Her dark eyes were like cool rapiers. Acidly she said, "We don't need any colored help today."

You see, Miss Hall was "passing" too.   [*Opportunity* 17.1 (January 1939): 21]

A Street Car Ride

by Frances Eisenberg

"Hold still, now honey," his mother said, as she stuck Jerry's legs into his little trousers and began buttoning them around the ruffled white blouse. Jerry stopped twisting his head around, trying to see his back. Instead he looked down admiringly at his white shoes. They had belonged to a little boy in a house where his mother worked, but they were almost as good as new, and they were snowy with polish. Once when Mrs. Wilson didn't have enough change she had said, "Here, Katherine, you take these little shoes; Sonny's outgrown them, and you can have them for your little boy. They're worth a lot more than the fifty cents." And although his mother had needed the money more than the shoes, she had taken them, because she didn't like to say anything; Mrs. Wilson had always been so nice.

"Jes wait now, honey, you're gonna look cute as pie!" she exclaimed as she buttoned up the last buttonhole. Jerry's brown face was solemn, but it broke into a smile when his mother backed off exclaiming, "Jes look at him! You never did see anything prettier than that! Stan still, now, son, en don't get your pretty clothes dirty, nen we'll go jes as soon a mamma puts her hat on."

Obediently Jerry stood quiet with his arms still stuck out on each side. "We gonna ride on the street car now, mamma?" he asked breathlessly. He felt so splendid and glittering in his new clothes that he was afraid to move. He was afraid he would tear a hole in them, or the buttons would fall off or something. And yet the thought that pretty soon he'd be on the street car, sitting up straight, looking out of the window like the people he had seen lots of times from the street, made him dizzy with excitement. His head felt as light as a balloon. He had to step down hard to keep his feet still.

"Yeah, when mamma gets her hat on," his mother answered, puffing a little because she was wearing her corset and it made it hard to breathe. She had a different look now—a look that she had only when she was dressed up. All around her middle was as smooth as a board. She had on a black coat suit that sagged at the hem, and a stiff white shirtwaist with a big ruffle sticking out in front. She put a little black hat on top of her head. It was one of Miss Goldie's hats that Mrs. Wilson had given her. "Here, Katherine," she had said. "Here's you an Easter hat. It's almost as good as new." It was a little too small, but it had a bunch of flowers on one side, and a little veil dangled in front.

As she fixed the veil she kept talking to Jerry, warning him about his clothes, partly for the pleasure of talking about them and partly because she felt good to be taking him somewhere, dressed up so cute, on a sunny April afternoon.

"That's right, you stan still, son," she said, "en be real careful; they won't let you ride on the street car if you dirty, nen how will Granma feel, watchin for us en watchin for us en us not come."

"I ain't gonna get dirty, mamma," Jerry assured her, "But you got to let me sit by the window."

"Yeah, if you stay nice and clean you can," his mother promised. "Granma ain't gonna know her little man, honey, you've growed so since she was here. First thing you do, you go up and give granma a big hug so she'll know her little ole boy!"

But all Jerry could think about was the street car.

"When I grow up I gonna run a street car," he cried excitedly. "I gonna ride you en pappa en big granma en grandaddy en Aunt Minnie en anybody else that want to ride. You won't have to pay me nothin either—it'll be free!"

"Lord love him, what's he gonna think of next!" His mother burst into laughter. "Gonna run a street car!"

Jerry, exhilarated by her laughter, skipped along the dirt walk, humming. The mid-afternoon sun shone warmly down. Jim and Edsel were playing by the side of the street in the dust. "Hey, Jerry," they said, standing up and shading their eyes, staring at him. "All dressed up, ain't you? Where you goin?"

"He's goin to see his granma," his mother said, before Jerry had a chance to answer. "She's sick in bed with the flu."

Mrs. Pickett was scrubbing off her front porch. She had a towel pinned around her head; her face was narrow and black between its folds. She straightened her shoulders and waved to Jerry and his mother.

"How you, Mis Jones?" she asked in a high, polite voice. "How you, Jerry boy?" She came on down the walk and stood leaning on her broom. "My, my," she said, smiling down at Jerry, "all dressed up! Ain't he a pretty thing, though! He's gettin to be a sure nough big boy, ain't he?"

"Tell Mis Pickett how old you are, son," his mother prompted him.

"Four, goin on five."

Jerry twisted around and rubbed his feet in the dirt, looking up at Mrs. Pickett. Both the women laughed. "Tell Mis Pickett where you goin," his mother urged him.

"Gonna ride on the street car!" Jerry almost yelled it, forgetting to be shy. "Come on, mamma," he said, tugging at her skirt.

Mrs. Pickett kept beaming at him. "On the *street car*, my, my!"

"The child never has rode on a street car before," his mother explained. "Yes sir, four years old, and ain't never been on a street car! You know most of the time I'm at work en his daddy's at work, and they jest ain't been no chance to take him. He can't get his mind on nothin else. I'm takin him over to Lonsdale to see his granma. She's been laid up in the bed a week and she gets lonesome for company. "Listen, son"—she turned again to Jerry—"Tell Mis Pickett what you gonna do when you get big."

But Jerry wasn't listening. He was looking anxiously down the block where through the gaps between the houses you could see the street cars pass on the other street.

"Tell Mis Pickett what you told mamma jes before we left the house," she prodded. But finally she had to tell it herself, and Mrs. Pickett laughed heartily.

"He's a rounder, ain't he?" she said admiringly.

"He's been spoiled, though," his mother apologized. "The other children is growed up en left us en everybody's made so much over him he thinks he's cock of the walk."

"You gonna let me ride on your street car, ain't you, Jerry?" Mrs. Pickett asked with pretended anxiety.

"Uh huh," Jerry murmured, not listening.

"Uh huh!" his mother said sternly, "What kinda way is that to talk? Where's your manners at? If you don't mind out I'll take you back home without ridin on no street car."

"Yes mam," Jerry corrected himself hurriedly to Mrs. Pickett. Then he whispered, "Mamma, we gonna miss it," several times, but his mother paid no attention. She and Mrs. Pickett began to talk. Mrs. Picket did most of the talking while Jerry's mother listened. "Oh, hush!" she exclaimed every few minutes to show her surprise at what Mrs. Pickett was saying. Jerry couldn't hear, but he didn't care anything about grown folks' talk. He thought about the street car, and wished he could stand by the motorman, and wondered vaguely even, if the motorman liked him, if he would let him drive it. His mother always told him that if he didn't stay nice and clean people wouldn't like him, so he stood very still. And he wished his mother would stop talking and come on.

An old black man, pushing a cart, was coming along the street. He shoved his cart up into the shade and stopped and took off his hat, wiping his sweaty face with a blue handkerchief. He had on a long dirty blue coat with brass buttons down the front. He leaned against the handle of the push cart and looked over at Jerry; his wrinkled face broke into a smile.

"I bet you goin somewheres," the old man said in a high cracked voice. "You all dressed up, son; where you going in nem pretty clothes?"

Jerry walked slowly toward the curb. "I gonna ride on the street car," he almost whispered, finally.

"Sure nough, sure nough!" The old man sounded delighted. He put his hat back on his head and slowly pushed the cart off, chuckling all the time. His skinny shoulder blades stuck out in the back. Jerry was watching him when his mother said, "Come on, honey, we goin now."

As they went down the cross street toward the other street Jerry kept skipping. But when he got on the other street he didn't skip any more.

Once in a while Jerry got to go with his mother to the big store on this street. And he had noticed something funny. On Spruce Street she was talkative and gay, calling to the neighbors, walking so the loose flowers on her hat flopped gaily. But when they turned onto this street where the white people lived, she always pulled Jerry over to the side of the walk. She acted almost as if they weren't supposed to be on that street. And that was funny, because the white people were his mother's friends, and treated her nice. When she came home at night she would tell what Mrs. Wilson had said; and how Mrs. Wilson had given her things. Once when his mother had cleaned up after a party, Mrs. Wilson had given her a big piece of cake and some sandwiches to take home and said, "I don't know what we'd do without you, Katherine."

Jerry always meant to ask her why she acted so different on the other street, but he didn't know how to say it. Today he was too excited to bother.

"We'll be on that old car in a few minutes now," his mother told him. And just then a humming sound came from away down the track, and over the top of the hill came the yellow street car. Its wheels made a lot of racket on the rails. Jerry clutched his mother's hand and ran toward the stop. "Hurry, mamma," he begged frantically, "Hurry, hurry, hurry, we're gonna miss it!"

But they got there just in the nick of time.

The motorman on the three-twenty car was a big fat man named Gus Hinkle, and this afternoon his face was red and worried. A truck had got stalled on the track on his last trip in, and he had had to wait for a passenger besides. In all he had lost twenty-two minutes. He stepped down hard on the claxon and clanged down Henson Avenue, praying that the tracks would stay clear and that he could make it on into town without stopping much. He hated the Henson Avenue line—so many Negroes rode it—and if you didn't watch them in the afternoons they would take the whole car. And he hated his work anyway; he had been raised on a farm, and he hadn't ever been satisfied since he left it. All he wanted now was to get back to the country again, where you didn't have to be afraid of losing your job just because you got a few minutes behind schedule.

At the corner of Henson and Home Street he had to stop and wait for a colored woman and a kid. Frowning, he watched the kid pulling his mother along by the hand; and he clanged impatiently as they climbed up the steps. The woman gave him half a dollar, fumbling in an old black purse as if she didn't want to part with the money. He jabbed his thumb down on the changer and shelled out the tokens. She would want a transfer; they always did, he thought. He jerked one off the pad. All the time the little dark-faced boy stood staring at him, and grinning, holding tightly onto the iron rail. It irritated him. He thought the kid was trying to act smart, and if there was anything he hated it was a smart Negro, big or little. He frowned, but the kid kept on looking up at him until his mother grabbed his hand and pulled him along toward the back of the car.

Before they had got past the first three seats the kid jerked loose and plopped down in one next to the window. He sat up straight, looking up at his mother. "Here where I gonna sit, mamma!" he said loudly.

"No, son," his mother said in a shocked tone. "We going further back."

"No, I gonna sit here! You said I could if I stayed clean."

Before she had time to get him up the motorman had looked up in his mirror and seen him sitting there.

"Sassy little black boy," he thought in a burst of fury, "spoiled as hell. All diked up like a white kid; gonna grow up into one of them fresh niggers that's too smart for their britches!"

"You git that kid up from there and take him back where he belongs!" he yelled to the woman.

The woman opened her mouth to talk back, but she must have thought it wasn't any use, because all she said was, "Come on," to the kid.

Gus kept watching in the mirror and he could see the little boy's smile change to a shocked expression as he scrambled down and followed his mother through the swaying aisle to the last seat in the car. He kept turning his head and looking back at Gus as if he couldn't believe that he had heard him right.

Suddenly Gus's anger left him, and he would have given a lot not to have hollered out like that and scared the kid.

"Might as well learn his place now as any other time," he said apologetically over his shoulder to the man who was sitting behind him on the long seat. "Inspector come on here and find niggers sitting in the front of the car, my job wouldn't be worth two cents!"

He waited almost anxiously for the man to agree. But the man didn't say anything.

Gus turned his head quickly, and the fellow was looking at him with an expressionless face, but Gus could tell what he was thinking, and suddenly he could feel it all behind him in the air, the unspoken disapproval, and he was afraid to look around. Or course nobody could *say* anything, but he could tell, and he knew that a lot of white passengers were like that man; they were *for the little colored boy*. He could feel them thinking. "That was a mean thing to do, to scare that little kid and holler at the woman like that. She would of got him where he belonged in just a minute."

Gus was so surprised that his thoughts were in a whirl. White people taking up for Negroes! He kept his eyes on the track and tried to forget the passengers behind him. But the unspoken hostility made him uncomfortable, and he felt hurt that they should think him mean. He wouldn't have hollered so loud only his nerves were on edge, and everybody knew that it was his job to make Negroes go back where they belonged.

He'd worked colored hands down on the farm, and he knew how it was. As long as you didn't let them forget they were black it was all right. But give them an inch, and they'd take a mile.

"I wouldn't of scared that kid," he thought defensively. "I like Negroes in their places. I don't think you can beat a good old fashioned southern nigger. But damit, nowadays they're gettin too smart. You've gotta hold em down or they'll run all over you. These people don't understand 'em like I do, or they'd know how it is. They're thinkin about this kid here like he was a white kid, just because he's dressed up like a white kid. But clothes don't change his skin. The Negroes is gonna take this whole country if we don't pin down on 'em. They've got to be learnt their place, and the time to learn 'em is when they're young."

But he kept his eyes away from the mirror so he wouldn't see the rows of faces behind him, or the little dark-skinned boy who was now sitting in the middle of the long seat in the back. He didn't look as if he was enjoying the ride at all; his back was to the window, and his short legs in their white shoes and pink socks were stuck out in front of him. Whenever the car hit a rough spot he braced himself with both hands and nearly fell over. He had a puzzled look on his face, and you could see that he was thinking hard about something. [*Opportunity* 16.12 (December 1938): 362–365]

HALL OF LIBERTY

by Manet Fowler

All the while Miss Rauber was talking, there in front of Halton Hall—while white Miss Rauber was fumbling and struggling for words—brown Linda Payne was trying to think, and to avoid seeing the pictures. It was hard to think, to form the phrases that should answer, "*Yes, it's all right, Miss Rauber, I understand; I understand you're not to blame; yes, I understand your position perfectly!*" It was difficult to voice the phrases that would say 'all right' to Miss Rauber calmly, without revealing that the pictures were there now, pictures that went together to make it futile for Linda to listen, that made Linda want Miss Rauber to stop talking and please to go away somewhere, quickly.

Singly, the pictures had been important enough, and each had hurt at its own time. But now Miss Rauber was talking about her sorority. She was saying, "You know I'm sorry, Linda; you know it's not *my* fault; you know that *I* like you, don't you, Linda?" And as she talked the pictures blended into disquieting mental views of pervading scenery—quickly, consecutively, easily fused in the hazy autumnal blur, among the shedding campus trees, before the carefully-blocked entrance of Halton Hall. Together, merged one after the other like that, they hurt more.

If it had not been for what Mother and Father, at home in Lowie, in the South, had thought, and for what the Dean, here at Marston University, in the North, had said, the pictures would not have wounded so deeply. But Mother and Father had planned rigidly on Marston. They lived in a small Southern city, had a comfortable home, a fair income, a car, and some white friends who were very broad-minded. And they had Linda. But with all of their "position," they could not escape entirely the raw Southern prejudices—and when Linda was graduated with honors from high school, Mother and Father had decided to send her to Marston University: *she* would learn to feel the glow of Northern equality, even though her parents might never quite escape the hateful condescension of their homeland.

At the University the Dean was particularly respected and famous, for in a conservative world Marston was known everywhere as a liberal institution and for this he was largely responsible. The Dean was spoken of as a liberal, but not a radical. It was his opinion that one could be liberal and have brilliantly expressed opinions as to free speech and human rights (for all men *are* created equal, my friends) and even as to labor's persistent fight—as long, of course, as one didn't go too far....

As Miss Rauber swallowed her words, Linda remembered that it was on the first day at the University, in late September, that the Dean had made his initial address at the Freshman Assembly. It was difficult to forget its resolved impressiveness, for the Dean was liberal, and he spoke his views fearlessly and brilliantly.

On the first day of school the Marston University auditorium had been filled with young people—some eager, with believing naiveté, some nonchalant with the boredom of youthful sophistication. Their massed faces were like pale chalk areas in the hall's dark gloom—all some shade of white but Linda's—with all colors of hair, lips, and eyes, and all shapes of noses and chins. Linda's alone was the face distinctive for its tawniness—an oval with soft black eyes and small but opulent lips like inverted half-moons in vermillion.

All the faces were turned toward the tall, ascetically thin Dean, as he brushed the stiff gray hair from his narrow-lined forehead with one hand; the crowd was looking expectantly as his short triangular beard bristled, as the long bony fingers of the other white hand gripped tensely the pedestal-edges.

The first pep-talks had been not too interesting, nor the freshmen too attentive. A soft-voiced flow of polite inanities had been released by a correctly gracious Dean of Women, fashionable in navy with touches of white; a wisecracking 'hello,' had been offered glibly by the stocky, clean-faced, red-haired boy who was Student Council president; a brief welcome had come from the blue-eyed girl chairman of the Women's Assembly; and, before the Dean stood, one rousingly tuneful chorus of the University-song, *Hail to Marston, Hall of Liberty*, had been sung by the class. Then the Dean had spoken. The freshmen listened, for his voice was weighted with tones rich and full, and the splendor of his final phrases resounded against the dismal paneled walls.

"You should know," the Dean said slowly, "that Marston University is in its very essence a democratic institution. With a disregard for the world outside that pains sometimes, with understanding knowledge of some unpleasant conditions in Europe—of some, yes, in America—we at our University shall remain free and equal men and women.

"Our doors are open to all who come; to all who try to make the best of their opportunity. At Marston you are one body; one group of seekers for truth, without thought or concern for races, creeds, or religions. We welcome you all here; we invite you to make the most of what Marston has to offer!"

Linda's cheers had joined those of the other five hundred freshmen, with enthusiasm, with grateful joy for the Dean's words. His expression was confirmation for Mother and Father: this university was different; everything was different from home. How different was the Dean from Mr. Wagstraw, for instance!

Mr. Wagstraw was president of the white school-board at home, and Linda remembered his address at her high school commencement. When fat Mr. Wagstraw spoke to or of Negroes he always said "you people," for Mr. Wagstraw was the kind of Southerner who could know no black-*and*-white 'we.' Still, Dr. Hogan, the dark-skinned principal of Douglass, had been obviously pleased that Mr. Wagstraw had actually come to speak to the graduates. It was a fine thing for Mr. Wagstraw to do, just as it was fine for the city to let its Negro citizens use the Municipal Auditorium for the exercises, for the first time in history. Yes, Linda thought, the white Marston Dean was certainly different from white Mr. Wagstraw at home; that made being at Marston good.

After the Dean had finished his speech the freshmen had plodded toward the huge brass seal-engraved doors. Outside, as the chatting groups separated, the September sun was shining, a cool breeze was beginning to stir, and the sky was clean and crystal blue.

The crisp currents of air felt good on her cheeks as Linda walked briskly across the campus to Halton Hall, Marston's women's dormitory, to register for her room. She had been thinking about this during the assembly, though there was no real need to hurry; the deposit had been mailed the required three months before, the receipt returned, and her registration accepted.

At the Hall the clerk came quickly when she saw the colored girl standing near the warm glow of the desk-lamp, between the two dull green artificial palms. As she hastened, many incoming residents were passing through the lobby, filling it with their pleasant chatter. Reaching the desk, the clerk nodded, smiled mechanically at Linda, and asked, "May I help you?"

"Yes, thank you," answered Linda, proffering the deposit-slip, "I'm a freshman, and I came to complete arrangements for my room."

The clerk was surprised; she did not smile any more. Fingering the deposit-slip, she looked at Linda, troubled.

"I'm very sorry, Miss Payne," she stammered finally, "but evidently there's some mistake; I'm sure there is. I'm sorry, but we really have no room here; you see, we're always overcrowded; perhaps that's where the mistake came."

But Linda could not understand such a mistake; how could there be a mistake when the deposit-slip had been mailed to Mother three months before? How could there be a mistake when the slip said that all one had to do was pay the remainder of the fee and get the room?

"It *is* unfortunate," comforted the clerk, "but the University has a list of approved boarding-residences; we shall find you a room, I am sure. Oh, yes," she said, glancing at the list, "Mrs. Mae Johnson has a room; that's at 225 First Place, Rosemont. I'm sure you'll be happier and more comfortable there, Miss Payne, and the University will return your deposit."

Nothing else could be done. That was the first day, after the Dean's speech, and

Linda was a little tired, and now, a little worried; but she climbed aboard one of the tall buses at the edge of the campus and took a trip to Rosemont.

Mrs. Johnson's home was clean and pleasantly furnished, and Rosemont apparently was the city's most pleasant suburb populated primarily by Negroes. But Rosemont was an hour's ride from the University; Halton Hall only a few minutes' walk across the campus!

The three other girls at Mrs. Johnson's were all Negroes (was that what the clerk had meant by being 'happier and more comfortable?') and two years before, Linda soon found, they too had been sent to Rosemont from a Marston dormitory because of a 'mistake.' Now they no longer needed to be sent; they came automatically, and they revealed few collegiate ambitions.

"You'd better make yourself contented," one of them advised the newcomer, "with getting all you can from your courses at the University. Forget about activities; you'll only be shoved around politely if you go out for that sort of thing, and you'd have a better time, with less worry and expense, at a good movie!"

Linda refused to listen; had not the Dean spoken? It was simply a matter of personal initiative, the Dean had said, for they were all welcome. Some people were always trying to take the joy from life; pessimists!

It was only when the first letter from Mother came that she began to wonder. Mother said, quite proudly, that mild Dr. Hogan wanted to put a piece in the paper about Linda's going to Marston, and had written the University to discover how many of the students were Negroes. The registrar had written the Douglass principal that he was sorry, but "Marston University keeps no records of the races of her students."

Mother was happy. Dr. Hogan was too submissive, and that letter was good to show him what type of school Linda was going to in the North. But Linda was puzzled; she remembered clearly that one blank on the University's registration-card was for race, another for religion. She had filled the former blank with *Negro* and the latter with *African Methodist Episcopal*. She would not tell Mother, but the University did have a record. It was strange that the registrar should write Dr. Hogan that letter, though the Dean had said that they were one body ... without concern....

It was not long after Mother's letter had come that the pictures had begun to form, in rapid, periodic sketches. Linda had to believe finally the girls at Mrs. Johnson's. Classes had been all right—efficient, impersonal, but all right generally—and some of the Jewish girls, especially, were friendly. Some intervals were unbelievably pleasant, but even these were broken, and shadowed, and were now being erased, as the important hurting things formed the pictures. Marston University had given them quietly to Linda Payne. They were moving, character-ful pictures. They would not go away easily. Each had hurt at its own time.

There was one picture, in the registration room adjacent to the Marston Gymnasium—dreary, closet-like; an undraped window, a dark brown desk for the swimming-coach, a table for the gym-assistant, stiff wooden chairs for waiting registrants:

Linda stood at the desk, the admission-card for swimming in her hand. The coach, her stringy blonde hair closely cropped, was busily signing the cards, thrust before her in mechanical routine by young tapered white fingers. But this hand with a card—Linda Payne's hand—was slim-fingered, but dark. After a vacant pause, the coach's whispered, hesitant snatches of words came.

"It's highly unfortunate ... but Miss Payne, you, are, frankly, the first Negro girl

to register for swimming in several years ... so it's likely that you'll put in practice-hours—well, alone—under Miss Jones, coach at the Recreation Center's pool, Rosemont.

"Of course, it's not really the University's fault ... the University merely leases the Liberty Women's Association pool, and the LWA just will not allow Negroes to swim there. However, if you could come in once a week, with your hours signed by Miss Jones, the University ... will accredit them, I am sure ... without inconvenience."

Listening to the coach, Linda Payne wondered, why must the University lease only the LWA pool? There must be other pools the University could have leased! But she took her card to the Recreation Center in Rosemont, and met Miss Jones—and that was all there was to the first picture: she took the card; she went back to Rosemont; she met Miss Jones.

But there were more pictures; even in the gym there came another—in the gray-walled gym, where the hooped baskets were stretched high above Linda, sitting, excited and happy, with other blue-rompered, soft-shod girls on floor-mats, awaiting anxiously try-outs for the varsity basketball-squad. Linda was neither nervous nor afraid. She had been the mainstay as captain of the Douglass Girls' Five at home; while practicing in the gym, she had seen the other girls at Marston play.

The try-outs! Linda made the basket three times in five minutes. Playing vigorously forward, center, guard, by command. When she heard last year's observant varsity captain murmur to a companion, "That colored girl—simply stunning, the way she plays!" she was glad, and confident.

But when the coach read the list of those chosen—twice she read the list—she did not announce Linda Payne's name. It was in the shower rooms afterwards that Linda, disappointed, overheard the gym-assistant, absently commenting,

"It's a shame about the colored girl, isn't it?... Seemed to have great stuff ... but better, after all, I suppose, to eliminate her now, than to have all the row later with the Southern contracts!"

In a class was formed a third picture, one that wounded especially, because Professor Butler was one of Linda's favorite teachers. He had never done anything like this in class before. Professor Butler was interesting, and his classes were usually crowded; hundreds of seats, each taken, every day. But on the front row, Linda knew that this day's lecture was not going over well. Short, red-faced, his rapidly-graying hair fringing his bald head, the teacher's loud coarse voice droned monotonously, singsong, chanting. The class was restless—rattling papers, moving around, talking in undertones—until Professor Butler told the joke.

Worried Professor Butler told a Negro dialect-joke, about "lazy Rastus and his fat black Mandy"; of Mandy and her wash-tubs; of Rastus and his eternally occupied mattress. Professor Butler could not do the Negro dialect well—that made it worse—but he looked beyond Linda, staring at him from the first row, as he blandly continued his joke. Most of the people in the class were Jews: Adler, Blumenfeld, Cohen. Linda felt them all staring now, staring at the back of her neck. Professor Butler, red and nervous because they did not laugh, grinned himself, alone.

During one of the routine conferences Linda was talking with the Dean of Women in her office. Without mentioning Professor Butler's name, Linda spoke of this incident, telling the Dean of Women that the teacher's recitation of a Negro joke like that troubled and hurt her very much. The Dean of Women seemed a little annoyed as she answered Linda quietly, saying only,

"It is unfortunate, Miss Payne, that things are, well, as they undoubtedly are. I myself have some charming Negro acquaintances and I am very much in sympathy with the Negro people; but I believe that you will be much happier if you will learn to accept certain things without worrying about them. That's really the only consolation I know to give."

Linda went home to Mrs. Johnson's with a headache. The Dean of Women! She would never understand how 'Miss Payne' detested trying to accept the things, though the other girls at Mrs. Johnson's said that was the most convenient solution to the problem. But Linda could never truly accept them, not as they were, and she did not think she ought to.

There had come finally this latest picture. Because it was just formed, today in the Rose Lounge in Halton Hall, it was more searingly vivid than the rest.

It was Rush Week at school, and the note Linda found with her mail at Mrs. Johnson's yesterday had said, "Pi Zeta Phi invites you cordially to tea in the Rose Lounge, Halton Hall, Friday, at three."

Pi Zeta Phi? Marston's "sorority of the blessed," the girls said. Linda was overwhelmed. At three, she joined gaily the long trails of girls moving across the campus to Halton Hall. Lightly she walked up the low concrete steps to the Hall, and through the opened door of the Lounge.

The Lounge was beautiful. Soft lamp-light cast friendly shadows along the shrimp-tinted walls, and a large ivory floor-vase stood in one corner, with tall blue delphinium pointing. At the windows were the creamy heavy sateen curtains piped in rose and navy. There were the small navy and ivory leather lounge-chairs; the tea-table, decorated with the brass flower-bowl in its center, the tall lighted candles, and the tea-service, with the sorority-sisters standing carelessly, graciously superior, about it.

The room was filled with guests; some girls, sitting at small tables chatting idly, to stifle the nervousness of conscious social inspection, others standing and smoking.

Linda entered. The pleasant chatter ceased. Activity was interrupted. As she sat in a chair, the girls' eyes fastened upon her, until one of the group at the tea-table approached competently. That was Miss Rauber, Miss Rauber in the American history class.

Embarrassed, Miss Rauber spoke to Linda hurriedly, of class trivialities, of anything, until she whispered,

"Could I see you outside for a minute, Linda?"

They walked, casually on the surface, toward the entrance. Cool, efficient, brilliant Miss Rauber's face was flushed when they stood outside; she stammered even.

Now Miss Rauber was talking; groping floundering, trying to find the best words.

"You don't know how rotten this makes me feel, Linda," Miss Rauber was saying. "You just couldn't know.... Well—really—I don't understand how it could have happened.... It isn't that I mind—you know that, Linda—but, well, it's just a rule; it's just a rule of our sorority, that we don't have—mixed races!"

Linda Payne was hearing Miss Rauber. Stilled at the entrance, her back to the door of the Lounge, she knew that she should say something; she should do something. She was trying to think of the phrases that would say 'all right' calmly, but she could not answer Miss Rauber. She could barely raise her eyes and gaze across the campus—seeing only the mental pictures forming rapidly, together, merged in the fall shadow among the trees.

Miss Rauber could not look at Linda. It was terrible to have to break such news. Miss Rauber could only touch Linda lightly on the arm and go back into the now strained atmosphere of the Lounge.

Miss Rauber had gone. Why was Linda standing here with her back to the entrance, seeing only pictures, seeing only faces?—the Marston Dean, a mask of sincere belief; obese, coldly prejudiced, Southern Mr. Wagstraw; white-haired, coldly indifferent Northern Dean of Women; red, coarse-voiced, grinning Professor Butler; suffering, helplessly apologetic Miss Rauber—she had told Linda and now she had gone; and the blithely beaming chorus shouting in the beginning, on the first day, a loud, enclosing refrain, *Hail to Marston, Hall of Li-ber-tee!*

From the beautiful Lounge, where the sorority's "rushed" Italians, Spaniards, Russians, Americans, Germans, one Chinese, and a few Jews gracefully drank their tea—from the Lounge came to Linda's ears the unconcerned laughter of the girls, recovering now a pleasant time. She did not feel the hate at once, but instantly, sharply, spontaneously it came. She had never had it before, this bitter green hate the rising, cramping, from within her: stupid contemptible white fools—their frank open contempt was no worse than their smug insidious hypocrisy!

She must do something.... She must say something.... Don't stand here muted staring into the haze.... Linda heard the young happy white laughter behind her and she ran. She could suddenly voice the phrases, but there was no need—Miss Rauber had gone. She had stopped talking, she had gone, and Linda had stopped trying to think. Choking, blinded, and stumbling through the tall trees, across the green-grassed, cement-walked campus, Linda ran wildly, artlessly, down the short concrete steps, for there was nowhere she wanted to run. There was nowhere she could run, really. Everywhere—at home, at Marston—everywhere everything was the same.

[*Opportunity* 16.4 (April 1938): 112–115, 121]

INCIDENT

by A'lelia Ransom

The day had a dark, hurt look about it, as though the busy wind had lashed it too hard; and the countryside, stripped and barren, lay desolate. Down the narrow road a rickety bookbinder's wagon, with its gaudy advertisements, creaked along. Its driver suddenly bade his horses rest a while and turned lazily this way then that, surveying the land. Relighting his pipe with one hand, he pulled out his watch with the other and gazed at it speculatively. His face, hardened, yet with a self-satisfied expression, looked as though it had stood the lashing of innumerable strong winds and sharp cross-currents through the years.

A cry like that of a hurt dog stirred him into action. He hurried to the rear of his wagon, lifted the piece of worn canvas that covered it completely, and looked inside.

Two of the fugitive slaves he had picked up a few hours earlier lay huddled up against the cart-side, weary, hunted looks on their sleeping faces. The third lay in the center of the narrow space. Her young body now was racked with pain, her lips were raw and bleeding from her agonized biting of them. Low moans escaped her swollen mouth, while her skeleton-like hands pressed frantically against her body.

The man's weather-beaten face twitched unconsciously, as though he felt one of the quick spasms of pain that caught her at intervals. He roused one of the fugitives, an old crone, and commanded her to take charge of the situation.

Her hands moved swiftly; she had often served as midwife in the slave quarters. Besides, hadn't she had fourteen of her own, and only once asked help from neighbors?

But this creature was just a child. That added mystery to the situation. Why did she want to escape? Usually young slave girls were pets of the Miss or Mistress on the plantation. They had no drudgery. The old woman frowned as she went about her task. If she were young, she'd gladly stay down South.

The man turned away as the ugly little mulatto handful uttered its first cry. He spat contemptuously at the underbrush beside the road. The thought came to him vaguely that he was crazy to be shielding these fugitives from their pursuers; he was a Southerner through and through; he believed that colored men were made to work, colored women to be pawed and kissed.

He climbed up, perched himself on his seat, coaxed the horses to go, and spat again. Maybe he was just too sentimental! What fool notion made him want to shield from harm the weakened, dark-skinned creature being jogged along behind him, and her baby and her friends?

The thought came to him then of a warm spring night in the old slave quarters. And he heard again the low, melodious voice of a young girl as she crooned to him the songs from her heart that had no words....

So what? The baby was even yellow, it was bound to look like him!

He drew a plug of tobacco from his pocket, bit a slug as the horses rounded a bend in the road. Then he spat again. [*Opportunity* 16.5 (May 1938): 147]

NOTHING CHANGES

by Mary Louise Bohanon

Simon Reese swung from the door of the bus into the fine mist of rain which was obviously the residue of a long determined rainy season in Spring Junction, Alabama.

218 Nothing Changes (*Bohanon*)

The court square was practically deserted. There was one man to greet Simon—Lee Kirk, the colored and only taxi driver in the Spring Junction. Lee hailed Simon boisterously.

"Waal, if it ain't ole Si! What you doin' back heah? I thought you had gone to Detroit to stay," he said, taking Simon's suitcase and leading him to the little worn second-hand car. "Mah, but you've changed," he added before Simon could answer him.

"Well, you surely look the same," said Simon. "How are Ma and Pa?"

"Oh, they's fine," said Lee, starting the car. "In fact, I seen yo' Pa t'othah day. Come in to sell his cotton. Idd ain't changed a bit."

"Did he have much cotton?" Simon inquired.

"Quite smart," admitted Lee. "Although 'tain't much profit in cotton this year, you know. But what you doin' heah? Gonna stay now?"

"No, I just came back to see the folks and the place," Simon answered.

"Waal, 'tain't changed none. 'Less it's wuss. Folks jest livin' the best way they kin. Still workin' in the fact'ry?"

"Yes, but I got a few days off. Have the schools started here yet?"

"No, they hasn't. They nevah starts 'till aftah cotton's been picked. Listen at me! Heh, Heh! Tellin' you that, when you wuz bo'n and brought up heah. You hasn't forgot it, has you?"

"No, I'm sure I haven't."

"Le's see now, it's been 'bout fifteen years since you was heah, ain't it?"

Simon nodded. From the car he noticed the familiar landmarks as they jogged along. In the distance he could see the tall pine trees standing like huge green statues, unbending in their vigil.

"Yes, just fifteen years this Christmas."

"Went away foh yo' Christmas present, eh? I thought it hadn't been any mo' than that. You sho' must like it up there in Detroit."

Lee pressed the clutch down to the floor and eased his foot on the brake as he leaned far out the window trying to see into the little yard which they were approaching.

"I b'lieve that's Sylvy ovah there now. Yes, that's you Ma. Did Sylvy know you wuz comin'?"

But Simon was no longer listening to Lee's chatter. He had begun to pick up his bag and was waving frantically from the window of the car.

"I brought you somethin', Sylvy!" Lee called to the small wizened woman in the front of the yard.

The worn little car jerked to a stop and Simon jumped out. He jammed a coin into Lee's hand and dashed up the path to Sylvy, who was still unable to recognize just who he was. Then he had Sylvy in a big bear hug and was showering her shiny dark face with kisses. Sylvy was mumbling, "Son, Son," in a full voice. Lee yelled something about Simon's looking well, but seeing that no one noticed him he drove off down the road, in a hurry to spread the news he had gathered.

* * *

Simon had been in Spring Junction for one week. He knew everything there was to know. Sylvy, his mother, was growing older. Idd, his father, had always been old, but now his eyes had that sort of neutral color that is characteristic of age. The crop had been plentiful, but so had everyone's cotton crop. "Too much on hand," the man at the gin had said. "Can't pay much for it this year."

Idd was tired—no pain, just tired. Couldn't work like he used to. But he had managed to get the cotton planted and picked and peanuts all bagged and ready for selling. He hadn't been surprised when he had been unable to sell his crop at a profit. It had always been that way. Just when they thought they were getting along all right something happened. Seemed like they just had bad luck and would always have it.

Lee was right—nothing had changed, the same cornbread, the same grits, the same fat back. He didn't like fat back any more but he had eaten it because he hadn't wanted Sylvy to feel bad. She'd cooked a lot of it; the very sight of it had made him ill.

He'd also pretended that he was very anxious to hear all the Spring Junction gossip. Funny how unimportant Spring Junction news seemed now. Simon remembered when he would have been interested in Sally Lee's having another husband but not in her having another baby. Now what interested him most was what was going to happen to Sally's new baby. She must have about seven kids by now. He wondered if the latter ones walked on spindle-like legs as the others had. He supposed they did. Sylvy was asking more questions. He must keep her interested in what he had been doing.

"What did you say, Ma?" asked Simon, feigning interest.

"Ah said hain't it cold up there? You know Kate Davis sent foh Cress. She 'lowed she wuzn't goin' to let Cress stay up there. Aftah all, he's all she's got. She said we oughta send foh you but I tole her that you'd done been gone too long to wanta come back heah where there ain't nothin' but ole folks. But Ah ain't goin' to keep none o' mine back, as much as Ah'd like them to stay. 'Cose ain't none left heah but you. Johnnie and Mamie seems satisfied with Spring Junction. Sometime Ah wish you'd a' stayed ... seems like you don't never git home. And when you do 'tain't long befo' you thinkin' 'bout goin' back. Heah you are leavin' day aftah tomorrer."

"But, Ma, you know I've got to get back to my job," said Simon consolingly.

"Waal, anyway you can go to church with me tomorrer," continued Sylvy, as if Simon hadn't said anything. "Ah wants you to heah the Rev. Mr. Starks. He sho' preaches good."

* * *

When he was small Sunday had been Simon's one day of rest and fun. He had lived for Sunday when he could see everybody and talk about—well, just anything. Now he actually hated to see Sunday come. He hoped that Ma wouldn't prepare lunch and plan to spend the day at church as they had done when he was small.

This Sunday everybody was up bright and early and even Idd forgot to complain about the times or his hard luck. Mamie and Johnnie were coming with their families to dinner so Sylvy said that they wouldn't take a lunch to church. Simon was glad to hear this.

On the way to church in the old wagon, which was made into a vehicle with rumble seats of cane chairs on Sunday, and used for hauling on work days, Simon chose to sit in the rumble seat. The sun was very hot and the wagon rattled as if it would come apart any moment. Sylvy and Idd said little as they rode along and Simon began to wonder what they were thinking. Both their shoulders were stooped and grooved where sacks of cotton had lain and been toted from field to house. From where Simon sat there was scarcely a motion to indicate that Idd was driving the wagon.

Simon looked around the countryside for visible changes. There was a path which led to the spring. Many a time he had gone down that path. That was before Idd had had the well dug. Often he had had to go at night because he had forgotten to bring his water in. He would run most of the way, especially when it was raining. The nights were so dark then. Sometimes after he had gotten to the spring he would sit down, hating to come back into the open road. He'd never sat for long because it had been too dark.

"Is that spring still down there?" asked Simon, pointing towards the path.

"Huh?" said Sylvy, startled from her dozing. "Oh yes, but Mistah Ollie Schmitt owns that land now and we ain't 'lowed in there."

Sylvy went back to her dozing as the wagon rattled on. They were coming around the bend in the road and Simon caught sight of the little church. He could see the people walking from the other direction. He wondered how far they had come—eight or ten miles maybe. Then he smiled, thinking how seldom he went to church in Detroit and it was just around the corner from where he stayed. He supposed that he had gotten out of the habit of going.

By this time Idd had driven the wagon inside the churchyard and Simon could see small groups discussing his being back in Spring Junction. The youngest group didn't know him but they were being told all the particulars by the others. For the first time Simon felt as if the people were reading his thoughts. No one had looked upon him as a stranger but he had sensed that he was from the moment he had gotten off the bus. Now these children looked and saw what he had so carefully tried to hide. Simon hopped down from his chair and turned quickly to help Sylvy. In helping her he noticed how very small she was. He could see the pride in her eyes as she placed one hand on his arm and three of them walked across the yard into the church.

Inside the building Simon regained that self-assurance which the youngsters had taken from him. The Rev. Mr. Starks was sing-songing the hymn raised to common meter, while the audience followed in their differently pitched tunes. All heads turned to the back of the church to note the incoming members. Simon bowed and smiled to those whom he knew and stood waiting for Sylvy and Idd to be seated.

After taking his seat, Simon began to consider the Rev. Mr. Starks. He would have known "His Reverence" anywhere—not as Mr. Starks but as The Reverend. His stiff white collar and his ankle-length trousers gave him away. Simon would have bet that the Reverend Mr. Starks carried a brief case. At present he was warning the congregation about "the wages of sin," "Daniel in the Lion's Den," and "the eternal damnation" of those people who played cards and danced, all in the same breath. Somehow Simon found it difficult to follow him. He finally gave it up and went to musing about the people in the church.

He noticed the hungry look on their faces. They reminded him of small sparrows—mouths open—waiting. Large unseemly chunks were being poked down their mouths, yet they nodded for more and more. Choked to the bursting point, they yelled out for relief—shouting, moaning and crying. This was what the Reverend Mr. Starks wanted. His voice, which had been loud and accusing, now became soft and soothing in its picture of the streets of gold running with milk and honey. Slowly but deliberately he asked for money—hard earned money—cotton money. He needed a new suit—the convention would be meeting soon. Simon felt as he had when he had eaten Sylvy's fat back. He watched Sylvy's worn knotty hand reach into her shabby purse and draw out a dollar. He wanted to shout—not as they had shouted but in revolt against this religion, against this poor sustaining force which had once kept him going and which now bled his people of money needed for other purposes. He started as he felt a gentle tap on his shoulder. Sylvy was telling him to take the collection plate that the Deacon was passing.

As Simon put a coin into the basket Sylvy said, "He's sho good, ain't he, Simon?" Behind the tears deep-seated faith filled Sylvy's eyes.

Simon swallowed slowly, tears came to his own eyes as he answered, "Yes, Ma, I guess you're right." Then he added quickly, "I've got an awful headache, Ma. Do you mind if I go on and walk down the road a piece? The air might do me good."

Sylvy looked wonderingly at Simon. "Why yes, that's all right, son, but don't forget Mamie and Johnnie's comin' for dinner."

* * *

Simon walked slowly down the road, shuffling his feet in the clods of red clay. He now began to realize just how tired of it all he was. The little church had seemed so closed in—so smothering. The long road stretching in front of him made him feel free. Suddenly he began to run. How long or why he ran he never knew. Faster and faster he ran until the hot air seemed to push against him. He'd once tried swimming upstream, had fought the current bravely, then had given it up—run out of the stream and stood on the banks trembling. As abruptly as he had once stopped swimming, he stopped running now and stood trembling. He dragged his feet along the road, looking for a shady place to rest.

Finally he came to a little shack of a building sitting a short distance off the road. Surrounded by trampled pine brush, it truly resembled some lost article no longer hunted for. Coming closer to the little building Simon noticed an opening which faintly resembled a window. Strips of pasteboard had been tacked in the opening to keep out the rain and hail. Torn strips of a flour sack curtain hung from the window, beaten to shreds from constant flapping back and forth. Cut into the side of the shack which faced the road was a door. Just below the door was a sewer pipe, the flat kind, placed to break one step as he entered. Over the top of the door was a sign which read "Ward School No. 2."

Simon stood looking at the building as if he were seeing it for the first time. Yet he knew the building as well as anyone in Spring Junction. He had spent a large portion of his life here, before he had gone to Detroit. Until now fifteen years seemed a long time, but now he felt as if he had never gone away. Lee was surely right! There weren't any changes—same place—same ideas!

Simon walked into the yard of the little school and sat on the tile step. The little peach tree, nearly crowded out by those massive pines, was still there. He had planted that little tree. He remembered that the kids had laughed at him and had told him that it would never grow, that there were too many pines for his little tree to have a chance. There was always too many of everything! Once when he had wanted a job he had been told that there were too many whites out of work for him to hope. But the little tree had grown and Sylvy said that she had gotten a dozen peaches from it last summer.

It had been fifteen years since he had gone to Ward School No. 2. Miss Rush, who was still there, had been his teacher. He supposed that she taught the same things in the same way. Miss Rush had received a certificate for something, but Mr. Roberts, the county superintendent, had said that she would have to do something else to get a diploma. Simon wondered if Miss Rush had ever gotten her diploma. She never went to school or anything and she was always scared to death of Mr. Roberts. Especially that day when Mr. Roberts had come to visit the school.

Simon knew that he would never forget that visit. They had known somebody was coming because Miss Rush had been nervous all that morning. She hadn't gone over the new lesson either but had said that there would be a review. The children were all excited because the white superintendent never came. He always sent to the colored supervisor, who never said anything that Miss Rush seemed to understand. They generally argued when they got together.

Mr. Roberts had come about one o'clock. He was a huge man, very, very red. He had large paths on either side of this head which Sylvy called cowlicks. Simon had the sensation of trying to reach up to Mr. Roberts, and although Miss Rush was taller than Mr. Roberts she appeared to be trying to reach up to him too. Mr. Roberts had strode into the room and over to Miss Rush who quickly got up from her chair and gave it to him. Simon had been afraid that Mr. Roberts was going to teach the class. He could have said the review in his sleep but white people always tried to confuse you. He hoped he.... But Mr. Roberts had begun to talk.

"How many of you all washed your hands this morning?" asked Mr. Roberts. Pete Brack had been the first one to get up and to start to the desk. Quickly Mr. Roberts had stopped him.

"No, don't come up here. I just wanted to know," he had said.

Everybody had to scramble back into his seat because Simon, with the rest, had thought that Mr. Roberts had wanted to see the clean hands.

A funny little smile had come over Mr. Roberts' broad face as he asked, "What kind of books do you all study out of?"

This time Simon had been the first to get his books from under his seat.

"No, I don't want to see them," Mr. Roberts had said. "Just tell me."

Miss Rush had begun to tell him about the books but Mr. Roberts had cut her short. "Thank you, Lucille, but I was talking to the kids." Simon thought of the way he played with his cat—dangling a string in front of him.

By this time Mr. Roberts had risen from his seat and was walking around the room. "Do you help your people work?" As Peter started to answer him, Mr. Roberts had shaken his finger in Pete's face saying, "Never mind. I just wanted to see if you helped them."

Then he had walked smilingly back to the desk and, facing the children, had begun to talk. Simon had never been able to repeat exactly what Mr. Roberts had said, but he had always remembered that Mr. Roberts had appeared to be looking down at him.... He seemed to have trouble talking and would stammer and hesitate in the funniest manner. Simon remembered that he had wanted to help him but he was afraid to offer anything to Mr. Roberts.

After Mr. Roberts had gone, Miss Rush had been all smiles. She wasn't afraid any more. Simon kicked a clod of clay as he thought how Miss Rush must have hated Mr. Roberts.

* * *

Sounds that told him that the little church was dismissing made Simon hasten to get up from the school step and start off down the road. Sylvy and Idd would be coming out soon. He wanted to go further away from the church before they caught up with him. He'd talk to Sylvy and Idd and tell them to come up to Detroit with him. They'd surely like it there. He didn't make much but they'd get along—as well as they did here anyway. Yes, that's what he'd do!

Looking back Simon saw Idd driving the old rickety wagon toward him. He was glad when they reached him. Sylvy wanted to know about his head.

"Oh, it's much better, Ma," said Simon. "I've just been thinking."

"Waal, Ah'm glad it's bettah. Ah tole Willa Mae Lee that yo' head was hurtin.' She 'lowed that you wuz jest stuck up and that you'd be tryin' to get us away from heah pretty soon. Folks will talk, you know."

Simon give funny little laugh. So Willa Mae also knew that he was a stranger. He looked across the field at the bare cotton stalks and said, "Yes, Ma, people will talk."

* * *

"Waal, you gon' back," said Lee as he drove Simon to the bus station. "We ain't big 'nough to hold you, eh? Waal, maybe yu'll be comin' back again. Think you will?"

"I don't know," said Simon.

"Anyway we wuz glad to have you. But I know Sylvy and Idd'll be lonesome."

Simon didn't seem to hear Lee. Lee looked at him wonderingly. "Cose hain't none o' mah bus'ness, but didn't you and yo' folks git along?"

"What?... Oh yes, everything's all right," said Simon confusedly.

Lee brought the car to a stop as he drew up to the station.

"Waal, heah we are. Same ole station! Everything's jest like we left it. Heh! Heh! Nothing's changed."

"You're right," said Simon as he leaped from the car and swung onto the bus, "it hasn't."

[*Opportunity* 16.6 (June 1938): 177–181]

BLACK FRONTS

by Marita Bonner

Front A

He was a lawyer. He had not had a case since 1932. This was 1935. Ma and Pa had crossed the Alps of effort, carrying an elephantine load to advance him. Luther had quit high school in his junior year to go to work in a foundry so Big Brother could be a lawyer. Henry had taken a janitor's job after he finished grammar school because he could get $125 a month and they could send Big Brother to law school.

When Big Brother was a lawyer they would all be rich!

Big Brother went through law school. Big Brother passed the state bar. Big Brother did a fair-to-middling business among the razor-cutters and crap-shooters.

"I'll hit a big gun some day!" he would promise. "Just wait! Then I'll be in the dough!"

But he met Miss Rinky Dew first. Miss Dew had come to the big city to go to business college. She said that her father was a doctor down in the little southern town that had loosed her upon the city.

She never mentioned her mother. Perhaps because her mother was a big, black, bandanna-bound washwoman. Her father was the white doctor in the town.

You know Rinky. The skin of civilization which covers the black world has been erupting her type for years.

They have no back—no middle—all front. No genuine intelligence, no real education, no super-saturation of a rich over-flow of true culture. Nothing but an extra wave to the hair—an extra flop to the powder puff—an avalanche of self-conscious "ings" and "ists" (in the presence of the lesser lights) just to show how close "dis" and "dat" still are.

Rinky was one of those still so bedazzled with their own fresh varnish of diction and degrees that they cannot discriminate between those born to the manor and those born to the gutter. In short, too weighted and freighted with claptrap and blank rot to offer soil suitable for the culture of anything but the weeds of Living.

When she first came to the big city, she held herself a little aloof. She finished the business college and went to work for Big Brother.

She was well aware that Big Brother eyed her warmly. And a lawyer's wife surely was on a par with a doctor's daughter!

Gradually the aloofness melted.

Gradually Big Brother was entwined until he unraveled himself before a preacher. As befitted what Rinky considered a doctor's daughter should have, their bedroom set cost $750.

It made everything else in Pa's and Ma's home look shamefaced and outmoded. Rinky made the whole family look shamefaced and outmoded.

By the time Big Brother was two months beyond the altar, he was moving the $750 bedroom set out of Pa's and Ma's flat, with $3,200 worth of furniture added to it to match the $750 layout.

Before long there was an automobile.

After Big Brother had moved his Rinky, the family did not see him so often. Once in a while he'd drop in on Saturday night—with an excuse for Rinky's absence—a hungry look toward the supper table—and a grateful murmur for the few dollars Ma would pinch off and slip to him when nobody was looking.

Came 1929.

Everybody in the world—with the exception of a few natives still naked in their jungles—knows what happened in 1929.

1929 began stripping Big Brother and his Rinky. The overcarved walnut dining room set followed the baby grand piano down the back stairs one Monday morning. Big Brother's suite of offices shrank to desk space in an insurance firm. The table-top range joined the hegira and took the typewriter, the automatic ice box, the vacuum cleaner and all the lamps on the light bill along with it.

The landlord grew insistent. The landlord grew insulting. The landlord leeched on the front door like a nightmare. Big Brother and his Rinky took a shambled house near Ma and Pa.

"We're taking a studio," Rinky broadcasted, and proceeded to angle the residue of the $3,950 worth of furniture until the studio atmosphere was more apparent.

There came still further shrinkage and lopping off. Rinky manoeuvered a job as a typist with the Relief Commission. The $75 she earned there each month appeased the landlord intermittently—reduced the grocery bill occasionally—and kept her lawyer-husband sitting in his desk space from 1932 to 1935—waiting.

Luther and Henry lost their jobs. They moved their families in with Pa and Ma. All three families went on relief.

That meant that three coal orders, three grocery orders, three twenty-four-pound bags of flour and three boxes of canned goods went to Pa and Ma's each month.

With a little juggling and rearranging, the three families were adjusted. They had enough to eat. The house was warm. Ma found a roomer who worked in a private family but who "'preciated a good home." The twelve dollars a month Ma got for the room meant money for church, movies, and a new pair of stockings once in a while.

Less than $100 a month was not so much at Big Brother's. He took to coming over to Ma's on Sunday morning just before breakfast.

Rinky would have a cup of tea and a cigarette and stay in bed.

Sometimes Big Brother lugged a basket of coal and a basket of food back from Ma's. He could not go on relief.

He was a lawyer!

He had to keep up his front.

So did Rinky. She had to have her hair "done" and buy a new dress "on time" monthly.

"Can't let the folks think I'm ragged," she'd say to herself as the debts mounted.

Every once in a while she and Big Brother gave a splashing party. The liquor and sandwiches cost them several semi-square meals.

But they would have their "gang" over to the "studio" and holler and shriek shady witticisms to cover the hollows inside of their bodies and inside their thoughts.

"I want one of those new rose lame backless dresses for the next formal!" Rinky frequently shouted. She knew while she was saying it that there was no money for lame dresses, no money for formals, no money for rent, nor food, nor clothes, nor anything else she wanted or had to have.

But she shouted and everybody else yelled with her to keep from being blotted out and smothered.

All the time the shouting and the drinking and the cackling was mounting, Rinky would be thinking, "My God! The rents are almost due again! My God! What will I do! What can I do!"

But then she would laugh louder and drink one more whiskey-sour and caress somebody else's husband just to show that she was smart and up-to-date, carefree, prosperous and a leading light—some few steps beyond Luther and Henry and their wives whom she never invited to her Sunday nights.

And when the gang and the whiskey and the sandwiches were gone, Rinky and

Big Brother would lie in bed and rehearse the party, each bolstering up the other's confidence in the thickness of their smoke-screen of pretense which they were spreading before their tattered notions of living.

Then—finally—Big Brother would lie quiet so Rinky would think he was asleep and would stare out into the darkness and wonder, "How long will it be before I can earn even ten dollars a month again? Or even a dollar a week? When will I ever be able to pay Ma back all I owe her?"

And Rinky, breathing evenly so Big Brother would believe she was asleep, would be lying there, wracking her mind, trying to find a place to pinch off one more dollar to send a gift of some sort down home to her mother. It was not to be so much a gesture of affection as it was to be an indication of unlimited largess and affluence such as befitted a lawyer's wife whose husband had an office in the main colored business block in the main street of the colored section of a big city up North.

She did not dare think forward to the day when the landlord and the grocer and all the rest of them would not accept a part of their money, but would demand it all. There was nothing to which she could think back.

Nothing.

So—she only could cover—hide herself—away from life—beneath her front.

Front B
(The Top of the Design)

Yas'm! I'll jes' iron out these heah damp things and leave the rest 'til tomorrer! Whyn't you go lie down an rest? I kin look out after these babies! When I go to Mis' Bowers, she jes' leave everything to me and lies down and reads a book! She shore is one nice lady! An' ain't her husband lovely to her! Jes' buys her everything and gives her plenty! She pays good, too! Two fifty a day and carfare! She always gives me something to carry home, too. Her husband—he been to college. He's a fine doctor, too!

Ain't your husband never went to college?

Yas!?

Then how come he ain't a doctor or a preacher? He study "business!"

What he got to go to college to study business for? These Jews on every corner—they makin' money all day and all night with Sunday th'owed in and they ain't never need to study no business! They can't hardly read but they shore can figger the dough outa your pockets into their'n. There's you 'phone ringing! (Thank God that telephone did ring! Git her out a here! Always doin' something aroun' the kitchen! Must he scared I try to *take* something! What she got for anybody to take? Po' as Job's turkey, her! She ain't got nuthin' to take! Sure hope she stays out there so's I can git a little sugar and flavorin' to make that cake for Reverend's birthday! Ole Miss Lewis, she think she the only one can bring Reverend anything! She *so* rich, and they gonna read out the names of those that gives a gift this time...!)

Heah, you little devil! Leave that iron cord alone. I bet I'll smack yore head off!

What? Your mama don't let nobody hit you? I'll bet I'll give you to the boogy man!

Ain't no boogy man!

Don't say "Ain't!!"

You is the mannish somethin' I ever see for three years old! Here comes yore ma!

She callin' you! Better g'long! (Certainly glad them little devils is out of the way! Make you sick! Tryin' to be white! Don't say "Ain't." Don't say "Bust!" Don't say "Yas mam," say "Yes, Mrs. Jones!" All that foolishness! Gotta feed them brats spinach and carrots and fresh eggs in the winter time and special milk and God knows what all—an she wearin' cotton stockings! I bet I'd feed them kids some bread and gravy and git myself somethin' if I was her! She ain't got as much stuff in her house as my Ruthie has! Dan—he pay fifteen dollars down and git Ruthie five rooms full of furniture with a radio throwed in! Talk about she don't buy on the 'stallment plan! How anybody going to get a house full of furniture 'less they ask for credit? Whyn't she leave them little fools with somebody and go on out an' teach—she s'posed to have so much edjucation! Course, Mrs. Bowen, she don't need no money 'cause she got plenty and he make a lot all the time. This pore gal ought to try somethin! Her husband can't be makin' so much. Always talkin' 'bout she don't want to leave her children! Bet she can't get no school to teach in this town! Talk about she always wanted to do somethin' else that won't take her from home! Hope she ain't thinkin' of takin' up sewing! That dress she make herself look like something the devil give his wife! Wish she'd leave them brats to me! They wouldn't be able to set down when I got through wid them! These napkins shore is pretty! Guess I'll take one to put on the flower table in the pulpit! They don't need no six napkins for two people no how! I'll jes'—Lawd! she comin!)

Yas'm! I forgot and left the iron settin' on the napkin while I was fixin' my stockin'! I shore am sorry it scotched! Maybe ef you puts a little flour paste on it, it'll come out! Only five napkins! Only five? Guess the laundry lost one for you! That's what comes of sending your stuff to the wet wash! I always says a woman ought to wash her own things ef she ain't sick abed! (Hope that stung you!) What! I standing on the napkin? Where? (Ain't that the dog-beatenest! Wish she'd a stayed out 'a here!) Well...! Gettin' on to five o'clock! Guess I better start gettin' ready to get home! Doctor Bowen, he always drive me home when I work at his house. Y'all ain't got no car, has you?

My daughter Ruthie, she got a Cadillac! Yeah!! Dan, he pays his boss so much every week out of his salary for his ole car! They got the swellest car in their block! (You'd think anybody with all de edjucation they 'sposed to have would have a car! Her husband look like a half-dead fool to me anyhow! Tippin' his hat to me on the car, then settin' in a seat all by hisself like he ain't never knew me!) It's two dollars and a quarter. Yas'm. I tol you on the phone that day you call me at Mrs. Bowers' it'd be a quarter extra when the clothes need to be ironed! Two dollars any other day. Mrs. Bowers always pay me extra when I iron things, 'thout saying nuthin! (She better find another quarter! Ef she so broke, she don't need nobody doin' no work for her! Some women gits so *helpless* 'cause they got a couple of babies! I ain't but ten year oldern what she is an I'm 'bout to be a grandmother! I'se married when I'se fifteen! Ain't no sense to no woman going to school and all that foolishness like she say she been when all she going to do anyhow is have babies and housework on her hands. She too soft anyhow! He kissin' her goodbye every morning like he was going to Yoorup and pattin' her head like she was a baby 'stead of an old hard woman!)

Yas'm! Thank you! Guess I'll be gettin' along! (Hope she go out again! I think I'll take Ruthie some of that fancy underwear! She thinks I been workin' for rich white folks and they always has somethin' you can take home! Don' want nobody know I been workin' for colored! Shore be glad when this depression business is over and the white folk'll turn loose the money again and I can work like I wants to! Aw, she ain't never going out! Let me git out a here!)

Goodby, y'all!

Front B
(The Bottom of the Design)

Why doesn't she hurry up and finish that ironing and go home? It's too much to keep concocting little jobs that will keep me busy around the kitchen while she's here! But if I don't stay, everything we own will go home with her. Two teaspoons and the butterknife last time! I can't take a weekly inventory, and—) Junior! Take your fingers out of that sugar bowl! Baby! Don't hit the window with the milk bottle! Why not play with the clothespins! See? Nice! (Between her brick-bat insinuations and these babies—it's a wonder that I don't loop-the-loop out of that window and mushroom somebody's hat! I ought to get rid of her—but she *does* do some of the things that I hate to do—when she feels like it!)

Junior! I told you to let the sugar alone! Suppose you and baby go into your room and play! Say excuse me to Mrs. Jones when you step over her feet, sonny! You *don't want to!* (Is this the point where I use the hairbrush or reason with him? God! why isn't there a Glossary of Living with all the proper answers for mamas indicated with red ink, or red lights, or red buttons or something? Or did everything I ever learned fail to teach me how to dive for the answers in my soul quick enough? Thank God the telephone is ringing! Time out from the maelstrom!)

Oh, hello! Your call is just interrupting round two with that curse you wished on my house! I thought you told me she was a splendid worker? She ought to be with Ali Baba's gang! Who was Ali Baba? Don't you remember the old story of the forty thieves—the way they had to simmer them in oil to stop them from stealing? What? You knew she took things from you? How did you stop her?—You let Nature take its course? How many shirts did you say she took? Well, Nature can't course in my house! My husband doesn't own that many shirts.

I'm too fretty? Have to pay for what I don't want to do? I don't mind paying, but I can't give away the shirts off of his back just to keep her, can I?

No, I don't want to talk about your club. Crazy? Losing poise? I suppose I am. These children and that woman are poised on my nerves so—

Of course, I want to hear about your new dress! Mm! Mm!! Sounds lovely. Listen. The children have gone back to the kitchen! I'll just have to go! I'll call you later!

The iron is scorching that napkin, Mrs. Jones! (She's stolen one napkin while I was gone! Always snipping and nipping at what I haven't got then stealing what I do have! How can I search her?)

You're standing on the napkin! Yes, under your left foot. (Thankful am I, too, that it's five o'clock! If she takes the whole house while I am out of the room getting her money—I don't care! I'm just going into the living room and sit down with myself for five minutes! Wonder if I'll ever reach the place, once more, when I can sit down quietly a little while every day?

It's time to pay her! How many extras can she find today? How many days can I stand this? Well—it's time to unlock my nerves—open the door—meet the pain again.)

I'll call you when I want you again! (That pile of clothes does look small!) I'll call you! (If I *do*, it will be my final bid for a sanatorium or the "dark house" or "my long sleep.")

Good night! [*Opportunity* 16.7 (July 1938): 210–214]

SOUTHERN CIRCUMSTANCE

by Manet Fowler

Carl Brown pushed his body behind the fig tree and crouched on the ground. He was panting and trembling. The tongue in his brown head felt heavy and taut. His whole self was being filled with a fear that was numbing, chilling. His thin lips parted. The sound which came was parched, hoarse, and scraping:

"Mrs. Lewis, Mrs. Lewis!"

The woman on the back porch turned. She was chubby and brown, and her thick eyebrows lifted in surprise. She looked into the yard. She saw no one. The sound came again.

"Mrs. Lewis, Mrs. Lewis! It's me—Carl—Carl Brown."

It was a man's voice, and it *was* behind the fig tree. Marian Lewis drew her dressing-gown about her and looked into the darkness. It *was* Carl Brown; she used to teach him in high school; nice boy, Carl.

The man's face—brown, saffron-tinged, appeared stealthily from behind the bushy tree.

"Mrs. Lewis, you've *got* to help me. I just beat up a white man, and they're gonna get me."

"A *white* man, Carl? Oh my God!"

Two seconds. A muffled undertone:

"Give me that hat; pull off your coat and vest; go out in the barn. If they find you, let *me* do the talking, and listen to every word I say."

Carl Brown pushed the hat, a dusty black felt one, from his head, and handed the coat and vest in a bundle to the woman. He crouched along the fence, next to the bushes, and reached the barn. There he sat on the floor in the darkness, his body stiffened with terror. His skin was slowly turning a sickly olive, his lips white and dry. The nostrils of his broad nose were quivering. His incongruously hazel eyes, a heritage from his octoroon mother, he closed—to shut out the fright—and he moved his hands to push the black crinkly hair from his face.

The Negro sat there, waiting for the cries of pursuit to begin around him. He hardly dared to expand a muscle or to breathe. The sweat from his face mixed with his tears of dread as he cowered on the floor. Waiting.

Marian Lewis was a school-teacher and the wife of a Negro doctor. Her own family had been middle-class Negro folk, who had a fairly decent home in a small Southern town, and a few of the conveniences of life. She knew little of the rough-and-rowdy type of Negro, little of cutting, shooting scrapes.

When Carl Brown handed her his clothing through the screen-door, Marian Lewis was thinking quickly, but she did not know what to do. She had to help this boy. That was all she knew. If those white men were really angry they'd lynch him right in her yard. She shuddered.

Her baby, in the next room, cried. His chest—*there* was a place for these things.

Beneath the rows of dainty blue baby-things the woman crushed the battered black hat, the grey coat and vest. She patted the blue things on top and returned to the porch. She was just in time.

The screen-door was rattling so that she thought it would fall off the hinges. A white policeman, panting, angered, flushed, hammered at the frame.

Marian Lewis walked calmly to the door, her hand on the lock.

"What do *you* want?"

"Open this door! Who's in there? Did you see a yeller nigger with a black hat, grey suit, run through here?"

Under breath, viciously.

"Damn nigger beating up a white man. Open this door!"

"No, there's no one here but me and the baby. My husband, the doctor, is out on a call."

Mrs. Lewis breathed deeply and prayed for strength to lie convincingly.

"Well, you open this door; I want to see for myself."

"I'm sorry, but I will not open the door unless you present a warrant!"

The policeman glared. He was opening his mouth to spout invective when there was a thump on the soft earth of the back yard. A body rolled over on its side, achieved sitting position, suddenly stood, and ran to the door: Another policeman had arrived. He had jumped over the barn, from alley-way to yard.

There were a score of them there in the next moment. Running, breathless, looking for a "damn nigger," savage hunters ready for the kill.

"Where's that nigger? Is he in there? Open up that door!"

"I tell you, there's nobody here but me and the baby!"

The policemen were spreading into the yard. Nearer and nearer to the barn.

"O yes, I forgot." Marian Lewis swallowed in a dry throat, and gripped the bars of the door for support.

Loudly, "Carl Brown is out there in my barn fixing the lights. He's been here since he came by from work. Carl!"

Carl Brown could not move. He had heard the sounds. He had heard the cops. They would get him; they would beat him; they would lynch him. He knew it.

His thoughts came tumbling about him. He was not a "bad Negro." He had never been in trouble before. But out of the hell of this last quarter of an hour everything kept popping before his eyes:

On the trolley-car, crowded with blacks and whites, jogging along. The sign, "For Colored," and behind it sitting this sandy-haired red-necked cracker, refusing to move, while tired black working-women stood, afraid to ask him.

The old woman, black, grey-haired, wrinkled. Looked to be about seventy. Loaded down with packages. Stooped. So weak, so tired she could hardly stand.

She bent over the man sitting on the seat below the sign. Asked him if he would "please, son" let her sit down. The car lurched; the old black woman fell on the seat.

That damn white trash skunk pushed her off on the floor of the rolling car and called her a dirty name. And he sat there.

"God, I ought've killed him!"

The policemen were at the barn door. Carl Brown heard Marian Lewis call:

"Carl! Carl! Are you there?"

He could not answer.

The door was pushed open. Two hands, two dozen white hands were upon him. Pushing, shoving, throwing the Negro into the yard.

"All right, nigger, what you doing here?"

The lips of Carl Brown moved but no sound came. The legs moved, but as an automaton. His senses were dead; his body numb; he could not think. White hands were marching him to the front of the house, propelling him along by the strong force of their moving bodies.

The street was filled with activity. Negroes were standing in frightened groups in their front yards, close to home. Every house was lighted, and from the street the disorder wrought by the pursuers was apparent. Clothes thrown from closets to floor, dishes shattered, silver thrown about.

A huge old-fashioned battered touring-car was parked at the head of the street. Within it were relatives of the beaten white man. Their rifles projected from the car, a few of them operated a tremendous searchlight which revolved slowly from one yard to another. Behind bushes, behind trees, down the street. Over and over again.

The Lewises' front-yard was lighted as the brightness of day. Among the flowers and trees Carl Brown was standing rigidly in the center of a circle of twenty white policemen, uniformly with one hand at hip, the other projecting a flashlight. The twenty flashlights emphasized the greenish pallor of the Negro's skin—his muscleless face, the hazel eyes staring ahead.

The lights were getting Carl Brown. Shining steadily in his eyes, they beat down upon him. Accusingly. Ceaselessly. Cruelly.

He began to sweat again. The lights were hot. His dry lips parted. His mind was working dully:

I guess I better tell. I can't stand these lights any longer. I guess I better tell. I can't stand them looking at me, just waiting to kill me. I guess I better—

Carl Brown opened his mouth.

* * *

Marian Lewis rushed from the front door of her house.

No sound had come from the Negro's lips.

"You can't take him. You can't!"

The lights from the car were shining on Carl Brown, revolving steadily.

The woman was almost screaming now:

"He isn't the one. I know it! He was fixing my lights. He was fixing my lights, I tell you!"

One of the policemen turned his head a fraction, leveled his eyes at her coolly.

"If he isn't the one, it's all right. But if he *is*, by God, we'll beat his damn brains out!"

Slowly Carl Brown slumped to the ground.

"Beat his damn brains out!" That was the cry.

A small tow-headed white boy came running to the group in the yard. He had a hat in his hand. A black felt one, battered and torn.

"Hey, copper!" he shouted. "I found this behind our house. Maybe the nigger went that-a-way." Then the boy looked hard, suspiciously, grinning at Carl Brown.

"Say—thought you was looking for a nigger with a black hat. This nigger ain't got no hat and no coat neither."

One of the policemen laughed. Carl Brown began to feel a little air in his lungs again. Once more Marian Lewis began. This was a chance.

"I told you Carl wasn't the one. I *told* you he's been fixing my lights."

The policeman looked at her. He was the one who had laughed.

"Well ... maybe he ain't the one. This nigger *don't* seem to have nothing but hisself!"

"Get on up, nigger. Go on home. We got to find the nigger that *had* that hat."

Twenty policemen left the yard to go to another. The touring-car with the searchlight remained at the head of the street.

Marian Lewis went into the house and returned with an object. In the shadow of her front-door she handed it to Carl.

He took it—a boy's grey cap.

"Thank you, Mrs. Lewis." That was all.

"It's all right, Carl. You'd better go home now."

Dryly she whispered:

"You can come back about a week from now and get your things. I'm very tired."

Carl Brown put the grey cap on his head. He straightened his shoulders, but he still had a scared feeling inside. He looked up the street at the touring-car and for a moment watched the searchlight revolve. Then, taking a deep breath, he walked down the steps and into the street, towards home.

One of the men in the car turned to the other as he revolved the light.

"That sure wuz a scared nigger, warn't he?"

"Sure wuz. Good thing he *weren't* the one with that black hat, damn him."

He turned the light on Carl Brown. Its beams followed until he had turned the corner.

THE FUGITIVE

by Grace W. Tompkins

For hours the crowd had lingered in the dusty street. Threats and oaths still hung upon the hot, still air. The blazing sun lit the hard, baked earth with a blinding light, and irregular waves of heat rose from the pavement of the courthouse square. Through the barred windows of the little jail knots of shifting men outside caught brief glimpses of Zeb Tabor pacing back and forth across his office; from desk to door and back to desk again. His batted hat, with its sheriff's badge pinned to its band, sat far back on his grizzled hair, and he pushed it further back from time to time to mop his glistening forehead with a blue bandanna.

The men gathered in the street could see his lips move, but they couldn't hear what he was saying. He had stopped his pacing now to talk to young Rod Massey, who ran the filling station on The Square. They had sent Rod in to see him, as their spokesman. Rod and Zeb were good friends, but for once they minced no words.

Rod draped his lanky frame across a corner of the sheriff's desk.

"So you won't let us have him, Zeb?"

Zeb pulled his hat forward. "Give me time," he hedged.

Rod regarded him intently.

"Time—for what? You callin' out the State militia?"

"No." Zeb rubbed the side of his chin reflectively. "You see—" he paused, "here it is broad daylight—." He stopped. "Rod, you know how long I been sheriff of this here county?"

"Nigh on twenty year, I reckon."

"Twenty-three years exactly. I was made sheriff the same day young Whitney was born. I ain't lost a man yet. And I ain't aimin' to now."

They were both silent. Apparently Zeb had started a train of thought in the younger man's mind.

"What time you goin' home?" Rod asked.

"Not 'til late supper."

"We'll stick around." There was an ominous finality in Rod's voice.

As he left the jail and crossed the pavement, the men outside could not tell by his walk what Zeb had told him. Rod only said to them, "We'll have to wait until tonight."

There was a faint murmur of disapproval at the mention of delay, but finally the crowd broke up into smaller, whispering groups.

Zeb lit his pipe. He couldn't hope to fool the mob more than a few hours longer. But even that, he figured, ought to give Mat a good start. He sighed. All hell would pop when those men learned what he had done.

It was cooler now. The sun had sunk behind the courthouse, the post office, then Joe's Place; it had lingered for awhile on the flat concrete driveway where Rod's

Garage topped the summit of Main Street, and finally had dipped slowly into Piney Creek.

One by one the stars came out. Zeb looked at them—the symbol of his office. As long as he was sheriff, he assured himself, Edensville would have no lynching if he could prevent it. Of course everyone would know eventually that he'd helped Mat skip the jail. But he could take care of himself. And he felt sure he'd never be ashamed of what he'd done.

He thought he'd better get along toward home. The Missus would be worrying about whether Mat had got away or not.

Mat had been helping her with the gardening in his spare time when he was not working at Judge Whitney's kennels, out on the Nine Mile Road. For the past two years he had spent every afternoon cleaning the kennels and feeding and exercising the dogs. At nightfall, he had walked the winding road that turned at Peters Corners and descended over the rickety bridge across Piney Creek, to the ramshackle little house where his mother waited for him.

On Thursday night he had started home as usual. About half a mile past Peters Corners, where the willow trees on either side of the road dropped their graceful branches in a misty arch overhead, the narrow passage way had been shrouded in an inky blackness.

Suddenly a young woman had stepped out of the darkness and ran into him. She had screamed and fled down the road. Her sudden appearance had been almost like an apparition, and Mat had stood gaping after her long after she had vanished screaming into the night.

He had been at supper about ten minutes when the sheriff came. To his mother's frightened questioning Zeb had said. "It's safer for me to lock him up, Lou. That girl is Hank Barret's granddaughter. She's engaged to marry young Whitney. He was at the house when she run in. She was pretty badly scared, and there may be trouble." Hank Barret was the president of the Grover Bank and Judge Whitney's bosom friend.

Zeb knew, just as Lou knew, that to leave Mat at home was plain homicide. Later, talking to Judge Whitney, he had sensed that it would be hopeless even to hold Mat for trial....

Perhaps he had been wrong, but now Mat was gone, and he hoped he'd get across the line.

He walked slowly across The Square. Only a few loiterers were in sight. He saw Kit, his young deputy, sitting on the steps that led up to the jail. Kit didn't know yet that Mat was not safely locked in there.

At the crest of Main Street he stopped at Rod's Garage and went into the office. Rod was talking to two men. Zeb recognized one of them as Bart Henry. Henry was an agitator, always mixed up in a brawl of some sort. The other man was Henry's brother-in-law, over from Aaronsville. That was the place where they had lynched a man last fall.

Rod got up to meet Zeb.

"Going home, Sheriff?"

"Yeh. Just thought I'd drop in to see if everything's all right."

"What time you coming back?"

"'Bout ten-thirty."

"Where's Kit?"

"Up at the lockup."

"All right. Give my regards to the Missus."

"Thanks. Good night."

"So long, Sheriff."

Zeb set his feet toward Nine Mile Road. He looked overhead at the clear, deep blue sky. The stars had a cold, hard glitter. He singled out two, brighter than the rest. And as he watched, one of them stirred, hesitated a moment, and then, carving a wide arc in the sky, plunged into the blackness of the tree tops.

Zeb sighed and trudged on toward home.

II

The house oppressed her. The walls of the room closed in on her consciousness, smothering, stifling her. Would Mat make it? She looked at the clock on the bureau. Nine o'clock. How far would he be now? Out of the state surely ... perhaps in Ohio. She prayed he wouldn't lose his way and come out in West Virginia. That would mean the loss of valuable time. She glanced from object to object in the small, neat room. Her gaze rested on her son's faded picture hanging over the battered piano. His eyes looked calm and steady. She could hear him saying, "We just have to be patient, Ma. Things'll be better."

Lou smiled bitterly. Were things really getting any better?

She wasn't afraid for herself. If only Mat could make it safely across the line. She hoped no harm would come to Zeb because he'd helped Mat to escape. Zeb had always been a friend. Now she owed him Mat's life. She looked up at the photograph again.

"Zeb knows he never done it," she said softly. Her voice quavered and died away. Her work-worn hands fumbled blindly with her jacket. She walked to the window and stood looking toward the road. The house seemed strangely quiet without her son. About this time each evening he had read to her, sometimes from the Bible, sometimes from magazines he brought home from Mrs. Tabor's house. But tonight a ghostly silence in the five-room cottage seemed to presage sure disaster.

Lou shivered and pulled her jacket closer. She could see two bright stars from where she stood, glimmering through the lacy openings of the tall tree just outside her window. That tree sure looked queer now, in the moonlight. It was as if it and the stars were painted on a stage drop. Everything seemed unreal, theatrical. How far away the stars were, above the earth. Above pain and heartache and terror. Lou felt a sinking in her stomach. She dropped to her knees and lay her head against the window sill.

A vein throbbed in her lean, sunken temples. The dull beat, beat of her blood was like the muffled tramp of the inevitable mob. She got up slowly. The walls of the room seemed closer. She could feel the space grow narrow, narrower. Shadowy bars seemed to cover the window. The floor was like the hard clay earth of the jail. She had to get out!

She snatched her shawl from the chest in the corner and stepped into the yard. The cool breeze cleared her brain. She threw back her shoulders and looked up into the sky.

Two stars held her attention. Perhaps, she thought, Mat could see those same two stars. She gazed at them intently. And as she watched, the brighter of the two swung lazily out of its orbit, dropped in a wide arc, and went plunging down into the night.

The moon lit the scene with an eerie light. The only sound in the quiet night was Lou's anguished wail.

III

The dashboard lights cast a dim glow on Mat's rigid lower jaw. Eyes, staring from his tense black face, shifted momentarily to the speedometer and as quickly back to the winding road. His foot pressed firmly on the accelerator.

The trees were solid banks of murky smoke as they struck the outer edge of eyes intent upon the scar of road ahead. The speedometer's blunt needle wavered in the upper fifties. The trees became a blur. Something yellow loomed ahead, was upon him, gone. A stop sign. Another yellow blur, then long white fences on a snaky curve. The tires pinched at the second bend; the rubber made a snubbing sound. The car careened a hundred yards, righted itself, then settled down to a steady hum as its low-slung body hugged the cement road. The needle was well in the sixties now. The countryside was a dull clot of earth through which the car lights cut a wedge. The rush of air sang a sharp obligato to the engine's whine.

A red tail-light showed ahead. Mat passed it with misgivings. He sighed with relief as dim headlights fell away behind him in the distance. He slowed down as he passed through a small town. Houses were dark. Everyone had gone to bed.

Outside the town, the needle climbed again. The road stretched straight ahead for miles and miles. He settled back and glanced out toward the sky.

It was clean and there was a yellow moon. He could drive for a while with only the dim lights. He wondered if his mother was all right. Had they found out that he was gone? What had they done to her, to Zeb?

Another curve. He took that one at fifty. His hands were trembling on the wheel. In another hour, he knew, he would be across the line.

He was busy with his thoughts again. He did not blame the girl. Maybe he had scared her pretty badly. She didn't know how badly she had scared him, though. For a moment he had thought she was a ghost. No, it hadn't been the girl's fault. He wasn't sure that it was Mr. Barret's either. Young Whitney, more than likely, had started all the trouble. He hadn't liked the idea when his mother had hired Mat to tend the dogs. Mat wondered who would feed them from now on. None of the bulls would let young Whitney near them. And who would finish trimming that north hedge at Mrs. Tabor's? He had meant to do it Friday morning....

His eyes shifted to the sky again. Those two stars to the south were brighter than the rest. He looked at them with interest. What stars were they? He tried to figure their position. But as he gazed, one of them swung suddenly away from the other, hesitated, then fell in a wide arc into the quiet night.

In that fraction of a moment a road sign loomed ahead. In a single instant the sky seemed to turn upside down. The solitary star was now beneath Mat's feet. The earth rose overhead in jagged peaks of brown, paused for an age, the slowly crashed.

Flames bred of ignited gasoline flowered in the dark. The acrid smell of burning flesh mingled with the fragrant odors of the night.

Black Brother

by Cordelia T. Smith

As far back as Jimmy could remember, back into the dim remoteness of his boyhood, home had been a refuge, a fortress to which he could retreat from the wilderness of noisy streets. Mother was there, often too busy for more than a smile and a pat, but he could always creep into the parlor, still and scrubbed for choir practice nights, and look up, with shining eyes, at Mother's picture and talk to that. The picture was tinted, so that there was a rose-color in Mother's cheeks, shining through the brown, and her dress was a beautiful pink with blue buttons, big as half dollars. It was lovelier than Mother in a way, but it didn't say, "Go 'long now, son, cain't you see I'm busy?" and then give him a warm cookie right from the oven.

Home, at supper time, meant father too. Jimmy admired his father with a sort of shivering, blissful sense of belonging to this strong, laughing man who tossed him aloft and asked, "How's my bright boy this evenin'?"

"Bright," that was it—that was why Jimmy was so proud of his folks—they were "bright"—light brown in color—and when Jimmy walked out with them on Sunday afternoons, he always thought, "I sure am lucky!"

That is, when he thought at all. Usually he was just happily aware of his mother—in her white satin dress, maybe, with a little blue hat—and his father with his shiny stiff straw hat and his Palm Beach suit. Sometimes they'd meet the Reverend Washington, who'd stop them and say, "Good afternoon, Sister Turner, we sure did enjoy choir practice Friday night at your house! Howdy, Brother Turner—fine day for a walk! And how big this boy of yours is growing! He's a bright young man, sure enough!"

Jimmy always thought the Reverend Washington was referring to his color.

His mother told him about the new brother he was going to have—"Or it might be a sister, honey"—and they planned where he should sleep and what he should wear, and finally they brought up from the cellar the old baby carriage that Jimmy had ridden in long ago.

"Yo' Pappy'll paint it, an' then, when li'l brothah's old enough, you'll ride him down the street far as the drug store."

Jimmy waited, as for a new puppy to play with, never dreaming—

"Son, wake up!"

"What is it, Pappy, is it mo'nin'?"

"Yes, it's mo'nin,' son, and guess what?"

"Oh, he's come!"

"Yes, son, yo' brothah's come."

"Can I see him now?"

"Come on in, but be quiet now."

And Jimmy tiptoed to the bed, never guessing that this was the end of the old, the happy, the established world.

"That's not my brother! Who's that ol' black baby? I won't have an ol' black baby! Take him back and give me my own brother!"

"Son, hush, this *is* yo' brothah; this is Clarence. Look how cute he is."

"I won't have him, I won't. That ol' black baby!"

Days and months did not change Jimmy's feeling toward Clarence. His home, his refuge was gone. Where home had been, there now was only a cradle for the black baby. Mother didn't understand, mother wasn't ashamed of Clarence, mother loved the black baby—more—more than the "bright" one!

Only mother's picture was the same. Mother's picture said, "Yo're *my* boy, Jimmy, ma *bright* little boy. There ain't room for no *black* boys here."

"Jimmy, what you doin' in the parlor? Come out heah this minute and take Clarence fo' his walk!"

"Don't want to!"

"Jimmy, do what I say. Wheel Clarence up and down the street, 'till yo' Pappy come."

Two hours later, a forlorn little boy crept into the kitchen.

"Jimmy, whar you been? Yo' father been all the way to the church lookin' for you. And *whar's* Clarence?"

"Gone."

"*Gone?* What yo' mean? Tell me this minute!"

"I lef' him—up by the drug store—I don't want him here—ol' black baby!"

Months and years did not ease Jimmy's hurt. It was as though a dark pall had fallen on his life. Mother was too busy now to see how lonely a boy he was; mother was washing and ironing all day for enough to buy corn meal and potatoes, and sometimes neckbones and greens. Father seldom laughed, either. He walked half the day looking for a job, and then just sat and smoked his pipe. And the black baby grew and thrived. He loved his big brother, did Clarence, but Jimmy would have none of him. Clarence would have given his toy wagon, the pride of his heart, for one approving word from Jimmy, but Jimmy would say no word at all.

Only to his mother's picture would he talk, and pour out his bitterness and his love. And when words failed him, he would sing. For Jimmy was allowed the run of the parlor now. He was allowed to play softly on the old organ and to pour out the deep rich wine of his voice. For Jimmy's teachers had discovered that Jimmy had a voice.

"Jus' as if all of us cain't sing!" said his father.

"Nev' min,'" said his mother. "Let him sing if'n he want to; he's too quiet anyhow. And his teacher say he can make money singin' some day."

So Jimmy sang, and his dark-skinned brother helped mother with the dishes, and carried baskets of clothes, and everywhere trod softly that he might hear Jimmy sing and share somehow that other world that was created by Jimmy's mellow voice.

And before long Clarence was ten, and after school he ran errands for the druggist at the corner—the same corner drug store where Jimmy had left him years before. On Saturday nights he got fifty cents, and sometimes he'd timidly ask Jimmy to go to a show with him.

"No, thanks, kid. I'll stay home," Jimmy would reply.

"Here, *yo'* take it an' go by yourself. Honest, I want yo' to!"

But Jimmy would just shake his head and turn away.

Jimmy was in Junior High now—there were not very many colored boys there, but his voice marked him out even more than his skin. Everyone knew him, and sometimes the white boys in the Glee Club ate lunch with him. After all, it wasn't as though he were *black*.

One day there was word of a concert—Downtown. The best musicians from all the city's schools—everyone would be there—a wonderful chance—maybe a scholarship—anyway the pride of singing Downtown.

Jimmy rushed home to tell his mother the news. He was to sing a solo—"Swing Low"—that they had sung together many times.

He would not have been so happy if he had heard the quartet, who were also to sing, closeted with the music teacher.

"But Miss Carver, we can't take him with *us!* Why, he's colored. There'll only be white people there. Why does *he* have to go? Nobody wants to hear his old spiritual!"

"That will do, boys. James has the best voice in this school and he's going to sing. Charles, I want you and the other boys to meet Jimmy at White's Drug Store and take him down with you. I shall be there when you get there. Here are the tickets for all of you to get in the hall, and here are car tickets."

"Yes, Miss Carver," said Charles obediently, but he winked at the boys.

The day of the concert came, and Clarence, home from the drug store for lunch, gazed with admiration at his big brother in his new suit. How many washings and how many odd jobs had gone into paying for it!

"Here, Jimmy," he offered, "I brought you some throat lozenges. Mr. White said they'd help if you got hoarse."

"No thanks, Clarence, I won't need them."

"I just got my pay, you'd better take it, in case you need some extra money."

"No, Clarence, I won't need any extra money. Charles Spero and the rest of the quartet are going to meet me at the drug store at one and we're going Downtown together. The concert begins at two."

"They all *white* boys, son?" his mother asked, a little doubtfully.

"Why, yes, mother—why not?"

"Oh, nothin' son, only—"

"They sing near the first, but my song isn't 'till near the end. It's going to be on the radio."

"I'm goin' over to Reverend Washington's, son. We'll all be listenin'."

James was at the drug store at a quarter of one. When one o'clock came, he went outside and looked up and down. Then he began to walk back and forth. He looked at the clock again. It was five after one. He hummed his song to himself—"Jus' as easy," he thought—and pictured the crowded hall, full of faces, listening, listening and smiling.

One fifteen. Where *were* the boys? He went inside again. Clarence had gone out on an errand. Mr. White nodded and smiled and waved his hand at his little radio.

"We'll all be listenin,' James," he said.

Jimmy hurried back outside. It was one twenty.

By this time Charles and the other boys had boarded the street car.

"Look, there he is, waiting at the drug store!"

"Let him wait!"

"He's all dressed up, too."

"What'll you say to Miss Carver, Charles?"

"Say he wasn't there. Say his brother said he was sick."

It was almost two o'clock now. Jimmy walked up and down. What had happened? If he only had his ticket! It cost a quarter to get into the hall. He had two car tickets, but no card of admission to the hall. Where *was* Charles?

Two o'clock. The little radio in Mr. White's store blared out. Jimmy hurried inside. The announcer was talking.

"The hall is crowded to overflowing. The Superintendent of Schools—"

"What's the matter, James? Haven't you gone yet? You'd better hurry—"

Clarence wasn't back. That was good, anyway. Clarence wouldn't know—Know what? Know that he'd been left behind, at the corner drug store. Know that the white boys didn't want—their black brother!

"The concert will begin with a chorus of voices from the city school singing—"

No, that *couldn't* be it. There must be some explanation. Maybe Charles was sick; maybe he'd been hurt—

"The next number will be rendered by a quartet from Lincoln school—"

The quartet! They were there, they were singing; and he was here, in the drug store, listening to the concert over the little radio. Mother was listening, and the Reverend Washington, and maybe Clarence. Clarence—

As if in answer to his thought, a dark face was close beside him—

"Jim, what's the matter? What you doin' here?"

He mustn't let Clarence know—

"I—I didn't feel good. Couldn't go—"

No! That wasn't right—

"Clarence, your pay—do you still have it?"

"Yes! Here it is, Jimmy—fifty cents."

"Clarence, they went without me. If you'll lend me your money—"

"'Course I will, big boy! Here—"

"And Clarence, if you still have those throat lozenges—I may need 'em!"

"Where'd I put em? Here they are! You'd better hurry, Jim. You haven't got much time before it's your turn to sing."

Fifty cents—and *two* car tickets—they could *walk* home—

"Oh, Mr. White?"

"Yes, James?"

"Will you let my brother off for the afternoon? I'll help him, tonight, to make up. I want him to go to the concert—Downtown—*with me!*"

[*Opportunity* 17.4 (April 1939): 102–104]

CONDEMNED HOUSE: A SHORT STORY

by Lucille Boehm

Dusk was falling across the Harlem River like a blanket of cold mud. The sky was dirty with fog. You slipped on the freezing carpet of slush once or twice, but you didn't notice. You were too tired. A big ache filled your thoughts. You saw the street ahead of you, but it looked small—dingy—like it was far away. You stared at the kids teasing bonfires along the curb. Running their fingers through the flames. Chasing each other, dashing into the streets between great groaning trucks. Your nostrils widened, sucking in familiar odors—the oily smell of the fish store on the corner, cooking grease, cheap gasoline, "King Kong," garbage. The stale smells of poverty. On a nearby stoop a gang of boys and girls, giggling, yawning. Nothing to do. Not enough change among them for a tune on the piccolo. Somewhere a radio beat out the rhythm of Count Basie's "One O'Clock Jump." Music that throbbed at the pit of your stomach. Men lolled outside the candy store—no work, nothing to do. The thought of it burned fiercely in your brain.

You walked as far as your own stoop, down toward the end of the street. Across the way were the condemned houses. Half a block of them. They stood there sagging against each other like tired women in a subway jam—ready to collapse. Some of the windows were gaping black holes, where the boards had been chopped away for fire wood. An iron girder held two of the walls apart over a dark alley-way that looked like a missing tooth in the long row. In the end house was a big, jagged opening where the stoop used to be. Ruins of brick and plaster cluttered the floor. An ugly black seam scarred the face of the house from the ground almost to the roof. You couldn't make out if it was a crack in the wall or only a heavy dirt stain.

They, too, were out of a job—these rotten shells of houses. They were mean-looking, like people who get old and sick and useless.

Out of a job! You shivered. There were four dollars in your pocketbook. You'd been saving up for weeks, stretching the relief check like a worn rubber band over the rent and the food and the unpaid debts. It was like hanging onto a tuft of grass with a flood raging around you, but you had managed to get those four dollars together. You had hoped maybe you'd find a job in one of the Sixth Avenue agencies if you had money enough for the fee. But....

Something seethed in your brain. It had happened at that last agency, where you had gone after three hours of steady searching. You were too tired to stretch your eyes over the mob around the door reading the cards. You went straight in, climbed two long flights of stairs and asked for a house job, part-time, sleep-in—anything. The man behind the dark wood partition was sweaty in rolled-up blue shirt sleeves. He looked fagged out—stared at you with dead grey eyes.

"Now see here, girlie," he said in a tired voice, "You're just wasting your time and mine. If I *wanted* black girls I'd have said so on the cards, wouldn't I? Why don't you take the trouble to..."

You didn't hear the rest. There was hot acid boiling inside you, from your stomach to the nape of your neck. You rushed downstairs, hurried along the avenue, too mad to cry.

The four dollars were still in your pocketbook. You opened the change purse, took them out and counted them slowly. Then you rolled them into a tight little sausage and tucked them back. The rent agent would grasp at them like a hungry tiger. You couldn't hold him off any longer.

You stared through the boarded-up house across the way. It sulked there in the surly gloom of dusk. It wavered before your eyes like it was under water, with bright sun spots dancing around it. You backed up and leaned weakly against the stoop railing.

"Watch out!" bleated a shrill voice behind you, and you jumped. A square-faced little boy pushed you out of his way and scooted across the street like he was on wheels....

"Clarence!" you yelled, startled.

Clarence disappeared in the big black maw of the condemned house.

"Clarence, hey!" you shouted. "Didn't I tell you not to go in that there house? You stay away from there."

"Gramma sent me for wood!" was the reply from the yawning mouth of the old tenement. "She says if I see you to tell you she wants you upstairs."

You looked after him. A sick, worried feeling jumped in your throat. Kids shouldn't go into those houses, even for chopping up the rotten old boards. You wanted to call him back again but it was no use. He was your sister's kid and if she didn't mind—

You shrugged and turned for the door of our house. Your heels dragged at you. You hated to go upstairs, to face the hungry family without a job without food for supper. Hated to warm over yesterday's boiled rice while six pairs of eyes drilled through your back....

Suddenly something stunned you.

You had been glaring at that big-mouthed skeleton of a house across the way. At the evil-looking scar like a knife-slash up its face. Now you stiffened with a shock like a bolt of lightning. Your jaw fell open and you forgot to breathe. You saw that the dark seam in the wall of the old tenement was widening straining apart into a jagged crack between the bricks. The wall was quivering, crumbling. The house was going to collapse!

You felt like you were having a nightmare. Blinked. Didn't know if you should believe it. But there was the crack opening black and wide like in a movie earthquake. And Clarence was inside!

Your heart pounded hot blood into your throat. Your knees sagged and sweat prickled your skin. You thought you would drop before you could move. Then you wrenched yourself from the stoop and sprinted wildly across the street.

"Clarence!" you shrieked, "Clarence!"

The wide toothless mouth closed around you. Cans and broken bottles jabbed at your ankles. You stumbled through a chalky rug of fallen plaster and naily boards. In the back, under the rotten steps, Clarence looked up at you, scared.

"The house is falling!" you screamed, and grabbed him by the arms. Junk tripped you, held you back like in a terrible dream. You fought it—dragged yourself and Clarence across the floor. Out toward the dim light of the front opening. Into the slush of the street, splashing it on your legs as the two of you raced through puddles to our own stoop. You held Clarence tight against you. He hung on to your coat, whimpering with fright. You watched the old house, shuddered, waited for it to collapse.

The street lamp on the corner lighted, feeble against the evening fog. A truck rumbled up the block. The piccolo in the candy store rocked with Fats Waller's piano. The condemned house still stood in the darkness, like a naked old woman. Its wood and plaster guts lay in ruins on the floor. The ugly scar was slashed up its face like it had been ever since you could remember. You squinted at it but couldn't make out in the dark if it was really a crack or only a heavy dirt stain. You frowned, open-mouthed, and shook your head in wonder. Your arms slacked around Clarence's shoulders.

He had stopped whimpering. Was calm—had already forgotten the scare. He looked up at you, puzzled. Then he looked at the house.

"It ain't falling!" he exclaimed. He thought you had played a joke on him. "Aaa! You ain't so funny," he growled sullenly. With the sudden impulse of a child he slipped out of your grasp like an eel and dashed across the street, mocking you with laughter and yelling, "House is falling! House is falling! House is...."

His voice and his body were swallowed up in the greedy black mouth of the tenement. Worried, you watched again. The house was still there, crumbling, rotting, biding its time. Not today; perhaps tomorrow it might go. Maybe next day. Maybe next year.

Suddenly you hated the old house as you would loathe a person who slowly, coolly plotted murder. You wanted to claw it to pieces. You wanted to dig your nails into the cement and tear it brick from brick.

A heavy sigh rose and fell in your chest. Your throat made a flat sound, like a chuckle, and you shook your head and smiled. Why in the world should you have thought it was going to fall in when there it was—still standing big as life!

"I must be going nuts!" you told yourself.

You turned and pushed open the door leading to the hallway of your house. You climbed upstairs, wondering at yourself. What had put such a crazy notion into your head? Scaring the kid like that! What on earth made you do it? The useless old tenement had been there all your life. Why were you suddenly so sure that it must come down? What was it that made you feel deep inside that somewhere, somehow, you must some day help build decent houses where poor people like yourself could live?

[*Opportunity* 17.6 (June 1939): 168–169]

Two-Bit Piece

by Lucille Boehm

The red sun was sweating in a humid sky. It died fiercely, shedding blood-colored heat over the crowded block. The narrow sidewalks were alive with people, rocking on the peg-legged chairs they had dragged out early that morning, playing cards at rickety tables, squatting on the stoops and fanning themselves with soggy handkerchiefs. Even the boarded-up houses, bleached and rotting in the sun all day, had come to life. Kids swarmed through them, chased each other, screaming; flailed the old woodwork with their pocket-knives. Men going home from work dangled foamy cans of beer.

'Liz was playing Old Maid with Patsy Crews and Bea Sutherland on the front steps of her house. The three of them shrieked as Patsy picked the Queen from Bea's hand. 'Liz's wide, laughing lips drew back, stripping brilliant teeth and wet bluish gums. When her name was shouted through the hallways she trumpeted all the louder, pretending not to hear.

"'Liz! Hey, 'Liz!" It was her big sister, Louise, standing outside the kitchen in the rear flat. "Got some change on you, 'Liz?"

'Liz dealt the cards without looking up. Louise pushed her wide body through the dark, dingy hall and planted herself in the doorway.

"'Liz!" she bellowed, "ain't you still got that two-bit piece I gave you?"

'Liz squirmed around on her step and looked at her sister quickly.

"Two-bit piece!" Her lips exploded into a noise that was half a giggle, half a poop. "What you think I am? Brenda Frazier?"

"Don't be so fresh!" warned Louise, "what become of that two bits anyhow?"

'Liz gave an exasperated shrug. "I dunno."

"Ain't you got even a dime, huh, 'Liz?"

The girl shook her head until her hair flew in her eyes, Louise clicked her tongue and sighed. She turned, tramped back through the hallway muttering, "O.K. Don't pay *me* no mind. All you get tonight is boiled potatoes, an' if you don't like it—" she slammed shut the kitchen door—*"lump it!"*

The baby in the bedroom woke with a start and began to bawl. He was almost swallowed up in the wide sagging bed that four people shared at night. He wailed piercingly, wriggled like a tiny black bug pinned to the lumpy sheet.

"Shut your face!" snorted Louise. She dumped a few peeled potatoes into the water-filled pot on the stove. The baby yowled in the next room. He sounded like he would tear his guts out. Louise popped the cork off the gasoline flagon and poured some of its contents carefully into the stove tank. She screwed on the cap, pumped the tank and turned up a low flame.

Then she shoved through two red rags of curtains into the bedroom and grabbed the baby. "You gonna shut up?" she yelled into his sniveling face. She carried him back to the kitchen on one arm, gave him a piece of cold toast to keep him quiet. With her free hand she took a fork and poked at the potatoes....

There were six for supper that night. But Gloria, when she got there, said she couldn't eat. Sullenly she shoved her plate aside and got up from the table. Shuffled over to the bed, her knees rubbery under the burden of her expected child. The others ate the lukewarm potatoes in silence. No one but Boodgy dared to speak. He banged his fork down on the plate when he had finished his meager portion. "Is this all?" he asked.

The volcano that had smoldered in Louise's chest all day erupted. She rose to her full height and breadth, pushed away the table with spread hands. A bit more force and she would have shoved it clear out the window. Its thin legs quavered, the plates chattered nervously.

"Sure, that's all!" she exploded at her husband, "Maybe there'd be more if you didn't have enough in you already to smell the place up like a brewery! I been sweatin' in this kitchen all day! But I can't make sumpin' outa nothin'!"

'Liz ducked under the range of fire. She reached down quickly, jerked something out of her shoe. Then she scraped back her chair and bolted out of the room.

"Where you goin'?" screamed Louise, but 'Liz was already halfway down the hall. She scooted into the street, raced across the gutter like a fleeing thief, her damp fist tightly clenched around a coin. A gang of kids had already gathered in front of the candy store opposite her house. They were whistling, clapping, hopping to their own music when she bounced among them.

Two bits on a Saturday night, the gang and the piccolo! It would be worth six sacrificed suppers.

"Look what I got!" 'Liz held high the birthday money she had saved. There were cries of "Geez!".... "Where'd yo get it, 'Liz?".... "*Solid!*" A dozen hands pawed her raised arm. "Let's have a tune on the piccolo, hey!"

Proudly 'Liz mounted the candy store steps at the head of the group. "I want change of a quarter," she announced grandly, "an' I want *Panassie Stomp* on the piccolo with the Count."

The music throbbed out of the lit machine, groaning with the full undertone of the running bass. The kids jammed themselves into the little store and began to dance. 'Liz was at the hub of the excitement. The boys took her on in turns, sending her swiftly over the rough boards. Their dancing was agitated, quick with the restless rhythm of hunger. One by one the nickels plunked into the machine. *Wolverine Blues, Twilight in Turkey, Doggin' Around.*

Wearying, 'Liz and her partner broke into off-time. Slow, rocking, searching movement, at once hollow and full with the weight of hunger. Another partner broke in, on time. Again the world sped 'round, 'Liz flung out her body like they do at the Savoy. Routine. Break. Jig walk. Close together, far apart, together again. Teasing. Almost having and then not having. Her empty stomach was rumbling, beating wildly against the belt of her dress. A knot was tying itself around her heart, tighter, tighter. Together, apart, together. The street spun in all directions.

'Liz stumbled forward. She fell on her face.

"Aw, 'Liz!" ... "Cut it out, 'Liz!" ... "You gon' get your dress all dirty!" They thought she was kidding. Prodded her with their knees, poked her with the tips of their shoes. She lay still.

One or two of the girls tittered uncomfortably. The others stood around gawking, foolish. Rooster left a poker game nearby to investigate the trouble. He bent over 'Liz, chafed her wrists. Then he called to the man behind the counter, "Hey, Joe, give us a shot of King Kong for the kid!"

He lifted her over the doorway. Joe had poured out a jigger of the watery, yellowish liquid from a musty bottle stuffed with orange peels and kimmel seed. Rooster tilted the glass to 'Liz's lips. Whiskey dribbled down each side of her chin. She gulped, shuddered. Her eyes blinked open and she spat the stuff all over her dress. The first thing she thought of was Louise. If *she* ever found out what had happened tonight! 'Liz shut her mind against that awful possibility. Louise mustn't know!

"Say, you won't tell Louise about this, will you?" she begged. "Please, don't tell Louise!"

"No no," ... "It's O.K." ... "We won't rat," they all assured her.

She got up, unsteady, shivering. Started slowing across the street toward her stoop, shaking like a scared puppy.

Suddenly someone found a nickel that hadn't been used. Plunk, it was fed into the slot of the piccolo. *Fortune Tellin' Man* blared out. And in the darkness they moved again—thin shadows of hungry kids and their hungry dancing.

[*Opportunity* 17.7 (July 1939): 201–202]

THE FINE LINE: A STORY OF THE COLOR LINE

by Marian Minus

Cadie Culkey's slight childish figure, in the middle of the dusty South Carolina road, bent forward dejectedly, as if with each new step her knees would give way. The sun was half over the horizon, and the dusty road was thick with other poor-white workers who, like Cadie, were returning home after a long day at the mill. But Cadie walked alone. It was more than late-adolescent stubbornness that caused her refusal of their companionship. At sixteen she was contemptuous of her kind, and through them, by reflection, saw nothing for her future except weary acceptance of everything that seemed to lead, in the shorter or longer run, to defeat. Some long-forgotten time ago, she reasoned, her fellows on the road had wanted the answers to all the things she had come to question now, but that time was past and sunk in dreary resignation.

Cadie turned from the road to a gate in front of a small house. She stood there, her hand half on the latch, taking in the picture of her home. The sprawling, unpainted boards followed no pattern to form the house. Beside it was a seared garden patch, burnt by the hard beat of the sun, and at the garden's end was a pile of crumbling bricks which had lain there rotting for as long as she could remember. Across her vision, movement against the stillness of decay, ran the younger Culkeys, her brothers and sisters. Their bare feet scraped against the sunbaked earth. Cadie saw their sallow faces. She wanted to stay outside the gate forever.

The touch of her hand on the rusty latch made the thin man on the porch look up from the stick he was whittling. Lem Culkey was a confident consumptive, regularly denying the possession of normal strength in his lean body and living consistently by his conviction that he had fulfilled his mission in life when he gave his wife, Lucy, five dirty children. He dropped his eyes before Cadie's intense stare. Tobacco juice slid to the tip of his overhanging upper lip and hung there in glistening globules.

"Come on up an' set, Cadie," he said, breaking the bubbles on his lip and wiping the wetness on his knee.

Cadie stared at him, her slowly moving feet stopping altogether on the way from gate to porch. Lem looked down at the stick in his hand.

"Don't know what I'll whit' out next," he told her confidentially. "Your ma don't want no more can'lesticks. She don't want no more li'l pretties t' hold th' salt in." He looked up and went on, mournfully, "Says she got more'n she go any use f' now."

"Y'oughta get up off your behind an' go to work!" Cadie's voice shook.

Lem looked at her in surprise. "You know I ain't fitten t' do no work," he protested mildly. "I'm glad th' young 'uns ain't got no idea o' my weakness." He looked at the children playing in the yard. "An' by God I don't want nobody tellin' 'em their pa ain't fitten f' labor," he concluded belligerently.

"What diff'rence it make?" Cadie asked him. "Knowin' or not knowin' won't make no diff'rence soon's they big enough t' work in th' mill."

Lem broke the second set of bubbles which had formed on his lip. He slapped his wet hand on his knee.

"You been actin' mighty funny, Cadie, these las' few days," he accused her. "Aint' no call f' you t' carry on like you been doin'."

"No call 'cept I'm tired takin' care of a lazy ol' man, a ol' woman an' four yung 'uns! I'm tired a-coughin' out my gizzard in that dam' mill an' havin' niggers call me 'Cotton head.'"

"You ain't aimin' t' listen t' what niggers say, is you, Cadie?" Lem was grieved. "You don't care 'bout nigger talk."

"Nigger talk or not," Cadie snapped, "I *am* a cottonhead, an' I ain't no better off'n they are. Fact, some of 'em, live in better houses 'n this ol' shack!"

"Cadie," Lem rebuked her, "y' know that ain't true. Ain't no cause t' worry. Time's comin' when niggers won't have nothin' a'tall."

"Yeah, an' cottonheads like us goin' have nothin' a'tall right 'long with 'em." Cadie spat after the fashion of her father. "Ain't got nothin' now," she muttered.

"Th' Good Book says—"

"Don't you come tellin' me ag'in what th' Good Book says!" Her voice rose. "You ain't got nothin' t' do 'cept set here an' recollect what th' Good Book says. If y' got up an' did some work, you'd hafta put your mind on what's so now. Th' Good Book don't say nothin' 'bout cottonheads, does it? It don't say nothin' 'bout a house full o' dirty li'l brats runnin' 'round half naked, does it? What's it say 'bout a poor ol' woman wearin' herself out havin' dirty brats an' tryin' t' keep 'em from starvin' on the' four dollars I make a week? What's th' Good Book say 'bout all that?"

Cadie took a step toward the porch. Her voice was shrill, and people stared from the sidewalk as they passed. Lem had been straining forward in his chair. Now he sank back, sighing.

"You sure got a powerful way o' talkin,' Cadie," he said in admiration. He was about to continue when he saw the fierce look sharpen on her face. "Th' Good Book don't say nothin' 'bout what you ast," he admitted hastily. "It jus' gives comfort t' folks like us 'bout th' niggers." He leaned back and closed his eyes.

"You ol' fool," Cadie gasped. "You ol' ig'orant fool!"

She ran up to the porch and across it to the door, avoiding by habit the weak places in the boards. Lem heard her cursing and sobbing beyond the door.

"She oughten t' git upset like that," he said softly to himself. "It ain't fitten for a long life."

Cadie ran into the small room which she shared with the sister nearest her age. She slid down on the bed, coughing and cursing. The bed was hard and unyielding to the uncontrollable shaking of her body. Cadie fought its hard resistance as she fought the urgent gnawing in her throat and the pain in her chest.

Lucy Culkey came to the threshold, wiping her greasy fingers on a ragged gingham apron. She pushed a loop of hair out of her eyes.

"Heared you carrin' on, Cadie," she said wearily. "Ain't no need." She stepped across to the bed and put her work-heavy, floury-hot hand on Cadie's damp brow. "Ain't no need," she repeated.

Cadie tried to speak, but a new spasm of coughing overcame her. She began to sob, and tears streamed from her eyes while her throat opened convulsively against all efforts of her will for silence. Lucy ran from the room. She had seen Cadie like this before.

"Reely!" she screamed from the back of the house. "Reely, git me a pail o' fresh water from the well!"

A high, childish voice drifted back to her in answer. She turned and saw Cadie stumbling toward her, holding both hands hard against her flat chest.

"It's all right, ma," she said weakly. "It ain't so bad this time."

Lucy put her arm around Cadie's waist and let her into the kitchen. She brushed off a chair with her apron.

"Set down, Cadie," she said. "You set here an' res' an' drink a dipper o' fresh water."

She left Cadie and went to the door. "You Reely!" she screamed.

Cadie's hands went from her chest to her ears.

"Reely! Bring that water in this minute!" Lucy turned back to Cadie. "Them young 'uns outdo my soul." She jerked open the oven door and let it fall noisily on its loose hinges. "Don't you fret," she continued. "Reely'll be here in a minute." She snapped the oven door upward, slamming it hard so the latch would catch.

"Aw, ma," Cadie groaned. "Th' noise, th' noise."

Reely, a dirt-scratched boy of nine, burst open the screen door and thumped the pail of water on the floor.

"Git!" Lucy dismissed him. She pulled a dipper down from the wall and filled, then sloshed half its contents over Cadie's head and face. She handed her the rest, murmuring, "Drink it down slow. It'll do y' a heap o' good."

Cadie felt the water run through the tight places in her throat, and once she coughed, her face full in the dipper. Then the water settled in her stomach, cold and shocking to her fevered body.

"Feels like I got a lake inside me," she said. She stood up and hung the dipper back on the wall.

Lucy began to take pans from the top of the stove and from the oven. Cadie offered to help, but her mother, in one of her rare tender moods, made her sit down again.

"Set by th' air long as y' can," she said.

She brought out a pan of well-baked bones lying in a pool of grease and poured a pot of greens into a cracked bowl.

"I know y' like spare-ribs an' musta'd salat," she said, looking at Cadie.

Cadie nodded her head in painful agreement.

"An' hot hoecake." Lucy shook the pale white disc out of a heat-blackened pan.

Suddenly, the water seemed to bubble in Cadie's stomach. A flush of heat and the sight of the food sent her sick and stumbling to the door.

"Wish I had some milk," she said when the spasm had passed. "My stomach don't feel so good."

Lucy stared at her in amazement. "Y' know we ain't had no milk in over a year," she said. "That's a pretty notion f' you t' be havin'!" She pushed past Cadie out of the door.

"You, Reely! You, Meggs! All you young 'uns! Come on in t' your supper. Cadie been home near 'bout a hour. She wants somethin' hot in 'er belly!" She came back into the kitchen, pausing just inside the door to add, from ritual rather than necessity, "An' git your pa!"

"I ain't hungry, ma!" Cadie said unexpectedly, and hurried from the room before her mother could speak.

Lem had come quickly in response to Lucy's call. Cadie almost fell over him as she fled the kitchen.

"Y' comin' back t' eat, ain't you, Cadie?" he asked in surprise.

She went past him without answering. Out on the front porch she heard the clash of knives on forks in the kitchen. Once in awhile she could hear Lem sucking a spare-rib dry. She moved away from the sounds to the bottom step.

Twilight settled into night, and the moon came up. Red, the way it often is in summer in the hot South.

Cadie's solitary regard of the moon was broken by the younger Culkeys who came tearing around the side of the house from the back yard. Then Lem came out and sat on the edge of the porch, his legs dangling toward the ground.

"Y' shoulda took some nourishment," he greeted her reproachfully. "It ain't good t' work all day an' go t' bed on a empty stummick. Y' oughta take care o' yourself. Might hafta lose a day." He coughed deprecatingly.

"I didn't want all that hot grease inside o' me," Cadie told him.

Lucy, coming from the house, snorted, her tenderness past.

"She wanted milk," she said, settling in a creaking wicker rocker.

"Yeah," Cadie sighed. "A glass o' col' milk woulda made me feel good. It woulda kep' my stummick from cuttin' up." Her voice trailed away in confusion. She seldom revealed her desires to her family.

"'For ever' one that useth milk is unskilful in th' word o' righteousness, f' he is a babe,'" Lem quoted.

"I don't wanta hear nothin' out o' th' Good Book tonight," Cadie told him fiercely. "An' maybe I am a baby. I'm only sixteen, and' I'm doin' what *you* oughta be doin.' I'm takin' care o' seven folks." Her voice grew old as she repeated, "An' I'm only sixteen."

"Your pa's sick," Lucy reminded her from the darkness.

"I'm sick, too," Cadie cried, jumping up from the step. The moonlight fell on her pale hair, bleached by the long hours in the textile mill, and it looked more than ever like cotton.

"Set down, Cadie, set down," Lucy told her before she could speak.

Cadie sat on the step again, but she was not silent. "Workin' all day in that mill— I'm too young t' be coughin' fit t' die." Her voice choked, and she dropped her head in her hands.

"A woman's made t' be strong," Lucy told her. "A woman's burden ain't easy."

"Well, I ain't a woman yet!" Cadie raised her head. "I'm only sixteen." Pointing a quivering finger at Lem, she said, "What about a man? Ain't he suppose' t' be strong?" She stopped to cough. "He ain't," she went on, still pointing to her father. "Ain't a manly bone in his body."

Lucy began to hum a hymn. She was tired of the everlasting fight between Cadie and Lem. She felt sorry for the girl, but there was no denying Lem's consumption. She wasn't sure about Cadie's. Anyway, she couldn't go out and work herself. Thirty cents a day wasn't worth it since the young ones had to be looked after. The mumbled melody of the hymn drifted outward to the edge of the porch. Lem heard it and added his deep voice.

Over the sound of this, Cadie heard another song. Walking in the middle of the road before the house, a Negro boy was singing:

Boy, Oh boy, th' moon am red,
Dis ain' no night t' go t' bed—

Cadie looked up at the moon. Round now, it was still red.

"Th' moon sure is red," she said, agreeing with the figure already out of sight.

Lem and Lucy stopped their humming. "What you say, Cadie?" they asked in chorus.

"I said, th' moon sure is red."

Lem spat a stream of tobacco juice at a firefly that was winking on the ground at his feet. Lucy rocked on in the creaking chair, and the young Culkeys played noisily in the yard.

"Don't you go repeatin' nigger talk," Lem said finally, wiping the back of his hand against the side of his thigh.

"That's all y' ever done f' us, pa," Cadie said angrily. "Talk. Don't do this-an'- so 'cause niggers do it. Don't say this-an'-so 'cause niggers say it." She paused for breath and to keep the coughs from spilling out. "Niggers or not, I bet th' men help take care o' their families."

"Your pa's sick, Cadie," Lucy said sharply, not breaking the rhythmic rocking of her chair.

All at once, sitting there was more than Cadie could bear. She jumped up, cursed weakly, and walked from the yard.

"Guess th' gal's got growin' pains," Lem said without concern. When Lucy did not answer, he spat at another firefly.

Cadie went down the dusty stretch of road. The heat had not disappeared with the sun's sinking, and the moon, red as it was, seemed to make it hotter. She looked at it often as she walked. Her dragging feet stirred the dust, and soon it was in her nose and in her throat. She began to cough. Shaken and weak, she stepped over a narrow rut to the unpaved sidewalk and leaned against an unpainted fence which enclosed an unpainted house. Straightening up, she saw a blur of dark bushes beside the house.

"Figs," she said to herself. Without thinking she knew she wanted a handful. They would be cool now that the sun was down. She wished that she could get inside the yard unnoticed. Voices came from the porch, but she could not see the faces, and by sound alone she could not tell whether Negroes or whites spoke. At that moment, fatigue turned to hunger, and it did not matter who owned the leafy little trees.

She went to the gate and unlatched it. Hesitantly, she walked to the steps, then stopped. The faces a little above her on the porch were black.

"What you want?" The question came from the man. Cadie almost knew that he wanted to add, "white gal." His voice was suspicious and she could hear the woman murmuring.

"I wanted t' pick two-three figs," Cadie said in a rush.

The man and woman held a whispered conversation.

"Go pick 'em." It was the woman who finally spoke.

Without a word, Cadie ran to the side of the house. The first fig she pulled, wrenching it from the tree, was hot in her hand. The sticky milk, torn out where she had parted fruit from twig, ran over her fingers. She felt the fig lying heavy in her hand, and in the moonlight she could see the thick white fluid where it smeared her fingertips.

The woman came toward her. Cadie forgot the sticky smear on her hand and snatched the hot, pulpy fruit from the tree. She would take them home and put them in cold well water until they cooled. The woman touched the figs exploringly. Cadie saw the dark fingers pressed lightly against the fruit.

"These ain't fit t' eat," the woman said. "Too hot. Th' sun's been mighty hot an' it don't mean us poor humans t' forget it." She laughed and took her fingers from the figs. "Come on in th' house," she said. "I got some in th' ice-box."

She started walking away, but Cadie made no effort to follow. She stared after the woman, muttering, "Ice-box. She's got a ice-box." The woman looked back and called to Cadie to follow.

Cadie ran a few steps and reached her side. Without a glance at the man on the porch, she trailed after the woman through the little house to the kitchen. Now she could see that the woman was young. Somehow, Cadie had thought she'd be older than she was. It might have been memory of Lem's lament, "young niggers ain't polite t' white folks like th' ol' 'uns was."

The woman opened the door of a battered wooden ice-box.

"Ain't much t' look at," she said, "but it don't leak an' it ain't hard t' keep clean."

Cadie peeped over her shoulder and saw a jar of milk, blue-white through the blue glass of the jar. It looked cold. Cadie's desire for cold milk, to lie like a lake in her stomach as the water had, returned.

"Milk," she said in a low voice.

The woman stared at her, puzzled. Then her eyes went to Cadie's hands.

"Oh," she said. "That ol' fig milk sure is nasty when it gets a holt o' your hands." She hurried off to soak a towel in water for Cadie to wipe her fingers.

The figs which the woman took from the ice-box were firm and full inside their rich, dark skins. They were cold and almost black on the white plate.

"Take a handful," the woman said.

Cadie took two, then three, and, after a quick glance at the woman, she took two more. The plate was almost empty, and in the realization of this, hunger retreated before shame. She laid one back on the plate, but the woman shook her head in mild protest and put the plate down on the table.

"Ain't y' had nothin' t' eat?" she asked.

"Yeah." Cadie couldn't tell this Negro woman of her hunger. Lem always said no matter how bad off white folks got, niggers were worse off still, and lower in God's eyes. "Yeah, I had a good supper."

The woman looked at the pale hair, the thin face, and the flat body.

"Don't look like you had very many good suppers." She laughed companionably, sharing the unrecounted inadequacies of the past.

Cadie's face flushed, and the fig in her throat stuck there without warning. She began to cough. Her breath was short and she gasped and gagged. The woman slapped her on the back, tried to get her to drink water, and finally, in fright, called her husband.

The man came in. He stood just inside the door, his brows knit in suspicion and concern.

"Told y' to let this white gal go on 'bout 'er business," he complained to his wife.

The woman made a brisk motion for him to be silent, and wrung out a towel in which she put a piece of ice. She wrapped the towel around Cadie's head.

"She got a coughin' spell all of a sudden," she told her husband.

In the man's eyes was an urgent appeal to Cadie to leave.

"Must be nice havin' ice," Cadie said as soon as she could speak. The cold towel felt good against her head. She wanted to talk; to stay where ice could be pressed to her throbbing temples.

"Nice 'nough," the woman said, "but it costs a lot. It's kinda 'spensive f' poor folks."

Cadie looked around the room. The stove was newer than the one her mother had. Clean curtains hung at the window. And, there was the ice-box.

"You ain't really poor, are you?" she asked. "Don't look much like it," she added, looking around the room again.

Then she was silent. She did not hear the woman's amused denial or the man's bitter grunt. She was thinking about Lem. She wondered if he had failed to do his best within the limits of the poverty of his kind because he had known it would be insufficient, and if, in knowing, the very knowledge had driven him to defeat.

"She ain't listenin' to a word we sayin.'" The woman's observation cut through her thoughts. She smiled a little.

"Where y' live?" The man addressed his first words to her.

Recalling Lem's admonitions about treating Negroes as equals, Cadie could not tell them—she could not tell niggers—where she lived. She knew, painfully, what Negroes thought of the cottonheads who worked in the mills and lived in Mill Town. She named a street on the other side of town, away from the little houses all built alike on streets that looked alike.

She could see the Negroes looking at each other in disbelief. She wished that she hadn't made the neighborhood such a good one.

"If y' live over there," the man said skeptically, "guess y' jus' makin' fun of us when y' said we wasn't poor." He waited for her to speak, and when she didn't, he asked "What you pa do?"

"He's foreman at th' mill," Cadie answered after a moment's hesitation.

"Them mills!" the woman said quickly. "I 'clare I see young girls comin' outa there lookin' like ol' women. Poor folks sure have a hard time. Sometimes I don't know what this worl' is comin' to."

"Don't was'e no pity on them," her husband said. "What 'bout yourself? It ain't no worse on them t' work in th' mill than 'tis on you t' have t' take any ol' job Miss Ann hands out."

"Yeah, but even if it is a hard job," Cadie protested, "it ain't like workin' in th' mill. Y' don't get stuff in your lungs t' make y' cough out your insides."

They looked at her in surprise and comprehension. But Cadie was making swift comparisons and before they could speak, she went on.

"Y' got any young 'uns?"

"We got two," the woman said. "They're sleepin' now."

"They ain't sick?" Cadie asked, alarmed. Lem said there were things niggers caught and lived through that would kill white folks.

The woman laughed. "Lord, no," she said. "They jus as healthy as they c'n be. How come y' ask that?"

"You said—well—" Cadie stopped, then tried again. "What they doin' in bed so early?"

"She puts 'em t' bed right after it gets dark," the man said, pointing to his wife.

"Oh."

Cadie went on making comparisons. She thought of the young Culkeys who ran around the yard until the elder Culkeys went to bed. She thought about Lem. He had never cared whether his children lived or died. He didn't even care if Lucy starved them half to death to buy him chewing tobacco every day. She thought about the long hours she had worked in the mill since she was fourteen.

All of a sudden she wanted to ask Lem about whites and blacks. She wanted him to reassure her of her place, and the place of all her kind, in the system of things. Right now she couldn't understand the superiority Lem had told her she possessed because she was white. These blacks were better off than the Culkeys had ever been. And Lem could not say it was just empty nigger talk. She could see for herself. Evidence of all they said was before her eyes.

She stood up, dropping the figs from her lap.

"I better go," she said in a tense voice.

"Don't y' want th' figs?" the woman asked her in bewilderment.

Cadie didn't want the figs. She wanted nothing beyond the reassurance of Lem. If what he had told her all these years was false, what did she have to believe in?

She did not thank them for the figs. Nor did she wish them goodnight. She ran through the house and down the walk to the street.

The moon was white now, all its redness gone. The heat was still stifling, and Cadie thought, momentarily of the milk she had wanted. Some niggers had ice when it was hot. Some niggers had milk for their children.

Lem was still sitting on the edge of the porch. As Cadie drew near, he sent a stream of tobacco juice toward a firefly. The brown stuff was clearer now in the moon's white light. Cadie stopped. It was hopeless. Lem looked ageless and eternal sitting there. Even his insistent, regular efforts to drown a firefly were everlasting. She knew how he would answer her questions. He would tell her again that niggers were dirt beneath her feet, and he would not care that she had seen a Negro man provide better for his family than he had provided for his. He would sit there sending that inevitable brown stream curving without accuracy toward a winking light on the ground.

"Y' back, Cadie?" Lem broke the bubbles on his lip and wiped his hand on his knee.

"Where y' been?" Lucy asked simultaneously. She didn't stop rocking.

"Yeah, I'm back." Cadie went up the steps and into the house.

"Lem," Lucy said a few minutes later, "y' hear Cadie coughin'?" She waited until he spoke before she set the chair in motion again.

"Yeah," he answered. "She's coughin' hard."

He spat on the ground, toward a pale yellow light. The light went out, and Lucy rocked in her chair. [*Opportunity* 17.11 (November 1939): 333–337, 351]

UNCLE BEN

by Helen Faw Mull

Pathetic, uncomplaining, lonely, Uncle Ben lived out his meager days in the midst of a society which offered him no husk of sympathy or understanding. He was a town character, a quaint old colored man, a relic of the sixties, pointed out as impersonally to sight-seers as were the overgrown breastworks on Fort Hill and the time-healed cannonball wounds in the venerable trees of the National Cemetery. Few know where or how he lived. Occasionally a fair-haired child would watch his regular pilgrimage along Roswell Street with distant, impotent pity. On Sundays the congregation of the white Presbyterian church would take casual cognizance of his presence in the old slave gallery, where he would rise punctiliously for the hymns and stand alone in silent, solitary worship.

But it was around the railroad station that he was best known. Whenever the Dixie Flyer, southbound, would whistle from behind the saddle-back of old Kennesaw, there on the station platform would be Uncle Ben, dressed in his faded Yankee uniform, meeting the train. If there were white folks waiting for the train, too, Uncle Ben would stand at a respectful distance, holding his shapeless felt hat in his hand. His wispy gray hair was like steel wool, standing out in a wide nimbus above his antique-mahogany face. The station agent would halloo to him familiarly, and most of the white folks coming and going would toss him a "Howdy, Uncle Ben!" To each greeting he would reply with a stiff bow and a pleased smile. But no one would pause to hear how he did, because his presence at train-time was so customary as to indicate that things were as usual with him. Meeting the trains was his one business in life. Tradition had it he had not missed a south-bound train in forty years. When the station agent had nothing to do, he used to tell Uncle Ben that he was crazy to go to so much trouble. The old man would grin dubiously and nod his head. He never tried to justify himself by argument. But the reason for his pains was the simplest one in the world: he was expecting someone.

For two-score years he had been awaiting his wife's return. During the hectic days of Reconstruction, she had made fun of his loyal contentment and, slapping a new red hat on her head, had gone off with a dashing young buck in a handsome blue uniform. Uncle Ben had grieved, but he had never blamed her. She was young, and everything was topsy-turvy in those days. He knew she would not be happy among those fine-feathered Yankees. He knew she would come back to him by and by. And should she come at morning, noon, or night, he did not mean for her to be unwelcomed.

No one knew how he had come upon the old blue uniform. He always wore it, with its high collar hooked up neatly beneath his wrinkled brown chin. His thought must have been to equal the lure that had enticed away his beloved. During the years of a generation's rise, its color had dulled with dust and wear, and its shape had fitted itself affectionately to the slight, gnarled, rheumatic form of its wearer.

When it rained, the suit was brightened by the washing; for only in the hardest downpour would Uncle Ben carry his bent-ribbed black umbrella. He never wore an overcoat. When it grew cold, he would put on one layer after another beneath the soldier suit, so that by the end of February, the coat's creases would show only as worn lines on the smooth stuffed surface, and the brass buttons down the front would be straining to hold together the points of inverted scallops. Winter or summer, Uncle Ben was always on the platform when a train from the North was expected.

As the engine rumbled to a stop, Uncle Ben would grow palsied with anticipation. The light of other days would gleam in his faded eyes. Standing apart from the white folks, he could look over their heads and catch the first view of every colored passenger that left the train. There were seldom more than two. But the old man would wait, always hopeful, until the conductor boarded the train again and the wheels began to roll.

Then Uncle Ben would look around self-consciously, realizing that the joke was on him. If the expressman twitted him, he would grin a wide sheepish grin, enclosed by deep marks of parentheses in his withered cheeks. She had not come this time, but she would come sometime. No amount of banter could shake his confidence. Putting on the old felt hat, he would shuffle off, his shoulders drooping slightly more than before, but on his face already the reflection of his glad reunion with Mattie when she should come, possibly on the very next train.

Sometimes the big fast trains roared by without hesitating. This station was only a flagstop for long-distance travelers. Then, indeed, the futility of the old man's trip bowed him and slowed his gait. But he would not run the risk of missing the time that Mattie might be coming home from a far country.

One morning in the early spring, Uncle Ben was on his way to meet the ten-thirty train. A cardinal flashed from one young-leafed tree to another and filled the dingy station yard with the unquenchable expectancy of his song. The warm sun that glinted from the inside of the train-track's curve must have penetrated even Uncle Ben's many-layered bosom; for a smile lighted his weathered face, and the far-away look in his eyes, as he gazed beyond old Kennesaw to the north, held dreams of a gay, tantalizing young girl and a love mellowed with years. The train whistled languidly. This was neither the Flyer nor the new Dixie Limited, but the accommodation from Chattanooga. It would make a lingering stop and possibly half a dozen colored people would get off.

The first one Uncle Ben saw, steadying herself at the top of the steps, was a ponderous colored woman with a newspaper parcel under one arm and a baby under the other. She moved in such an odd, crab-wise manner, in her effort to keep her three tagging children close to her skirts, that she blocked not only the passage but the sight of the other passengers in the vestibule of the jim-crow car. At last the conductor became impatient. But Uncle Ben, who had waited forty years, could wait without vexation. He watched the family party through their difficulties and saw, waiting to descend the steps behind them, a gay, laughing girl in a red hat. At the sight of her, Uncle Ben, unnoticed, gave a squeak of delight and stumbled forward. He pushed his way through a group of startled white folks. He waved his hat to make her look. She did not see him yet. She'd wonder how he knew which train to meet. Quivering with eagerness, he reached the place where the young woman in the red hat was just stepping off the train.

He stood before her, grinning. "Well, Mattie," he said, "you're back!"

"Who's this ole fool talking to?" the young woman asked indignantly as she stepped aside to go past him.

"He won't hurt nobody," soothed the conductor. "His wife ran away. Went North after the War. Been forty years, I reckon, but he's always lookin' for her to come back."

"Doan yuh know me, Mattie?" pleaded Uncle Ben piteously. "Been lookin' fer yuh."

The colored girl spoke insolently: "Be your age, Gran'pa! Your ole lady ain't comin' back now. If she ain't dead, she's too ole to travel."

"Then—then you ain't Mattie?" he asked, bewildered. "When she comin'?"

"She ain't comin', I tole yuh." The girl laughed carelessly and went off up the street.

The vestibule was empty now and the platform was already clearing. The conductor climbed back on his train and soon it rolled leisurely on. Uncle Ben was left alone in his confusion. As he stared after the slowly disappearing train, tears tracked across his wrinkled brown cheeks. He whimpered like a deserted puppy.

The station agent called to him in an effort at kindness, "Don't mind, Uncle Ben. Prob'ly she warn't worth waitin' for nohow."

The old man looked dumbly in the direction of the well-meant words. He still clutched his hat in front of him as if it were the only familiar thing left in his world. He could not speak. He bowed in acknowledgment of the station agent's attempt. Or perhaps he only seemed to bow, because something within him that had supported him through the years had suddenly wilted. His thin legs, bent with rheumatism, looked almost too frail to carry him. From long habit, he lifted his eyes once more to the north. Then shaking his head sadly, he turned his back toward Kennesaw and trudged wearily away.

That night when the 9:17 whistled mournfully around the mountain, the station agent noticed that Uncle Ben was not on the platform to meet it. He chuckled to himself. "Guess he's given up hope. Humph! Forty years! Poor ole fellow!"

Two days later, the white-folks' weekly paper noted briefly that Uncle Ben, familiar character around the railroad station, had been found in his cabin, dead. The coroner, it reported, had issued a certificate of death. The cause assigned: old age.

[*Opportunity* 17.12 (December 1939): 370–371]

The Woman in the Window

by Ramona Lowe

The employment agency sent her to a place that wanted a cook. Fifteen a week, they paid. Twelve hours a day, but after all fifteen's good wages.

When the proprietor, Mr. Parsons, saw her he was delighted. He rubbed his hands and showed her the kitchen. There was no need for a prolonged interview. He could see that she was just the thing. And the rest of the establishment was invited to take a peep to see what a treasure had been found.

Mrs. Jackson went right to work frying chicken with a lofty unconcern for the curious faces peeping in at the door and the proprietor's nervously evident pleasure. The tenth time the proprietor appeared in the kitchen he was accompanied by a stout man with an appraising eye, apparently a partner in the restaurant.

"Mr. Kraft," Parsons said loudly by way of introduction, "this is our new cook."

Mrs. Jackson turned her broad back indifferently on the two men. This was not the expected reaction. Parsons cleared his throat for attention. "I didn't get your name."

"You never asked it," Mrs. Jackson corrected him brusquely. "My name's Mrs. Jackson."

"What's your first name?" asked Kraft, surveying her with the brazen air of a master.

"Where I works," Mrs. Jackson replied with finality, "I'm known as Mrs. Jackson."

Kraft, trying to overlook this show of dignity, simply remarked, "She'll be a beaut in the window, Mike. A beaut!"

The proprietor rubbed his hands and addressed Mrs. Jackson. "You look straight from the South," he said.

Mrs. Jackson, suspicious of the compliment, was noncommittal.

"I'll bet your home's in Georgia," continued Parsons chaffingly. Without waiting for this conjecture to be confirmed, he turned to his partner. "How soon can you get the equipment up?"

"Couple of weeks for everything," Kraft replied.

"Good. Good. Mrs. Jackson, we're going to make a few alterations, but business will go on just the same. When the alterations are complete, you will be cooking in the window!"

Shock ran through Mrs. Jackson. Her mind had not followed the trend of their remarks to this conclusion.

"Yes, ma'm," Kraft rocked on his heels. "You'll be displayed just like the pancakes and the waffles."

Mrs. Jackson was verbally not quite equal to the unexpected. She knew where she stood, but she didn't know how to express it. "The 'ployment agency jus' tol me cookin'," she floundered.

"That's all it is," said Kraft. "Cookin'."

"What you talkin' 'bout a winda?" she wanted to know.

"We're gonna let you do your cookin' in the winda," Kraft explained.

"I doan like nobody watchin' me cook," she protested.

The proprietor sensed the need of tact. "It should be a privilege," he assured her, clipping his words and using his hands for emphasis.

"Humph!" was Mrs. Jackson's wordless comment. Signs of anger were becoming evident.

Kraft selected a piece of chicken from the freshly cooked pile.

"I ain' one for a show, Mr. Parsons," Mrs. Jackson explained; "so if it's a show you want I reckon you'll have t' get somebody else."

But the proprietor's zeal could not recognize lack of enthusiasm in anyone else. "We're gonna have all new equipment," he announced. "Everything new. You can see everything that's going on in the street. Our customers will see how clean and tempting everything is. We'll run the frauds that advertise Southern cooking out of business."

Mrs. Jackson was not interested.

But Kraft, eating his piece of chicken, knew a formula for compulsion to his will. "We'll make it eighteen a week—give you a vegetable preparer and a dishwasher," he offered.

Mrs. Jackson did not take long to consider. A family that had to be supported, when jobs were scarce and poor-paying, made duty triumph over pride.

Parsons beamed. "Then it's eighteen a week. All settled."

Kraft wiped his greasy fingers on a dish towel with the satisfied and confident air of a man who always knows how to settle all things. "Anybody who can cook chicken like that is worth a million," he said.

When the alterations were complete, Mrs. Jackson was moved into the window. She was wearing her neat blue cover-all apron. But she hadn't reckoned with enterprise.

Parsons hovered about, rubbing his hands.

"Mrs. Jackson, that's fine. Now. I wonder if you have a skirt. Green or purple. And a big white apron. Then we'll have to have a bandanna."

Mrs. Jackson was appalled. She drew herself up indignantly. "No, sir!" she said. "I ain' got none of the them things."

Parsons was not discouraged. "Well, we'll have to get them, Mrs. Jackson. We'll have to get them."

And he did.... He got a voluminous dark purple skirt, a big white apron, a loose snowy blouse, a green shawl and a red bandanna. "Now," he cautioned, "no corsets, Mrs. Jackson, and we're made."

Mrs. Jackson, who had always minimized her bulk with the soberest of colors, was stubborn. "I'm cookin' in this here winda, but I ain' gonna look like no circus freak."

"This is Southern," said Parson brightly.

"The South ain' never had nothin' looked like that," averred Mrs. Jackson.

Parsons, convinced of his infallibility, was heedless of criticism. "Now I'm just going to make you a present of this," he said.

But Mrs. Jackson would have none of his generosity. "What I want with that stuff?" she snapped.

Parsons, baffled by this ingratitude, was reduced to one word, "Please."

"Why, folks'd laugh," argued the offended woman.

Parson was exultant again. "That's just it! That's just what we want! We want people to laugh."

Mrs. Jackson put down her cooking fork with a look that predicted resignation from a distasteful occupation.

"Twenty dollars a week," offered the resolute Parson, remembering how Kraft had achieved his success.

Mrs. Jackson had a conscience quickened by four little children who had to be clothed and fed and who belonged to her. She grumbled, "Ain' *nobody* ever wore no such foolishness!" But she accepted.

Parsons was jubilant. There was his bright spot to attract, his mass of color to display, his invitation to new volumes of business. He arranged the bandanna-ends to stand up like two impudent ears. His caricature lacked but one detail.

"Now if you could just smile, Mrs. Jackson."

But Mrs. Jackson couldn't. "I spose you think smiles is put on like cloes," she said. "I ain' no actress, Mr. Parsons."

So she set to work in the window. Children trooped past, just out of school. One of the white youngsters, sighting her, cried out gleefully, "Oooh lookee, Aunt Jemima!"

"That Aunt Jemima?" queried another.

"Sure that's Aunt Jemima. Hey you, Aunt Jemima!"

One of the colored youngsters, flattening his dusky face against the pane, saw his mother.

The blood ran molten from her throat to the pit of her stomach.

"Oh black mammy! Oh Aunt Jemima!" shouted the white children. And one broke out in song,

> *"Nigger, nigger in the pot.*
> *Stew him till his bones all rot."*

The dark youngster ran on, his companions following with their tormenting ditty.

Mrs. Jackson wondered if her other children would pass by. The perspiration stood out on her forehead. She had no strength to wipe it away. She leaned against the table and looked out, and the world looked in curiously at the embodiment of a fiction it had created. But then three round, dark faces appeared at the pane who had never imagined this fantasy before them. They gazed with wonder. With an almost imperceptible movement of her head, she ordered them away. They started to run, but the youngest looked back and asked, "What's Mama doing there?"

Coming out of the alley-way, her day's work done, Mrs. Jackson was confronted by a huge new neon sign in front of the restaurant. It bore the legend: *Mammy's*.

What could she say to the children? Should she take advantage of her superior position and force them to an unquestioning subservience to the indignities of human life, or should she make them comrades in her battle for a livelihood? When she reached the door of her flat, she paused. She was so ashamed. Four pairs of eyes were wide open as she tiptoed into the room. "You wake? she asked.

"Yes'm," replied the eldest.

Mrs. Jackson took off her coat and hat busily, wishing vaguely that they had been asleep and she might defer explanation till morning at least. But her young son allowed her no leeway. "Mama, that wasn't you in the winda, was it?" He asked the question with a downward inflection, as though convinced that it couldn't have been she.

"Yes, honey, that was me. Why ain' you children sleep?" There was silence for a moment. Then another question.

"What you in the winda for?"

"I got t' work. Tha's my job."

"I thought you did cookin', Mama," remarked one of the girls.

"Tha's cookin.'"

Her son thought. Then he spoke. "I don't like that kind of cookin'."

"Now you children jus' lissen t' me. There's some things you got t' unnerstan'. Some work's dignified 'n' some ain' so dignified. But it all got t' be done. My work's cookin' 'n' there ain' nothin' wrong with that. If I didn' cook you wouln' have no shoes 'n' I wound' have no shoes 'n' we wouldn' have nothin' t' eat 'n' I 'speck we'd jus' lay up here 'n' die." She paused for breath, then went on:

"The owner man where I works thinks he gonna dress me up t' look like a ol' Southern mammy 'n' get a lotta business—

"What's a ol' Southern mammy, Mama?"

"A Southern mammy's a ol' colored woman who had the nursin' of all the little white children t' do in the South doin slavery times. Sometimes you hears folks talkin' big 'bout their ol' mammy 'n' how powerful much they loved her 'n' all."

"Is that good, Mama?" asked her son, doubting that a mammy was to be approved.

"Well, when you hears such talk you jus' say, 'uh huh,' 'n' let whoever's talkin' talk on."

"Then what happened after you was a Southern mammy, Mama?" The little girls were impatient.

"Then I had t' do my cookin' in the winda. 'N' when you go pas', you can speak, but doan you linger. 'N' if your little fren's asks questions, you tell'm, that's your mama all right. She's got t' work for a livin.'" She paused. *"N' son, doan you never let me see you run no more when a body say nigger. You turn roun' 'n' give'm such a thrashin' they woan never forget. Unnerstan'?"*

The youngster remonstrated. "They said in Sunday school we wasn't to fight—"

"You got t' use a little horse sense bout some things, son," his mother replied tersely. "Now you all go t' sleep."

The little boy went back to his cot and the little girls snuggled against each other under the thin blanket. Mrs. Jackson was about to lift her weary self from the edge of the bed when the smallest girl, as if divining the trouble stirring in her mother's soul, crept up to her and whispered, "Mama, I thought you looked pretty in the winda. Real pretty."

A DAY'S PAY: A SHORT STORY

by Elise D. Challeno

Someone had been at work on the colored advertisements and the white-painted walls of the subway station. Fatuously smiling ladies disclosed blackened gaps in place of teeth and laughing children sprouted full-grown moustaches and beards. Nasty little innuendoes adorned the borders of the advertisements and in a final burst of genius the wag had scribbled, *This way to the Bronx Slave Market.*

Jessie got off here, clutching her tabloid nervously, and found her way out of the station and onto the bright sunlight of Westchester Avenue. For a moment she stood looking up and down the street, then hesitantly she walked a block, glancing curiously at the other colored women who were strolling leisurely along. Some of them were neatly dressed, others were run-down at the heels and badly dilapidated, but each carried a familiar brown paper-wrapped bundle or a telltale bag. By the time each had sauntered down the avenue and back, a prospective employer would appear, usually dragging a small child by the hand. Having idly surveyed the shop windows, chatting brightly to the child meanwhile, the white woman would presently approach one of the strollers and accost her. For a few minutes they would haggle over wages, both seemingly disinterested and both obviously distrustful of each other, then they would go off together, followed by the envious stares of the other women.

Struggling to appear unconcerned as one after another worker was hired—even some who had joined the ranks much later than she had—Jessie continued to plod up and down the block. A storekeeper came out to perk up his vegetables with a sprinkle of water, and he stared at her curiously, ogling her slim figure with greedy eyes.

"Hey, you!" He jerked his thumb in her direction. "You wanna come upstairs and work for my wife?"

Jessie glanced up at the curtained windows of the apartment above the store and then looked down hastily. He was appraising her ankles now.

"No," she stammered, "I was just waiting for someone I know."

The fellow shrugged his shoulders and turned back to his fruit and vegetables. Picking up a duster, he gave them a gentle flick or two.

Jessie took her fears around the corner. She was beginning to grow discouraged. Perhaps the vegetable man was a perfectly harmless simpleton with a fat wife and three children upstairs—perhaps she had turned down a good job—perhaps nobody would hire her anyway, she was so thin and anxious. But if she didn't get a job today, how could she go home and face Ma and Aunt Emma? Ma had always had a job until her rheumatism got the best of her. Aunt Emma could always get a job. All the other women down of Mulberry Street could get jobs, except those who didn't want to work, and they knew how to get along too.

She was on a side street now, a street with neat brick houses in rows, and hedges evenly clipped. As she passed, she hoped desperately that someone would come out of one of them and ask her to come in to work. Then as she neared the end of the row, a wrinkled little old woman did come out.

"Girl, girl!" she called in a shrill voice.

Jessie's heart leaped. A job at last.

The old woman offered twenty-five cents an hour, and Jessie in her relief would gladly have accepted, but she remembered in time the advice from home. "Always be sure to bargain." At her timid protest, the woman raised the bid to thirty cents an hour and carfare, for an eight-hour day.

"And maybe you come again next week, yes?"

After the little frame house on Mulberry Street, this house seemed beautiful to Jessie. In the living room there was heavy, square modernistic furniture, covered with a brocaded fabric. Rich velvet draperies hung from the windows and bookcases lined two sides of the room. There were several books and magazines strewn about.

Jessie tied her head with a cloth she had brought and began at once. To her inexperience it seemed a back-breaking monotony of sweeping, scrubbing, dusting, polishing, bending and dragging and lifting until her breakfast rose up and coiled itself into an unpleasant lump in her throat. Living room, dining room, the stairs and hallway and "just a few small things to be washed for the children." The children, Jessie surmised, were the two grown girls and a boy whose pictures she had seen in the living room.

After a long while it was lunch time. Her employer produced some warmed-over potatoes, a few cold beets and a fried egg, at which the lump in Jessie's throat turned over rebelliously. As soon as the old woman's back was turned, she slid it off the plate into the garbage and buried it deep in the pail. She was grateful for a cup of warm tea and a couple of dry cookies.

Three bedrooms, kitchen, bathroom and a small foyer in the front of the house. The woman followed her from room to room, peering at each piece of furniture, finally picking up Jessie's newspaper and settling herself in the most recently dusted chair until Jessie was ready to move on to the next room.

The last hour seemed to be endless. Jessie felt that she could not drag the mop another inch. But the thought of two dollars and fifty cents sustained her. Lift, pull, push, shove—only one more room to go. She was moving mechanically now, she could not feel the motion of the dust cloth in her hand nor see clearly the outline of the countless small objects on the hanging shelf in the foyer. She picked up something, dusted it, and returned it to its place on the shelf, something else and then something slippery and roundish which slid from her numb fingers and splintered into a hundred pieces of china on the hardwood floor.

Her employer came rushing out. She gathered up the fragments and held them in her lap, tenderly, like a favorite child.

"My vase—my precious Ming vase—fifty dollars it cost me!" She moaned over and over again.

For a time she seemed not to see Jessie, who was standing there transfixed. Then she jumped up to face the girl, letting all the pieces tinkle to the floor unheeded. Her face mottled with rage.

"You—you—you dumb girl!" she spluttered. "That was a very valuable vase you broke! Get out of my house!" Her voice rose higher. Get out of my house before I call the police!"

As in a daze, Jessie had been standing there listening to this tirade. At the mention of the police she was terrified. Stopping only to get her hat and coat, she took the woman's advice and fled. Hurrying down the street, she expected any minute to hear the voice of a policeman behind her. Where could she get fifty dollars to pay for a vase if they arrested her? Not until she was safe on the subway train did she recover from her fright.

Sitting in the train with other people going home from their day's work, Jessie clutched an empty pocketbook. She had spent her last nickel for the ride home. She was sweaty and grimy, her shoulders ached, her hands were blistered, her finger nails were broken. And she had nothing to show for her day's work. She fought to keep back the tears.

The other people on the train were unconcerned. They were stupidly gazing into space or reading their newspapers. A man directly across from her sat with his toes turned in. He was reading about a chorus girl who had been found slain in bed. His mouth hung open and he licked his lips slowly as he took in the implications of the case.

Jessie thought of going home empty-handed. Ma and Aunt Emma would call her a fool for working all day for nothing. For the first time the thought came to Jessie that the woman had been glad for an excuse not to pay her, that she had wanted to cheat her and that she had indeed found an easy mark. Jessie had not even stopped to examine the vase. For all she knew, the precious Ming vase might have been bought at the five-and-ten. She began to feel very sorry for herself. Her arms ached unbearably, her legs hurt, her hands, her knees. Tears of self-pity trickled slowly down her brown cheeks.

When she got off at her station, the winter twilight had closed in. It was chilly. But an idea had come to Jessie that made her cheeks burn in the darkness. She was not going home with an empty pocketbook. If she could not earn money like Ma and Aunt Emma and the good women on Mulberry Street, she would have to take care of herself as the others did. She wiped the tears carefully from her face and then, emerging from the subway, she began to saunter idly up and down the same street, much as she had done this morning. Only this time she peered searchingly into the face of each male passerby.

[*Opportunity* 18.5 (May 1940): 136–137]

THE RED DRESS: A SHORT STORY

by Grace W. Tompkins

Lily hummed softly to herself as she expertly flipped the corn dodgers in the big old iron spider. The afternoon sun had left the stoop and it was getting along towards six o'clock. It was almost time for Zeke to come shuffling up the cinder path. One mean man—that Zeke! The hum grew deeper, throatier.

Baby Zeke climbed the stoop and sat down carefully on the door sill. Lily stopped humming and watched him. That child certainly was a caution. He methodically pulled the legs off a grasshopper. Next he tackled the wings. Soon the ravished insect lay jerking crazily on the step. When it was quite still, the child wiped his grimy hands on his shirt and said slowly,

"Dat hoppuh's daid. Sho' nuff!"

Lily stood lost in thought. A swish of the old broom would remove that small corpse. A dead husband would be something else again. She reached for the broom.

"Look out, honey," she said softly, and brushed the stoop clean. She cast a sly look at the shelf above the table. There was an untidy array of cans up there. Her "seasonings," she called them. A new can sat there and she had carefully pasted a label on it. The label said "Soda." The humming started again.

She turned back to the big coal stove and shifted the battered, greasy pots about. Savory steam was pushing up the top on the biggest one where collards and salt pork were boiling. She removed the evenly browned dodgers and poured more batter on the spider. From the shelf she took a pinch of soda for the greens, but she didn't take it out of the new can.

A soft shuffle on the path warned her of Zeke's sullen approach. Tiger, the mangy dog who had been asleep in front of the stove, made a wild dash for the door and disappeared under the house. Zeke despised Tiger. Baby Zeke looked up and said, "Pop."

Lily busied herself setting the table while Zeke stopped at the pump to splash water over his face and hands. He entered the kitchen with a grunted greeting and sat down at the table. She picked up the baby, wiped his hands with the wet dish rag, and set him on his packing-box high chair. She put the steaming food on the table and filled Zeke's bowl with thick black coffee. He ate in silence, shoving the food between his thick lips and washing it down with long draughts of the scalding coffee. His eyes never left his plate.

As the shadows drew deeper, Lily pushed back her chair and lighted the lamps; one for the table and one for the window. Satiated, Zeke leaned back in his chair and stared at her. She dropped her eyes, hastily.

"S'pose yuh goin' tuh meetin' 'gin tuh night, huh?" he said.

Her reply was a whisper.

"I been heahin' things," he snorted ominously. "Yuh bettah be keerful."

A sharp retort died on her lips. Baby Zeke, sensing something familiar in the tone of his father's voice, began to whimper.

"Shet that bawling brat up!" roared Zeke, sending his chair tumbling backward from the table.

Lily grabbed the child quickly and disappeared in the sleeping room. Zeke righted the chair and was soon asleep at the table, head buried on his arms.

Tiger put an inquiring head in the door, but hearing Zeke's snores, retreated to his hiding place under the house.

II

The house in which they lived sat at the end of Cranston's pasture. It was built of non-descript boards and consisted of two large rooms and a lean-to. The kitchen faced the west. By passing through the pantry, one entered the sleeping room. It was necessary to cross the stoop to get to the lean-to where Lily did her washing when the weather was too bad to use the yard.

The kitchen, where she spent most of her time, contained no part of Lily. The large coal range took up most of one wall and an old-fashioned safe filled the rest of it. Here she kept her dishes, an assorted lot, donated by the Cranston's cook from time to time. A table with a red-and-white-checked cloth was pushed against the opposite wall and over it hung the shelf of "seasonings." The remainder of the foodstuff was kept in the wide pantry except ham and bacon, which hung in the lean-to, and strings of red pepper and garlic, which decorated the curtainless windows. The bare wood floor, worn with many scrubbings, was still far from clean. Two chairs and a few packing cases completed the furnishing.

But the sleeping room was different. Here was Lily. Its two small windows were hung with a red cotton print purchased at the Square. A large, much washed, but still beautiful rag rug completely covered the floor. This was a gift from the Cranston house also. A low rocker had a gay red cretonne cover and a home-made footstool had a cushion of the same material. Lily loved red. The large brass bed had a snowy white counterpane while beneath it, in the day time, was hidden Baby Zeke's pallet. Between the windows was a marble-topped table on which sat a portable phonograph which she never dared play while Zeke was in the house. And last, there was a huge full-length mirror with a gaudy gilt frame that held the place of honor opposite the door.

The yard surrounding the house was swept daily, and near the fence each year Lily tried to encourage a garden which usually sprang up with hope in the Spring and died in despair before Summer was a month old.

Although the house was owned by the Cranstons, it belonged to the Mobleys as long as they wanted to stay there.

III

Zeke Mobley was a coal-black Negro with heavy features and thick wooly hair. He stood six feet in his bare flat feet and his breadth of shoulder was startling. His evil little eyes were set close together and bored into one without blinking, while the muscles in his heavy jaw knotted and writhed. He was known throughout Cranstonville as a hard worker, but a "bad Negro." His temper was poisonous and it was whispered that he had once almost torn a section hand apart with his bare hands. He carried neither gun nor knife as most of the dock wallopers did. His reputation was his safeguard. Whatever attracted Lily to him always remained a mystery, for Lily had "class"—or at least she had had before she married Zeke.

Lily was a "high yaller" type with course, wavy hair. Her oval face held dark frightened eyes, a rather thin nose and wide full lips. Her teeth were even and well-cared-for. Although she was slim, her breasts were heavy and rounded. Her feet were long and narrow and her hands thin and tapering.

Lily liked pretty clothes. Before she had met Zeke she had worked in the Cranston house. Many bits of finery had come her way. She had learned by precept how to keep her teeth white and her hands well groomed. Whenever she had been to the stores in the Square to market for the House, the odor of old Mis' Cranston's gardenia perfume had lingered behind her. Yes, Lily had had class!

Then, Zeke had come to town. A big, swaggering, over-bearing male. It must have been his shoulders that got Lily, for in a short time she had married him and set up housekeeping at the foot of the pasture. It wasn't long before little Zeke had come along and she had stopped working at the Big House.

And now she was tired. Tired of being browbeaten and bullied by Zeke. Even little Zeke was not going to interfere with what she had fully made up her mind to do.

IV

Lily came into the kitchen. She stopped in the pantry door to look at Zeke, sprawled grotesquely across the plaid cloth, snoring. Disgust and loathing crept into her eyes. She moved noiselessly about, cleaning the table and stacking the dishes on the safe. She would wash them later. When this task was done she returned to the sleeping room. Baby Zeke was sound asleep on his pallet, his little fingers curled in his thick hair and his mouth slightly agape. She pulled her dingy apron over her head. Standing in front of the long mirror, she appraised herself coldly. Yes, she was still good-looking, but another year with Zeke would end that. She examined her roughened hands and broken nails. Chunking fires, splitting wood, washing and ironing had all too soon taken toll of the slim hands that had been Lily's. She shrugged and went to the corner, where a curtained-off recess held her meager wardrobe. She took down a neat dark blue calico dress and slipped it on. Rummaging in the table drawer she found a neatly pressed red ribbon (it had been salvaged from a candy box) and tied it at her throat.

The red ribbon brought memory and hot resentment. For weeks now she had eyed, longingly, a bright red lawn dress in a shop window in the Square. It was only six ninety-eight, and Zeke could easily afford it. But broaching the subject had only resulted in a long blue bruise on her jaw where he had struck her with his huge fist.

She rubbed her jaw thoughtfully. "The big bully," she murmured. Many times since then, she had thought of murder. She could poison him. He was such a glutton he'd never notice. Or she could stab him. But she didn't have a knife small enough to be concealed. The butcher knife was too conspicuous. Or she could drench him with kerosene and throw a lighted lamp at him. No, she might not be quick enough.

Suddenly she thought of Baby Zeke and the grasshopper. She smiled ruefully. She dusted some pink prepared chalk on her face. She blew out the lamp and slipped through the pantry. Zeke stirred uneasily. She stopped short, undecided whether to wake him and say she was going, or slip out.

She slipped out.

V

Pleasant Green was the most pretentious church the Negroes had in Cranstonville. It was a single-story red-brick building with rows of windows on each side. Seven stone steps led up to the glass door entrance. The uncushioned wooded benches were sturdy. A narrow red carpet covered the single central aisle. The low rostrum held three red plush chairs, and flanking either side of the white-pained pulpit were tubs of artificial flowers. To the left of the rostrum was a shiny upright piano, behind which were three rows of chairs for the choir.

When Lily arrived, the church was half-filled. The noise was deafening. Everybody was laughing and talking at once, for "meeting" was where you exchanged all the gossip you heard between-times. This was the fifth night of "revival." The Reverend Dabney, a city minister visiting relatives in Cranstonville, had "condescended" to conduct a ten nights' revival to renew the spirit in the sin-laden, gin-crazed population that the regular shepherd could not reach. His eloquence on the first night must have been widely discussed, for on the ensuing evenings there was not even standing room inside. Crowds gathered in the yard, where his sonorous tones floated out to them through the rows of opened windows.

This night, when he mounted the rostrum, the church was filled again. The Reverend Dabney was about 35 years old. He was tall and showed the evidence of too much good eating in the slight bay window and the heavy pouches beneath his eyes. He affected a gold pince-nez which kept falling and dangling at the end of a thin chain as he waxed more gymnastic in his discourse.

Now, before he opened the Bible, his eyes searched the congregation until they rested on Lily sitting at the end of the fourth row of seats. He cleared his throat and gave out a hymn. The meeting itself was pretty much like all others Lily had attended in Cranstonville. There was much snorting and cavorting on the part of the minister, much moaning, groaning and foot-patting on the part of the congregation. Occasionally someone was "seized by the spirit"—and either screamed and fought, or fainted and had to be fanned vigorously by the Helping Hand Sisters. Sinners crowded to the "Moaners' Bench" and were prayed for, and finally the meeting was over.

Lily found herself, as on previous nights, drawn against her will to the pulpit. She shook the Reverend's hand and murmured something about how much she had enjoyed the sermon. But tonight, unlike the previous night, the Reverend Dabney asked her to wait so that he could walk down the pasture with her.

She wondered how he knew where she lived, but made no comment. When the crowd had thinned he got his hat from a nail beside the piano and left the church with her.

VI

Revival was over, but still the Reverend Dabney remained in Cranstonville. Tongues were wagging, and every now and then bits of gossip came to Zeke's ears. Lily had stopped her brooding and was like nothing more than a watchful cat biding her time at a rat-hole. Baby Zeke noticed it too, for she often caught him staring at her intently as though listening for the humming she had ceased to do.

Saturday night. Pay night. The Square was filled with people doing their weekly marketing. Noisy Negroes congregated on the corners. Zeke walked up Main Street and paused in front of a store. The red dress was no longer in the window. On a sudden impulse, he entered the shop. The keeper asked him gruffly what he wanted. Zeke explained that he had seen a red dress in the window and he wanted it for his wife. The storekeeper shook his head.

"Sold that dress some days ago to that colored preacher that's visitin' here."

The sudden rush of blood to his brain made Zeke stagger. He made his way uncertainly out of the door.

"Must be drunk," the storekeeper said to himself.

When Zeke reached home, the lamp was burning in the kitchen window. Lily was bathing young Zeke in a big tin tub on the kitchen table. One look at Zeke's bloodshot eyes and she picked the dripping child up in her arms and fled to the sleeping room. He did not follow her at once. He searched the kitchen methodically, then the lean-to. He even went down the yard to the outhouse.

Returning to the house, he entered the sleeping room. He searched the curtained recess—beneath the bed, under the mattress, the table drawer, beneath the covered rocker. He did not find the red dress.

Lily watched him, fascinated. Then she began to laugh. Her laughter mounted until it became hysterically shrill and only ceased when a blow from his fist felled her.

Neither of them slept that night. Lily lay stiff with fright on her side of the bed. Zeke sat on the edge, nursing his suspicious until the sun came up over the pasture trees.

Young Zeke awoke with a whimper and Lily sprang out of bed. She slipped his shirt on him and carried him to the kitchen. She laid the fire and cooked the baby some mush. When he was fed, she turned him out in the yard to play with the dog.

Zeke came into the kitchen. He pulled a chair to the open door and sat down. Without looking at her he said, "You ain't goin' to meetin' tonight."

She did not say anything.

She peeled potatoes and set them to boiling over the stove. She "picked" the salad greens and immersed them in cold water to crisp. When the salt pork was tender she put the greens in the pot.

She went to the shelf above the table and took down a small tin can. Removing the top, she took a tablespoon and put some in the greens. She began to hum. The sound made Zeke turn around.

"Watcha puttin' in them greens?"

"Soda."

"Why yuh put so much?"

"They're tough."

He turned again to watch the empty cinder path. Lily, smiling secretively, hummed deeper and deeper.

Dinner was ready.

"I'll feed you, Zeke, and while you eat I'll clean up the baby."

Zeke grunted.

Lily heaped his plate with greens and pork. She put a plate of pone bread on the table and poured his coffee. When he sat down at the table she picked the baby up and went into the sleeping room. She left him there, after a few moments, and returned to the kitchen. Zeke's plate was nearly empty. She walked to the stove and busied herself with the pots. A sudden noise at the door made both of them turn around.

From beneath the house Tiger had pulled a package and was trying to drag it up on the stoop. Lily was rooted to the spot. She tried to cry out, but her tongue clove to the roof of her mouth. Terror had paralyzed her. Zeke crossed heavily to the door and, picking up the package, tore the wrappings from the red dress. When he turned upon her a savage fury was in his eyes.

The strength was leaving his fingers now, but still he pressed and pressed. The gurgling sound that had come from Lily's lips had ceased. Her soft, frightened eyes were bulging and suffused with blood. There was a sharp snap. Zeke heard it as if from a great distance. Lily suddenly hung limp in his hands. He saw her through a dark haze. There was a drumming in his ears and the room was growing dark. He was falling through black space.

It was the Cranston cook who found them there on the kitchen floor, and Baby Zeke bawling lustily because he couldn't wake his mother.

Of course, she told the neighbors later, the poison saved the county the expense of hanging Zeke. But the red dress didn't do Lily any good.

Who ever heard of a crimson shroud?

[*Opportunity* 18.6 (June 1940): 170–173]

HALF-BRIGHT: A SHORT STORY

by Marian Minus

The scattered settlers in Ridge Clearing said that Sonny Blue wasn't quite bright, and often his parents, exasperated and fretted, agreed. Hattie Blue watched him fitting his big feet into the deep-cut ruts before the house.

"Th' oldes' one," she complained aloud, "an' he hasta be silly actin'."

Sonny, twelve and raw-boned, black and good-natured, was carefully turning in his dusty tracks. He flinched occasionally when the sharp-baked edges of the clay cut his bare feet. He hummed and his high-pitched voice delighted his audience of younger brothers and sisters.

Hattie took her eyes away from him and looked toward the road where she heard the creak of wagon wheels.

"Sonny!" she called sharply. "Your pa's comin'. Go to meet 'im."

Sonny looked regretfully at the dissolving imprints of his feet and went toward the road without answering.

An old brown horse, pulling a small wagon with unsteady wheels, drew his father into sight.

"Hey, there, Sonny!" Jim Blue called.

Sonny waved and walked on to meet his father.

"Got a pile o' things," Jim shouted above the creak of the wagon. "A new han' plow, some seeds, an' that mail-order wire f' th' chicken house."

"Y' got 'em already?" Sonny asked.

"Yeah. Spring come rushin' like it did, sorta put me to it in a hurry. Hot weather done come t' stay, an' it come so quick, a man ain' got time t' let things git a head start on 'im."

The wagon drew abreast of the boy and Jim brought it to a protesting halt.

"Jump on the wagon," he said to Sonny. "Nellie ain' had such a hard trip she oughta min' haulin' another carcass."

He reached out and affectionately patted the horse's rump.

"Your legs gittin' so long," he said companionably, turning to Sonny who was awkwardly climbing in the wagon, "you 'bout th' mos' clumsy thing ever in my fam'ly."

He chuckled and nudged the horse with the reins.

"I'm bigger'n the' res'," Sonny said.

"Didn' mean jus' my own chillun," Jim said, laughing. "Meant all the' folks I ever knowed in my whole fam'ly."

Sonny smiled uncertainly, then looked over his shoulder to the wagon floor.

"I don' see no han' plow in there," he said casually.

Jim jerked around in his seat. "Sure 'tis. Got t' be. Bought it at Simpson's on time."

"I still don't see no han' plow in there."

"Is, to. Got t' be."

They faced each other. The horse turned into the road that led to the house without urging from Jim. Then it stopped and Jim jumped down. He looked into the back of the wagon. He did not see the plow, so he pulled out the burlap bags that were piled in a heap in one corner.

"You c'd see it if 'twas under them crocus sacks," Sonny said sensibly.

"You hush your mouth!"

Jim searched fruitlessly. Hattie came out into the yard, demanding an explanation of his behavior.

"That boy," Jim told her, pointing an accusing finger at Sonny, "says there ain' no han' plow in th' wagon. An' I know 'tis. Got t' be, 'cause I got it at Simpson's. Got it on time. Paid 'im a dollar down."

Hattie ran her eye over the wagon floor.

"Ain' no han' plow, or any other kin', in there, sure 'nough," she said. She watched her husband's strong black hands lift and drop the burlap bags. "No need t' carry on like a fool, Jim," she admonished. "You c'd see it if 'twas underneath them bags, 'thout raisin' all that dus'. It jus' ain' there."

Jim finally admitted the absence of the plow. He climbed back on the wagon and sat down, staring moodily before him.

"How come you carryin' on so?" Hattie asked. "You jus' f'got t' take it out t' the wagon after you bought it." She waited for him to speak. "You 'member takin' it out the store?"

"Naw," he said disconsolately. "That's jus' it. Mr. Simpson an' some other white folks was sittin' 'roun' in th' store doin' nothin' when I went in. I tol' 'im what I wanted, ast if I had credit good 'nough f' me t' get it on time, an' when he said Yes, I paid 'im the' dollar."

He stopped talking and looked at his wife and son thoughtfully. The younger children crowded around the wagon. Jim shook his head and clamped his full lips together in stubborn refusal to talk more.

"Well," Hattie demanded, "what happen' after that?"

Jim shook his head again. "Things is kinda mixed up in my head," he lied. "I can' seem t' remember."

"Jim Blue," Hattie said slowly, "you lyin', sure's you born."

Jim did not answer. He stared with exaggerated interest at everything about him. The sky held his attention and he looked at the sun until he was momentarily blinded.

"Jim!" Hattie said severely. "Y' better get on with whatever kin' o' story y' got t' tell."

"Well," he said finally, grudgingly, "Mr. Simpson said he thought he'd do me a favor. He said colored folks always totin' f' white folks, time white folks did some totin' f' them." Hattie snorted. Jim rushed on. "He picked up th' plow I picked out an' tol' me he'd carry it out t' th' wagon th' way he carried stuff out f' 'is white cust'mers. I didn' follow 'im right away. I stayed inside talkin' t' th' others. When I went out, I didn' look in th' wagon. I jus' clucked t' Nellie an' got away fas' as I could."

Sonny laughed, his high childish voice stinging his mother out of her speechlessness, which had increased as Jim's tale progressed.

"You make me sick, Jim Blue," she said with feeling. "You let them white folks make a fool outa y' like that. They figga'd you'd feel too outa place to look in th' wagon an' they was right. Ol' man Simpson jus' took that plow out th' front door an' carried it right roun' to' th' back."

"Maybe I los' it on th' way," Jim protested weakly. "Maybe it fell off when I took a bump."

"It didn' have no bizness bein' where it c'd fall off goin' over no bumps," Hattie snapped. "It shouda been put right down on th' wagon floor. 'Sides, bigger things 'n a han' plow's been in this wagon an' they ain' fell off."

"It ain' but three miles t' Clinton," Sonny said unexpectedly. "I'll go an' ast Simpson what happened t' th' plow."

Hattie stared at him in amazement.

"Ain' no use goin' back t' ast 'im," Jim said heavily. "If he done what your ma said, ain' likely he'd 'mit it." He sighed. "No use t' go back."

"'Course 'tis," Sonny disagreed. "I c'd fin' out easy if Mist' Simpson put th' plow in th' wagon."

Jim's frustration became anger. "You ain' gonna' do no such thing," he said irately. "You gonna' stay here an' act like you got some sense."

"The boy's right," Hattie said. "He c'd ast Simpson 'bout it if he don' come 'cross it on 'is way t' town." She went on scornfully: "You willin' to' let th' white folks make a fool outa you an' cheat you, too?"

"Likely Mist' Simpson'll give me th' plow or my dollar th' nex' time I go in town," Jim said hopefully. "No need stirrin' up trouble sendin' Sonny back."

"If y' don' get that plow today," Hattie predicted, "you'll never get it no other time. An' stidda gettin' your dollar back, you'll be havin' t' keep on payin' f' a plow you ain' had your han's on."

"I c'n go now," Sonny said to his mother. "Ain' gonna take me long t' walk t' town an' back. I c'n go th' short way."

"I'm f' y' goin,'" Hattie said quickly, "but not th' short way. Go by th' road. Won't take y' but five more minutes."

"Yeah," Jim said, "do what y' ma says." He yielded to their common will that Sonny go into town. "You better hurry," he said, looking at the mounting sun. "If y' go quick, y' c'n get back in time f' mid-day dinner."

"He can't make it that quick," Hattie disagreed, "but he c'n get back while 'is food's still warm."

Sonny re-rolled the slipping, frayed bottoms of his overalls and walked to the road without further instructions.

"Ain' true Sonny's all silly," Hattie said thoughtfully. "He's got a heap sense in 'is kinky head."

"Yeah," Jim agreed, abashed. "he's got more sense'n his pa,"

Sonny's laughing eyes explored the familiar countryside as he walked over the rutted country road. He hesitated in the sparse shade of a clump of scrub-pines.

"After I fin' out 'bout that han' plow," he addressed the trees, "I'm comin' back an' set under you awhile."

He came to the trestle that carried the railroad tracks. He wanted to jump, perilously, across the wooden ties. The trestle was a quarter of a mile nearer than the little bridge that ran over the shallow stream spotted with sharp rocks. It was the short way, but Sonny remembered his mother's admonition and continued to the bridge.

The sun was directly overhead, hot and enervating, when he reached Clinton. A few wagons and high-bodied automobiles were lined up at the station. The streets were almost empty.

Sonny walked directly to the general store on the main street. He pushed open the screen door and went in. The transition from bright sunlight to the dim interior of the store blinded him for a minute. He stood just inside the door, blinking and collecting his senses.

"There's Jim Blue's half-bright boy."

Sonny looked in the direction of the derisive voice. He screwed up his eyes, then opened them wide.

"That you, Mist' Simpson?" he asked.

"That's right."

A wiry man of about forty came forward. A half-smile was on his weather-beaten face.

"Reckon y' know what I come for," Sonny said. He looked at the two men who were seated in the rear of the store. "Reckon y' all know, too," he said, addressing them directly.

"Don't you go interferin' wit' my customers, silly boy," Simpson drawled warningly.

"Pa didn' have the han' plow he bought here this mornin' when he got home," Sonny said.

"So what y' want me t' do?" Simpson asked sarcastically.

"Ma says y' likely took th' plow out th' front door an' brought it in th' back." Sonny looked straight into Simpson's eyes.

There was an unrestrained shout of laughter from the seated men. Simpson looked at them warily.

"You ma mus' be crazy, too," he said lazily.

"An' pa said y' musta done jus' that," Sonny continued. "Ma said y' ain' gonna cheat pa out th' dollar an' th' plow both."

A hot flush covered Simpson's face. He stepped towards Sonny with clenched fists.

"You ain' got sense 'nough t' know what you sayin,'" he whispered hoarsely. "If y' wasn't a idiot-boy, I'd knock every dam' one o' your teeth down your black throat."

Sonny's eyes lost their childish, good-natured light. They clouded and his black throat constricted. His bare feet scraped slowly over the hard floor.

"I ain' crazy," he said slowly. "I ain't near as crazy as folks think I am. I ain' crazy one bit, an' my ma ain' crazy."

Simpson looked appealingly toward his friends. Sonny's behavior was incredible. The men rose and came forward.

"What's all this?" one of them asked brusquely.

Sonny looked at his narrow eyes, his thin cold lips, his forehead with its abnormally depressed temples.

"Was you here this mornin' when my pa bought a han' plow?" he asked.

"Yeah, I was here," the man admitted challengingly.

"Did y' see it on 'is wagon when he got ready t' go?"

Simpson interrupted, his voice thick.

"By God," he said furiously, "this kid's got a hell of a nerve—to ask a white man questions!"

"I'm only tryin' t' fin' out th' truth," Sonny began. "I—"

He stopped as the men drew closer to him. His eyes measured the closing gap between him and their moving, stocky bodies. His throat suddenly went dry. He wanted to run out of the store, to escape the blows he knew were coming.

"Go on," Simpson jeered. "You ain' nowheres near through."

"I ain' scared of you," Sonny said quietly. "I jus' can' stan' bein' hit. But it ain' 'cause I'm scared. Bein' hit hurts me inside."

"Sure it does," Simpson said softly. "Like it would if I was t' tap y' like this."

His hand shot out, but Sonny had sensed its coming. As Simpson moved his arm, the man next to him shifted almost imperceptibly. It was enough for Sonny's quick twisting body. He went through the opening between the two men and shot toward the door. He reached the street. Simpson followed, shouting. A half dozen youngsters who had been lounging on the curb outside the store jumped up to see what was causing the excitement.

"You boys git 'im," Simpson shouted. "I'm too old t' be runnin' in all this hot sun."

Sonny looked back once and saw boys, hardly older than himself, running after him. The heat made his legs drag, but he could not stop to rest. He ran past the station, and the crowd which had collected in the yard to meet the twelve-thirty from Columbia yelled encouragement to the pursuers.

"Git a autymobile," Sonny heard someone call out behind him.

"I'll go the short way," he decided hastily.

He ran along the train tracks. Stumbling around a curve, he saw the trestle just ahead. He looked back in time to see one of his pursuers leave the tracks. A whistle sounded somewhere far off, and the tracks began to shake. Sonny hesitated for a moment, then started across the trestle.

"That kid's gonna be killed," he heard, then the sound of excited voices was shut out by the blanket of the train's whistle.

Sonny looked up and saw it speeding toward him. He knelt and threw one arm over a wooden cross-tie just as it started across the stream. He lowered his body between the ties with a jerk that almost wrenched his skinny arm from its socket. Frantically he threw his other arm over the tie above his head and closed his eyes. The train thundered above him. Hot cinders fell on his clinging hands. He bit his lips until they bled.

A slow, hot billow of smoky air moved over Sonny's head in the wake of the train. Tearing his arms and legs with splinters, his eyes popping with pain, he patiently pulled himself up to the tracks. His legs wavered unsteadily as he walked to the end of the trestle.

On solid ground again, he examined his wounds. A thin whimper rose high in his throat. He rolled his overalls down to cover the scratches on his legs and sucked at the broken skin on his arms and hands. The steady, hard beat of the sun aggravated his pain. He began to run. His one thought was to get home as quickly as he could.

Sonny's bare feet shrank from the red-ocher earth as he crossed the yard. He stumbled up the steps and into the house.

Hattie was washing dishes in the kitchen.

"God have mercy!" she exclaimed. "Where you been, boy?"

Sonny wanted to explain but the words would not pass his dry lips. His head and stomach were whirling.

"Don' you hear me talkin' t' you? Where you git them scratches?"

Sonny licked his lips. "Tres'le," he answered in a low voice.

Hattie stared at him until her anger allowed her to speak.

"You been on that tres'le after me 'n your pa tol' you t' stay off it!" she exclaimed fiercely. "You been playin', tha's what you been doin'; Playin'! I'm goin' t' give you a beatin' you ain' gonna f' get easy."

"Where's pa?" Sonny asked beseechingly.

Hattie paid no attention to him. She marched into the little room she and Jim shared with the youngest child and returned with Jim's razor strap. Sonny whimpered and backed into a corner. Hattie caught him with a strong hand.

"We shoulda knowed better," she panted, wielding the strap. "We shoulda knowed better'n to sen' you to town. Y' always was silly actin'. Y' always will be." She paused, the heavy strap uplifted, "An' you the' oldes', too."

Sonny fell forward on the floor. He buried his head in his arms and cried. It was like he had told Simpson. He wasn't afraid of the blows the way a coward was; it was just that....

Sonny twisted on his belly. He raised his tear-streaked face, grimacing as he tried to understand his tortured, unformed thoughts. Maybe they were right about his being silly-acting. Someday he would be a grown man. Maybe, then, he would understand. He dropped his head again, and his wounds tormented him. It was such a painful, troubled world.

[*Opportunity* 18.9 (September 1940): 271–274]

Mammy (A Short Story)

by Dorothy West

The young Negro welfare investigator, carrying her briefcase, entered the ornate foyer of the Central Park West apartment house. She was making a collateral call. Earlier in the day she had visited an aging colored woman in a rented room in Harlem. Investigation had proved that the woman was not quite old enough for Old Age Assistance, and yet no longer young enough to be classified as employable. Nothing, therefore, stood in the way of her eligibility for relief. Here was a clear case of need. This collateral call on her last employer was merely routine.

The investigator walked toward the elevator, close on the heels of a well-dressed woman with a dog. She felt shy. Most of her collaterals were to housewives in the Bronx or supervisors of maintenance workers in office buildings. Such calls were never embarrassing. A moment ago as she neared the doorway, the doorman had regarded her intently. The service entrance was plainly to her left, and she was walking past it. He had been on the point of approaching when a tenant emerged and dispatched him for a taxi. He had stood for a moment torn between his immediate duty and his sense of outrage. Then he had gone away dolefully, blowing his whistle.

The woman with the dog reached the elevator just as the doors slid open. The dog bounded in, and the elevator boy bent and rough-housed with him. The boy's agreeable face was black, and the investigator felt a flood of relief.

The woman entered the elevator and smilingly faced front. Instantly the smile left her face, and her eyes hardened. The boy straightened, faced front, too, and gaped in surprise. Quickly he glanced at the set face of his passenger.

"Service entrance's outside," he said sullenly.

The investigator said steadily, "I am not employed here. I am here to see Mrs. Coleman on business."

"If you're here on an errand or somethin' like that," he argued doggedly, "you still got to use the service entrance."

She stared at him with open hate, despising him for humiliating her before and because of a woman of an alien race.

"I am here as a representative of the Department of Welfare. If you refuse me the use of this elevator, my office will take it up with the management."

She did not know if this was true, but the elevator boy would not know either.

"Get in then," he said rudely, and rolled his eyes at his white passenger as if to convey his regret at the discomfort he was causing her.

The doors shut and the three shot upward, without speaking to or looking at each other. The woman with the dog, in a far corner, very pointedly held the small harmless animal on a tight leash.

The car stopped at the fourth floor, and the doors slid open. No one moved. There was a ten-second wait.

"You getting out or not?" the boy asked savagely.

There was no need to ask who he was addressing.

"Is this my floor?" asked the investigator.

His sarcasm rippled. "You want Mrs. Coleman, don't you?"

"Which is her apartment?" she asked thickly.

"Ten-A. You're holding up my passenger."

When the door closed, she leaned against it, feeling sick, and trying to control her trembling. She was young and vulnerable. Her contact with Negroes was confined to frightened relief folks who did everything possible to stay in her good graces, and the members of her own set, among whom she was a favorite because of her two degrees and her civil service appointment. She had almost never run into Negroes who did not treat her with respect.

In a moment or two she walked down the hall to Ten-A. She rang, and after a little wait a handsome middle-aged woman opened the door.

"How do you do?" the woman said in a soft drawl. She smiled. "You're from the relief office, aren't you? Do come in."

"Thank you," said the investigator, smiling, too, relievedly.

"Right this way," said Mrs. Coleman leading the way into a charming living-room. She indicated an upholstered chair. "Please sit down."

The investigator, who never sat in overstuffed chairs in the homes of her relief clients, plumped down and smiled again at Mrs. Coleman. Such a pleasant woman, such a pleasant room. It was going to be a quick and easy interview. She let her briefcase slide to the floor beside her.

Mrs. Coleman sat down in a straight chair and looked searchingly at the investigator. Then she said somewhat breathlessly, "You gave me to understand that Mammy has applied for relief."

The odious title sent a little flicker of dislike across the investigator's face. She answered stiffly, "I had just left Mrs. Mason when I telephoned you for this appointment."

Mrs. Coleman smiled disarmingly, though she colored a little.

"She has been with us ever since I can remember. I call her Mammy, and so does my daughter."

"That's a sort of nurse, isn't it?" the investigator asked coldly. "I had thought Mrs. Mason was a general maid."

"Is that what she said?"

"Why, I understood she was discharged because she was no longer physically able to perform her duties."

"She wasn't discharged."

The investigator look dismayed. She had not anticipated complications. She felt for her briefcase.

"I'm very confused, Mrs. Coleman. Will you tell me just exactly what happened then? I had no idea Mrs. Mason was—was misstating the situation." She opened her briefcase.

Mrs. Coleman eyes her severely. "There's nothing to write down. Do you have to write down things? It makes me feel as if I were being investigated."

"I'm sorry," the investigator said quickly, snapping shut her briefcase. "If it would be distasteful—. I apologize again. Please go on."

"Well, there's little to tell. It all happened so quickly. My daughter was ill. My nerves were on edge. I may have said something that upset Mammy. One night she was here. The next morning she wasn't. I've been worried sick about her."

"Did you report her disappearance?"

"Her clothes were gone, too. It didn't seem a matter for the police. It was obvious that she had left of her own accord. Believe me, young woman, I was relieved when you telephoned me." Her voice shook a little.

"I'm glad I can assure you that Mrs. Mason appears quite well. She only said she worked for you. She didn't mention your daughter. I hope she has recovered."

"My daughter is married," Mrs. Coleman said slowly. "She had a child. It was stillborn. We have not seen Mammy since. For months she had looked forward to nursing it."

"I'm sure it was a sad loss to all of you," the investigator said gently. "And old Mrs. Mason, perhaps she felt you had no further use for her. It may have unsettled her mind. Temporarily," she added hastily. "She seems quite sane."

"Of course, she is," said Mrs. Coleman with a touch of bitterness. "She's old and contrary. She knew we would worry about her. She did it deliberately."

This was not in the investigator's province. She cleared her throat delicately.

"Would you take her back, Mrs. Coleman?"

"I want her back," cried Mrs. Coleman. "She has no one but us. She is just like one of the family."

"You're very kind," the investigator murmured. "Most people feel no responsibility for their aging servants."

"You do not know how dear a mammy is to a southerner. I nursed at Mammy's breast. I cannot remember a day in my life without her."

The investigator reached for her briefcase and rose.

"Then it is settled that she may return?"

A few hours ago there had been no doubt in her mind of old Mrs. Mason's eligibility for relief. With this surprising turn there was nothing to do but reject the case for inadequate proof of need. It was always a feather in a field worker's cap to reject a case that had been accepted for home investigation by a higher paid intake worker.

Mrs. Coleman looked at the investigator almost beseechingly.

"My child, I cannot tell you how much I will be in your debt if you can persuade Mammy to return. Can't you refuse to give her relief? She really is in need of nothing as long as I am living. Poor thing, what has she been doing for money? How has she been eating? In what sort of place is she staying?"

"She's very comfortable, really. She had three dollars when she came uptown to Harlem. She rented a room, explained her circumstances to her landlady, and is getting her meals there. I know that landlady. She has other roomers who are on relief. She trusts them until they get their relief checks. They never cheat her."

"Oh, thank God! I must give you something to give to that woman. How good Negroes are. I am so glad it was you who came. You are so sympathetic. I could not have talked so freely to a white investigator. She would not have understood."

The investigator's smile was wintry. She resented this well-meant restatement of the trusted position of the good Negro.

She said civilly, however, "I'm going back to Mrs. Mason's as soon as I leave here. I hope I can persuade her to return to you tonight."

"Thank you! Mammy was happy here, believe me. She had nothing to do but a little dusting. We are a small family, myself, my daughter, and her husband. I have a girl who comes every day to do the hard work. She preferred to sleep in, but I wanted Mammy to have the maid's room. It's a lovely room with a private bath. It's next to the kitchen, which is nice for Mammy. Old people potter about so. I've lost girl after girl who felt she was meddlesome. But I've always thought of Mammy's comfort first."

"I'm sure you have," said the investigator politely, wanting to end the interview. She made a move toward departure. "Thank you again for being so cooperative."

Mrs. Coleman rose and crossed to the doorway.

"I must get my purse. Will you wait a moment?"

Shortly she reappeared. She opened her purse.

"It's been ten days. Please give that landlady this twenty dollars. No, it isn't too much. And here is a dollar from Mammy's cab fare. Please put her in the cab yourself."

"I'll do what I can." The investigator smiled candidly. "It must be nearly four, and my working day ends at five."

"Yes, of course," Mrs. Coleman said distractedly. "And now I just want you to peep in at my daughter. Mammy will want to know how she is. She's far from well, poor lambie."

The investigator followed Mrs. Coleman down the hall. At an open door they paused. A pale young girl lay on the edge of a big tossed bed. One hand was in her tangled hair, the other clutched an empty bassinet. The wheels rolled down and back, down and back. The girl glanced briefly and without interest at her mother and the investigator, then turned her face away.

"It tears my heart," Mrs. Coleman whispered in a choked voice. "Her baby, and then Mammy. She has lost all desire to live. But she is young and she will have other children. If she would only let me take away that bassinet! I am not the nurse that Mammy is. You can see how much Mammy is needed here."

They turned away and walked in silence to the outer door. The investigator was genuinely touched, and eager to be off on her errand of mercy.

Mrs. Coleman opened the door, and for a moment seemed at a loss as to how to say good-bye. Then she said quickly, "Thank you for coming," and shut the door.

The investigator stood in indecision at the elevator, half persuaded to walked down three flights of stairs. But this, she felt, was turning tail, and pressed the elevator button.

The door opened. The boy looked at her sheepishly. He swallowed and said ingratiatingly, "Step in, miss. Find your party all right?"

She faced front, staring stonily ahead of her, and felt herself trembling with indignation at this new insolence.

He went on whiningly, "That woman was in my car is mean as hell. I was just puttin' on to please her. She hates niggers 'cept when they're bowin' and scraping. She was the one had the old doorman fired. You see for yourself they got a white one now. With white folks needin' jobs, us niggers got to eat dirt to hang on."

The investigator's face was expressionless except for a barely perceptible wincing at his careless use of a hated word.

He pleaded, "You're colored like me. You ought to understand. I was only doing my job. I got to eat same as white folks, same as you."

They rode the rest of the way in a silence interrupted only by his heavy sighs. When they reached the ground floor, and the door slid open, he said sorrowfully, "Good-bye, miss."

She walked down the hall and out into the street, past the glowering doorman, with her face stern and her stomach slightly sick.

The investigator rode uptown on a north-bound bus. At One Hundred and Eighteenth Street she alighted and walked east. Presently she entered a well-kept apartment house. The elevator operator deferentially greeted her and whisked her upwards.

She rang the bell of number fifty-four, and visited briefly with the land lady, who was quite overcome by the unexpected payment of twenty dollars. When she could escape her profuse thanks, the investigator went to knock at Mrs. Mason's door.

"Come in," called Mrs. Mason. The investigator entered the small, square room. "Oh, it's you, dear," said Mrs. Mason, her lined brown face lighting up.

She was sitting by the window in a wide rocker. In her black, with a clean white apron tied about her waist, and a white bandanna bound around her head, she looked ageless and full of remembering.

Mrs. Mason grasped her rocker by the arms and twisted around until she faced the investigator.

She explained shyly, "I just sit here for hours lookin' out at the people. I ain' seen so many colored folks at one time since I left down home. Sit down, child, on the side of the bed. Hit's softer than that straight chair yonder."

The investigator sat down on the straight chair, not because the bedspread was not scrupulously clean, but because what she had come to say needed stiff decorum.

"I'm all right here, Mrs. Mason. I won't be long."

"I was hopin' you could set awhile. My landlady's good, but she's got this big flat. Don't give her time for much settin'."

The investigator, seeing an opening, nodded understandingly.

"Yes, it must be pretty lonely for you here after being so long an intimate part of the Coleman family."

The old woman's face darkened. "Shut back in that bedroom behin' the kitchen? This here's what I like. My own kind and color. I'm too old a dog to be learnin' new tricks."

"Your duties with Mrs. Coleman were very slight. I know you are getting on in years, but you are not too feeble for light employment. You were not entirely truthful with me. I was led to believe you did all the housework."

The old woman looked furtively at the investigator. "How come you know diff'rent now?"

"I've just left Mrs. Coleman."

Bafflement veiled the old woman's eyes. "You didn' believe what all I tol' you?"

"We always visit former employers. It's part of our job Mrs. Mason. Sometimes an employer will re-hire our applicants. Mrs. Coleman is good enough to want you back. Isn't that preferable to being a public charge?"

"I ain't a-goin back," said the old woman vehemently.

The investigator was very exasperated. "Why, Mrs. Mason?" she asked gently.

"That's an ungodly woman," the old lady snapped. "And I'm god-fearin'. 'Tain't no room in one house for God and the devil. I'm too near the grave to be servin' two masters."

To the young investigator this was evasion by superstitious mutterings.

"You don't make yourself very clear, Mrs. Mason. Surely Mrs. Coleman didn't interfere with your religious convictions. You left her home the night after her daughter's child was born dead. Until then, apparently, you had no religious scruples."

The old woman looked at the investigator wearily. Then her head sank forward on her breast.

"That child warn't born dead."

The investigator said impatiently, "But surely the hospital—?"

"'T'warnt born in no hospital."

"But the doctor—?"

"Little sly man. Looked like he'd cut his own throat for a dollar."

"Was the child deformed?" the investigator asked helplessly.

"Hit was a beautiful baby," said the old woman bitterly.

"Why, no one would destroy a healthy child," the investigator cried indignantly. "Mrs. Coleman hopes her daughter will have more children." She paused, then asked anxiously, "Her daughter is really married, isn't she? I mean, the baby wasn't—illegitimate?"

"It's ma and pa were married down home. A church weddin'. They went to school together. They was all right till they come up N'th. Then *she* started workin' on 'em. Old ways wasn't good enough for her."

The investigator looked at her watch. It was nearly five. This last speech had been rambling gossip. Here was an old woman clearly unoriented in her northern transplanting. Her position as mammy made her part of the family. Evidently she felt that gave her a matriarchal right to arbitrate its destinies. Her small grievances against Mrs. Coleman had magnified themselves in her mind until she could make this illogical accusation of infanticide as compensation for her homesickness for the folkways of the South. Her move to Harlem bore this out. To explain her reason for establishing a separate residence, she had told a fantastic story that could not be checked, and would not be recorded, unless the welfare office was prepared to face a libel suit.

"Mrs. Mason," said the investigator, "please listen carefully. Mrs. Coleman has told me that you are not only wanted but very much needed in her home. There you will be given food and shelter in return for small services. Please understand that I sympathize with your—imaginings, but you cannot remain here without public assistance, and I cannot recommend to my superiors that public assistance be given you."

The old woman, who had listened worriedly, now said blankly, "You mean I ain't a-gonna get it?"

"No, Mrs. Mason, I'm sorry. And now it's ten to five. I'll be glad to help you pack your things, and put you in taxi."

The old woman looked helplessly around the room as if seeking a hiding place. Then she looked back at the investigator, her mouth trembling.

"You're my own people, child. Can' you fix up a story for them white folks at the relief, so's I could get to stay here where it's nice?"

"That would be collusion, Mrs. Mason. And that would cost me my job."

The investigator rose. She was going to pack the old woman's things herself. She was heartily sick of her contrariness, and determined to see her settled once and for all.

"Now where is your bag?" she asked with forced cheeriness. "First I'll empty these bureau drawers." She began to do so, laying things neatly on the bed. "Mrs. Coleman's daughter will be so glad to see you. She's very ill, and needs your nursing."

The old woman showed no interest. Her head has sunk forward on her breast again. She said listlessly, "Let her ma finish what she started. I won't have no time for nursin'. I'll be down on my knees rasslin' with the devil. I done tol' you the devil's done eased out God in that house."

The investigator nodded indulgently, and picked up a framed photograph that was lying face down in the drawer. She turned it over and involuntarily smiled at the smiling child in old-fashioned dress.

"This little girl," she said, "it's Mrs. Coleman, isn't it?"

The old woman did not look up. Her voice was still listless.

"That *was* my daughter."

The investigator dropped the photograph on the bed as if it were a hot coal. Blindly she went back to the bureau, gathered up the rest of the things, and dumped them over the photograph.

She was a young investigator, and it was two minutes to five. Her job was to give or withhold relief. That was all.

"Mrs. Mason," she said, "please, please understand. This is my job."

The old woman gave no sign of having heard.

[*Opportunity* 18.10 (October 1940): 298–302]

THE BISHOP AND THE LANDLADY

by Patsy Graves

Emma Ramsey bent lower and gave her whole-souled attention to the collar of the white shirt she was ironing in order to keep the gleam of satisfaction on her face from being too evident. So they had come after all! Who else in Peach Creek would have kept the Bishop when the conference met? Wasn't she the best cook in the whole place? Wasn't her house the tightest built, with the only glass windows, in town? Hadn't she been to Columbus, Mississippi; Pensacola, Florida; Atlanta, Georgia; and Birmingham, Alabama, to church meetings—the only woman in all of Peach Creek who had ever done such a thing? What was the use of them stewing around, putting on airs like there was a dozen different places for the Bishop to stay, when everybody knew there wasn't but one?

"Well, lemme study now, Sis Rose...."

She peered close at the shirt for an imaginary cat face. "I declare, I meant to jes' cool my heels and enjoy this meetin' without bein' bothered with nobody like no Bishop. Tell you the truth, I ain't achin' to wait on nobody while Conference is goin' on."

"Sis Emma, I know you ain't," the visitor said sympathetically, while thinking to herself, "She woulda died if we hadn't asked her—now look at her, playing like she ain't bothered."

"You see," she continued aloud, "we thought maybe a woman of your standing would be better able to entertain a man like the Bishop."

Emma Ramsey didn't look up. "Well, I'll ask Willie when he comes in. I can't give you no answer without talkin' with my husband, you know."

"I know Brother Willie won't have no objections."

"Naw, Willie don't never object to nothin' that means work for me." Emma set the iron on the stove with more than accustomed vigor. "I'll let you know at missionary meetin' Friday."

Emma hoped, by her manner, to let Rose know that the little affair budding between Rose and Emma's husband had not escaped her notice. She had not moved in the direction of breaking it up, as thoughts of the impending church meeting had occupied all her time and energy. She was well aware that it was a mistake to let things go too far. In her long years of breaking up budding romances between her husband and other women she had developed a technique, the essence of which was not to delay striking until the iron was hot, but not to let the iron get hot in the first place. The trouble with her technique was that it did not give her sufficient time to be sure that her husband was not trying to "go with" every woman with whom he was the least bit friendly. She was wrong as many times as she was right, but that had never deterred her from pouncing like a duck on a June-bug on every woman who got more than a passing glance from Willie. Breaking up one of his affairs was a job requiring so much time and adroitness, however, that Emma felt this time it would simply have to wait until Conference was over.

After Rose's departure, Emma's work-worn face broke into a frank smile of satisfaction. She would not even admit to Willie how much she longed to entertain the Bishop. Life does not hold many high spots for a woman living in a rural Alabama town of seven hundred souls. That an Annual Conference of the African Protestant Church would meet there was in itself an occasion of unusual importance. To be asked to sleep the Bishop was an honor coveted by many, but only realized by the select. And not only was Emma being asked to sleep him, but in deference to her culinary abilities, the sisters wanted her to feed him too.

Right away, Emma's mind began turning; making menus, cleaning house, airing bedding, frying chickens. "I'll set some vittles in front of that Bishop he won't never forget," she mused, "I'll put on the big pot and the little one too." Fried chicken—every preacher loved fried chicken and a Bishop was no exception. She would have Willie begin fattening no less than six fryers at once. Maybe they would kill a hog. No let's see.... Bishops and other big men like that had to be particular. Ofttimes fresh meat sent their blood pressure up. Oh, but suppose the Bishop did get sick. Wouldn't it be wonderful to have him all to herself! She would wait on him hand and foot. She would say, "Now, Bishop, you just say what you want, and I will be too glad to fix it for you." Oh, Lawd, naw. The Bishop couldn't get sick in her house because her toilet was outdoors. Her spirits fell to zero. What a terrible thing an outdoor toilet was. They had been wrong to invite the Conference to Peach Creek anyway. How could they expect the Bishop and the presiding elders and the big preachers from Mobile and Birmingham and Pensacola to go outdoors to the toilet. Suppose the Bishop asked where the bathroom was, how on earth could she tell him, "Right straight down by the chicken house, under the chinaberry tree." Oh well, it was too late now. The invitation to the Conference to come there had been extended and accepted. There was one good thing: the Negroes in Peach Creek were all shades, all sizes, and of all degrees of righteousness but there was one thing none of them had and that was a bathroom, so she would just stop thinking about that.

She would plan all her meals in advance. Emma was on surer footing there. "I'm going to feed the Bishop so well he won't notice the other things I ain't got," she comforted herself. Besides an abundance of fried chicken she would have chicken and dumplings, greens, white and sweet potatoes, macaroni and cheese, salad, sweet potato pie, and egg custards. The Bishop would say, "Madam, in all my travels I never had more appetizing vittles." Emma would reply, "Bishop, I'm highly honored that you find my cooking pleasing to your taste."

Emma wondered if the Bishop would want a bath while he was there. He was just going to be there four days and wasn't no need of nobody taking a bath in that short length of time. Well, she would buy a Number 3 zinc tub anyway, but if the Bishop didn't say anything about a bath, she wouldn't say anything either. Emma put down her iron to go and look at the bed the Bishop would sleep in. That cornshuck mattress would never do! No matter how much she shook it up, it would be all lumpy the next morning. She had been begging Willie for months to buy a tacked mattress for her company bed. He would have to do it now. Nobody in their right senses could ask a Bishop to sleep on shucks. She would write a card to the furniture man right away, and tell him to bring her a mattress on his next trip. She could pay him a dollar down and fifty cents a week until the trumpet blew. Wasn't no need of waiting to have a fuss with Willie; he wouldn't see the need of buying a mattress. He might only pay on it for two or three weeks if he consented to buy it, and it would be hers to finish out anyway.

If Willie only cared anything about helping her! She could make it so pleasant for the Bishop. But Willie never showed the slightest interest in doing anything that was uplifting. Her grandmother had been right thirty-eight years ago when she had said, "Em, that boy Willie ain't after nothin' but makin' a dog outa you." Yes, she had been all too right. "I shoulda listened to her, too," Emma said half aloud, but thoughts of that kind never remained with her long at a time. Willie as a young man had been the handsomest creature she had ever seen in her life. She knew that nothing on earth or heaven could have kept her from marrying him.

At that very moment, Emma heard Willie come up the steps. She hurried to set his dinner on the table, but refrained from mentioning that their home would soon be graced by a Bishop.

"I saw Rose last night and she was asking me if I thought you'd keep the Bishop when Conference met." Willie looked steadily at his plate as he spoke.

"Saw Rose last night? Where?" Emma's voice was on edge.

"At the church, where you reckon?" Willie looked up in an exasperated manner.

"What was goin' on at the church last night? I didn't hear no bell ring."

Willie called himself a fool for forgetting the bell.

"We had a committee meetin' to make 'rangements for the Conference." He spoke in a patient manner as if he were addressing a recalcitrant child.

"Aw, Willie, don't tell me that stuff. How can the African Protestant Church have a committee meetin' and I don't know nothin' about it? You mighta seen Rose last night, but it wasn't no committee meetin' less you and her were the only members present. Or if it was a committee, I got my own idea 'bout the kind of meetin' it was. No wonder she come sneakin' in here today talkin' 'bout, 'I know Brother Willie won't have no objections.'"

Emma was holding onto a stew kettle by the handle while she let Willie have the verbal deluge of her anger. He pushed back his chair with an angry movement, both because it infuriated him to know that Rose had been there and because the stew kettle looked threatening. He hoped he was successfully hiding his chagrin over being caught in a web of his own making. Rose had been teasing him for a beating three weeks ago. He'd let her have it Saturday night.

"That's enuf, now. I don't wanna hear no more about."

Willie gathered up the table scraps for his dogs and went out of the kitchen door.

Emma went back to her ironing without stopping to clear the table. She needed to slam something around, and her supply of dishes was rather low. Her anger vented itself on another of the fourteen shirts she had in her white-folks' washing that week. Committee meetin', committee meetin'—the two words whirled around in her head. "I ought to be shame," she said to herself finally.

"That rascal done been runnin' after women these thirty-eight years we been tied together. I shouldda learned not to care by now."

She never had learned not to care, though. Maybe that, in part, accounted for her passionate devotion to the African Protestant Church. Willie had never given her the respect and care due a wife, particularly as she had supported him since the beginning of their union. She didn't mind working for him, but it was a bitter pill to feed a man and then have him cheat on top of that. Out of the welter of bitter thoughts, her mind settled once more on the anticipated visit of the church dignitary. She forgot Willie and his defections, marital and otherwise, as she reveled in her plans for the entertainment of the Bishop.

She should meet him at the door and he would say, "Why, my dear Mrs. Ramsey, what a very great pleasure to see you again." Emma had seen him at a distance at the Atlanta meeting; by what alchemy she expected him to remember her, only she knew. "My, my, this is a nice room," he would say as she ushered him into the company bedroom. And she would reply, "Now, Bishop, just make yourself right at home and anything you want, just ask for it." Pray God he would not want anything her wages as a washwoman could not afford. As she served him his meals and chatted he would be moved to observe, "Why, Madam, I don't see how a woman of your intelligence would stay in a small place like this," and then her cup of joy would truly run over. Willie would hear what he said, and forevermore he would understand how fortunate he should be to have her for a wife, and would thenceforth be kind and good to her. The years stretched out in halcyon peace after the Bishop's stay with them.

There would be no more women in Willie's life. The Bishop would talk with him, advise him, and above all point out Emma's merits as wife and helpmeet.

A few days later, Emma broached the subject of the mattress again.

"Now, Willie, we jus' got to get things fixed up a little better befo' conference. Mr. Woods say we can pay him jus' like we want for what furniture he let us have." She talked unhurriedly and friendly-like in hopes of getting Willie on her side of the question.

"Emma, don't go gettin' up to your eyelids in debt to these white folks for no lot of stuff to entertain no Bishop or nobody else." Willie's voice sounded like a nutmeg grater. "You done paid twenty-seven dollars in interest on that twenty dollars you borrowed from the insurance man to go to the missionary meetin' in Atlanta, and ain't touched the principal yet."

"Well, it woulda been paid long ago if you hada helped me a little, Willie. If I could jes' get a small part of what you make at the sawmill, I could do a thousand times better."

"What you mean, a small part? If you don't get what I make, I'd like to know who do."

"I don't have to go to no conjure woman to answer that one!" Emma's anger was rising slowly, like a pot of turnip greens fixing to boil. "Everybody in town know that Rose gets whut she wants from you."

"Everybody in town jus' know a lie then!" Willie's voice was a little weak and unconvincing.

This was getting out of hand. It was not Emma's intention of gettin' too deep into the subject of Willie's girl friends. Experience had taught her that accusing a man of having another woman was a poor way of starting out after what she herself wanted done, particularly when he was not too anxious to do it.

"Maybe everybody do be lyin'; that ain't what I'm talkin' 'bout now. What I want to know is this: is you goin' to help me git a mattress for the Bishop to sleep on, or not?"

"Naw, by God, I ain't, and that's the word with the bark on it. Goin' in debt for a Bishop is jus' pure crazy. I sleeps on shucks and anybody who comes to my house kin sleep on shucks, not scusin' the Bishop. A Bishop ain't nuthin' but a dam man jes' like me, nohow! Hand me them specs."

Emma meekly removed the family spectacles from her own nose and handed them to Willie, whereupon he took up the Southern Ruralist and promptly forgot her.

"Leastways I know where I stands now, and what I got to do," Emma said to herself. She promptly forgot Willie as she tried, mentally, to make two and two equal more than four.

Came the glorious October day before Conference was to convene. Emma had almost worked herself into a state of exhaustion. The windows sparkled, the floors were scrubbed, the tacked mattress was in place—a splendid affair with a ticking of red roses on a blue background. Covering the bed was a resplendent spread of gold and green, with a brilliant red fringe. The coat-hangers swung behind the door, waiting submissively for the ecclesiastical black robes of the prelate. A white bowl and pitcher entwined with more red roses sat on the washstand waiting the ablutions of the reverend gentleman. About everything there was an air of importance and dignity as if even the inanimate objects of the bedroom knew that no ordinary personage was to be in their midst.

In the kitchen cabinet there was a chocolate cake, a white cake, and a "hasty" cake—simply layers spread with tart plum jelly—a lemon pie, an apple pie and three sweet potato pies, stacked one upon the other. There were three egg custards, deeply and richly yellow, with little flecks of brown on the top. There was a grated sweet potato pudding, muffin cakes, and two loaves of store-bought bread for fear the Bishop did not care for corn bread.

By the time for the Bishop to arrive next day, there was a pot of cabbage, cooked low and greasy until it had changed from white to a dull brown, a plate heaped with fried chicken, beautifully browned and crisp, a large dish of rice, every flakey grain of which stood to itself, and a bowl of gravy, neither too thick nor too thin, filled with delectable bits of gizzard and liver chopped fine. A pot of field peas bubbled slowly on the stove. On top of the peas Emma had dropped a few pieces of the last okra to be had in the garden. Her corn bread was crackly and yellow; two eggs instead of the usual one had gone into its making. And at the last moment she had stirred up flour bread because everybody loved a good hot biscuit, dripping with butter, to sop chicken gravy with.

The honk of an automobile horn took Emma hurrying to the front door, and there stood the Bishop's limousine. My gracious, it looked like a hearse. The car was so long it extended nearly the length of the front yard. Even the dogs were awed, and they did not utter a single bark. The sight of it was enough to tax your breath away. But who were those women? There were two of them, and man driving the car. "The name of God!" Emma breathed, "where all those folks going?" And there was the bishop himself—a fat man with skin of undiluted black. If it had not been for the white of his collar, Emma could not have determined where the Bishop stopped and his dark blue suit began.

"Har-r-r-rumph, good afternoon, Madame." The Bishop's voice started low and went up the scale as if he were saying do, re, mi, fa, so, la, ti, do. "I presume this is the place provided for me and my party." His eyes almost hidden in his fat cheeks, kept darting about.

"Why, why, they only told me to prepare for one person, Bishop." Emma was so confused she almost failed to greet her guest.

"Har-r-r-rumph, har-r-r-rumph, this won't do at all! My party cannot be divided. I have my chauffeur, my secretary, and my wife." The Bishop herded them in as if the very magic of their presences would make more room in the little house. The wife was thin and faded—the result, no doubt, of years of self-effacement in the august presence of her spouse.

"Sit down and rest yourselves, and after dinner I'll make arrangements." Emma was in despair. The women, each looking as if she smelled something—and that chauffeur!

"Willie, for God's sake, do you know that Bishop's brought everybody and his cousin along with him! There's three other folks out there besides him, and I ain't got nowhere to put 'em." Emma could hardy speak above a whisper.

"Now ain't that a pretty howdy-do!" Willie was not very helpful.

Emma prepared the dinner in gloomy silence. The guests filed in and took their places. There were two kinds of plates and three kinds of knives and forks on the table, but there was no help for it. The table groaned under the weight of all the good food but alas—"Cabbage hurts the Bishop, he never eats it"—the little wife hovered around him like a hen with one chick, tucking his napkin around his neck. "Oh, don't let the Bishop get a piece of that hot pepper." "I believe the gravy needs just a speck of salt." "Yes, he would take a spoonful of rice, just a teeny spoonful." "Oh, my, the coffee is too strong for the Bishop to drink at this time of day!" "Now, dear, you know you shouldn't eat those peas." "Bishop, no sweets now, you know your doctor forbade it." The wife was like a brown bird pecking, and just as worrisome. She looked at Emma for her understanding of the Bishop's digestive eccentricities, but Emma's hurt was too deep to return her even a glance of sympathy. But the chauffeur made up for what the Bishop could not enjoy. Everything on the table disappeared down his throat like magic. Mounds of cabbage, piles of peas, slabs of pie—and Emma stopped counting the pieces of chicken he consumed at the fifth.

Emma served the meal in a sort of vacant stupor. How could she endure this for four days? Where were those women going to sleep? She wasn't putting up that car driver; he could just go and find him some place—greedy hog, swallowing her vittles down like he was starved! And that long thin secretary woman—tall as a horse and just as ugly! What a bitter disappointment! Gone were the visions of her sparkling, intimate conversations with the Bishop. He had scarcely noticed her. How could she get real chummy with that ugly little wife around? Four days of this and she would be dead!

Tonight, while they went to church, she would have to clean out her room for those women and that meant that she would miss the opening meeting of the Conference when the mayor of the town would make the visitors welcome. What had been a rosy vision of a four-day drama, with her and the Bishop as the principal actors and with Willie in the supporting role, now became a miserable farce to be endured as best she could. Her thoughts turned from the Bishop to her own errant husband. If Willie would just behave and help her try to keep face for these four days, she could bear it. If he would let Rose alone and give her a helping hand, everything would come right. Partly because she wanted to put him in a good frame of mind, but mostly because she was so thoroughly convinced, her last words before she drifted off into troubled slumber on the hard floor were, "Willie, honey, you was right! That Bishop's nuthin' but a dam man!" [*Opportunity* 19.4 (April 1941): 105–109]

Excess Baggage

by Helen Faw Mull

Light of skin and light of heart was Lucretia, traipsing gaily up and down the red clay lane, "totin'" a sober brown baby under her arm. But this afternoon as she sat on the steps of her grandmother's cabin her face was troubled.

"What about Anthony?" the "bandannaed" old woman asked accusingly. Her beady eyes searched Lucretia's sullen back.

"You can have him," the girl answered insolently.

"I doan want him," averred the old woman, removing the peach twig snuff-brush from her mouth and spitting emphatically into the bareswept dooryard. A chubby brown child in tan overalls chased a chicken around the corner of the cabin. The grandmother rumbled on:

"I done kep' yore ma, after her pa went off and lef' her, a two weeks ole baby. I wuz young den, like you. But I nursed white folks' chillun and took in washin' so's to feed an' keep her. I wuz proud of my baby, an' yo' ma wuz always dressed jes like white folks' chillun. She growed up so pert an' lively there warn't no girl in town had as many fellars as she did. I can heah her laughin' now on dis same front porch while her mammy tried to go to sleep. Jes fifteen she were when I asked her when she war goin' to work. She tossed her head an' said, 'I can't work. I'm going' to have a baby.'"

The girl on the step looked furtively to either side, making sure no passer-by might be hearing this family disclosure. Her grandmother took note of her anxiety.

"Oh, doan you worry, Lucrisha honey, yo' ma was married proper when you was born. I guess nobody ever knowed how bad I felt after she tole me dat; 'cause next Sunday when we wuz all in church waitin' for service to begin, I hearn a commotion behin' me an' looks an' dere I see yo' ma, jes' a slip of a girl an' so purty it took my breath away. She was standin' in the open doorway like a picture in a frame, an' beside her was a tall, good-looking young fellar I didn't know. She was tossin' her head like a young colt, an' holdin' on to the fellar's arm. When everybody had turned around to look, that pair pranced up the aisle an' ast the preacher to marry 'em. He wuz surprised, but he said he wouldn't refuse the sacraments of de Lord to nobody wantin' to enter de holy state; so he laid away his sermon for another Sunday and turned that meetin' into a weddin'. All afternoon folks wuz comin' to my house to congratulate dem two, an' stid of being a reproach to me, here she were a pride agin. I helped her get ready for you an' you wuz born right here in my house....

"Your pa wuz a steady sort of fellar an' he had a good job. I thought they wuz doin' well. But yo' ma had new-fangled ideas. She said she warn't happy wid him. So when you wuz four years ole, she got a divorce. She went away, to New York she say, an' she ain't never been home since. I started raisin' you jes like I raised your ma, an' seem to me like there weren't no difference. You wuz jes like her, headstrong and lively, wid lots of friends all time having a good time. But you wuz in school. You had lots better chance than yo' ma had, an' I thought you'd want to stay an' graduate before you got married."

The indifference which had cloaked the girl's desire to hear about her mother dropped from her when her grandmother's harangue became familiar. She moved down a step. But the older woman thwarted her escape.

"Jes heah me through, now Lucresha. It's for yo' good Ise speakin'. You say you want to get married again, an' I say dere's no good in it. I'd think you could see yourself. I done did my duty by you. "Member yo' weddin'?" I ain't never seed a finer. An' you wuz a purty bride."

Lucretia's black eyes softened and lost some of their defiance. But the old woman spat out her next words with sharp rancor.

"Where yo' husband now? You doan even know. Not nineteen yo'self, lamb, an' Anthony big enough to traipse after you everywhere you go."

"O Granny, you doan know how tired I get of having him go everywhere I go!" An angry jerk of the girl's head drew her back up stiff, and her shoulders rose and fell rapidly with her breathing. She fretted appealingly: "If I go the park with the rest,

Anthony go, too. If I go to a dance, Anthony go an' sleep on two chairs. Seems like I can't remember when I didn't have him."

Feeling a stab of pity for the girl mother, the old woman hardened her voice with anger.

"Well, he ain't never kep' you home from nowheres you wanted to go. I warn't no older than you, honey, when I waz stayin' home nights takin' care of my baby and workin' days makin' a livin' for her. You ain't never done neither for Anthony, you an' him both livin' off a me, an' every girl in yo' class helpin' you nurse—"

"But Granny, they doan mind." Her voice was plaintive. "It ain't half as hard on them as it is on me."

"They gets plenty tired of him, too," broke in her grandmother. "I've heared 'em say so!"

"Well," defensively, "they all had a good time out of my wedding. They shouldn't oughter kick!"

"So you want to make another payment, so to speak, by givin' 'em another wedding'?" The old woman grinned at her gibe.

"No, Granny," urged Lucretia hopefully. "I'm not asking you for another wedding. You just take Anthony, that's all. Howard and me'll get married quiet-like and you won't have to support me any longer. He has plenty. He'll give me the things I've always wanted." As visions of grandeur danced in her head, she added sulkily, "He'd a-taken me sooner if it hadn't been for Anthony.... Looks like you'd want him. I named him for you."

Aunt Phoeby Anthony looked with pity on the audacious young thing before her. Lucretia's clear skin was flushed with color. Her glossy bobbed hair was well-groomed. Her shapely body had the fresh firmness of a girl's still. It was hard for the old woman to deny her. But the grandmother shook her kerchiefed head and spoke with an effort at finality.

"I tell you I doan want him an' I ain't goin' to take him. Howard has plenty to take care of him, too."

"But Granny, I asked him, and he said he won't let him come in his house.... Please, Granny,"

"You've asked me, too, an' I say no. If Howard doan want you wid yo' baby, den you can go to work an' take care of yo' own, de way I did."

With a rheumatic grimace, she got up out of the old rocker.

"Granny!" called Lucretia desperately. "Don't go yet. I got to tell you something."

The old woman stopped but did not sit down. Misgiving haunted the depths of her leather-set eyes. Life had worsted her before at argument.

"I thought sure you'd take Anthony for me," repeated Lucretia, faintly hopeful yet. The lines on her grandmother's face set darkly. After a silence, Lucretia added, "Howard thought so, too. We were married today at noon. He's looking for me to be at his house when he comes from work."

The grandmother leaned heavily against the doorjamb. At last she spoke in a voice old and spiritless.

"Go 'long, Lucresha. I gotta git supper for me an' Anthony."

SALLY

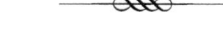

by Duanna Dungye

I met her in Kentucky. She maintained a kind of boarding house in the camp. Nobody called it a boarding house, but that was what it really was. Sally had eight boys in her four-room house. Some of the boys worked at night and some worked during the day. None of them minded in the least sleeping two in a bed, sometimes three. They enjoyed getting into a bed still warm where someone just got out of it. Yes, the boys were glad to be living at her house. They were very considerate of her, and that's why Sally did everything she could to make things nice for them.

On her way to the store—that's where she was going—she went over in her mind her program for the next two or three days. This meant considering what the boys wanted to eat. Sally tried to give them exactly what they wanted. They paid her well and she fed them well.

Sally walked on by the big store. She had to draw some scrip on Kola Davis' time before she could make any purchases. She drew checks on any of the boys whenever she wanted anything from the commissary. The amount was subtracted from their board.

Sally took her place in the line after speaking to most of the other colored folks, mostly women, who were already in line. A colored woman stood just in front of Sally; a white woman stood behind her. White and colored were in the same line. Sally and the colored woman talked. The white woman stood, saying nothing to anyone. There were Negroes in front and in back of her in the line. Sally didn't have anything to talk about, she had too much to think about. The colored woman's turn came. When she left, Sally faced the scrip writer. The writer glanced at her but he didn't ask her what she wanted. Sally and all the other colored members of the community were accustomed to scrip writers and their ways. She had not expected a greeting.

"I want to draw some scrip on Kola Davis," she informed him.

He consulted his records for a minute. "What's his number?" he asked.

"64-K," Sally replied. The writer looked at his records again.

"Kola Davis' number has been changed," he said, "and you must get on his new number. You're not on the new number and until he puts you on, you can't draw any scrip on him." He looked past her at the white woman who stood next in line.

Sally was plainly vexed at what looked like a hitch in the forward progress of her plans. "What must I do now before I can draw on Kola," she asked, annoyance showing in her voice. The writer handed her a card. "Take this card home and have him sign it, or have him come back down her with you and we'll put you on his number if he says so."

Without another word Sally took the card and stepped out of the line. She did not leave the office immediately, but stood looking at the card, wondering how she could avoid the long walk back home.

"Good morning, Mrs. Bradley," said the writer to the white woman who was next in line. "What can I do for you this morning?"

"Well, you see, Mr. Nelson," began the woman nervously, "my old man's number has been changed and I haven't been put on the new one yet. Can I get some scrip?"

"Certainly, Mrs. Bradley," said the writer without hesitation. "How much do you want?" Several women looked at Sally who now stood with a frown on her face, watching the proceedings. "Two dollars," the woman said. The writer hastily wrote out the scrip and handed it to her. The woman stepped from the line. Ignoring the others who stood in line, Sally stepped up to the cage.

"Say, here! What do you mean giving that woman scrip and not giving me any!" her voice filled the office. The writer's face flooded with color. The crowd in the office became silent. Two other scrip writers in the cage stopped writing and stood waiting to see what was going to happen. Everything had stopped. Sally spoke again.

"I heard that white woman tell you that she wasn't on that number. Why did you give her scrip and wouldn't give me any?" she demanded.

The writer finally found dignity enough to bellow, "Do you know who you're talking to! Get out of here!"

Sally did not move. "What am I supposed to do now? Run? I'm not going anywhere until I get that scrip!" A volley of well-chosen oaths followed her last statement.

The writer's anger at the insults being heaped upon him by the Negro woman knew no bounds. However, there were too many black men in the office and in the streets just outside the office for him to forget himself completely and give her the thrashing he was certain she deserved.

"Woman," he thundered, "Stop sassing me!"

"How can one grown person sass another grown person!" came her reply.

The writer took to his last haven. "If you don't shut up and get out of here I'm going to call 'the law!'"

Sally grew louder. "The law!" She knew "the law!" She had washed "the law's" Sunday shirts for fifteen years!

"You can call up 'East Hell' if you want to," she said, "I ain't going nowhere!"

Five minutes later "the law" came into the office. The excited line swayed backward to give the officer a chance to get to the window of the cage where the woman and the writer stood glaring at each other.

"Well, I'll be John Dobby!" he said when he saw Sally. "What the deuce is the matter with you, Sally?"

"What does it look like is the matter with me?" she demanded, control gone. "This writer won't give me no scrip!"

"She's not on that number," the writer hastened to explain, seeing the glance the officer had thrown him. The writer was beginning to feel ridiculous since "the law's" arrival.

"I was on the old number," explained Sally, "and I ought to be on the new one."

"The law" turned to the writer. "Give her what she wants," he ordered. He turned to Sally again. "If I had known it was you they called me for, I never would have come. Stop the racket when you get that scrip and get on out of here!" With that the officer walked out of the office.

Turning to the writer who was nervously handling his pencil inside the cage, Sally ordered, "You give me five dollars on Kola Davis' number."

"What's the name?" asked the scrip writer in as steady a voice as he could muster.

"You said there wasn't any name on the number, so, you give me five dollars on that 'no-name' number!"

The other writers had commenced issuing scrip. Their hands shook. The office was alive again. Lines were moving towards the windows. People were talking. The words "race riot" came from a group of Negro men. Somebody said something about "that crazy woman."

As soon as Sally obtained the desired scrip, she left the office and hurried towards the big store. She was an hour behind with her plans and she was expecting a crowd that night. All the boys were bringing their girls in for soft drinks and sandwiches. She had to hurry if she was to have things ready when they came.

[*Opportunity* 19.11 (November 1941): 334–335]

THE LITTLE THAT IS EVERYTHING

by Elsie A. Parry

Mr. Philip LeBeau stared at the open letter that shook in his fingers, and knew that miracles can happen. The printing on the sheet—the impressive letterhead belonged to a world-famous hospital—wavered before his eyes, mild, dark eyes set in an ebony face, so that he had trouble with the words:

"...on Dr. MacLean's urgent recommendation it gives us great pleasure to invite you to our staff as an assistant in tropical disease research...."

It was incredible! North ... To New York—away from this tiny Caribbean island.... Away from the poverty and the superstitious ignorance, from the malnutrition and the medical inadequacies that made his practice so difficult and so discouraging. Here was God-given opportunity that would enable Philip to serve his fellowmen as he wanted to serve them....

Philip marveled. What astonishing fruit his meeting with Andrew MacLean had borne! Ten years ago he and Andrew—big, clever, ambitious Andy—had studied together in Edinburgh University, but after graduation Dr. LeBeau had returned to Dominica to practice in the jungle hinterlands of his birthplace; Dr. MacLean had gone to New York. Last May a vacation jaunt to the West Indies had landed Andrew at Roseau, where he had run smack into Philip, in town for the weekly mail steamer. The two men had talked as only people can who must bridge the hiatus of years. Andrew had listened with interest to Philip's half-apologetic account of his professional doings. Polite interest, Philip had thought at the time, but apparently he'd been wrong. MacLean's interest had been avid and penetrating.

With sudden shock Dr. LeBeau came back to the waterfront's steamer-day bustle. Naked heat shimmered over the corrugated iron roofs, the dusty roadway, and the high-flung palms; seaward lay the mail steamer, white against the blues of sky and water. Philip had been dreaming of well-equipped laboratories, of immaculate operating rooms, of libraries where a man could fortify himself with the accumulated experience of his fellows.... He thought, wryly, of his two-room, palm-thatched house, perched high on a mountain-side, which was laboratory, operating room, office. Not much to show for ten years' unremitting labor!

Phillip stuffed the letter into his pocket. He must tell Zena Boissevain the glorious news. The doctor hurried away from the waterside toward Morne Bruce, Roseau's landward bulwark. Almost immediately the road began to lift toward a settlement of white houses on the mountain's flank.

Philip found Zena in the garden. Over her dusty head a frangipanni tree shed its prodigal delicate fragrance.

"Philip!" the girl exclaimed. "You here—at this hour? How grand...!" There was shy welcome in her smile, then she sobered. "But didn't you see Paul? He's only just gone."

"I haven't seen him. What...?"

"Ralph sent him for you," Zena said: "Francillia's baby, you know...."

"I see.... Then I ought to cut along." Philip consulted his watch. "The newcomer won't hurry, though—it's Francillia's first!" He paused. "Zena, I ... I must talk to you...."

Zena looked at Philip, startled by the excitement in his voice. He was pulling a letter from his pocket.

"Zena, this came today!"

The girl's eyes hurried over the typewritten page.

"Why, Philip—how marvelous!" she burst out. "A chance to study in New York.... It's what you've always wanted. But ... your patients?"

"Oh, Hugh Sibley can take over. He's competent."

"Mm–mm, competent..." Zena agreed, "but unsympathetic. You'll be missed, Philip...!"

"Zena," Philip's voice was suddenly unsteady. He took the girl's cool brown hands in his. "I've wanted a chance like this—for professional reasons, of course, but most of all for you. My scrabbly practice here is nothing to offer you. But New York has infinite possibilities. Think what it will mean to us—life in a big city, a fine home...!"

Philip stopped, alarmed by a strange stillness in a girl whose hands he held.

"Zena, what is it?"

"Philip, you mustn't count on me," she said quietly. "New York isn't for me. Dominica is my home, my people are here, I belong here. In New York I'd be a lonely alien forever."

"But, Zena, you'd soon fit in!"

"No, Philip, it would never do. I'd die of homesickness."

"But, Zena, I thought...."

"I love you, Philip. You know that..." Zena said gently, "but I can't tear myself up by the roots. But *you* must go!"

It was fortunate that Philip's mare could pick her nimble-footed way up the mountainside to Ralph's wattle-and-daub cabin without much guidance, for her rider paid her scant heed. He was wrestling with the sudden alarming complexities of his problem. It had never occurred to him, even remotely, that Zena would balk at leaving Dominica. True, she had never set foot off the island, except for a school term in neighboring Grenada. Her whole world was encompassed by Dominica's three hundred square miles. But to Philip, since his momentous stay in Edinburgh, Dominica had shrunk to an insignificant dot in the sea. To leave it would be heaven! But to leave without Zena ... without hope of Zena following him...? That was completely fantastic. They'd been in love for years. All Philip's ambitions had centered around her ultimate well-being—the decision to become a doctor, the try for the Edinburgh scholarship, his patient work with Dominica's poor to gain knowledge and experience for advancement....

Philip shook a troubled head. Bury himself forever on this island? That was fantastic, too! Jog over these mountain trails day after day to help Francillia or Clarice or M'lissa give birth to a squalling youngster? Fight yaws and rickets and witch-doctors and dirt? Teach, year in and year out, the A-B-C's of hygiene and diet to the blissfully ignorant? True, he was making headway.... Here was Francillia defying her family in demanding that "doctuh-suh" attend her instead of Big Angy, the witch-doctor. And old Sebastian was actually wearing shoes now to protect his feet from yaws! Something, but so painfully little....

Zena couldn't have meant what she'd said! The sudden shock of Philip's news had frightened her. She'd get used to the idea of leaving Dominica, given time and the chance to miss Philip.... It was a consoling thought, and the doctor felt suddenly cheered. He clucked to his mare, suggesting more urgency in her leisurely jog.

Day was marching steadily across the shadowed gorges and down the steep, green-clad slopes before Philip headed home. He was dead-beat, but in Ralph's cabin Francillia's son was trying out lusty new lungs. He'd been born, moreover, without benefit of black pepper blown into his mother's nostrils or hen feathers burned on glowing coals!

Philip hoped, sleepily, that Paul had thought to prepare breakfast at Valcour. The stewed plantain at Ralph's had tasted of kerosene and there'd been hairs in the goat's milk. Suddenly Philip jerked upright in his saddle. Good Lord, Paul...! In his anxiety about Zena and his preoccupation with Francillia, he'd clean forgotten Paul. Whatever would become of the lad if Philip went north? He had no home but Philip's, and no family.

The doctor groaned. God, what a mess! Ever since he'd rescued the half-starved waif from a marauding shark eight years before, Paul was never willingly out of Philip's sight. But to take him to New York was impossible. As well cage the eagle's free flight. Paul belonged in Dominica's mountains, whose trails his splayed feet knew as he knew the palm of his hand.

Well, Paul's future would have to be arranged somehow....

Abruptly, Philip realized he hadn't seen Paul the day before. Not in Roseau, nor at Zena's. And Paul hadn't showed up at Ralph's, which was strange. Well, no matter. The boy would be at Valcour.

But Paul wasn't at Valcour. The house was empty and there was no breakfast....

Before the week was out Philip was nearly frantic. Zena refused to see him—*I mustn't influence your decision*, had been her message—Paul was still inexplicably missing, and the letter of acceptance was still unwritten. The day the northbound steamer was due, Philip flung himself at his desk.

"God, I'm going mad!" he groaned. "But mad or not, I'm going to New York!"

His pen began a furious scratching.

Someone knocked timidly.

"Come in!" Philip called impatiently

He looked up and gasped. The doorway, the steps, the garden, and all the slope beyond overflowed with people and bundles and animals. The excited babble was punctuated by bleatings, squeals, and a cock's excited crow. What in Heaven's name...? Why, these were his patients! And there was Paul....

Old Sebastian, glistening shoes on his feet, stepped forward.

"Doctuh-suh," he began, and the crowd quieted. "Paul yonduh don' bring us de bad tidings he oberhear—ob de letter ... an' we's grieved. Paul say yuh lak leave us ... 'cos' we's pore."

Blood rose hot in Philip's face.

"We's pore, sho' nuf," Sebastian's voice was gentle, "bu,' doctuh-suh, we loves yuh! An' so we's come wid what little we hab...."

He waved an arm at the scrawny chickens, the grunting porkers, the plantains, the handfuls of mangoes, the pitiful stalks of sugar-cane.... The little that was their all!

Philip looked down at the eager, anxious black faces turned up to him with a child's helpless entreaty, and sudden unbearable pain caught at his throat. These were more than his patients, they were his people.... They belonged here, Paul belonged here, and Zena.... And he, himself! Serving them would bring neither fame nor money ... only honor, as God measures honor—*Inasmuch as ye have done it unto one of the least of these....*

Ten days later Dr. MacLean frowned over Philip's letter.

"Good Lord, what gets into people?" he exclaimed irritable. "Imagine LeBeau turning down such an opportunity—the sentimental fool!"

[*Opportunity* 20.6 (June 1942): 179–181]

PORTRAIT OF A CITIZEN

by Zora L. Barnes

Dear Jane,

At last the day is here—the day I worked for, the day you dreamed of, the day Mom and Pop slaved and sweated for. Yes, sweated is the word for it 'cause the easiest job Mom had during the whole time was that scrubbing job at Sears and Co. I can still smell the lye in that yellow soap as the steamy hot water gushed and slopped over it and you could feel the heat from it a yard away. I can still see Mom flinch every time she'd first stick her hand with the big stiff-bristle brush in that pail of hot water. They advertise lotions from dishpan hands, but I wonder did they ever think of advertising anything to help scubwoman's hands—yes, scrubwoman's hands, red and rough and riveted with countless callouses and careless splinters, scrubwoman's back knotted about the shoulders with muscles hard as only a stevedore's should be, scrubwoman's shame that her normal school diploma was just a piece of paper yellowed with age and gnawed by mice somewhere down in the bottom of an old trunk.

I used to wonder when I was a kid why Mom would look so queer after some of her old school friends had been to visit. She didn't linger on the porch and watch them out of sight as she did other folks who came. She'd shake hands if they were men or kiss them on the cheek if they were women, smile kinda gentle like and then go quickly back into the house and mend socks faster than fury. All the time she was mending she'd be whispering to herself "blessed something or other." I never knew exactly what she was saying until one day it came to me she must have been saying the beatitudes. I asked her and she said yes, that if she said it often enough soon she'd believe it and that's all that mattered anyway.

It wasn't easy for Pop either, 'cause the whole time it was up in the morning to go to work and back home in the evening to get ready to go to work the next morning. The only time he had to rest in was on Sunday and that eleven months he was out of work. That eleven months he spent trying to find work and going after surplus commodities. Surplus commodities—that was the only thing I ever saw get next to Pop. He never could understand why they thought he was coming there for food. He wanted a job. He could work as well as the next one, in fact, Pop could put out a day's work better than some fellows my age. And he was one of the best carpenters that ever spit into a sawdust pile. The thing that beat Pop was that he didn't have the "right attitude" for a man on relief. He could speak more than three sentences without saying "yassah, Boss!" so he was one of those "smart niggers" who needed to be shown his place and kept there. Besides, he was clean and had on whole clothes and he owned a house although it was in Mom's name. He didn't even look as if he needed a job, so the "powers that be" decided he needed a dose of the "clients' entrance" in the rear.

"Clients' entrance"—that's a laugh. I always had the idea that a client was someone who was having some professional services done for them. I finally looked it up and I guess they picked the right word because one meaning given is "anyone receiving habitually the protection of a person of influence; ... sometimes, a hanger-on." Pop thought he was under their protective influence, but they cased him as a hanger-on. He sat out there with overripe bananas, squashy oranges, moldy celery leaves and prunes confiscated by millions of gnats.

For eleven months Pop sat back there, damp in the spring, sweltering in the summer and frigid in the winter. He sat back there with a lot of hungry devils who were too hungry to care whose tobacco they shared and too cold to see what color was the man sitting so close to them. I bet Pop found out more about the kind of people they were inside, what they did for fun when they had any, where the biggest blue-gills were caught, why the crippled woman left California. Pop almost proved that winter that hate and bigotry and racial prejudice are digestive disturbances.

For eleven months, Pop would get up every morning, go to the employment office and look around for odd jobs, then come home to stick his old black pipe with the stem in the corner of his mouth, rest his chin in his hand and just sit looking into space. Finally, after supper he'd puff a little longer, then knock the ashes out on the heel of his shoe, blow through it a couple of times, get up and say, "Well, Mama, we better go to bed. I 'magine I'll get that call to go to work in the morning."

Every night he said it. I thought he was either the dumbest man alive or else the stubbornest. I even teased him about having a one-track mind. He just grinned a little and said, "I s'pect that makes things right simple and easy, Son, 'specially if the track's in the right direction."

Maybe smart folks would say that's the line of least resistance. Maybe clever people depend on knowing that people are like that. The only thing that they don't consider is that sometimes people with one-track minds do get where they are headed for.

Every night he'd polish his work shoes, lay out a clean work shirt and pants. He said there was nothing like clean clothes to prove you'd done a day's work; said you couldn't get very dirty just standing around doing nothing so if at the end of the day you had worked some there'd be some evidence of it. Too, he believed that a thing belonged to you more if you had worked for it because if it had been given to you it always partly belonged to the other person. I remember when I was a kid if I wanted money to buy something or to go somewhere, he'd always say, "I can't give it to you, Son, but I think we can find a job for you to do that's worth that much."

I had everything I wanted but I always worked for it. I never learned any short cuts. I guess that's why it has taken this day so long to come.

Then one day, Pop saw a different man. He must have been new on the staff. Probably he was some kid just out of school, full of ideals of sociology and humanitarianism. He must have talked to Pop in a different way or something 'cause Pop had a livelier step when he came home that evening. His eyes were kinda misty-like and he had the old one-sided grin on his face. At supper he said, "Son, it's the educated young folks in this country what's going to steer this ship of state into home port. We old working men are in it all right, but it's you fellows that are going to give the orders. That's why I wanted you to go to college."

"Yes! Pop was a happy man that night. He teased Mom and told me I was just like him—getting uglier every day. Next morning, he couldn't get there quick enough. Went off in a downpour of rain without his rubbers or umbrella and got pulpy wet. Well, this nice young man forgot about him or went to a luncheon and stayed all day or something. Anyway, Pop sat there all day in that mess of wet clothes. Of course, I don't need to tell you about that. I don't need to tell you how sick he was for a while until finally the doctor said that he was fixed for this time and as far as physical and medical laws were concerned he ought to get well. Oh, Jane! What can physical laws do for a man who finds his life's journey is a dead end road? What can physical laws do for a man who has discovered too late that patience is a virtue for animals alone? What virtue is its own reward because that's all you have for being so? The world teaches axioms and proverbs for a man to follow and then forgets to tell him not to depend on them. The big fellows throw an arm of protective benevolence around the little fellow and then lock the door they dare him to try to get in. God! Jane! What can physical laws do for a man whose hope has gone up in smoke before he even gets a good blaze kindled?

What did Pop do? He kinda smiled and said, "Your Mother always said I didn't have sense enough to come in out of the rain."

As for Mom, she never said very much anyway. Now that Pop's gone she says even less.

The day you dreamed of has come. Fellows aren't supposed to know what girls' dreams are like, but Jane, my darling, there's a light in your eyes when you look at me that tells me. It tells me that you're still a little girl dreaming of a knight in shining armor. And to top it off, you think you've found it in me. If it weren't so terribly frightening to me, it would be ridiculous. King Arthur would have thought all the sorcerers in his kingdom had been turned into one awful spirit if they had ever unmasked and found a black knight in the bunch. That crowd was more, if possible, "lily-white" than a certain Southern senator, was worse that the "main liner" in *Kittey Foyle*. (By the way, I lost yours, I'll have to get you another copy.) Too, I guess most of the knights were good-looking and the most that even the kindest people could ever say about my face is that I have a "friendly smile." Yet, you say I'm your dreams come true.

Yes, Jane, you're still a little girl. If you weren't you would not trust me as you do with your every dream of life and happiness. You're still a little girl, Jane. If you weren't you wouldn't believe that people can still "live happily ever after." You're still a little girl, Jane! If you weren't you'd know that the meek do *not* inherit the earth because the earth is the Lord's and most meek people would be scared to death if they ever got a chance to meet anyone as decent to them as that.

Only a very young girl, Jane, would sign a contract to teach in a little back-wash school like ours. Even if they paid you what they promised it isn't half what the white teachers are getting, yet before the school year is over, the funds run out, the school board looks distressed and apologetic, you feel sorry for the children who don't have half a chance and sign for another year. Yet, as I sit here looking from my window I see a world of beauty that would make the sorriest heart a gay and gleeful thing and I am glad from the bottom of my heart that I didn't let you give up that job. I wanted to take you away from a place where you couldn't go to the public library and read or even borrow a book, where you couldn't sit on the benches in the park when you wanted shade and quiet, where you didn't dare try on a hat in a millinery shop or tell the man in the shoe store that the reason the shoes didn't fit was because he wouldn't let you fit them on. I'm glad you still have even that job because your three sisters can still go to school in whole clothes; your Mother can still have a best dress to go to church in. Yes, at least, she can go to church.

You're a little girl, Jane, but you're a better man than I am. You would have given up that job. You knew you couldn't keep it afterwards. You knew, too, that as the wife of a struggling young colored architect that I'd be building more air-castles than I would low-cost houses. You knew, too, that you'd have to pay for those air-castles of mine with worry, with fear, with maybe, disillusionment—yet, *I looked like a knight in shining armor to you.*

So, Jane, my dear, my darling, I drew my sword, I challenged every foe, I conquered the enemy. I laid the aurel wreath of success at your feet. That firm decided to hire me. Though it was not their policy to hire colored persons to their staff they felt my excellent training and promising work merited their attention. Of course, the salary was lower than was customary because I would not be doing the usual contact work with clients. That was all right, because I don't want to sit at a client's dinner table or drink cocktails with him at his club or take his daughter out to lunch. I was content to know that at least I had what Mom and Pop had planned and worked and sweated for, what you'd dreamed of, what I'd hoped for, but—

This cup of success contains a bitter draught, Jane. I received my first pay check from that job today, but I also received notice to report for selective service duty four days from now.

I'm not a praying man, my darling. It would take a man Pop's size inside to pray after all I've seen and gone through. I'm afraid that circumstances have stunted my inner growth. But I have a faint consolation. Four days from now I'll have on a uniform and *I'll be citizen!* I'll be one of that vast crowd of young men who are postponing their dreams, their hopes, their loves to join hands and hearts to form a chain of courage and determination for their country. No, I'm not a praying man and now I'll have even less time to learn how, but my darling while you're praying for our little dreams to come true will you say something about hoping that after I get out of that uniform that the "citizen" part will stick."

Lovingly,
Tom.

[*Opportunity* 20.9 (September 1942): 274–276]

THE SIMPLE ONE

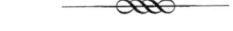

by Alice I. Murray

The room was filled with beauty. And the small black boy of fourteen years standing so simply before that class of forty-odd white children was the creator of it. His audience was lost to everything but a voice. It's rich cadences poured like liquid gold from the young throat, soothing and comforting ears attuned to the blatant noises of restless, clamoring life lived with speed and recklessness in an atmosphere of poverty and squalor.

After the youngsters had passed into my room for their reading lesson, the requests came thick and fast.

"Please let Andy read to us."

"Can't Andy go on with the story from where we left off last time?"

I nodded an assent and joined the eager class. The colored boy stepped forward with his book. A hush descended over the group. The miracle began.

Andy's life, like that of the rest of the pupils', was hard. He lived on the fringe of a society where Life spreads her largess very thin. But unlike the others, Andy faced his world calmly in a simple, unobtrusive manner. His gentility and poise, his courage and humility set him apart. Many of our pupils acquire polish as the years go by. Andy never has. He didn't need to. Yet in him can be found the simple, natural ways of one to the manor born.

But before Andy finished the eighth grade, he had to quit school. A father of seventy-two whose days as a driver of a dilapidated ash cart were over, relinquished its rickety seat to a firmer, younger body. And so the cares of a family that long had troubled the boy, became for him, stark reality. His younger brother, over-age for his grade and constantly in hot water, proved too difficult for the invalid step-mother to handle. So Andy spent much time placating irate neighbors. The older brother, a nonchalant Lothario, had taken unto himself a wife and thereafter never could be counted on for financial assistance. In fact, he often appealed to Andy to bolster his constantly depleted larder. But the boy never whimpered and his young shoulders only seemed to grow firmer and more stable with the increasing weight thrust upon them. Although Andy has never seemed to grow much physically, he had assumed a mental stature far beyond his years.

But as time went on, Andy's grasp on the economic tiller of his small craft became weaker. Gathering up the ashes of dead fires brought in precarious financial returns. It took a great deal of conniving to eke out the meager income with various other small jobs. Old Bill, the faithful slat-sided horse, as rickety as the wagon itself that bumped along behind him, became too great an expense. Maybe Old Bill's keep could have been managed some way if the new fangled oil burners and gas furnaces hadn't come into style just them. And as if that were not enough at this crucial time, a license must be bought so that the business of hauling ashes might be carried on lawfully. It was the last straw. No more on my way to school would I see a ragged but valiant figure sitting so meekly behind wobbly Old Bill as he plodded along a snowy street, leaving behind him a thin film of dust, sifted from his load of ashes.

The collapse of Andy's business and the loss of his horse were severe blows to the youngster who was the head of this house and the captain of his soul. It was at times like these that one of Andy's talents stood him in good stead. Much as the sun's heat encourages the bud to flower, so Andy's thoughts under adversity bloomed into poetry. At least he and I used that word in speaking of his efforts.

Even before the boy left school, he would bring me his poems. And once on a late spring afternoon when the air had been made sweet with the fragrance of lilacs that the pupils carried with them from class to class, Andy wrote:

> TO A LILAC BUSH
> *Soft, green petals of velvety hue,*
> *Pale purple flowers tinted with blue,*
> *Dark green stems, tapering to thin,*
> *Half flower, half tree, the children's friend.*

Andy never told me much about his difficulties. But I guessed things became increasingly difficult, for after a long absence, I looked up one day from my work at my desk in that schoolroom, quiet at last, to find Andy sitting in one of the seats waiting for me to finish. He is like that. Quiet, patient but never apathetic. One turns in relief to such a personality after a day filled with demanding, aggressive youngsters. He was dressed in his 'best' which was poor indeed.

"How glad I am to see you," I said to him. "Why have you been gone so long?"

"To tell you the truth, I just wouldn't come over until I got something decent to wear." My heart warmed to the direct look he gave me.

"But you know that I'm interested in you, Andy, not your clothes. Don't let them bother you for an instant."

"They do, though." The quiet voice continued proudly, "I've never visited you in my old clothes and I never will."

Finally one autumn with the bed-redden father gone, Andy had to ask for relief for his family while he went hopefully off to CCC camp. But he wasn't there long. I received a note from him after his return home telling me that he had come back. Later, I gathered from bits injected into his conversation that he had been placed in a camp with a group of white southern boys. He could not tolerate their treatment of him. They could not understand his attitude towards them. A fight resulted. Andy was discharged.

But the trouble and turmoil brought out the soul of the poet and a whole note book of poetry appeared on my desk. This is typical of what he wrote at that time:

>   AUTUMN
> When I dreamed of autumn,
> I visioned pomp and charm,
> A mallard winging swiftly south
> Fleeing a hunter's harm;
> A wild goose flying high and fast
> Over swamp and moor,
> A weasel weaving through the grass,
> Training a rabbit's spoor.
> But autumn as I saw it,
> Was not like this, alas,
> The duck is in the haversack,
> The goose lies in the grass.
> The rabbit hangs in the market,
> And the weasel will never pass.

Along about Andy's nineteenth birthday, he fell in love. Almost from the first, the affair was doomed and Andy knew it. I never saw the girl but his glowing poems of her told me much. Told me more than he suspected. Her father would have none of the boy. He was poor and he had no prospects. The girl as the daughter of a prominent colored pastor had a better future before her. Andy's days and nights were colored with dreams of his loved one. But always those dreams were smudged by the wispy, trailing fingers of melancholy. His heart spoke to me in simple rhyme that poured into my room thick and fast. His sweetheart was flattered by his attention. Not every lover has a poet's soul. But verses are simple things. So when another came along with money in his pockets and a promise of security, she married him and Andy's heart broke.

The lonely boy with the potentialities of an artist needed encouragement and an appreciative audience. And I always tried to see that he got both whenever he came to visit me. I long ago learned to let the mechanics of his art alone. Andy's outpourings were so natural to him, so much a part of him, that correcting their metre, giving them polish and finish, only confused him. It seemed as meaningless as telling him how he must laugh or weep. Occasionally when he asked for it, I would help him to clarify his thoughts or correct his punctuation. A copy of Dunbar's poems, a dictionary and a book of Shakespeare's plays were handy to his bed where he spent many of his evenings, reading and writing. I gave him lists of books that he could easily borrow from a nearby library. But 'hands off' was my policy.

A change was coming over my friend as time passed to which he was oblivious. He was reaching a maturity even emotionally that surprised me. Possibly the opportunity to travel furthered this process, for Andy's luck changed. He was fortunate enough to meet a well-to-do colored couple who owned a large car. Neither one could drive but as they were eager to go to New York to see the Joe Louis–Schmeling fight, they hired Andy to drive them. In the boy's past, one of his precarious jobs was that of plumber's assistant. And the kind-hearted Jew had allowed him to learn to drive his old jalopy between jobs.

The offer of the job as chauffeur carried Andy to the very peaks of happiness. The trip turned out to be a very extended one. He had a wonderful opportunity to see cities both north and south and his mental horizon was considerably extended. His poetry at this period was full of enthusiastic descriptions of the large eastern cities. In a letter to me at the time he wrote: "These verses will tell you of my actual experiences and thoughts while on my trip."

Not only did that wonderful trip widen the scope of his thoughts but it showed him how much better off he was even in his dubious financial state than the colored folks in the South. And it swept the tag ends of his old love affair from his heart. When he came to visit me on his return, I saw a new Andy. One more vibrant and free. He smilingly said, "You told me a long time ago that some day I'd meet another girl that I could love. I have."

And so one day last week when the telephone rang, it was Andy inviting my husband and me to his church on Saturday. He was going to be married. I was consumed with curiosity. What was his sweetheart like? Were Andy's love poems to her just stuff with which to feed her ego? Or had he met his equal at last?

George and I sent a box of spring flowers to the bride and Saturday night found us sitting in a long hall brightly decorated in vivid blue and white crepe paper. There was a piano but no music. A choir but no singing. This was a poor man's wedding. The seats of the auditorium were filled with the 'small fry' and elderly. The young people stood in the rear and filled the aisle. The audience was bubbling over. An air of carnival prevailed. The jollity and lack of music bothered me. Andy's new life should be ushered in with music and solemnity.

In a perfect hubbub of talk and laughter, Andy and his bride quietly entered and ascending the platform, faced us. She was a pleasant, mature looking girl with a soft, loving expression. She wore a black dress and carried our gift of flowers. Andy looked younger than she, his short, slight figure was attired in a neatly-pressed suit, faded and blue. One that I have often seen over a period of years.

The suave, affable minister entered into his duties in much the same spirit that gripped the congregation. When the large handsome man asked Andy to repeat after him the old, old lines, 'On thee I bestow all my worldly goods,' the effervescent spirits of the genial audience knew no bounds and there was much laughter and joking. But through it all, the two principle characters kept their natural dignity and poise. An undercurrent of derision that ran like a thread through the conduct of the onlookers, bothered me but not those two. In a discussion with my husband later in regard to it, he assured me that it was the logical expression of a group of people who were out for a good time and in a gay and happy mood which certainly was suitable to the occasion. The explanation sounded sensible but not satisfying.

Yesterday, a colored boy and former pupil of ours came to school to call on us teachers. He also had been at the wedding. When I asked him why the people laughed all during Andy's wedding ceremony, his lips curved into a sneer as he said, 'Oh that simple guy.' To him it seemed perfectly lucid answer to my question. But still I felt disturbed.

"I don't understand you," I said.

"Say, did you ever hear him talk?"

"Yes," I replied, "many times."

"Well, then you know. She talks the same way. They're both a couple of simple ones."

"I'm glad," I thought as my visitor left, "that Andy's wife talks his language. He can tell her of his hopes and dreams and she will understand." I looked after the retreating form swaggering so cockily down the hall and murmured to myself:

"It's all a matter of what one considers, 'simple.'"

[*Opportunity* 20.10 (October 1942): 302–304]

CITIZEN IN THE SOUTH

by Ruby Rohrlich

The train pulled out of Pennsylvania Station. Melanie Thornton smiled as her small son pressed his nose against the window. Eleven hours, she thought, that's less than half a day, practically nothing in time. When you're in the hospital working, it passes quickly; but on a train, when you haven't seen your husband for six months— eleven hours is a lot! Still, she thought, as she mused lazily on the relativity of time, still it's only hours ... and her breath quickened.

Billy climbed on her lap. "The wheels are singing, mum—gonna see da-dee, gonna see da-dee." Billy heard a song, rhythm in everything. Melanie pictured Randall's amazed delight when he saw the boy. "How he's grown!" he would say, and measure him. At five they grew so fast they needed new shoes before the old were half worn. Billy straightened his visor cap, pulled down his soldiers coat, and raised two finger to his forehead. "Is this it, mum, is this how pop does it?" The white baby teeth gleamed through the slightly pendulous lips, the dark eyes dilated in excitement.

In her loneliness for Randall the sight of Billy never failed to comfort her—to comfort, and yet to wrench her heart, too, for the boy looked so like his father. It was hard this separation, their first separation in seven years of a marriage that had made her complete, sane. They were both physicians, they loved their work and shared it closely; they had their boy, and their delight in him. Randall, who had taught her to love life and people—how she missed him.

She had wept when his Christmas furlough had been cancelled, for she had not seen him since his enlistment in June. But he had phoned the next day, urging her to come to him instead, and her laughter became frequent and easy. It had been hard for her to arrange her own leave—so many doctors had already left for the Army that the hospital was seriously under-staffed. But they knew Randall's regiment might be sent overseas any day, and by pleading she had wrested a week from them. One week, 168 hours, and twenty-two of them had to be spent in traveling. And then—when again would she see him?

The sound of the wheels came to her muted, and sad, and monotonous. Melanie shook herself impatiently—they, the three of them, would have a along week together, and it would begin in about ten hours.

Dreamily she made her son comfortable with a cookie and a picture book.

"Tickets, lady."

Melanie started, and showed the conductor her tickets. The wheels were screeching to a stop; they had reached Philadelphia.

"You'll have to change cars at Washington, lady."

Melanie was puzzled. "I thought this was a through train."

The conductor did not meet her inquiring look. "It's a through train all right, but from Washington on colored folks have to sit in a separate car."

Melanie sat up straight, her bronze face resuming the impassive mask of the time before Randall. "My boy and I are going to Fort Bragg. My husband's in the Medical Corps there."

"That's the rule, ma'am. They haven't changed the rule." The conductor kept toying with his ticket-punch.

Her voice deep with firmness, Melanie said, "These are reserved seats. I paid for them, and I'm not changing."

The conductor shrugged his shoulders as he walked away, but his eyes were sympathetic.

Billy tugged at her hand, her stern face frightened him a little. "What'd the man want, mum?"

"It's all right, Billy."

The joy had run out of her, but she managed a reassuring smile and motioned to a double seat where three children were playing. "Why don't you play with the children, dear? Show them your book."

For the next two hours, until they reached Washington, she would have something to think about.

The children were laughing at something Billy was saying. He was probably telling them one of his made-up stories. Now he and a little girl began to bounce a ball against the plush back of the seat. Melanie's face softened as she looked at him. Then she frowned, and her hand flew out toward him in a small, unconscious, protecting gesture. How had she dared bring Billy to the South. He would be burned deep, would never forget. She *had* remembered the South, but she had thought, now?... surely not now.

Suddenly she felt confined, cramped in this train. It was so narrow, so close. She wanted to stretch her legs, walk somewhere, fast. The even spacing of the seats, their faded bilious green irritated her. Melanie passed her hand wearily over her forehead and through her thick, short, curly hair. She stood up, straight and slim, and walked to the water faucet, lurching with the movement of the train. She thought, shall I move? Randall, what shall I do?

When she returned, she found the children playing on her seat. Billy was whirling his spinning top for them. As she watched how naturally these children accepted him, she realized again that the rejection of her people was not instinctive, was not transmitted in the genes and chromosomes. Poor little Billy. And yet she and Randall couldn't have protected him much longer. He would have to learn in the usual, the bitter way.

Melanie swallowed an aspirin for her aching head. She gave the children some of the sandwiches she had prepared that morning, and milk from a thermos bottle. Billy's eyelids were drooping, he needed a nap. Melanie asked his playmates to go. She held her son on her lap, and he soon fell asleep. The afternoon sun was strong and hot in the train. She drowsed a little, then fell into a troubled sleep.

The train stopped. Melanie awoke

"All 'board ... Washington."

She waited.

"You gotta change cars here," the new conductor said, as he waited for Melanie to get up and leave.

"These are my seats," said Melanie quietly. "I reserved them and paid for them."

"That don't make no difference. Colored people sit in their own car down here." His light-blue, middle-aged eyes looked hard at her, unashamed.

"My husband is in the Army. We're going to visit him at Fort Bragg," Melanie explained, very patiently. Billy stirred in her arms, and opened his eyes.

"That don't make no difference. You gotta change cars here. Come on now."

Billy clung to her. He looked with blinking eyes from his mother to the conductor. Melanie tried to conceal her growing anger. "I'm an American citizen, I've got the same rights as anyone else. I'm not giving up seats that I reserved and paid for."

"You'll leave this car if I have to put you out." His face an apoplectic red, eyes furious, he left the car, almost running. He returned in a moment, with two men of the train crew.

"Here she is, the nigger woman. Now let's get her out of here."

He put his hand heavily on Melanie's shoulder. She threw it off. "Don't you touch me." Her voice shook with the outrage she was damming up. Billy burst into tears. She thought, I mustn't cry ... please, I mustn't cry.

The other passengers were craning to see what was happening. Melanie said to the men, who looked uneasy and helpless, "I'm not moving, do you hear." Her eyes were wide with determined hatred.

One of the crew tugged at the conductor's arm. "Look, you can't fight a woman and a kid." They left the car, the conductor reluctant, trailing threats: "Sassy Northern nigger ... they'll show her what's in Virginia ... she won't get away with it there."

Billy was hiccupping with sobs, the tears oozing through his tightly-shut eyes. His fists clenched. Melanie held him tightly. "Don't, baby ... Mama's here ... nothing will hurt you ... don't baby."

It was quiet in the train. The clicking of the wheels sounded subdued, futile. Melanie gritted her teeth, and ached from the thumping violence in her heart. I hate ... I hate ... I hate. Billy in the South, and little girl Melanie in the South. From her scarred memory came the ghastly resurgence of the scene—her father bleeding on the floor of the hut and with his last breath urging his wife to take Melanie and get out of the South; the anguished words pouring out of her mother, "That's enough—you'll kill him. For Jesus' sake, that's enough." And the white man, sated, "You niggers gotta learn your place: I tell him what's comin' to him—he don't tell me." But he *had* killed him. A little girl of seven, with the first crust of hardness.

Then the Harlem room, her mother coming back bone-tired from the cleaning of white folks' homes. But now the glad renewal was before her, and even on the way to church her step grew lighter. Night after night Melanie watched her mother and the others in the room of intricately-blended smells, thick sweet and rotten: the sweat, the stale sour cooking from below, the exaggerated flower perfumes. Proudly they wore the white, loose angels' gown, clapping hands and stamping feet to the hot rhythm of the hymns.... I been saved all the day, and I'm glad. The voice of the preacher, ear-hurting, sense-beating ... the moans, the swaying, the testimonials ... "I been wicked, Lord, but I'm gonna keep my mind steadfast on Jesus."

Billy, exhausted by his sobs, was clutching her in his sleep. Melanie looked at the dull, flat greenness of the passing Virginia fields.

She remembered the awe she had felt in the beginning, and the wild, forgetful soaring from the hymns. But with slow understanding had come pity, then boredom and shame. After that her mother went to church alone.

A few seats ahead a man turned on his portable radio, and Melanie heard the beat of boogie-woogie. This was Harlem singing, singing in the night, Harlem black and red, stepping fast to the crashing of juke-hymns-radio from Swingland and church and whorehouse. Whores they make of us, whore or servants, with music in the night to make us forget.

It was good this hatred, it strengthened and hardened you. The first clear consciousness of it had come in high school, when it had driven her to win prizes and honors. Grimly triumphant, she had silently challenged the white girls: Can you do better? Her turbulence swept fiercely over the people in the moving train, all the white people she had ever known: Can you? Can you?

But then the warning of defeat through loneliness when her mother had first coughed up blood. The pity and love she had buried welled up and spilled over. With her mother she waited at the clinics, watching incredulously, afraid, as day by day the skeletal form emerged. It was then, brooding the long hours in the crowded, antiseptic waiting rooms, that she had first determined to be a doctor. Terror of loneliness had forced a feeling of identity with her people, and then had come the will to fight for them, to succor their poor flesh in the name of her father and her mother.

The train was speeding through the country, hills in the distance vague with the first grayness of night. She wrapped a coat around Billy against the chill, and remembered the winter bleakness at the employment agencies, the hard oblivious eyes ... we can't do anything for you, don't bother to register ... no office jobs for colored. So college student Melanie scrubbed the floors of white homes, and medical student Melanie washed the diapers of white babies. Did I discriminate? Was Mrs. Brown's white baby less to me than Bessie's black?

No, Randall, you're wrong. I believed you; to become soft and whole I wanted to believe you. But you're wrong, Randall, wrong. Unto the third and fourth and fifth generations do they destroy us. Why are you fighting, Randall? You've given up everything. Your practice, slowly and patiently built up, it's gone now. And why did we have Billy? My little boy, crying his heart out. You may die, Randall ... you may die for democracy, die with the white men. My life may be emptied like a white wife's, my boy fatherless like a white boy. But why? For what, Randall?

Billy woke up, restless, fretful. "I'm hungry, mum." Melanie glanced at her watch—7:40. She gave her son the last of the sandwiches and milk. "We'll see Daddy soon, darling."

The train stopped—Richmond, Virginia. Melanie thought tiredly, again it will happen.

The conductor paused at her seat, immensely surprised. "What you doin' here? Didn't you change cars at Washington?" His lips remained stupidly open.

Melanie felt Billy become tense. She stared straight ahead of her, and said evenly, "I saw no reason to change cars. These are the seats I reserved and paid for."

"You saw no reason to change! Why, woman, get out of this car." Incredulity had raised his voice to a high falsetto. His eyes blinked rapidly, and his mouth stayed open.

Melanie wondered dimly if she had the physical strength to oppose this one, too. She clenched the arms of her seat to brace herself.

"You just let her be, buddy. She's had enough." The voice was deep, angry. Melanie looked up. Why, it was a white man, a white man in uniform, thrusting his face challengingly close to the conductor's. She memorized unconsciously the wheat-colored hair and large, firm mouth.

"That's right, leave her alone."

"It's disgraceful, hounding a woman and child like that."

"This is a free country, she's got her rights like anyone else."

But these protests were coming from all over the car! Unbelievingly, Melanie searched the faces nearest her; yes, she *had* heard the words. The conductor backed away toward the exit, as if afraid to turn his face from this anger. His mouth still open, he left the car.

The soldier watched him until he had gone. Then he raised a finger to his cap in a half-salute. "Sorry you've been bothered, ma'am. I should have spoken up before, but...." He stopped, embarrassed by her brimming eyes. "You see, the uniform ... I wondered if I should ... then I decided, yes, *because* of the uniform...."

She whispered, "Thank you."

The soldier sat down opposite Billy. "Hello," he said. "I've got a brother about your age. His name is Billy."

"That's my name!" said Billy, astonished. He smiled shyly. "We're going to see my pop, he's a soldier, too." And he settled down to talk.

Now Melanie let the tears fall, tasting the salt, her heart slowly easing itself of the heavy burden. You fool, she thought, letting yourself go blind with the old hate.... Randall warned you against it ... save it, he said, save it for the real enemy.

Her mind was washing itself clear now. Never again must she let herself go blind and deaf from the red haze, the wild drumming in the ears. In her paean of hate she had pushed far back in her consciousness the certainty of their friendships, the sure warmth of the many who did not think in terms of black and white. She had ignored, too, her knowledge of the others, her patients—the wives of workers, white and black. She had heard them talk together, borrow and lend of each other, solace each other in pregnancies and childbearing. She had seen their children play together, naturally as children play.

She turned to the soldier, her voice strong. "It was knowing that I wasn't alone any more that made me cry. And that I could stop hating."

His mouth widened in a smile of admiration, tribute. "You really didn't need help. You'd make a good soldier."

"I come from a tough family." Her pride was in her eyes. "My great-grandfather was a runaway slave, and his son fought against the South in the civil War. My father was killed fighting for his crop. You see we do need help, we can't get anywhere alone."

"Yes. I often wonder why so many of your men enlist, the way things are."

Melanie spoke with quick eagerness. "That's wrong. Though a while back, I was feeling that way myself. But things are better now than they were. I'm still sitting here, isn't that so? It's the slowness you're thinking of. But now at least we can fight to make it come faster. If we lose this war, we won't be able to fight at all."

The soldier's voice was doubtful. "It's a hard thing for many Negroes to see, and I can't say I blame them. You certainly need a long-range point of view."

"We're fighting for two things." Her words came more slowly now, as if she was clarifying it for herself, too. "We're fighting for a country which does give us a chance to solve our special problems. I know it's slow, but we are not powerless to make things better. While if Hitler wins, we'd be slaves again, and even our friends would find it hard to help us. The other thing is that in fighting Hitler and defeating him, we'd beat those elements that are keeping us down."

The soldier said, "Putting it that way, we're really all in the same boat, I suppose." He got up and held out his hand. "We'll be in camp in a few minutes. I hope I see you there, ma'am."

Melanie clasped his hand. "We'll all meet again soon." And he left.

She hugged Billy tightly, with sudden exuberance. I'm going to the other extreme, she thought, but it's such a relief.

As the train slowed to a stop, Melanie felt herself sharing the general excitement and bustle, and she smiled at her vision of a train crowded with people of many colors, talking together and laughing. [*Opportunity* 20.12 (December 1942): 366–368, 388–389]

"Faith"

by Doris Peters

"Pete" was a tall, dark, slender Negro boy twenty-one years old. Life had been unkind to him in many ways. First, he was black! Being black to "Pete" was the worst thing that could have ever happened to him. He cursed his father for the heritage and hated the woman who had borne him. Ofttimes had he heard the expression: "There is nothing worse than a 'nigger'—born at the bat, two strikes against him, the ball sailing towards him—nothing to do but to strike out!"

Secondly, he was poor! Black and poor—Oh! what a combination! To be black was bad enough but he had to be poor and poverty-stricken in the bargain. How often had he crunched a piece of hard bread between his strong white teeth, feeling the awful crumminess of the stuff as he tried to swallow it.

His father, who drank to excess, was in plain terms "no count." His mother was a hard-working, patient woman. Her lot had been cast and she bore it bravely with a hope within her heart that a better life awaited her "on the other side." This philosophy she tried to instill into her son but he would have none of it. Thus it was on her dying bed, she tried one last feeble attempt to make him "see the light." But to no avail, he gently patted her on the head, looked wryly at the state in which she had to die, thinking of the dreadful drabness of it all. He watched her die for three days, powerless to do anything about it. What could he do?

Bitterness arose in his heart. If only he could have the simple childlike faith she had possessed. Perhaps then, he could endure his black face and the poverty into which he had been born and from which there seemed no escape. But where did one get such a faith? He did not know. Too bad he had not asked his mother, but she was dead now.

This attitude of "Pete's" was not something that he acquired over night. It was something that had been constantly eating into his very bone. When he was a small child, he was pushed into the far corner of the crowded bus. Why? Because he was black! He was forced to attend a rural segregated school with inferior equipment and with teachers interested only in the monthly check. Whether he attended or not was optional. Why? Because he was black! He could not attend college and here entered his other obstacle—he was poor!

To overcome these things, he needed what? That he did not know. And so it was on a warm July day, he sat under a tree, a youth, a black youth, motherless and without hope, idly watching the Rural Free Delivery man make his deliveries. He knew there would be no mail for him. Who was there to write to him? He was acquainted with no one outside his community. He brushed a fly away and continued to gaze lazily at the mail man. To his unbelieving eyes, he saw him deposit a long, white envelope on his doorstep. What could it be? Rather hastily, he scrambled to his feet, half ran, half walked to his house, looked at the long envelope, picked it up rather gingerly and in heavy typewritten words saw his name, Peter Rye. In the upper left-hand corner, he saw, United States Government. What could it mean? Slowly he opened it and pulled forth numerous pages. He examined them and saw any number of questions. There was one person who might know what this was all about and that was the "reverend." So without much ado, he hurried up the road to the kindly old minister's house. The old man was home and "Pete" presented his envelope with its numerous papers to him.

The minister explained that this was a call to the United States Army. Slowly the implication came to the youth. He clenched his fists, his dark eyes smoldered, he trembled slightly as he leaned over, facing the minister squarely.

"The United States Army!" Why should I go? Look at me! I'm black! I'm poor! I've never been given a chance! What has anyone ever done for me besides shove me around and push me into the background? I've been stepped on all my life and now the Army needs me, does it? Well, I ain't goin'! I don't need the Army!"

The lovable old man who had seen his people suffer for various reasons or other, slowly arose to his feet and asked the boy to follow him. He took him by the arm and led him out of the house, down a path and toward a small brook.

"Sit down," he said.

The youth obeyed and the old man likewise sat down beside him.

"I used to come here when I was a boy," he mused, "and my problems were much the same as yours. I was black and for that matter still am. I was also very bitter, very bitter, my son...."

The boy stirred uneasily and thought, "What was the old man going to say? Wish he would come to the point."

His aged friend noticed this and continued, "I'm going to try to show you that the resentment of your color and your economic situation is wrong."

"How can you do that?" muttered the youth. "I am what I am. Nothing can change that. God! why was I ever born?"

The old man looked at the young lad by his side and wondered if he could show him, if he could convince him, that some day there would be an equal chance for all. The process would be slow, but eventually, probably over a century would have to elapse before the great change would be noticeable. He and this boy beside him would not be here to see it, but at present, they were the ones to contribute to the slow, but inevitable change. If only he could show "Pete" that and make him realize the importance of it all.

He spoke again in a voice that made the lad look at him attentively.

"Jesus of Nazareth," he began, "was a great mystic, the one and only. He associated Himself with the whole of humanity. It was He who helped the good and bad, the black and white and the rich and poor. Everyone needed Him and His wisdom."

The boy looked at the old man, bewildered. What was he saying? Puzzled, he asked Reverend Carter, "What are you talking about?" This language was new to him. The words fell like so many pieces of cotton on his ears, feeling very pleasant but making no impression. Reverend Carter realized this and knew that he had forgot, knew that his was not an educated youth but one with undeveloped innate ability, and so he started afresh. He did not want to give this boy the elementary faith possessed by those in the rural community in which he worked. Instead, he wanted to give him something bigger and better.

"Let me tell you a story," he began, "about Jesus. You know He was a wonderful storyteller and this story I am going to tell you is one that He told many years ago. Now listen closely. There was once a man who had a vineyard and he needed men to gather the grapes. This day, he went out to the market place and hired some men early in the morning. Later on during the day, he needed more men and hired them accordingly. In the late afternoon, he hired more men. When evening came, he paid all the men the same amount of money. Now, the men who had worked all day were angry because they received the same amount of money as the men who had worked only half day. The man explained to the laborers that he had given as much to the last as he had given to the first. The same is true with you, "Pete." You think that you have been last but, my lad, some day you will be first. It is a situation such as this present day one. This war and the implications involved will make you first. Do you understand?"

The youth nodded. Slowly he turned his head toward the old man.

"Yes," he said, "I think I see. If only..."

"If only what?" prompted the minister.

"If only I could have a son—or a daughter who could..." he fumbled for the right word.

In his mind he knew that he wanted to leave something on this earth to profit by what he was going to help thousands of other Negro youths to do.

A week later, he left for the army. He adapted himself very well and, although he did not rise above a private, he was well-liked. The Chaplain, Father Holmes, especially liked him because he felt that this lad had an inner something nobody could take away from him. He seemed to have a goal in mind and was striving to attain it. What it was, Father Holmes did not know but he was determined to find out.

One day he stopped "Pete" and by way of conversation asked him how he was getting along.

"Fine," was the reply, "only I can't find the right girl."

"The right girl?" asked the puzzled Chaplain.

"Yes, I want to get married."

"To ask you why would be impolite."

"No Sir, you see I want to get married so I can leave a child here. Then when the change comes, my child will be different."

Father Holmes was now thoroughly puzzled. Here was something that he had not seen before. The boy's language was crude and his vocabulary was limited but there was some idea that he had that was valuable and the Chaplain sensed it.

"What change?" he asked.

"Why, don't you know the story Jesus told about the vineyard? Don't you know that some day we shall be first and not last?"

Father Holmes saw it then. This was what the youth had. This was why he wanted to get married. This crude, ignorant, black boy had an inner conception of something great, something intangible, something heart-rending and still something stable and strong!

"Find your girl, my boy, marry her and God be with you. Yes, we shall be first some day."

A year passed and "Pete" finally found the "right girl" whom he loved in a simple way. They were married and three months later he was sent to the front to fight. He had been gone a month when he received his first letter from his wife telling him that she was to become a mother.

"Thank God," he prayed, "now I have something to fight for. Whatever my child is, a boy or a girl, this world will be a better place for him to live in because I have fought to make is so. Jesus said the last shall be first. My child shall be first.... My child shall have a chance!"

"Pete" was killed in action a few weeks later. A black youth! A poor youth! However, though, one who had been given a reason for fighting. He believed in his reason. He believed in the words of Jesus as told to him by the old minister. He left a part of him on American soil and he died with a peaceful heart, believing that he had contributed his share in helping to move the slowly, changing nature of a complex society in which his race was the underdog!

Those who saw him, dead in the muddy "dug-out," wondered at the serenity of his face. Little did they know that when he fell, he had heard a voice saying—

"You, my son, have helped to make the last first!"

[*Opportunity* 21.1 (January 1943): 11–13]

Two Worlds

by Helen Bayne Anthony

> *"There are two worlds: the world that we can measure with line and rule, and the world that we feel with our hearts and imagination."* —Leigh Hunt

Crystal Brown watched quietly the other high school girls and boys as they danced at the regular Friday afternoon "gym frolic."

She had no desire to dance with any of the boys even had they asked her, which they did not. In their stumbling adolescence, they bore no resemblance to her brother, Jim, a college soph, who taught her all the smooth new steps whenever he came home.

Occasionally a girl, meaning to be kind, asked her to dance, but Crystal merely shook her head abstractedly.

The girls were known to wonder why she came each week when she did not dance. She always sat there listening to the music, watching the others with a far-away soft look in her eyes.

Crystal was not a plain-looking girl. On the contrary, an artist might have found her beautiful. But she was different.

Only Crystal knew how really different she was from these other giggling, whispering girls.

To what she was on the outside she did not pay much attention. But she cherished dreams of what she was on the inside. She moved amid the dancing merriment to a part of the gymnasium where she could look through an opposite window and see the hazy Pennsylvania hills whose rosy, floating mists seemed a fit setting for her enchantment.

Entranced, she knew herself to be blue-eyed and golden-haired: all the fairy princesses in story-books were blued-eyed and golden-haired.

She was Cinderella. These girls, her stepsisters who accepted good times as their right and threw her a crumb once in a while; they would be surprised some day when the prince chose her above them all!

Or, she was the Sleeping Beauty. She almost stopped breathing when she thought of the cool, damask fairness of her check as it awaited the awakening kiss of the great, good prince!

Today the prince did not seem so shadowy as usual. He had always been tall and dark in outline, but today he seemed to be taking a more material shape.

She sat up with a start. Her eyes lost their abstraction and focused upon the figure of a boy in the doorway.

It was the tall new boy who had come to town this week. The girls had all gone ga-ga over him, whispering about his "Spanish air," his "patent-leather curly hair," and his "deep, dark sad eyes."

Usually the girls made her tired with their "boy-talk,"—the boys they chose to rave about fell so far short of her own "great, good prince." But this time, she had agreed with them. She had been secretly pleased that he did not seem to pay any attention to their obvious approaches. Yesterday she had watched him stride home alone after school in the direction of the best residential district before she herself had slowly turned in the opposite direction toward her own humble home.

Now his appearance seemed only a continuation of her day-dream. He stood in the doorway until the music stopped; then he came directly to her.

"You're Crystal Brown, aren't you?" She nodded, mutely, thinking how natural her name sounded in his deep, soft voice.

The dream continued, it seemed. Without words, she rose and found herself floating over the floor to the perfect rhythm of fairy music, supported by strong, gentle arms.

It seemed natural, too, to look up into an olive face bending over one's own. "I AM the Sleeping Princess," she murmured.

"For a sleeping princess, you dance very well," he chuckled.

The schoolgirl awoke to reality. She became aware of the dancing couples about her and of the fact that a number of her schoolmates were watching her progress with what looked like unflattering amazement.

"That's because I'm Cinderella," she told herself, not him. "Now is the time to show them."

She laughed up at him as she had seen the movie stars act while dancing.

"Dance well? Oh, yes, my big brother and I dance whenever he is home from college."

"From college. I knew, just to look at you, that you came from an educated family. Where does he go?"

She named a Southern university.

"I hope to go to college, too," he said eagerly. "My uncle has promised to help me if I help him now while he is recovering from an operation. By the way, we live at the Madison Apartment House. They have a swell party-room there. Some time when no one is using it you'll have to come over and we'll try some fancy stepping."

She remembered that she did not even know his name.

"My name? Oh, I'm sorry. I should have introduced myself. My uncle told me to look for you and I just naturally forgot you didn't know who I am. My name is Raoul."

She'd known he'd have a fascinating name.

"Raoul what?"

"Just Raoul Lee. Dan Lee is my uncle."

Dan Lee was the janitor at The Madison. Then Raoul was—

He must have seen the question in her eyes.

"Of course. You don't suppose I'd have had the nerve to ask you to dance if I didn't know we could be friends."

The hour of midnight had struck She *was* Cinderella, indeed! Only Cinderella.

"You asked me to dance because I was the only...?" The music had stopped and she stood there unheeding the curious looks of those about them. The music started again and he swept her into his embrace away from those who must not see her quivering face.

"You little fool!" he looked down at her with two years' superiority in age and even more years' experience in a puzzling world. "You *are* a sleeping princess, I guess. Aren't you ever going to wake up? All the king's horses and all the king's men couldn't have dragged me here this afternoon if you had not been good-looking."

"But," she faltered, "how can you say that? I haven't fair skin and blue eyes and golden hair."

"Who wants cold, ice-bound beauty like that?" he asked, rather savagely. Then he held her away from him, looked down deep into her eyes and demanded: "Say, what kind of fairy tales do you read, anyway?"

She made him let her hide her face under his chin. "You don't suppose I still read fairy tales, do you?"

"You dream them, it seems. But if you must dream fairy tales, I'll get you a copy of Arabian Nights. That's the kind I dream—the princesses are all like you."

She fled to the dressing room but she did not get her wrap immediately. She sat down before a corner mirror and gazed at herself.

He was going to take her home—her, Crystal Brown, the only girl whom the magic slipper which he held could fit!

The girl in the mirror had smooth, brown skin. She had dancing dark eyes and black permanent curls. She was dressed in orange, with an orange ribbon in her hair. Warm, vital, vivid!

The girl in the mirror stretched her arms upward as if reaching for life.

With that stretch, the princess really awakened. And upon her awakening, the cold granite walls of the Germanic castle-in-the-air crumbled into oblivion. In its stead appeared the rightful abode for her spirit: a soft-tinted canopy in an Eastern garden, swept by fragrant breezes under a sky hung low with fairy lights.

It was good to be—different.

It was good to be—colored.

[*Opportunity* 21.2 (February 1943): 56–57]

REQUIEM

by Zora L. Barnes

As I lie here in the huge white bed, through the triple mirror on the opposite wall I can see the topmost branches of an old oak tree whose branches are just beginning to waken again. The rusty forsaken look they had worn since fall is smoothing off to a moist sheen. Leaves have not yet begun to peer through, but even from here I can almost see the tiny greenness which will burst forth. The day nurse says any day now. Then, in the other side the indifferent outlines of the door through which I've been carried—in and out, in and out—so many times and the neat white screen that guards the door reflect only a cold implacability that remains always the same.

I like best the side mirroring the ancient oak. I never am certain whether the marathon I'm in will end with me the victor or whether I shall go out of that door for the last time still not knowing if the tiny greenness breaks through all at once. Or, if twig by twig, limb by limb the tree will flaunt its leafy banners and proclaim another spring.

That mirror reveals to me six other things. Sometime in the queer haze that filters through the window-pane just at dusk, I seem to see six people—three of them me and three are those I might have been.

The first time I saw myself, 'twas on a bitter afternoon. The wind had howled and shrieked and rattled madly at the windows the whole afternoon. Then just as evening came, the wind hushed away and a golden red fringe of light escaped from the sunset to paint itself across my mirror.

The light took form and shape. I saw a long-legged, round-shouldered girl of fifteen. Her black hair was tied with a bright red bow. And in her dark brown face was reflected all the glory and wonder of the picture she was painting. It was a huge piece of silken cloth—not white, but of the subdued shade of golden that years of waving bravely in a desert sun might softly mellow. At her side was a smoking pot of wax rimmed 'round with many brushes—large, small, fat, lean, of every variety. And on this ivory cloth she painted with smooth dexterity a carnival scene. Beneath her brush in wax the outlines of a sickle moon, a Moorish temple, a balcony fretted with ornament and carving sprang to view. Then cobble by cobble between the row of quaint dwellings she built a street. And upon it she placed a man of Spain and beside him with head thrown and arm upraised to the turn of the fandango she placed a girl. I could see them dancing there upon the silken cloth. Though it may have been the wind—I seem to hear the click of castanets, the beat of feet, and the laughter of onlookers in the street.

Then—like the pieces of kaleidoscope which are shaken, then fall into alien pattern, I saw the thin girl look up in blank surprise. Perhaps, it was again the wind—but I heard voices, a voice raised in angry accusation.

"Mary Brown! Where is the leather book you were making?"

"It's there, on the table, Miss Hanson. With my notebook. Why?"

"Lillian Moore can't find hers. It isn't in the drawer where she left it."

Still with no notion of what was yet to come, the girl answered, "I'm sorry, but I haven't seen it."

And back to her smoking wax pot and dripping brushes she turned her attention. Like a moving picture, I could see the face of all those who were in that room. From the first there had been a strangeness in it. And as I gazed closer and still closer, I discovered the strangeness. The little girl with the brushes had the only brown face.

The tall, straight person with the accusing voice looked vaguely about the classroom then walked to a table on which reposed a single notebook and—a leather book. Picking up the little leather book, she opened its cover and peered closely at an inscription written in it. After a moment, she came with the book to the girl.

"This is not your book."

The girl put down her brush and turned to the person. Quietly, she contradicted, "But it is. See? It has my name in it."

"You could have put that there any time. This book has been marked 'Excellent.' Yours would not have been so well done."

Again the girl contradicted, "You marked that in mine yesterday. And I took it home last night to show to my father."

"You may have taken it home, but it isn't yours. It's Lillian Moore's *You stole it!*"

The girl winced as if struck and retorted sharply, "That's a lie! I don't steal!"

The person's eyes narrowed to malevolent slits and her pointed tongue flicked once or twice across her lips as she hissed, "Get out of this class! Get out of this school and stay out! We don't want any thieving niggers in this school!"

The branches of the tree waved flirtatiously and their reflection brushed the gay carnival scene from my mirror.

The second time the mirror caught the magic of *now* and turned it aside to reveal the past, I saw another girl. This one too was small, but not fifteen and her shoulders were straight and her eyes were dauntless. In her hands she held a square of paper. It seemed some kind of report. About her were many other girls. And strangely enough this girl, too, had the only brown face.

The girls laughed and chatted in friendly banter. And again the wind seemed to speak.

"Mary, you go first! You got the highest marks, so you will get the best job."

"It seems like strutting too much to walk in there with all these 'perfects' on my report. Somebody should have given me 'poor' if only in mending. It would seem more natural, really."

"Go on. You can't help it if you're a genius. Go ahead. Maybe she'll make you assistant librarian."

"And maybe she won't," the girl retorted as she knocked at the door marked PRIVATE.

There was a tiny, gentle-looking woman with snowy hair and candid blue eyes sitting behind a desk. She looked up with a friendly smile and said, "Have a seat, Mary."

"Thank you, Mrs. Wright."

"Have you enjoyed the apprentice class with us this summer? With your college training and teaching experience, you must have been able to contribute a great deal to the class. We're glad to have had you with us."

Without looking at the square of paper the girl had placed before her, she continued, "Now what are your plans?"

"I was hoping to be able to work here in the library. It's my home town and I'd like to work where I'd be near my parents."

This time it was the other person who looked up in shocked surprise, "But you wouldn't be able to do that. That is, I mean ... you seen there are no positions open here at the library."

"I understand that three of the staff are leaving. Two to go to school and one to be married. Their places will be open, won't they?"

"Not exactly. You see ... our budget is smaller this year and we'll have to work with a smaller staff. If you really want to do library work, I think you'd be happier working with your own people, say at Hampton or Wilberforce. But if you think you'd rather stay here at home and work ... my housekeeper has left and we'd love so much, Mr. Wright and I, to have you come take care of us."

The piercing scream of the ambulance as it turned the far corner on the way to an emergency broke the spell of the second picture.

For days I lay here remembering those two scenes. For some reason they wiped out the blank horror I'd been feeling ever since they had carried me back in here that last time. The doctors had been too hearty about telling me that soon I'd be up and able to fall and break something else. The nurses had been too cheerful and too solicitous about how I felt when they knew as well as I that I hadn't felt anything at all for days. They'd shot enough dope in me to make the whole yellow race dream of their ancestors.

Then just a little while ago, this afternoon, I realized that I couldn't feel or move the fingers of my left hand. And I didn't know I was crying until I looked in the center mirror. There I saw great blobs of tears coursing down my face. As I lay here alone with my eyes all drowned with crying, my reflection in the mirror blurred and I saw the last picture.

There was another girl—her shoulders not so straight, her eyes not so glorious, her head not so high. Yet there lingered some faint resemblance to the other girls. She was atop a tall ladder reaching toward a huge lighting fixture overhanging a balcony. In her roughened hands she held a wet rag and with it she was industriously wiping at the large globe. From time to time the ladder swayed precariously over the three flights of stairs. As she worked she sang a song in odd contrast:

"Oh, Lord! I don't feel no-ways tired,
Children, Oh, Glory! Hallelujah!"

From below the stairs came a tall fair man with the blue line of his freshly shaven jaw in splendid contrast to the wind-whipped pinkness of his cheekbones. His blue eyes glittered in anticipation and persuasion. He ran his hand through his bright hair and rumpled it becomingly. He paused at the foot of the ladder.

"Mary, you don't want to be a cleaning woman all your life. Do you?"

"Of course not, Mr. Gordon I applied here for a sales job. The ad said a college graduate with a knowledge of art for the gift department."

"I know, I know. But you see, the customers might not like the idea of a colored girl for a saleslady. Not when there are so many white girls who need jobs."

"I understand, Mr. Gordon. It doesn't really matter much any more."

"Now, now, Mary! I just have to be careful. You see, this is my first big manager job and I have to ease my weight in at first. So to speak. But to show you I'm a good scout, I'll tell you what I'll do. I'll talk to the owners and try to change their policy a bit.... but you'll have to be kinda nice to me, Mary. I'll really be sticking *my* neck out, you know."

He reached up and ran his finger up and down, up and down the seam of her stocking.

He grinned confidently, "You wouldn't mind that. Now would you?"

The girl jerked away from his exploring finger and as she moved the ladder swayed. She caught futilely at the light, but its glassy strength slipped from her fingers and like a plummet she hurtled to the floor below.

I've known them all—those three. And too, I know the three they might have been—artist, librarian, or even salesclerk.

But life has eyes for choice too keen. Of late, I have thought perhaps this frizzly hair which might have gone incognito beneath a patterned turban but for the too-thick lips and flattened nose might be ironically rejected even by death. Then to the legend company of Flying Dutchman and Wandering Jew there might have been added—a Weary Pilgrim. But from the hearty greetings and muted footsteps and evasive eyes I learn the first small bit of hope: Death is blind and knows not of race or creed or color.

This, then, is the first fruit of them that sleep. And as I lie here shrouded in white against that time and rimmed in by the gloom, I only wonder if perhaps tomorrow the tree—.

[*Opportunity* 21.2 (February 1943): 74–76]

BIG JOE: A SHORT SHORT STORY

by Stella Kamp

Big Joe stood near the saloon door looking out at the rain. Big drops like melted wax from an inverted candle dripped down the plate glass door. It was autumn and the last few withered leaves rustled and shone in the wet wind. The streets were empty. Joe heard a gentle scratching at the door. He looked down into the brown eyes of Fritz, the Kessler's dachshund. His nightly chores performed, Fritz was demanding re-entry. Joe teased him by opening the door a little, but not enough for Fritz to squeeze his soft body through. The night was wet and cold so Joe did not play long. He picked the dog up and felt the cold body tremble against the warmth of his own. He found a clean towel behind the bar and rubbed Fritz dry. Then he wrapped him in an old woolly sweater and put him down to sleep near the heater at the end of the bar.

Big Joe began to clean up for the night. He wiped the top of the bar carefully. He put away a bottle of Martin's V.V.O. Scotch and a pottery bottle of Jamaica Rum. He emptied the ash-tray of pulpy cigarettes. He took a linen towel from the stack of clean ones and began to dry the glasses. The wind from the opened door blew the paper napkins into ugly little piles. Big Joe looked up and saw the thin, little man at the bar and hoped he wouldn't stay long. Joe knew his customers—and this one looked like the pathetic quiet kind of a guy who came to a bar to talk his heart out the way he couldn't to his wife at home. But the little guy took his Scotch neat and prepared to go out.

"Bad night, eh, boss?" Joe figured he could be polite because the little guy was going now.

"Every night's a bad night for me." The little guy turned up the collar of his thin coat and went out.

Big Joe was only acting when he used words like boss and dat. Big Joe was eligible for Phi Beta Kappa and had won two prizes for his poems. But then when you were carrying bags or waiting on table or mixing drinks, it was better for people to get the dancing-feet-smiling-all-day long picture, than to be reminded that the six feet three of black man serving was a college graduate.

Now came the hour Joe loved best. This was the time when his heart began to sing until the song overflowed into his mind so that the music was captured forever on the little white pad in front of him. He could forget that once he had dreamed of the wonderful things he would do when he was through with school. His greater knowledge would be his strength, his weapon. His dreams were all tied up with the shining ribbon of idealism. There was so much he was going to do to uplift his people. His awakening was swift and bitter. He soon found that there were only certain ways to earn a living when you are black and the honorary gold key he wore might have been a cheap bauble, instead of a reward for mental merit—fourteen carat gold. There were two things you could do—fight back and break your heart, or take it as it came and break your back. So Big Joe fetched and carried, had borne passively the sneers, the hard words that bit like sulfuric acid. But there was always the precious time of day when he was set free to make his music. And he knew someday—somewhere—the melody would be heard first by one—then by many—and his music would become the means to bring glory to his people.

Joe put out all the lights but one. He sat in the half light while mosaics of things remembered began to form a pattern in his mind. The silver look of the sea in the early hours of a fog-veiled day ... a gull wheeling over a tramp steamer ... a gray-haired man on the wharf watching the boat pull out ... his eyes sad with memories ... words stood straight and tall in his mind's eye. The gray probing fingers of fog ... wail of a tug-boat siren ... like a lost soul doomed to live without love.... Big Joe's mouth worked as he rushed to get it all down.

It was done. He read the poem through and a feeling of exultation pounded through him so strong that he had to clutch the table top to keep from falling. He felt dizzy and faint. He walked to the bar for a drink to tighten that loose feeling in his stomach. His hands shook even after the whisky had plummeted in a hot biting rivulet to his stomach. The music of his poem began to repeat itself in his mind and he felt calm again. For a moment he was clairvoyant and could see the thin books of his poems standing in years to come as a lyrical lasting monument.

The rain still clattered against the panes with monotonous insistence. The dog stirred in the warm sweater. Overhead a board creaked, breaking the late-at-night silence. Joe walked to the door and fastened the bolt. He clicked off the lights and walked slowly, saying the words of his poem aloud in the empty darkness of the bar, as he went up the back stairs to his room. [*Opportunity* 21.4 (April 1943): 164]

Tell It to Us Easy

by Eleanor Simms

Frank drove up in his very pre-war car and paralleled the curb. It had been a hard day, and he wondered whether he would have all the strength he needed for the rally tonight. It wouldn't be just a political meeting—well-organized, with an alert and civic-minded audience and glib smooth-tongued candidates, each expounding, orating, and convincingly promising more advantages to the city and this particular community—promising more than his rivals. No, it was going to be, he knew, a meeting of very tired people who were going to be there in order to be reassured that they would receive the usual gratuity tomorrow,—or else they would not vote. Three or four handfuls of people that didn't realize what a powerful weapon their ballot could be. And those candidates who would be there, would be there to reassure their ignorant audience that they would be paid. Knowing full well in their small selves that if they paid tomorrow, they would never have to grant at a later date a single improvement to this community sleeping so peacefully on the other side of the tracks.

Frank sighed. "Oh, God, if he could only get his people to realize. This was the 1940s—today, shadow of tomorrow. Not a fancy, a foolish whim. Not a glass of beer not a surprise for supper."

War had shifted Frank's job from a well-organized urban community to this almost forgotten town. Here he had found several disinterested but well-like leaders, content with their own comforts and directing with too careless a hand.

Frank had been patient, watchful, observant—in fact, he had almost succumbed to the lackadaisical attitude of the community until something (he knew not what) had given him a jolt.

Frank banged the car door. A car was whizzing down the street. Frank looked over at the boys who were using the side of his house on which to bang their ball. Suddenly the ball bounced over the heads of all of them and into the street. A be-sweatered lad rushed to retrieve it. Frank ran and roughly pulled him back. The automobile meteored past.

"Say, son, why don't you and others stop playing in street? You know better. You'll have all the little chaps in the street, too. Someone's bound to get hurt."

"Mister," the boy shook himself from Frank's clutch and stammered, "there's no place else to play ball. We haven't got a playground."

Frank didn't have any answer. He felt ashamed that this community couldn't have all the advantages that the city gave its white children. He realized months ago that when the 120 families would move into the Defense Settlement that the streets would be swarming with children trying to release their healthy energy. There had been no land left for a playground. And to date, the city was doing nothing about the matter. The children of the taxpayers in the colored neighborhood didn't have play space before the war, and evidently, no one thought it imperative now. "No excuse for playing in the street," he called to the lad, although he did not believe it himself. "Say, sonny, you'll have a playground next month," he called over his shoulder.

Louise had prepared an exceptionally good dinner and Frank had eaten heartily. But in attempting to correct his speech he soon forgot this. Finally, he folded up his typewritten speech and tore it in two. The incident with the boy had upset him. He got up, arranging his tie as he did so. He took his coat out of the closet and put in on. Then he tiptoed over to the crib and leaned over the sleeping child. The baby's half-emptied bottle was still in the little brown hand. "Dad's going to get you space enough to play, too. It will be all ready when you're big enough to crawl." Frank looked over at his wife and smiled.

The hall was not even a third full when he walked in. He nodded to several people and went over to the chairman. Three of the candidates were already on the platform, laughing and conversing. Frank reached for the chairman's hand. "Glad you're here, son," said the little fat man. Frank took a seat in the front.

An hour later the meeting was at its best, that is, at the highest point of the evening. Frank was tired of listening. The speeches were all the same. Great praise and respect for the Negro people. They had such patience. Such courage. They were so dutiful. The speeches were long and flowery. Frank wondered if such tribute would be paid Negro servicemen when they returned. Everything was so general. No promises. No actual plans. All of them sounded like school boys in a declamation contest. One or two new aspirants were nervous, those already in office, far from sincere.

When the chairman called for comment, Frank arose. Without hesitation he looked at each candidate and he told the story of the boy and the playground. Brief as it was, the candidates readjusted themselves several times. Two left, after fingering their watches nervously. Frank finished, and turning to the audience said, "The candidate who promises a playground is the man for whom you should vote." Frank sat back down.

Confusion was noticeable. One of the candidates began to speak. Apologetically, he admitted no knowledge of such lack. He wished to know more of the community's needs. Frank smiled to himself. "The acquirement of the playground, Mr. Candidate, is of more importance than anything else."

Then another candidate took the floor. Within the next twenty minutes the audience listened to a discourse which led from the need of supervised recreation through the needs of the entire city and back to the inspirational power which the Negro has given to America; from Africa to World War II; from the power of prayer to the Allied Nations. The playground was deliberately forgotten.

* * *

Another day's work was finished. Frank drove his car through the main street, across the tracks, and down to the polling booth. A few minutes later he had marked his ballot and handed it to the officer. Two men spoke to him as he left the building. "Hello," Frank replied. He walked over to the car and opened the door.

There lying on the front seat were two crisp one-dollar bills. Frank closed his eyes tight for a second. He pushed them out of his way. His foot on the gas and his hands gripping the wheel tightly, Frank drove to the highway. This wasn't the way home, but drive he must.

Out along the road he lowered the car window. Then he let first one bill, then the other fly out, like symbols, like meaningless words. Frank kept driving.

Each candidate had reassured himself and how cheap it was: for a head of cabbage or a bottle of soda, for a smelly cigar, or a package of gum. Frank knew that many people would accept this degrading situation. You couldn't yet show some of them that the blood their boys were shedding every day was worth much, much more. You couldn't yet get them to see that they had a weapon in their ballot. He felt so sick inside. He must turn back. Louise would be wondering where he was. He slowed down and turned the car. In other parts of the country people were fighting in court to vote. And here.... "Son," he thought, "I'll tell it to you easy. There'll be no playground this year."

[*Opportunity* 22.4 (April 1944): 172–173]

ONE BLUE STAR

by May Miller

He did not give me a chance to open the door. Even as I hesitated there separating from the ring the right key to fit into the lock, he swung the door vehemently inward and barred the way, waving exultingly in his hand a letter. I knew without questioning its import. Not recognizing one symbol, I read each word as though it had been magnified tenfold.

The President of the United States
    To————————————Greeting:

Transfixed, I attempted to utter no sound, to make no movement. His strong arms encircled me and drew me into the hallway. I stood convulsively clutching him, digging frantic fingers into his firm young flesh. And I, who had but once conceived, who had for one brief period only felt life within my womb, knew the stirring of generations within me, suffered the agony of multitudinous birth. Life of dim eras, of far-flung continents swept through and over me, engulfing my entity. I was one with timelessness—I became the black mother of the fighters of the ages.

* * *

I was Zipporah, the black wife of Moses, standing amid the alien corn of my mate's new land of adventure, cuddling my wounded dark boy from the taunts of Miriam. I experienced with him the hurt and bewilderment of childhood and held back the puny arms that would have struck at his tormentors, the young of Hazeroth who found his dark skin strange.

"Hush, my beautiful golden boy, your brothers of tomorrow, older and far wiser than you, will fight that your tawny head shall not be bowed in shame."

* * *

With Simon of Cyrene, my strong fighter offspring, born to lead insurrectionist slaves, I dreamed a dream of freedom, of freedom snatched through blood and burning. Then by his side climbing the hill to Golgotha, I glimpsed with him for one brief second the light in a doomed man's eyes; and I felt the bitterness and rebellion die in my son's soul as he humbly shouldered the cross and trudged beside his Savior.

"Don't hear their jeers, Simon—Don't look up to the gaunt cross now fixed against a leaden sky. The crown of thorns is there; the purple robe lies in a crumpled heap on the ground; the torn bleeding form hangs limp now; but we know—you and I—that it has housed the secret of the ages—love of human kind."

* * *

In my frail body I have cradled the sperm that came forth dark heroes of distinction. Down the ages, I marched, rode and tented with them—my warrior sons. I call the roll and from the dim corridors of time they answer century after century, from continent to continent:

Antar the Lion—Arabia's black warrior bard, conquering with artful lance and nursing in his soul a poet's vision.

Angelo Soliman—defender of the Holy Roman Empire, snatched from his African hut to be at last courted by Emperor Francis I, himself.

Henrique Diaz—invincible general in the Portuguese army,—on his breast the "Cross of Christ" and in his heart the hope of a free Brazil.

Toussaint L'Ouverture—native governor general of Haiti, whose rule the mighty Napoleon could break only by cheap chicanery.

Chaka—stern military chieftain of the Zulu tribes, building of the uncivilized one of the most effective fighting machines in history and leaving unto his unheeding native land, one rule—"Conquer or die!"

Antonio Maceo—Negro general and hero of Cuba's wars of independence, whose deeds the imposing monument in Havana calls a free people to do honor.

"Stand there in life, my generals, my chieftains, my rulers, robed in your odd vestments and babbling your many tongues and hear me. Know you that neither time nor space; not greed, nor prejudice can snatch your prestige nor eradicate from your countries' histories the names you have etched there for immortality."

* * *

On these shores of my native Africa I stood when the strange ravishing horde bore down and snatched my strong young sons. With them I traversed an ocean in the stench hole of a slave ship. I huddled near them on the auction block, their great strength bound in irons, their firm gleaming bodies naked for appraisal and barter.

I watched them bend their backs in foreign fields beneath another stretch of sky, toiling to bring the soil to flower. Down to the swamp they crept when stars were hazy and the moon dripped blood—there to nurse a faint hope and seek a God who seemed to have forgot them.

"Make your plans. They will fail, for even your own may prove traitors and bloodhounds have keen scent. But never, never forget that swamp flowers bloom too."

* * *

Blood of my blood spattered on the dignified sod of Boston Commons to christen a baby country in its first stretch for liberty. Crispus Attucks, bound though he was by shackles of color, died to bring to liberty a new meaning, a breadth that must eventually encompass a continent and all thereon.

"Crispus, the shot that fell you penetrated to the bowels of a nation. Rest well in your honored grave."

* * *

That lank, lean thing that dangles grotesquely on the gallows in yonder clearing—he's mine too. That's Nat Turner—my poor impatient Nat.

Where's the proud army he raised, armed with makeshift weapons, and fired with the promise of freedom? Some captured and punished; others deserted and gone back sniveling to their masters. And now he hangs there alone with only me lurking in the shadows and around him the wise wind howling, "Too soon! Too soon!"

"It's all right, Nat. They have yet to stifle a dream by killing the dreamer. A dream such as yours never ended a broken limb on a skeleton tree."

* * *

And here again I am, my dark form silhouetted against a vast white amphitheatre, marble columns rising behind me and below me flowing the lazy Potomac; but I see none of this. The omnipresent thing is the severe white sepulcher, and I claw and claw to scratch my way to the carrion flesh within.

Can he be mine, too? He might; he well might; and I have a message:

"Son of min, or son of fairer hue, you are mine, too. Do you not lie here because you believed in a world safe for democracy? That bond at once makes you mine. It mustn't be for naught that you gave up the acrid smell of soil, the feel of soft flesh in the moonlight, the laughter of children at play, even though your brothers returned to a land still shackled by fear, want, and prejudice.

"Time slid rapidly over your alabaster box; and so soon they are at war again, for oppression is a cancer that eats at the vitals of mankind. They are fighting again, mark me, with the word freedom whizzing around them and filling the air.

"Murmuring Potomac, don't drown my whisper; let him hear me."

Dig, dig—I can reach him. Claw, claw—the hard stone softens.

* * *

"Hey, Ma, you're scratching me. You're not going to faint, are you?" Gently my son shook me, bringing me back to the stark reality of the present with all my fears and self agony—my yesterdays and todays and all time hereafter bound up possessively in his eighteen-year-old body.

"No, son," I answered steadily, "I don't think I am."

"You were standing there looking queer, staring through me out into space."

"Yes, I know. I saw many things; I had a vision."

"Come on, Ma, don't carry on like that. You're not sick, are you? You want me to fight, don't you—fight for those four freedoms we live for, don't you?"

"Yes, son, yes I do." I studied his unlined face marked by the conflict that was tearing him between solicitude for me and the age-old yearning for vindication, for accomplishment. I knew he bore in his young heart the harvest of all those others:—their fierce pride, their feel for power and the inward knowledge of their own capabilities and the relentless yearning to realize the world that Simon had envisioned when the scourged Man had spoken.

And he bore their burden too—their burden of frustration and rebellion, for now he was boastfully announcing as if to quiet his own secret misgivings, "And this time there'll be no quibbling. We mean those four freedoms for everybody, everywhere—for Negro boys like me right here in America."

His voice faltered; the grand pronouncement dribbled to a pitiful personal plea; and I felt a gnawing pain for the doubt that clouded his great vision. He must go to battle freed from nagging doubt. He must keep throbbing within him the promise of a better world. His untried youth must nurse a dream, if he is to fight for fulfillment. And eager to quell his inward questioning, I answered quickly, "And that's something well worth fighting for. I shall be proud of you, my son." I had given him up, and spent from the wrenching effort, I sank on the hall seat.

His eyes cleared; the dear swagger returned as he reached in his pocket to draw out a bit of cloth. "Look," he said boyishly, "after I got the letter, I went out and bought this for you to hang in our window."

He tossed in my lap a tiny white silken banner bearing in its center a single blue star. [*Opportunity* 23.3 (March 1945): 142–143]

THE SOULS OF WHITE CHILDREN

by Mary Capotosto

Martha knew almost right away that trouble was brewing at the school. Even while she was still in the hospital they couldn't keep that from her.

First, on her third day in bed, Mr. Stuart dropped in to see her on the way home from school.

"A girl who never crosses roads against traffic lights, never runs for streetcars, never pushes and shoves in crowds," he scoffed, "so you end up flat on your back in a hospital bed!"

"But he was almost a foot taller," Martha shot back, laughing, "And he weighed about twice as much—and I certainly didn't expect him to land on top of me!"

The streetcar had not been crowded. In its favor, Martha had missed two others. But suddenly a small car shot around a corner, and, to avoid colliding with it, the motorman halted abruptly—too abruptly. Martha couldn't remember anything after her first shock of surprise at being jerked and thrown from her seat. Afterwards she discovered that she had gone down under that man sharing her seat.

So here she was now, somewhat bruised and battered, with her left arm in a cast, "a nice clean break that won't give you much trouble," the doctor had told her cheerfully.

Mr. Stuart took a small packet of letters from his pocket.

"I promised to do postman duties. Mrs. Branch said—"

"Mrs. Branch," Martha began quickly. But she did not go on.

Mrs. Branch always spelled trouble. Though Martha did not know her very well, she had met the elderly supply teacher once. She remembered the day.

The youngsters from her class had entered the room in an odd manner that morning: apprehensive, curiously tense, suddenly filled with relief when they saw her standing at her desk. On being asked what was wrong, one child blurted out:

"We saw Mrs. Branch down in the hall!"

"Well?"

"We thought maybe you were away."

"Oh—"

And now she was away, and they did have Mrs. Branch.

Martha sighed.

The letters from the children were not particularly reassuring. She had to laugh over Betsy Worth's "Weer sorry you got hurt on the car and weer sorry we got Mrs. Branch in our room. She ain't nice to us like you are and she has big mussels in her arms and she has lots of lipstick on." Martha had to laugh, too, at the letter from George York. "I can't come and see you in the hospital. My mother says they won't let me in because I'm only ten years old. I told my mother she should come instead of me because it's a good thing to visit the sick. My mother says it's a good thing they won't let us in because then you would be really sick. Would you, Miss Jordan? I hope not because we all miss you so much and want you back quick."

But Martha's laughter was touched with tears, because from Barbara Anthony's neat little correct note to Roger Maines' almost illegible scrawl, all the letters contained such bewilderment and discontent and unhappiness that they made her ache a little.

Mrs. York did go to see Martha.

"I suppose George wouldn't give you any peace until you agreed to 'visit the sick?'" the girl teased.

Mrs. York laughed. Her laughter was gay and young, almost boyish; it went oddly with her massive figure, her interestingly ugly face, her graying thin hair caught back so tightly from her face.

But Mrs. York sobered abruptly.

"He decided this morning that he wasn't going to go to school until you went back—"

"Oh, no—"

"Of course he went. But unwillingly, and under pressure."

"But why? What happened?"

"I don't know. He simply said he didn't want to go just because he didn't want to go.... They all miss you horribly. It makes them feel completely lost not having you there."

"Children always feel lost with a new teacher," Martha said sympathetically.

"Miss Jordan, this is different. This is—strange—a little frightening. I can't quite understand it. I wish I could."

For the next few days, Martha heard nothing disturbing. Temporarily her fears of trouble at the school were lulled into non-existence. She even laughed at herself for having worried about the situation there, scolded herself derisively, "Worse than a mother hen fussing over her chicks, even if it was only mental fussing!"

But the day Martha went home Miss Grey from grade four visited her, Miss Grey with something-has-happened-and-I-can-hardly-wait-to-tell-you oozing from every pore of her plump small body. At sight of the older teacher, all of Martha's previous nebulous anxiety assumed very definite substance, and her heart sank within her.

Martha didn't know just what she expected, but she certainly wasn't prepared for the announcement that none of the girls and boys from grade five had been at school that afternoon.

Forty-three children not at school? Forty-three children playing truant—or what had it been?

"But where were they?"

"You'd never guess—"

Impatience surged through Martha Jordan. To "guess" was about the last thing on earth she wanted to do just then. Her soft full mouth tightened a little. She didn't "guess."

"It really was funny, Martha," Miss Grey continued. "There was Mrs. Branch at one-thirty, alone in your room. Finally she came down to ask me if I knew where they were. Of course I didn't. Then she went to Mr. Stuart. The first thing he wanted to know was if anything had gone wrong during the morning—"

As if taking a cue, the principal appeared in the doorway.

"More company, Martha."

Without waiting for preliminaries, Martha asked directly:

"Mr. Stuart, where were they?"

"In the basement of the church."

"But why?"

The man threw up his hands in a gesture of helplessness.

"Martha Jordan, *are* they bad?"

"No—"

"Are they impertinent and rebellious and stubborn?"

"No!"

"All year people have been remarking on how good they are—It was rather a shock to discover that Mrs. Branch thought them one of the worst classes she has ever worked with."

"But what happened?"

Again Mr. Stuart threw up his hands.

"I don't know yet. We didn't find them until almost three-thirty. Of course when they were all missing I felt that they were probably together, and there was no use in alarming anyone."

"What did you do?"

"I tried several things. At last I got a lead from O'Reilly. He said he had seen an unusual number of children go into the church while he was at the corner after lunch. The reason he notices them especially was that they carried books. Since they weren't in the church, naturally we tried the auditorium. That's where they were, working away as quietly as if under supervision. You really do have them trained to work on their own," he interposed. "But they weren't willing to tell me why they were there—"

"That's not like them," Martha contended. "They aren't like that at all."

"What struck me was that they didn't seem in the least guilty or ashamed. I felt they couldn't look like that unless they were innocent. So I said we'd attend to the affair in the morning and I sent them home."

But Martha could not wait until morning, especially when she knew that she would not be at school then. The doctor had decreed at least a week at home before she went back.

As soon as Miss Grey and Mr. Stuart left, Martha called George York. "I'm home. Would some of you like to come over and see me?" She called Barbara Anthony, too, and asked her the same thing.

Shortly after supper the children began arriving, some on bicycles, some by streetcar. They crowded as close as they could get around Martha, all aquiver with excitement, all talking at once, and they hadn't been with her long before Jim Borowski volunteered, "Miss Jordan, we weren't at school this afternoon."

"I know," Martha told him soberly. Only that and nothing more.

A curious stillness fell over the youngsters. The air throbbed with the stillness, and their faces were intense with it, and their eyes were aware of it.

"We don't like Mrs. Branch."

And, when Martha did not say anything, Kenneth Andrews told her:

"But we wouldn't have done it if she hadn't started it first."

"Started what?"

"Well—well—she's ignorant!" Jim blurted, his ruddy face drained of color and his eyes hot with fury.

"Jim, you can't say things like that," Martha began; but Barbara Anthony said quietly and with conviction, "But, Miss Jordan, she is. We haven't said anything to anyone else—But she's really horrible."

For a few moments Martha looked into Barbara's face, a pale small face with too-grave eyes very clear and direct, but with outrage in their dark depths. Martha looked around at the other children. The same violence was mirrored in all their eyes, and it was a little frightening to see. Suddenly, and chillingly, she remembered the admission of Mrs. York some days before. "Miss Jordan, this is different. This is strange—a little frightening. I can't quite understand it. I wish I could."

"We haven't said anything to anyone else," Barbara had just said.

They had kept it among themselves—until now, when they were sharing it with her, and of their own accord.

"But you can't say things like that," Martha repeated, "unless you have something with which to back them up."

"It was about the pictures we have in our music gallery."

They had been studying the voice of Paul Robeson. Their enthusiasm over him and that for which he stood had known no bounds. In newspapers and magazines, the children had found dozens of pictures to supplement Martha's own collection, and their display was one of which to be extremely proud.

"What about them?"

"Mrs. Branch said she felt like tearing them all down."

"She said we ought to be ashamed to have pictures of *niggers* in our room."

"She said," from white-lipped Dennis Butler, "That nice white children shouldn't have to sit looking at dirty black people all day."

"She was always saying nasty things about the Negroes."

"And she called Paul Robeson an *ugly nigger*—"

As the children were making their accusations, too contained, strangely calm, there came to life within Martha a sickening sensation which started at the pit of her stomach and flooded her entire being until, at Barbara's "And she called Paul Robeson an *ugly nigger*—" it seemed to explode in her head, blinding her with uncontrollable fury.

"—and Miss Jordan, we couldn't let her say that about Paul Robeson," Barbara was saying. "We just couldn't! All the other times, when she said all the other things, we kept quiet—"

"Even though we felt like traitors," George interjected, "we kept quiet. We didn't want to, but Mrs. Branch wouldn't let us talk to her about it. So we talked it over outside, and we knew we couldn't make her change her mind about the way she feels about anything because she's too old and stubborn. But we couldn't keep quiet any more when she called Paul Robeson an *ugly nigger!*"

"No," Martha assented. "No, of course you couldn't."

"Barbara told Mrs. Branch that Paul Robeson is a handsome man, not an *ugly nigger.*"

"Then Mrs. Branch got mad and called Barbara an impertinent young snip and she gave her the strap."

Martha's sound arm went out, drawing the little girl close and hard against her.

"I didn't mind much," Barbara maintained stoutly. "I was proud to have it, because it was like fighting for something good."

Martha saw it as clearly as if she had been there. The small figure, head flung back, black bangs hanging still and straight above eyes filled with outrage decency and the fire of justice; eyes touched with dread, too, for never before had anyone strapped her.

Inwardly Martha cried out, "Oh Barbara, Barbara!" and her arm tightened around the child.

"Then she strapped me," Jim declared, "because I told her that we don't call Negroes niggers, not ever."

"But what," Martha wanted to know, "made you tell her that then? I mean, you let her say it before—"

"This was different. Mrs. Branch said, 'All this fuss and bother about some dirty niggers.' She had said it so often, and that was like the last straw, Miss Jordan. I thought if Barbara was brave enough to take a punishment for Paul Robeson, I was willing to take one for all Negroes."

"I've taught them well," Martha thought, tears stinging behind her lids, her throat full and tight. "I've taught them better than I know."

"I understand," she said aloud.

"But it was when Mrs. Branch did take down all the pictures in the music gallery," George offered, "that we decided we couldn't go back while she was there. Do you think Mr. Stuart will make us go?" he ended anxiously.

Martha shook her head.

"I'm sure that he, too, will understand." [*Opportunity* 24.1 (January 1946): 18–20]

Mrs. Millennium

by Frances Evans Layer

Kathy Julian sat back in the corner of a rear booth in Brown's Drug Store, just off the campus, sipping a milkshake and eating a toasted cheese sandwich. The radio up in the front of the store had been turned low, for once, and the smell of freshly boiled coffee filled the place pleasantly.

The store was unusually empty this rainy day and the voices of the two girls in the next booth came quite distinctly to Kathy.

"I heard her sorority was going to break Marcia Whitman's pledge."

"I don't believe it!" Why?"

"Because of her making such a friend of that colored girl—what's her name?"

"Katherine Julian?"

"That's it."

Kathy shrank back in the corner, horror taking her breath away. She heard the rest of the conversation as in an evil dream.

"They'd be awful silly to break *her* pledge. She's the most attractive member they've ever had—the Governor's daughter, voted the most popular Freshman on the campus...."

"I wonder how she ever happened to pledge that sorority, anyway, instead of one of the big five? She could have joined any one she wanted."

"A cousin she liked was a member."

"That's carrying loyalty pretty far."

"They say she's awfully independent."

"The play she and that colored girl wrote won first place in the Dramatics Club contest."

"Really?"

"It's going to be produced by Dramatics Club next month."

"Hurry up, we're late...."

The two girls left and Kathy leaned against the wall, trying valiantly to calm herself.

There was only one thing to be done, of course: she'd have to quit seeing Marcia. She was to meet her in the hotel in half an hour.

Well, she'd enjoy every minute of this last afternoon. Then she'd tell Marcia it was all off. She must.

She got up, put on her worn raincoat and faded babushka, paid her check, walked unhappily out of the drugstore and started down the hill to town.

They sat on the bed in the hotel room with their shoes off—Kathy leaning against a pillow at the head, Marcia at the foot.

Marcia was reading aloud from "The King's Henchman," by Edna St. Vincent Millay. She came to the lines where the two brothers swear friendship "'Til Life and Death be friends."

"Gee, that's nice," Marcia said. She went back and read it over again slowly.

The hotel room had been Marcia's idea. The two girls sat next to each other in Creative Writing, when Marcia suggested they collaborate on a play to enter in the Dramatics Club contest. Kathy was particularly good at plotting, settings and thinking up bits of business to provide for the actors. Marcia excelled at contriving natural-sounding dialogue.

"Say, I'll bet together you and I could write a winner! Let's try it, will you?" Marcia cried.

"All right," Kathy said, a little doubtfully. Where would they work?

As if she'd read Kathy's mind, Marcia said, "The trouble is, we'd have to have a good place.... We could go to my sorority house, but we'd never get any peace there. Someone would come crashing in all the time...."

Kathy looked out the window. "If the weather was nice we could work on the campus...." But the weather had been chilly, with frequent rains. "We'd never have any peace at my place, either." Kathy roomed with three other girls in a boarding house on the wrong side of the tracks. Maybe Marcia wouldn't like to go there, anyway.

"We could go to my Aunt Prue's if she was in town," Marcia said. "But she's away just now."

Aunt Prue—that was Mrs. Thompson Payne Hamilton, who lived in a regular mansion on the stylish East Side. Imagine her, Kathy, at Mrs. Hamilton's!

"I know—we can rent a room in the hotel?" Marcia cried.

Kathy protested. She was in college on a scholarship and she couldn't afford to pay her share.

Marcia had said, "Don't be silly. I can pay for it."

Kathy was aware from time to time of the words that Marcia was reading aloud. But mostly she was thinking about her and Marcia's friendship.

Let's see, they must have spent about twelve Thursday afternoons together by now. They'd written that play that won the Dramatics Club Contest. They'd written a short story. And now they were beginning another play.

Only once, the first day, had anything been said about the unconventionality of their friendship. Kathy herself brought it up. "Maybe your sorority sisters wouldn't like your being friends with me."

Marcia looked her square in the eyes. "You mean because you're colored." They both felt better to have the word spoken. Marcia leaned back on the bed and looked up at the ceiling. "Nuts!" she said indignantly. "You and I like each other. We can have fun reading and writing stuff together." She got up briskly, dismissing the matter. "Let's outline our play today and start working on the first two scenes."

Kathy's colored friend, Lulabelle Marvin, had been skeptical. She had warned, "I hate white people, Kathy. You can never trust 'em. You're a fool to be friends with that Marcia Whitman. She'll hurt you sure."

"How?"

"I dunno. But she'll hurt you sure some way or 'nother."

Kathy thought this over. Then she said gently, "I reckon white people are like colored people. Some you can trust and some you can't. I'm takin' a chance I can trust Marcia."

Marcia had finished reading the scheduled portion of "The King's Henchman" and laid it down. "S'pose we'll ever write anything as good as that?" she laughed.

"Sure," Kathy smiled.

They got off the bed and got their paper and fountain pens and the outline of their play.

"Let's see. I was to do the first scene and you the second. You get yours done?" Marcia asked.

"Mmmm."

"Okay. I'll start reading."

They read their scenes through first, then acted them out, cutting, re-phrasing, re-arranging.

Kathy got so absorbed she almost forgot the need to tell Marcia what she must.

Suddenly she glanced at her watch. Four thirty! At four forty-five she really must tell her; they always went home at five.

It seemed to her her watch was taunting her, laughing cruelly at her, the hands rushing to the dreaded minute. "So you and Marcia thought you could be good friends!" it seemed to sneer. "You didn't feel like a colored girl and a white girl—you just felt like 'two congenial human beings'? Well, you're colored and she's white and in a very few minutes, you'll see...."

She looked at Marcia, frowning and muttering over a bit of dialogue. She wore a familiar costume of blue sweater and grey wool skirt; her clothes, when they were together, were never more elaborate or expensive-looking than Kathy's own. And who but Marcia could have made her completely forget her natural shyness and self-consciousness in the warmth and purposefulness of their relationship? "I love her. I love her just as much as if she was colored," Kathy thought. The tears were stinging behind her eyelids.

Marcia looked up, smiling her ready smile; then seeing Kathy's disturbed expression, her smile melted. "Hey! What's the matter with you?"

Kathy got off the bed and began gathering up her things. Here it was. The minute had come. She took a deep breath. "We mustn't meet like this any more," she said.

Marcia stared. "What?"

Kathy repeated herself in a dull, patient voice.

Marcia said, "Well, we don't need to. We can use Aunt Prue's library after this. She got home last night and I asked her."

Kathy forced herself on. "No. It won't do. I overheard some girls up at the Drug Store saying your pledge was going to be broken because you'd been friends with me. It's been wonderful.... We've had fun, but...." The tears were trembling in her voice now. She turned quickly into the bathroom, and jerking on the hot water, began to scrub the ink from her leaky fountain pen off her hands furiously. Over the sound of the running water she could faintly hear Marcia's protesting voice. (Of course loyal Marcia would resist, but she must pay no attention to her.)

It was all over now. If she could only keep from crying, tell Marcia goodbye, and get away quickly, quickly....

But Marcia had come to the bathroom door. "Did you hear me, silly?" she demanded. "I said I'd heard that rumor myself. So when the District President of our sorority was here last night, I went to her and tried to turn in my pledge pin. She wouldn't take it."

Kathy steadied herself against the washbowl. "She wouldn't?" Her voice seemed to be coming from a great distance.

Marcia went on in her warm, sturdy tones. "She told me the Chapter was proud of the work we'd done together. That she thought you and I were both to be congratulated for having the good sense to recognize a congenial friend when we found one, even if she did happen to have a different-colored skin!"

Kathy sat down suddenly on the side of the bathtub. A stunned moment went by. "She did, *really*?"

"Really."

Another stunned pause. Then Kathy asked, "What's that woman's name?"

Marcia thought. "Mrs. Robinson, or Robertson, or something. I forget. Why?"

"Should be Mrs. Millennium," Kathy said, and a tremulous smile began to grow amongst her threatening tears.

Dark Quarry

by Babette Stiefel

Evening, spawned of a sudden day, slowly enmeshed Gary's Flat, Georgia, in a horizontal band of pallid grey. The spool of the sun unraveled of all but a few last filaments of light, rolled off the edge of the horizon, leaving the evening sky pale and empty. The interlude of stillness that usually accompanies the descent of evening was broken suddenly by the excited baying of hound dogs. Twilight hadn't come to Gary's Flat but it found the little town painfully indifferent, for every man and boy was following the lean ragged road that twisted around and through the colored section. The air was nervous with their tramplings, and their whispers that frayed the clean surface of the stillness. Anyone who was observant at all knew that a lynching was in the offing.

Chester Janik, son of the South, was talking rapidly with Bert Falk, County Sheriff.

"Man, don't be a fool!" he argued forcefully. "The people want that nigger and they are going to get him despite all the proclamations you will ever print. Don't waste your time and you know as well as I it'll save the State a lot of money. Trials cost a lot, don't you and the people want it this way? Election comes up next month, too, you know, and they might get funny ideas about you being a nigger lover if you go too far with your ideas of justice. Now, c'mon and be sensible. WE'LL handle it proper and right."

Bert stood there uncertainly, the last shadow of strength hovering for a minute and then crumbling.

"Yeah, I gis you're right about the money part. Trials sure do cost plenty. Wal I gis ah'd better wish you all the luck, eh?"

Chester hoisted the barrel of his shotgun in his hand and continued down the twisting road that led into a patch of lean cottonwoods, distorted by wind and age. Beyond the clump of trees there was Finch's mill, an old cotton mill tilted angularly against the sharp rise in the ground. Beyond this knell there was a stretch of land known as Sparrows', once having been a prosperous farm of a gentleman of that name. Now it was worn and disheveled. The land was rotten with disease and ragged growth. Just the place, Chester thought, for someone to hide in. Just the place.

As he walked down the path, overrun with weeds and patches of fallen leaves, he had the curious sensation of being watched. Evening, a silvery blue, lay as a piece of bright paper across the sky, as thin, as uneasily tugging at its moorings. The land lay fallen in grotesque heaps with no purpose, no pattern. Just a tumult of massed shadows and scampering strips of light where the very last glimpse of daylight lay. Chester was too intent in purpose to be afraid, yet he had a feeling suddenly of strangeness. He should have been with the others but he had to remain behind and argue with Bert. Now the men had gone far ahead and Chester decided to strike out on his own.

He wasn't certain he was doing the right thing. There was an odd feeling of humility in him as the bridge of quiet was interrupted with the quick rasping noise of crickets, the soft downy flutter of birds, the irregular plucking stir of wind among the trees. Wasn't it a bit old-fashioned, he began to wonder, to think of saving the whites from the blacks? And wasn't it a bit strong-armed to dispatch the mechanics of justice with the uneasy bleat of hound dogs and Winchester '38s? He wavered in twilight's first ruffled stir, thinking maybe he was wrong. But then he remembered the people. Randy Turner, Willie Lester, Grannie McGee, and all the others. They expected him to demand their kind of rights, and to achieve them by Southern white purposefulness. A lynching in this case was the only thing.

So Chester dismissed the strange wariness in his mind and continued through the field. Yet something was hidden in between the layers of the coming nightfall, some tiny thing that pricked his ease and scratched at his conscience with a feeling of guilt.

As he entered the old house he thought that perhaps much of the despair of the South had its beginnings when this old house lost its look of grandeur. A king, dethroned, remembers the ermine and silks, and until his death remains snarling at the present and silent grieving for the past. The house had once known greatness and wealth and now, its sides bulging, its windows broken, its fine columns blackened with age, its floorings warped and ugly, it had the appearance of an uncouth ragged beggar, a pauper who was once a prince.

From somewhere in the eaves the wind moaned, pressing to its flat desolate breast the empty hollowness of Sparrows' house. Something fell in one of the deserted rooms, rolling over and over again, spinning violent webs of sound in all the stillness. Chester felt certain someone was here. He could hear the man think, could feel his own blood freeze with a kind of shuddering excitement.

He reached the top part of the house, the rooms slanting beneath the slope of roof. He was certain he would find the nigger. There was breathing in this house not his own. Caution, labored, frightened breathing. The nigger had to be there.

In the front room, lodged in the ragged leaves of darkness, he was aware at last of confronting something tangible. A shadow stirred, something hit sharply against the floor with deliberate thud, almost like the sound of a friendly dog wagging his tail. The beam of his flashlight caught it at last. The nigger! The nigger with a dog, simple-minded hound pup beating its tail in welcome. The dog had as much sense as niggers, wagging its tail to an enemy. Chester was caught off guard by the irony of it. If the animal had snarled or bared its teeth it would have fitted better into the picture. But this way it made it much harder. At best this was all a mess anyhow.

"You've come for me, mistah?" The Negro lay rigid on the floor, his eyes reckoning with the inevitable. By this time he had gotten used to the other's presence, knowing from the first creak of the door he would be discovered. Chester wondered why he hadn't tried getting away, then he noticed the boy's leg. The ankle was tremendously swollen.

"Hurt your leg, boy?" he asked almost kindly.

"Yissir, fell while runnin'."

"Your name Saunders Bates?"

"Yissir, that's mah name."

"Well, nigger, looks like they're getting a party ready for you." The two were caught in a breach of silence. Was that all there was to be said, Chester wondered. All between the two men, the one living, the other already tasting death?

Whatever there was that was honest in Chester suddenly could no longer find himself flagellating this Negro youth with his sternness. In all fairness, he thought, let's hear the story out. We are stooping to murder, certainly there are privileges one must grant the dying.

"Look," he said, "are you guilty of shooting Mr. Watson?"

"Yisser," the Negro said, tiredly, as if he had been all over this many times before.

"How come, nigger, how come?"

"We was crossing Main Street," the boy said, "I was just behin' him. Someone pushed me and I knocked again' him. He shoved me back and said, 'look here, you bastard, jest you watch where you're goin'."

"I said, 'I didn't mean to.' It was at the corner of Main and Peach. It's real crowded there and while we was at the corner someone bumped up again' me and I knocked again' him. 'Look,' he said, and suddenly pulled out a gun. All I could think of was stoppin' him from shootin' me so I wrestled with him some and got the gun away. In all the tuggin' we was doin' to each other I reckon mah hand pulled the trigger. The next thing I knew, Mr. Watson, he was lying there, blood comin' out of his head and him dead!"

Chester wondered what he should do. The story, he felt, was most likely the truth. Lem Watson was hotheaded as they come and quite likely pulled the gun on the kid. Too bad, Chester thought, too damned bad.

He didn't have time to reflect, for suddenly the boy was talking.

"Look, mistah, ah knows you hate me and mah people and I know I don't have no chance. But before I die I'd like to say somethin' and you seem like a fair enough white man. I'd just like to ask you a question. What it'd be like if things was different and you and your white folks was in the position us black folks is in. Kin you imagine how it would be for you?"

The question was startling. Chester felt the roots of his mind twinge. He wondered what it would be like if he were a white man in a black world.

* * *

Chester found himself walking sullenly down the street, his mind bristling with resentment. He was bitterly conscious of his pale, colorless face, his limp yellow hair...

He hated it, but it was everywhere he went, the same thing. The Negroes hated them all, called them "white trash" and jeered at their conspicuous anemic coloring. Their rich, vital bodies, their full-blooded vigor made Chester feel he was as vapid, as weak as a fish flapping vainly on a beach. God he hated it, but there was nothing to do. Even walking down the street he felt it, their stony glances, their disdain. He was always aware of it. They said white people smelled funny and he wondered if they really did.

The bands of helplessness seemed to pin him down to the point of inertia. Even in school it had been the same. The teachers saying he was too stupid to learn, indifferent to his eagerness. He was a white boy, what could be expected of him! He was suited to putting a top on a can, had enough intelligence to wield a broom or drive a car. No more than that, not really.

Now he walked the streets fighting with himself. Where could he go, where would he be allowed to find himself? Not certainly in this town where his job of janitor in the mill permitted his use of body muscles in the constant task of cleaning, but never admitted the use of his mind. "White trash" haven't got minds. They just are smart enough to know when to say "yes sir" and "no sir."

He came to a drinking fountain in the middle of the square. There it was bubbling merrily. Beside it was a sign "Negroes only." Good God, he thought wearily, are Negroes the only ones who get thirsty! He lived in a world, he decided, that accepted him and his people only as necessary evils. Since they could not be destroyed wholesale—at least no attempts had been made in that direction so far—the fact of their existence had to be minimized as much as possible. Unspoken lines marked them as unwanted creatures, misbegotten offspring of a time that had lost its seed in the crumbled caverns of ancient days. They were a lost people finding no rest anywhere in a world that swung with the mighty rhythms that beat with the thickened pulse of a dark race.

The center of the town flashed with silver beauty. The windows of the stores were resplendent with figures of slim, haughty Negro girls dressed in expensive gowns and suits. Negro people everywhere, Negro advertisements, Negro movies, the land of liberty, the pursuit of happiness dedicated only to the swarming throngs of dark people. Where did he fit in, where?

He looked dismally into the throng of people, the rage of sea of dark faces, the surge and pound of black feet, the dark stretches of black laughter, the splash and sting of black voices.

His eyes, caught in the gay colors, suddenly noticed a girl crossing the street. She was walking in a dream it seemed, her dark eyes clouded in a mist. Perhaps she was thinking of her lover, he thought, or the magic of being young. She seemed so poised and graceful.

Suddenly his heart shivered. The girl didn't see the car but it was coming straight at her, moving down the street at a terrific speed. Quite obviously the girl didn't see it. She would be hit.

Chester spun for a second, in a vast revolving world of indecision. Then he found strength and motion, and feeling that he was holding back the edges of time by his racing toward her, he lowered his body and stretched out his legs. He must get there in time.

It seemed he would never reach her, but he did. He pulled her toward him, lifted her lithe young body close to him and stumbled back to the pavement. She was safe, and to him standing there, the plume of the sun catching them in its magic, flashing like peacock feathers, he felt clean and proud of having done a deed of valor.

He did not realize he was still holding the girl till he became aware of voices crashing upon him.

"Hey, white trash, put that girl down. Have you no respect," a burly man shrieked, "for Negro womanhood? Put that girl down, you white bastard, and be quick about it."

Chester was dazed by what happened. Gradually his mind stopped spinning and he was able to refocus it on where he was and what had happened. The girl was struggling in his arms.

"Let me go, do you hear, let me go." She scratched and pulled at him. He didn't want her, didn't want to have anything to do with her. But he had saved her life. How else could he have done it if he hadn't picked her up? His mind stumbled at the rumble of voices.

"I bet he was going to rape her," someone said, quite obviously forgetting that that would have been a superhuman task, considering the time and the circumstances. "I bet he was gonna rape her." The talk gained momentum, became surly, ugly. The crowd gathered and formed a circle of metallic black eyes and grim slashes of mouths. "He was gonna rape her, sure."

Their ill humor, their rage speared him with helplessness. He would have no chance to even explain. They pressed closer and closer. The flat of someone's hand stung his cheek. He felt the blood rush to his face. But he was helpless, there was nothing he could do. Some men behind him grabbed him by the arms, "Let's take him for a ride, let's beat him up. Beat him up, ram curses down his throat, strangle his self-respect, stamp upon his mind and soul. Kill the bastard, slit open his lily-white skin."

Chester stood there, lashed at, despised, tormented and knew there was nothing he could do. He was only "poor white trash."

* * *

A finger of wind found a sagging shutter and slammed it against the side of the house. Chester returned to the room with a start. He suddenly remembered the Negro boy's question. He wondered if that was how the nigger felt. Could it be that bad for them?

There were the trolleys and buses, Negroes crowded into the rear. There were the things they couldn't do, the places they couldn't go. There was the constant smug of superiority of those blessed with white skins. Sustained mockery of men exalted by the whiteness of their faces. It must be awful.

He turned to the boy. From the window he could hear the far off baying of hound dogs. The crowd of men was moving off to the left, down to the streams and beyond to Saunders Hollow. The lights from their lanterns flickered and danced like so many fireflies. But the air was heavy and shadowed and the echo of men's voices rang out, etched firmly with hate. If they found this boy he would be lynched, of that there was no doubt.

You cannot erase so suddenly a prejudice fostered in the flesh, as imbedded as the scarlet veins, as taut and rigid as the muscles. But Chester had never been quite sure how he felt about the Negroes. To all appearances he regarded them in the same light as his white contemporaries did. But beneath the surface of this disdain and scorn there had always been something else. Caught in the madness of the evening when the people of Gary's Flat determined to catch the nigger who shot Lem Watson, he had to go and even had to assume leadership. Somehow he could not extricate himself from the eyes and questions and demands, for he was a banker's son and a banker himself and therefore one of the leaders of the Flat's rapid, torpid, mentally sluggish society. But inside himself he had faltered and almost longed for the courage to refuse or, better still, urge the people to pursue a more noble, less impulsive course. Justice could never be defined, he felt, by a rope strung up by a band of hysterical men and boys, wounded with violent running sores of self-imposed hate. They wanted to kill the nigger, they wanted to blame him, even though he was completely blameless. They were full of despair, maddened with the slow currents of their lives, the dust-blown dark corners of empty lives and the dull methodical pursuit of bare wages and the ragged shadow of comfort. A lynching acted as a screaming catalyst in the lives of these men who vented rage, disappointment and sorrow on the body of a black boy, though he was far more innocent than they.

Chester turned to the boy, knowing what he was thinking.

"Look," Chester said gruffly, "here is thirty dollars. It's all I have on me and it won't take you very far, but it will help. Perhaps you'll find friends who will be able to take care of you for a while." The boy mutely nodded.

"Then, look, the men are going down towards Saunders Hollow. I'll take the chance and drive you out to Dalton. You couldn't get very far with your ankle in that shape. After that it will be up to you. Now come and let's get started. The boy lay there, huge tears running down his cheeks. He sobbed and turned his head away.

Chester felt he could not stand it any longer. He suddenly found himself quite a different sort of man. He had never participated in a lynching before and had never concerned himself at all with human emotions that did not arise from whiskey sours and the passion of a kiss. But this was different. This was a youth who had stared at approaching death and now lay shivering with relief. The boy had courage, Chester suddenly realized, and more. And in the boy's sobs he detected all the passionate misery and despair of generations. He never knew life could be so ugly, so bare of beauty and hope.

"C'mon," he said, "don't be afraid of me. You trust me, don't you?" The boy managed a feeble smile.

"Well, c'mon then," Chester tried to be hearty as he helped the boy rise, urging him to rest his weight on his arm. The boy was frightened and uncertain, but almost blindly he limped beside Chester, down the stairs webbed in darkness, across the fields, both of them careful to remain enshrouded in the shadows. The dog whimpered, not understanding, following uneasily.

They at last came to blacker mounds of darkness, automobiles parked on the twisted road. Chester found his and helped the boy get in, all the time wondering if anyone had seen them. But the night was dark and all the men were far away, stumbling over the rocks and tall tufted grass in Saunders Hollow. They were far away, and through the ridge of silence that separated the Hollow from eternity there came the thin blades of sound of hound dogs giving tongue. Everything else was reproachfully quiet.

* * *

The boy would be safe. He had some relatives at Dalton. They gratefully took him in and promised they would look after him. Now Chester was alone, driving back over the rutted road to the Flat, the land resting its quiet open palm up towards the sky.

Chester wondered what he should to, what he could do. How far dared he go, what could he hope to accomplish? All things that had seemed right before seemed twisted and bent with tinges of what now appeared wrong. His mind was bitten with a new, great doubt and in all the silence of the night he wondered where he could find help. But gradually there came to his mind and despair a gentle coolness. He had saved the boy's life and at last he knew he must save others. He would have to finally break with tradition and habit. He saw at last that all men must live and breathe beyond the measurements allotted. They must grow and fill the sky with their magnitude, none excluded willfully by others.

When he returned to the Flat he saw what apparently was the lynching party gathered in the local saloon. He entered and found them all quite disgruntled, licking their wounds. "Hey, Chester, where the hell you been? What happened to the damn nigger? Chester, the lousy son of a——got away!"

The place was clotted with smoke and stale air and dispositions with fatigue and shifting, burning annoyance. The men turned to Chester, and he stood there, calm and unswerving.

"Yeah, I know he got away." He looked at them steadily, the gentle coolness still inside him. "Yeah, I know he got away," he repeated—"Thank God!"

[*Opportunity* 25.1 (January 1947): 18–21, 36]

Concerto

by Shirley Nelson Shuman

Before the Conservatory concert began, Gordon Jones, a Negro, stood apart from the white students in the back stage room. His large eyes in his painfully thin face took in their flushed and excited faces as they discussed their guests, but they also saw beyond them. They were the eyes of a visionary, yet at the same time, those of one who knew exactly what he wanted.

Suddenly a girl called out to him, "And you, Gordon, is your family out there too?"

"My mother," he said.

The girl said, "That's nice," smiled at him brightly. The others upon perceiving him likewise threw quick smiles at him before resuming their talk among themselves.

Precisely at that moment, the program director entered and said to Gordon, "I'm sure you'll start us off well."

"Thank you, sir."

"Good luck, Gordon!" the group called.

"Thank you all."

He glided through the left wing on to the stage. For just a second, the grand piano with its raised top, standing alone in the center of the bare stage, assumed Brobdingnagian proportions. But the applause that greeted him spurred him on.

As his finely tapered fingers touched the keyboard, an angry voice shattered the stillness. "I'll be d—if I'm going to sit around to hear a *nigger* play! Down South they wouldn't dare!"

Gordon turned around slowly. His eyes, no longer that of a visionary, burned with a bright intensity while his mouth struggled for control. At the same time, he knew what he had to do at once.

Pursing his lips and straightening his shoulders, he struck a chord softly, and having turned the magic key, opened the door wide, only this time it was not at all the composition he was supposed to play. The melody, with which he wooed the irate Southerner, was "Dixie."

When he finished, two astounding things happened. First, the dissenter slid neatly into his seat. Second, the audience did not applaud. What had happened was as profound as Lincoln's Gettysburg address.

Presently there was a suspended waiting for those hands, still resting on the keyboard, to perform another miracle. Soon afterward it happened. As the audience held its breath, Mendelssohn came astoundingly to life, not the society favorite, but the grandson of Moses Mendelssohn, the hunchback, who fought the good fight against derision and ostracism. In his playing the yearning of Mendelssohn became identified with his own. Then when he swung into the joyousness of the *Rondo Capriccioso*, it was as if he had found the answer.

When it was ended, the audience forgot its Yankee sobriety in a thunderous applause and with cries of, "Encore! Encore!" Again and again he was recalled. Each time the boy bowed gravely and finally withdrew without giving an encore.

When he stood in the wings, he could hear the applause meted out to the players with a gradual awareness that it did not compare with that accorded him.

When the concert was over, he greeted his mother, a quietly dressed, middle-aged woman who said, "You handled the situation like a gentleman. That's what counts, Gordon."

"Thank you, mother."

Not a word about his playing.

Taking his mother's arm, he led her up the aisle, stopping from time to time to acknowledge congratulations.

Outside, the wind was icy, the streets were wet and people walked carefully. As Gordon guided his mother, he noticed that those who had showered him with applause, now passed him by without recognition. For a moment his eyes clouded, but in answer to his mother's gentle pressure, threw up his head and walked on.

[*Opportunity* 25.3 (March 1947): 135]

THE BONES OF LOUELLA BROWN

by Ann Petry

Old Peabody and Young Whiffle, partners in the firm of Whiffle and Peabody, Incorporated, read with mild interest the first article about Bedford Abbey which appeared in the Boston papers. But each day thereafter the papers printed one or two items about this fabulous project. And as they learned more about it, Old Peabody and Young Whiffle became quite excited.

For Bedford Abbey was a private chapel, a chapel which would be used solely for the weddings and funeral of the Bedford family—the most distinguished family in Massachusetts.

What was more important, the Abbey was to become the final resting place for all the Bedfords who had passed on to greater glory, and been buried in the family plot in Yew Tree Cemetery. These long-dead Bedfords were to be exhumed and reburied in the crypt under the marble floor of the chapel. Thus Bedford Abbey would be officially opened with the most costly and the most elaborate funeral service ever held in Boston.

As work on the Abbey progressed, Young Whiffle (who was seventy-five) and Old Peabody (who was seventy-nine), frowned and fumed while they searched the morning papers for some indication of the date of this service.

Whiffle and Peabody were well aware that they owned the oldest and the most exclusive undertaking firm in the city; and, having handled the funerals of most of the Bedfords, they felt that, in all logic, this stupendous funeral ceremony should be managed by their firm. But they were uneasy. For Governor Bedford (he was still called Governor though it had been some thirty years since he held office) was unpredictable. And, most unfortunately, the choice of undertakers would be left to the Governor, for the Abbey was his brain-child.

A month dragged by, during which Young Whiffle and Old Peabody set an all-time record for nervous tension. They snapped at each other, and nibbled their fingernails, and cleared their throats, with the most appalling regularity.

It was well into June before the Governor's secretary finally telephoned. He informed Old Peabody, who quivered with delight, that Governor Bedford had named Whiffle and Peabody as the undertakers for the service which would be held at the Abbey on the twenty-first of June.

When the Bedford exhumation order was received Old Peabody produced an exhumation order for the late Louella Brown. It had occurred to him that his business of exhuming the Bedfords offered an excellent opportunity for exhuming Louella, with a very little additional expense. Thus he could rectify a truly terrible error in judgment made by his father, years ago.

"We can pick 'em all up at once," Old Peabody said, handing the Brown exhumation order to Young Whiffle. "I want to move Louella Brown out of Yew Tree Cemetery. We can put her in one of the less well-known burying places on the outskirts of the city. That's where she should have been put in the first place. But we will, of course, check up on her as usual.

"Who was Louella Brown?" asked Young Whiffle.

"Oh, she was once our laundress. Nobody of importance," Old Peabody said carelessly. Though as he said it he wondered why he remembered Louella with such vividness.

Later in the week, the remains of all the deceased Bedfords, and of the late Louella Brown, arrived at the handsome establishment of Whiffle and Peabody. Though Young Whiffle and Old Peabody were well along in years their research methods were completely modern. Whenever possible they checked on the condition of their former clients and kept exact records of their findings.

The presence of so many former clients at one time—a large number of Bedfords, and Louella Brown—necessitated the calling in of Stuart Reynolds. He was a Harvard medical student who did large-scale research jobs for the firm, did them well and displayed a most satisfying enthusiasm for his work.

It was near closing time when Reynolds arrived at the imposing brick structure which housed Whiffle and Peabody, Incorporated.

Old Peabody handed Reynolds a sheaf of papers and tried to explain about Louella Brown, as tactfully as possible.

"She used to be our laundress," he said. "My mother was very fond of Louella, and insisted that she be buried in Yew Tree Cemetery." His father had consented, grudgingly, yes, but his father should never have agreed to it. It had taken the careful discriminatory practices of generations of Peabodies, undertakers like himself, to make Yew Tree Cemetery what it was today—the final home of Boston's wealthiest and most aristocratic families. Louella's grave had been at the very tip edge of the cemetery in 1902, in a very undesirable place. But just last month he had noticed, with dismay, that due to the enlargement of the cemetery, over the years, she now lay in one of the choicest spots—in the exact center.

Before Old Peabody spoke again he was a little disconcerted. For he suddenly saw Louella Brown with an amazing sharpness. It was just as though she had entered the room—a quick-moving little woman, brown of skin and black of hair, and with very erect posture.

He hesitated a moment and then he said, "She was—uh—uh—a colored woman. But in spite of that we will do the usual research."

"Colored?" said Young Whiffle sharply. "Did you say 'colored'? You mean a black woman? And buried in Yew Tree Cemetery?" His voice rose in pitch.

"Yes," Old Peabody said. He lifted his shaggy eyebrows at Young Whiffle as an indication that he was not to discuss the matter further. "Now, Reynolds, be sure and lock up when you leave."

Reynolds, accepted the papers from Old Peabody and said, "Yes, sir. I'll lock up." And in his haste to get at the job he left the room so fast that he stumbled over his own feet and very nearly fell. He hurried because he was making a private study of bone structure in the Caucasian female as against the bone structure in the female of the darker race, and Louella Brown was an unexpected research plum.

Old Peabody winced as the door slammed. "The terrible enthusiasm of the young," he said to Young Whiffle.

"He comes cheap," Young Whiffle said gravely. "And he's polite enough."

They considered Reynolds in silence for a moment.

"Yes, of course," Old Peabody said. "You're quite right. He is an invaluable young man and his wages are adequate for his services." He hoped Young Whiffle noticed how neatly he had avoided repeating the phrase 'he comes cheap.'

"'Adequate,'" murmured Young Whiffed. "Yes, yes, 'adequate.' Certainly. And invaluable." He was still murmuring both words, as he accompanied Old Peabody out of the building.

Fortunately for their peace of mind neither Young Whiffle nor Old Peabody knew what went on in their workroom that night. Though they found out the next morning to their very great regret.

It so happened that the nearest approach to royalty in the Bedford family had been the Countess of Castro (nee Elizabeth Bedford). Though neither Old Peabody or Young Whiffle knew it, the Countess and Louella Brown had resembled each other in many ways. They both had thick glossy black hair. Neither woman had any children. They had both died in 1902, when in their early seventies, and been buried in Yew Tree Cemetery within two weeks of each other.

Stuart Reynolds did not know this either, or he would not have worked in so orderly a fashion. As it was, once he entered the big underground workroom of Whiffle and Peabody, he began taking notes on the condition of each Bedford, and then carefully answered the questions on the blanks provided by Old Peabody.

He finished all the lesser Bedfords, then turned his attention to the Countess.

When he opened the coffin of the Countess, he gave a little murmur of pleasure. "A very neat set of bones," he said. "A small woman, about seventy. How interesting! All of her own teeth, no repairs."

Having checked the Countess, he set to work on Louella Brown. As he studied Louella's bones he said, "Why how extremely interesting!" For here was another small-boned woman, about seventy, who had all of her own teeth. As far as he could determine from a hasty examination, there was no way of telling the Countess from Louella.

"But the hair! How stupid of me. I can tell them apart by the hair. The colored woman's will be—." But it wasn't. Both women had the same type of hair.

He placed the skeleton of the Countess of Castro on a long table, and right next to it he drew up another long table, and placed on it the skeleton of the late Louella Brown. He measured both of them.

"Why, it's sensational!" he said aloud. And as he talked to himself he grew more and more excited. "It's a front page story. I bet they never even knew each other and yet they were the same height, had the same bone structure. One white, one black, and they meet here at Whiffle and Peabody after all these years—the laundress and the countess! It's more than front page news, why, it's the biggest story of the year—"

Without a second's thought Reynolds ran upstairs to Old Peabody's office and called the *Boston Record*. He talked to the night city editor. The man sounded bored but he listened. Finally he said, "You got the bones of both these ladies out on tables, and you say they're just alike. Okay, be right over—"

Thus two photographers and the night city editor of the *Boston Record* invaded the sacred premises of Whiffle and Peabody, Incorporated. The night city editor was a tall, lank individual, and very hard to please. He no sooner asked Reynolds to pose in one position then he had him moved, in front of the tables, behind them, at the foot, at the head. Then he wanted the tables moved. The photographers cursed audibly as they dragged the tables back and forth, turned them around, sideways, lengthways. And still the night city editor wasn't satisfied.

Reynolds shifted position so often that he might have been on a merry-go-round. He registered surprise, amazement, pleasure. Each time the night city editor objected.

It was midnight before the newspaperman said, "Okay, boys, this is it." The photographers took their pictures quickly and then stared picking up their equipment.

The newspaperman watched the photographers for a moment, then he strolled over to Reynolds and said, "Now—uh—Sonnie, which one of these ladies is the Countess?"

Reynolds started to point at one of the tables, stopped, let out a frightened exclamation. "Why—" his mouth stayed open. "Why—I don't know!" His voice was suddenly frantic. "You've mixed them up! You've moved them around so many times I can't tell which is which—nobody could tell—"

The night city editor smiled sweetly and started for the door.

Reynolds followed him, clutched at his coat sleeve. "You've got to help me. You can't go now," he said. "Who moved the tables first? Which one of you—" The photographers stared and then started to grin. The night city editor smiled again. His smile was even sweeter than before.

"I wouldn't know, Sonnie," he said. He gently disengaged Reynolds' hand from his coat sleeve. "I really wouldn't know—"

It was, of course, a front page story. But not the kind that Reynolds had anticipated. There were photographs of that marble masterpiece, Bedford Abbey, and the caption under it asked the question that was later to seize the imagination of the whole country: "Who will be buried under the marble floor of Bedford Abbey on the twenty-first of June—the Countess or the colored laundress?"

There were photographs of Reynolds, standing near the long tables, pointing at the bones of both ladies. He was quoted as saying: "You've moved them around so many times I can't tell which is which—nobody could tell—"

When Governor Bedford read the *Boston Record*, he promptly called Whiffle and Peabody, on the telephone, and cursed them with such violence that Young Whiffle and Old Peabody grew visibly older and grayer as they listened to him.

Shortly after the Governor's call, Stuart Reynolds came to offer an explanation to Whiffle and Peabody. Old Peabody turned his back and refused to speak to, or look at, Reynolds. Young Whiffle did the talking. His eyes were so icy cold, his face so frozen, that he seemed to emit a freezing vapor as he spoke.

Toward the end of his speech, Young Whiffle was breathing hard. "This house," he said, "the honor of this house, years of working, of building a reputation, all destroyed. We're ruined, ruined—" he choked on the word. "Ah," he said, waving his hands, "Get out, get out, get out, before I kill you—"

The next day the Associated Press picked up the story of this dreadful mix-up and wired it throughout the country. It was a particularly dull period for news, between wars so to speak, and every paper in the United States carried the story on its front page.

In three days' time Louella Brown and Elizabeth, Countess of Castro, were as famous as movie stars. Crowds gathered outside the mansion in which Governor Bedford lived; still larger and noisier crowds milled in the street in front of the offices of Whiffle and Peabody.

As the twenty-first of June approached, people in New York and London and Paris and Moscow asked each other the same question, Who would be buried in Bedford Abbey, the countess or the laundress?

Meanwhile Young Whiffle and Old Peabody talked, desperately seeking something, anything, to save the reputation of Boston's oldest and most expensive undertaking establishment. Their talk went around and around, in circles.

"Nobody knows which set of bones belong to Louella and which to the Countess. Why do you keep saying that it's Louella Brown who will be buried in the Abbey?" snapped Old Peabody.

"Because the public likes the idea," Young Whiffle snapped back. "A hundred years from now they'll say it's the colored laundress who lies in the crypt at Bedford

Abbey. And that we put her there. We're ruined—ruined—ruined—" he muttered. "A black washerwoman!" he said, wringing his hands. "If only she had been white—"

"She might have been Irish," said Old Peabody coldly. He was annoyed to find how very clearly he could see Louella. With each passing day her presence became sharper, more strongly felt. "And a Catholic. That would have been equally as bad. No, it would have been worse. Because the Catholics would have insisted on a mass, in Bedford Abbey, of all places! Or she might have been a foreigner—a—a—Russian. Or, God forbid, a Jew!"

"Nonsense," said Young Whiffle pettishly. "A black washerwoman is infinitely worse than anything you've mentioned. People are saying it's some kind of trick, that we're proving there's no difference between the races. Oh, we're ruined—ruined—ruined—" Young Whiffle moaned.

As a last resort, Old Peabody and Young Whiffle went to see Stuart Reynolds. They found him in the shabby rooming house where he lived.

"You did this to us," Old Peabody said to Reynolds. "Now you figure out a way, an acceptable way, to determine which of those women is which or I'll—"

"We will wait while you think," said Young Whiffle, looking out of the window.

"I have thought," Reynolds said wildly. "I've thought until I'm nearly crazy."

"Think some more," snapped Old Peabody, glaring.

Peabody and Whiffed seated themselves on opposite sides of the small room. Young Whiffle glared out of the window and Old Peabody glared at Reynolds. And Reynolds couldn't decide which was worse.

"You knew her, knew Louella, I mean," said Reynolds. "Can't you just say, this one's Louella Brown, pick either one, because, the body, I mean, Whiffle and Peabody, they, she was embalmed there—"

"Don't be a fool!" said Young Whiffle, his eyes on the window sill, glaring at the window sill annihilating the window sill. "Whiffle and Peabody would be ruined by such a statement, more ruined than they are at present."

"How?" demanded Reynolds. Ordinarily he wouldn't have argued but being shut up in the room with this pair of bony-fingered old men had turned him desperate. "Why? After all who could dispute it? You could get the embalmer, Mr. Ludastone, to say he remembered the neck bone, or the position of the foot—." His voice grew louder. "If you identify the colored woman first nobody'll question it—"

"Lower your voice," said Old Peabody.

Young Whiffle stood up and pounded on the dusty window sill. "Because colored people, bodies, I mean the colored dead—"

He took a deep breath. Old Peabody said, "Now relax, Mr. Whiffle, relax. Remember your blood pressure."

"There's such a thing as a color line," shrieked Young Whiffle. "You braying idiot, you, we're not supposed to handle colored bodies, the colored dead, I mean the dead colored people, in our establishment. We'd never live down a statement like that. We're fortunate that so far no one has asked how the corpse of Louella Brown, a colored laundress, got on the premises in 1902. Louella was a special case but they'd say that we—"

"But she's already there!" Reynolds shouted. "You've got a colored body or bones, I mean there now. She *was* embalmed there. She *was* buried in Yew Tree Cemetery. Nobody's said anything about it."

Old Peabody held up his hand for silence. "Wait," he said. "There is a bare chance—" He thought for a moment. He found that his thinking was quite confused, he felt he ought to object to Reynolds' suggestion but he didn't know why. Vivid images of Louella Brown, wearing a dark dress with white collars and cuffs, added to his confusion.

Finally he said, "We'll do it, Mr. Whiffle. It's the only way. And we'll explain it with dignity. Speak of Louella's long service, true she did laundry for others, too, but we won't mention that, talk about her cheerfulness and devotion, emphasize the devotion, burying her in Yew Tree Cemetery was a kind of reward for service, payment for a debt of gratitude, remember that phrase 'debt of gratitude.' And call in—" he swallowed hard, "the press. Especially that animal from the *Boston Record*, who wrote the story up the first time. We might serve some of the old brandy and cigars. Then Mr. Ludastone can make his statement. About the position of the foot, he remembers it—" He paused and glared at Reynolds. "And as for you! You needn't think we'll ever permit you inside our doors again, dead or alive."

Gray-haired, gray-skinned Clarence Ludastone, head embalmer for Whiffle and Peabody, dutifully identified one set of bones as being those of the late Louella Brown. Thus the identity of the Countess was firmly established. Half the newspapermen in the country were present at the time. They partook generously of Old Peabody's best brandy and enthusiastically smoked his finest cigars. The last individual to leave was the weary gentleman who represented the *Boston Record*.

He leaned against the doorway as he spoke to Old Peabody. "Wonderful yarn," he said. "Never heard a better one. Congratulations—" And he drifted down the hall.

Because of all the stories about Louella Brown and the Countess of Castro, most of the residents of Boston turned out to watch the funeral cortege of the Bedfords on the twenty-first of June. The ceremony that took place at Bedford Abbey was broadcast over a national hook-up, and the news services wired it around the world, complete with pictures.

Young Whiffle and Old Peabody agreed that the publicity accorded the occasion was disgraceful. But their satisfaction over the successful ending of what had been an extremely embarrassing situation was immense. They had great difficulty preserving the solemn mien required of them during the funeral service.

Young Whiffle and Old Peabody both suffered slight heart attacks when they saw the next morning's edition of the *Boston Record*. For there on the front page was a photograph of Mr. Ludastone, and over it in bold, black type were the words "child embalmer." The article which accompanied the picture, said, in part:

"Who is buried in the crypt at Bedford Abbey? The Countess, or Louella, the laundress? We ask because Mr. Clarence Ludastone, the suave gentleman who is head embalmer for Whiffle and Peabody, could not possibly identify the bones of Louella Brown, despite his look of great age. Mr. Ludastone, according to his birth certificate (which is reproduced on this page) was only two years old at the time of Louella's death. This reporter has questioned many of Boston's oldest residents but he has, as yet, been unable to locate anyone who remembers a time when Whiffle and Peabody employed a two-year-old child as embalmer—"

Eighty-year-old Governor Bedford very nearly had apoplexy when he saw the *Boston Record*. He hastily called a press conference. He said that he would personally, publicly (in front of the press), identify the Countess, if it was the Countess. He remembered her well for he was only thirty-five when she died. He would know instantly if it were she.

Two days later the Governor stalked down the center aisle of that marble gem—Bedford Abbey. He was followed by a veritable hive of newsmen and photographers. Old Peabody and Young Whiffle were waiting for them just inside the crypt.

The Governor peered at the interior of the opened casket and drew back. He forgot the eager-eared newsmen, who surrounded him, pressed against him. When he spoke he reverted to the simple speech of his early ancestors.

"Why they be nothing but bones here!" he said. "Nothing but bones! Nobody could tell who this be."

He turned his head, unable to take a second look. He, too, some day, not too far off, how did a man buy immortality, he didn't want to die, bones rattling inside a casket—ah, no! He reached for his pocket handkerchief, and Young Whiffle thrust a freshly laundered one into his hand.

Governor Bedford wiped his face, his forehead. But not me, he thought. I'm alive. I can't die. It won't happen to me. And inside his head a voice kept saying over and over, like the ticking of a clock, It will, It can, It will, It can, It will.

"You were saying, Governor," prompted the tall thin newsman from the *Boston Record*.

"I don't know!" Governor Bedford shouted angrily. "I don't know! Nobody could tell which be the black laundress and which the white countess from looking at their bones."

"Governor, Governor," protested Old Peabody. "Governor, ah—calm yourself, great strain—" And leaning forward, he hissed in the Governor's reddening ear," Remember the press, don't say that, don't make a statement, don't commit yourself—"

"Stop spitting in my ear!" roared the Governor. "Get away! And take your blasted handkerchief with you." He thrust Young Whiffle's handkerchief inside Old Peabody's coat, up near the shoulder. "It stinks, it stinks of death." Then he strode out of Bedford Abbey, muttering under his breath as he went.

The Governor's statement went around the world, in direct quotes. So did the photographs of him, peering inside the casket, his mouth open, his eyes staring. There were still other photographs that showed him charging down the center aisle of Bedford Abbey, head down, shoulders thrust forward, even the back of his neck somehow indicative of his fury. Cartoonists showed him, in retreat, words issuing form his shoulder blades, "Nobody could tell who this be—the black laundress or the white countess—"

Sermons were preached about the Governor's statement, editorials were written about it, and Congressmen made long-winded speeches over the radio. The Mississippi Legislature threatened to declare war on the sovereign State of Massachusetts because Governor Bedford's remarks were an unforgivable insult to believers in white supremacy.

Many radio listeners became completely confused and, believing that both ladies were still alive, sent presents to them, sometimes addressed in care of Governor Bedford, and sometimes addressed in care of Whiffle and Peabody.

Whiffle and Peabody kept the shades drawn in their establishment. They scuttled through the streets each morning, hats pulled low over their eyes, en route to their offices. They would have preferred to stay at home (with the shades drawn) but they agreed it was better to act as though nothing had happened. So they spent ten hours a day on the premises as was their custom, though there was absolutely no business.

Young Whiffle paced the floor, hours at a time, wringing his hands, and muttering, "A black washerwoman! We're ruined—ruined—ruined—"

Old Peabody found himself wishing that Young Whiffle would not speak of Louella with such contempt. In spite of himself he kept dreaming about her. In the dream, she came quite close to him, a small, brown woman with merry eyes. And after one quick look at him, she put her hands on her hips, threw her head back and laughed and laughed.

He was quite unaccustomed to being laughed at, even in a dream; and the memory of Louella's laughter lingered with him for hours after he woke up. He could not forget the smallest detail of her appearance: how her shoulders shook as she laughed, and that her teeth were very white and evenly spaced.

He thought to avoid this recurrent visitation by sitting up all night, by drinking hot milk, by taking lukewarm baths. Then he tried the exact opposite—he went to bed early, drank cold milk, took scalding hot baths. To no avail. Louella Brown still visited him, each and every night.

Thus it came about that one morning when Young Whiffle began his ritual muttering: "A black washerwoman—we're ruined—ruined—ruined—," Old Peabody shouted: "Will stop that caterwauling? One would think the Lock Ness monster lay in the crypt at Bedford Abbey." He could see Louella Brown standing in front of him, laughing, laughing. And he said, "Louella Brown was a neatly built little woman, a fine woman, full of laughter. I remember her well. She was a gentlewoman. Her bones will do no injury to the governor's damned funeral chapel."

It was a week before Young Whiffle actually heard what Old Peabody was saying, though Peabody made this same outrageous statement, over and over again.

When Young Whiffle finally heard it, there was a quarrel, a violent quarrel, caused by the bones of Louella Brown—that quick-moving, merry, little woman.

By the end of the day, the partnership was dissolved, and the ancient and exclusive firm of Whiffle and Peabody, Incorporated, went out of business.

Old Peabody, retired, after all there was no firm he would consider associating with. Young Whiffle retired, too, but he moved all the way to California, and changed his name to Smith; in the hope that no man would ever discover he had once been a member of the blackguardly firm of Whiffle and Peabody, Incorporated.

Despite his retirement, Old Peabody found that Louella Brown still haunted his dreams. What was worse, she took to appearing before him during his waking moments. After a month of this, he went to see Governor Bedford. He had to wait an hour before the Governor came down stairs, walking slowly, leaning on a cane.

Old Peabody wasted no time being courteous. He went straight to the reason for his visit. "I have come," he said stiffly, "to suggest to you that you put the names of both those women on the marble slab in Bedford Abbey."

"Never," said the Governor. "Never, never, never!"

He is afraid to die, Old Peabody thought, eyeing the Governor. You can always tell by the look on their faces. He shrugged his shoulders. "Every man dies alone, Governor," he said brutally. "And so it is always best to be at peace with his world and any other world that follows it, when one dies."

Old Peabody waited a moment. The Governor's hands were shaking. Fear or palsy, he wondered. Fear, he decided. Fear beyond the question of a doubt.

"Louella Brown visits me every night, and frequently during the day," Peabody said softly. "I am certain that unless you follow my suggestion she will also visit you." A muscle in the Governor's face started to twitch. Peabody said, "When your bones finally lie in the crypt in your marble chapel, I doubt that you want to hear the sound of Louella's laughter ringing in your ears—toll doomsday."

"Get out!" said the Governor, shuddering. "You're crazy as a loon."

"No," Old Peabody said, firmly. "Between us, all of us, we have managed to summon Louella's spirit." And he proceeded to tell the Governor how every night, in his dreams, and sometimes during the day when he was awake, Louella came to stand beside him, and look up at him and laugh.

He told it very well, so well in fact that for a moment he thought he saw Louella standing in the room, right near Governor Bedford's left shoulder.

The Governor turned, looked over his shoulder. And then he said, slowly, and reluctantly, and with the uneasy feeling that he could already hear Louella's laughter, "All right." He paused, took a deep unsteady breath, "What do you suggest I put on the marble slab in the crypt?"

After much discussion, and much writing, and much tearing up of what had been written, they achieved a satisfactory epitaph. If you ever go to Boston and visit Bedford Abbey you will see for yourself how Old Peabody propitiated the bones of the late Louella Brown. For after these words were carved on the marble slab, Louella ceased to haunt Old Peabody:

<blockquote>
Here lies
Elizabeth, Countess of Castro
or
Louella Brown, Gentlewoman
1830–1902
Reburied in Bedford Abbey June 21, 1947
"They both wore the breastplate of faith and love;
And for an helmet, the hope of salvation."
</blockquote>

[*Opportunity* 25.4 (April 1947): 189–192, 226–230]

GOLD IS WHERE YOU FIND IT

by Alberta Thomas

The bank president leaned back in his chair and, smiling, looked at the other four members of the board of trustees. The others stared at him in utter astonishment.

"Jonathan Covery! Are you losing your mind!" James Jarrett exclaimed, with a puzzled frown on his usually placed countenance. "Why, this man is a Negro, and he has no collateral. He has already lost his sheep. He can't pay us what he owes now. We can't take a chance on a Negro."

"My friends," Jonathan answered, "Will you let me tell you a story?

"It was the first day of the big snow, the day the Prairie Blossom children were lost. It was also little Black Billie's first day in a white children's school. His parents had just lately come from the Sunny South. Billie was strong, though small. He had picked much cotton, dragging his long heavy sack all day. When he had played "Fox and Geese" with the other colored children in the Southland, he'd always won, for he could run very fast on those black skinny legs of his.

"Had he been white, he would have looked pale that day: but Billie was very black, like his maternal grandmother; so he only looked ashy. Here in the North the other children had never seen a colored boy in school before. To them he was comical as he rolled his big brown eyes. 'Saucer Eyes,' they called him.

"'The school will come to order and stop snickering,' Miss Ramsey commanded.

"About ten o'clock it began to snow. At recess the children huddled around the stove to keep warm. Billie sat shivering in his seat. Then the hectoring started. The children began to sing 'Wall-eyed nigger came to town, came to town.' A big bully struck poor Billie across the face. The little colored boy did not fight back, for he remembered how his old mammy had told him, 'Never hit a white child. They don't understand.' Billie told himself that his mammy had taught him to pray, too. So he bent his head low over his book and silently asked 'Please God, help me to show them *I is white inside.*'

"By noon the snow was a foot deep. Miss Ramsey walked from window to window with a worried look on her face. All around the little school house was a vast sea of whiteness. No sagebrush, no cactus, no road. It was getting colder, too.

"'Put the bucket of water on the stove—we must get started,' she said. 'Everybody get their coats and overshoes on.'

"At first the bus refused to start, but after putting hot water into the radiator, the engine turned over and off they rolled towards home.

"The bus must have gotten off the road, for several times it almost turned over, but on they went. Why didn't they come to some house? Miss Ramsey knew now that they must be off the main road. Soon it grew dark. There were no stars, moon, road, nothing to guide them. Then it happened. The bus stopped. Miss Ramsey tried again and again but the starter only growled. The smaller children began to cry. 'Someone must go for help,' she said. 'Who will volunteer?' No one answered. They were all frightened and most of them were crying. Miss Ramsey began to sing 'Onward Christian Soldiers' and made them march up and down, stomping their feet and slapping their hands together. Then Little Black Billie said, 'Miss Ramsey, I'll go,' and before she could answer, he opened the door and disappeared into the deep snow and the ominous darkness.

"God, in His great mercy, must have guided little Billie's feet, for there was no road, no landmark of any kind, not even a star, but he *got through* and that night the ranchers found the bus with its precious load, cold, and hungry, almost frozen in the terrible cold, but *alive.*

"That's my story, gentlemen."

Jonathan Covery spoke into the inter-office phone, "Tell Mr. Brown to come in," he said. A timid knock sounded at the door and then a small middle-aged man came into the room limping, quite painfully.

"Friends, this is Mr. William Brown. You will notice he limps. Well, gentlemen, that is because his feet are made of wood. The doctor took them off because they were frozen that night when he went for help. *This is little Black Billie Brown.* He needs to borrow some money. Shall we lend it to him?"

James Jarrett wiped a tear from his eyes. He seemed all choked up as he said, "I'm sorry, *I*, you see, was the big bully who struck Billie that first morning at school."

"And I was one of the little ones who cried," the president of the bank replied.

In less than five minutes, all had voted for the loan, and each one shook hands with Brown, the Negro. Whom they now all honored and respected. They wished him luck on his sheep ranch. Said they would see him through. Here was pure gold where they had least expected to find it. [*Opportunity* 25.4 (April 1947): 196, 230–231]

A Change of Scenery

by Rosalie Lieberman

Amanda Pattley rang the bell of the gracious Colonial house, and suddenly thought herself a fool. True, Dr. Barstow had ordered a rest, and she'd always been clumsy with leisure time. But to come eight hundred miles to see a former pupil ... in a way, it was ridiculous. Yet, she so wanted to know about this boy Dick Mattson ... one of the keenest minds she'd ever taught ... spoiled when he'd first come to her—convinced that his ideas as given to him by his parents were the only ones. Gradually though, he'd changed ... the quick mind had become eager to learn—to adjust where he'd been wrong.

The door opened. A Negro butler stood there. "Yes, ma'am." His voice was low and courteous, though it was obvious from his expression that strangers didn't often arrive at the Mattson door.

Amanda hesitated. "I've come to see Mr. Richard. I'm Miss Pattley, a former teacher of his, and I was just passing through Roxford...." A lie, of course, but a pale one.

The butler made no direct reference to Richard, but asked her to come in. "I'll tell Mrs. Mattson you're here," he said.

Amanda was annoyed. If Richard weren't there—if he'd run off with the girl from the other side of the tracks—whatever he'd done, why didn't someone say so? She bristled at all the vagueness, and in spite of her irritation, the house with its soft-toned curtains, its mahogany furniture catching the sun, had a soothing effect on her. She listened for Richard's quick, young steps. But there was no sound at all. The room was distractingly still.

Then suddenly, the stillness was broken by a high, shrill voice. "No, let me go down. I want to see her. Let me go by myself."

Amanda looked toward the stairway. A woman was running down, swiftly, fluidly almost as if she were being pursued. She rushed rather than walked into the living room. Her features were beautifully chiselled, but her mouth was drawn to the thinness of a pencil line, and the hands were interlocked so tightly that the veins were prominent. "Miss Pattley?" The voice was hard and piercing.

"Yes, I ..."

"I'm Dick's mother. And I'm *glad* you came." The hysterical tone didn't match the words. "I want you to know what you've done. Dick's gone. He was all we had, and now...."

Richard Mattson dead! The room for all its sunshine and warmth went suddenly lifeless, too.

"I want to know why you did it? Why?" The meaningless words spilled out frightening, angering Amanda. But before she could question the trembling women, an efficient-looking nurse came noiselessly into the room. She looked pleadingly at Amanda for cooperation.

"It's time for your medicine, Mrs. Mattson." The nurse took the older woman's arm with a gentle, practiced touch.

"But I haven't finished with her yet. I want to know what right she has to send Dick away."

Suddenly, a new thought jagged through Mrs. Mattson's brain. The tone of her voice was softened—there was a brief, hypocritical smile.

"Maybe if you have so much influence with Dick, you might get him to come back. He might listen to.... I want you to try."

"All right, Mrs. Mattson. You take your medicine now." The nurse began nudging her away from Amanda. "And then you can talk things over with Miss Pattley some more."

The nurse looked at Amanda again. The look asked her wait.

Amanda felt little tremors shoot through her entire body. What had happened to Dick?

In a moment, the nurse was back. "I'm Miss Drake," she said, "and I'm terribly sorry this happened. But Mrs. Mattson gets incoherent when she hears your name."

"But why?" Anger tinged Amanda's words. "And what's happened to Dick?"

"I'll tell you," Miss Drake said. "Listen."

And then Amanda heard. Richard had stopped off in Chicago on his way home after graduation. He'd heard about conditions in some of the Negro tenement districts there, and well, he'd gone to see for himself. The unspeakable way many of the people lived in these districts had stirred him so that he could talk of nothing else when he got home. His family thought it was just a phase. But it wasn't. He said he couldn't live in solid comfort with a solid future ahead of him—not when he'd seen so much misery with his own eyes.

"But what exactly has he done?" Amanda asked.

"He's done plenty, Miss Pattley. He's doing plenty. Dick has a job in Harlem. He's working on a committee whose sole aim is to improve the Negroes' living conditions.... And Dick is living in Harlem, too—in a house with Negroes because he feels that's the way he can understand them and their problems best."

Amanda let her body relax now. So that was the explanation of the mystery. Oh, she pitied that hysterical Mrs. Mattson more than she'd ever pitied anyone. But could she really be sorry for what she'd taught Richard. She couldn't. Instead, her heart slipped over inside her. Richard had started on his great adventure, and through him, she'd begun one too. And there'd be other Richards....

Amanda stood. She thanked Miss Drake and walked briskly out of the house. Dr. Barstow *had* prescribed a change of scenery. And it had turned out a better prescription than he could ever have given. [*Opportunity* 26.3 (March 1948): 95, 104]

NOT IN THE RECORD

by Elizabeth Walker Reeves

The little old woman leaned way over the side of Heaven and peered down into the world. She held on tightly so that she wouldn't fall, because she was never quite sure of herself whenever she had to use her wings. Except when she was in a hurry, she rarely flew. And she was seldom in a hurry. Most of the time she just kept her wings folded across her back and shuffled along the gold pavements of Heaven—taking care not to slip when it got too misty.

It was still a novelty to her—to be able to look down through the clouds and watch the mortals rushing between hither and thither, busy about the business of living their lives. She would focus her eyes in order to watch the earthlings with that last-row-in-the-balcony effect. That wasn't hard to do. She'd been used to last rows in balconies until she'd moved up to New York. Then when she got there, she just never had enough time to see movies. Often at night she was the last operator to leave the stuffy little beauty parlor and the first to arrive in the morning—even then, some of the smoke from the night before still lingered.

The little woman smiled contentedly and breathed deeply. That was one thing she liked about Heaven. It was nice and airy, and the air was sweet. She didn't have that racking pain in her chest anymore that once made her cough up little specks of red. Funny how she'd known she wasn't going to return from the hospital to that dingy two-room apartment that she and her son shared. There were rows and rows of beds in the hospital, and they were almost jammed up against each other so that if anybody came to visit anybody, they hardly had space to sit down by the side of the bed and talk. Of course, nobody ever came to see her, though, 'cept Jimmie and Mrs. Davis. It had been kind of Mrs. Lottie Davis to have taken care of Jimmie so long and to have tried to get help for him from the social agencies. Each day that Lottie got off early from work, she had walked up and down the pavements of New York looking for aid for Jimmie. Saint Peter had written Lottie's name in his book for that.

Lottie was awfully poor, though, and the little woman had been glad when her Jimmie had found a job. He was now seventeen and until recently had been living in a rooming house and putting money aside to finish school, out of the twelve dollars a week he was earning working at the grocery.

But while she was focusing her eyes to pick out Jimmie's rooming house, a voice kept droning in her ears. It was very annoying; the nearer she came to the rooming house, the louder the voice became until, finally, she just had to listen to it. "The People of the State of New York versus Harry Brooke, Charles Bailey, and James Wilson." Her heart pounded when she heard Jimmie's name. She switched her eyes to the courtroom downtown that sent forth the voice. Then she knew it was useless to look in Jimmie's room, because there he was, standing before the judge's bench. Bewildered, she turned her eyes toward a woman sobbing softly. She recognized the woman as Lottie Davis, when the woman lifted her head to say something to the person sitting next to her.

"Jimmie was like a child just throwed away when his mother died," Lottie was saying to her seat mate. "I tried to get help for him but it was no use. Nobody wanted to watch out for him. He was like a child just throwed away."

Her Jimmie on trial? The woman in Heaven trembled as she heard the prosecutor saying, "...to show that these three boys, while committing a robbery, killed one Albert Silver on the night of...." She couldn't believe it. Something was wrong. The little woman knew that her Jimmie would not kill. Jimmie was never a bad boy; he had always said he wanted to get ahead and maybe go to college some day. What could have happened to cause him to be in such a situation? Quickly she made use of her heavenly power to will Jimmie to retrospect so that she could know what had happened.

Her Jimmie watched the prosecutor go through the motions of a fiery address, but he scarcely heard what was being said. He knew that his man with the smooth words and the big talk was trying to take away his life. It was odd. It was odd because he'd hardly even got a good look at the man that "Moe" and Charlie had mugged. Gosh, he'd only known *them* about two weeks. Then he thought back.

He had lost his job and stretched out the money he'd saved until he was living on practically nothing each day and sleeping in parked cars. He was sleeping in somebody's car that night when his two newly met acquaintances shook him awake. At first he'd thought it was the cops.

"Hey, Jimmie, wake up. C'mon, we wantcha to go wid us."

"Where ya' goin'?"

"We just goin' out on a little 'mugging' job."

"Aw heck, Moe, whyncha do it by yourselves? I wanna sleep."

"He wants to sleep," Charlie sneered. "Ain't dat somepin'? I told ya he'd be scairt, Moe."

"Naw, I ain't no scarder than you are, Charlie," threw back Jimmie. "I just gotta sleep, dat's all. Mr. Rosenberg said maybe I can deliver groceries tomorrow, since it's Saturday."

"Well, now ain't dat real sweet," jibbed Charlie again. "How much is dat big fat slob gonna give ya—five cents an hour?"

"Aw, cut dat, Charlie," snapped Moe. "Don't pay no 'tention to him, Jimmie. He's just kiddin.' Listen, kid, it ain't gonna take ya long. All we need is a look-out guy, see? And when we get through, maybe you'll have enough so ya won't have to worry 'bout no job for awhile. Shux, we'll prob'ly catch a guy who'll never even miss the dough."

No, the guy never missed his money. An ironic smile curled Jimmie's lips as the District Attorney put the finishing touches to his case.

They'd tucked down back streets and finally come up in Morningside Park.

It was pretty exciting at first, sorta like a funny-book adventure, until they had to sit around and wait for somebody to come by. Moe told him that if he did a good job as look-out, they'd let him help out in the actual "mugging" next time. He didn't think much of the idea, but he kept his mouth shut. Anytime he said anything that made him sound like decent guy, Charlie would dive right into him with some sarcastic remark. He got tired of Charlie and his ribbin'. Some day he was gonna bust him.

"Hey, watch it," Charlie hissed, "here comes a guy all by himself. Just what we been waitin' fer."

"Okay, Jimmie, you mosey on up to the corner and make like a cat howlin' if ya see somebody comin'," whispered Moe out of the corner of his mouth.

"Moe gave him a shove and he sauntered on off, like he'd just said good-bye to them. Moe and Charlie moved on down toward the man. When Jimmie looked back, Moe had got behind the man and grabbed him around the neck, and Charlie was going through his pockets. Then Jimmie turned back to look around the corner to see if anybody was coming. He was watching the other street, when the boys suddenly ran past him. "C'mon, Jimmie!" Jimmie caught up with them. In Charlie's hand was what looked like a suit. Jimmie glanced back. The man was lying on the ground in his underwear. Suddenly there was a funny sick feeling in the bottom of Jimmie's stomach.

"Hey, whatcha'll do to the man?" demanded Jimmie. They were slowing up now, feeling fairly safe.

"Aw, he's just unconscious. Moe just tapped him lightly."

"Well, watcha take his clothes for?"

"Aw, dat sucker didn't have no more'n seventeen cents," sneered Charlie. "We hadda git *somethin'* out dis job."

"*Seventeen cents*? Well I'll be.... Didn't he have no wallet?"

"Naw!" Moe glared at him. "Look, we got his suit, ain't we? If he had a wallet, we'da seen it, wouldn't we? Now, here, I give you dis two cents. I gits ten and Charlie gets five. We gonna pawn da suit tomorrow, and you'll git part of what de man give us for dat."

"Two cents...!" Jimmie turned up his nose. "Dat ain't near as much a Mr. Rosenberg would give me, is it Charlie? You said maybe he'd give me only five cents, remember, huh? Two cents! And I done lost some sleep besides."

"Aw, shet up and git da hell outa my sight," said Charlie. "And tell Mr. Rosenberg I said to go choke hisself!" he heard Charlie yell at his retreating back.

Charlie must have had choking on the brain. He'd figured Charlie out to be jealous, anyhow, 'cause Mr. Rosenberg wouldn't let some guys work around his store. Old man Rosenberg wasn't such a bad guy, nohow. During the war he'd worn a badge with four red stars on it, and Mrs. Rosenberg was now a Gold Star mother. Mr. Rosenberg said you didn't have to wait aroun' for the army to come and get you like Moe and Charlie had told him. You could go on down and ask them to let you in, like three of Mr. Rosenberg's sons had done. Jimmie wondered if it was true that the pay was good. Best of all it would be swell if they really did help a guy to go to school after he got out, because that's what he wanted most of all. Well, he'd go down there

Monday and find out. He was getting tired of bothering with Moe and Charlie, anyway.

But that Monday never came. He'd worked hard all day Saturday and made himself a nice pocket-full of change; night had come and he'd just dozed off to sleep in a parked car when somebody grabbed him by the arm. This time it really was the cops! They weren't kiddin' neither. Heck, if he'd gone on and done like Mr. Rosenberg said, he'da been in the army. He wouldn't have been in none of this mess. No matter what Moe and Charlie said—being in the army was better than being in jail.

He looked at the man talking now. That was the defense lawyer, the man who had come to his cell and asked him all about everything. Jimmie was kind of proud of him. He was colored, but he seemed just as smart as that white man who wanted to take his life. He didn't understand much of what this man was saying now, either, as the defense counsel intoned, "...but nowhere on the docket do we find listed as accessories before the fact the names of the social agencies, public and private, which refused to help this boy when his life might have been guided in another direction. Not in the record can we find the weak refusals of aid for this boy that Mrs. Lottie Davis received when over a year ago...." Mrs. Davis had found this lawyer for him. She had been really a good friend of his mother. She had looked out for him real swell and had even told him he could come upstairs and sleep on a mat on her floor when he lost his room. But he hadn't wanted to impose on her any more; Maw had told him before she died that he had it in him to make it on his own. Gosh, he guessed Maw would be sore at him if she was him now.

"No, Jimmie, no. Don't think that, please," the little old woman whispered down from Heaven. "You know I can't be sore; I understand. You mustn't worry any more, Jimmie, honey. I'm watching over you and I'm going to see if I can help. Yes, gonna see if there ain't some way I can get ya free. Don't worry," she whispered, and the words floated down to settle in a sort of mist on the frown in Jimmie's forehead. Before she drew her eyes from the courtroom, she noticed that the tense lines in Jimmie's face had eased somewhat.

The little woman didn't know exactly what she could do. But first she was going to tell the Lord about it, and maybe He'd see what He could do. Everybody knew that the Lord had the complete record before Him and could handle any situation. Look at what the Lord had done for her and helped her do for others. She turned quickly away from the spot where she had looked over the side of Heaven and she headed toward the main entrance. She rushed past the big gate so fast that she almost forgot to wave to Saint Peter. He was a good guy. He didn't look to see what color you were before he let you in.

It had grown misty and the gold pavements were sorta slippery. She had quite a little way to go before she reached the throne of the Lord. So the little woman took to her wings—because she was in a hurry.   [*Opportunity* 26.3 (March 1948): 105–107]

Index

Africa 4, 23, 26, 80–82, 88, 104, 105, 178, 282–284, 321, 323
African Methodist Episcopal 213
African Protestant Church 282–284
Alabama 186, 217, 281–282
Aladdin 76, 78, 82
Algiers 5, 26
Alps 223
Amazon 105
Amen 123, 155, 160, 201–202
America 13, 87, 104, 126, 176, 179, 211, 321, 324; Americans 37–40, 42, 44, 64, 85–86, 89, 102, 128, 178, 180, 215, 305–311
Anderson, Sherwood 102
Antar the Lion 323
Arabia 23, 314, 323
Army 12, 31, 304–305, 309, 311, 323, 355–356
Art 5, 13, 14, 54, 66, 77, 78, 84, 95, 104, 301, 312, 317
Atlanta 281, 284–285
Attucks, Crispus 323
Austria 180

Banjo 7–8
Baptist Church 126
Bayou 44
Belgium 79, 88
Bell-hop 141
Bible 83, 109, 126, 235, 267
Birmingham 281–282
Boston 4, 61, 64, 78, 176, 323, 340–344, 346, 347, 349
Brazil 176, 323
British Museum 85
Bronx 29, 261, 275

California 296, 348
Cambridge 178

Cape Haitien 80
Caribbean 4, 292
Cellist 7–8
Celts 179
Chaka 323
Charleston 29
Chattanooga 173, 256
Cherokee Indian 77
Chesapeake 95
Chicago 4, 133, 136, 178, 205, 352
Chinese 138, 216
Christ 35–37, 85, 87, 323
Christ Church 85
Christening 83
Christian 82, 87, 105, 123–124, 126, 159, 164, 181, 323, 350
Christian Science 79
Christmas 21–22, 78, 150–151, 218, 303
Church 4, 21, 35–36, 85, 123–126, 154–155, 159, 181, 195–197, 199, 219–221, 223, 225, 238, 254, 267, 280–284, 287–288, 298, 302, 306, 327
Civil War 38–39, 42, 178, 308
College 4, 30, 88, 109, 157, 176, 188, 194, 205, 224, 226, 297, 306, 309, 312–313, 316–318, 331, 354
Columbus 281
Composer 13
Concert 13, 14, 112, 239–240, 339–340
Conjure 44, 46, 48, 56–57, 64, 98, 104, 285
Creole 4, 38, 40
Cuba 323

Dance 7–9, 8–9, 10, 11, 18–20, 29, 35–36, 47, 61, 68, 82, 88, 92, 122, 136, 143, 146, 152, 154, 161–163, 165, 220, 242, 245, 289, 312–313, 337

Danes 138, 179
Daniel in the Lion's Den 220
Delta 166
Department of Welfare 275
Detroit 218, 220–221, 223
Devil 68, 72, 134, 140, 154, 160, 164–165, 182–185, 187, 200–202, 226–227, 279, 281, 296
Devilment 201
Diaz, Henrique 323
Discrimination 4, 42, 306, 342
Disease 157–158
Dixie 254, 256, 340
Doctor 12, 14–15, 78, 89–90, 104, 129–130, 143–146, 163, 172, 176, 180–181, 194, 212–213, 224, 226–227, 229–230, 280, 286, 292–295, 297, 304, 306, 317, 325, 327, 351, 353
Dominica 292, 294
Dream 19, 21–23, 27–28, 37, 42, 45, 46, 50, 54, 62, 80, 82, 84–85, 88, 100, 131, 137, 237, 243, 256, 293, 295, 298–299, 301, 304, 312–314, 317, 319, 322, 324, 330, 336, 348, 349
Duluth 132
Dunbar, Paul Laurence 112, 301

Eastern Europeans 179
Eatonville 67
Edinburgh 292, 294
England 38, 42, 65, 77, 80–81, 86–88, 128, 148, 154, 158, 179, 182
Europe 4, 84–86, 179, 211
Evansville 173–175

Farm 47, 105, 179, 193–194, 208, 210, 333; farmers 4, 88, 109, 112, 114

357

Florida 45, 47, 67, 281
Food 9, 58, 62, 86, 126, 146, 154, 166, 168–171, 175, 177, 185–187, 193, 225, 241–242, 249, 264–265, 272, 280, 286, 296
Fort Bragg 304–305
France 80, 85, 88
Freedmen 79
Freedom 10, 26–27, 32, 36, 38–39, 42, 59, 61, 73, 79, 80, 82–83, 90, 96, 98, 100–102, 105, 113, 125, 127, 129, 140, 147, 169, 179, 182, 186, 198, 206, 211, 221, 245, 294, 302, 307, 309, 319, 322, 323, 324, 356
French 38–39, 82
Freud 86
Funeral 34, 61, 123, 124, 180–181, 341, 346, 348

Gauls 179
Georgia 7, 9, 68, 159–160, 257, 281, 333
Germany 4, 147, 176–178, 180, 216, 314
Ghost 13, 15, 134, 137, 159, 193, 195, 236
God 13, 24, 30, 36–37, 62–64, 85, 94, 98–99, 101–102, 105, 112–113, 117, 123, 125–126, 128, 133, 138, 143, 145, 147, 151, 154, 156, 159–165, 168, 171, 179–181, 184–185, 187, 198, 200–202, 225–229, 231–232, 247, 252, 273–274, 277, 279, 281, 284–286, 292, 294–295, 297, 310, 320, 323, 335–336, 339, 345, 350
Goddess 47
Gods 81, 87, 131
Gold coast 87
Golgotha 322
Grandmother (Grandma, Granma, Granny) 16–29, 46, 104, 106, 200, 206–207, 227, 283, 287–289, 350
Greek 78, 138
Grenada 294
Grieg 10
Guadeloupe 38
Guitar 32

Hair 9, 14, 17, 23, 25, 34, 38, 64, 69, 71, 73, 77–78, 86, 90, 96, 107, 109–110, 112, 121, 132, 135–136, 141, 143, 145–149, 159, 168, 172–173, 176, 178, 182, 193–194, 205, 211, 213–214, 216, 224–225, 228–231, 233, 244, 248, 250, 252, 254, 262, 265–266, 278, 289, 304, 307, 312, 314–317, 326, 335, 342–343
Haiti 4, 323
Hampton 316
Hankow 84

Harlem 3–4, 29–30, 67, 76, 165, 241, 275, 277, 280, 306, 352
Harvard 176, 178, 342
Hat 29–30, 39, 69–71, 74, 76–79, 92, 101, 122, 124, 139, 153, 155, 156, 160, 168, 172, 174, 176, 182, 186, 189, 200, 206, 208, 227–230, 232, 237, 254–256, 260, 263, 267, 298, 347
Hathaway, Anne 85
Haviland, John 143
Hayti 80
Health 37, 40, 42–43, 46, 79, 82, 93, 253, 280, 320
Health care 4
Heaven 14, 21, 104, 118, 124, 127, 135, 138–139, 142, 144, 147, 156, 160–163, 166–169, 180, 182, 283, 294–295, 353–354, 356
Hebrew 99
Hell 33–34, 76, 101, 138, 195, 197, 199, 202, 204, 209, 230, 233, 273, 278, 291, 339, 355
Hercules 20
High school 37, 46, 154, 156, 176, 211–212, 223, 229, 306, 312
Hitler 308
Holy 21, 72, 159, 164, 288, 323
Holy Christian Saints 159
Hymn 160, 181, 201, 220, 250, 254, 267, 306

Indian 77, 180
Ireland 61, 77, 86, 88–89, 177–178, 180, 345
Ironing 125, 153, 164, 193, 226–228, 238, 266, 281, 282, 283, 284
Italian 138, 182, 184, 216

Jacksonville 45–46, 48, 54
Jamaica 318
Janitor 62–65, 156, 224, 313, 335
Jesus 109–110, 126, 129, 142, 160, 161, 164–165, 181, 184–185, 201, 305–306, 310–311
Jew 138, 147–148, 213, 214, 216, 226, 302, 317, 345
Jim Crow 175, 256
Jungle 10, 87, 105, 166, 292

Kentucky 290
Killarney 89
Kitchen 46, 49, 51, 63–64, 69–70, 74, 104–107, 133, 141, 147, 150, 149, 153, 159, 166, 169, 171, 173, 188, 199, 200, 228, 244–245, 248, 265, 268, 274, 278, 279, 284–285

Landlord 62, 167–168
Laundress 344

Laundry 346
Law 58, 82, 83, 109, 119, 132, 178, 291
Lawd 16, 20, 33, 47, 53, 68, 71, 73–74, 116–117, 131–132, 164, 184, 282
Lawyer 164, 356
Lenox 72, 170
Library 78, 293, 298, 301, 316, 332; librarian 85, 316–317
Lincoln, Abraham 123, 340; Gettysburg Address 340
Lisconnel 88
Liverpool 86
London 128–129, 344
Lord 62–63, 129, 131, 159, 160, 168–171, 177, 179, 181, 198, 206, 253, 288, 294–295, 298, 306, 317, 356
Louis, Joe 302
Louisiana 21, 81, 134
Louvre 85
Luray 144
Lynching 230, 234, 333–334, 337, 339

Maceo, Antonio 323
Madrid 87
Maitland 19
Mammy 97, 129, 135, 173, 259–260, 275–278, 278, 280, 288, 350
Mardi Gras 37, 40
Maryland 109
Mason Dixon 77
Massachusetts 64, 178, 341, 347
McNeil Institute 142
Mendelssohn, Felix 340
Michigan 178–179
Millay, Edna St. Vincent 330
Minister 113, 125, 161, 267, 302, 309–311
Minnesota 132
Mississippi 102, 281, 347
Mississippi River 134
Mob 169–170, 198–199, 233, 235, 241
Mobile 79, 282
Mom 110, 129, 295–299
Moorish 315
Moscow 344
Moses 99, 105, 168, 322, 340
Mother 10, 11–13, 17, 22, 25–26, 44, 46–51, 59, 80–83, 85–86, 88, 96–97, 104, 109, 117, 122–123, 128–129, 132–133, 139–140, 142–145, 147–148, 153, 157, 160, 166, 173–174, 177–181, 189, 194–198, 200, 202, 204–209, 211–213, 218, 224, 226, 229, 234, 236–240, 249, 252, 259–261, 269, 271–272, 278, 283, 288–289, 297–298, 300, 305–306, 309, 311, 322, 326, 339–340, 350, 354–356
Mother Earth 28

Index 359

Mulatto 5, 38, 77, 80, 166, 217
Music 4, 7–8, 10, 11, 12, 13, 18, 21–22, 36, 70, 72, 78, 88, 122, 139, 140, 166–167, 202, 239, 241, 245, 302, 306, 312–313, 318–319, 328–329

Napoleon 323
Navy 49
Nazareth 310
New England 79
New Mexico 4
New Orleans 4, 38–39, 42–43, 79–82, 126
New York 39, 67, 75, 175, 288, 292, 293–295, 302, 344, 353–354
Nice 84
Nordic 85, 88, 182, 205
Norseman 136, 179, 226, 255, 292
North 16–17, 61–62, 67, 85, 123, 136, 144–145, 201, 211, 213, 226, 236, 255–256, 280, 292, 294, 302, 350
North Sea 84
North Star 95

Octoroon 79, 81, 83, 229
Opportunity 42, 80–81, 87, 104, 116, 174, 194, 205, 211, 292, 295, 302, 341
Orchestra 88
Oriental 29, 80, 161–162, 179, 182
Orlando 16

Paint 22, 23, 35, 55, 58, 109, 167, 121, 155–157, 235, 237, 261, 315
Painting 80, 315
Palm Beach 237
Paris 344
Pennsylvania 100, 102, 303, 312
Pensacola 281–282
Philadelphia 304
Physician 129, 145, 179, 303
Pianist 13, 14, 67
Piano 10–13, 15, 67–68, 70, 72–73, 92, 224, 235, 243, 267, 302, 339
Piccolo 241, 243, 245–246
Picts 179
Plantation 56, 95, 97, 104, 131, 133, 136–137, 217
Poet 301, 323
Poetry 88, 112, 114, 300–302, 318–319
Poland 88
Police 29, 78, 126, 163, 182, 230–232, 263, 277
Porter 62, 89–90, 92–93, 174
Portuguese 88, 323
Potomac 324
Pray 53, 66, 117, 127, 145, 147, 152, 161, 168–169, 181, 200–201, 208, 230, 235, 267, 171, 284, 299, 321, 350
Prayer 23, 105–106, 112, 125, 168–169, 171, 321
Preacher 201, 219, 224, 226, 268, 282, 288, 306, 347
Prejudice 174, 177–178, 180, 197, 211, 216, 296, 323–324, 337
Presbyterian 254
Promised Land 101
Protestant 4, 282–284
Psalm 112, 140
Pupil 102, 109, 112, 299

Quadroon 77, 79, 80–82, 104, 108, 178
Quaker 102
Queenstown 88–89

Race 23, 29, 36, 39, 42, 59, 61, 77, 80, 82, 88, 101, 117, 138, 174, 177, 180, 182, 194, 197, 205, 212–215, 221, 275, 311, 317–318, 336, 342
Race riot 4, 169, 292
Radcliffe 79
Reconstruction 39, 255
Religion 36, 201, 212–213, 221
Reverend 159–160, 164, 180, 219–220, 226, 237, 239–240, 267, 285, 309–310
Richmond 307
Robeson, Paul 328–329
Roland 85
Russian 138, 216, 345

Sahara 5, 23
Sahil 27
Saint Peter 353, 356
Scheveningen 84
Schmeling 302
School 4, 21–22, 25, 29, 35, 37, 46–47, 62, 68–69, 77, 87, 102, 106, 109–111, 124–125, 131, 153–158, 160–161, 176, 178, 187–188, 199, 204–205, 211–213, 215, 218, 221–224, 227, 229, 238–240, 259–260, 269, 280, 288, 294, 296–298, 300, 302, 306, 309, 312–313, 316, 319, 321, 325–328, 335, 350–351, 354–355
Scots 77, 179, 180, 318
Scrubwoman 20, 35, 165, 207, 262, 265, 285, 295–296, 306, 332
Seamstress 40
Seeress 130–131, 133
Segregation 309
Sermon 123–124, 267, 288, 347
Sewing 17, 124, 227
Shakespeare 154, 301
Sickness 36, 41, 64, 115, 144–145, 148, 156, 194, 200, 206, 227, 229, 240–242, 249, 253, 271, 276–277, 279–280, 282, 297, 321, 324, 326, 328, 355
Simon of Cyrene 322
Singing 7, 12, 15, 21–22, 24, 29, 32, 66, 88, 102, 111, 114, 136, 168–169, 171, 200, 201, 238–240, 250, 302–303, 306, 318, 350
Skin 9, 17, 35–36, 67, 77, 81–82, 85, 87–88, 96, 130, 143, 157, 167, 174, 178, 189, 194, 196–197, 199–200, 205, 210, 212, 217, 224, 229, 231, 238–239, 242, 274, 286–287, 289, 314, 322, 332, 337, 342
Slave 4–5, 39–40, 55–56, 58, 80–82, 95–102, 104–105, 217, 254, 260–261, 295, 308, 322–323
Soldier 82, 255, 303, 307–308, 350
Soliman, Angelo 323
Song 8, 11–12, 21, 24, 28–29, 53, 70, 89, 102, 105, 109, 111, 113, 168–169, 200–201, 211, 214, 217, 220, 239, 250, 255, 280, 301–305, 308, 317–318, 333–334, 339, 350
South 9, 13, 16, 21, 23, 28, 65, 77, 124–125, 132–133, 183, 201, 211, 212, 217, 236, 249, 257, 259–260, 304–305, 308, 333, 339, 350; Southern 7, 10, 12, 61, 67, 78, 116, 125, 133, 178, 196–197, 210–211, 214, 216, 224, 226, 230, 258–260, 277, 285, 298, 301, 313, 334, 340
South America 126, 176
South Carolina 246
Southland 123, 350
Spain 18, 42, 86–87, 216, 312, 315
Spell 9, 44, 46, 48, 53, 64, 115, 130, 252, 316
Spellbound 9
Spirit 18, 20, 22, 57–58, 61, 77–80, 102, 111, 112, 114, 118, 124–125, 151, 159, 161, 173, 194, 201, 239, 267, 298, 302, 314, 349
Spirits 18, 34, 56–58, 137, 282, 302
Stenographer 64
Stevedore 72, 75–76, 296
Stitching 31, 40, 143, 146
Streetcar 77, 154, 205–208, 239, 325, 327
Students 21, 84–86, 157, 213, 306, 342
Sunday 67, 71, 87, 90, 115, 125, 143, 152, 154, 158–159, 161, 219, 225–226, 237, 254, 260, 288, 291, 296
Sunday school 22, 110, 260
Surgeon 128–129
Susquehannah 99
Swedes 138

360 Index

Teaching 38, 46, 68, 77, 88, 109, 111, 147, 222, 227–229, 294, 297–298
Teachers 25, 77, 84, 85, 97, 103, 109, 124, 154, 156–157, 199–202, 214, 222, 238, 239, 302, 309, 316, 325–326, 335, 351
Texas 193, 195
Thames 85
Theatrical 235
Toussaint-L'Ouverture 80–82, 323
Turner, Nat 323
Typewriter 61–66

Under Ground Railroad 102

United States 7, 322, 344; government 309
University 77–78, 86, 177, 205, 211–214, 292, 313

Violin 7, 36, 109
Virginia 144, 305–307
Voodoo 82

Washington 179, 237, 239–240, 304–305, 307
Washwoman 16–17, 64, 70, 104, 125, 159, 165, 169, 193, 214, 224, 227, 266, 285, 332, 348
West Indies 4, 38, 292
West Virginia 235

Westchester 29, 261
Westminster 85
Witch doctor 104, 294
Witchcraft 44, 46, 105, 136
World War II 4, 123, 321
Writing 13, 65–66, 79, 84, 85, 93, 97, 99, 109, 113, 118, 150, 166, 173, 178, 195, 198, 203–204, 213, 276, 283, 290–292, 294, 301, 309, 315, 320, 330–331, 347, 349, 353

Yeats 88

Zipporah 322
Zulu 323

www.ingramcontent.com/pod-product-compliance
Ingram Content Group UK Ltd.
Pitfield, Milton Keynes, MK11 3LW, UK
UKHW050544150426
5217IPUK00026B/2062